Derik's Luck

Derik's Luck

t'Sade

Curious Cabbit Press

This book is a work of fiction. Names, characters, places, and incidents are the product of the author's imagination and are used fictitiously. Any resemblance to actual events, locales, and persons, living or dead, is coincidental.

This book contains scenes of graphic and explicit sex in a fantasy context. There are topics and scenes that will make many people uncomfortable or may be illegal in some cultures. If you are someone uncomfortable with this, in a place where reading this would be illegal, or a minor in your locality and/or culture, then *do not read it.*

There is sexual assault in the first chapter along with chapters thirty-four through thirty-six. Thirty-four has a content warning in front of it.

Derik's Luck was written in the heady days of 2007-2008 on a couple image boards: 99chan/elit and 7chan/elit. At the time, I used the handle *tSade!O9S.2cqv5k.* The Kusaba image boards weren't designed for writing stories so this novel was written in its entirety without being able to add chapters, correct typos, or even expand on things that were missing. One post and that was it. The only thing that kept me going were the comments folks posted after each chapter. Sadly, their names have been long forgotten through board resets and technical issues that inflict any site over thirteen years, but without those encouragements, this story would have never finished.

In the years that followed, Derik's Luck was almost abandoned. Every few months, someone would track me down and ask for a copy. That kept the fires burning because every time, I was reminded that I needed to do *Derik's Luck* justice and get it properly edited. I didn't have the opportunity to do so, but you wouldn't let me forget. Thank you.

Finally, in 2019, I finally found a wonderful editor who was willing to work with all my perversions and ideas. They went through and polished my little fantasy. Thank you, Shannon, I couldn't have done this without you.

And finally, I got a push with a wonderful review out of the blue. That was what I needed to finally finish this story that I started thirteen years ago. For that, Plaguehound, you have my deepest thanks.

Introducing Derik

Derik watched the full lips of the prostitute slide down his cock with a wry smile on his face. Even at her exorbitant rate, she was worth every mark just from the heat of her mouth, the tickle of her tongue, and the tits caressing his legs. He leaned back against the headboard and sighed. "This is a fucking good life."

Her eyes flickered up to him and then back down to his length before drawing up. Her bright red lips left a smear along his cock, darkening the swollen shaft, as she bobbed her head up to the top of his member. When her bright brown eyes lifted back to him, they were wide-eyed and innocent.

He didn't care that she had probably spent months on the street. The look brought a surge of heat to his length. He tightened his muscles just to feel his hardness press against the soft heat of the top of her mouth. In only a few moments, he would paint the back of her throat.

Derik reached down to stroke her hair. He wanted to enjoy the texture of the bleached strands, a far cry from his own soft hair.

She jerked away, shoving down in the process, grinding her lips against the base of his cock and burying her nose in dark hairs already matted with pre-cum and saliva. The tip of his length rubbed the back of her throat, and he almost came at the slick pressure of her mouth.

"Oh, fuck, that feels good."

She slid up and let his shaft escape her lips with a pop. With a smile only slightly faked, she dove back down and pressed her lips tight against his base. Her tongue caressed the bottom of his cock as he filled her mouth. On a midweek night, eighty marks could buy the best.

He gave up trying to touch her and slumped back, a happy moan slipping from his lips. He tilted his head back and admired the silky skin of the whore's backside. Muscles in the tight rear flexed with every stroke as she bobbed the entire length of his cock, pulling him closer to the edge.

With a smile, he lifted his attention to the mirror where he could see a black thong nestled against her shaved pussy and ass. Her swollen lips bulged over both sides, the folds dark with her excitement. She had refused to take it off, but he couldn't help but admire her shaved pussy. He loved bare cunt lips sliding along his cock and he couldn't wait to bury his entire length into her to enjoy every centimeter.

Derik glanced back to his own cock where his dark hairs tickled her lips. As much as he loved to see a shaved pussy, that was for women, not men. He admired his own thatch of pubic hair before gazing at her blonde hair that spread out across his lap and the sheets.

He touched a strand of hair hanging in her face, and she flinched. Pulling off him with a pop, she pointedly looked at him. "No grabbing my hair," she reminded him with the faint burr of someone who grew up on the southern side of the country. Her other rule had to do with touching her throat while fucking but that didn't bother him. He wasn't into perverted stuff; he just wanted to ram his cock into her mouth until he came. Then, in a few minutes, do the same in her pussy.

Leaning back, Derik decided to enjoy the blow job. In a few minutes, he planned to fuck her, and he could wait. "Life is—"

The door slammed open, wood cracking as it snapped off one hinge.

Derik jumped. The movement caused his cock to scrape against her teeth, and he let out a high-pitched scream as he scrambled to be free of her toothy maw.

She did the same, her hands against his thighs as she pulled herself off. She sat up and spun around so fast, her large breasts smacked Derik on the side of the head, and the momentum carried her top-heavy figure to slide off the side of the bed. She landed with an inarticulate screech that ended in a swear.

Whimpering, Derik grabbed his crotch and felt for damage. Shaking, he glanced down in fear that he would see blood. He only saw her lipstick at the base of his cock and let out a sigh of relief.

The door creaked open before landing heavily on the ground. The impact shook the wooden floor and the sturdy bed Derik had rented for an hour. He looked up as he saw movement on the other side. "I paid for an hour! It's only been three...."

The words died in his throat as a thriban squeezed through the door frame. A distant cousin to humanity, thriban were large and gray-skinned. Every one Derik had known was muscular, hairy, and smelled like a skunk. Compared to his own slender size, it looked like an ogre entering the room.

He gulped and pushed himself up against the headboard. "What the fuck is going on?"

The thriban looked at him with yellowed eyes. His skin shone darkly, making the shadows on his gray face deep and evil. He stepped aside to let a large human entered the room.

At the sight of the leather jacket and dirty blond hair, Derik clamped his mouth tightly. A ripple of fear tightened his sphincter and his cock wilted underneath his hand.

It was Rick Thrantas, also known as The Man Who Ran The Entire Underworld In Town and Shouldn't be Fucked With.

Derik stammered as he sat back down with whatever dignity he could muster. With a shaking hand, he grabbed a sheet from the bed and jammed it into his crotch. "R-Rick!? What are you doing here?"

Rick looked around the room with a scowl on his face. He had a rugged face, kind of a dark shadow under his unwashed hair that somehow still looked good . He filled his jacket like a body-builder, and it creaked with every movement. The floor shook with his footsteps, the heavy, steel-tipped boots punching the ground with every step as he entered the room.

He had a presence, not only as the King of the Underworld but something about him made Derik want to shut up and do whatever he said. More than the threat of death or beatings, Derik had the disturbing sense that Rick was more than a man.

Derik started to open his mouth to say something else, but Rick silenced him with a glance.

The intruder's dark blue eyes bore into Derik. The scowl never changed but the air in the room grew tight and suffocating.

Gulping, Derik tried not to think of the horror stories about Rick. Being pinned to the headboard with nothing but a glare brought a sense of humility and fear to Derik. He struggled to breathe so he opened his mouth to pant.

Rick continued to say nothing as he looked around the room. His eyes focused on the pile of clothes scattered on the floor, then up at Derik, before sliding over to the trembling whore in the corner.

Derik breathed a sigh of relief when Rick stopped looking at him. He glanced at the window to his side. It was cracked open, Derik made sure of that when he rented out the room. It was always important to have an exit planned.

As if knowing his thoughts, the thriban walked over to the window and stood in front of it. He flexed his powerful arms over his chest. At the sight of the pectorals jumping with the movement, Derik glanced away. No escape there.

In the corner, the whore whimpered and crouched behind the corner of a dresser, her thong offering little coverage and her large breasts quivering with her fear.

Rick's mouth twitched for a moment, almost a smile.

Derik blanched. He had never seen Rick smile. He had never heard of Rick smiling.

The powerful crime lord reached down and picked up the door with one hand. One foot slipped back and the muscles of his leg tensed with the effort to brace himself. Without taking his eyes off the whore, he jammed it back into the frame.

Even with the minor flaw of balancing himself, the action was terrifying.

Derik's vision blurred. He took a deep breath, trying to find some way to escape with all his limbs intact. "L-Look, Rick, I have another week—"

Rick's eyes snapped to the side to glare at Derik, silencing him.

Reflexively, Derik pushed back against the headboard in an attempt to escape.

"The deadline was last week, Derik." Rick had a deep, powerful voice.

"Last... last week?" Derik shook his head. "What do you mean? I own you money on the 7th—"

"It's the 17th, idiot. We have a ten day week and you are exactly a week late." His voice had a deep rumbling quality to it as he sat down on the end of the bed. The straw mattress sank down heavily.

Derik started to slide toward him and let out a whimper. He grabbed the headboard as if it would stop him. His cock wilted even further as he imagined being killed in the bed and left naked for the maid.

He silently counted the days. He had done the Silthsdotter job on the 9th, then the.... He let out a low groan. Fuck. "Look, Rick—"

"Shut up."

Derik snapped his mouth closed so fast he bit the end of his tongue.

Rick glared at Derik as he dug into his pocket.

Derik, terrified that Rick would bring out a knife, cracked his knuckles against the headboard.

Rick pulled out a small notebook. "Look, you own me fifty thousand marks last week."

Derik whimpered and clutched his balls through the sheet. Oh, shit, oh shit.

"And I'm not known for being pleasant with people who forget to pay me."

"Rick—"

His voice cut me down, "Say another word and you'll be choking on your dick."

Derik closed his mouth with a snap.

Rick open the notebook to a bookmarked page. "Now, I know you are a damn good thief, Derik, but you are a fucking idiot. More importantly, you are a fucking idiot with my money."

Derik almost said something and then whimpered.

Rick looked at him sharply.

Trying to look away, Derik found he couldn't escape the dark blue eyes.

"And you've done a few good jobs for me in the past, so I am giving you one," he spat out the word, "more chance. You have three weeks to get my money back, plus interest."

Interest? Derik groaned inwardly but he wasn't stupid enough to say no to Rick when he was naked and helpless.

"Understand?"

Derik nodded. He was already planning on escaping. Just stop by the safe house and grab his lock picks and then right out—

"And if you run, I will send Bruk here to break your legs and arms before dragging you back."

Derik gasped and blushed. He nodded frantically. He glanced at Bruk, the large ogre that happened to be a thriban.

Bruk smiled broadly back, the tiny tusks of his mouth peeking up from his lower lip. With deliberate slowness, he cracked his knuckles; it sounded like someone breaking a tree in half.

Derik shivered, then looked back at Rick. Seeing his piercing eyes, Derik looked away like a child being beaten.

"Three weeks, bring what you can, it might save your skin. Might let you walk out of my place."

Derik shivered at the memory of the last person who owned Rick too much money and couldn't pay it. He saw her every time he walked past Rick's tower. It looked like a stone statue but he knew that it wasn't exactly hollow inside. Derik was there when the poor bitch was transformed and the screams still gave him nightmares.

Realizing that he attention had slipped, he looked up at Rick who had turned his attention to the prostitute.

"You done with her?" asked Rick.

Derik glanced over at the whore.

She stared back, frightened and terrified. Her pretty, brown eyes begged him to say no, to make Rick go away.

He looked over at Rick.

The powerful man slowly turned to face Derik. The sharp gaze stole the thief's breath away with the powerful gaze.

Unwilling to face Rick's wrath, Derik nodded. "Um... yeah."

The whore whimpered, but Rick just grinned at Derik.

"Thanks, man, threatening pussies like you always makes me horny."

Derik's sphincter tightened even more.

Rick motioned for her to approach.

She shook her head and she crawled further into the corner, her naked leg curling over her protectively. Tears ran down her cheeks.

He just sighed. "I'm not going to hurt you, I just haven't been introduced. I'm Rick and I own all the whores in this town. I own all the asses that sin in this town, including Derik's."

Reaching out, he snapped his fingers and held out his hand to help her up.

Despite the fear on her face, she cringed but took his hand. She let out a gasp as she was pulled to her feet.

Rick looked her over, his eyes and fingers probing at her naked body. "You look too good to be on the streets. What are you charging?"

"F-Fifty marks."

"No, charge ten times more, do you hear?" His rough voice was almost comforting compared to the threatening tone he had given Derik. "Who do you work for?"

"N-No one."

He smacked her lightly on the cheek.

She whimpered. "Y-You."

"That's right. After all this, I want you to head over to Kerlis—"

Derik flinched at the hated name.

"—and tell him to treat you right. Do you understand? No less than five hundred a fuck."

The whore blinked and wiped the tears. "Y-Yes... sir."

Rick reached back to thread his fingers into her blond hair and force her to turn her toward Derik and the bed. "Mind if I enjoy myself on your tab?"

Derik knew that she would be begging if he looked up. But he wasn't going to tell Rick no to anything, he might wake up in the morning hanging from his balls outside of Rick's tower. With a gulp, he gestured to her tight, fuckable ass. "G-Go ahead, Rick."

He chuckled, and grabbed her head tightly with both hands. Without even trying, he angled her head up so they were looking at each other. "On your knees and unzip me."

Whimpering, she reached up to his crotch. Her fingers worked at his pants, unbuttoning the fly and pulling his cock out. She sank to her knees before it finally came out. The heavy length thumped down against Rick's thigh and on the whore's shoulder.

Derik gasped. "Holy fuck!"

He considered himself reasonably sized, but Rick was gigantic. To Derik, it looked like the arm of a small child with a huge, swollen fist, easily twice as long and double the girth of Derik's rapidly shrinking cock.

The whore let out a gasp. She tried to pull away, but he just grabbed her tightly before forcing his swelling cock into her mouth.

"Both of you need to remember, I own this fucking town. You don't work on your own, you work for me." He yanked her down, driving half of his length into her tightly stretched lips. He relaxed slightly, letting her pull off with a gasp, but only gave her a mere moment before yanking her back down.

Rick hadn't heard her "no grabbing my head and neck" rule, but he wouldn't have cared anyway. He forced his cock further into her mouth until it seemed to buckle at the back of her throat. Gagging, she struggled against the thickness. Then, there was an audible pop as he drove her face down into the thick thatch of his pubic hair, her throat bulging with his massive member.

He let out a moan and leered at Derik. His hands held her skull tightly, grinding her down into his base, suffocating her as she struggled. Her hands pounded against his thighs as he let out another long sigh, still watching Derik's face.

Slowly, he let her pull off. She gasped for air, drool dribbling down her chin. Rick gave her only a few seconds again before he forced his cock back into her throat. This time, it only buckled for a second before popping in. He held her down again for a long count before letting her up for air. Then impaled her once again. Hard and brutal, he fucked her mouth until tears shone on her cheeks. Her makeup ran in black streaks as she gasped for air between thrusts.

He continued to fuck her, driving her down faster and faster, holding her down longer and longer until finally he let out a grunt and ground down on her, pinning her on his cock as he came inside her.

She struggled, her face turning red then almost purple as he finally released a long shuddering sigh.

His rough fingers finally released her, and she yanked herself off his cock, choking and gasping for air until cum and drool dripped from her painted lips.

As she started to regain her breath, Rick forced her to her feet by pulling on her hair. She let out a shriek of shock as he picked her up and threw her into the bed. Her face hit the sheets, her breasts slapping against Derik's legs, they were as soft as he had hoped. Earlier he had hoped to enjoy them, but it didn't look like it would be an option any longer.

Rick kicked apart her legs.

She started to push up from the bed when he grabbed her hair, spinning it once around his left hand like reins, and then slammed his hips forward. Derik couldn't see what happened, but her eyes opened widely, bulging as a strangled scream erupted from her mouth.

He drove his massive cock into her with one stroke.

Derik shuddered from the impact with the bed.

She grabbed at the sheets as her eyes bulged out. Her fingers caught Derik's thigh and she dug in, fingernails breaking the skin.

Rick just drove into her, no foreplay, no nothing but hard, brutal thrusts.

The whore's mouth opened into a wide "O" as he vented his passions, filling the room with wet slurping noises as he drove into her.

Derik could only watch, pinned by him using her. Then, he realized Rick wasn't fucking her pussy. Instead, his massive rod tore into her ass, plunging into it with hard strokes that must be ripping her open.

Rick pounded her for close to five minutes before letting out a bellowing grunt. He shoved forward, his muscles bulging as he rammed as much of his inhuman cock into her colon and came hard inside her.

Derik jerked with each of the whore's cries, knowing that she was responding to hot jets of cum filling her.

With a grunt, Rick pulled out.

The whore slumped forward, whimpering into the bed. Cum poured out of her gaping asshole. It splattered against the sheets and dripping down to the floor.

Rick eyes focused back on Derik, then he reached for him.

Derik let out a cry and tried to dodge but Rick easily caught him by the throat.

With a wrench, Rick yanked him out of the bed and threw on the ground into the puddle of rapidly cooling cum. Derik managed to scramble to his knees before Rick grabbed his long hair and twisted it around, just like he had done with the whore's. With a snarl, the powerful man yanked Derik closer.

Derik found myself staring at his cock, huge and massive, dripping with cum. He had balls the size of fists. The dripping length looked more like some sort of weapon than anything that belonged attached to any living being. The thick veins pulsed with Rick's heartbeat and it darkened visibly as Derik watched in horror.

Rick leaned down to snarl at him. "Three weeks, Derik. If you don't have my money, I'm going to fuck you like this whore. But I'm not going to stop because I cum. I'm going to rape that pretty little mouth and ass of yours one day for every fucking mark you owe me!"

He threw Derik against the wall.

Derik struck it and slumped down. Stars floated across his vision.

"And I won't be as gentle."

Derik whimpered. Rick had been gentle? Trembling, he glanced at the woman on the bed, cum still dribbling from her gasping asshole.

She slid to the floor and tried to push her naked body away from Rick. Black raccoon eyes and tears marked her face as she stared up with a look of abject fear.

Rick looked down at her, and the corner of his lips twitched. Slowly, he lifted his gaze back on Derik. "Where's your money?"

Derik really didn't want to answer, but he pointed to his pants.

Bruk lumbered over and pawed through them, pulling out a black wallet. Derik had nearly a thousand marks in there. The thriban took it all, tossed the empty wallet aside, and handed the bills to Rick.

Rick counted it for a moment, then handed all of it to the whore —over twenty times what Derik paid her.

She stared at him with surprise, but her fingers clutched the bills tightly.

"Services rendered. Talk to Kerlis, and blackball Derik here for at least a month while you are at it. No, make it a year. This little fuck doesn't deserve to hire a pretty ass like yours."

Derik's lips tightened into a thin line. Fucking bastard.

Rick pointed at him and Derik dropped his look. "Three weeks, Derik, or you're going to be choking on my cock for a long time."

He walked out, shutting the door behind me.

Derik sat on the floor for a long moment, before getting to his feet.

The whore took longer to get up, shuddering as she pressed one hand against her no doubt aching ass. She glared at him with her no-longer innocent brown eyes.

Derik glanced away. "S-Sorry." It wasn't his fault that Rick had fucked her.

She slapped him. Before Derik could recover, she kicked him in the balls repeatedly until he collapsed in half with stars blinding him.

Then she did it again.

The Family Silver

Derik groaned as he cracked open one eye. He peered at the ceiling of the cheap hotel. A piercing headache throbbed in the back of his head. It was too much effort to fight it and he drifted in and out of a daze. His gloriously long, black hair spread out in a sunburst around his head, rippling off the edges of the straw mattress and touching the floor. One of his sheets had wrapped around his leg, but he couldn't find the energy to crawl out of the warm covering.

He pressed one delicate hand against his face, still peering at the ceiling through his fingers while his other fumbled with the rickety nightstand that leaned against the wall. Catching the edge of a bottle of rotgut with his fingertips, he pulled it closer, then sat up to drink it. His face wrinkled with distaste as he finished the bottle and tossed it aside. It hit the wall, but didn't break.

He snarled silently and flopped back down on the bed. "Damn, I could use a whore right now."

He scratched himself, working his fingers around his shaft. Idly masturbating for a moment, he finally got the energy to sit up again. His long black hair pooled in his lap and he ran it through his fingers, enjoying the silky strands along his sensitive fingertips. In the back of his mind, he remembered how the blond woman's hair caressed his thighs and a smile crossed his lips. Almost instantly, he remembered Rick's invasion and the smile disappeared.

"Fuck it. Better get moving, only eighteen days left."

Over a week had passed. He already tried to pick up a pair of cheap prostitutes, but they snubbed him as soon as they realized he was blackballed. Derik pulled another face and glared at the room in general. He couldn't even get a street urchin to give him a hand-job, not that he would after the latest crackdown on loli sex. Consent, the child goddess, running around and slaughtering everyone for raping little children did wonders for making anyone even close to age of eighteen not even remotely interesting.

Staggering out of bed, he found a clean pair of clothes and pulled them on. Tight jeans—dyed black—clung to his ass and a white shirt showed off the nearly flawless skin of his chest and shoulders, with just a bit of chest hair, to show he was a real man. He grinned and brushed his hair out and tied it back with a simple black leather tie.

Feeling presentable, he admired himself in the mirror, then abandoned his room. He considered locking it, but dirty clothes, empty wine bottles giving the burn of a three-day old brew, and a dirty sheets weren't worth the effort to steal. He chuckled to himself as he took the stairs, his boots rapping sharply on the wooden steps.

In the entry hall, he looked around for his ever-present thriban shadow. Bruk, who dogged him every step for the last twelve days, couldn't be found, and Derik let a smile cross his lips. Without grabbing breakfast, he hurried out of the main hall and into the busy streets. His destination was the Bone Gate, not the closest gate, but one near the poor district of town. He carefully avoided the guards wearing the uniform of Baron Hamel, the local lord known for his intolerance of thieves, and the known spots where Rick's underworld thrived with business. He actually hummed as he slipped through the crowds, relieving some of a few marks as he passed. By the time he reached the Bone Gate, he was a hundred marks richer and almost floating across the hard-pounded dirt.

Reaching the gate, he looked around for his shadow and let out a sigh of relief. Ducking his head, he pushed his way into a thick knot of farmers and followed them as they made their way out of the gate.

He almost made it.

Just as he reached the shadows of the Bone Gate, a deep clearing of a throat froze the entire crowd. As one, everyone looked at the massive thriban standing in the center of the opening while looking pointedly down the center of the lane.

Derik swore to himself as the crowds parted, instantly melting away to leave him standing alone in the center, with Bruk chuckling as he hefted a large, metal-banded club in his hand.

"Morning, Derik."

Derik blushed and laughed as smoothly as he could. "Bruk! How are you? I was just going for a stroll."

It didn't even sound like a real lie.

Bruk shrugged and let the club head drop to the ground. Even from the ten paces away, Derik could feel the impact through the ground. "Just going for a brisk walk?"

A casual question, but the thief could hear the menace. A cold shiver dripped down his spine as he stared at the bulging muscles and the evil grin.

"Um, no, just checking out a mark."

Bruk scanned the gathered crowds with yellow eyes. A quarter of a hundred farmers desperately wanted to get out of the gate but didn't dare pass the thriban. Even the other thriban farmers were unwilling to pass him. A few of them glanced at him and their attention grated on Derik's senses; he was not in a position where he wanted to stand out from the crowds.

Derik backed up slightly. "Look, I'm going to check out somewhere else, okay?"

Bruk nodded, "You do that. Wouldn't want you to get hurt."

Threat delivered, Derik grunted in acknowledgment and fled back into the city. As soon as he disappeared from sight of the Bone Gate, he ran. Dodging between tightly pressed bodies, he managed to gather up another fifty marks before hopping on a straw cart. Before the driver or the mule pulling it could notice, he jumped up on the awning of a store and then up to the roof.

Grinning gleefully, he sprinted across the rooftops, heading for another city gate, the Shell Gate, which stood right at the junction of the river and the city's northern wall.

Thirty minutes of flat-out running left him gasping for breath as he leaned against a chimney and stared at the massive gate. A carved shell in the center of the door represented the namesake of the door, but he was more focused on the thriban who stood in front of it, hefting his massive club and looking around curiously.

Fuck! How did he get there so fast!? Bruk wasn't even breathing heavily.

Derik groaned and leaned against the brick, catching his breath as he tried to estimate how fast he could get to the Wood Gate.

Wasn't worth it.

"Fuck," he repeated.

Slower this time, he hopped back along the roof and started to walk back toward the poor side of town. His mood darkened, despite the sunny day, and he found himself spitting at pedestrians below as he followed the line of stores and houses.

By the time he reached the Buggered Unicorn, his favorite tavern, he was in such a foul mood that a raincloud almost literally followed him. Hopping on the sign, he jumped down and landed on the ground neatly. Pushing open the door, he ignored the sign that said they were closed until sunset and disappeared inside.

The Buggered Unicorn smelled like home to Derik, and he let the scents of the old wood, bourbon, and beer fill his nostrils. A ghost of a smile crossed his lips.

One end of the tavern held a large wooden bar, lined with glasses and bottles. Behind it, an older man in his thirties peered over a small set of glasses and smiled sadly. "Wondering when you'd show up, Derik."

A blush colored his cheeks. He stepped carefully over to the bar and sat down. "Hi, Storn, how are you doing?"

Storn shoved a few glasses out of the way to pour Derik a beer, then pushed the glass toward him. "Kind of sad actually, wished you'd been here last week."

"Why?"

"I heard about your troubles with Rick."

Derik's good mood evaporated instantly. His fingers clutched the handle of his glass and he let out a long sigh. "Fuck."

Storn said nothing so Derik looked up.

"How'd you know?"

"Everyone knows, Derik. He's the king of the underworld and someone you don't screw with. And you blew every mark you owned him on whores and booze. We all know. Every damn thief, hustler, and fence."

Derik groaned and lowered his head to press his forehead against the glass. "Fuck me more."

"Rather not, it would piss off Wendi."

Derik raised a delicately arched eyebrow. "How is your sister?"

"Still wants to castrate you."

"And your mother?"

"Still wants to fuck you."

"Well, I guess that always—"

Storn cleared his throat, "And if you flee to her, I'll tell Wendi and my brothers where you are."

Derik shivered. "That's cold."

The older man shrugged, "You left her at the altar, Derik."

"I panicked."

"And took the family silver too?"

Derik blushed deeply and he rapped his head against the glass, feeling the cool beer against his face. "I really panicked, okay?"

Storn reached over and pressed two fingers against the bottom of Derik's chin.

For a moment, the thief resisted, then let his friend tilt his head. He found himself staring into the green-brown eyes of the bartender.

"Look, Derik, I love you as a brother. That is the only reason that I still talk to you after everything you did. But, you need to get a handle on your life."

Derik's blush deepened.

Storn released his chin before sighing. "Look, why didn't you come here after Rick? I could have helped you."

"I-I-", Derik sputtered for a moment, "I hate asking you for help, Storn."

"But you always come here. I heard about your troubles and managed to line up a couple of jobs. Would have gotten you free and clear in a week, but someone else grabbed them."

"Who?"

"Some new thief on the block, calls himself the Shadow Wasp."

Derik snorted with laughter.

Storn, on the other hand, didn't look amused. "Problem with the name, 'Silk Spider'?"

The icy tone silence Derik. He pouted for a moment. "I haven't used that name in three years, Storn."

"Yeah, but all new thieves go through it. And he's moving pretty fast up the ranks. Less of an acrobat as yourself, but a pretty good boxer."

"I hate safes."

"Yeah, and I found a great job for you. But then you didn't show up for a week, and he took it. Damn it, Derik, get a hang of yourself and stop doing this two-bit crap!"

Derik could hear the frustrating in Storn's face, but couldn't say anything. He turned away as the door to the tavern opened. Seeing the bulk of Bruk, he groaned and turned back to his beer.

The thriban sat down next to him.

Storn nodded. "Morning, Gluk, how's things?"

Derik looked up. Gluk?

He considered saying something else wittier, but it came out as he thought. "Gluk?"

Bruk, or Gluk, he wasn't sure how, chuckled dryly as Storn handed him a large beer. Unlike Derik, the thriban pushed a few marks over the counter in return.

"Yeah, didn't you know?"

Derik looked at Storn, then at the grinning thriban. "Um, know what?"

"Gluk is Bruk's brother."

"Brother...."

Gluk grinned and drained his mug. Slamming it down, he sighed happily. "Delicious, Storn."

Storn grunted.

Derik let out a soft whimper as he looked back and forth. "You mean, there are two of them?"

Gluk laughed for a moment, "Three, actually, but Truk is the pretty one."

Derik looked at the massive muscles on the thriban, then focused on the fangs that peeked out from the lower lip. A face that only a mother could stomach, despite the raw strength of Gluk, and apparently his brothers.

"P-Pretty one?"

"Yeah, Truk is the pretty one, but she's also nastier than either of us."

The idea of a female thriban left Derik feeling cold. He shuddered at the thought of the few naked thribans he'd seen. All muscles and hair; he suspected that he didn't want to see a shaved thriban in his life, but it might be better than the mess of curls between their legs.

Gluk chuckled, "Pretty boy is getting sick."

Derik blushed and looked away. "I am not."

Gluk just laughed again, a booming laugh that vibrated the glass.

Derik waited until it grew softer, then looked pleadingly at Storn. "Is there anything?"

"Only the nasty jobs."

Derik almost got up, then he looked over at the thriban enforcer. "Fuck, I need the money. Fifty thousand."

"Eighty," corrected Gluk.

Derik's heart stopped for a mere moment and he clutched the glass tighter. "Eighty thousand marks?"

Gluk gave him an apologetic shrug, "Sorry, interest."

Derik groaned and bowed his head. "Fine, any job over eighty?"

Storn nodded, "Three of them, but you really shouldn't do any of them."

"Hit me."

He glared at Gluk, just in case the thriban took it as a suggestion.

The tall creature chuckled and drained another beer.

Storn rolled his eyes. "Well, there is the longest one. Survive Shiel. Two hundred thousand if you can make it past the month, a hundred days. An extra ten thousand for every month after that."

Derik choked, "Shiel? She's a monster!"

"No, she isn't, she's just a good bounty hunter."

"She broke Baston's legs and arms, and that was because he managed to evade her for a week! A week! Do you know what she would do to me if I managed to escape a month!?"

Gluk chuckled. "Probably rip your arms and legs off, turn you into a pillow boy."

Derik snapped back, "That isn't even funny!"

Gluk grinned. "It is to us. Truk says she would love sleeping on your pretty little body."

For a moment, Derik growled, then his face froze. "Us?"

Gluk grinned, "Yeah, we're triplets. Got that whole mind-reading thing going on. Psychic siblings."

It took another long second for that to register. "God damn. That is why you kept showing up; you can talk to each other."

"And you can't run faster than thoughts, boy. Face it, you screw up and your ass is Rick's."

Derik's anal ring clenched up at the thought. "I don't want that."

Gluk shrugged, "I don't want that. It will take weeks to get your screams out of my head."

It sounded sincere, and Derik stared at him in surprise.

Gluk shrugged. "What? You are going to be like a little cunt when he breaks you. High-pitched and with all the sobbing. We're just betting how long it takes before you ask one of us to take your life."

Derik's mouth closed with a snap. "Thanks, you bastard."

Gluk grinned, "Thank you."

Ignoring the thriban, he turned back to his friend. "What else that isn't suicide?"

"Well, the Eye of Hamel."

Gluk gasped. "You mean the fist-sized sapphire that is perfect for enchanting. The one hanging from the baron's constantly occupied great hall?"

"Yes, everyone knows that."

"No, I'm reading it on a poster behind you." The thriban pointed to a torn piece of paper nailed to one of the boards.

Storn rolled his eyes. "Two million marks, I could have a buyer in three days."

"There are standing orders to torture anyone who tries. No thanks, what else?"

Storn looked away suddenly, grabbing a mug to polish.

Derik frowned, feeling a very bad sense of danger in the pit of his stomach. "Storn?"

Storn glanced over to Derik, "Why don't you go for the Eye, Derik? You are a great thief, you can make it."

"What's the third?"

Storn hesitated. "Wendi."

Derik's mouth dropped as Gluk roared with laughter. The peals of laughter filled the room for a long moment before Derik cleared his throat.

"E-Excuse me?"

Storn sighed, "Wendi. She'll clear your debt if you hand your ass over to her. She made the offer herself when she heard about you."

"That would be a living hell! She'd kill me!"

Storn shook his head, "Probably not. Dad's a necromancer, remember?"

Gluk burst into another roaring laugh.

Derik just groaned and dropped his head to the bar. "Fuck. He's involved?"

"You fucked my mom on your wedding altar a few minutes before the ceremony, and the entire family walked in. That's kind of hard to put aside."

Gluk bent over with laughter, clutching his side as he fell to the ground.

Derik, blushing brightly, looked down at the thriban.

He sighed. "Fuck."

Ignoring the thriban rolling on the floor, he looked up in depression. "Eye of Hamel, huh?"

In the twenty minutes that followed, Derik got the details he needed, and Storn promised to send more with Gluk.

The thriban staggered back to his feet and sat down on the stool, smirking as he ordered a round for him and Derik.

Slightly buzzed, Derik finally pushed himself away from the bar. Groaning with the weight of the world, he waved to Storn.

Storn called to him. "Look, Derik. After this, why don't we sit down? You really need someone to help you stop screwing up your life. This should have never happened."

"Yeah, yeah. I'll make a good score, then I'll settle down."

Gluk snorted, but said nothing.

Derik turned quickly but instead of striding through the door with his dignity, he ran ran into someone. Reflexively, he held up his hands to stop himself and his palms pressed tightly against a pair of very large breasts. He squeezed without thinking. The size and heft were familiar, but it wasn't until the hard nipple with a the tiny cross piercing that pressed into his palm that he realized he knew the owner of the magnificent tits.

His eyes focused on a surprised woman standing in the door. "Wendi?"

Wendi was a curvy woman, not skinny but not fat. She wore leather armor and a corset, which gave her an hourglass figure that nearly stopped Derik's heart again. Her dark hair shimmered in the light of the fading sun as a flame burned in her eyes.

Her look of surprise turned into one of fury. "Derik," it came out as an epitaph, a year's worth of hatred burning in a single word.

"Um, hi. How are you?"

"Suddenly better."

Behind her, two large men glared at him. They were nowhere near the size of Gluk and Bruk, but much larger than Derik's slender form.

He groaned. "And your brothers, brought them too?"

She shoved him back and he fell to the ground. Winching at the impact, he crawled backwards, his hair mopping the floor as he looked between the three siblings with growing fear.

"Um, can't we talk about this?"

A clear flame rose up around Wendi as her eyes turned incandescent. Power beat on the air as the battle mage, the girl he once loved, brought her powers to bear.

"You fucked my mother!"

Gluk laughed loudly again. "Stop, this is killing us!"

For a brief microsecond, Derik remembered the feeling of the soft breasts wrapped around his cock, and their shared grunting right on the altar. However, the brief flicker of a smile on his lips only ignited Wendi's anger even more.

Snarling, she pulled out a long hunting knife and lunged for him.

Derik let out a scream as he tried to dodge it, but his feet caught on his hair and he fell to the ground.

A ham-sized hand grabbed her wrist, halting her.

Shuddering from fear, Derik looked up to see Gluk holding her hand.

"No knives," announced the thriban in a low, amused tone.

Derik let out a gasp. "Thank you, Gl—"

"Just beat him up properly, no broken bones though."

Derik gaped, "What!?"

Wendi grinned at Gluk, then favored Derik with an evil smirk. "Doing a job for Rick, huh? I never thought you'd get that desperate."

Whimpering, Derik nodded.

Wendi bent over, her massive breasts almost obscuring his vision. She whispered to him, "You know, I'll bail you out. No matter the cost."

The very idea of selling his soul to Wendi terrified him more than anything else. He looked over at the bar, pleadingly toward Storn.

His long-time friend shook his head. "My family owned that silver for nine generations, Derik. Nine generations. You may be a friend, but you aren't that much of one."

Wincing, he turned back to Wendi who cracked her knuckles. Whimpering loudly, he took a long breath and shook his head.

Wendi looked almost disappointed as she cracked her knuckles again. The raw, beating power silenced though as she prepared to beat him to the ground using nothing but her anger. Her two brothers, still furious over the minor thing he did had done on the altar, closed the door and locked it.

She turned to him as she stripped off her leather top, revealing a silk blouse under her corset. The nipple piercing pressed against the fabric, a black cross of the battle mage. "This is going to hurt you a lot more than me, Derik."

Wendi cleared her throat. "Who am I kidding, this is only going to hurt you."

The Master Thief

High above the Baron Hamel's great hall hung an incredibly beautiful and flawless sapphire, a perfect sphere without a single facet
along the brilliant blue surface. Rumor said it was polished on the
thighs of a hundred virgins. Derik suspected closer to thirty, and
probably only technical virgins. And maybe not even their thighs.

He didn't care if they sat on it like an egg. The gem was flawless.

In a world where perfect objects had the ability to enhance magic, the sapphire was the most desired crystal in all the country. The
two million marks offered for the job was a fraction of its true value.

He sighed softly as he stared at its beauty, almost the same color
as his eyes, but somehow more ethereal than he could ever imagine. Four massive statues, each one easily ten meters in height,
stood around the sapphire. Carved in the shape of a dragon-like
ferret, it somehow gave the impression of strength and absurdity
that marked Hamel's belief that you should never take him for
granted. Each statue held out a paw toward a single point where
the gemstone was balanced on all four points.

Above the crystal burned an intense magical flame, a pinpoint
opening into the realm of fire. The brilliant white light was hot
enough to ignite flesh for anyone who lingered more than a second
underneath it.

Below the sapphire, the statues held a large sheet of stained
glass parallel to the floor. The baron had the entire barony
mapped out in lead so the magical light that shone down would
cast a blue-tinted image of the map on the floor of his great hall.
Stealing the sapphire would turn the map a different color and the

six, heavily-armed guards who patrolled the great hall at all hours would instantly notice something messing with the priceless treasure.

The sapphire was perfectly displayed in plain sight, but only the stupidest thief in the world would risk stealing it. If the guards with crossbows weren't enough, the statue arms, a seemingly perfect stepping place, spewed both magical flame and acid with the slightest of pressure. The flame above the gem was just as dangerous, able to burn away flesh and bone in seconds but inflict no damage on the priceless gem.

Derik let out another chuckle of amusement as he crouched in the shadows of the great room, balanced on a thin ledge five meters above the ground. His slender body was wrapped in dark gray fabric, clinging to his body so tightly he couldn't even wear underwear. The only other color were his blue eyes and the intricate stitchery along the hands and feet of his outfit.

He swallowed, mentally preparing for the worst. But, he couldn't make a mistake. There was too much at stake, including his own life if he screwed up.

There was also the fear of Rick.

Or even worse, Wendi. If it wasn't for Gluk paying for the healer while adding the cost to his debt, he'd still be in traction and she would be gloating. She and her brothers had worked him over pretty hard, and his bones still ached from their beating.

He shuddered at the thought and inspected the ceiling. Despite the guards patrolling, he had managed to cross the mosaic ceiling a number of times to place nearly invisible brackets made of glass into the cracks in the stone. Another few trips gave him the opportunity to thread a transparent rope through each of the brackets. They rope hung down into air, their length almost invisible.

The rope was the most expensive available. He had stolen it from an artificer's shop two nights ago.

He gazed across the space. From his perch, he knew more than saw the short lengths before him. Grab the rope there, swing there, catch the next one. A series of short swings would bring him under the flames, above the glass, and right in the perfect spot to swap the crystal out. He couldn't see all the ropes from his position, but he knew where they were. Just a few simple swings, and he would be millions richer.

Beyond the stone, a small ledge on the far wall marked ten openings into the ventilation system. He had opened them all to make it harder for anyone to follow him, but he had his plans set on the fifth from the right.

He worked a large blue glass sphere from a small bag at his waist. It was not as perfect as the sapphire above, but it would be close enough to avoid the guards' attention for a few minutes. By then, the magical flame would have melted the glass or they would notice the changed color. He planned on being long gone before either happened.

His eyes probed the floor below, watching the guards moving in their almost graceful patrol, shifting and turning almost unexpectedly. A dance that left no moment with the floor unprotected. Except one.

Derik had watched the patrol for hours to find the pattern to their movement. He would have the longest moment of uninterrupted movement, less than a minute, when both of them would have their backs away from the map. Then, he would replace it.

Imagining the swing in his head. he hefted the glass and held it firmly in his left hand. With his right, he stroked the translucent rope and prepared to swing out into empty space. If he missed once, he would fall five meters to either death or imprisonment.

Heart pounding, he took a deep breath and stepped out into space.

Gravity yanked him down, but he held the rope tightly. It jerked against his shoulder but then swung him forward. He took a deep breath and waited until it hit the length of the pendulum swing before releasing it. He snapped his hand out where the next rope should be and easily caught it.

Halfway across the room in less than a second, the sapphire rushed up, and his heart seemed to slow as he reached out to grab the priceless stone.

His hand passed through the beam of light shining down on the gem, and pain exploded along his wrist. The light was so bright that he saw his bones. Stifling a scream of pain, he grabbed the hot sapphire and swung out of the light. When he reached the apex of his swing, he swapped the glass and gemstone in his hand. His wrist already burned red from an instance in the light.

Shuddering, he swung back. This time, he braced himself and pulled his hand back. He tossed the glass into the light, careful not to expose himself to the burning agony once again.

He swung to the end and then back again. By the time he reached the next rope, he had carefully placed the sapphire in a pocket, and he could maneuver to safety with both hands.

Derik swung a few more times before landing lightly on the narrow ledge on the opposite side of the room. Heart still pounding, he wasted no time racing along the ledge and diving into the opening. One edge caught his uniform and it tore from the momentum.

He came to a halt inside the ventilation of the baron's castle by bracing himself against both walls. He grinned to himself, shaking with the adrenaline pumping through his veins. It would take hours before they found out–

A faint popping noise interrupted his congratulations. He glanced back down the shaft in time to see a large hunk of the ceiling break off and plummet, shattering the map glass before slamming into the floor with enough force to shake the entire building.

"Fuck," he breathed. "I got to—"

A burning sensation on his thigh interrupted him again. He looked down to see his clothes smoking violently. The super-heated sapphire was burning his stealth outfit. Swearing silently, he jerked and the gemstone dropped to the bottom of the vent, smoldering as he tried to quietly pat out the flame.

It took a few precious seconds for him to put out the flame. By the time he finished, the heat filled the vent and sweat prickled his body. The noises in the great hall increased as more guards came running.

Derik imagined an hourglass counting down the seconds until he was discovered. He grabbed for the sapphire, only to touch the side of the vent. Surprised, he looked around and saw the priceless sapphire rolling down the vent, picking up speed as it disappeared into darkness.

"Fuck!" he whispered as softly as he could and crawled after it.

Dust burned away from the gem as it casually rolled just out of his reach.

He crawled after it, winching with every crunch of dust against his knees.

Five minutes of frantic crawling in the narrow vent left him sweating and gasping. The sapphire would roll to a stop only to start moving again just as his fingers touched it. He swore softly and chased after it.

Finally, it came to a halt, and he let out a sigh of relief. Sweat dripped from his brow and soaked into his clothes. As he stared at it, the sapphire rolled back and forth as if taunting him.

The precious stone had caught on the edge of a vent. A vent with an opened grate.

"Aw, fuck..." he whispered as the sapphire balanced on the stone edge, dancing on the edge of the dark pit below.

The flawless sapphire casually rolled over the edge and Derik lunged forward, fingers clutching. His slender body slid along the stone and he braced his feet on both edges of the opening as he caught the sapphire.

He didn't have a second to spare, dangling above the darkness of an unknown room, before the heat of the sapphire began to burn at his clothes. He stared at the dim flames as they rose up along his shirt. Flames roared up his arm, igniting it as if the magically treated cloth had been doused in oil.

Biting back a whimper of pain, he clenched his stomach and tried to roll up.

That is when, in a spat of terrible luck, the injuries Wendi gave him flared up, a spasm that sparkled along his back and made his muscles lurch. Derik's feet started to slip into the opening of the vent. Hissing, he managed to pull himself up long enough to shove the sapphire down the vent, in a safe direction he hoped, before his feet slipped off the edge. Blindly, he grabbed at the edge of the vent to pull himself up, but his clothes flared into full flame and he slipped, plummeting into the darkness, lit only by his flaming clothes.

A Bad Place

He only fell a few meters before smacking hard against the surface of some pool. Despite the agony that surged along his back, in that mere moment before he slipped under the surface, he realized that he needed to worship one of the gods, if just to curse them.

Now to find a list of gods he hated the least.

The hot water washed over him, and he hoped it would extinguish the flames on his stealth suit. It rushed against his face and nostrils, he clamped one hand over his nose to prevent from drowning and flailed around for the surface of the pool. To his surprise, his feet caught the bottom of the pool seconds later; it was only a meter in depth. Kicking up, he gasped for air as soon as his face broke through the silky surface.

He couldn't see anything, his eyes still adjusting from the brightness of the flames. Unsure if any guards were rushing toward him, he lowered himself until he remained just above the water's surface with his black hair billowing out in a cloud. He patted along his side to where his knife was, not that he knew how to fight with it, but he only encountered sensitive bare skin. The flames had destroyed his suit, and he lost his weapon in the process.

Rolling his eyes with frustration, he lowered himself into the water until it lapped at his lips and the bottom of his ears. He waited the long, painful seconds while his eyes grew accustomed to the darkness by feeling around.

The pool was relatively wide and long but shallow. It took a moment to get to the marbled edge and press his cheek against the smooth stone. The smooth, perfumed water felt luxurious against his skin compared to the harshness of the water he usually used for bathing. The scent was unusual, delicate but complex, like a mixture of many different scents he had enjoyed over the years. It also smelled slightly of sex, the musky rasp of spent passions.

His back ached from the impact. Working blindly, he explored his outfit along his side. His fingers caught the scorched edges of many rips and tears. The fire had all but destroyed the suit and only a few straining threads kept it from falling off his body. He cringed at the idea, it would be hard enough to explain why he was in the pool much less why he was in the pool naked.

Derik's questing fingers found his back. He found a lump already forming along his spine but otherwise no discernible injuries. He breathed a sigh of relief that rippled the water. He could handle a few burns along his smooth skin, but a serious injury would make it impossible to pay back Rick.

Rick scared the fuck out of him.

He lifted himself up and then gagged at the burning smell. There was no way anyone could miss smelling him if he was above the surface. With a silent snarl, he bobbed back down and breathed in the perfume.

Looking at the dim light, he tugged at the remains of his outfit from his body. The thin shreds wouldn't do anything to protect him, and he didn't think wearing smoldering rags would be any better than being naked. He ran his fingertips along his shaft before yanking the fabric clear from his tight buttocks. His long hair caught on his hands but he shook them free as he stripped.

A loud yawn interrupted his efforts.

Derik froze and looked up over the edge. At the far end of a hall he saw a light growing brighter. It bobbed slowly from a young woman carrying a lantern. The beams of brilliance that speared out from it lit up parts of the room. Derik looked at it and then when he saw the floor covered in naked women, he did a double-take.

Dozens of them, all gloriously nude, naked, and very female. There were breasts and pussies on display, some of them sprawled out on pillows while others were bent over in the casual relaxation that only sleep could bring. The women slept on blankets. Some stretched out across each other. He gasped, feeling his cock twitch to life as he stared at shadowed nipples and shaved pussies.

His eyes focused on the only one moving, a woman probably in her late teens or early twenties. She wore nothing but a silk robe that did nothing to hide her beautiful body. Yawning, she held a magical lantern over her head as her eyes drooped sleepily. Her bare feet moved with practiced grace as she made her way between the naked limbs that obscured the floor. Reaching the edge, she yawned as she disappeared down a hall and the room once again plunged into darkness.

Derik promptly decided that he needed a god to thank.

As he realized where he was, he revised his opinions again.

The baron's harem.

The forbidden harem.

The "if I get caught, I will lose my balls painfully" harem.

Baron Hamel refused to marry himself, holding out for the "perfect" wife to hang on his arm. Instead, he had a harem of nearly a hundred women, each of them living a life of sensual comfort. While most of them selected from the cream of society, the baron also accepted exotic women as part of negotiations and treaties.

Remembering the sheer amount of naked bodies before him, Derik decided that Hamel was very good at statecraft.

Slowly, he pushed himself out of the water, wincing as the water dripped off and the last ruined remains of his stealth suit slipped from his body. As the water sheeted off, the warm air caressed his bare skin. He turned around to strain as much of the remains from the water to hide his presence.

By the time he gathered up as much of his outfit as possible, nearly choking from the burnt smell, his eyes managed to adjust to the dim light. Peering around, he could only see the shadows above him, where the priceless sapphire rested inside some ventilation.

He breathed in the smells of naked women and promised he would find a god to hate later.

Creeping as quietly as he could, he sneaked to the edge of the room, hiding behind a pillar. To his luck, he found a mirror reflecting just a hint of light and used it to inspect the damage.

His slender body looked unharmed, but he missed a few strips of cloth. A burnt patch caught along his hips, barely hiding his manhood, and a few more strips held on the rest of it. Swearing in a whisper, he shrugged out his outfit and tried not to think about losing such an expensive tool of his craft.

Expensive if he actually paid for it, of course.

Despair filled him as he shoved the remains into the bottom drawer of a nearby dresser. In the dim light, he carefully fumbled around, trying to find something to cover his now-naked body. His cock, hard at the thought of the harem just steps away, bounced with each movement as he pulled open the drawers.

Soap and perfume, not even a strip of silk to cover himself.

"Fuck," he whispered. Standing up, he looked back and forth for another dresser when he caught the reflection of a woman staring at him in shock.

She had sandy brown hair and a silk robe that, spread open, revealed small, perky breasts that left him breathless. His eyes drifted down as he turned around, a blush rising up in his cheeks. Focusing on her, he saw her shaved pussy framed by her perfectly delectable legs. His cock surged to full height, swelling until it ached, as he lifted his eyes to stare at her.

"Um, hi," he whispered as softly as possible.

She cocked her head as she took a hesitant step forward.

"Why are you naked?" she whispered back.

Derik let out a sigh of relief. She didn't yell for help as the first thing. "Um, I fell down."

She glanced up and he almost managed to step out of the light of the lantern, but she stepped to the side to keep him centered on the pool of brilliance. "Okay, but why are you naked?"

Her whisper had a hint of amusement.

Derik blushed hotly and pulled his long black hair around to cover his groin, one hand holding his hardness tightly as he looked around for some escape. He gave her a helpless glance and tried to step away from her.

A sudden grin on her lips made his heart skip as she stepped forward again, following him as he tried to duck behind a pillar. "The guards will kill you if they find you."

A heat rose to warm his cheeks as he glanced up. The opening to the vents stood above him, three meters and just out of reach. Even climbing the wall, she would have too much time to call for help.

Her head still cocked, she grinned. "You're desperate, aren't you?"

Derik's head snapped to stare at her. "Um..."

She took another step toward him, the grin turning into an evil mask, the type of playful mischief that sent a shiver down his spine. "Admit it, you're fucked."

Derik tried to back away, then realized that she was almost illuminating the rest of the harem. One may play with him, but if the entire room woke up, he was screwed.

The flush burning on his cheeks, he turned back to her and nodded.

She grinned triumphantly. "Want me to help?"

Surprised, Derik just stared at her with his mouth gaped open.

The harem girl motioned for him to come back around the pillar. He obeyed, keeping his eyes locked on her as he inched his way back.

She looked in both directions. "You have to do something for me."

"Anything."

She grinned and looked down at her tight body. Her nipples were standing up straight and he caught a whiff of her pussy. "Lick me."

Derik froze, staring at her with wide eyes. "Um, what?"

She grinned, "I just went into the bathroom to frig myself, but couldn't get off. I bet you could do a perfect job, those slender hands, that pretty face."

Derik's lips parted in shock. The heat grew with every word she said. His hands trembled as he risked a glance down to her shaved mound. "I... I never did that."

She rolled her eyes. "You have to be kidding?" she whispered, "You never went down on a girl?"

Derik nodded, whispering back, "It's dirty and smelly. I mean, that's what whores—"

She interrupted him with a glare. "Well, if you don't want me to scream, you better get on your knees."

When he didn't answer, she inhaled sharply.

Wincing, Derik forced himself to his knees, feeling the warmed tile against his naked skin as he stared at the swollen lips of the harem girl. He froze, he didn't mean to, but the idea of sticking his face in there disgusted him. He looked up in hopes of finding some compassion.

She just looked down with an evil grin. She gestured with one middle finger toward her sex. "Now."

A whispered command, just on the edge of being a spoke word.

He shuddered, wincing at the sound of it. Carefully, he leaned forward, breathing in the smell of sex from her pussy. He gingerly reached up to stroke against the soft, warm skin that slid sexily against his palms.

She sighed loudly.

He inched forward, steeling himself to do it when she reached down with her other hand, twisted his hair into her fingers, and yanked him forward.

Derik couldn't even yelp before his face was pressed against her vulva, soft and slick with her juices. He gasped, pressing his palms against her thighs, but she ground his face against her pussy, spreading open her lips until his lips pressed against the tangy pinkness of her sex.

"Start licking," came the whispered command.

His cock aching with heat, he started to draw his tongue against her folds, tasting woman for the first time. It was overpowering, the smell of sex and juices. He cringed at the wetness soaking his face, but the hand in his hair refused to let him pull away.

Instead, she ground him harder against him.

"Use your tongue, damn it," she hissed loudly.

Fighting back the shame and humiliation, he used his full tongue to lap at her pussy, from ass to clitoris. At her moan, he hoped it would be enough, but her guiding hand kept him tightly against her pussy until he started to lap harder, tasting every fold until her juices dribbled down his face.

He held her thighs, feeling the muscles flexing as she adjusted in position. Derik heard a click, then her other hand pressed against his head, guiding him as she whispered commands.

"Lick there... oh... yeah, use your tongue... there..."

Her lust-filled whispers filled his hearing as he lapped and sucked, obeying to the best of his ability even as he fought down a shame of being forced into such a position.

Then she came.

Derik had never had his mouth so close to an orgasm, and he choked on the flood of juices that splashed against his face. He tried to pull back, but she held him tight against the soft flesh.

She let out a high-pitched gasp of pleasure.

He didn't know what to do, so he stopped licking. When she jerked him tightly against her, he resumed his lapping, pinned by her iron grip.

She came again, her juices splashing off his chin, before she relaxed her grip, giving him a chance to pull back. She gasped happily, "Oh... that was a good start."

Derik made a face as he wiped his mouth. He could taste her juices. It was tangier than he expected, but not entirely unexpected from the inevitable scents that came up when some whore lowered herself on his shaft. His cock, dripping hard, bobbed with each movement as he looked up at her.

She smiled, then her smile dropped when a third voice whispered over.

"Teri, what are you doing—"

Derik's head wrenched around.

Teri's hands pulled his hair down as they both looked over at another girl.

The new girl was a blonde. Her hair cascaded off her wrists as she rubbed her eyes clear.

A shiver started deep inside. It grew into a sick feeling that blossomed when Teri's hands tightened in his long black hair.

"I found him trying to escape, Sherrel. He's really desperate for some help and he's willing to earn it with his tongue."

Derik's eyes slid to look up at Teri, her swollen sex right on the edge of his vision and her juices in the back of his throat.

Fuck.

Sherrel pushed back her blond hair and peered at him. A slow smile crossed her lips as she regarded him. Derik, caught by Teri's grip in his hair, could do nothing but look back at her with pleading, helpless eyes.

"Really? How desperate?" Sherrel stood up straighter and lowered her hands. Her breasts were much larger than Teri's, swollen mounds that would fit perfectly in his palm and wrap around his cock. She would have been the perfect whore, but Derik wondered if he would ever see anything besides a prison after he escaped.

Double fuck.

In Plain Sight

Derik's tongue hurt. He looked up from the fifth woman he had been forced to service. He could still feel Teri's hand in his hair, guiding him. Her touch might have seemed comforting, except she kept holding his head against the plump pussy lips. Letting out a sigh, he opened his aching jaw and began to lap.

Soon, soft moans of pleasure rose from her body, another hand grabbed his head to guide him to her special places of pleasure. Knowing what to do, he worked his slick and slender fingers up between her legs, easing them into her slick sex and pumping with short strokes. His fingers dripped with the liquid that flowed out of her, and he curled his fingers, trying to find that spot of pleasure. He didn't at first, then he brushed against it, his fingers working in the dripping depths of her pussy, and rubbed it as his tongue lapped against her clitoris.

She came, hard.

Derik, with the embarrassment of being recently and forcibly taught how to pleasure women, continued to lick and pump until she pushed him away, letting him sit back on his haunches as he looked up pitifully.

His face dripped with sweat, and he couldn't get the taste of woman out of his mouth. Around him, five of the harem members giggled and whispered to each other, passing a bottle of wine between them as they leaned against the walls and pillars. The dim lantern, the one Teri first held, remained on a hook right above Derik's head, highlighting his rather precarious position between the women.

Teri lifted her hand, the streamers of his long black hair slipped out between her fingers and she smiled. "You do have beautiful hair."

Derik didn't know what to say. He worked his tongue in his mouth, trying to get the tangy sweet taste out, but it refused to go. He could feel it in his throat and his senses, the scent of pussy overwhelming him. It clung to his face and drowned out his sense of smell.

Teri grinned and handed him the bottle. "Here, you deserved it."

Gratefully, Derik stood up shakily and had to lean against the pillar. His knees hurt, his back hurt, and most importantly, his dripping cock hurt. A small puddle of pre-cum between had formed between his knees, and thick droplets ran down his length.

Taking the bottle, he carefully drank from it, watching Teri as he did.

She smiled playfully as he drank. As soon as her expression changed slightly, he stopped.

No getting drunk.

But the drink did somewhat clear the taste of girl-flesh from his mouth.

"T-Thank you," to his surprise, Derik's voice was rough.

Sherrel worked the bottle out of his hand and leaned against him. Her soft body felt wonderful against his skin, he would have been attracted to her if it wasn't for the nearly an hour he spent licking, lapping, and slurping between her and the other's legs.

"So, why were you naked?" she whispered.

The others giggled and looked at him.

For a moment, Derik considering the various lies he could say. Instead, truth was stranger than fiction. "Um, my clothes caught fire."

Five women stared at him in shock. Then burst into a whispered giggling.

Sherrel took a swig of the bottle and handed it to the next woman, a short-cut, raven-haired woman with a tattoo right above her slit. When her hand was free, she gestured at him. "Fire? You can't be serious."

He blushed before he sheepishly pointed to the chest of draw-ers. Sherrel padded over to drawers and opened each one until she found the remains of his burned stealth suit in the bottom.

Wrinkling her nose, she looked back. "You're serious."

A third woman, one with thick red hair named Graf, a nickname to be sure, stared at him in shock. "Why are you here?"

"I, um," he blushed even hotter, "I fell."

As one, they looked up at the ceiling. Derik glanced up as well, seeing how all the vents were open, but then glanced around as he considered running. Catching Teri's sharp gaze on him, he gave her a sheepish grin and leaned back.

His eyes scanned over her. Her perky breasts still got a rise out of him, but his balls ached from nearly an hour of no release. And none of the five women around him looked inclined to release the pressure or let him walk out.

Feeling Teri's eyes still on him, he looked at her again.

She held the bottle again in her hand as she regarded Derik, then took a swig before handing it to him. "A deal is a deal."

Derik almost dropped the bottle. "You'll help?"

Teri grinned, "Of course, I mean, you've been giving head for—"

She stopped in mid-word as she cocked her head.

Sherrel gasped next to him as a brighter light appeared across the room. "Shit, Madre!"

All five women looked surprised as they stared at Teri.

Teri thought for a moment, then yanked the bottle from Derik's hand. With her other, she grabbed his hand and pulled him. "Come on, you got to hide."

Graf whimpered as she stepped back. She had thick hips and huge breasts. The look of fear in her eyes frightened Derik. "Where?"

Teri suddenly grinned and then pulled Derik to his feet. As the light grew brighter, the other harem women were stirring, groan-ing as they lifted their heads, their naked bodies still sprawled out on pillows and blankets.

Derik cringed like a cockroach as Teri dragged him near the cen-ter, carefully stepping over the stirring women, then sat him down on the pillows.

Right in the middle of the room.

He looked around in confusion. "What—?"

She silenced him by pushing him back.

Despite the sick feeling growing in his stomach, exposed and vulnerable, he flopped down on the scented pillow.

Sherrel came up. When Teri yanked her closer, she whispered. "What—?"

Teri hissed, "Sit on him!"

Derik opened his mouth to say something, then looked up to see Sherrel straddling his face. He barely had time to take in a deep breath before she set her pussy on his face, knees on each side of his head.

He tried to jerk away but more sat on him and pinned him to the ground. He wanted to say something, but the soaked folds were pressed against his mouth, smothering anything he could have said.

Sherrel gave a coo and rocked her hips back and forth, smearing her wet pussy against his mouth and nose.

Seconds later, he was completely covered in soft, womanly flesh.

Except for his cock. Warm air caressed it, reminding Derik of his exposure.

He struggled, but Sherrel just ground her cunt against his face and he had to open his mouth more to relax the pressure.

Then, the most incredible sensation of a hot, soaked pussy sliding down his cock, pulling it into the wet, steamy depths of some woman and hiding him completely. He was trapped, pinned, and helpless. He was also almost on the edge of an orgasm in his helplessness.

Sherrel's thighs blocked his hearing and he lost himself in a world of liquid silence.

The pussy wrapped around his cock squeezed, and he twisted. Sherrel's juices flooded his mouth as she ground down, unconsciously at first, then a soft rocking. Moving as he was recently trained, Derik extended his tongue and began to lap. She grabbed his chest tightly, but only to grind down harder on his face, nearly smothering him.

He could barely contain himself, his cock buried in the sweetest pussy he could ever imagine. It was indescribable pleasure, compared to the torture of lapping at woman. But Sherrel was hiding him, so he lapped harder.

The other girls must have noticed it since hands guiding his fingers into wet places. He obeyed, sliding and pumping in and out with slow movements. Even one of them rocked against the ridge of his foot, hiding him even as they used him as nothing but a toy.

Shame and helplessness flooded his thoughts and he imagined being caught at any seconds. Only the pussies wrapped around him, the hottest on his cock, distracted him for the endless minutes.

Sherrel came, a silent shuddering that suffocated him before she lifted her body enough for him to get some air.

Then, the girl on his cock came herself, squeezing down wetly, soaking his shaft as she ground down.

Heart pounding, the ache in his balls, the growing need for orgasm, and the clenching pussy was all he needed.

He came so hard, stars exploded in his vision, his body tightening hard as his shaft exploded in a white-hot burst of flame and pleasure. Surge after surge pumped into the girl, the intensity growing with the realization that he had come inside one of the baron's private harem.

Drained, he relaxed more for the endless seconds before Sherrel's hips lifted and he breathed in the air scented of sex and perfume. He looked down to see Teri sliding off his swollen shaft.

"You were fucking him!" whispered Graf, shocked.

Teri shook her head in sharp denial. "Was not!"

"You were fucking! And he came! I can see the cum on your thigh. Madre's going to kill you!"

Teri blushed and held her fingers between her legs, raising them up to see the white fluid dripping down. "Well, fuck."

Sherrel chuckled before whispering sharply, "Well, what did you think would happen? You get pregnant and the baron's gonna have your tits for dinner!"

Teri started to say something when one of the other harem girls looked over at them.

"What are you whispering about... who's that?"

Looking around sharply, Teri suddenly got a grin on her face. "Oh, we found him."

As she spoke, she stepped over to Derik. He stared up at her, feeling helpless as more of the women perked up, staring over at him.

Teri straddled his head, and he looked up to see her swollen lips, oozing with his cum. The very thought of lapping at his own cum nauseated him, and he tried to get up, but Teri slapped her pussy against his face and pinning him down.

The taste of their combined juices was almost too much. Derik's hands clenched the pillows tightly as she ground down, overly wet from his orgasm.

"And he's really good at giving head, too," she said with a giggle and a grind.

Tears burning in his eyes and his heart pounding in his chest, Derik opened his mouth to lick her clean.

Bathroom Confrontation

Derik cracked open one eye, feeling an ache in his very bones. And a taste that clung to the back of his throat that he couldn't immediately identify. His eyes stared up at a mural ceiling meters above his head. For a moment, he wondered how he could afford such a large hotel room before he realized he had three separate bodies pressed against him. Soft bodies. Soft bodies with hard nipples. Turning his head, he looked to his right. Teri slept against his side, her breath tickling the hairs on his chest. There was an innocent look to her face, playful and sexy.

He groaned softly, not really willing to move his tongue or his fingers. Everything hurt; he never realized exactly how much work it could be to please every single woman in a harem.

Derik wondered how the baron did it.

And it was every single one. Over the night, they had forced him into service, his mouth and lips pressed against countless pussies and his fingers shoved into dozens of wet holes. His brief moment of release, emptying his aching balls into Teri's tight pussy had passed into memory.

He could see the morning coming, a false dawn coloring the sky above the harem. He considered climbing up to the ventilation or even the skylights, but the aches in his muscles made it hurt to twitch. Between Wendi's brutal beating and a night of servicing, he didn't feel safe climbing anything higher than his knees.

Sighing, he looked over at Teri. Her sandy brown hair tickled her nose as she snored softly. On the other side, Sherrel curled up with her back against him, her curvaceous ass pressed against his thigh. He could feel the heat between them, teasing his senses as much as their individual scents imprinted in his senses. His cock twitched to life, his balls aching even more as it took up to full height.

Then he realized he had to pee.

Carefully, he slipped out from the two women and staggered to his feet. In the morning light, the dozens of women sprawled out in silk and pillows, their naked bodies displayed for his pleasure brought a sigh to his lips.

"Even if I die today," he whispered, "this sight was worth it."

Scratching his head, he wrapped his long hair into his hand and made his way down the hall Teri took the night before. The feelings of exposure—knowing that someone could walk in at any moment—faded with the need to find a toilet. His bare feet whispered against the tile as he made his way down the hall.

Beyond, he found a large bathroom which he made use of, sighing with pleasure. He considered returning to the room, but his self-preservation rose up, and he decided to explore the suite of bathrooms.

A few doors down, he found a huge set of soaking tubs, each one four feet in depth and lined with wood. Steam rose up from the surface, highlighting the softly glowing runes that kept the water heated. They were design to ease the ache of bones and injuries.

He grinned at the thought of his tongue and fingers needing to soak. Then, he tasted his lips. Realizing that the flavor in the back of his throat was all the women from the night before, their juices fermenting in his throat, he found a sink and washed off his body using a rag. Then, he returned to the tub and slid into it, moaning as the hot water covered him.

"Oh, fuck, that feels good."

He considered jerking off to release the pressure in his balls, but moving his hands took much energy. Instead, he leaned back and prayed no one would come in for at least an hour.

Naturally, a few minute later, he heard the scuffing sounds of bare feet coming down the hall. He groaned and lowered himself until just his head remained above the water. His hair spread out over the water's surface, obscuring him. More feet came into the bathroom and he listened to the harem women talking to each other. Their words were soft and playful, and he started to doze before a voice spoke next to him.

"There you are."

Her voice surprised him and he looked up to see Sherrel peering down at the tub. She smiled with sleepy eyes and shrugged off a thin silk robe before slipping into the water.

"I almost thought I dreamed you."

Derik's heart thumped against his chest, his eyes dropping to the water that swelled against her breasts.

She caught his gaze and smiled. "Last night was fun, wasn't it?"

He could only groan.

Her eyes flickered for moment, then she slid over to him to press one hand against his hardening cock, "I bet you didn't get any release, did you? Well, Teri helped you but you were going hours after that."

Unable to speak, he shook his head. Then, leaned back when she caressed his length with her fingertips. "Why don't I help then?"

Sherrel purred, her hand jacking him with slow movements. Derik took a deep breath, letting the first flicker of a smile cross his lips. Her soft hand slid up and down in the scented water, bringing him closer and closer to an orgasm until he started to gasp.

Then a second body slipped next to his as Teri sat down heavily and splashed him. "Still here?"

Derik jumped, then blushed. He sat up and Sherrel pulled back her hand, abandoning him as his pressing orgasm faded quickly.

Teri grinned, her perky breasts standing out of the water. "Sorry about last night."

He could only groan again.

"I'm impressed you made it so far, you were a really good sport," she smirked, "Are you sure you haven't given head before?"

Humiliation rose up inside Derik, reminding him of his helplessness as she forced him into action. Each woman who woke up and that act of pressing her sperm-filled pussy to his mouth. Tears filled his eyes and he looked away, vowing to never think of this moment in his life again.

Teri leaned back, spreading her legs out into the water. He watched as her hand swished along the surface, playing with his long, black hair.

"Well, you are a fast learner anyway."

Suddenly, she sat up and pulled him close. Derik tried to look away, but she pulled his chin to face her. Before he could pull back, she kissed him, closing her eyes as she did. He lost himself, his hands twitching as she wrapped her soft, perfumed body around his, grinding her hips against his side. One hand delved down into the water and brushed against his aching member.

When she broke, she purposefully glanced down. Her fingers teased his length for a moment, circling around the swollen head. "Oh, you enjoying this."

Sherrel giggled. "I think he needs to come."

Teri started to jack him, sliding her palm up and down. "This help?"

Derik shuddered and nodded.

Sherrel pouted for a moment, then reached over, joining her hand with Teri and teasing his balls, tugging on his hairs and running her finger in the area between his ass and base.

He clenched, shifting her out of position.

Sherrel chuckled but pulled her fingers away from his anus.

Just as he almost reached another orgasm, he heard three more enter the room.

"Oh wow, he's real!?"

"What is Madre going to say?"

"Here, let me in."

Hands pulled away from his aching cock as the newcomers joined them in the water, sloshing as they wiggled next to each other. Five pairs of eyes focused on him, then more as more of the women filtered into the room. Seeing him, they stared in shock and remembered pleasure as they filled all the tubs. More bodies slid into his own tub and he was jostled into the center, surrounded by breasts, bodies, and teasing hands. They caressed him, fingertips against his manhood and balls, but never giving that release he desperately needed.

"What is your name?" asked Graf.

"Um, Derik," he answered.

"Oh, sounds pretty."

"How did your hair get so long?"

"Why are you here?"

"Why were you naked?"

More questions came and he tried to answer them, avoiding the exact reason he was in the harem in the first place.

"Are you going to spend the night?"

The idea of pleasuring all of them again, being shoved into pussy after pussy, left him cold inside. He ached and he wanted to forget this as fast as he could. "I... I'd rather not."

Teri ran her fingers through his hair. "We should probably help him out, he did," she grinned, "pay for our services."

One of the women made a dramatic pout. "I didn't come last night."

Another woman crawled over Derik, her slick breasts teasing his cock for a moment and causing it to twitch, before slipping into the speaker's lap. "I'll make you come."

They giggled and started to kiss, which did nothing for Derik's aching hardness. Derik watched, his body growing hotter and his cock screaming for release.

Sherrel leaned over him, speaking to Teri. "What are we going to do?"

Teri cocked her head for a moment. She ran a finger along her breast before answering. "I say, we hide him until Madre does her rounds, then wrap him up in clothes and sneak him out the back door. It's early morning, so Tornsin is on duty and easily swayed with a little bit of tit."

To make a point, Teri reached over and hefted one of Sherrel's larger breasts, thumbing the larger nipple until it perked up. They both giggled and regarded Derik.

"Sound good?"

He had no clue. "Um, yeah."

Teri glanced down, then sighed. "Oh, sorry. You still need to come?"

Derik let out a soft whimper that halted the conversation.

Teri reached down and started to slide her palm down his shaft again. In two strokes, he was ready to come, then a frantic whisper cut through his pleasure once again from someone at the entrance to the tubs

"Madre is coming!"

In a flash, Teri's hand pulled away from his cock, and he was shoved into the back of the tub, away from the door. Women scurried to stand in front of him, pinning him against the back tightly with their slick bodies. He was thankful and claustrophobic at the same time.

A few heart-pounding minutes later, he heard someone coming into the tub area. She, this Madre, wore heels. The clicking on the tile sounded slow, measured, and infinitely dangerous to his well-being. One wrong thing and he would be slaughtered.

Despite his fear, he could only focus on the asses pressed deliciously close to his body. He shifted slightly, moving his aching cock to slide down the crack of the nearest one, Teri he guessed. In response, she pressed back to stop him, but didn't move his aching length from her firm ass.

He considered working his cock in, when they all spoke up.

"Good morning, Madre!"

"Morning!"

Madre had a cheerful voice, with a slight northern accent of the Belkim region. He guessed she was in her thirties and could almost imagine what she looked like.

Someone asked her a question but it was quickly followed by others.

"What happened last night?"

"How was the baron?"

The room quieted down and he could imagine her gesturing for silence.

"Hamel is actually in a very good mood. His trip went well, and the girls are still sleeping off the trip back in the carriage. When you get finished, help them into the room and let them get some good sleep. The baron laid into them most of the trip and they are quite sore."

A round of giggles.

"But, it appears that the roof collapsed in the great hall last night. Looks like supports failed under the weight of the mosaic."

Derik's ears perked and he froze to make it easier to listen. The distraction of naked women made it hard, but he heard Madre's next words with chilling clarity.

"Two guards were killed when it collapsed."

Ice filled his heart as tears started to burn his eyes. Slowly, he whispered to himself. "Fuck."

There were gasps of shock. Teri's ass pulled away from him.

A suicidal urge to stand up filled him and he struggled to contain it.

One of the women spoke up. "Who?"

"Tornsin's brother, Thomas, and Old Gaff."

He listened to the cries of sorrow and more of the women pulled away from him. His hands balled into fists as he stared at their backs, sinking into the water.

Madre, her voice brimming with sadness, spoke carefully. "It wasn't anyone's fault. I mean, it wasn't a thief or anything, otherwise they would have taken the Eye of Hamel. But, just in case, with so much damage, they are tripling up all the guards. So, stay in the rooms, I don't want our little family to cause any troubles. Do you understand?"

Agreements filled the room and Derik couldn't help but smile at the joy of knowing his decoy sapphire remained in place. After a few more questions, he listened to Madre leaving, her shoes clicking on the floor as she left.

But, just as he started to relax, he heard her turn around.

"Who is he?"

Derik's heart froze in place and he gasped softly.

Teri looked around. "Um, who?"

"The man in the tub with you."

Fuck, fuck, fuck echoed in Derik's thoughts as he tried to crouch down. He wormed his away among naked limbs in an attempt to disappear. The sounds of her shoes coming closer, unerringly seeking him out, pounded in his heart as he cringed.

"I can hear him whispering behind you." She spoke in a threatening voice, "I can hear his sighs. I can smell him in the air and I know he's behind you, Teri."

There was a ripple through the bodies pressed against him before Madre finished, "Let me see him unless you want to see how pissed I can get."

His heart nearly burst in his chest. Letting out a whimper, he tried to crawl into the bottom of the tub. The women shielding him hesitated, then he watched as they crawled out of the tub. Naked bodies dripping with water. Too soon, he was alone in the tub, naked and helpless, his black hair sprawled out over the surface and looking up at Madre, the mistress of the harem.

She had curves, was the first thing he thought of. Short, probably only a meter and a half in height, she had hair with red highlights, pulled back into a tight, professional bun. Two sticks stuck out of both ends of the bun; he thought he could see metal points on the end of them. Her dress, clinging to every curve of her body, stuck against her skin in the humidity. It was silk brocade, something Derik could easily have stolen from the most expensive of import business. Her shoes, matching perfectly in color, had relatively short heels, but they looked as serious as the stare she focused on him.

"Stand up."

When he didn't respond, she repeated it, barking it out as a command. Derik staggered to his feet, water dripping off his body and streaming down his hair as he stood on a step.

Her eyes narrowed and she snapped her fingers, pointing to the ground in front of her.

Derik, blushing hotly, covered his groin with his hands and exited the tub, standing where she pointed.

"Don't move," she commanded.

Derik shivered with fright, looking around at the others. They watched, sprawled out on the sides of the room or in the tubs. Naked bodies and curious eyes, all focused on his nude form.

Madre said nothing more, her eyes scanning over him. Her gazed burned directly into his chest, as if she could see his very soul.

An uncomfortable silence filled the room.

He squirmed, noting the depressingly few exits.

"Who are you?"

"D-Derik."

"Derik who?"

"J-Just Derik... madam. I don't have a family... name."

She stepped forward. As she did, she lifted her hand and a translucent blade of force appeared in her hand. Beats of sweat formed on his body as she pressed drew it down and sliced away a few of the hairs on his chest.

He could feel force rippling off the blade, stirring the damp hairs on his stomach. He tightened his muscles, feeling terrified at the sharp end nearly pierced his skin.

"Did you fuck my girls?"

A single question, and he knew he didn't have more than a heartbeat to answer. Remembering the whispered conversation between Teri and Sherrel, he shook his head as he swallowed hard.

The tip of the knife never twitched.

"No, madam," he lied.

"And that is the only reason you aren't bleeding on the floor. And if you ever try, I'll gut you and the girl who lets you."

He didn't know what to say. "Y-Yes, madam."

She glared at the others, her hair frizzing slightly in the humidity. "Right?"

As one, the women in the tub area spoke. "Yes, Madre!"

She turned back to him, jabbing him slightly with the magically created blade. "Now, what in name of the Seven Gods, are you doing in my harem?"

"I... um, fell, madam."

"Madre."

"Madre," he repeated.

"Fell from where?"

"The ventilation shaft, actually."

"And how did you end up naked in the tub? Fall into that?"

She raised an eyebrow, but when she didn't stab him, Derik stuttered an answer.

"No, but I... I spent the night, but I wasn't planning on staying. I-I was trying to get out before someone saw me, then s-someone said I had to help them before I could get out."

Her eyes narrowed again.

"That doesn't explain how you got in here," she glanced over at Teri, "but that response does sound like one of my girls."

Teri giggled and Madre focused back on Derik. "So, you spent the night here? Getting blow-jobs and hand-jobs from the pretty girls?"

She spat out the words, stabbing a bit deeper until a single droplet of blood formed at the tip of her knife.

"No! I mean, no, I didn't get a single one, madam."

"Madre."

"Sorry, I didn't, I swear, Madre."

"Then what did you do?"

"I... she made me lick them all."

"You gave head to my girls?"

Around him, the girls nodded in assent along with a couple sighs of pleasure. He spotted a few of them stroking each other as they watched. Madre looked around in surprised, her eyebrows arched.

"Seriously? All he did was blow you?"

"And fingers, Madre, He has very long and nice fingers," supplied Sherrel with a smile and a twist of her hips.

"He didn't get anything?"

Derik saw Sherrel look sharply at Teri, then shake her head. "No, I was giving him his first hand-job when you came in."

Madre's eyes looked down to Derik's crotch, still covered by his hands. Her knife lowered as she gestured with it.

"Let me see."

The last thing Derik wanted to do was expose his cock to that knife, but he hesitantly pulled his hands away from his throbbing erection.

Madre grunted, "A cute little cock, I see."

Derik blushed hotly. Little?

The point of the knife went dangerously low as she used it to ease his cock aside to inspect his balls. "And you are telling me you broke into the harem, with a lame excuse of falling, to just pleasure these girls all night?"

Derik spent a mere second to consider his answer. It seemed safer to admit to that instead of accidentally killing guards with his efforts to steal the Eye of Hamel. Once again, he lied and very carefully said, "Yes, Madre."

Around him, Teri and the others giggled and laughed, hands touching each other as they watched.

"Seriously?"

"Y-Yes, Madre, that is all I wanted," he said while putting as much effort as he could into concealing his lie.

She stared at him and an icy ripple of fear ran down his back. Her eyes pierced him, holding him still as energy seemed to ripple off her. More sweat beaded her brow, then she lifted both hands, the knife suddenly gone.

"You're an idiot, Derik."

"I-I know," he said with complete and utter honesty.

She took a long deep breath before speaking up again.

"You also picked a very bad time to do this, boy."

He flinched at the title, but said nothing.

"With the great hall in ruins and the Eye nearly unprotected, they are arresting any and all unknown people. And you, Derik, look very suspicious in this room."

"I-I didn't steal anything."

"I know, otherwise you'd be on a pike right now."

He shivered at the thought. His body tensed at the memory of the sapphire just meters above his head.

She stared at him, then around the room. "So, the question is, Derik, do I turn you over to the guards, where you'll spend the next week in the dungeons as they ask why you slept in the harem?"

Derik let out a tiny squeaking noise. He clutched himself tightly, giving her a pleading look.

"Or," she grinned at him, "do I let you play with my girls, earning every night until you can leave safely?"

The thought of days and nights at the mercy of the women send a cold shiver down his spine. He glanced over at Sherrel and Teri. At the sight of their grins, his fear and anxiety spiked.

He almost asked to be taken to the dungeon, but he regained his wits before his mouth opened. "I-I... please let me stay here?"

She regarded him seriously.

"You know that means you'll be pleasuring these girls almost every moment you are here, right?"

A twitter rippled through the room and he swallowed before nodding.

"Yes, Madre."

"And you'll obey every command I give, every rule I state, no matter how much you don't want to?"

He nodded, feeling like he stood at the entrance to hell. She stepped next to him, the knife reappearing in her hand to press against his throat. "And if I ever, even for a second, think you have something else in mind, I'll have you throw in the dungeon or gut you myself. One attempt to escape, one hurt girl, one finger raised in anger, and you are dead."

Swallowed in fear, he nodded.

"Y-Yes, Madre."

After a second of holding his gaze, she stepped back and the knife blew away like mist. "Very well. You may stay."

A cheer filled the bathing area but Madre wasn't done.

"And, to prevent you from being caught, you are to be treated like one of the girls."

Derik nodded.

"That means you will dress like them—"

He froze in mid-nod, suddenly flushing.

"—and exercise with them, bath with them, and you will act like them in every way like a pleasure slave until the day you leave."

She circled around him before stopping in front of him. "Understand?"

"Y-Yes, madam."

"Madre. You are always to call me Madre. That isn't my name, that is my position here."

"Yes, Madre."

"Good. You accept?"

It was better than torture or death, even if he would suffer with the dirty task of pleasing them.

"Yes."

Madre suddenly grinned. "I suppose the best way to keep an eye on you, Derik, is to make you the 'new girl.'"

He didn't understand, but one of the girls behind her suddenly let out a sigh of relief as the others giggled. Madre grinned. "That means you some special duties starting tomorrow morning."

Fearful, he just nodded.

"And the first is your hair."

Derik clutched his long black hair tightly, looking fearful. It was his only point of pride, the long black length that cascaded down his back.

Madre shook her head sharply.

"No, that is beautiful and worthy of a truly gorgeous woman instead of you," he flushed at that, "but I'm talking about this," she pointed to his chest, "and this," her finger lowered to his balls.

"It all has to go."

Derik whimpered, "No..."

Madre's face twisted in a scowl. Her hand snapped out to grab his chin, turning him to look at the others.

"Do you see hairy women here?"

Looking over the dozens of naked breasts and the swollen pussies he had lapped, he knew there wasn't a single strand of hair below their necks. "No."

"Then it would look strange to have a hairy girl in the middle of my room, wouldn't it?"

"Y-Yes, Madre."

"Then, the hair has to go."

Derik let out a sob as tears dripped down his cheeks, and his balls tried to crawl up into his body.

Waking Up Nude

Derik settled down between the sprawled bodies of Teri and Sherrel. He sighed unhappily as he rested against an overstuffed pillow, looking down at his hairless body. His cock, purple and half-hard, twitched slightly as he focused on the wrinkled balls.

It disgusted him.

For his entire adult life, the difference between the him and whores had been hair. Tiny short hairs and a thatch right above the legs. It was his mark of importance, his manhood. With his slender body and no hair, he almost looked like the harem women spread out around him.

Thinking of that, he glanced over at Teri who took his hair removal with a giggle and a night of forced licking. The smiles and the giggles burned against his cheeks like a brand.

But when she slept, there was an innocence to her sweet body. A delicateness that almost made him want to wake her up in the way she wanted most, with his mouth between her legs.

"Good morning," said a sleepy Sherrel.

He shifted slightly to glance at her. She smiled and reached out, stroking one fingertips against his cock. "It's beautiful."

Her voice barely carried over to him.

He shook his head. "It's disgusting."

Her hand wrapped around his shaft, and it warmed in her palm. He could feel, and see, his balls twitching, tightening up against his skin as she brushed her palms against her side. Sherrel looked up at him. "No, all of you is beautiful. Your hair, your body, even your cock."

"But..." he let his voice trail off for a moment, "I..."

Sherrel shifted slightly until her large breasts pressed against his thigh. Her hand trailed down, dragging the smooth ends of her fingertips along his wrinkles. His cock twitched with his humiliation.

"What? Just because she removed your hair?"

Unable to form the words, he just nodded.

She raised an eyebrow, her fingertips teasing his cock as it stretched up to full length, a throbbing ache burning inside him. "Give me a man without hair any day."

He couldn't understand it. "W-Why?"

Sherrel smiled and reached over to suck lightly on the side of his shaft. The warmth and liquid heat sent waves of pleasure coursing along his entire body.

"Because it is clean, it is pleasure. Every little touch," her mouth worked down the side of his cock, to suck lightly on his sack. A burning wetness that sucked one ball in, then the other.

He clutched the pillows next to him.

"And you don't have to pull hairs out of your mouth. I mean, the baron is huge, but it is just worse when your face is buried in that forest of hair. Y-You can't really breathe around it."

He shivered at the thought, suddenly remembering Rick's cock.

Sherrel let out a giggle as his cock surged even hotter. She pulled her mouth from the base of his cock and giggled. "Thinking about the baron?"

Derik shook his head sharply. His cheeks burned and he refused to admit it. "No!"

She giggled again then dragged her tongue up his length, to tease his cock-head. "I bet you just masturbated in the bathroom?"

Derik nodded as he looked over the harem. It was late in the morning, but everyone remained asleep. With Madre back in charge, the harem woke up closer to noon and drifted to sleep well after midnight. He always preferred sleeping until afternoon, but in a room with three dozen harem members doing the same, it was both familiar and surreal at the same time.

"Did it feel good?"

He looked down, then gave a little nod. It was an okay orgasm, just enough to take the edge off his aching balls, but nothing else.

"As good as this?"

She lifted her body over him, nipples teasing his legs as she pressed her lips against his cock. Her hand reached down to tease his balls as she drew his length into her mouth.

He let out a soft moan of pleasure, feeling the liquid pleasure taking him.

Sherrel smiled at him and began to bob, sliding up and down with her firm lips caressing every millimeter of his length

Please, please, please let me come, echoed in his head as he watched her swallow him. Lips to his base, then sliding up his glistening shaft to kiss the tip. Soft, almost gentle, slurping noises filled his hearing as he watched.

His orgasm stared to burn inside him, almost ready to crest when Teri touched him without warning.

She smiled as she stood up. "That looks like fun."

He closed his eyes, praying she wouldn't interrupt him. He didn't hear her moving. When her thighs stepping on both sides of his head, he jumped in surprise. Looking up, he watched as she straddled his face, pinning him back against the pillow. He opened his mouth, automatically now, lapping at the soft mound of her pussy as Sherrel continued to blow him.

Not being able to see Sherrel pleasure him intensified the experience. He gasped, lapping at the familiar taste of Teri's pussy.

Teri moaned softly, grinding against him.

Derik surprised himself by reaching up to cup her buttocks, pulling her tight.

Sherrel rewarded him with deeper, wetter strokes.

His cock swelled painfully hard. Then, his pleasure crested inside him, a powerful orgasm that consumed his thoughts. He could only clutch to Teri, lapping frantically at her slit. He barely registered her grabbing his hair as she came.

She pulled away with a gasp. "Wow, you are getting good at that."

Derik flushed at the compliment, then looked down to see Sherrel cleaning off his cock with her mouth, a tiny bit of cum oozing out of her full, red lips.

She smiled at him as she licked her lips. "As I said, beautiful."

Teri grinned and patted his head as she headed into the bath-rooms, her feet stepping over the others. Derik watched her, then turned back to Sherrel.

"Um... do you want me...?"

Sherrel grinned. "Give me some head?"

Cheeks hot, he nodded. She shook her head and sat up to press her back against his chest. She spread her legs and let one hand drift down.

"Just hold me, okay?"

Derik held her and stroked her breasts with his thumbs. His fin-gers touched and stroked her as she jerked in his grip, both hands buried between her legs as she arched her back in pleasure. Derik's cock surged back to full heat as she brought herself to a silent, powerful orgasm right against his body. He could just stare, mar-veling at the intensity of her actions.

When she finished, Sherrel slumped against him. She looked up at him with a smile. "Sometimes, my own fingers are the best."

He chuckled and then said nothing. She held his arms around her and soon he heard her breathing slow. Together, they drifted back to sleep.

Teri woke him up again, and Derik automatically opened his mouth for her pussy.

To his surprise, her fingers pressed lightly against his lips. "That's sweet, but you need to get up."

His eyes focused on her as she stood above him. Slowly, she drew her fingers from his lips and leaned down to kiss him. It took his by surprised, but he melted into her embrace. His hands reached up, clutching her body against him until her perk breasts pressed tight-ly to him. A kiss so sweet and powerful Derik was utterly lost. When she broke it, he could barely catch his breath.

"Come on, you have 'new girl' duties."

With a giggle, she helped him up, and he followed her toward Madre's room.

The New Girl

Teri drew him down a different hallway with a grin.

Derik, naked as her, just followed, his hand in hers until she stopped in front of a gilded door.

"Here we go, Madre's room."

Derik looked around and blushed. "Um, what do I do?"

Teri kissed him on the cheek, then on the lips. "Don't piss her off. She will probably cut off your balls if you do."

"Oh." He sighed and reached for the door.

Teri stepped back, then cleared her throat. "Derik?"

"Yes?" he turned to look at her tight body, with pert breasts and a slightly worried look on her face.

"Look, we all went through this, um, what you are about to. So, don't get too upset."

A shiver of fear filled him. "Um, what?"

Teri looked away and quickly walked down the street.

He watched her disappear, then turned to face the door. His hand trembled as he reached out. Before he could knock, a voice cut through the door.

"Just come in, girl."

Derik froze at being called a girl. A flush rose in his cheeks and he looked down at his naked, hairless body. His hand continued to tremble, but he pushed open and stared into the dim light inside.

Her room smelled of perfume, but a muskier one than the rest of the girls used. A few candles flickered in the darkness, a dim cave, of Madre's room. He took a deep breath and stepped inside.

He froze in the door, his eyes catching the reflections of an immense tub in one corner, a wall of drawers in another. Turning slightly, he spotted her form on a bed large enough to house five people comfortably.

Madre slept under a sheet, the fabric draped over her body. Her back was to him, but a mote of light hovered in the air above her head and he could see a book in her hand.

"Door, please."

Blushing even hotter, he shut the door quickly, then looked around. Finding no seat in the room, he stood near the center, unsure what to do.

Languishingly, Madre folded her book closed and sat up. A silk robe rippled along her body, black in the dim light as she regarded him. "You're late."

"I-I'm sorry, Teri didn't wake me up until—"

"Doesn't matter. You are still late. I don't care if there are a dozen men begging to fuck you,"

Derik's blush hot even hotter and he whimpered softly at the thought, disgusted but also terrified.

She grinned at him, "But, still means you'll get punished. There is only one person who can keep you away from your duties, girl, remember that."

He couldn't decide to take offense at the 'girl' comment. Instead, he quietly asked a question. "Who?"

"The baron, of course."

Derik let out another tiny whimper. "H-He wouldn't... you know, with me?"

Madre scooted along the bed to sit on the edge. The mote of light followed her, bobbing slowly in the air. She said, "You better hope he doesn't. I don't know how he would take to finding a man in his harem. But, if he does, there is nothing I'll do to stop him or save you."

"I-I better make sure that won't happen."

Madre chuckled dryly and stood up. The silk robe parted down the middle and his jaw dropped at the sight of her body. At first, he could see her large breasts and the swell of her belly. She was old, but not fat, just comfortably plump. Then, his eyes adjusted more to the light, and he saw scars on her body.

She almost looked sad as she stepped up to him. With a shrug of her shoulders, the robe slipped off her skin to puddle at her feet. Derik gasped, staring at the hundreds of scars that crisscrossed her body, the gouge of a knife fight, and even three parallel lines of some creature that took a chunk out of her side. His eyes snapped up to her light, then down to face her as realization dawned.

"You're a battle mage, aren't you?"

Another chuckle, this one more amused. "Bright boy. How did you guess?"

"M-My financée was one... Madre."

She cocked an eyebrow, looking over him. "I would have pegged you for being utterly gay," that brought another flush to his cheeks which only deepened as she stroked a hand along his chin, chest, and hips. "You have the body of a woman, Derik."

"I-I'm not gay," he sputtered, "I wanted to be here, didn't I?"

She looked at him, her brown eyes piercing him again as the air seemed to beat around them. "No, you don't. That isn't the reason you were in the harem."

Fear burst inside him as he stared at her. His hands trembled as they formed fists and he desperately tried to remember the exits.

Madre cocked her head slightly and held out her hand. A ball of faint flame appeared in it, hissing loudly as it spat sparks in the air.

Derik swallowed hard, feeling his testicles crawling up into his body.

Madre closed her fingers and the flames dissolved into incense. "You are very frightened, aren't you? Desperate?"

Shaking, Derik said nothing.

Madre looked him over, then glided across the room. Stepping into the tub, she looked over at him. "I'm not going to report you. You have a secret. I can hear your heartbeat speeding up every time I talk about it."

He stared at her in shock.

She gestured for him to come closer.

He obeyed, stepping into the steaming hot water next to her.

She nodded in approval and sat down, her back to him.

He stared down at her battle-scarred back for a moment, then up at the soap she held in her hand. No directions were needed.

Not finding a washrag, he soaped up his hands and began to rub them against her back. Even through the suds, he could feel her scars. They terrified them, but they also reminded him of the scars he used to caress along Wendi's body. The thought of his former fiancée sent a shiver down his spine. He distracted himself by rubbing, listening to the grunts of pleasure as he cleaned her back.

When he finished, he started to get up, but she leaned back against him, hooking the back of her head against his shoulder. He looked down at her glistening body. Her nipples were hard as she looked up at him, saying nothing.

Soap dripping from his fingers, he took a deep breath and started to clean her front. His cock twitching as he rubbed his slick hands against her breasts, hefting them as he worked the soap along her curves. His palms teased her nipples and she just smiled.

Encouraged, he soaped up more of his hands. As he worked in silence, his hands moved further down until his hands brushed against the puffy mound of her sex.

"Go on," came the command and he delved his fingers between them.

Her clitoris was hard and hot and he teased it. A bit too rough, and she shifted her position. Thinking furiously, he thought back to Sherrel masturbating against him. Moving his other hand around her waist, he closed his eyes and recalled how she moved. It took him a moment to find a rhythm, but the intake of breath and the soft moans of pleasure guided him.

He slid his fingers into her pussy, working them with long, slick strokes until she arched her back. His cock pulsed against the base of her spine, but he struggled to keep it still as he brought her to a shuddering orgasm.

As she came down from her high, she lifted her leg and he obediently washed it. She lifted the other and he worked his fingers along her toes, washing each one before she let it splash into the water.

"Good, one of the rules I have: you never wash yourself."

"Um, why?"

"Because we are sisters."

He started to interrupt her, but she turned to look at him.

"We. Are. Sisters."

A hot flush on his cheeks, he nodded.

She sat up and turned around. At her gesture, he mimicked her movement until his back was to her. He leaned forward as she began to soap up his back, working his hair to the side as she cleaned him.

"I'd rather you have all your orgasms at their hands too, but I already know everyone jerks off. Just... keep it to a minimum or at least share it with someone."

"Why?"

Her cleaning was harder than his, scrubbing at his back. He jerked with every movement until he could relax enough to enjoy it like a massage. Slowly, he closed his eyes.

"Because it isn't just one girl here. There are thirty-eight at the moment, including you and me. And there are times when we are called to perform together."

His cock surged with the thought of multiple girls making out for someone's pleasure. Then he realized he had already experienced it.

Madre chuckled as she finished and pulled him toward her. Her large breasts pressed tightly against his back as she wrapped her arms around him, soaping him up and cleaning his hairless skin.

"The baron usually has three to five girls a night, he is very large and wears them out."

"I-I won't have to, will I?" Every muscle in his body tensed.

"If he commands it, yes." She spoke in his ear as she scrubbed him, "If he commands it, I'll spread you out and let him fuck that ass of yours until it bleeds."

He let out a whimper and she chuckled.

She reached down to grab his cock, working her slick fingers around his length and balls. "But, that won't happen."

He let out a tiny sigh of relief. She chuckled as one of her hands left his cock to work around him. Her fingers teased his hips and he tensed. She continued to caress his side before working down to his buttocks and then to slide one digit up between the curves of his ass.

"Um," he squirmed, "I don't really WANT TO!"

His last words came out as a yell as her finger brushed against the wrinkled opening of his ass and delved inside. It was hot and uncomfortable as he squirmed, trying to pull away.

She flexed her arms, squeezing down on his cock as she pulled him back against her. Her breath tickled his ear, "Because you won't bleed after I'm done stretching you out, that's why."

Derik whimpered pitifully as she pinned him against her. Even the slick, soft body of Madre couldn't distract him from the finger worming its way into his sphincter, pumping with tiny strokes. The heat gathered in his cock, the shame of being turned on by such a debased act. She just breathed into his ear, working her finger deeper until his body started to adjust to her.

She pumped with her other hand, stroking his cock until it almost exploded, then she drove the finger deeper into his ass.

Against his will, his body exploded into an orgasm and he let out an inarticulate and humiliating grunt. Hot cum poured into her hand as she fucked him with her finger, using him like nothing but a common whore.

Derik sobbed as she pulled away from him.

She pulled her invading digit from his anal ring and wiped both the finger and her cum-soaked palm on a small table. When she looked back, she sighed. "It's a start. You are very tight."

Unable to look at her, he continued to cry. He felt dirty, used, and helplessly. Wallowing in his own feelings, he didn't realize Madre had started to wash his hair until he felt the shampoo against his scalp. Wiping away the tears, he looked at her.

She had almost sad eyes as she worked her fingers through his hair, combing it with the shampoo. "You'll get use to it. They all do."

He sniffed, tears still burning in his eyes. She just scrubbed his hair, then pointed to the edge of the tub. Slowly, his eyes looked over to see an array of dildos resting on the edge, the largest easily dwarfing even Rick's cock.

"Once we get you loosened up, I'll be using some of those on you."

Derik trembled, unable to tear his eyes away from the immense toys.

She washed and rinsed his hair. Then, she stood up and pulled him out of the water. "You are to serve me, Derik... actually, we need a new name for you."

Derik looked at her, his mouth opening softly.

Madre looked him over, cock still hard and dripping water at the edge of his tub. "Can't use Deri, that's too close to Teri. How about Dora?"

"W-Why can't I be Derik?"

She responded as a matter of fact, "Because you are a girl in the baron's harem. And soft, little sluts like you don't have boy's names. You have slut names, lover names," she leaned forward, "woman names."

The door to the room opened, flooding it with light from the hall. Derik looked up to see one of the other members of the harem walk in.

"Madre, we're ready."

"Give me one second, Nightingale, I have one more thing."

Nightingale nodded and started to turn, but Madre stopped her. "No, please stay. I just have to punish Dora."

The girl looked quizzically at Derik, "Dora?"

"Her new name."

Derik's blush burned hotly, searing his cheeks as he looked away.

The girl smiled and nodded in approval. "It does fit her."

Madre glided back to her bed, then motioned for Derik.

He obeyed, unable to match either of their eyes. He started to sit down next to her, but Madre gestured to her lap.

"Bend over."

Frightened, Derik looked at her.

Madre gave him a stern look. "You were late."

"B-But, it wasn't my fault."

"It doesn't matter, so bend over."

"I-I, please don't!"

"Every time I give a command, I'm going to add to your punishment."

"But—"

"This is four."

More tears in his eyes and he shook his head. Madre stared at him, her voice hard.

"Five."

He looked helplessly at the girl who just shrugged.

"I wouldn't get to ten, she starts to use the paddle," added Nightingale.

Paddle? Derik looked at Madre who nodded.

"Six."

Tears running down his cheeks, he forced himself to bend over her lap. The softness of her thighs cradled him. Both of their bodies were damp from the perfumed water of her tub.

Then, her hand stroked his backside. He cringed, praying she wouldn't force her finger into his most private of places.

What she did was far worse.

A single crack filled the room as his ass blossomed into pain. He gasped, jerking against her as she raised her hand and slapped his other cheek. He tried to stand up, but her other hand pushed him down, pinning him as she spanked him hard again. His ass burned with heat as she smacked him hard, her fingers spread out to cover as much of his delicate buttock with a single strike.

Five more came, each one smarting more than the one before it. Even in the moments between her spanking, a searing feeling refused to subside. The discomfort and stinging somehow ignited his cock once again. Hot tears dripped down his face as he realized he was growing hard at being spanked.

Two more came, each one powerful enough to drop him to his knees. He could barely balance on her lap as she spanked him mercilessly, driving her hand against his buttocks until he screamed out at the humiliation, shame, and the burning heat.

Then it was over.

She held him to his feet as she stood up again.

"Tomorrow, don't be late."

Sniffing at the tears that wet his cheeks, he nodded.

Her eyes trailed down to look at his cock, hard and dripping once again. Madre chuckled dryly. "We'll have to work on that one later."

She turned to the girl. "Gale, help Dora get a little release and dress her. Her new outfit is on the corner of my desk."

Pulling her silk robe back on, she walked out of the room, leaving Derik alone with a burning ass and a flush on his cheeks.

71

Courage

As the door shut behind Madre, Nightingale's pleasing smile dropped instantly. He could almost feel the temperature in the room dropping as she turned to glare at him. Her eyes, a lighter brown than her hair, looked over him.

Ashamed, he gingerly covered his hard-on with his hands.

She sneered at him. "You are pathetic."

His jaw dropped open as she stepped toward him. Her gaze seared across his skin, withering his cock instantly as she gestured at him. "Nothing but a fucking pretty boy, aren't you? And you just 'fall' into the harem? And she doesn't throw your ass to the guards!?"

Her icy voice slammed into him and Derik let out a whimper.

"And then, you just roll around with the girls, like a fucking bloody wolf who just crawled into the sheep. But, she still doesn't report you. She should have cut off your fucking balls and dragged your carcass in front the baron!"

Derik whimpered and stumbled as the back of his knees smacked against the edge of Madre's bed.

Nightingale suddenly shoved him hard, throwing him back on the bed.

He yelped as he flipped over and landed face-first on the thick blankets. When he looked up, she just growled at him.

"And if you think I'm going to jerk, suck, or even fuck you, regardless of what Madre says, you can just drown yourself in her damned tub and rid of us of your fucking presence. As far as I'm concerned, the second I find a damn guard, I'm going to make a pervert like you gets his dues!"

Her voice reached a shrill point.

Derik trembled as he stared up at her. The peace of his afterglow had faded under the assault of her anger. Only the pain in his reddened ass cheeks complemented the rage in those burning brown eyes.

"Now get your fucking clothes on and go serve Madre. I have better things to do than deal with a cross-dressing fuck."

Spinning on her heels, she yanked the door open and slammed it shut behind her. The air blew past Derik and he whimpered, trembling as he stared at it.

He heard footsteps and the door slammed open again. Nightingale peered inside. "And if you fucking mention this to Madre, I'll cut your balls off personally!"

The door slammed shut again and Derik blinked back the sudden tears that formed in his eyes. Trembling, he lifted himself to his knees. Madre's bed was soft—very soft—and he had to struggle to get back to the edge of it. To his surprise, his legs trembled as he set them down on the cooler ground. Glancing at the door, he stood up and turned around, unsure what to do.

Rubbing his shoulder where Nightingale hit him, he was surprised to see a bit of blood where her fingernail caught him. Moving as gingerly as he could, he returned to the tub and sunk into it, rubbing the wound to clean it. Sitting back up, he stared at the water for a long moment; he held his fingers against the cut waiting for the blood to stop flowing.

A tear burned down his cheek and he sniffed, wiping it away. He tried to understand why he was upset. He was a thief, only taking advantage of their kindness to prevent himself from being thrown in the dungeon or execution. It was a role, he knew that, but the venom in her voice and actions still brought tears to his eyes.

Derik sat for a long moment, wondering what was wrong.

He finally stirred from his thoughts, rising out of the water. "I-I better get going."

Slowly, he got out and found a large towel. His soft cock was sticky, but he didn't want to get back in the water. Instead, he wiped it down as much as possible. Cleaned up, he carefully set the towel on the edge of the tub and padded over to the desk.

Hundreds of papers, orders, and accounting statements. He noticed some of the paperwork for invoices, but most of it was beyond his cursory skill to understand. On the corner, he spotted a set of silk clothes and picked them up.

The first piece was obvious. A pair of sapphire-tinted silk panties. He blushed hotly as he stared down at the rest of the sapphire silk and wondered if Madre knew something about the theft.

Unwilling to risk her wrath, he put on the panties. They were snug, holding his cock tightly against his body and clinging to every curve of his buttock. He shivered at the feel of silk on his shaved skin and his manhood twitched with every movement.

When he picked up the bra, Derik was hit with a serious epiphany.

Madre was turning him into a woman.

It was obvious, but there was something about holding up the silk bra that brought everything into crystal clarity. He started to shake as he fingered the fabric between his fingers, staring at the door. Madre had no ventilation shafts in her room for him to escape. Looking down, he saw a shadow outside of the door. Someone waiting for him. No doubt Nightingale to threaten him again. If he came out not wearing clothes, she would know instantly, and he trembled at the thought.

It was the coward's way out, but he licked his dry lips and stared down at the silk bra. After a long minute of consideration, he took a deep breath.

"Just a few days, what is the worst that can happen. Just… stay away from Gale and keep Madre happy, then I can get the fuck out of here."

Encouraged, he fumbled with the bra. It was an elastic one, not with the wires that he was used to watching whores take off. It took him a moment to pull it down over his flat, hairless chest. To his surprise, it fit snugly against him just like the panties.

It also felt very good.

He pulled up a silk top. Working it above his head, he let it slid down his skin. It brought a different type of flush to his cheeks as it settled into place, the two thin straps over his shoulders and the fabric fluttering against his skin. His cock grew from the slick material, tenting the delicate panties and soaking around the tip of his shaft.

The final piece was a matching silk robe, not unlike the ones most of the harem wore. Slipping it on, he caught sight of himself in the mirror.

For a brief moment, he could almost imagine himself as a woman. That tiny spark of realization sent a shiver down his spine and he turned to stare fully at the mirror.

Except for the lack of hips and breasts, he could suddenly see why the others kept calling him gay. He fingered the robe, considering throwing it aside, but he needed to keep the charade for just a few more days.

The, he promised himself, he would sprint away with the sapphire and never return.

His eyes scanned her room, and he remembered being in a very similar situation once before, standing in a room with Wendi and her mother screaming on the other side of the door. Wendi had just caught him fucking her mother against the altar and responded with the full rage of a battle mage. Only her mother's quick spell saved them both from having their flesh sloughed off in an instant. The same dread filled him as he looked at the shadow of the door, the same feeling of something terrible outside.

Derik didn't know what to do. He had no clue. He was trapped. Caught by his own lies. Somewhere beyond that door was the baron, his men, and a battle mage who knew his secret. And the guards who may be waiting for him as soon as he stepped outside.

He was nothing but a thief. A thief wearing silk panties. A practical slave of an entire harem.

He chuckled at the thought. It gave him a brief respite and he looked at himself in the mirror. His long black hair cascaded down his back and he looked back with the face of a man who could be a woman.

Soft.

Delicate.

He sighed, "She's right. I am pathetic."

He ran his fingers through his hair. "I'm also a coward."

He padded to the door. As his fingers reached the handle, he spotted a bit of deep blue cord on a shelf. Looking back at the mirror, he got a sudden idea. Picking it up, he gasped as a tingle traveled up his arms, but nothing else happened. Shrugging, he returned to the mirror and began to braid his hair.

It seemed like the right thing to do.

It took him nearly twenty minutes to finish. But his hair became a magnificent black line with the deep blue rope woven in to keep everything in place. He smiled as he looked at himself, feeling at bit more in control of his life. He also relished stealing something, even if minor.

Cleaned up and dressed, Derik stood in front of the door. Beyond was the great unknown. It could be the baron, Madre, or even guards with sharp swords. But, it could be nothing but pussies and sex. There really was only one way for him to face it. Only one way to keep together the lies he trapped himself with. Only one way to open that door. Only one thing to do.

He opened the door not as Derik but as Dora.

Dressing Down

There were no guards on the far side of the door. Nor did Madre, Nightingale, or anyone else wait for him. Instead, Derik found himself staring at an empty hall. The reddish tiles below cast the room in a warm light and he blinked for a moment. His heart pounding painfully in his chest, he took a hesitant step forward and closed the door behind him. It closed with a click and he jumped at the sound.

Feeling like any second would bring rushing guards, Derik padded down the hall toward the main room. He could hear Madre barking out orders and his buttocks tighten with the realization of how long he took to dress; he didn't want to get spanked again. Blushing, he hurried down the hall.

As he turned the corner, he briefly saw someone running toward him. Unable to dodge, he collided with Teri and they both yelped as they tumbled to the ground. Landing on his still sore ass, he whimpered and rolled over, tearing up at the pain that radiated from his buttocks.

Teri had rested her hand against the small of his back.

"Aww, poor baby, Madre really got your ass?"

Nodding through his whimpers, Derik carefully got on his knees, then stood up. His braided hair flopped against his shoulder as he stood up, one hand rubbing his pained butt.

Teri looked concerned as she helped him up, then straightened the silk robe on his shoulders. She wore a similar outfit: panties, bra, and a tight-fitting top but no robe. The dusty pink color matched her skin almost as much as the sapphire fit with his eyes.

She leaned closer. "Are you okay? Are you hurt?"

He nodded, then gave a pained smile as he shook his head.

Teri grinned and rolled her eyes. "Sorry. I assume you got spanked, right?"

Derik gave her a hurt look, and Teri grinned.

"Don't worry, Derik, if you obey, you don't get it much. And don't piss her off, you only got swatted. There are times when she'll come hard from breaking your ass. Then you just have to lick her out. But if you really piss her off, she starts to use magic and then it really starts to hurt."

Still rubbing his butt, Derik sighed, "I think she did that already."

Teri raised an eyebrow as she tugged on his shirt. She leaned to the side to look at his ass and then back to grin at him. "You got fingered? Up the butt?"

A hot blush rose up in his cheeks and he nodded.

She looked sad for a moment, then kissed him on the lips. "You'll like it up the ass, it's a great view."

To make a point, she turned around and flipped up her top, revealing her shapely ass.

Derik let out a tiny whimper as his cock made a different type of reaction.

She turned back. "See, all better. Don't worry, you'll get used to that. After a while, it feels good."

"There is more?"

Shaking her head in amusement, Teri said, "Lots more. Every night and every morning until she can stuff her whole hand—"

Derik let out a whimper.

She hugged him. "—into that tight bubble ass of yours."

Teri finished by clamping her hands on his butt cheeks, sending a bolt of discomfort and sudden pleasure through his system.

His cock, trapped in its silk prison surged to life and pressed up against her.

He gulped. "H-Her whole hand?"

Teri nodded and stroked his butt. He could feel her fingertips caressing the cleft of his rear and he squirmed with discomfort. She giggled softly and nuzzled against his neck.

Derik gingerly held her, still trying to escape her fingers. He whispered, "Why?"

"The baron, silly."

At the mention of the baron, Derik froze. "Um..."

"He is really huge. Like this thick tree branch huge. Even if she could jam her fist into your hole easily, he's still going to stretch you out."

Derik shivered at the thought.

Teri grinned evilly. "Just be glad you don't have a pussy too."

One hand released his stinging cheek and caressed against his silk-clan member, teasing it. "He can't get his monster into this little thing, so you only have two holes to please him."

Another whimper.

Grinning evilly, Teri teased his shaft for a moment before withdrawing. "I'll protect you. I'll make sure that thick, drooling cock doesn't slam into that tight little hole of yours. The only people getting into that hole is Madre."

Derik let out a sigh of relief.

Teri skipped back with a smirk. "At least until I get a chance at it."

He froze, staring at her with hopes she was joking. His eyes glanced down, wondering how she was going to get a cock between her legs. He spent enough hours between her thighs to know that part intimately.

She giggled. "Silly, with a strap-on. I got this nice little thing that would open you right up. Sherrel says it feels really good up her shitter."

Fighting the intense blush on his face, he shook his head. "I... I'd like to pass, please?"

"Rather have Madre do it?"

"No! I mean, I don't want it, you know, in my... ass."

She laughed cheerfully. "You say that like you have a choice."

Stepping back, she started to say something, then she frowned. Her eyes scanned over him, and he cringed with embarrassment.

"What?"

"Didn't she have someone help you dress?"

A flash of Nightingale screaming at him and Derik lied, "No."

Clicking her tongue, Teri reached up and pulled off his robe. Letting it pull to the ground, she tugged up on his shirt.

Unsure, he just lifted his arms as she pulled it up.

Spotting his bra, she giggled. "Little flat for that?"

Self-conscious, Derik crossed his arms over his chest.

Teri grinned and tugged on his wrists.

He resisted for only a moment before she pulled them apart. The heat of his embarrassment seemed to grow every passing second she looked at him.

A frown furrowed her brow. She whispered something under her breath before speaking louder, "Give me a second."

Trotting past him, she disappeared around the corner.

Derik stood there, in the middle of the hall, wearing nothing but a bra and panties. From his vantage point, he could see Madre ordering the girls around. Most were exercising while others headed into what she called the classroom. On the very far side, he spotted Nightingale speaking with an armored man and an icy sensation sank into his gut. She whispered as she gestured toward him, and he fled behind the corner. Heart pounding in his chest, he peeked around to see the guard walking toward Madre.

"Derik?"

Derik let out a yelp as he jumped. Turning around, he flushed as Teri looked at him curiously.

"What's wrong?"

"Nothing!"

Teri stepped past him and looked into the main room. "You know Madre hates people who lie, right?"

Derik said nothing.

Teri turned around and brandished two handfuls of silk. All of them were the same color, dusty pink. "Stand up."

He stood up straight as she pulled up the snug bra.

With childish glee, she began to stuff the silk panties into his bra, filling the cups up. It only took a few seconds before he almost looked like he had a set of small breasts. Teri held up her finger, then trailed her fingers up her side. He watched as she lifted the hem and pushed down the panties she wore. There was one ribbon nestled in the furrow of her slit.

"And one warmed for your heart."

His own heart pounded as she worked the slightly damp, fragrant panties right against his skin. His body heated up quickly, his cock swelling, as she smoothed over his bra. His eyes delved lower to catch a sight of her hairless pussy peeking underneath her silk top as she stepped back.

"You almost look like a woman."

Pointedly, she looked down at his cock. He blushed and started to cover it, but she gave him a warning look. "Look, normally it's your job to please me, but just this once...."

As she spoke, she lowered herself to her knees and pulled his cock out of the blue silk panties. Kissing the top, she drew it into the warm heat of his mouth. He let out a long moan of pleasure.

Looking up at him, Teri slowly worked her mouth down his cock, burying his length until he could feel it teasing the back of her throat. With a slurp, she drew up his glistening shaft and he let out another moan. Teasing his balls, she sucked him back in, bobbing back and forth.

With the pressure building, Derik leaned back and leaned against the plaster. It was cool compared to the liquid heat of her mouth. His hands hovered in hair, unsure what to do.

She ignored them as she trailed her fingernails against his sack, playing with them until they tightened on his base. Then, her finger worked back, along the skin between his balls and his ass.

He let out a soft whimper and started to reach down, but her other hand snapped up to catch his wrist, pinning it to the wall.

Still sucking on his cock, she wormed one finger along the tightly clenched cleft of his buttocks. He tried to stop her, but it was hard to concentrate with the shameful pleasure of being penetrated. The pleasure mixed with discomfort as she circled around his ring, working it open even as her tongue lapped at his shaft.

Despite his efforts, between one slurp and another, he relaxed just a tiny bit and she speared him, plunging one finger into his tight ring and sending a shudder of indescribable ecstasy coursing through his body.

He strained to move his pinned wrist, but she held him down as she sucked and fingered him. A hard edge of an orgasm rose up inside him, powerful and intense, as stars swam across his vision. Just as his body strained to hold it in, he exploded in a single flare of pleasure. His free hand scraped against the plaster wall as he let out a soft whine of release; hot jet after jet of cum poured into her mouth. The very feel of her swallowing sent him over another edge of pleasure.

Teri slurped and bobbed, filling the hallway with wet, juicy sucking noises. She continued to pleasure him until he slumped with release.

Gasping for breath, he looked down to see her pulling away, a tiny strand of saliva connecting them before she licked her lips. His cock, sucked dry, flopped down.

She smiled. "There we go. Now, try not to get excited."

Moving his sensitive member with her fingertips, she tucked it back into his panties and eased his balls into place. When she smoothed the fabric over his mound, it almost looked like he had a pussy himself.

"Now," she stood up, "You look like a proper harem girl."

Still lost in his afterglow, Derik could only nod.

Teri grabbed his top and held it up. "Now, this you had on backwards. You see this slit, it goes in front so it stays flat on your tummy. This curve, that is where your ass goes."

He flushed, realizing he wore such a simple thing wrong, but Teri just helped him into it, sliding it into place. His cock twitched slightly and he clamped his thighs tightly against it. After a few moments, it seemed to soften.

Teri smiled as she helped him put on his robe. "You are really beautiful, Derik."

"Dora."

He didn't know why he said it, but she looked at him with surprise.

"What?"

"Madre said I was to be called Dora."

She grinned, "Did she now?"

A nod. He swallowed hard before responding. "She said it was more of a woman's name."

"Well, Dora, I'll tell you what. Normally, Madre has the new girl spend the night with her for the first week, but if she doesn't," she leaned forward and pressed one finger along his faux pussy, sliding a finger down his length, "If she doesn't, I'll get my strap-on and make you a real woman tonight."

She kissed him, giggling at the helpless and stunned look on his face. Slipping her hand into his, she drew him down the hall and toward the others, to rejoin the harem.

Spanking

Derik groaned as he padded down the hall. His back hurt as did his neck. The first part of the morning became a whirlwind of physical conditioning and impromptu lessons about anatomy. Madre knew a stunning amount about the human body, and she was a harsh mistress when it came to his exercises. He couldn't help but wish she had been involved when he had first started as a thief, she would have taught him a lot about moving.

"Just the right balance of keeping you in shape and not too swollen with muscles. In your case, Dora, we don't have to worry about that one, but you work out like the others."

The giggles that followed brought another hot blush to his cheeks, but he ran and worked with the weights with the others. He almost found it pleasant, losing himself with the others.

Except for the guard. Derik spotted him talking to Madre for a long moment and he wanted to crawl into a dark pit. But, instead of calling for more guards, Madre just dismissed him, gave Derik a brief glance, and then returned to her instructions.

He let out his breath but curiosity and confusion made it impossible to relax. His worry grew more when he saw Nightingale's smirks directed at him. He just passed through the morning classes and fell right into being forced into pleasuring every girl who came to him. Teri sat next to him, riding his face before he could have a breather and talking about how she was going to fuck his ass if he didn't spend the night with Madre.

By the time he headed to Madre's room, he was exhausted. Three in the morning, and he was getting tired. Outside, the summer crickets bitched at each other as a wet, warm rain poured down off the gutters. Behind him, he passed the sleeping harem without even trying to talk to Teri or Sherrel.

At the door, he knocked softly.

"Come in, Dora."

The name still didn't fit, but he opened the door. Madre sat behind the desk, doing some paperwork. Looking up at him, she gestured for him to enter the room. He did, shutting the door behind him. Without commands, he didn't know what to do, so he looked around. The bed was a mess and the towels were everywhere. Glancing back at her, he noticed Madre continued to work, so he padded over to her bed.

Without asking, he started to make the bed. He didn't know why, but he needed to do something besides stand in the middle of the room.

"Normally, I'd prefer if you just stand there, Dora."

Derik stood up, holding her blankets.

"I'm sorry, I wasn't—"

"In this case, go ahead."

"Yes, Madre."

He worked in silence, folding the blankets. He barely knew what to do, but his hands guided him as he straightened the bed, then stood up.

Madre looked at him and gestured in front of her desk. "Right there, please."

Derik obeyed, standing there fretfully.

Madre continued to work in silent for a long moment, then casually asked. "Did Nightingale help you out when I left?"

She didn't look up from her writing.

Derik swallowed before lying. "Yes, she did."

She wrote for a few seconds. "That's one."

Sweat formed at his brow. "W-What?"

"You're lying to me, Dora. That's two."

Her eyes never rose from the papers, her hand never stopped writing with the pen, but somehow the force of her presence beat against him, her eyes invisibly staring at him, piercing his soul as he stood there. Squirming, he looked around.

"The longer you go, the more it will hurt. And that's three."

Derik let out a soft whimper. Clenching his hands tightly into fists, he looked away before answering. "No."

Finally, her eyes lifted up from the desk. "No, you won't answer me? Or no, she didn't help?"

He tightened his jaw, remember the threat Nightingale gave him.

Madre sighed. "That's four."

Derik's eyes snapped toward her in surprise.

Madre just lifted one eyebrow. She spoke in a hard voice, "Not answering me is the same as lying. And we'll make that six."

Fuck.

Derik forced himself to open his mouth, to crack a whisper. "She didn't help me."

Madre chuckled dryly. She set down her pen. "That part was obvious, I saw Teri redressing you in the hall. Very sweet, actually, though the blow job was a bit much since you were already late."

He flushed hotly, but didn't look away.

Madre smiled softly as she stood up. For a moment, she leaned against the desk before stepping away. "Pleasure slaves, unlike the rest of us, don't always have common sense in their heads. Everything they do involves shoving something into one of their holes."

As she spoke, she came around the desk. He watched her as she came around, inspecting him. She stopped behind him and tugged on his braid. "Where did you get this?"

For a moment, he was confused, then he remembered the blue rope he found the room. "I... I saw it in your room, and it was the right color, Madre, I hope you don't mind. I can take it off."

She toyed with it for a moment, "No, keep it. It matches your eyes."

He exhaled with relief.

"Now, as I was saying, your newfound mistress Teri is a pleasure slave. She was born as a consort, raised as one, and has all the common sense of a palace cat."

Derik turned to her.

Madre smirked then gestured to herself. "Whereas half the harem is like me, a trophy of the baron."

"Trophy?"

Madre guided him to the bed and sat him down. She raised one foot and pressed it in the space between his legs before she started to remove her boot. Derik reached out to help as she worked the laces. He saw more scars on her body as her dress parted, revealing a distinct lack of underwear. She was shaved, just like the others, but there were even scars along her inner thighs and over the puffy mound of her sex.

"I was on the wrong side of an attack against the baron. I was the only female in the battle mage squad, and we actually took out about half of his army, but he showed himself to be a brilliant tactician and left most of my squad dead. I got this." She parted her dress to show the three lines on her side. "Bleeding to death, our leader begged for surrender."

Derik slid off her boot, and she swapped feet.

He started to work the laces. "What happened, Madre?"

"The baron sent his healers to help his enemy, to heal me, then demanded me as terms of surrender. The general I followed, an ex-lover actually, gave me up, and I found myself the new girl of the enemy's harem."

Derik tugged at the laces, parting the leather as he worked her foot out. He didn't know what to so, so he spoke demurely. "Must have been hard."

"I was trapped, helpless. A prisoner for so long."

The sadness in her voice made Derik look up, unsure of what to say. Madre's eyes were soft, unfocused. After a moment, she cleared her throat and looked down. "The baron won me over, Dora. He fucked me like a slut and treated me like a queen. Unlike the general, I knew that every word out of his mouth was the truth, and he proved it time and time again. After fifteen years of this, I became Madre."

Unsure what to say, Derik finished pulling off her boot.

She nodded in approval, then stood up. Looking purposefully down at the ties that held her dress, she waited.

Derik got the hint and started to remove her dress, letting his fingers brush against her textured skin as he did.

"Now, you are different, girl. You aren't a pleasure slave like Teri or Nightingale. You aren't a conquest like me and Sherrel."

Derik froze, "Sherrel?"

Madre explained briefly, "She was a princess, but the baron has a high price for his help. Her father is one of the Shattered Kings."

The Shattered Kingdoms, the multitude of kingdoms that appeared between Franome and Emberka after the war only a few years back. They were rough and violent, trapped between the two large nations. Derik shivered at the thought and tried to imagine Sherrel as a princess.

"But, that's enough explanations for tonight. I believe you owe me six."

Fear clutched his heart, but he stood up as she sat down. At a silent look, he stripped down, piling up his new silk clothes at his feet before taking his place over her lap. His heart pounded in his chest as he tried to anticipate the swats.

"Now, remember. It doesn't matter what you do, the punishment will always be worse if you lie to me."

And with that came her hand, slapping hard against his upturned ass. He let out a loud whimper as the crack echoed in the room left a stinging impact. She drew back and smacked him again, no doubt leaving a red mark against his ass as she spanked him hard.

A third came down on the first cheek, right over the first handprint. He let out a yelp from the sharp pain blossoming in his ass. His body lurched forward and he ground his cock—hard and dripping—against her thigh even as shame filled him.

Madre didn't give him a chance. She laid a powerful blow against his ass, cracking it loudly against his skin. The pain burst along his skin. It echoed loudly in the room, then redoubled as she smacked him hard again.

He clutched her as his legs shook with the agony. He struggled with the heady mixture of his burning ass and a remarkable pleasure that burned in his loins.

The sixth blow came, smacking hard against his ass and leaving a fiery trail as he let out a scream of pain. It was intense, so intense he almost came on her leg.

When the seventh didn't come, he stood up. Winching from the heat that radiated, he found himself shaking as Madre stood up.

She cupped his chin and he was helpless as she drew him to her, pressing his naked body against her own.

She spoke in a whisper he barely could hear. "If you are honest, there is no pain."

It would have been a matter of just leaning forward to kiss her. A heat rose up as he looked into her eyes, feeling the forceful personality pinning him in place, holding him with her presence. He wanted to kiss her, but he couldn't move.

Madre released him with a soft sigh. "Just stand by my desk."

Somehow feeling rejected, Derik returned to the desk as Madre opened her door. He saw a brief aura of power surround her and sweat dripping off her body.

"NIGHTINGALE!"

The force of her voice trembled the papers of her desk and kicked up tiny whirlwinds of power. It pushed against him as her voice echoed deeply off the walls, rumbling through the harem. He shivered from the power of it, then looked away as Madre returned to her bed.

Moments later, Nightingale came to the door. She spotted Derik first, and he saw anger burning in her eyes. She was naked with a star-burst tattoo around her navel that he barely noticed before. She glared at him as she entered the room, plastering a false smile on her lips as she faced Madre.

Madre seemed angry as she regarded Nightingale. "Did you help Dora when I asked you to?"

Derik stared at Madre with surprised, then fear from the direct question.

Nightingale glanced at him, fear suddenly in her face, then back at Madre. "He didn't need help."

Chuckling, Madre cocked her head. "Truthful, but not really truthful. Dora was reluctant to give me a clear answer, so I'll ask you. Did you help Dora with the release she needed?"

Nightingale's jaw tightened. "He didn't need it."

"She didn't need it?"

The girl shook her head.

"So, you decided that she didn't need help with an obvious sexual need, and she didn't need help dressing?"

"Yes, Madre," came the terse reply.

"Then why did I see Teri redressing him in the hall?"

Nightingale looked surprised, then glanced at Derik.

Derik couldn't match the questioning look and turned away, blushing hotly.

"Plus, I was quite surprised to see Teri giving Dora oral pleasures when I would have expected Dora to be sated by then."

"I was wrong."

"And why did it take Dora a half-hour to come out?"

"I-I..."

Madre's voice turned icy, "Be very careful how you answer."

Nightingale's jaw clenched for a moment. "I left him, Madre."

"You just left her?"

"I... I screamed at him... her, then left."

Madre gestured to Derik and then to the door. "I got that impression since I heard you from outside. I heard it rather clearly from the other room."

It was Nightingale's turn to look away.

Madre shook her head. "You know I have supernatural hearing when I want, Gale. You also know I could have heard you screaming at him before you even left the room."

"It isn't fair," came the muted response.

"What?"

"Him!" She pointed a finger angrily at him, "He's a fucking pervert! He's either a murderer, a thief," Derik's heart jumped at that, "or he's a wolf! And you are just letting him pretend to be one of the girls! Just like he's one of us!"

Madre stood up sharply, her body glowing around the edges. "She is one of us!"

"He's a fucking guy!"

"As long as I say he's... she is one of us, then she's one of us!" came the bellowing response. Madre's hair rose from her head, wafting on the waves of power rising from the battle mage. Madre took a deep breath and some of the redness faded from her face. When she spoke, it was still forcible. "I am Madre. And you better be damn sure when you disobey me on this. Because if you go to the baron with this, then you stand alone, Nightingale. And if you are wrong, this will be the last time you enjoy this harem."

"He's a fucking guy! The baron doesn't want a damn guy in his harem!"

"Willing to bet your life on it? Are you willing to risk everything on that anger?"

Nightingale's jaw tightened again. She looked angrily at Derik, then to the door. Then, slowly she turned to Madre.

Madre stared at her for a long moment, a battle of wills before she spoke in a hard, commanding voice. "Your choice, Nightingale. Either you obey me, or you go to the baron. Your life, your choice."

Her hands in fists, Nightingale answered, "You are Madre."

Madre let out a long shuddering breath. Her body seemed to relax slightly. "And what happens when you disobey Madre?"

Nightingale sullenly looked away. "She punishes you."

Madre patted her lap.

Nightingale crossed the room as if Derik weren't there, taking a slightly circular path to avoid him. She leaned over and pressed her stomach against Madre's lap, her breasts hanging over the far side. Her legs parted for balance and Derik's cock jumped at the sight of her naked pussy.

Madre ran her hand along the tight buttocks, circling them as she looked down at the submissive woman across lap.

Derik couldn't understand how she could have so much anger toward him and then bend over Madre's lap for punishment without hesitation.

Madre patted Gale on the right cheek. "This is going to hurt."

Nightingale said nothing as she looked fixedly forward, staring at the wall. Derik's breath caught in his throat as Madre lifted her hand. It came down with a crash, smacking her loudly. Derik flinched at the noise, his own burning cheeks clenching in sympathy.

The hand came down again, cracking loudly. Derik flinched again, but Nightingale just stood there. He could see a bright red hand print on her ass. Madre struck again and he watched the ripple of the impact coursing up her body, but she said nothing. Not even a flinch.

When the fourth blow came down, he had to look away.

"Don't," came a warning from Madre.

Derik looked back to see his mistress looking at him.

"Don't you dare look away, Dora. Better yet, come around to watch her face."

Her hand came down again, smacking against the bright red point. Derik flinched, but didn't look away and obeyed the command.

Nightingale's eyes flashed with pain, but another swat came down, then another. They started to rain down, hard and powerful, smacking into her ass until it glowed red.

Derik whimpered, tears forming in his eyes as he watched Nightingale clutching tightly against Madre.

A tear rolled down her cheek, but she kept her jaw clamped shut.

On the next impact, the air moved around him unnaturally. Surprised, he stared at Madre. To his horror, he saw a ripple of energy coursing up Madre's hand as she raised it, surrounding her palm as it impacted against Nightingale's upturned ass.

The impact echoed in the room, the air itself beating against Derik.

Nightingale jerked forward.

Derik shook his head, unable to look away. When he realized she would be punished, he was almost happy, but now, seeing Madre's hand fill with energy and the crack of power as it impacted against the ass left him feeling sick.

Each blow was worse. Nightingale's eyes burned with pain as Madre's hand came down. Each impact blew wind past him as it cracked painfully against her ass. Hot tears poured down his cheeks as he mentally screamed for her to stop. He couldn't count the blows as they came down, one after the other. The magic in the room blew papers from the desk, and beat against his body with every blow. He looked into Madre's face, hoping for mercy, but Madre's eyes held only sadness. This wasn't for anyone's pleasure, not any more.

When he saw blood, he couldn't take any more. Tears soaking his face, he screamed out. "Stop! Please stop!"

Madre's hand froze in place, energy rippling off her fingers as she looked up. She looked surprised as she regarded Derik.

"What?"

"Please!" he wiped at the tears on his face, "Don't hurt her anymore."

Nightingale looked up from her lap, tears running down her cheeks. She looked at him with a mixture of utter confusion and resentment.

Madre lowered her hand as the energy faded. "Why? She risked everything. She risked your life by telling that guard."

Nightingale looked up sharply at Madre, but Madre's eyes were focused on Derik.

"I passed it off as petty jealousy, but you were seconds from being dragged to the dungeon, and you want me to stop?"

She rested her hand on Nightingale's ass, covering up the blood and bruises.

Derik had to think for a moment, looking down at the girl who almost got him arrested. He swallowed hard and let out a shuddering breath. "I... I..."

"Well, spit it out!"

Derik closed his eyes as another tear rolled down his cheek. "Yes, damn it."

There was a long silence before Madre spoke again. "Why?"

Derik opened his eyes to look at Madre. His throat was dry, and he wanted to throw up. "Look, she's right. I am pathetic. I mean, look at me." He gestured to himself. "There is no question. She was right. I'm a spineless coward. I'm terrified the guards are going to come; I won't lie about that."

His words seemed to relax Madre slightly and her finger tapped against Nightingale's bruised skin.

"But, please don't hurt her like this. She got the idea, I don't think she'll do it again."

Madre raised an eyebrow and looked down.

Nightingale looked away until Madre grabbed her hair and twisted her to look.

"Are you going to do this again?"

Nightingale, forced to stare at Madre, shook her head. "No," came the broken whisper, "Madre."

Madre stared at her for a long moment, before giving Derik a hard look. "She has three more. Would you take one of them for her?"

Derik froze, "Um, what?"

"Would you take one of her swats? Would you be willing to take the blows for her?"

His heart slammed against his chest as a cold wind blew past him. He started to tremble, staring at the bloody ass before him.

Nightingale wouldn't look at him, pointedly looking away as he stared at her.

The world spun around him, lurching his stomach to the side as he trembled.

"That's one."

Derik whimpered, his body tensing painfully.

"Two," came Madre's hard voice.

"Fuck! Yes, I will!"

His voice echoed shrilly against the walls, even as he wanted to crawl under the desk or run away screaming. Hot tears blurred his vision as he fought against his fear.

"Very well."

Her hand came down with a force of a thousand storms, an explosion of wind blowing the papers off the desk and collapsing three shelves. The energy slammed into him as Nightingale finally let out a single shrill scream of pain. It echoed against the walls as she straightened out in agony and her bare feet kicked off the ground.

Madre lifted her hand and Derik saw the energy building, massive and powerful as the air around her palm seemed to twist on itself.

Nightingale's scream had barely died in her throat when it came down. The force of the blow threw Derik off his feet as Nightingale let out another wail of pain which faded with the echoes in the room.

Derik scrambled to his feet to see Madre helping the shaking Nightingale to her feet.

Blood dripped down her buttocks as she glared at Derik.

He shook violently at the thought he was going to experience the same agony himself.

Madre helped her lean over the bed, suddenly compassionate again. "Just let me do this, Gale, just one more thing."

She sat back down and looked pointedly at Derik.

He almost ran away as his balls tried to crawl up into his body. He took one shaking step forward, then one back. Madre's stare never wavered, and he made his way to her. Slipping next to the bent-over Nightingale. He heard her sniffing as he bent over Madre's lap. His heart crashed against his ribs in hard, brutal beats. He positioned himself over her damp thigh.

Her hand brushed against his back, rubbing against the red mark of his ass from his prior spanking. He parted his legs as his cock pressed against her thigh. He let his hand dangle until she whispered to him.

"Grab my leg, you can't hurt me."

Madre's hand gently rested against his heated ass. She circled it with her palm. She appeared to hesitate and the anticipation of her blow grew stronger. He adjusted his position again as he cringed with the thought of when she finally struck.

"This is one for Nightingale."

The tears blurred his vision. It took all of his willpower to make a grunting noise in acknowledgment.

Madre spoke again softly. "Now, she's a pain slut, which means it will probably hurt more than you can imagine."

"You mean, she was enjoying this?" The revelation somehow made it worse.

On the other side, Nightingale sniffed hard and Madre shook her head.

"No, this was a real punishment. I can't allow you, her, or anyone else threaten my harem."

The hand rose up from his ass, and he tensed, waiting for the blow.

"And if there is one thing I can't stand, is people who lie to me."

He didn't know when her hand came down, but his entire world exploded in agony. His spine burned sharply, as if she had shattered it, and his vision turned to stars. He tried to scream, but his throat refused to move as pain seared through his system, burning away his world until he thought he would be blown away with dust. Time compressed down to a single point, a singularity of suffering.

Derik woke up on Madre's bed, face down and sobbing.

Madre stroked his hair. All the hardness had faded from her face. "Hurts, doesn't it?"

Still sobbing, he nodded. His hand bent back to touch his buttocks, hissing at the pain, but thankful that he could still move his legs. He couldn't imagine how Nightingale could take so much without screaming out.

"More than you thought possible?"

He nodded again.

Madre bent over and kissed the back of his shoulder.

Shocked, he stared at her first demonstration of affection.

She whispered in his ear. "There is spanking for pleasure and there is spanking for punishment. Many of my girls are turned on by the mild stuff, just like you," he let out a whimper as her breath teased his ear, "but there is a very hard line when it isn't to turn you on. Nightingale passed that line when she threatened you. She passed it again when she told the guard instead of talking to me."

She stroked his cheek.

He turned his head to look at her with bleary eyes.

She had a smile on her lip as she kissed him on the cheek. "Now, go out with the others. I suspect you aren't in the mood for sex, and I'd rather you enjoy it instead of dreading it."

She helped him up.

He stumbled, clutching to her as he regained his feet.

Nightingale had not moved, still bent over the edge of the bed. He could see her tears soaking the sheets and the blankets. Trickles of blood ran down her thighs and along the furrow between her legs.

Despite the threats and everything, he spoke up, surprised that his voice cracked. "What about her?"

Madre picked up his robe and slipped it over his shoulder. Even the touch of silk against his burning buttocks sent a hiss of pain from his throat. He shuddered at the feeling.

"She's going to spend the night here."

Surprise and fear bolted through him as he looked at her. "You said—"

Madre held up a hand, "Her punishment is over. That doesn't mean that I can't feel some sympathy for her. Once punished, the topic is dropped. Period."

Derik thought about it for a moment, and Madre repeated herself.

Then she continued, "Period. You don't mention it to the others, you don't complain about my decision. You can talk about what I did to you, but neither you nor her will ever," she growled out the word, "have this issue again. Do you understand?"

Nodding frantically, he agreed.

"Now, get some sleep. Nothing that can help that pain except sleep. If the girls try to ride your face, you don't have to unless you want to."

Dismissed, Derik limped out the door and shut it quietly behind him. The summer rain on the roof mimicked the tears rolling down his cheeks. As he stumbled down the hall, he realized two things:

One, the guilt of stealing the Eye of Hamel had risen to an unbearable point. He had never experienced anything so emotionally painful before. He wanted to burst back into the room to tell her, but his lies wrapped around his throat and choked him into silence.

And two, he really, really wasn't in the mood for Teri to ride his burning ass with a strap-on.

Pillow

Limping painfully, Derik had to lean against the wall just to move. The coldness from the tile beneath his feet did nothing to soothe his burning ass from Madre's single magical blow.

Outside, he could feel the patter of raindrops splattering on the roof, rolling down gutters, and splashing beyond the walls of the harem. The ceiling and walls shook from the rain hitting them.

He looked out at the harem, the sprawl of naked women. Somewhere in the sea of flesh rested Teri with her evil thoughts and Sherrel with her compassion. His eyes scanned up to the skylights. Flashes of lighting lit up the room and, he blinked at the brightness.

Outside.

His life had changed already. Just a few days had passed, filled with abuse from Teri and forced lapping at the pussies of the rest. Somehow, he had this strange feeling of comfort that he never had outside.

He sighed, his eyes sliding along the shadows of the ceiling to focus on one of the many open vents above it. Somewhere above him, the most precious gem in the country waited in a vent. Or it had fallen and was underneath or behind some furniture. Remembering how it seemed to move with its own will, he grimaced. It was probably waiting to drag him into some other annoying situation, like the guard barracks filled with horny men.

He shivered at the thought, then blushed as he realized his cock twitched at the thought. Blinking, he looked back up at the vent.

It would only take a second. A rapid climb, and he could be running in the streets with the gem and his freedom.

Slowly and painfully, he limped around the harem, circling the naked flesh. He found the chest of drawers and the fountain, knowing that right above it was the gem. His eyes, adjusted to the light, stared up at the darkness.

"D-Dora?"

He jumped as Sherrel groggily spoke up from the pillows. He looked guilty as he turned around.

She had lifted herself slightly off the pillows, her full breasts teasing the soft velvet.

"Are you okay?" she whispered.

Derik turned his back to the vent of his freedom and limped over to her.

Sherrel sat up as he got closer.

He started to sit down, then let out a groan as his abused ass protested.

Realization flashed across Sherrel's face and she pressed a hand against her mouth. "My god, was that you being punished?"

Derik whispered back, "Yes and no."

"I don't understand."

"I foolishly took one for Gale."

Sherrel stroked the side of his face. "Why? She's a bitch."

Derik sighed as he tried to sit down again, but the pain in his ass was too much. Even the thought of the soft velvet against his buttocks caused a twinge of pain to rise up his spine. "Because I'm an idiot."

She shook her head and smiled. "You aren't an idiot. Here…"

She shifted on her back, spreading her legs like a lover. Arching her back and shoving forward her breasts, she situated some pillows behind her back. Then, with a grin, she placed one precisely on her sex, covering it. "Lie down, on your stomach."

Derik frowned, but obeyed, wincing as he knelt between her legs. His strength failed him and he landed on her, his nose bumping her forehead. Her skin was warm and soft compared to the chill teasing his exposed backside.

Sherrel's breath blew hot across his skin. She wiggled into place then wrapped her arms around him. "Just use me as a pillow, Dora."

He settled down, one hand against her right breast and the other on her hip. His cock, the traitor of flesh, rose up to grind against the pillow, and he rested his chin her shoulder.

She suddenly stroked his hair and he jumped in surprise. When she only ran her fingers along it, he relaxed again.

"I used to do this with Teri, you know," whispered Sherrel.

"Really?"

"Yes, she was always getting in trouble. She'd come limping out of that room, her ass practically on fire and trying not to cry. Though, I never thought you'd be a troublemaker."

She giggled and Derik found a grin crossing his face. Then, guilt grabbed him and the smile faded. He pressed his face into the pillow under her, his thumb teasing the hard nipple in his palm. "Why are you doing this?"

He wasn't sure why he asked, but he had to.

Sherrel stroked his hair and shifted her hips under the pillow before she answered. "Because, there is something about you. When I first saw your eyes, I didn't see a pervert."

His heart skipped a beat. "What did you see?" he asked.

She turned her head, and he lifted slightly to look at her. Her bright eyes shimmered in the light of the storm. "I saw someone who belonged here."

A tear formed underneath one eye. He opened his mouth to say something, then closed it. Derik tried to say something again, then just pressed his chin against her shoulder, staring into the pillow.

Sherrel stroked his hair softly.

Derik sniffed. "It can't last, you know."

She shook her head. "No, it can't. Sooner or later, the wrong person will figure out you're a guy. Then, you'll be taken away, or you'll leave us."

He sighed, blinking back the tears.

She smiled sweetly at him. "I was lying here a little bit ago, and you know what?"

He leaned against her, drinking in the scent of her body and the feel of her skin. She was soft and compassionate, beautiful and comforting.

"What?"

"I wished you were one of us, a real woman."

Silence pooled around them as he stared into the pillow. Then he slowly lifted himself again to look into her eyes. "Why?" It came out as a soft, broken whisper.

She smiled up at him, like a true lover in his arms. "Because I like you. You are sweet and compassionate. Just the right amount of submissive and slut," he blushed at that, "and you belong here."

He stared at her in shock.

She lifted her head to kiss him.

He froze for a moment, then kissed her back. Her lips were so soft and delicate, but they were hot and powerful. He followed her down, resting her head against her pillow as their lips embraced, moving against each other, sending wonderful pleasures burning inside him.

The hand on his head held him firmly, holding his mouth against her own as their tongues caressed, teasing with the flavor of another in his mouth. It was hot and tender and he never wanted it to stop. He gasped but she held him there, their kiss growing hotter as she twisted her head slightly so their noses brushed against each other.

Underneath him, her body arched up, pressing the firm mounds of her breasts up to him. His fingers wrapped around her breast, teasing the hard nipple and trailing his fingers along the puckered tip. She moaned, deep and throaty. He curled his hand under her back, holding her tightly to him. His cock, hard and aching, ground against the pillow. Without, he would be violating one of Madre's laws. Instead, he just pumped into the pillow as she ground her hips from the other side.

Soft whimpers escaped her throat as she jerked up against him. Then, she released his head and pulled away. Looking up with smoldering eyes, she parted her lips. "Finger me."

He said nothing, but his hand slid around the pillow, delving along damp fabric to plunge his fingers into her wet pussy.

She let out a low moan of pleasure and arched her back.

He trailed his lips against her collar and throat, moving down to take a hard nipple in his mouth. His fingers drove into the smooth, soaked folds of her womanhood, driving up into her as she let out gasps of ecstasy that filled the room.

Wet and slurping, he drove into the molten core of her being until she arched her back sharply and brought in a long, shuddering breath.

Her body squeezed his fingers while she ground up against him.

He continued to pump, his fingers dripping with her juices. Just as he started to withdraw, she grabbed his head and brought him into another kiss, grinding her lips against his and stealing his breath away.

Derik kissed her as if she were the only woman in the world. His fingers toyed with her entrance and he ground his cock into the pillow, feeling how his own juices had soaked the surface in sticky cum. He didn't even remember coming, but the passion of the kiss brought another orgasm in his loins, and soon he was pumping more seed into the pillow.

When she released him again, he was gasping for breath. She panted, looking into his eyes, then looked around.

He followed her gaze to see three others watching them, fingers delving between their legs as they lost themselves in their own fantasies. Derik's eyes widened but Sherrel made no attempt to move.

"Look at them, all pretty little things," she whispered.

They watched the others as one of them, a raven-haired woman came with a shuddering gasp of her own. She blew both of them a kiss before rolling over to return to sleep. The other two continued to finger themselves, their eyes closed tightly.

Sherrel cocked her head. "Let's go help them."

It was a command, but a playful one. He wiped his cock on the pillow and set it aside before crawling toward the nearest. His ass, still on fire, protested as he brought his fingers to her pussy.

She welcomed him, and he brought her pleasure as Sherrel pleasured the other.

Later, much later, he sank into the tub and yawned.

Sherrel slid in next to him, her body sinking under the surface of the water before surfacing. "I'm not sure how those things get started, you start licking one woman, then another wakes up and joins. By the time you know it, you are wrists deep in pussy and your fingers hurt."

Derik chuckled as he gingerly tried to sit. Uncomfortable, he rolled over and let himself float in the water. "Story of my life lately."

Water splashed as she came up to him, rubbing her hands against his back. "It isn't that bad, is it?"

Derik thought for a moment, "Actually, no. It's very pleasant."

He flinched as she trailed a finger down his ass crack. "I'm glad."

Neither said anything for a long time. Then he spoke abstractly. "Are you really a princess?"

Sherrel's finger froze on his back. "Yes, three years ago. A different life."

"What happened?" It was the wrong thing to say. He knew it the second it passed his lips.

Her fingers pulled away, and she turned her back to him.

Ashamed, he turned over and sat up, wincing as his beaten ass pressed down on the tile. Trembling, he reached out with his hand. "I'm sorry."

Sherrel looked back, with tears in her eyes, and leaned away from his hand. "I just can't talk about that right now."

She stood up to leave.

He held out his hand, feeling sorrow and guilt inside him. "Please don't go."

"Stay here, Teri should be back soon." Her voice was lower and had lost all the tenderness.

Derik watched as she walked out of the room, dripping with water but not looking back. He listened to her fading footsteps and every step made him feel more horrible than the previous. He waited for nearly twenty minutes, half hoping she would return. When she didn't, he crawled out of the tub himself and used a towel to dry. His ass remained sore, but some of the heated pain had finally faded. Half fearing of what he would see, he inspected himself in the full-length mirrors that lined the bathroom.

It looked like he had avoided serious damage. Curiously, he stroked his fingertips along the curve and enjoyed the warmth against his tender skin. As he reached near his tailbone, he stroked down just to enjoy the pleasure and pain that teased his senses.

When he straightened up, his member was, once again, at full mast, and he had a flush on his cheeks.

"Damn it, I don't like being spanked," he lied to himself.

Deciding to keep that bit of knowledge to himself, he wrapped the towel around his body and padded back into the main room. For a moment, he didn't know where to go, but then he spotted Sherrel back in her place, legs spread and a pillow placed on her sex. Just like before.

Relieved, he returned to her and knelt between her legs. After a moment hesitation, he leaned his hip into her. She tensed up for a moment, and he thought he did the wrong thing, then she reached up to stroke his head. He rested his chin against her shoulder, his cheek pressing against hers, and sighed. "I'm sorry."

She didn't say anything, just stroked his hair.

Embarrassed, he tried not to think about his failings. Instead, he concentrated on the warmth and softness of her body caressing his. "I didn't want to hurt you."

Sherrel finally answered, "I know. I'll tell you when the time comes, but you need to sleep a bit. Madre will want you in her room come noon."

Her other arm wrapped around his back and he pressed his arms against her. Embraced, he gave her one kiss on the lips, a soft brush of pleasure, and they both drifted to sleep.

Morning Duties

Madre woke him with a frown and an angry tapping on his shoulder. He looked up, sleepy and exhausted, into her tense face. She gestured down at Sherrel, and he looked at her. Asleep, she smiled as she groaned and spread her legs a bit more.

Derik sat up, thankful his ass didn't hurt as much. His eyes looked down to the junction of their beings, where the velvet pillow kept them safely apart. He picked up the pillow and held it up to Madre.

To his surprise, she suddenly smiled and gestured for him to follow.

He scrambled to his feet, not wanting to wake up Sherrel. Hurrying up, he picked his way across the room, cleaned up, and hurried to Madre's room. Instead of knocking, he entered and looked around the room.

Nightingale was there, curled up on the foot of the bed. Leather straps held her arms behind her back and pulled her knees up to her chest. His mouth slowly opened as the sight of a large dildo driven up in the cleft of her being, glistening with rivulets of excitement that soaked the blankets. Her eyes were half-focused, looking out into nothing as she worked her lips around a bright blue gag in her mouth.

Madre chuckled dryly next to him. "I suspect she didn't get much sleep last night."

He found himself staring at her splayed open pussy. She seemed to respond to his look by rocking her hips, moving the dildo back and forth as a fresh river of pussy juices dripping along the member. His throat was dry. "Is... Is she okay?"

Madre laughed, "Never better probably. Nightingale is happiest bound at the foot of my bed, with something shoved into that cunt of hers."

The flush on his cheek spread to his ears as he stared at her. He knew his mouth was open in surprise, but he couldn't tear his eyes away from her face. He could see her mouth working around the ball gag and drooling into the blanket.

Then, for a brief moment, he wondered what it would feel like to be in her position and his cock almost exploded right there. With a groan, he turned away with his cheeks burning with embarrassment.

Madre chuckled dryly. "Come on, we need to do one more thing, and then I'm putting her to sleep in the main room. Teri and the others should be back from their night with the baron, so its going to be a quiet day."

He looked at her with surprise, "Baron?"

"Yes, I sent five of them over to keep him company last night. He was in a mood, and best to keep your master happy, right?"

Derik blushed as he helped Madre pull Nightingale toward the edge of the bed. Her skin was slick with sweat and hot with excitement. But, at his touch, he could feel her tense.

Madre tugged her off the bed, forcing her to her knees right off the edge. The dildo slipped out and bumped against the ground. As he watched, Nightingale's legs spread out slightly to drive it back into her glistening slit.

To distract himself from the girl impaling herself, he swallowed before asking Madre a question. "Does he need that many?"

Madre answered with another question, "You mean, does the baron really need to fuck five women in a night?"

"Um, yeah."

"Yes," came the simply reply.

"Really?"

"As you no doubt heard, he is very large. He is also very hard and can easily go five or six hours without growing soft."

The flush that was almost fading ignited in his cheeks. His jaw tightened as he listened.

Madre spoke as she brushed out Nightingale's hair, tender and caring despite the bondage and gagging. "And... well, it's hard to explain, but they get tired. Drained, if you will."

"Drained?"

"Yes, I was one of the few who has ever done a single night with the baron by myself, a 'solo run' as they call it. The more he plowed every hole in my body, the more exhausted I became. By morning, I couldn't even find the energy to crawl out of bed."

The last bit ended with a grin and a laugh, but he wondered if he would escape before he suffered the same fate.

"Now, I think it is time for Nightingale to be reminded of something."

Madre worked the blindfold off Nightingale. The girl looked up at Madre with shimmering expression, which instantly hardened as she spotted Derik. Madre reached down to cup her chin and spoke softly, but firmly. "Now, my love. I know you promised you wouldn't put anything of Dora in your mouth, but I want you to suck her off, okay? Then you can sleep."

Both Nightingale's and Derik's eyes widened with surprise. Her eyes focused on him, anger and frustration burning brightly. He could see her twisting and shifting, rocking on the dildo driven in her pussy and her own desire to lean away from him.

Madre, on the other hand, wouldn't have any of that. She drew Nightingale's eyes back to hers. "I am Madre."

A nod and frustrated tears in her eyes.

"And she is going to fuck your mouth."

Another nod.

Derik's cock jumped up at the thought as he looked back and forth. He cleared his throat. "Um, Madre? I don't know if I'm comfortable with this."

Madre looked up with a curious expression. "I wasn't aware I asked you, Dora."

He flushed as Madre used her fingertips to work the ball gag out of Nightingale's stretched lips. Nightingale gasped with breath, licking her lips as she stared at Madre with pleading eyes.

Madre shook her head and motioned for Derik.

Helpless to obey her, he stepped in front of Nightingale with a throbbing cock already dripping with pre-cum.

Nightingale looked at it with all the disgust of someone coming up to a half-rotted corpse.

Madre walked behind him, then held his hips firmly. "Now, grab her head."

Ashamed, he obeyed, his heart pounding in his chest as he aimed his cock toward her mouth.

Nightingale glared at him and kept her mouth sealed shut. Her short hair teased his palms as he held her head firmly.

Madre pushed him forward, and he pressed his cock up against her lips. The pressure built before her jaws parted. His cock slipped past her lips and scraped past her teeth. He gasped, shuddering as Madre held him down.

"And tell me if she uses her teeth," came a wry but playful whisper.

Instantly, Nightingale's mouth opened more, and he lurched forward, driving her nose into the base of his cock and his entire throbbing length into the moist depths of her mouth. She swallowed his length, her tongue trying to shove him out and he shuddered with the pleasure.

"Now, Dora, I want you to fuck her mouth, but if you come, you'll be punished."

He let out a whimper. Looking down, he just saw Nightingale silently glaring at him, with a look that could cut the throat of a god. He shuddered as Madre shoved him forward, grinding the base of his cock against her lips.

"Move."

Holding her head tightly, he rocked back and thrust into her mouth.

She threatened to close her jaw.

His heart lurched in fear, but her teeth never touched him. Nervous and frightened, he just held her tighter and thrust into her mouth. With every stroke, he ground her face into his stomach. His balls slapped against her chin, and he pulled out. Each thrust brought more anger to those eyes that refused to look away from him, and he suddenly wanted her to stop hating him.

Using the only weapon he could, Derik began to drive into her, fucking her mouth with hard, almost brutal strokes. He could feel his balls slapping against her, the tickle in the back of her throat. Tears formed in his eyes as he held her gaze, silently begging her to stop hating him. His cock, glistening with her saliva, plunged in and out with a wet slurping noise and he almost came from the sounds alone.

Then, something cold pressed against his ass.

He gasped, lunging forward to bury his length, but Madre just pulled his hips back, and a pair of lubricated fingers worked their way into his anal ring.

"Don't stop," came the command.

He whimpered and saw a look of triumph on Nightingale's face as he found himself in a different type of movement, driving into the wet depths of her mouth or pushing back against the slick fingers that pierced his most private of places. As he drove into Nightingale's hot mouth, Madre's hand would pull him back, impaling him on her slick fingers.

The intense sensations in two different places filled him with a burning heat.

He tried to slow down, but Madre pushed and pulled him, forcing him to fuck Nightingale and himself at the same time.

With horror, he realized he was about to come and tried to stop it, squeezing down on muscles he didn't realize he had in a desperate attempt to stop. His cock betrayed him and he started to orgasm, but the pressure in his rectum prevented the cum from spraying out. He let out a whimper as his body betrayed him by trying to come again and again. The ring of his ass tightened on her fingers but he kept on fucking his cock and ass between mouth and fingers.

The intensity of his orgasm rose up higher and higher, a knife edge of pleasure. Finally, it was too much and he let out a strangled sob as he began to flood Nightingale's mouth with his searing hot cum.

She gagged for a moment, then swallowed down as Madre shoved him forward. Nightingale's nose ground against his base and he let out more surges of pleasure against the back of her throat.

Madre sighed, "I didn't give you permission to come, Dora."

Then she drove a third finger into his ass, pumping in and out of him with the same hard, rough strokes he had fucked Nightingale's mouth with. He bent over Nightingale's head and planted one hand on the blanket behind her for balance. As Madre pounded her three slick fingers into his body, he whimpered. Feelings of being used and violated filled him. She pumped him in the same manner that she had forced him to use against Nightingale. Now he was the victim of her lusts.

His hardness surged again, flooding Nightingale's trapped throat as he came a second time. This time, he saw stars in his vision as Madre drove the fingers deep into his rectum and held them there. He sobbed from the pleasure and pain, caught between Madre and Nightingale's hot, churning throat.

After an infinity of time, Madre allowed him to pull his dripping shaft from Nightingale's mouth.

She breathed deeply, gasping actually, as he withdrew, but his cock came out glistening clean. Her eyes burned a hole in his heart, the icy glare scraping against his senses as she look up.

Madre unbound Nightingale and helped her up.

Nightingale was unsteady, but ignored Derik's offered hand. Deliberately, the harem women turned away from him as Madre whispered to her. A few moments later, the dildo dropped to the ground and Nightingale limped out of the room.

Madre watched her, then turned to Derik with a disappointed look on her face. "Tonight, you are taking her place."

Derik could only whimper.

Refusal

Derik had hoped sex wouldn't be in the cards. As the new girl, he found himself in Madre's tub, washing her body as she explained the plans for the day. His fingers worked at the curves and even teased her sex, but she wasn't in the mood for anything beyond a quick flick against her clitoris and a pat on his head.

He, on the other hand, suffered with Madre washing him and scrubbing his hair. He hoped to get out of her fingers sliding into his ass, but she bent him over her lap in the tub and fingered his hole until he came hard into the soap bubbles.

Then, he was presented with a fresh change of outfit: all the deepest blue he had ever seen. Panties, a bra with padding.

Madre gave him a grin as she handed it over. "This way, you won't be wearing Teri's sloppy underwear against your skin. I kept smelling whenever I was close to you."

He blushed hotly as he struggled with the bra.

Madre helped after a moment, smoothing over his curves.

Then he dressed himself in the silk top while remembering which direction went in front.

Madre nodded in approval, then offered to brush and braid his hair.

Thankful, he found she was a rough, but very fair mistress when it came to his appearance.

Madre spotted him with perfume, a delicate apple-scented one that was almost enjoyable, and they went out into the harem. She announced the plans for the day, away from the six sleeping women in the corner. "Okay, today is marking day."

Derik sat next to Sherrel and frowned, but he didn't want to say anything to embarrass himself. Instead, he just listened.

"We'll use the massage room. Forbis and his apprentices can handle up to five of you. Remember, after this, it does mean you can play with Dora the way some of you want—"

She pointedly looked at Teri who still slept in the corner. The room filled with giggles and Derik blushed hotly as Sherrel patted his lap and slid a hand up his thigh.

Madre paused for the laughter, then continued. "But, please remind the little palace cat not to do it in public?"

One of the others spoke up. "Is, um, Dora going to get marked?"

Madre though for a moment, "It would look strange if she didn't have the same markings as all of you, so yes. But, I'm going to need to talk to Forbis about that, ideally he'll keep it a secret for a few days."

The presence of more than thirty women focused on him.

Derik cringed slightly against Sherrel.

Another question: "Is he—"

"She—" corrected Madre.

"Fine, is she going to get the female one or the male one?"

Derik had no clue what they were talking about. He continued to listened as some of the women turned to look at him.

Sherrel just kept her hand on his thigh, teasing him slightly as they listened.

Madre sighed unhappily, "Forgot about that. I better talk to Forbis. The male one is pretty obvious, isn't it?"

"Blue geometric instead of the yellow weaving," said one of the other girls in a confident tone. "It also uses the fifth pattern of Hugo's—"

"Damned gods, I'll figure out something. Dora will be last of course. Once that is done, you have the rest of the day to yourself."

As one, the room looked up to stare up at the rain rapping against the skylight, the shadows of clouds pouring ahead.

Madre arched an eyebrow. "Wish you could run out, but the baron is holed up in negotiations. I think..." she looked around the room and picked out some of the harem members, "you six should go up to him come midnight. He's going to need to blow some steam."

"And something else."

The room dissolved into giggles and Madre joined them before heading out.

Derik blushed hotly as he looked over at Sherrel. "Um…"

She smiled at him, her fingers delving between his legs to stroke against the base of his tucked shaft. "Something?"

"What is marking day?"

Sherrel cocked her head quizzically, then smiled again. "No idea? It's this rune that goes on the base of your spine, right at the small of your back."

Derik gaped slightly as he realized what she was talking about. Most whores had them, a circular disk-shaped marking on their base. There were different colors, but he knew to always pick the pink and yellow ones, they were the safest. "Oh, you mean whore mar—"

The word froze in his throat. Suddenly frightened, he saw Sherrel stare at him in shock, then her expression turned stormy. Slowly, she got on her knees and leaned over him. He tried to pull away, but she pinned him down with her weight and her fingers curling up between his legs.

Her voice was icy as she spoke curtly to him, "Are you calling me a whore?"

For a moment, fright flooded his thoughts and he had to look away. "No."

Sherrel held him in place until he began to shake and the nearly ever-present blush burned at his cheeks. Then she lowered herself down, the yellow silk of her robe fluttering. "I don't recommend you ever call it a whore mark again, Dora."

"Sorry," came his sullen response.

He couldn't look at her until her fingers caught his chin. He tried to pull away, but she dug up between his legs. Wincing, he let her catch his chin and turn him to face her.

"Now," she said more cheerfully, "there are three of them. They are the magical runes of sterility, protection, and containment.

There is also entrapment, but I highly recommend you never get that one."

"Entrapment?"

Teri dropped down next to him, naked and yawning, "It means that when they come in you, it doesn't come out. Even if your belly gets full and you think you are going to explode."

Derik jumped but Teri giggled and wrapped her arm around his waist, pulling him close so she could rest her head on his shoulder.

"Pretty useless when you got one or two guys, but someone like the baron who comes in buckets or a really good gang bang can make you really full in a hurry."

Derik tried to consider the idea but he couldn't imagine it. Neither of them seemed to say anything, so he asked another question. "Do you, um, we get all three?"

Sherrel nodded, "Yep. Sterility is why Teri will be able to play with you, means you won't get pregnant. But, there is a version for guys—"

Teri interrupted with a giggle, "Or slutty boys pretending to be girls."

Derik blushed hotly, and Sherrel rolled her eyes.

"And protection means you don't get diseases. Containment means you don't have to worry about things coming out."

He realized that the pink and yellow runes were sterility and protection, but he didn't think he understood containment.

"I don't get it."

Teri leaned up, pressing her breasts against his arm. "It means, when the baron fucks that tight little ass of yours–" Her fingers teased his ass cheeks and he squirmed away. Teri followed him, her finger resting against his anal ring before she whispered evilly, "—then no poop comes out. It will be as clean as he shoved it in."

Derik's cock twitched at the thought and he wondered if he could blush even more.

Teri teased his opening, but withdrew after a second.

Sherrel, a faint blush on her own cheeks, swallowed before she said, "It also means he can safely go from ass to mouth without anyone getting sick. Since the baron ride our holes pretty hard, it's an important thing."

"I-I can imagine," he said even if he couldn't.

Teri yawned again. Without asking him, she curled up against his lap, her head resting on his thigh and proceeded to go back to sleep.

Derik held out his hands for a moment, then rested it on her breast. Underneath, her nipple hardened but he made no additional effort to please her.

Sherrel grinned as she stood up. Gesturing down to Teri, she said, "Looks like you have pillow duties now, Dora."

He ducked his head but he couldn't help but notice her presence in front of him. Looking up, he lost himself in her smile, then looked down at her slick pussy right in front of his mouth. Without being asked, he opened his mouth and drew her in, one hand stroking Teri's breast while the other held Sherrel's ass to lap at her sex.

Sweet and tangy, he thought, his tongue delving between the heated folds. Sherrel held his head, gentle, not grinding as he brought her to a slow, smoldering orgasm. Then she withdrew, leaving him with a glistening face and a smile.

Derik wiped her juices off his face with her hand, but remained on the pillows, comforting Teri as he watched the rest of the room.

Forbis showed up just under a half hour later. He was an older man, maybe in his fifties, with bushy eyebrows and a scowl on his face. He had a black bag in his hand and Derik saw runes flickering along the outside. In specific, he saw a few warding runes to discourage any thieves from stealing the contents.

Not that it would have stopped Derik.

The older man had five assistants, all barely dressed females in clothes at least two sizes too small. Their breasts were huge, the size of pillows, and they had puffy lips and wide hips. Derik stared at them in shock—they looked like cheap whores on Pipe Street more than assistants. They passed them on their way to the massage room, and he almost choked from their perfume.

Any desire to move fled as the doctor and the assistants frequently entered into the main room, gathering up the members of the harem or asking questions. Derik kept his head bowed and waited, staring at Teri if one came closer.

When they woke Teri, one of the last, he finally stood up and fled behind one of the columns. He was terrified. Looking up, he stared at the vent above his head. Just thirty seconds. Looking around, he could see a few within sight, but he realized he couldn't stay. Taking a deep breath, he reached up for the hook to pull himself up.

"You okay?" asked Madre as she came around the pillar.

He jumped at her voice, and backed up against the wall. "Um, yeah."

"You look frightened, Dora."

Sweat dappling his brow, he could only nod.

Madre looked at him curiously, then glanced up at the ceiling. His heart pounded against his chest for a moment, then she returned her gaze to him. "Well, it's time."

When she took his hand, she held it firmly.

He took a deep breath and followed, pulling the sapphire silk robe around his chest to cover himself as she drew him toward the massage room.

Inside, the room was mostly dark and lit by candles and floating lights. In the far end was a pond with a trickle of water, icy cold but relaxing to listen to. Forbis stood by one of the tables, finishing up Nightingale's markings. He had four sticks between his fingers, each one sparkling with magical power as he drew on her back. Derik watched as his sure hands traced out lines and obvious energy poured down the sticks into the tips. One hand was between her legs, obviously fingering her as he held her still.

Nightingale just had her eyes closed, an expression of annoyance and apathy plain for everyone to see.

"Ah, ah, there we go. Lovely as ever, my lovely Gale."

He had a southern accent, kind of a drawl with a hint of Carium gentry in it.

Derik clutched himself tighter as Madre strode over to him.

"Forbis?"

"One moment, Rachi, one moment."

He finished with a flourish and a twist of his wrist as he delved his fingers deep between Nightingale's thighs.

She jerked, then sat up when he pulled away. Spotting Derik, she smirked. Hopping off, she walked past him and left Derik alone with Madre, Forbis, and his assistants.

Madre watched her leave, then turned to Forbis. "Could I have a moment alone?"

"Oh sure, Rachi, just..."

His voice trailed off and he just waved to the voluptuous women. They shrugged indifferently and filtered out of the room.

Derik couldn't meet their gaze as he stepped away, trying to keep to the shadows. His stomach lurched right and left, as if it was being twisted in a storm.

Forbis looked at her and a creepy grin crossed his lips. "Oh, a new girl? A new toy for Forbis?"

"No, she's special."

"Ah," he nodded sagely. "A virgin for the baron? No shoving fingers in her wet pussy?"

Derik blushed hotly, feeling his puckered opening clenching at the thought of him.

Forbis regarded her for a long moment, then turned back to his bag. His voice lost some of the playfulness instantly. "What is it, Rachi?"

Madre actually sounded uncomfortable as she glanced at Derik. "I-I need to you to mark her as a woman."

"But, she is a woman..." it only took a single heartbreaking moment for him to realize it. "A guy?"

Madre nodded, "Yes."

He gave her a quizzical look. "I wasn't aware that the baron was into guys."

She said nothing for a moment. Then she glanced away. "He isn't."

"And yet, here he is."

Derik's face burned as he looked away.

Forbis stared at him, unseen but the man's presence burned Derik's skin.

After a second, Derik glanced over his shoulder to see a look of disgust on the older man's face. Then, he turned and started to pack up his things. "Won't do it, Rachi."

Madre put a hand on his shoulder. "Please? For me?"

Forbis shook his head. "No, I don't approve. Why is he here then? Not for you, I know that."

Madre blushed herself and withdrew her hand.

The older man slammed his stuff into his bag. "So, there is something else going on. There is a man in the harem, a man the baron doesn't know about."

Madre started to say something, then closed her mouth with a snap.

Derik trembled, feeling that he stood on the edge of a cliff.

"I will not mark him as a woman, that is an offense to my trade. And I will not let any man ruin the baron's goods."

"Damn it, please?"

"No, Rachi, this is wrong. Utterly wrong and an offense, and you know it. He should be in the dungeon or somewhere else, not ruining the baron's goods!"

His voice rumbled as he spoke.

Madre clenched her jaw for a moment, before she spoke curtly. "You owe me, damn it."

Forbis froze for a moment, then shook his head. "Not this big, Rachi. You're asking me to violate the trust of the baron, my guild, and my profession. Even that... that incident isn't enough."

"It wasn't that small!"

He didn't budge for a long moment, two forces of personality glaring at each other. Then, Forbis relaxed slightly. "But, you called that favor, and I can respect at least part of it. I won't tell anyone, but I won't mark him as a woman."

She said nothing for a long time.

He finished packing his bag. "Take it or leave it, Rachi, you won't find another marker in this town that will do it."

"Damn it. I'll take it."

He snapped his bag shut loudly. He gave Derik a hard look before turned sharply to Madre. "Get rid of him, Rachi. He's a bad egg. He cannot bring anything good this place and you know it."

"But-"

"Nothing."

As a final word, he stormed out of the room, brushing past Derik roughly as he disappeared.

Derik's jaw clamped down tightly as he heard the footsteps fading with the distance, then him calling for the others to leave.

Slowly, he looked up at Madre. "What did he mean?"

Madre tried to visibly relax. She let out a long shuddering breath. "About what, Derik?"

She used his real name and the sound branded his skin. "About me not being for you?"

"Because he knows I'm in love with someone else."

With that, she stormed out of the room.

He could feel the heat of her anger blasting him as she left, and he leaned against the wall for a long moment. "Well, fuck."

Alone in the massage room, he opened his hand. Most of Forbis' marking tools rested in his palm, crackling with soft power. He regarded them for a long moment, wondering if he could fake the markings at least. He lifted one up and drew along his hand, holding it lightly as he saw Forbis do. No color touched his skin, but he could feel the power tingling inside the tools.

Then Madre called for him.

Loudly.

Sighing, he padded over to one of the massage tables and pulled open a drawer, putting the stolen marking sticks into the back before answering her call.

Oral Sex

"You didn't get marked."

Teri sat down next to the sullen Derik and stared at him with her clear eyes. She had a plate of food in her hand, which she delicately picked at. Her robe fluttered to the pillows, hanging off her left shoulder.

He glanced at her and shook his head.

She popped a piece of raw fruit into her mouth, staring pointedly at him. "Why?"

"Forbis refused."

Teri patted him, then held a slice of apple to his mouth. He looked at her and she arched an eyebrow. Opening his mouth obediently, she set it down on his tongue and trailed her fingertips on his lips. "And yet you are here."

He enjoyed the apple before saying, "What do you mean?"

"I would expect Forbis to run to the baron as soon as he left here."

Derik wasn't sure what to say, "I'm sure Madre talked to him about it."

Teri nodded in approval and held up a strawberry to his lips. He opened his mouth and she grinned as she set it inside, caressing his lips before he closed his mouth. "Madre is a great woman."

"I heard she spanks you a lot."

Teri grinned and rolled her eyes. She gestured at him with a wet finger. "Yeah, but I bet you get turned on by it too."

He shifted slightly as his cock started to twitch, caught in the confines of his thighs.

Teri giggled and held up another apple.

He took it, kissing her fingertips.

She grinned happily. "I missed it? She get your ass last night?"

Derik shook his head, "No, Nightingale spent the night in there."

"Oh?" She sounded excited for a moment, then she pouted, "You mean I missed a chance to make you a real woman?"

Derik's muscles clenched, but he was secretly overjoyed. "I guess so."

Teri sighed unhappily. She rolled one of the strawberries along her fingers before squeezing it. Dripping juices, she brought it to Derik's lips.

Caught in her gaze, he opened his mouth obediently. When she swirled the tangy juices in his mouth, he sucked on her fingers to clean each one.

She just cocked her head to the side, saying nothing.

He looked around for a moment with a blush growing on his cheeks. "What?"

"You are so pretty, you know that?"

He twisted his hands in the deep blue robe that clung to his shoulder. "Thank you."

They had no more to say as she fed him the rest of the plate, letting her fingertips trail along his lips and sending tiny bolts of pleasure through his system. His cock rose up against the confines of his panties, tenting them as she teased his lips, tongue, and throat.

Too soon, the mood was broken with the empty plate.

Teri sighed and set it down. "Madre have plans for you tonight?"

Derik gazed over at the hallway leading to her office. "She says I'm going to be bound at the foot of her bed for the night."

"Oh?"

At the evil, delighted tone, he didn't want to look at Teri. She giggled and caressed her knuckles along the back of his hand. "Your first puppy night. It's going to be a treat."

His stomach did a slow roll to the left. "P-Puppy night?"

"Didn't you ever have a dog sleeping on your feet?"

"No, I grew up in..."

Instead of reliving the memories of his childhood, he closed his mouth.

Teri regarded him for a moment, then shrugged. "Well, I didn't either. But we call it a puppy dog night because you sleep at the foot of her bed, warm up her toes, and if you are lucky, she lets you lick them."

"If I'm unlucky?"

"Well, then you get a big plug shoved up your ass, a gag in your mouth, and you get to figure out how to sleep while something is vibrating in your butt."

Derik stared at her with a mixture of horror and surprise, despite the pre-cum that leaked out of his cock.

Teri looked down at her plate, then held up a finger. "Hold on, I want some desert."

He leaned back as she left and looked up at the ceiling. In the shadows, he could imagine the Eye of Hamel just meters away, taunting him. Needing to tear his thoughts away, he let his eyes drift up to the skylight. Rain splashed down, drumming a beat of gray and lighting. He smiled as he watched the rivers of water rolling down the side, to the gutter system he already scoped out when he went to steal the Eye in the first place.

Around him, the harem continued to thrive. For lunch, a pair of servants set up tables of fruits and vegetables and some delicately cooked meats. Sherrel confided that they only got the fried and good stuff once a week, if everyone was good. He chuckled at the thought.

Casually, he arched his back over the pillow to watch everyone moving. It was peaceful: women chatting with women, a pair of them making out in the pool, and even Madre talking animatedly with Nightingale who pointedly ignored him. He focused on Madre, wondering what the favor she just called in and why she was doing so much for him.

He was an outsider.

Relaxing, he sat back up and just stared at the skylight more. Lighting flashed in the sky and a deep rumble shook the room with the rumble of the weather gods. He chuckled.

Life was good.

A large cock appeared over him.

He nearly choked as he stared up at it, his mood evaporating instantly. Teri giggled as she stepped forward, the fake cock sprouting from a leather harness around her hips. From his vantage point, he could see the large fake balls and how her pussy lips were already glistening with excitement.

"Um, what is that?"

He didn't need to ask the question, but it distracted him from the distinct sensation of his asshole trying to tighten into a singularity. His cock, on the other hand, seemed to get a different idea as it strained against his silk panties and he clamped a hand over it as he stared up in shock.

Teri looked down around the shaft and beamed happily. "Desert!"

"That isn't desert!"

"Gonna be sweet for me."

He scrambled to his feet, accidentally bopping his head on the fake cock before he backed up against the column. "Not for me!" He whimpered.

In response, Teri used a hand to jack off her pretend cock. It was slightly longer than his own and about as thick as three fingers held together. In her other hand, she held a small vial of lubricant.

Derik looked around for support, but he was already the center of attention. A few of the girls set up pillows around them while Teri favored him with an evil grin.

"Come on, you said you were spending the night with Madre—"

"But—"

"—and you know she's gonna shove something up that ass of yours," she continued.

He whimpered, "You don't know that."

In response, almost every single woman in the harem nodded.

He looked at them, then let out another whimper. "But—"

"Your butt is going to get stuffed. Now, either you can let the nasty, old lady—"

From across the room, Madre loudly cleared her throat.

Teri rolled her eyes and amended herself quickly. "—who is the most beautiful woman in the room do it, or you could let me lovingly, sweetly, tenderly," she gave him a beaming smile, "ream that ass open for you."

"What kind of choice is that?" he wailed.

Stroking her fake cock, she answered, "Well, its the kind where I really want to be the one who takes that virginity of yours. That and I'm betting you'd rather it be me."

He glanced over at Madre who just leaned back against the wall. She had a playful smile on her lips.

Next to her, Nightingale grinned cruelly and held up a fist, miming it being shoved up something that could not be anything but his ass.

He whimpered, looking back at Teri who continued to jack her cock.

"Come on, I'll be gentle."

Around him, the other women cheered for him even as they shed their clothes, delving fingers between their legs, and otherwise getting ready for a show.

His fingers clutched the column, but his cock stood up at full mast, drooling with the thought. He whimpered again, eyes gaze going from Madre to Teri and back again. No mercy came from either, but Teri beckoned to him from her position near the center of the room.

It took all his will not to race up the column and dive through the vent. Instead, he forced himself to release the column. He stepped forward to the cheers of the room as Teri continued to motion him closer. His panties soaked with his juices, he hesitantly covered the distance between them. Teri smiled and reached up, stroking the side of his chin.

"You are so beautiful, Dora."

He blinked back the tears before he whispered softly. "I'm scared."

She whispered back, "I won't hurt you."

Her hand stroked his face, soft and gentle and so tender. Then, she nodded her head and gestured down with her chin. "We'll start slow, kneel."

His heart pounded in his chest and his stomach twisted into a knot, but he slowly lowered himself in front of her. His eyes refused to leave her own as he settled down on the cushions, right before the fake cock that jutted from her hips.

She smiled sweetly. Bringing her fingers down to his chin, she rested her thumb on the front before gently pulling down.

Terrified, he obeyed and opened his mouth. He couldn't look down, but he watched as Teri stepped forward. The rounded tip of her fake cock brushed against his lips and a sob slipped out of his throat. Burning bright in the center of attention, he closed his lips on his first cock. The thickness forced his mouth from closing and the heavy tip rested against his tongue. The taste of the well-used toy flooded his mouth, of pussy and sex. Hot tears splashed down as she eased her hips forward, sliding it deeper into his mouth.

Trembling, Derik just opened his mouth more, accepting her as she drew back, sliding it in and out of his lips with those tender movements. Shame and helplessness burned him but so did the fire in his cock.

Teri's breath came loudly, deep and excited. Her scent flooded his own, the tangy sweet smell of her sex as she drove the fake cock in and out of his lips.

The world was just them.

Teri and Derik.

Lovers of sorts.

She plunged in and out of his mouth, working deeper as her hips rocked back and forth. The head slid along along his tongue, then up against the back of his throat.

He started to choke but she eased back almost instantly.

A moment later, it bumped up against the back of his throat again, a steady thump was easier to adapt once he choked the first time. Derik struggled with gagging for a moment. The shaft that slid out of his lips dripped with saliva and he heard it slurping, but her insistence continued to bump it against him, working it deeper into his throat.

Trembling, he reached up to caress the back of her thighs.

She moaned, sweat sparkling along her skin, as he leaned forward more. He kept his eyes locked on her as he held her, guided her.

Sweet tears in her own eyes, she drove into him deeper.

He managed to swallow it, choking on the unfamiliar feel of something in his throat, then to his surprised, it just sort of... slipped deep inside.

For a brief moment, he panicked, his fingers digging into her thigh, but she withdrew quickly, holding the fake cock head at his lips until his breath quieted, then drove forward again.

He choked on it, struggling but this time he pulled on her thighs, pulling him into her, to force that cock into his throat. His eyes burned with tears and his skin burned, but he wanted to please her so badly.

It was love that drove him forward, love that urged him to take that hard, thick cock into his throat. Elation flooded through him as it impaled him, and she plastered her stomach against his face with her entire length seated inside his body.

She crushed his nose against the soft, perfumed skin.

For a long moment, the war of senses assaulted his thoughts: the burning in his throat, the need for breathing with the indescribable feeling of fullness, the lust that curled his toes. When she withdrew, he coughed and gagged, but he couldn't help but smile from the intense pleasure that seared through his veins. She grinned and stroked her fingers through his hair, holding his head to ram forward again.

It violated his throat again with a delicious feeling of surrender as he once again reached the base of her cock. His own manhood surged twice, then he came in his panties, soaking the silk as Teri, his mistress, fucked his face. Wet slurping noises filled his ears as her hips drove the shaft into him again and again, burying it completely into him. She gripped the back of his head and held him still while she pumped.

Soft grunts interrupted his pleasure and he blinked to see Teri driving for her own pleasure, fucking his mouth harder and harder until the fake balls slapped against his chin. She pumped faster into him, gasping as her eyes rolled into the back of her head.

He reached up, fingers clutching her ass. Her legs spread as she stroked her false cock even deeper.

Then she drove deep into him, grinding her stomach against his face as a flood of juices dribbled down her thigh.

He gulped at the hard intruder buried in his throat as his fingers dug into her thigh. Her scream echoed shrilly in his ears, burning away the humiliation of being pleasured and pleasuring.

"Oh, fuck!"

Teri only held it there for a few seconds before she withdrew the dripping shaft from his lips.

He panted hard, gasping for breath.

Above him, she breathed heavily and looked down at him. Her parted lips closed into a smile. "I," she panted, "I think I just came like a boy."

And the room burst into applause.

A Real Woman

Applause? For him?

He looked around with a blossoming confusion, staring at the women around him. They were spread out on pillows and blankets. Most of them focused on him, cheering him on. Others bent over pillows or curled up in the cracks between the cushions, fingers frantically riding out the last shuddering scream of an orgasm. He saw Madre in the far back, leaning back in the wall with Nightingale's head buried between her legs. She had her eyes closed and mouth open in her own silent orgasm.

Derik fought a brief pang of jealousy before he brought his attention back up to Teri.

Panting hard, she reached down to pull a strand of his long black hair from his face. He could see sweat dripping down her cleavage and her body.

He worked his fingers along her damp inner thighs and the very feeling of it brought a smile to his lips. His own cock dripped with cum, soaking and overflowing the delicate sapphire thong. He actually felt sexy for a moment.

Teri gasped between breaths. "I still want your ass, you know."

His cheeks heated, but it wasn't from embarrassment. Instead, he looked around to where Teri had dropped the lubricant in her passions. His stomach lurched as he reached down and picked it up, holding it up to her.

Teri looked surprised as she stared at him. "You sure?"

He didn't trust himself to speak, so he just nodded. When she didn't just take it, he held it up with both hands, on his knees before her.

She smiled, a single tear in her eyes. "Bend over, love."

Handing the lubricant to her, Derik did the one thing he didn't think he could have ever done. He turned around and spread his legs, leaning forward to plant his hands on the ground.

Instantly, the room grew silent.

Heart pounding in his chest, he pressed his face against the ground and held up his ass.

Someone moved before they pulled him up into a sitting position. He opened his mouth to protest, but it was Sherrel with a pillow. Grinning from ear to ear, she kissed him on the lips and shoved the large pillow under his chest. Another pillows went under his hips and he adjusted with each one until he was spread out along the pillows, his trembling ass high in the air and poised right in front of Teri's cock.

He had never been so helpless.

Nor had he ever been so turned on.

Groaning softly in pleasure, he adjusted his legs to brace himself as his anal ring clenched in anticipation.

Hands stroked against his backside. He closed his eyes and let the tiny trembles fill him.

More hands stroked his legs, his back, and his ass. There were more than two sets of hands touching him, but he refused to let his eyes open. More of the fingers teased at his sphincter. The tight ring had already been opened by Madre. His cock drooled with excitement, soaking the pillows as he tried to quiet the pounding of his heart.

The room grew terrifying silent, a held breath as he laid helplessly before Teri's plans to take his virginity. Hundreds of images flew past in his mind as he rested on the pillows, clenching and relaxing his fingers around the edge of the pillow.

Sherrel was there, he could feel her fingers in his hair, stroking him with the tender gentleness he remembered so well from before.

The lubricant hit his asshole with an icy splash. He jumped, mouth opening to let out a shuddering breath.

Fingers, anonymous and questing, pushed it around, slopping up his opening before the first one plunged into him.

Derik let out a moan, a soft sobbing moan.

Sherrel stroked and held him as fingers penetrate his ass, working in and out with tiny pumping movements. Every thrust violated his nether ring. It was uncomfortable, but he also knew that he wanted it almost bad enough to beg.

A third finger pushed in, moving unlike the others. A second woman was fingering him, and he gripped the pillows tightly. Tears of fright, anticipation, and lust dripped from his face as they worked him open, pumping in and out until he could feel the knuckles slipping in and tugging out.

Sherrel cooing in his ear, he tried to relax. His hips rocked against the pillows as the three fingers plunged in and out, fucking him like tiny cocks. He leaned into each one, trying to imagine what it would be like with another man, the baron or, a shudder, Rick's immense cock poised at his entrance.

Another sob escaped his lips.

Sherrel's hand worked her fingers into his palm and he clutched it, refusing to open his eyes.

In his ass, the fingers slowly pulled out until there was only one, pumping its entire length into his asshole, fucking him like a woman. Every knuckle plunged in until it was buried and he could feel the knuckles at his entrance. His unseen lover would twist before withdrawing, then slide it back in.

A pleasure smoldered in his loins, a burning ember that started to grow inside him. His balls tightened against his skin as the finger pumped more.

Then, the finger pulled out, and the thick, rounded tip of Teri's fake cock replaced it.

Panicked, he tried to pull himself away from the cock.

Sherrel held him down, holding his hand as she cooed to him. She whispered for him to bear down if he wanted, to squeeze as tightly as he could.

He wanted to and tried to, squeezing down, but her voice never changed from that loving tone.

The cock at his ass circled around his slick, lubricated entrance. It was immense, a rubber violator of his body. He wanted to cry out as it eased into his ring. The head of the toy slowly spread the muscle apart, stretching it tautly around the rounded tip. It wasn't plunging fingers, it was thick and irresistible. It was hard and soft at the same time. His ring spread out even more, swallowing the fake cock until his insides protested at their limits.

Derik let out a sob and squeezed down on Sherrel's hand.

She whispered soft nothings to him as he tried to breathe.

The cock worked deeper, and his ring expand around it. Reaching the apex of the thick head, the tight muscles swallowed up the cock head and pulled it deeper into his body until they clamped down on the ridge behind the glans.

He was impaled.

Just a bit of the head, but there is was.

He was fucked.

Teri's hands rested against his hips.

She held him tightly as she leaned forward. At the first intense feeling of something sliding into him, he shook his head. "No! Too much, too much!"

His voice sounded pitiful, but Sherrel just crooned to him, and the cock kept impaling him. Slowly it buried deeper into him, filling his rectum with thickness that never seemed to end. The tiny ridges that were barely visible were immense canyons as the cock slid into his ass. He found he couldn't breath; too many sensations, burning bright with ecstasy and humiliation, filled him. His cock jerked in an attempt to orgasm but nothing came out as the shaft continued to plunge into him.

Teri said something, but he couldn't hear it through the rushing in his ears and the soft breathy voice of Sherrel. He clung to her as Teri began to withdraw her cock. He couldn't help but focus on every millimeter sliding out, the motion puckered his opening and tugged his insides.

Sherrel whispered, "You are doing great."

He opened his mouth widely to cry out but any sound refused to come out. When Teri slid it back deeper into his body, he leaned forward as he tried to adapt to the thick intruder impaling him.

Sherrel squeezed his hand as Teri pulled back.

Then...

Then she fucked him.

She was gentle at first, just a rock back and forth of a few centimeters, but then her thrusts grew harder and deeper. The cock drove deep into him, plunging deep until her soft hips slapped against his ass and the fake balls smacked against his own.

He let out a pitiful sob as the cock drove in and out of his tightly-stretched ring.

Spearing deep, his opening clung to every ripple along the length as Teri fucked him, her body slick with sweat as she drove the fake cock into his clenching asshole. Derik wanted to scream out, but his throat refused to make a sound.

Every plunge jerked him forward, rocking him against the pillows. He kept one hand planted against the ground, but it just made each thrust more intense. Hands gripped tightly on his hips, drawing him back as she speared him. The rest of the world faded away, leaving him adrift except for the hardness that violated his very core.

Finally, the cock impaling him started to feel good. He gasped with each lunge, not from pain or discomfort, but from a growing pleasure.

Finding strength, he shoved back against the cock, impaling himself instead of just accepting Teri's thrusts.

Soft sounds of surprise and pleasure rippled across the room.

Sherrel held him tightly as Derik fucked himself on the shaft, driving back as Teri impaled him. The pleasure growing inside his body only intensified.

He whimpered when it became too much for his delicate frame. He didn't know if he could survive the explosive orgasm.

Every thrust filled his rushing ears with the sound of slurping and the realization he was being fucked, something he swore would never happen, even after falling into the harem, but there he was, taking a long, hard cock into his ass and wanting more.

Teri's fingers dug into his hips painfully as her thrusting grew faster and harder, slapping against his skin and driving the cock so hard into him that his cock surged with each. And then, the withdrawal, he almost sobbed as it pulled out, readying to ram back into his willing, aching body.

He screamed as he came harder than he every had before. Not a localized explosion of his cock spewing cum on the pillows, but something that shook his entire body, set it aflame, and send it into the abyss of ecstasy.

Teri slammed his ass repeatedly, sending more bolts of searing pleasure coursing through his system, and he just kept coming and coming. His endless surges splattering against the pillow. The intensity stole his breath away and he clutched at Sherrel until his body shook once hard and he lost control of his senses, an aftershock of pleasure that blinded him.

Teri slumped over his body, draping his form with her own sweaty one. As the blindness of pleasure took him, he heard her whisper through her rapidly panting breath. "Now," she gasped, "you're a real woman."

Date Night

His senses came back to him with a rush. He clutched Sherrel and the pillows. Tremors raced along his body. He vibrated from the intensity of his orgasm.

Teri's naked body, slick with sweat, clung to his back. Her rapid breathing, panting actually, blew hot air along the nape of his neck, but his senses were drawn down to the hardness that remained quivering in his backside. Her dildo still impaled him firmly. Every twitch of Teri's body sent an identical tremor through his insides and his cock surged again hotly, but nothing came out.

He just closed his eyes again and leaned into the pillows. He couldn't stop his legs from trembling.

Distracted, he barely registered the others making out in the room, the muted and loud screams of orgasms and even the slapping sounds of others who wielded their own strap-ons into willing flesh.

He found it oddly inspirational.

Teri stirred. "Okay, you are a good fucking lay."

Sherrel giggled and Derik smiled.

"I feel... full."

Teri chuckled as she sat up, her movements driving the cock deeper into his reamed ass.

His feet rose up against the feeling, his cock trying to find one more surge of cum to splatter against the pillow. Every movement filled him as she planted her knees on the pillow.

Slowly, she pulled the cock from his ass. No longer in the throes of passion, he enjoyed every ridge as it slid out of his rectum and past his anal ring. As the head popped out of his body, a strange sense of emptiness filled him.

"Oh, wow, you came a lot!"

He needed Sherrel's help to sit up and all three of them stared at the pillow, dripping with his cum in sheets of milky white. More than he ever though possible soaked the fabric and puddled on the padded ground. In shock, he stared for a long moment and just remembered the intensity of being fucked, fucked as a woman.

Teri patted him on the hip. She said, "Come on, I need a bath and a nap."

Tiredly, he followed her into the bath area and sank into the first tub. She joined him, hand stroking his thigh but not touching his cock.

Sherrel slipped in on the other side, kissing his neck as he and Teri just relaxed. She seemed content to just stroke and touch. After a few minutes of soaking and holding each other, all three of them crashed in the corner of the room, well away from the wet spot he had made. With Sherrel's ass against his hips and Teri draped on his back, they fell asleep together.

When Teri woke him up, it was dark. He sat up with a bolt of fear.

"Shit, am I late?"

Teri giggled, and he noticed she had changed into a form-fitting dress. Her smaller breasts formed a shadow of cleavage. "Now, you got about twenty minutes to clean up before new girl duties. Madre is still in her room with Nightingale, but I wouldn't be late."

"Um," he blinked, "Why are you dressed? You weren't going to the baron, were you?"

She giggled and kissed his nose, "No, silly, it's Marking Day."

As if this explained everything, she hopped across the room and out the door that lead into the place.

Derik groaned awake and pulled his hair into a loop around his hand. Peering around, he noticed about half the room was empty. "Um, what's going on?"

Sherrel yawned, stretching out on her back and spreading her legs. "Marking Day. Since we can't get pregnant for a while, and the baron doesn't need us, we get to wander around the palace."

A strange prickle of jealousy rose up. As he looked down the hall, Teri disappeared. "To do what?" he asked.

"Boyfriends, girlfriends, affairs of the body, and maybe a couple screaming orgasms."

She giggled as she saw up, her heavy breasts swinging as she watched Derik through hooded lids. He knew that there was something else in her thoughts but he couldn't imagine what.

"Boyfriends? I'm confused."

Laughing, she helped him up. "Look, Dora, the baron is one man. And he owns our bodies utterly, but Madre lets us fool around on occasion. She always makes comments about cats in heat and letting them play. As long as we don't get pregnant or in trouble, and she approves of our dates. And Marking Day is the first day that we know we can't," she empathized the word, "get knocked up. So, no danger of pissing off Madre and getting sold off."

She drew him into the bathroom to give him a proper bath, with soapy breasts and a hand job that left him a bit warm under the collar. Then, she had him do the same, nuzzling against his neck as he pumped his fingers between her soft folds. Sated for a moment, they helped each other brush their hair.

"Does this mean," he blushed as he looked away, "you are going somewhere tonight?"

Sherrel stared at him for a moment, then made a cooing sound. "Aww, is Dora jealous?"

"No!"

"You are! You are sweet on me!"

He fought the burn in his cheeks. "No, no I'm not!"

She laughed playfully. He ducked his head, but she grabbed his hands, plastering his palms against the soft mounds of her breasts. Her hard nipples ground against his skin and a different type of flush rose up in response. "Don't worry. You have Madre all night. By the time she lets you go, we'll be back. And then you can hear about my night with a certain lesbian aristocrat and Teri's night with her boring scholar."

He stroked her breasts until she giggled again.

"Come, help me get pretty."

"You already are," he said.

She playfully batted at his noise. "Flirt. Don't worry, we have tomorrow."

Fighting a tiny flame of jealousy, he helped her into a stunning sheaf dress that left very little to the imagination: a canyon of a cleavage and a slit that went a hand-span past her hips. Crossing her legs, he could see a brief flash of her hairless pussy and his cock came to life again.

Sherrel lifted her eyes from his crotch with a grin. "And I see you approve."

He nodded, but couldn't find the words.

She helped him back into his padded bra and panties before draping the sapphire robe over his shoulders. The feeling of silk did nothing for his excitement and it took him a few tries to tuck his cock in between his legs.

Sherrel pulled out a small bottle of the apple perfume from his drawer—there was one for each of the women in the harem—and spritzed it on Derik. Her own perfume, a fruity exotic scent, dusted along her body before she finished.

Together, they walked to the entrance of the harem, where two guarded men protected the door. He ducked his head away from them, then blushed again when Sherrel kissed him goodnight.

"Take care, my little puppy."

He watched her leaving but a feeling that someone was watching him distracted him. Glancing up, he saw the guard's deep green eyes in the shadows of the full helmet and blushed hotly, fleeing before the gaze could determine the full extent of Derik's disguise.

At Madre's door, he slowed to a stop. Through the wood, he could hear grunts of pleasure, apparently going strong since his show on the floor. Gasping whimpers echoed in the hall and the rapid slapping of skin against skin meant that Madre and Nightingale were still fucking each other, hard and fast. Each slap of skin caused the door to flex with a pulse of magic.

He almost walked in, but something held him at the last minute. His hand rose up to knock, but as he raised his knuckles, an intense feeling of being trapped slammed into him. It grabbed his heart and squeezed the breath out of him. He froze, mouth open in surprise, as he could imagine eyes of a thousand men staring at him, seeing through his nakedness.

A sob tore from his throat as he fled.

Prayers

He cowered in the massage room for almost an hour. In his hand, he held the tools stolen from Forbis. Rolling them in his hand, he could feel the power but didn't know how to tap it. It was frustrating on more levels than he really wanted to understand. Part of him desperately wanted to be marked like the others, to join them and be truly part of the harem, while another screamed him to take the sapphire and run.

Derik still couldn't figure out why he struggled with his heart. There should be no conflict, there should be no question. He stared down at the tools that could be used to mark him as a woman, then down at the deep blue silk panties and bra. "What am I?"

He sighed as he rolled the sticks in his fingers. "Who am I?"

Staring down at the sticks, he was disgusted with himself. A coward. Hiding among naked women. Rolling around like a good slut and pretending it could last. An anger rose up inside him directed inwards more than anything else. Flinging the marking sticks into the pool at the back of the room, he swore in an angry whisper, "Fuck this, I need to get out before I-I-I..."

His voice cracked, and the surge of anger drained out of him as fast as it filled him. He sunk to his knees as a sob caught in his throat. "Damn you gods, why do I want to be here?"

Hot tears splashed the tile floor of the massage room. The scent of his own perfume, apple and delicate, and the tinkling of the fountain both teased his senses. He could feel his heart in his chest, squeezing through a tightness and straining against the silk that bound his non-existent breasts. He so desperately wanted to belong in the harem, to keep this life of passion, sex, and really belong.

But he was an outsider.

A thief.

A male.

Above him, he could feel the Eye of Hamel staring down at him, the sapphire gaze of something far more than himself, and he just couldn't tear himself away from it.

He sniffed loudly and wiped the tears from his eyes. Staring down at the tiny puddles he created, he whispered brokenly. "Isn't this the point I'm suppose to find an answer? Isn't this the point where the stories always have a god showing up?"

He looked up to the ceiling. "Well, where the fuck are you?"

No shining champion came down to him. No gods split the heavens. Instead, it was just Derik standing with his image of Dora in the center of a room. Talking to the ceiling. "Well!?"

Outside the room, he could hear someone heading to the bathroom. Mundane and perfectly normal, it was the opposite of what he desperately wanted. No one to give him the answers, no one to save him from himself. He felt so tired and broken, split and bound by the very lies he created.

Staggering to his feet, he padded to the far end of the room to gather up Forbis' tools. He looked down at them and sighed sadly. "I'm a coward."

Replacing them in the drawer, he turned his back on the room and the gods who forsook him and headed back to his duties, as the new girl.

"A god-damned coward."

Puppy

"You're late."

A simple statement and a fact. Told from a naked woman sitting on the edge of the bed. He looked up at her and flinched at the stern look on Madre's face. His eyes caught the red marks of a harness, no doubt used to pound a fake cock into the purring Nightingale behind her.

Nightingale rocked back and forth, her red ass up in the air and hummed to herself playfully.

Madre stood up and walked to him.

Derik held his position, letting his eyes drop to the run he stood on. "Why?"

"I," he sighed and almost lied. At the last moment, the truth came out, "I panicked."

She lifted his chin to force him to look at her. "Seconds thoughts?"

He nodded, feeling the tears rising in his eyes.

"Do you want to leave?"

Derik saw Nightingale raise her head curiously, staring at him with an expression that bordered on a glare. Sweat soaked her front and cleavage, and her intense gaze sent a shiver down his spine.

"No, Madre."

He didn't. As he stared into the warm, comforting eyes of Madre, he realized guilt burned at him. Guilt of being a thief. He opened his mouth to blurt out the truth, but no words came out.

"What is it, Dora?"

Trying again, his voice refused to make a sound, and he looked away, tears rolling down his cheeks.

"You can leave right now, Derik."

At the sound of his real name, he looked back at her. He knew it was a pleading, desperate look, but it was the only emotion he could feel.

She caught his hands, holding them to her slick breasts. "We can sneak you out right now. No one will ever know there was a Derik in this harem. If that is what you want. What you really want."

He opened his mouth, surprised and shocked. He forced his mouth to close and shook his head. "N-No," he stuttered, "I want to be here. I want... I want to belong."

Nightingale let out an annoyed grunt and shoved her head back against the blankets.

Madre ignored her and smiled. "Sherrel said you belong here, something about feeling it in her heart."

She reached up to stroke the side of his cheek and then tugged on a tiny strand of long black hair.

He sniffed and wiped away the tears. "Thank you, Madre."

She swept him in a surprise hug, and he instantly wrapped his arms around her, feeling the scars of her battles but also a strange feeling of comfort in just being held. Madre held him for a long moment before she stepped back. "Now, if you do plan on staying, you must realize something."

From the bed, Nightingale rolled over sharply. She had a grin on her face.

"What, Madre?" he asked.

"You owe me twenty for being late, having second thoughts and panicking, and coming without permission."

He blushed hotly as the wry grin spread across her face. He bowed his head, but his cock twitched with excitement, drooling at the very thought.

"Now, this is a proper punishment, since you appear to be going the same route as Teri."

"I'm sorry."

"It's what I expect of pleasure girls. So, tonight, I think we're going to use the paddle."

Trepidation grew inside him, but Madre wasn't done.

"And I think Nightingale is going to administer it."

He started to tremble at the thought as Nightingale looked up with surprise. Then a slow smile filled her face as she regarded Derik.

Derik looked at her, then Madre, but the older woman shook her head. "You have to remember, I am Madre, and we have rules, Dora."

To his surprise, his body relaxed in relief when she called him by his other name. "Yes, Madre."

"Good. Nightingale?"

Gale hopped off the bed, almost vibrating with excitement.

"Get the small one."

Nightingale raced to a large cabinet. When she flung it open, Derik saw an array of floggers and paddles of all shapes. There were cuffs and blindfolds. He spotted a pair of something that looked like pony tails. His stomach twisted with fear as he watched Nightingale yank a square paddle about twice his hand-span across and bounded back, gleeful as a child opening presents.

Her ass smacked the bed as she got into the same position as Madre, gesturing to her lap.

Derik looked at Madre but the older woman just shook her head.

"Just take your punishment, girl."

Despite Nightingale's glee, he padded over to her and stripped down. The silk of his outfit puddled to the ground as he stood naked before her.

Nightingale reached up and pulled him down over her lap, yanking him forward until his ass stretched into the air and his crotch ground into the softness of her thigh. She pressed one hand against his shoulders, pinning him. Leaning forward until her nipples just teased his back, she whispered sharply. "Don't you fucking dare come on me."

He held his breath in anticipation. The wooden paddle had been smoothed from heavy use, there wasn't even a ripple of a grain as it tapped against his ass. Each caress against his skin brought a skip to his heart and a heat growing in his loins. Despite his best efforts, his manhood rose to full mast and ground against her thigh.

She shifted slightly, then tapped his other cheek. "Twenty, Madre?"

"Twenty."

A tiny tap, then he wouldn't feel the paddle.

Anticipating the strike, he tensed up but she didn't bring it down. He whimpered, clutching her leg as he closed his eyes tightly.

SMACK!

His ass exploded in an intense burst of pain that quickly turned into a heated flush on both sets of cheeks. Nightingale chuckled happily, brought up the paddle, then down in a powerful smack against his other cheek.

Derik gasped with the pain, struggling with an intense desire growing inside him. His cock leaked pre-cum on her leg as she brought down another smack, right on the first one. The stinging pain jerked him forward as his leg straightened, but Nightingale kept him pinned against her thighs.

The fourth blow drove down on his right cheek, reigniting the burn along his ass. He gasped from the intensity of it, balancing on a world of pain and pleasure.

She brought it down hard on his buttocks. He could feel her putting all of her strength into it. Each one burned more than the last, but each one also left a searing mark across his senses, an intoxicating knife's edge of pleasure and pain.

Nightingale continued to smack him hard, then slow, each one more powerful than the last.

He whimpered and writhed on her lap, trying to escape but with little real effort. He writhed against the hand that pinned him. Her breath came as rapidly as his and he was flooded with the scent of her excitement. He held her tightly, eyes closed to take the blow of his punishment.

Despite the pain radiating from his ass, the burning that seared his cheeks, his cock grew harder and hotter with every smack. An orgasm began to build as she beat him again and again with short, powerful strokes.

When the paddle came down the next time, the fifteenth blow he guessed, his body spasmed once and he came. It splattered against her thigh.

She let out a disgusted growl. The last five blows came hard and fast, breaking the skin as she vented a sudden anger into his poor, burning ass.

As soon at the twentieth blow struck, she shoved him hard off her lap. "Fucker!"

"Nightingale!" came the sharp reply.

Nightingale gestured to the river of white cum that dripped down her thigh. "He came! And I told him not too."

Madre didn't seem as upset as Nightingale. "You come with the paddle too."

"On me!?"

"Calm down."

Nightingale dropped the paddle on the ground as she struggled to control a rage.

Derik winced as he tried to get to his feet, but Madre rested a hand on his shoulder, holding him kneeling on the ground. He watched as the cum dripped down her leg slowly as the girl regained her composure.

"Better?"

Nightingale let out a long sigh. "Yes, Madre."

"Now, tell him to clean you up."

Derik looked up, but Madre only had eyes for Nightingale.

Nightingale stared back for a moment, then she looked down at the ground as she fought with her emotions. "Der-Dora."

"Y-Yes."

"Clean this up."

He tried to get to his feet, but Madre held him down. He stared at her, but she just smiled.

Nightingale took another breath, then suddenly grinned evilly. "With your mouth."

Derik froze, a trembling shaking through his body as he looked up at Nightingale.

Madre's hand released his shoulder as he found himself staring at his own cum dripping on her leg. She spoke softly, "If it touches the ground, Dora, it will be another twenty with the bigger paddle."

Nightingale motioned for him with a finger. "Come on. It's time for you to learn how to swallow like the rest of us."

Derik had to force himself to crawl toward her, staring at his own spunk as it inched toward the ground. He swallowed hard, not even realizing that he found a new low.

Nightingale's breath came hard as he brought his mouth within centimeters of it. He could smell it, a tangy and salty scent of his own being.

Fresh tears burned down his face as he closed his eyes tightly and gingerly lapped at it. It was hot and slimy against his lips, but Nightingale's hand reached down to pull him against her thigh, grinding him against his own cum.

Swallowing down the bile, he lapped at it as he shook with humiliation. He tasted it in the back of his throat as he cleaned her leg with his tongue, moving up her thigh with her hand pulling his hair. He obeyed her, his shame matching the heat of his burning ass.

He finished and made a face at the taste of himself.

Nightingale pushed him away, as if she couldn't stand his touch on her skin.

Madre's hand stroked his chin for a moment, before pulling his gaze to her. She used her thumb to push a blob of cum into his mouth.

"I'm Madre."

A simple statement.

"Yes, Madre."

"Tonight, you take her position."

"Y-Yes, Madre."

He saw the ball gag in her hand. He whimpered in his throat as she pressed it against his lips. He could taste the rubber fighting with the flavor of his own cum. Somehow, he found the strength to open his jaw and accept the rubber ball as Madre fitted it into his mouth. As soon as it settled into place, he tried to close his mouth but couldn't. He squirmed at the unnatural state of being unable to press his lips together.

"Tonight, you sleep at our feet."

Our feet? He looked up as he worked at the ball with his tongue. Nightingale looked just as surprised as him as she stared at Madre. Madre cocked her head.

"New girl is getting me rather horny, and I want to try a different strap-on tonight."

Nightingale cooed as Derik's cock almost exploded again. He stood up as commanded, his body shivering with anticipation. The gag in his mouth gave every touch a sharp edge as Madre tied his wrists behind his back, forcing his back to arch forward as she bound his elbows together. He tried to shift in the increasing sense of helplessness, but Madre expertly bound him in place.

He was guided to the foot of the bed, right against the wooden foot board. He whimpered, muted by the gag wedged into his mouth. Madre's hands were firm and fast, bringing his knees up to his chest and tying them tightly to him. Curled up in a fetal position, he was helplessly exposed as the cool air that teased his burning ass and throbbing cock.

In a matter of minutes, he was bound at the foot of her bed. When he saw her hold up a blindfold, he let out a muffled whimper and shook his head. Madre nodded her head.

"You had your chance."

More tears splashed down as she blinded him, tying it back firmly across his face.

He was helpless.

Utterly helpless.

He could hear them moving and whispering. Breezes of their motions caress his skin. He tried to shift position but his body refused to obey him. The straps around his back and knees held him tightly in place. More straps held his ankles together as tightly as his wrists were bound. He couldn't move a single muscle except for his head. Blinded and gagged, he let hot tears wet his cheeks.

Then, something teased his ass. He tried to squeal out, to scream out, but the smooth, slick intruder already found its target. He wiggled but couldn't stop as something hard and smooth pushed into his rectum. While nearly as thick as Teri's cock, it was thankfully gentle. No doubt Madre was working it in and out of his body. It pushed in all the way.

The base of the cock seemed to flare out, and he whimpered loudly as it stretched his entrance to its limit. Then, with a wet slurping noise, it popped into his body and plunged deeply into him. Hard and long, it filled him completely. His tightly stretched anal ring found a notch or indent to hold it tight inside him. When it settled into place, it forced another moan to rise up.

He shifted to the best of his ability, but every movement only rubbed the hardness against his insides. His cock, full mast and drooling all over him, just bobbed with every movement. No matter how he clenched or twisted, the thick intruder refused to move.

Time stretched into forever as he tried to escape his bonds. Then, movement on the bed interrupted him as they shifted positions. It started slow, but soon the bed was rocking. Nightingale's screams of pleasure beat on the room, no doubt for his own humiliation, as Madre fucked her. He tried to focus on their movements, to distract him from the intensity of his own bondage. He soon realized, he couldn't tear his senses away as they fucked.

Just as he thought Nightingale finally came, they started again. He lay helpless, feeling the incredible sensations of being impaled, powerless, and focused at the same time. His cock surged, but the pressure in his rectum prevented him from spurting cum. Instead, just more pre-cum pooled on his thigh as he prepared for a very long night.

Sleeping

He couldn't sleep.

Despite his best efforts, he kept shifting in place, fighting against his bindings and trying to find some comfortable position. His wrists burned from where he twisted, but Madre's knots were far beyond his ability to slip free. After a few moments, he would try to settle down, but his movements nudged the hard plug in his ass against his delicate nerves, sending up tiny flares of pleasure coursing through his system. Sweat beading on his forehead, he tried to force himself to hold rock-steady, but then Madre or Nightingale would move and the maddening sensations would ignite once again.

His burning ass cheeks glowed in his mind, a distraction of stinging pain and the glow of warmth that made it impossible to concentrate. He tried to move his focus away from his rear but then his blind helplessness magnified every other touch. Even his beating heart caused the plug in his ass to twitch, igniting uncomfortable pleasures to ravage his mind.

To make things worse, the bed shook hard as Madre fucked Nightingale, no doubt with some strap-on. He could smell their excitement and he could feel the body movement, but it only increased his feelings of being trapped. He struggled with focus on his body, but then he would feel the pressure in his rectum, filling him like... like a man would fuck his ass. Pleasures curled through his thoughts starting fires in his loins. Pre-cum dripped from his shaft, soaking his leg. He tried not to think about it; he could still taste his own juices in the back of his throat.

If he focused on their movements, he started to imagine their position. How Madre's buttocks would flex as she rammed some huge cock into Nightingale's pussy. Just the thought of it increased the heat in his shaft, forcing it to drool even more across his leg and soak the blankets underneath.

Damned no matter how he focused.

They fucked for hours. Hours of pounding and shaking, of the muted moans that drifted past his senses. He could feel them changing position and hear the wet slurping of fingers and tongues. And he was helplessly. So utterly helplessly.

And it only turned him on more.

Maddeningly, he could feel each breath escaping around the ball gag. His mouth ached with the ball prying his teeth apart, but like the plug in his ass, he was utterly helpless to remove it. Chunks of his sanity crumbled under the assault of pleasures on his body. Striving to protect it, to defend that last bit of his own dignity, he desperately tried to find something to distract him.

Then, he found something. The Eye of Hamel.

He hated it.

He hated how it rolled away from him, teasing him almost.

But, it kept his mind away from the thick intruder buried in his rectum.

He thought about the great hall, the four statues holding up that glass map. For a brief moment, he didn't feel the discomfort of his bondage or even the solid slamming of cock into pussy. Grasping on the thought, he just imagined himself jumping around the room, racing to avoid the acidic traps or swinging across the room. He reviewed the entire theft and expanded on it. He counted the tiles in his mind and even the footsteps of the guards. He threw all of his imagination into that room, in desperate hope to not suffer through his bondage.

It only partially helped, but it passed the long seconds of the night.

Somewhere, sometime, Nightingale shifted position and slid down.

Madre let out a guttural moan.

Nightingale's feet teased his stomach.

He clenched up, tightening his gut as her soft toes strokes around his belly button. Her body moved with short, rhythmic movements, and he imagined her head lapping up between Madre's legs. His delicate imagination of the theft shattered as his cock grew harder, soaking his leg again.

As she pleasured Madre, Nightingale's feet worked lower until her toes pressed against his groin.

He whimpered softly, wondering if she found some measure of forgiveness for him.

When she ground his cock against her feet, he realized there was no god. He whimpered and tried to escape, but she caught him, twisting his cock with her feet even as she brought Madre to one orgasm, than the other.

She didn't move when they finished. She kept her feet pressing down on his cock and balls, increasing the pressure of the thick plug buried in her ass. He could almost imagine her smile as she shifted into a comfortable position and drifted back to sleep.

He tried to follow, but a few seconds later, she twitched and brought him to full wakefulness again.

Whimpering, he tried to twist away, but she kept him silently pinned with just her feet.

The long night turned even longer. Every time pre-cum dripped down his shaft, she would grind down. Every time he twitched or shifted position, she would squeeze his balls on the sole of her feet or between her toes. Every movement would bring pleasure and pain storming through his thoughts.

Every second passed with glacial slowness.

Every pulse of his heart seemed to slow down more than the one before it.

Every moment turned into an eternity of discomfort, balancing on the edge of some pleasure and the agony of Nightingale's tortures.

And he cried. Softly to himself, muffled by the ball gag and helpless to escape, he just cried.

Morning came after centuries, when Madre pulled the blindfold from his eyes and he blinked at the light. Somehow, he missed Nightingale's parting from the room and he tried to lift his head.

"Did you sleep?"

Lips still tightly stretched around the ball gag, he could only shake his head.

She smiled softly and reached behind his head, unbuckling the gag and giving him the first feeling of freedom.

His jaw seized up and his muscles trembled with the effort to budge.

Madre worked his bonds, freeing him even as she whispered to him. "Now, don't move right away. Just hold still."

He obeyed, despite the screaming need to move that built up over the night. When she reached the bounds of his ankles, her fingers briefly stroked his cock.

"Was Nightingale playing with you?"

He wasn't sure of torture was playing, but he nodded anyways.

"All night?"

Derik didn't want to answer. He looked away, but he nodded anyways.

"Did you enjoy it?"

Tears burned at his face as he remembered her torture. He almost nodded, then once again Madre's demand for the truth compelled him. He shook his head.

"Damn, I was hoping she would finally get over this. Too much to expect from her in such a short time." With surprising strength, Madre picked Derik completely off the bed.

Pins and needles screamed through his limbs as he collapsed against her, holding her tightly as tears streamed down his face.

She brought him to the tub and lowered him in. "There you go. It will pass. It will pass..."

He sobbed while leaning on her, helpless as a baby. His limbs refused to move for the longest moment, flame burning at his senses. He could feel the thick plug still up inside him, but his fingers refused to unclench. His jaw spasmed for a moment, but he managed to calm down before the muscles in his throat tightened up.

"It will get easier, you know. Next time, it will be just you and me. No more Nightingale," she spoke sadly, "I hoped that she would get over this, but these things take time. And she is a very angry kitten, always hissing about something."

As she spoke, she stroked him along the cheeks and shoulders, not sexual but comforting.

His body relax minutely.

She brushed her cheek against his own. "I won't do that again, Dora. Next time, just you and me."

He grunted noncommittally.

She reached up to grab his cock, holding it firmly until he looked at her. "Excuse me?"

His voice came out as a hoarse whisper, "Y-Yes, Madre."

"Good."

She grinned and soaped up her hands, standing him in front of her as she bathed him. At the feel of the slick soap and her hands, his body began to respond despite the long night of torture. His balls, aching from a night without release, seemed to grind themselves into his cock.

Madre continued to lather him up. Her fingers finally reached his sore buttocks and he spread his legs obediently. Fingers working up into him, his cock surged to full mast as she pulled out the immense plug from his ass.

Letting out a groan, he collapsed.

Madre caught him and pulled him to her. His cock press against her thigh as she steadied him. Looking down, she raised an eyebrow. "Did you come?"

He shook his head.

She looked around the room at no one, then took her soapy hands to lather up her cleavage. Pressing his cock between them, she squeezed her breast around his shaft. "Enjoy your chance."

It took him a second to register, and he rocked against her. She was soft and smooth against his member. He clutched her shoulder, not daring to touch her hair as he began to fuck her breasts. After a night of torture, he was surprised how long it took him to come, but he finally did, adding his cum to the soap of her breasts.

Once he slumped against her, she let him sink deep into the water. "Finish washing me and get some sleep."

Exhausted, he found the strength to do his duties as the new girl. Out of the tub, he struggled to dress and needed Madre's help to pull the bra and panties on, to once again hide his masculinity from the world.

"Go on, get some sleep."

This time, he obeyed without question or hesitation.

"Yes, Madre."

Secrets

The handle to the door was warm as he opened it. Derik stepped into Madre's room feeling nervous for the upcoming night, but he froze in the door as he saw flickers of light filling the room. In the center, Madre stood with her hands reaching up into the air. Sparkles of light flowed around her naked form, lighting up the deep valleys of her breasts and thighs. He swallowed as he stepped forward; the air seemed to resist him for a moment but he managed to step through it.

Once inside the room, pulses of energy beat against his skin, flooding his senses with a strange euphoria. Unsure if he should stay, he turned and closed the door before pressing his back against it.

Energy pulsated powerfully in the air as Madre held out her hand. It collapsed into a singular point in her hand, eldritch forces boiling into a storm of violence and power. He watched it with fear as the pressure in the room built up quickly and a tightness spread across his chest.

She closed her hand around the energy, and he watched as it spread out from the cracks of her hands. One of the beams slashed toward him, and he stepped aside quickly. It shuddered against the door, and he smelled burning smoke. He kept his eyes ready for the next ball of force. Another lash arced out, slicing the air as it came screaming toward him.

Derik reacted without thinking. Muscles and reflexes of an acrobat-thief kicked in and he leapt out of the way, hopping off the shelf next to the door and flipping over the energy as it crashed into the door with a thud. He came down lightly on his toes, ready for more. Instead, Madre looked over at him with surprise as his hair fluttered down around him.

With a snap, she closed her hand and the power in her palm popped with shock wave of power.

"You're early," came the wary but expected response.

Derik stared at her hand, then blushed. "Sorry, I thought you'd appreciate it since I'm always late."

Madre chuckled while she walked to him. "I am surprised actually. But, it can be dangerous coming into my room early."

He looked away. "Sorry, Madre."

She said nothing as she stopped in front of him. Her gaze seared him and a blush rose to his cheeks. "You are very agile, Dora."

"Lucky."

"Luck doesn't do back flips."

More a side flip, but he didn't correct her. Instead, he kept his gaze away and said nothing. For a long, painful moment, there was silence. Then, her hand rested on his cheek.

"Do you trust me?"

The question surprised him, and he glanced at her, quickly looking away from those compassionate eyes. "Y-Yes, Madre."

Her hand never left his cheek as she traced the line of his chin. "You are hiding something."

His jaw tensed, and he forced himself to relax. He trembled softly, his heart pounded in his chest. Her hand trailed down his throat, and a different type of heat rose between his legs. Her hand pressed against his heart.

"I can hear your heart, you know. I can hear it speed up when I say certain things. You have a secret, don't you?"

Derik opened his mouth to confess, but he quickly asked another question. "How? How can you hear it?"

Her hand remained firmly against his pounding chest.

Strange emotions bubbled up, confusing him as he tried to understand how the touch could invoke them.

"I'm a battle mage, Dora, trained in colleges where the instructors and other students attack you constantly. In a school of three hundred, only the top thirty graduate and the bottom thirty dies.

Every year, for ten years. In that environment, you learn to enhance your senses or you end up at the bottom of a grave."

Heart skipping frantically now, Derik whimpered as he realized she could hear every lie he said. He closed his eyes tightly, waiting for the killing blow.

"Because of that training, I survived the baron's attack. I got very good at remote sensing, like here in my room or in the bathrooms. The girls know, but I don't think they really understand. I also can hear the heartbeats of my enemies, knowing what lies in their eyes more than themselves."

"S-So you know my secret?" As he spoke, his chest ached as if a dagger had been shoved under his sternum. For a moment, he waited for the killing spell with fear and guilt pounding in his veins.

"No, but I do know you are hiding. Something is keeping you here, and it is more than just a fear of being caught. You are tied here, Dora... Derik."

A single tear rolled down his cheek. "I'm sorry."

Her hand lifted from his heart. "I won't push, but you need to let that secret out before it becomes too late."

He said nothing.

"If you wait too long, the consequences will be far and away worse than if you just come forward. It is how the baron lives his life and, as his women, it is how we must live as long as we stay in his harem."

The words came out of his mouth before he could stop them. "Even if it is a terrible thing?"

Her fingers caught his chin and he was powerless to stop her from bringing his gaze to hers. She stared into his eyes, emotions storming through her eyes before she found her own words. "You aren't a killer, or at least you don't have the aura of a murderer. You aren't a danger to the baron or the girls, that part I'm absolutely sure."

His heart nearly exploded as he remembered the guards who died. He shook his head. "No... I never wanted.... I didn't. I swear."

A sob ripped out of his throat.

She suddenly pulled him into a hug, wrapping her arms around him as he let the tears fall. No matter how much he wanted to, his confession refused to leave his lips. Slowly, he sank to his knees, and she followed until they were on the floor.

When the last tear fell on her shoulder, his heart finally eased. There was hope for a moment, though he still feared a killing blow.

Madre kissed his forehead. "Eventually it will come out, and the longer you wait, the worse it will be. That is the baron and that is his way. There can be no lies."

"W-Why?"

"I don't know, really. He can't tell a lie. The previous Madre told me he was cursed. Laid on him as a child: if he lies, he dies. And everything I've seen, both the magical energies that surround him and the way he lived his life, I have no doubt in my heart that he is incapable of lying."

"And why do you?"

She smiled as she brushed a strand of hair from his face. "Well, if he's honest with me, I should be honest with him. Part of being a mage is knowing who you are. Even if it takes you bleeding to death on the battlefield and having a," her voice got soft for a moment, "strong man promise to save you, even though he's the enemy."

She kissed him again. "It takes more strength to be honest than to lie, just remember that."

He sniffed and nodded. He still wanted to confess but he couldn't admit to it. It was death to say anything, despite the comforting words.

Madre's eyes searched his face for a moment, then she pulled him up. "We'll talk later about that. I want to apologize for how Nightingale treated you last night."

A bit of hope rose up.

"H-How?"

"By fucking that ass of yours with a nice thick strap-on."

He froze in place as the hope popped like a bubble.

Madre grinned wryly. "What? Time for this old lady to show you what she can do."

"I'm not really sure," he said with a sigh, "how that is an apology."

Madre drew him into the bathtub, sinking down into the bubbles. She pressed the soap into his hands before answering. "I'm not going to use the spiked one. Now, new girl, you know what to do."

He did. He washed her carefully, stroking and teasing her. She nestled against his chest, spreading her legs for him to bring her pleasure with his fingers. Then, standing up, she pressed his mouth to her dripping slit and he lapped at the soap and juices until he found her clitoris. Sucking on it, he brought her to a soft, shuddering orgasm.

Switching places, she soaped him up, teasing his cock and ass until his manhood ached for release. She washed his hair and bound it into a thick rope of blackness. Her hands were firm and teasing and commanding, pushing him down to his knees or pulling him up as she explored every inch of his body.

He watched, trembling from the growing pleasure as her heavy breasts rubbed against him.

Finally, she stood up and motioned for him to do the same. Water and soap dripping from his naked body, his cock an angry red under the bubbles, he stood up.

She smiled. "I can see why Teri likes you so much."

"T-Thank you, Madre."

Instead of pulling him from the tub, she turned him around and bent him over the edge. His feet slid for a moment, but her hand forced him to kneel over the edge of the tub. He trembled with anticipation as she moved behind him.

Her hand came down on his ass and he jumped. Chuckling, she pushed him back down and smack his other cheek. "You always get so worked from that."

"Sorry, Madre."

"Fuck sorry. I love it when you get off. I nearly came when you splattered Nightingale's leg."

His hardness lurched at the thought. "T-Then why did you make me clean it?"

She whispered in his ear, "Well, I did come when I saw that submissive crawl of yours. Then you cleaning her with your mouth. You have the perfect lips for being pressed against my slit."

Her breasts pressed against him as she leaned against him, lifting one leg than the other to put on the harness.

He could hear the leather against leather, then the heavy weight rested on the base of his spine. His heart and cock beat harder as she drew it back until the rounded tip pressed against his soapy entrance.

"Now, my Dora, you won't be cleaning this up."

She entered him slowly, pushing the thick intruder into his body. He couldn't help but focus on every centimeter working its way past his tightness. Thicker and larger than Teri's, it sank into his body as if he were made for it.

He groaned out in pleasure, leaning forward.

She wrapped her hands in his hair and pulled him back, impaling him on the fake cock.

"This is bigger than Teri," she moaned, and he agreed with a moan of his own. She tugged on his hair and the pleasure arched from his scalp to his ass.

His muscles tightened up around the shaft and his balls grew tight with pleasure.

One hand on his buttocks, she pushed him off until only the thick head remained inside him. Then, she pulled on his hair, and he arched his back letting the thick cock once again impale him, filling him. She shoved his head down, fingers still in his hair, and began to thrust hard into him. Water and soap splashes as he was fucked, pounded into the side of the tub with hard, powerful strokes that made him feel more loved than anything else in the world.

Each stroke stuffed him to his limits, stretching him out until he groaned with the pleasure, then left him empty and aching for more. He quickly found a rhythm, but she thrust harder with each stroke, slapping and pounding.

Derik was nothing but a hole to her, an orifice for her fake cock.

He almost came, but Madre's thrusts kept coming. Energy curled around them as the bubbles popped and floated in the air. The wet impacts shot through his chest as she rode him. The momentary discomfort passed into a sheer wall of pleasure as she drove into him, pinning him to the side of the tub until he let out a cry of pleasure.

His cock surged, desperately trying to come, but the pounding pressure rubbing against his insides, sliding in and out with slick movements, prevented him from release. It built up, hot and intense, swamping his sensations with a desperate need to come. His ears throbbed with the pounding of his heart and the rush of ecstasy that flowed through his veins.

When he came, a single star burst of light that blinded him. He let out another strangled scream as she impaled him with a thrust that lifted him to his toes. He clutched the air as he finally found a release, splattering the side of the tub and the walls with his essence.

She matched his surges with thrusts of her own, pumping him dry with nothing but the hard, slick member driving in and out of his clenching hole.

Madre rode him for a few more minutes, as if trying to reach her own orgasm, but eventually she stopped. Panting against him, hard nipples grinding into his back, she chuckled. "And that, in your mistress' words, is a tender reaming."

"T-Thank you, Madre." And to his surprise, he actually meant it.

Trying Again

"I'm not done with you."

She withdrew the fake cock from his body and he slumped down against the side of the tub. Feeling drained, he stared at his own cum splattered on the wall and managed to stand up.

When he turned around, he was shocked into stillness at the sight of her there, wearing nothing but a harness and a large cock bobbing from her hips. For a moment, she was the most beautiful creature on the planet. His mouth opened in surprise and tears blurred his vision.

"What is it, Dora?"

"Nothing, Madre."

"Are you lying?"

He hesitated, "Yes."

"That's one."

"Sorry! I just thought you were beautiful."

She beamed as she slipped out of the harness. He saw that the cock had a protrusion on the other end, glistening and soaked. No doubt pushing up into her. He blushed as she handed it to him.

"Thank you."

He cleaned the cock off in the water and drained the tub. Getting out, he dried her off, but she remained naked. She did the same for him before drawing him to the chairs by the bed.

Instead of fucking him again, she surprised him by pulling out tools for working nails. He watched as she trimmed and polished his nails, giving them almost a womanly elegance that he always admired.

"Do you like sapphires?"

His heart jumped and he thought about the Eye, but he managed to calm himself. "Y-Yes."

"Madre. And I'm glad. I never asked you what color you like, but with those eyes of yours, all I could think of was the Eye of Hamel."

He fought back a whimper as he stared down at the sharp file she used to bring his nails to a rounded peak.

"Too bad it is so large," she looked up with a smile, "it would look so beautiful in your hair."

Derik opened his mouth to say something, then closed it. He tried again after a few heart-pounding seconds. "Thank you?"

"You'll notice that most of the girls here follow a color theme. It isn't required, I just happen to prefer it so I normally start them off with a solid color. After a while, most of them may change the color but they stick with the same. Others, like Nightingale and Sherrel, sometimes change colors or patterns every couple days or weeks."

"Oh."

"Just telling you, you'll have a chance for other colors if you desire. How do you like your nails?"

"I... I..."

Madre grinned, "I bet you never had them colored in your life."

"Um, no."

"Do you like a style?"

He thought back to the girls he grew up with. Few of them could afford nail color. He remembered one whore he used, she had some of the most striking nails he remembered. "I-I like the ones with the white tips, like a curve."

"You're blushing," Madre chuckled which only made his blush hotter.

"I—"

"—don't worry, just teasing. Sometimes, it really is hard to believe you don't belong here. You are thinking of a Karith Crescent. I'll show you how to do it..."

It took longer than he expected but soon he had both fingernails and toenails in striking sapphire, with a thin white strip along the polished edge. He stared at them in shock, surprised at the feeling of happiness that filled him.

As they waited for them to dry, Madre told him about her youth, in the battle school. He remembered some of the cryptic statements Wendi made and realized that both Madre and Wendi grew up in very similar places. It scared him and fascinated him; it was a way of getting close to his former financée in a way he never thought possible.

At least not after fucking her mother on the altar.

And stealing the family silver.

And then lying about telling everyone he sold it.

He chuckled at the thought. Madre relaxed and they just chatted about nothings. She didn't push him for his secret and he was content to refer to his life in veiled details.

Soon, it was late and they were both yawning. He admired his nails, hardened and crystalline. He smiled as Madre put away her tools.

"You like?" she asked.

"I... they're beautiful."

"You are."

He blushed, "Thank you, Madre."

Derik looked up as she came back, then stared in shock at the rope in her hand. His eyes widened as he shook his head. "Not another night, please?"

Madre leaned forward, her naked breasts teasing his thighs. "Last night was my mistake. I should have never trusted Nightingale to forgive you so soon."

"But..."

"Do you trust me?"

He said nothing and she repeated her question.

"Do you trust me?"

"Y-Yes, Madre."

"Then tonight, you will enjoy this."

He feared for the endless hours before him, but he stood up with a bowed head.

She caught his chin and lifted him gaze to her. "And smile, you have such a pretty smile."

He did his best.

She raised an eyebrow. "That's it?"

"Sorry."

"That's two."

His cock jumped at the thought of being spanked.

She pointedly looked down. "At least something likes being paddled."

Derik chuckled, "Sorry."

"And there is my smile. Come. And that is three, you aren't sorry."

She pushed him to the bed, placing him on the bottom half on his back. He was confused as she trailed the end of the rope along his cock, sending a surge of pleasure. Pushing his left leg up, she pressed his ankle near his buttocks, then tied his folded leg together. Pre-cum oozed out of his cock as she did the same to his other leg, pushing them near his chest and leaving him exposed.

"Now, I enchanted these ropes not to bind or to cut off circulation. They won't hurt in the morning, but you'll be just as helpless to escape them."

He tried to shift his legs, but they refused to budge. All he could do was spread or tighten his legs. Looking at her eyes, he kept them spread, exposing his cock and asshole to her.

She nodded in approval. "Now, give me your hand."

He held out his hand, and she pushed it against his leg, spreading him wide before tying his arm along the side. In a matter of seconds, he was fixed in place, his arm preventing him from closing his leg. Pre-cum pooled on his belly as she did the same for the other side, binding him in place, spread for her enjoyment.

He moaned as she started to tease him. Trailing her own polished nails against his inner thighs and cock, teasing his balls and down around his anus. His breath came out as panting as she playing with the streamers of pre-cum from his cock and stroked along the swollen member.

"Now, can't have you coming tonight."

She spoke with a playful whisper but he could do nothing as she took a thinner rope and wrapped it around his balls, separating each one and wrapping it around his base.

"But in the morning, you are probably going to come like no tomorrow. If you're good, I'll let you come somewhere good."

He wondered if she had Teri in mind, but the rope around his base seemed to magnify his cock, swelling it up to an angry red and throbbing with a sudden need to come.

"You have two tonight, and that means I'm going to fuck your mouth and ass twice tonight."

He gulped. "T-Three."

Her eyes lit up and she grinned happily. "You are right. Three. Well, I'll find something for the third. Something nice since you're being honest with me."

Derik let out a whimper, then his eyes widened as she pulled up something that looked like a two-headed cock with a strap in the middle.

"But it isn't your tongue, I'll be using."

He shook his head as she brought the penis gag to his lips.

"Trust me."

It took all of his effort to part his lips, to feel the rounded head sliding past his lips. He wondered what it would feel like with a real man and his cock bobbed with the thought. It filled his mouth and tickled the back of his throat by the time the middle reached his lips. He whimpered, looking up at her with pleading eyes, but she just strapped it around his head.

"No blindfold, though. Just enjoy tonight."

She left him along, wiggling at the bottom of her bed. It left him feeling helpless but not exposed. There was a tenderness in her movements, and he didn't feel as trapped.

Not having a huge cock in his ass didn't hurt either.

He watched as she bustled around her room, finished up some of her paperwork, and even straightened her clothes. Despite watching her do everything but pay attention to him, a lust grew inside him. It was the anticipation that rose into a hungry desire. His breath ran along the length of the cock gag and when he leaned back, he just saw himself looking up at fourteen centimeters of hard, rubber cock. He swallowed at the unfamiliar feeling of something in his mouth. Using his tongue, he played with it, working it in his mouth as he grew used to having something stuffing his mouth.

When she finally turned off the lights, dread rose up. She just crawled into bed and ignored him. His heart pounded as he listened and waited for her. She settled into a comfortable position and drifted to sleep, leaving him on the knife's edge of anticipation.

He just leaned back and settled into his own place. His pre-cum dripped down both sides of his balls and he managed to drift to sleep himself.

Hours later, Derik woke up with a start, blindly trying to move as his bound body refused to budge. He groaned, then leaned into the fingers holding his cock.

She jacking his slick member as the rounded end of a dildo pressed against his entrance.

He trembled with lust and lifted his hips to accept it.

Moaning, he concentrated on it sliding into him.

The lubricated and slick length filled him completely. She stroked with both hands, pumping the thick member in his ass and stroking his cock until it pulsed but didn't give him release.

He pushed down with every stroke, enjoying the pleasure that came from the wide intruder. His body seemed to rise up to the crest of an orgasm, but she withdrew just as he almost reached it. Then, ignoring his whimpers for more, she dropped it on the floor and settled back into her sleep.

He found himself vibrating on the edge of excitement, his body shaking with every beat of his heart. Every breeze in the room set afire more passions but soon sleep took him again.

Again, she woke him, this time straddling his face. The pressure on his lips and jaw increased as she sank down on his cock gag. Her perfumed thighs surrounded his head and he drowned in the smells of her cunt. The end in his throat pushed down, gagging him, but he could do nothing as she ground down.

When she finally bottomed out, his face was buried in her pussy, and his nose touched her hard clitoris, so wet it soaked his face. She let out a guttural moan of pleasure, rocking back and forth before pumping herself up and down on his gag. She drove his head into the blankets and the cock deeper into his throat. The intensity of it was overwhelming, and he tried to reach up to her, to find some other way to bring her pleasure, but she just used him, fucking his face like a midnight toy. He shuddered with the edge of pleasure, but she came to her orgasm before he could and slipped off.

His whimper echoed in the room as she crawled back to her spot and returned to sleep. He was left alone, his face slick with her juices and the taste of her cum seeping past his lips. He swallowed and tried to ignore the ache of his manhood as it danced and throbbed with every pulse.

This time, he couldn't sleep. He thought about everything he could, from pretend explorations of the grand hall to how he pleasured Teri and the others that first night. He relived being spanked. No matter what he thought about, the anticipation of being used again just brought him up to a slow boil.

Much later, she moved again and he wondered if it would be his ass or mouth. She answered when she straddled his face again. He couldn't see in the dark, but the pressure pressure on his gag was unmistakable. This time, it was a tighter pressure as she slowly slid down his cock. He squirmed, and she grabbed his cock; he realized she was facing the other way this time.

Then she pushed down, and his nose pressed against the smooth curve of her ass. He tried to imagine her position as she fucked herself again on his mouth, driving long and deep, a slow orgasm that seemed to take forever to build in her.

When her wet pussy pressed against his chin, he realized she was fucking her ass on his penis gag. His eyes opened with surprise, but he could see the magical rune on the small of her back flickering just on the edge of his senses. Her hands reached down to hold him steady, moving faster. He surrendered and used his neck to thrust up into her, fucking her ass to the limit of her ability.

She came before he did. When she slipped off, she rewarded him with a hand job, bringing him almost to the edge of orgasm before she crawled back to her sleeping spot.

He wondered if he would get any sleep.

To his surprise, he did. He woke up as she slipped off the bed. He moaned softly, raising his hips in anticipation of being impaled once again. He heard her wry chuckle in the darkness, then his world exploded into sparks of surprise pain as she spanked him twice.

"Greedy little slut?"

He moaned as his cock pulsed, desperately trying to come. The rope around his base held him like a vise as he tried to come again and again, but soon his body surrendered in a shuddering sigh. He swallowed at the cock in his mouth as he waited.

It came, huge and thick. A massive member dripping with lubricant that dwarfed his tiny opening, but she worked it in and out of him, fucking him until he relaxed enough to take it. He gasped at the sensations, feeling how it stretched him to even further limits as it sank into him, burying deep. Then, a ridge stretched him even more. She kept pushing as he whimpered and writhed in place.

Slowly, his body took in the thick butt plug, and it slurped into place, cementing him as the thickness stretched him to his limits. His cock surged and drooled. Derik whimpered at the thought of a long night, but Madre wasn't done.

When her pussy pressed against his swollen, aching head, he realized what she was doing. His body froze solid as he drew every iota of attention to the heated velvet that slid down his cock, swallowing him into the sacred place of her body. He groaned and moaned, shaking with the intensity of her hot pussy wrapped around his cock. The rope and plug in his ass only making it more intense as she rode him.

Up and down, in and out, slow and steady. He concentrated on every movement until her pussy was his entire world. His cock pulsed and surged, screaming with lust as he tried to fill her womb with his seed. But, nothing came out but more pre-cum. He groaned as she took her time, fucking him for hours.

When she loudly came, grinding her pussy against his stomach until he whimpered with need. He thought she would pull up, but she continued to ride him to another, then a third orgasm, using him even as he screamed out with his desperation for an orgasm.

Finally, her torture ended when she came to a halt, still impaled by his cock. Their shared breath came in shudders. She leaned forward, settling into the position of his body and bringing her lips to his ears. "Did you enjoy that?"

He moaned and nodded.

She smiled in his ear, then shifted slightly, still impaled by his cock. Then, she drifted to sleep.

He remained there, pinned and cradling her weight, holding her soft wonderful body against his own. His cock surged in the confines of her pussy, but he was nothing more than her pillow.

Derik didn't want to sleep anymore. For some reason, he wanted to spend the rest of the night just being hers.

When he woke for the last time, she was pulling his swollen cock out of her pussy. It dripped with juices as she chuckled and ran a fingernail along it.

"So thick, I bet you have to come, don't you?"

He blinked at the light in the room and groaned. His cock ached like a sausage ready to split at any second. He watched as she worked a huge plug out of his ass and set it aside.

A disappointing void remained inside his body as she released his binds and then his gag; he wanted to be filled again.

Her fingers delicately worked out the rope around his base, freeing his cock. He gasped at the ache deep inside.

Madre gestured down with her fingers.

"Go on, come."

He stared at her, then wrapped his hands around his shaft, pumping hard and furiously. His fingers slurped through their combined juices as he brought himself to an orgasm. It took longer, but when he finally found release, he let out a long gasping groan and sank to his knees, splattering his cum on the floor behind him as the world spun around.

He kept on coming as he pumped. His fingers dripped white as he pressed his forehead to the ground, praying to the ground and hand working in a blur.

Each surge took forever to be forced out of his body, but soon he was empty. Gasping, he looked up to see Madre standing over him, smiling broadly.

"I bet that felt good too?"

Speechless, he could only nod.

Madre reached down to stroke his face. "You should probably get some more sleep. So, clean that up and head into the other room."

He looked down at the puddle of his own cum. He thought about what she said. Then, he made another decision in his depravity. Fighting back the feeling, he leaned down and began to lick up his cum.

Madre gasped as he did it. He swallowed the taste of his own seed. He thought about other men, wondered if it tasted the same, then almost came again. The taste wasn't as bad this time, not as forbidden, and he licked the floor clean. His hand stroked his shaft slowly as he finished up.

Then, he realized he was almost enjoying it and a flush of shame burned his cheeks at the realization. He sat back to look up at Madre.

She had her hands between her legs, stroking hard as she stared at him with open lips and lust in her eyes. "I-I meant, fuck it. Fuck me. Now!"

She grabbed him and pulled him to the bed. Spreading her legs, he stared down at the swollen opening of her pussy. Her folds glistened with her juices. Madre growled and pulled him into her.

He sank into her pussy with a sigh of long forbidden pleasures. Velvet and smooth, he was there as a man, not as a woman. Her hands were frantic as he pumped, driving into her until they both came to a screaming orgasm and he flooded her pussy.

Madre gasped as she clutched him. "Goddess, you are the hottest damn submissive I have ever known."

This time, he got to sleep in her bed.

One of Them

After that night of bondage, he finally did start to trust her. When she pulled out her paddle or the rope, his cock surged to full mast and a heat grew inside him.

Whenever he staggered out of Madre's room, Teri responded with her own bondage and strap-ons, pushing him as much as Madre to find his limits.

Everyone wanted to tie him to pillars and use him as a pillow. His shame slowly faded under the assault of lips, strap-ons, and dildos. Being pressed into one pussy after the other, lapping until his mouth ached, brought an appreciation for the number of ways women could be pleasured. And, as he learned them, he found that they were distinct and wonderful on their own, a realization that made him suddenly wonder how he could have ever been content with just thinking them as whores.

For Madre, and only Madre, did he clean himself up off the floor or her leg with his tongue. Every time it set a fire in her eyes, but she never lost it like the first time. He cherished that memory, a point when Madre broke down and treated him as a man.

For Teri, he found that slurping juices from her slit brought her to the strongest orgasm he could, baring fucking his poor ass with a strap-on. She enjoyed every time he accidentally bent over in the shower or over a pillow.

On the other hand, Sherrel preferred masturbating against him, her body shuddering as she came. He would just stroke her as she focused on her body.

Then, there was this moment when it wasn't him on the bottom, but another of the harem. Teri jumped him, and a tickle fight quickly became a gang-bang of fingers. He joined in, just as one of the women. As he pumped his own fingers into her soaked pussy, he realized he never wanted to leave.

His nights turned into days, then orgasmed into weeks. Time slipped by so fast as he slipped into a routine, a feeling of belonging.

One morning, he passed another step. A sleepy morning where he woke up with his legs sprawled out over Sherrel's back. He could feel the delicious curve of her ass against his toes as he looked up from where he laid on his belly. He tried to move his arm, but Teri moaned in her sleep and wrapped tightly around it, holding him down.

He looked at her, through the curtain of his long black hair and smiled. His free hand reached up to move the strand to better see her innocent face. He held his hand up there, staring at the sapphire nail polish and the thin crescent of white at the very tip.

His eyes trailed along her body, where his long black hair had spread out like a web over her beautiful skin. Carefully, he started to pull them to him, drawing the delicate strands across her skin until she moaned and shifted in her sleep.

She smelled differently, and he frowned. Beyond the scent of perfume, there was the taste of beer and smoke on her skin. He inhaled it, instantly reminded of the Buggered Unicorn and Storn.

It hit him like a sledge in the center of his back.

Rick. Rick's deadline had long since passed, and he was still in the middle of the harem. A cold sweat spread out along his skin as he stared up at the ceiling, suddenly afraid.

Madre took that moment to step in front of him, a flicker of concern on her face. "What's wrong?" she whispered.

He answered quickly, tearing his thoughts away from Rick. "Nothing."

"You're lying."

He didn't even try to hide it. "Yes, Madre."

"That's one."

He said nothing.

"What's wrong?"

"I... please don't make me tell you."

Derik was terrified that she would press. He kept feeling the words on the tip of his tongue, that madding desire to spill every secret he had.

She searched his face for a moment, then carefully stepped around his hair. "Come."

It was a whispered command but he couldn't disobey. He tried to pull his arm from Teri, but she clutched it tighter.

Madre chuckled and reached down, sliding her finger down the small of her back and into the crevice between her legs.

Teri shuddered and released his hand, curling up against the pillow as her hand delved between her legs.

Grinning, Derik managed to gather up his hair and pull it back. His cock safely confined in his silk panties, he padded after Madre, wondering if he was late for his duties.

She stopped at the door to her room and turned to him. "We... better... damn, forgot your robe."

Her hand reached up, and she straightened out his bra, smoothing it down to give him his feminine appearance.

He blushed, not at the shame or humiliation, but just that feeling of being loved.

She reached into her bedroom to pull out one of her black silk robes and put it on him. It looked striking against his sapphire nails and the clothes underneath.

Madre chuckled and said, "Come on. You have a visitor."

"A..." He gulped, fearing that Rick had found him. "A visitor?"

Madre nodded, her eyes still focused on straightening his outfit. "We have to pass some guards, so no speaking until we do."

Cold sweat prickled his brow. "Y-Yes, Madre."

His heart pounded in his chest as she drew him down the hall, out of the hallowed halls of the harem. They passed the two guards at the entrance, and he could feel eyes following them as they went down one unfamiliar corridor, then the other. He tried to remember the map of the palace, but he never memorized this wing. There was no need, he was just going to grab the Eye and flee.

That thought brought a sardonic smile to his lips. Then, he let it fade as he remembered Madre's words of hearing his heart.

She glanced back at him, then pulled him up to her before slipping an arm around his waist. She spoke to the guards, "Relax, I asked her to come."

He stumbled for a moment, then let out a long sigh of relief.

She squeezed him for a moment, then lead him along the tiled floors toward the main hall. He wondered if he would ever be able to walk along the smoothed edges of the floor without feeling growing fear or trepidation.

"You were afraid it was someone else, weren't you?"

Madre spoke casually, but he could feel her attention on him as she did.

He swallowed and nodded. "Yes, Madre."

"Who?"

He couldn't answer. He just concentrated on his feet as he walked.

She slowed down, prolonging the agony. "That's two."

He winced, but kept his mouth shut.

"Three."

"P-Please?"

"Four."

"Please, Madre, don't make me."

"Five." A moment later. "Six with the paddle."

He managed to keep his mouth shut as she counted up in time with her steps. When she hit thirty, he broke down and let out a pitiful sob. Choking on the words, he named his fear. "R-Rick."

She stopped and turned in front of him. Her eyes looked down the empty hallway as she stared down at him. "Rick? The only Rick I know is Rick Thrantas, the baron's—"

At the sound of Rick's full name, Derik's heart nearly exploded. He stepped back in fear, shocked into silence.

Madre froze in mid-word, staring at him first in confusion, then into concern as she took the step to him.

He tried to step away from her, but he slammed up against the warm plaster wall.

Her hand pressed firmly against his pounding heart, and he tried to say something but no words came out.

"My gods, is that who you are hiding from?"

Tears ran down his face as he started to deny it, then nodded.

She kept her hand firm against his chest, feeling his heart slamming against his ribs. "Oh, my little Dora, Rick is a very dangerous man."

"I-I..." He swallowed back the sob. "I know."

"Yes, I think you do," she whispered and slowly lifted her hand from his body.

He stared at her, not knowing if she was going to finally turn him in.

Compassion filled her eyes as she sighed. "You picked a very bad enemy, Dora. Rick is the baron's good friend and he frequently borrows girls from the harem for days at a time. He's rough and a bit of a sadist, but some of the girls like him and the baron allows it."

He trembled at the thought.

Madre sighed unhappily. "And he owes me no favors, none at all. That means I have no recourse other than to bring it up with the baron himself. And then I'm asking my lord to choose between you and a friend."

Her voice trailed off and he sniffed at the tears, closing his eyes tightly. She said nothing as she cupped his chin and tilted his head. He opened his eyes, staring at her through the shimmer of tears.

She was centimeters from his face, her breath hot on his lips. "Dora, I will fight for you, but there is a price."

It took him a second to find the words. "W-What?"

He already dreaded what would come out of her mouth, but the actual words were spikes driving into his gut.

"There can be no more secrets between us. I need to trust you absolutely. I need to trust you as much as I trust the baron before I will stand before him to defend you."

"E-Even as a guy?"

"If I trust you that much, I will defend your right to be in my harem. These last weeks have proven that you belong there, even as a rooster in the hen house."

He blushed deeply at that.

She stared at his eyes, but he didn't need to say anything for her answer. She sighed. Stepping back, she sighed again. "I will do everything I can, but I will not go to the baron for you if you have this secret between us."

More tears rolled down his cheeks as guilt pierced his stomach. His body trembled as he spoke softly. "I-I'm sorry, Madre."

Neither said anything for long painful moments.

Then she sighed with obvious disappointment but held out her hand. "Come on, I already blew a favor for your visitor, no reason to waste it."

Fragile from their conversation, he held out his shaking hand. His painted nails slid along her palm, then she took it and lead him along the hallways until they found a room he recognized from the map, a conference room. Knocking once, she opened it up. He got only a second to look inside before he was pulled in.

A statuesque woman waited by the far wall. She had a light blue habit on, a priestess of sorts he guessed. In the light shining through the window, he could only stare in shock at her imposing profile and blonde hair before she turned her warm eyes toward him.

Madre shut the door behind him, and he stared at the new woman.

The priestess glided toward him. With every sway of her waist, the dangling part of her rope rocked back and forth. He noticed her habit was slit up both sides, revealing a black garter with every step. She stopped in front of him and stared at him with piercing brown eyes that bored into his spirit.

He blushed.

"Rachi is absolutely right, you are stunningly beautiful, Dora." She had a seductive voice, a purr that sent a strange flickering in his stomach. It wasn't pleasure or lust but something else. A voice that begged for him to drop to his knees and confess his sins.

"I-I'm, um," he stammered.

When she smiled, he could only stare up at her in shock. Her smile so brightened the room, he nearly didn't realize she stood ten centimeters taller than him.

"Don't worry, I know your little secret."

As to make the point, she reached out with her plain fingers to run a fingertip down the seam of the pitch-black robe. "In fact,

Rachi owned me a little favor from some years ago. And she asked me if she could owe me a bigger one, if I could help you."

Derik looked at Madre who blushed slightly on her own. She caught Derik's gaze and gave him a hard look. "You," she empathized the word sharply with one raised finger, "will continue to call me 'Madre.'"

"Y-Yes, Madre."

The priestess laughed, a sparkling laugh that left him feeling dizzy, before stepping back to admire him again. "Amazing how much they listen to you now, Rachi. I remember when you struggled to just keep Nightingale in line. Is she still here?"

"Yes, but currently being punished for arguing with me."

The priest laughed again, "Fighting is just foreplay for her, and you know it."

Madre blushed again and looked away from Derik. She spoke curtly after a moment. "Can you do it, Hime?"

"Always impatient, my Rachi."

Hime turned her attention back to Derik who couldn't shift from his position. She held up one hand and he stared at it. She had no scars or callouses, but there was a sense of comfort as she held her hand right above his forehead. "Just try to relax, Dora."

He couldn't relax, but he could stare at her.

Hime whispered softly, and it took him a second to realize she was chanting. Whispered prayers, just on the edge of his senses, seemed to overlay with his thoughts. Above him, her hand flickered with white wisps of energy rising up off it. He swallowed hard as he stared at it, terrified and curious at the same time.

She pulled her hand back after a moment, then gave him a warm smile. "I can do it. She has the right energies that the side effects will be minimal. Maybe a bit of emotional breakdown, but nothing as serious as bleeding or internal damage."

Derik looked back and forth between Madre and Hime, still confused.

Madre caught his confusion and explained. "Hime is a priestess of Bridget. But, she also can mark you like the other girls. So, you'll look like them."

"B-Bridget?"

He tried to remember the goddess, but nothing came to mind.

Hime laughed again, a sparkling laugh that made him want to smile. She leaned over to him and whispered in his ear. "Bridget is the patron god of cross-dressers... Derik."

He didn't think he could blush that hotly without exploding in flames. A tiny squeak noise escaped his lips as he stared up at her with shock, fear, and surprise.

She laughed cheerfully and stepped away, releasing him from her presence. "I can do it. I didn't bring the right marking stylus though. Her energies will corrupt it, so I need to find a good quality set that I'm willing to lose."

"How much?"

"Probably a hundred marks, if I'm lucky."

Derik swallowed, "What is a stylus? You mean those sticks that Forbis used?"

Madre nodded and Hime expanded on her assessment.

"They focus the energy of the mage, or priestess in my case, into a specific purpose. You have one stylus—the stick as you call it—for each color. Typically, you have a set of six, but you don't need that for what you use, three would do. A good quality set will cost a couple hundred marks while the best sets can easily go into the thousands."

Derik shifted on one foot as he tried to think about the to the styluses he stole from Forbis. "C-Can you use any set? No, um, restrictions?"

"Yes, mages don't normally—"

Madre interrupted Hime with a hand gesture.

"Dora, what is it?"

"Um..."

"Thirty-five."

He grumbled, "Fuck."

"That will also happen, forty. Ten more and I start using magic."

Feeling like the situation was quickly growing out of control, he blurted out as quickly as he could. "I stole some of those from Forbis."

A stunned silence followed as both the priestess and his mistress stared at him.

Derik, feeling in center of two powerful forces, shuffled his feet as he looked sheepishly at him. "He was an asshole. And... and I-I was kind of mad at him, so I stole them from his bag when he shoved past me."

Madre cleared her throat before speaking very carefully. "Der-Dora, you stole them from Forbis? From his bag?"

"Yes, Madre."

Madre's face paled. "Forbis had me enchant his bag with my best warding spell. That should have stripped the skin off your bones if you stuck your hand in there."

Oh, crap. He swallowed hard as he looked at Hime. To his horror, the priestess just grinned before bursting out laughing.

"Wow, beautiful and with some interesting talents for sticking your foot in your mouth. So, how was Rachi's deathly trap?"

"Um..."

Hime leaned forward, smirking. She folded her fingers together. "Oh, please be honest. I want to hear this."

"T-They were," he swallowed again as he glanced over at Madre. He could almost see the emotions rolling off her, just like Wendi right before she blew her temper. He thought back on the little twist of movement he used to bypass charms and wards with a bit of hope, speed, and luck.

"T-They were..."

Madre snapped out angrily, "Forty-five."

"Sorry! They were actually pretty, just easy, um, fuck, they weren't that good, Madre. I-I didn't eve... even feel a tingle."

Sweat poured down his neck as Hime burst into laughter, her musical mirth echoing in the room as she clutched her stomach from a stitch in her side.

Madre glared at her, then at Derik as the temperature of the room dropped a few degrees.

He shivered and backed away. "I-I'm sorry."

Madre looked away from him as she stepped forward. His heart pounded as she pressed right up to him and spoke softly in his ear. With the soft, hard voice of a killer. "One hundred."

He whimpered, "I'm so sorry, Madre."

"Ten thousand if you ever," she nipped his ear, "ever tell anyone else."

He swallowed hard, but his cock nearly burst with excitement. "I'm sorry."

Madre stepped away and glared at the still laughing priestess. "Oh, shut up, Hime."

Hime, tears streaming down her cheeks, staggered back into a standing position. One hand pressed against her stomach as she struggled to control her laughter.

"Sure, Rachi, I'll-oh, I can't. Didn't even tingle!"

And she burst into laughter again.

Derik swallowed as Madre's glare figuratively stripped away his skin.

Marked

"Show them to me?" asked Hime.

They were alone in the massage room, just the two of them. Derik slid forward and pulled open the drawer of the table. Reaching back, he pulled out the four styluses he stole from Forbis and held them out.

Hime delicately picked them up from his hand, brushing her fingertips against his palm as she did. He watched she held them out, then frowned in concentration.

Tiny colored sparkles dripped out of the ends of them: pink, yellow, and green. From the forth just came bright white sparks.

Hime's eyebrow arched and she smiled. "You stole the right ones, Dora," she fingered the one that dripped white, "The perfect ones actually. That should say something for someone randomly grabbing into a trapped bag."

He ducked his head. "Um, what do I do?"

Hime gestured to the nearest table. "Might as well get started. Strip down and hop on up, I take it the other girls here already know."

Derik slipped the jet-black robe from his shoulders and let it puddle to the ground. His padded bra and panties followed quickly, leaving him naked and bare. He blushed, feeling the eyes of someone new on him.

Hime just admired him for a moment, then patted on the padded table. "Just as beautiful as before. You are very lucky."

He sighed as he slipped on the massage table. Settling into place as he rested his chin on the end. "T-Thank you, priestess."

"Just call me Hime, Dora. Neither of us were born with our names."

Her hand slid down his back to the base of his spine. Her touch was sure and confident. His muscles flexed reflexively, lifting his hips but she pushed them down.

"I'm not going to fuck you, don't worry about that. Now, be silent, it takes a bit to corrupt these."

Hime's hand grew noticeably warmer. Within seconds it was hot.

He held his breath. It sent tiny ripples along his skin, forcing the tiny hairs on his back and arms to stand up on their own. His longer black hair, still unbound from waking up, rose slightly in the air as the energy filled him. It ended with the sensation of a bubble popping and he gasped from the unexpected sensations.

"Now, these can never be used by anyone else. If they do, someone will get sick. That does mean keeping them away from Forbis, but I think you already know that."

"Yes, Hime."

She giggled softly. "You say that like I was your Madre."

"Sorry."

"Don't be, it's been a long time since I had a Madre."

The first stylus tapped on his tender skin and then quickly began to trace lines along his skin. Tiny quakes seemed to ripple in his stomach as he groaned. His hips shifted until she pressed one hand down on his thigh, holding him in place as she drew on him. The feeling of energy being worked on his body increased, and he spoke to distract himself.

"What do you mean?"

"About what, having a Madre?"

"Y-Yes."

"I used to be part of this harem, actually. Back when Rachi was the new girl."

Curious, he wanted to ask more, but didn't know how.

Hime continued to mark him as she spoke in a soft voice. "She was so young and so angry when she came in. Older than me, but I was one of the harem kittens as Madre used to say. I didn't know about the outside world then."

She let out a bitter laugh and switched styluses. A different trembling grew in his loins, stirring a storm in his testicles, and he groaned in discomfort.

"I was our Madre's Hawk, then, a different time of my life."

"H-Hawk?"

"Madre's lover. She called me a hawk because I always pointed out the flaws in everyone else. Plus, I was kind of a snitch and a major bitch. We always joked that Rachi would be the next Madre because she was in love with Nightingale. Bird lovers unite."

"What happened?"

"Madre died. Her heart stopped one day while talking to the baron. It was sudden and a surprise, and..." her voice trailed off for a moment as the stylus stopped, "I went a little crazy with grief."

She resumed marking with a third stylus, this one set his entire skin on fire, a burning blush that refused to go away. He groaned and wiggled but she pinned him down even tighter.

"After that, I asked to leave. The baron knew how much I loved Madre, and I simply didn't have it in my heart to serve him anymore. So, he actually let me go instead of selling me off as he usually does. A bag of money and the clothes on my back. Then, well then I found out what the real world was like."

He could barely hear her over the rushing in his ears but he forced himself to listen to her words, if just to distract himself from the flush searing his skin.

"I had no skills as a kitten, so I ended up being a stripper. Then Bridget found me."

"H-How!?" His word came out in a cry when the stylus burned him.

"Sorry, little hot?" She switched to a stylus that left quakes in his belly before speaking again.

"When you give a lap dance to a god, they have ways of making their nature known. In my case, it changed me physically."

He whimpered as she switched to the fourth. This one ignited a cutting pain across his chest, tightening it painfully as he clutched the edge of the table. A second band of agony wrapped itself around his waist, tearing at his senses like a flail. "Ow!"

"Hold on, this is going to be the painful one."

Derik whimpered as he closed his eyes tightly. He managed to belt out a word through his clenched teeth, desperately trying to distract him.

"Changed?"

She didn't say anything, just marked terrible things against his spine.

Derik imagined his skin sliced open from the tip of the stylus, but that did nothing to help his growing discomfort. He knew she wasn't cutting into him, but the raw sparks of pain made it impossible to think of anything else.

She worked in silence for a long moment before switching to the stylus that churned his balls.

"Reach between my legs."

"What!?"

"Go on, it will help distract you when I switch."

Hesitantly, and feeling a bit disrespectful, he released his trembling fingers from the edge of the massage table and slid his hand along her inner thigh. Hime's legs were soft and he trailed up the garter, following the thin strip of fabric until he reached her satin thong. She switched to the one that set his skin on fire and he gasped, working his hands toward the junction between his legs. When his fingers wrapped around a large cock clad in satin, he froze, and Hime giggled.

"Bridget is the god of cross-dressers, Dora, he protects and provides for those who desire the cloth of women. But, the key part is a man in the dress. Since I was already a woman, he made me also a man, a priestess of his faith. I have the breasts but I also have the cock. I can never have children though."

"D-Didn't it hurt?"

"It was the single best orgasm of my life," came the simple reply before she switched to the truly painful stylus, "and finding faith was probably the single best moment I've had ever since."

He groaned and accidentally gripped the large shaft tightly. It grew harder but she didn't even flinch. Instead, she rocked forward, holding his hand there as she traced delicate lines against his spine, filling him with pain and discomfort. It went on for a long time.

Between one stylus and another, he finally released the satin-clad shaft and clutched the table again.

Hime chanted softly as she worked between the four styluses until his ears rang with the various spells being laid out on his body.

Just when he started to whimper loudly in pain, she stopped. "Don't move yet."

"It hurts."

"It won't next time. Your body is getting used to magic. I gave you four runes, but no one can see the fourth. All of them will wear off in three months, just like the other girls."

He slumped his head down on the padded pillow. "I'll have to do this again? It really hurt."

"Yes, but longer spells can have side effects. I could make them permanent, but I feel that you aren't ready yet."

She slid her hand up his back, through the sweat the beaded on his skin, to trail along the nape of his neck. "This will also cause some changes. You might get more emotional. For a few weeks, I recommend you don't do anything that would devastate you, otherwise there is a chance it will embed itself in your psyche."

"W-What?"

"You weren't born a woman, but this sterility rune is going to force you to become sterile like one. It... is rough the first couple of weeks as it changes you. Madre knows that, she'll protect you. I think she's quite fond of you."

Somehow, he could accept being changed closer to a woman through magic.

He let out a sigh before grumbling. "Then why am I getting a hundred swats?"

"Only a hundred? Rachi used to get block of a hundred from Madre every couple hours. She was quite angry, and Madre quite often got into the thousands. Took days to spank the hell out of her and days for Rachi to sit down again. We had to take turns with the paddles."

Derik chuckled at the thought. "She likes to spank, doesn't she? Did she like being spanked?"

"Hated it, actually. It was degrading for a battle mage."

"I... I kind of like it." He started to blush.

Hime giggled and helped him sit up. He started to look down, but Hime caught his chin and forced his gaze up. "Don't look down yet."

A prickle of fear flooded his stomach. "Why?"

"Because I made a change without asking you or Madre. I highly suspect that one of you is going to look at it and scream at me very loudly."

He trembled at the thought. He tensed his muscles trying to feel what she did. "Um, why?"

She smiled, her blond hair dancing in the air. She leaned forward to kiss him on the cheek. "Because faith told me too. And when Bridget gives me the exact tools I would need, I use my best judgment."

She grinned sheepishly and gave him an apologetic look. "Just sometimes my best judgment gets me and others in a lot of trouble."

The prickle of fear turned into a full-blown torrent of terror as he tried to look down. The hand remained on his chin, forcing him to look up.

"What, what did you do?"

"I made it easier for you to pretend to be a woman."

He kept trying to look down but she strained to hold him.

"What?"

"Remember, it will wear off in three months."

"What is it?"

Hime actually sounded a bit nervous as she forced him from looking down.

Panicked, Derik spoke louder. "What!?"

She just released his chin.

He looked frantically down, staring at the valley between his legs, afraid she took away his balls or cock. At the sight of his member, half-hard and just as he remembered it, he let out a sigh of relief.

Then he noticed the two perky breasts tipped with perfectly little nipples.

On his chest.

His chest.

His nipples.

His breasts.

Derik stared at them for a long moment, then decided Hime was a fortune teller. He opened his mouth to say something, but all that came out was a single shrill scream of terror. He could hear it echoing in the main room and the sounds of someone rushing in.

Then he passed out.

t'Sade

Therapy

Derik woke screaming, a muffled scream from having his face buried in the deep cleavage of Sherrel's breasts. He clutched at her, sobbing and keeping his face buried even as he struggled for air.

She cooed to him as he struggled with thousands of new emotions and twinges, new impulses that sent electric tremors through his body. He could feel his breasts, things he should never have, rubbing against her thighs. The tiny nipples, hard for some god-forsaken reason, rubbed against her skin and his traitorous cock grew harder with every passing second.

"It's okay, Dora. It's okay. Just calm down."

He struggled to calm himself, but just as he would relax, his mind would flash on the image of the perky little tips, and he would feel anxiety and horror rising up once again.

"Calm down, please?"

Sherrel spoke to him, but he was lost. Tears soaked his face as he curled up, trying to find some way to not feel the mounds on his chest. It was nearly impossible, even the smallest bit of wind seemed to set off the hypersensitive nipples.

"I say we fuck his ass until he stops screaming, then spank him until he screams for the right reasons."

"Teri!"

"She'll get over it, one good fucking, and that submissive little mind of hers will handle the rest."

Teri, with her practical response of sex, was enough to free him from his horror. He shivered at the thought of being impaled on

Teri's fake cock. A single slid down to the base of his spine and his nipples and cock ached with anticipation.

Struggling with a storm of emotions, Derik finally let Sherrel push him into a sitting position. He panted, dreading looking down. Even without an inspection, his body moved differently. It was wrong, as if his balance had been subtly changed. He shivered and a new jiggle caressed against raw nerves. There was only thing it could be, though he didn't know how she had given him breasts.

Panic surged through his veins. They were wrong. They weren't him. It was too much for this farce he played.

He blinked when he realized that Teri had disappeared, then let out a gasp as two strong hands came under his arms to cup his new breasts. Her touch burned along his skin and he could feel her excited pulse through the swollen mounds that were now part of his body.

A heat connected her touch to his nipples and then straight to his dick with a burning web of unexpected pleasure. A frail whimper escaped his throat as he tried to shift away, but Teri just held him tightly, rubbing his aching nipples with her thumbs until he was writhing from her touch.

Her whisper echoed in his ear, "Oh, they are nice and sensitive too."

"P-Please stop."

Her smile teased his ear. "Make me."

Moaning, he fought with the storm of emotions and feelings inside. Everything she did was intense, right on the edge of pleasure and pain, but it was ecstasy and his cock ached with a sudden, desperate need to come. "I-I can't."

She pinched his nipples, just a hard, little twist. It sent a stinging flash through him, not unlike being spanked by Madre.

He gasped and twisted, arching his back, grinding his sensitive nubs harder against her fingers.

Teri purred as she pressed her own nipples against his back. "Then I won't stop." She pinched them again, and he whimpered.

He reached out for something, but all he got was satin-covered pillow and blankets. "Please?"

Her fingers spread out over his left breast, digging the fingernails in. Every new touch, every caress against newly transformed skin was both wonderful and terrible. Her mouth teased the ridge of his ear as she whispered. "And you are nothing but my submissive little toy, Dora. And, right now, I'd like to fuck these cute breasts of yours with my fake cock, then grab your hair and fuck that pretty little mouth of yours."

As she whispered, the heat inside him redoubled. He writhed and twisted, trying to escape, but Teri just held him down with nothing but her fingers clutched to his breasts. Swamped, he sobbed as he tried to escape.

"Go on, Dora, tell me I'm wrong."

A hard pinch that arched his back again. His balls almost burst from the bolt of pleasure and pain that coursed through his system. "I-I can't!"

"Then I'm going to fuck you."

Her breath heated his ear.

He moaned and closed his eyes tightly, fighting with a hunger that grew inside him.

"You want that, Dora? I bet one orgasm and that slutty little mind of yours will accept these as if you were born to them."

"N-Never!"

He yelped as she pulled him back, standing up at the same time. He quickly tried to scramble out of the way, but Teri just pushed firmly on his back and sat on his stomach. Her hands worked at the straps of a harness. He stared down at a thick rubber cock sprouting from her hips.

His breasts, still unfamiliar, stood at attention, a valley for her to line up her strap-on. She grinned as she shifted forward, pressing it in the channel of his tits. He gasped, pinned on his back but no longer trying to struggle. Excited, Derik couldn't help but notice that the lust boiling inside him wasn't much different than the liquid heat pouring out from between the straps of her harness.

"Go on, touch it," commanded Teri.

He hesitated, but then he watched Sherrel slip behind Teri. With a smile on her lips, she slid down Teri's back until his cock slid into the steamy depths of her cunt.

"Oh, fuck!" he said, arching his back at the wet slickness of Sherrel's pussy wrapped around his member.

Teri grinned and took his hands, pressing them against the delicate smooth sides of his mounds. She squeezed them together around the slick fake cock. "Now, just hold them there."

The feeling of having of his breasts touched was nothing compared to the feeling of something hard and slick sliding through them. When he saw the head bobbing toward his mouth, another surge of lust flooded his mind. He watched with fascination, his body racing toward an explosion as Sherrel rode his cock and Teri fucked his breasts. He moaned, gasping for breath, and squeezed tighter.

She rewarded him by thrusting harder. Sherrel's hand snaked around to grab Teri's own breasts, holding them tightly as Teri drove forward, painting a line of her juices against his stomach.

As the rounded head of the cock brushed his lips, he opened them without thinking. It slid into mouth as if it always belonged there. Before he could get adjusted to the thickness on his tongue, Teri began to fuck his face. He swallowed the cock, releasing his fingers on his breasts as the cock drove deep into his mouth. His own member burst inside Sherrel, flooding her insides as he wished Teri could flood his mouth.

A few minutes of pumping and Derik finally leaned back with a flush of an orgasm and a giggling Teri sprawled out over him.

"See, once a slut, always a slut."

"Bitch," he said affectionately.

"I'm still wearing this, Dora, and you have a very pretty ass I bet."

Derik shut up, even though part of him pushed to say just one more thing. He let out a long shuddering breath.

Sherrel slid next to him and plastered her body along his own. She reached over to tilt his head toward hers and then she kissed his bruised lips. "I'd probably panic also if I had a cock just spring up."

"I-I didn't know she was going to do that."

Both Teri and Sherrel laughed. Teri nodded toward the massage room and Derik looked up to see a crowd gathered at the entrance.

"We heard. Madre bitched out that lady for the ten minutes. Man, they both have a set of lungs."

He wondered why he didn't hear it, then realized the pounding of his own heartbeat had overpowered his ears. Tenderly, he reached up to stroke the sides of his new mounds.

Sherrel caught him, and he snatched his hands away. She grinned and just ran a casual finger along the side, teasing as she watched him.

Teri spoke wryly, "Apparently, Madre would rather have your boyish figure than one of a proper woman."

"I would rather have my body back."

Sherrel spoke softly, her finger circling around his nipple and sending terrible feelings of pleasure to all corners of his body. "Would you really?"

He opened his mouth to agree, then he froze.

Sherrel cocked one eyebrow. "It means you won't be wearing a padded bra. Your hips are wider, but just by a little."

Teri blinked. She peered down at Derik's chest. "They are?"

Sherrel rolled her eyes. "This girl only sees a hole."

Teri bopped her, but Sherrel giggled before continuing.

"And you can now be mostly naked in the main room, which means you don't have to wear the robe all the time. Yeah, it looks weird, but you are the same person you were before, you just have a few new parts."

She finished with a gentle pinch on his nipple. He arched his back, gasping.

Teri finally noticed and pouted for a moment. Then, she grabbed his other nipple and played with it, sending maddening erotic thoughts to fill his thoughts.

Madre appeared before them, looking down with storm clouds in her eyes. "Girls, off."

At the sound of her voice, both Teri and Sherrel quickly scrambled off him.

Derik got to his feet, anger washing over him.

Madre pointed at him. "My room in five minutes. You owe me two hundred."

Before he could question the additional swats, she stormed off.

Nightingale followed with a smirk and a wiggle of her ass. He watched her disappear into the shadows and shivered. One hand protectively went to cover his ass, but there was a glove-covered hand already resting on it.

Hime giggled softly as she spoke in his ear. "Ah, let her vent some steam. I was right, and she knows it."

Teri gasped.

At the sight of Teri staring at him and Hime, he blushed a bright red.

Hime slithered around to hold his shoulders, staring directly down at his breasts. "I didn't do a bad job, did I?"

He shivered as her thumbs stroked his nipples. Hime smiled but didn't take her hands away. "Very nice. A handful, I'd say. Perky with good heft."

Teri grumbled, "Did you have to make them bigger than mine?"

Hime smiled warmly, and the room seemed to light up. "No, but this is what I think Bridget wanted."

She hefted Derik's breasts and he flushed. Her eyes slid over to Teri, admiring her. "Besides, you are beautiful on your own without magic. An acrobat's body. You would look beautiful balanced on a wire."

Teri opened her mouth to respond but then snapped it shut. She looked away with a flush on her cheeks.

Hime glanced around, then ran her finger up the channel between his mounds. At his shiver, she smiled happily. "Take care, Dora, and if you ever need me, just ask."

He couldn't move as she sailed right out of the room, looking like she had all the time in the world.

Teri gaped. "Who was that?"

"Hime, she used to be in the harem."

Sherrel purred. "She is beautiful."

"I know, why did she ever leave?"

He spoke up suddenly. "She's got a dick."

There was a brief moment of silence, then Derik slapped his hand over his mouth.

Teri and Sherrel grinned at him and he blushed.

Teri stepped next to him, trailing a finger along his right mound. "And how do you know this?"

"Did you fuck the priestess too!?"

"You slut!"

He blushed hotly as they teased him. Sputtering, he stepped away from the fingers stroking him and their grins. "I-I better be going!"

And he fled himself for Madre's room and his two hundred spankings.

Backstabber

He staggered out of Madre's room. His ass burned with a flame that wouldn't go out. Even the slightest whisper of Madre's silk robe, which seemed more like his own now, brushing against his backside sent a sparkling pain along his skin. He was hot and excited, drained from coming so many times against her leg. He swallowed back the taste of his own cum, lapped from her leg, floor, and pussy after she mounted him twice. He smiled as he stopped to lean against the tiled walls. "It was worth it."

Night had come and the girls of the harem were speaking quietly amongst themselves. The hour before sleep and everything was quiet. He walked past Nightingale, propped up on her pillow, hoping she wouldn't say anything.

Thankfully, she just gave him a smirk and watched as he painfully made his way, burning ass and all, across the room to Teri and Sherrel's sleeping spot.

Teri sat with her back against a mound of pillows, her strap-on set aside and glistening.

Sherrel purred on her lap, wiggling her rounded ass happily as they talked.

Seeing him, Teri patted her on the shoulder. "He's back," she whispered.

Sherrel sat up, brushing her hair from her face before whispering. "How you doing?"

"My butt hurts."

"We heard. She used magic this time, didn't she?"

"Yes, that impact palm of hers. I can feel it clear in my bones."

Sherrel slipped off Teri's body and laid on her back, her knees held apart. She held up her hands, offering him the comfort of her body like she did before.

He almost sobbed in thanks and sank into her, pressing his body against hers as he tried to not think about his burning ass.

Teri reached up to touch it, but Sherrel cleared her throat. Teri flinched and pulled back. "What? I love it when its so hot you could melt butter on it."

Sherrel chuckled. "Just go to sleep, you bitch."

"Slut." But she settled down next to Derik and Sherrel, resting her hand on Sherrel's shoulder as she looked up into his blue eyes. "Derik?"

His name sounded foreign to him now. "Y-Yes?"

"Thank you for falling into the harem," Teri sounded genuine as she smiled at him.

"Why?"

"Because you make me smile. And you make Sherrel, Madre, and everyone else smile too."

"Not Nightingale."

Sherrel shrugged, "No, she smiles when you are being spanked."

Derik rested his head on Sherrel's other shoulder. "Okay, I make everyone smile."

Teri reached over to stroke his cheek. "I just wish this could last forever."

He sighed. "Me too."

Both Sherrel and Teri drifted to sleep after a few more words.

Derik, on the other hand, couldn't sleep with his searing buttocks. His cock rested against Sherrel's cleft, but he was sexually drained to take advantage of the situation. It didn't matter though, he was happy in her arms. He reached over as gently as he could to stroke Teri's face.

Happy with her too.

Not fully asleep, he half-dozed, watching them. The sounds of the harem died off as the lights grew dark. Shifting and moans gave way to silence, and he sighed happily.

Then, he heard a pair of voices in the distance. At first, he thought they were guards, but they grew louder with every moment. He picked out Madre speaking, cheerfully despite being well past six in the morning.

Then, a bright light speared across the harem, startling him. Groans and moans rose up from the women and Sherrel shifted underneath him. He winced against the pain still burning in his ass as he pushed himself up to his hands and knees, cock bobbing in the air.

Sherrel smiled at him and sat up.

At the far end, Madre spoke loudly as she clapped her hands. "Rise and shine ladies, we have someone special this morning."

As they struggled to wake up, a deep booming voice rang out over the harem. It resonated inside him, sending off tiny quakes in Derik's stomach as he blinked his bleary eyes. "You know what would perk them up? A proper fucking for every single one. Maybe I should get some guards to help?"

Teri's eyes snapped open as she sat bolt straight. "Oh fuck, it's the baron!"

Her voice echoed in the room, and silence pooled across the harem.

Then, a burst of booming laughter. Derik's blood ran icy cold as he froze, terrified to turn around as he heard the baron laughing with everyone else. "And that would be my little Teri-cat waking up."

A slow shiver ran along Derik's spine as he listened to the baron speaking. His voice rumbled like a storm, a purr of a hell cat, and the growl of some beast at the same time. Derik cringed at the thought of the baron approaching.

"Teri!" snapped Madre. "Come right here!"

Teri grumbled as she blushed hotly. Lithely jumping to her feet, she slowly walked across the sprawl of waking women, blankets, and pillows.

Derik didn't watch her, too afraid to even look toward the booming voice. Slowly, he lowered himself to the pillows, spreading his legs until his manhood ground against a pillow and his ass disappeared among the pillows.

Sherrel groaned as she got to her own feet, waking up slowly. He noticed her eyes were alert as she watched Teri stand in front of the the baron. Then, she held out her hand. "Come on!" she whispered furiously.

Terrified beyond belief, he took her hand, and she drew him past the pillows, into the protective shadows and away from the casual gaze of the baron.

Panting, he leaned against the cool stone and groaned. "Fuck. Fuck, fuck."

Sherrel's eyes flashed, "Yes, and in a prison cell if you don't shut up!"

Derik's mouth clothed with a snap. He looked down at his body, naked from head to toe. His breasts, still foreign and horribly perky, rose up with their sensitive nipples. His shaft, for once, remained sleeping with his fear of being exposed. "Fuck, what do I do?"

"First, we get you some clothes, then you spend the night hiding in the massage room or the bathrooms. But not the tubs, he likes to go in there."

She disappeared out of sight, leaving him alone.

He whimpered softly, clutching the stone pillar as he struggled to calm his racing heart. On the other side, he could hear the rumble of his voice, the very sound of it twisting his insides.

"Don't worry, Rachi, I'm sure Teri-cat is just looking forward to a bit of play."

Teri playfully said, "Meow," and the baron laughed cheerfully.

Derik worried his bottom lip as he looked around, still feeling exposed and wondering where Sherrel disappeared to. His heart pounded against his chest as he peeked around, steadfastly ignoring the gathering of women and the baron to look for his own clothes.

Spotting a pair of his own panties—the sapphire-colored silk was unmistakable—he glanced over at the crowd. Only the baron's head, a shock of white, could be seen over the array of naked asses and backs. A few wore their robes or underwear, but mostly they were laughing and gathered around their lord and master. Risking everything, he scrambled over to grab his underwear. He spotted Madre's black silk robe and also grabbed it before diving back behind the pillars.

Panting, he quickly pulled up the silk around his hips, tucking his cock and balls back in between his legs. His breasts were slick with sweat and fear as he finished donning the robe. It had no tie, leaving a gash of naked flesh between the valley of his breasts. Closing it as tightly as he could, he prayed it would be enough and pressed his back against the cool stone of the pillar.

Madre spoke over the crowds. "And who is to please you tonight?"

The baron rumbled for a moment before answering. "After that last negotiation session, I'm actually thinking about starting with every girl here, then finishing up in your room actually. It shouldn't take more than a day," a pause, "for you."

He finished with a cheerful laugh.

Derik's stomach twisted again and he whimpered softly.

Madre exclaimed with a purr of her own, "Oh, baron!"

At the sound of her flustered and excited, Derik froze. His lips parted with curiosity and he peered at the side of the pillar.

"One peek," he whispered.

His pulse crashing in his veins, he pressed his stomach against the pillar and slid his head around. He spotted Madre first, with a flush on her cheeks and giggling. There was a fire in her eyes that he only saw a hint of when he served her. However, he couldn't clearly see the baron through the women in front of him. But, he could tell that the baron was a large man, and very broad from the large arm he had wrapped around Madre's waist.

The baron cleared his throat. "Why don't we line up my ladies by the pillars and let me get a good look at them? Been a while since I've seen my lovelies."

Derik gasped and flung himself back behind the pillars. His heart slammed hard and he heard a rushing in his ears as he looked around for some method of escape. Then, he remembered the ventilation shaft. Looking up, he got ready to climb up the pillar.

Then someone came around the pillar toward him.

Blushing, he looked up expecting Sherrel or Teri, but it was Nightingale who favored him with an evil smile.

"Fuck," he whispered.

"Not if I can help it," came her sharp reply and a nasty grin. Behind her, more women filtered around the pillar, circling around to gather up in front of it. They gave him a curious look but then just kept on walking as they lined up. Derik backed up toward the pillar, but Nightingale motioned with her finger.

He whimpered, shaking his head.

She snarled silently, whispering harshly as she reached for him. "You come with me or, baron help me, I'll make him come here—"

A strangled noise escaped his throat.

"—with swords."

With every word, her eyebrow twitched with annoyance. Her hand caught his wrist and pulled him away from the stone.

He whimpered again, his fingernails clutching the stone, but Nightingale just yanked him away, forcing him around the pillar.

To his relief, she stopped after only a few steps and jostled him against the pillar and facing out into the main room. She stood behind him with her fingers resting on his shoulders. Her nails dug into the flesh and he whimpered again with sweat beading his brow.

It dripped down his neck as he frantically looked around for Teri or Sherrel. He spotted Teri standing next to Madre, looking impatient as she danced from foot to foot. She caught his eyes and she looked apologetic, then they narrowed as they caught sight of Nightingale behind him.

Derik whimpered, eyes flashing back and forth as the crowds thinned in front of him.

"Sherrel's in the bathroom, Derik," whispered Nightingale in his ear, "there is no one to save you this time."

"W-Why?"

"Because I told her that Madre needed towels."

He bit his lower lips. "Why would you do that?"

"Because you don't belong here," came the hissing reply, "and I think Madre has been blind to that."

"What are you going to do?"

"Nothing, nothing at all," but even as she spoke, her fingernails dug deeper into his shoulder.

He praying that someone would save him. Instead, the baron cleared his throat.

"Okay, ladies, I'm feeling pretty damn randy. And the only thing I can think of is fucking each and every one of you until I pass out happy. Screw the guards, they can have the sloppy seconds."

A wave of cheer filled the room but Derik felt only ice-cold claws gripping his heart. In front of him, a blonde with short hair bounced up and down as she waved for the baron's attention.

"Gonna do a theme again!? Even/odds? Last ass standing?"

It was a joke, from the laughter, but Derik couldn't focus on the humor of the moment. Instead, he moaned, trying to duck despite the attention drawn to his presence.

Nightingale hissed and dug her claws in tighter, almost breaking the skin as she forced him away from the pillar.

He whimpered but every little movement seemed to be controlled by Nightingale's fingers.

The baron's voice drowned out Derik's whimpers. "Why not? Got any suggestions?"

His voice continued to send flutters through Derik's stomach, each word vibrating against his chest, a deep base drum to the rapid-fire pattering of his heart.

Derik trembled as he clutched the side of the pillar, trying to slow his frantic breathing or his beating heart.

From behind him, with a voice that froze his heart, Nightingale called out, "Why not the newest girl first?"

The baron seemed to think about it, then a laugh. "Break them in early? Sure! Now where are my new girls?"

Derik realized what she was doing and shook his head. His fingers dug into the side of the pillar as he whispered frantically. "No, no, no, no—"

On the other side, standing at the far wall, Madre's head shot up, concern and fright flashing across her face. She looked around, scanning the women quickly. Her eyes passed over the women standing in front of him and tears blurred his eyes.

Behind Madre, Sherrel came out of the bathroom hallway with some towels and an expression of confusion on her face.

Derik planted his feet, still whispering desperately. "—no, please don't, no, no—"

Nightingale leaned forward and whispered in his ear, anger burning in her voice. "Time for you to meet the baron, Derik."

He screamed out. "No!" It was too late.

Nightingale's finger dug tightly into his shoulder and she shoved with all her might.

He grabbed for the stone pillar, but the force of her shove cracked his painted nails, and he stumbled out into the girls before him. They melted away with exclamations of surprise and annoyance and he found himself staggering out into the clearing of the harem, into the exposed area of pillows and blankets.

His foot caught on a thick pillow, and he tumbled hard on the ground, catching it with his knees and lurching forward. Planting his hands on the ground, he barely managed to avoid smashing his face on the ground; even padded, it would have hurt.

Derik's long black hair fluttered to the ground, a spiderweb across the pillows as he froze. His heart crashed hard in his chest, and he shook violently from the fear welling up inside. Hot tears splashed down his nose as he prepared for the worst, expecting something far worse out of Nightingale.

It didn't come with her crying out.

It didn't come with Nightingale calling attention to him.

It came with footsteps.

Heavy footsteps of the only other male in the room approached him, shaking the floor beneath his bare feet. The baron stopped in front of him. Through the curtain of hair, he could see the heavy boots, weathered and black. Each foot was huge, easily twice the size of his own. He shook, unable to tear his eyes away from the feet of his doom. With a start, he realized he was sobbing silently. His mind spun with the future possibilities of what would come next: him fleeing for his life, being throw in the dungeon, or even the thought that brought another sob up, the guards killing him right there.

"Look up, girl." The command came from the rumbling voice of the baron. He felt it in his stomach and chest, filling him with a power he couldn't even imagine, a presence that made him want to obey despite his fear.

Tears burning on his cheeks, he fought his sanity for a long moment. To either side, he glanced for someone to rush to him, but he was alone in the center of the room, too far to hide among the women.

"Look up," came the repeated command, this time with a hard, forceful tone.

Derik's eyes blurred, and he shook with silent sobs as he lifted his eyes to look up at the one man he never wanted to meet.

The baron.

The Baron

"Look up," he repeated. Derik whimpered as the baron's words rumbled inside his chest as much as they assaulted his ears. It seemed to echo deep inside, like tiny quakes coursing through his body, and he shook from the force of those two words.

Shoulders shaking from his silent sobs, he had to force himself to lift his eyes. He focused on the heavy boots, then on the trousers. Underneath, the baron had legs of a weight-lifter, thick and corded. His pants strained the fabric with every movement and Derik shivered at the thought of touching them.

A tear ran along his jaw as he focused his eyes on the baron's crotch. He didn't mean to, but as soon as his gaze found the immense bulge under the fabric, the rest of the world disappeared.

His lips parted as he stared at it, far larger than anything than anything in Madre's room, longer and bigger than even her fist. An errant thought cut through the fear storming inside him, just the idea of it being pressed against his naked ass. His cock twitched, hot and excited, and Derik had to clamp his legs tightly together to avoid exposing himself.

He didn't know why, but it was important.

The baron cleared his throat. "My eye is up here."

To pull his eyes away from the massive member took as much effort as to first look up. Derik shuddered with the thought, forcing his eyes up along the heavily muscled chest of the baron. The other man was huge, easily twice as wide as Derik's frail form and half a meter higher. The shoulders were strong and corded just as the legs; he could see it flexing as the baron looked down at him.

Finally, he managed to look completely up at the giant, terrified and frightened as the figure loomed over him.

The baron only had one eye, a single sapphire pupil that looked down at him, piercing his very heart with an intense, steady stare. The other eye had an eye patch over it, embroidered with the baron's seal. The face behind it was smooth, like a young man's, but his burning gaze held a sense of age. The shock of white hair seemed to blur his face, giving Derik an impression of ancient powers just beneath the kind-looking face.

Derik let out a shuddering breath, his fingers clutching the pillow underneath him. His cracked nails caught on the edge, but he was already trapped and horribly exposed. He wanted to look away, to stare at anything else, but he couldn't tear his eyes away from the baron's eye.

Time became meaningless as he stared up at the baron. It wasn't until the baron reached down and brushed the hair from his face that he realized he was holding his breath. The first touch, a caress of skin against skin, sent a bolt of pleasurable lighting to connect his sensitive nipples directly to his cock. The shock ignited an instant inferno deep inside. Derik's thighs clenched together as baron ran his finger along the length of his chin.

"I don't remember you."

The very words rumbled through their bodies, pinning Derik down by the weight of them. He whimpered softly but the baron's eye crinkled in the smile.

"Has Teri-cat been telling you horror stories?"

"I-I—"

Derik couldn't get any other word out.

The baron chuckled and brushed the rest of Derik's hair from his face, hooking it behind his ear.

Derik shivered at the touch, the fingertip trailed along the ridge of his ear.

"But you are a pretty one, aren't you?"

"Uh..."

The words refused to escape his throat. Derik cringed mentally at the touch of the larger man, but when he brought his finger to trace Derik's lips, he had to strain to prevent his cock from bursting right then and there.

The baron stroked his finger and then caught Derik's bottom lip. He slid his digit in and out of Derik's mouth for a moment before pulling out. The baron's smile faded minutely as he hooked the crook of his finger under Derik's chin. "Poor little blackbird, you look so frightened."

Pressure built up under his chin, and Derik, helpless as he was to everyone else who did the same, stood slowly as the baron drew him up. His hands clutched at the robe, protecting him as he came to his feet. Sweat dappled his brow as the baron smiled again, stroking the side of his face. The electric touch arced down between his legs and fanned the inferno growing with every passing heartbeat.

Reaching his feet, the baron smiled warmly. His hand trailed down from the line of Derik's jaw, tracing the side of his neck.

Derik shivered with each caress, half-closing his eyes as the large fingers followed his collarbone. Then, two fingers at the opening of his robe. He whimpered, clutching the black silk tightly.

"My goodness, you really are frightened." The baron's voice sounded amazed with just a tiny hint of hurt. His eyes stared into Derik's gaze as a warm smile stretched across his face. "I bet you Teri-cat did frighten you with stories, didn't she? I wonder if she needs a proper spanking?"

From his side, somewhere on the other side of his universe, he heard Teri gasp, then let out a sigh of excitement.

He trembled as the baron's finger delved down, parting the jet-black robe like a finger parting labia. He shivered, goose pimples rising up on his skin, and clutched the robe short.

The baron chuckled wryly and let his eyes flash down, breaking the spell that froze Derik's body.

Derik whimpered, still shivering, and clutched tighter.

The baron reached up with his other hand, the large palm pressing against Derik's trembling check and hooking his fingers into the gap of his robe. "This is my robe, you know."

"I-It is?"

Derik's voice rose in pitch, higher than he thought possible. A heated blush filled his cheeks, as he swallowed. His eyes shifted down, to stare at the heavily muscled chest, then the large hands that parted his only protection.

Swamped with vulnerability, he could only tremble as the baron's thumbs parted the robe until Derik's soft, perky breasts were brought to the cool air. Nipples, hard as the glass windows he had broken through, quivered in the air and he had to fight back a moan.

The baron spread out his fingers, cupping each of Derik's breasts. Derik gasped at the feeling of his sensitive nipples dragging across his palm. The sensitive nub caught on every crevice and seam, reporting pleasure from the assault against the rough skin. It fanned the fires inside him to even higher heights. He squirmed to keep his cock buried between his legs, and he could feel the pre-cum soaking the bottom of his panties.

The baron caught one pert nipple between his fingers and pinched it. The bolt of pleasure and pain burst inside him and his cock surged for a moment before he bore down with his inner muscles. He gasped, clutching the man's arm as he leaned into it. Derik closed his eyes tightly as he fought his own body, trying to regain control over the terrible pleasure that burned inside.

"These are very nice, though," rumbled the baron. His fingers teased the sides of his breasts. To Derik's horror, one hand slid further down, trailing strong fingertips along his taut belly and toward the junction of his legs. Panic rose and he whimpered. When the baron's fingertips slid under the silk panties, the sound died in Derik's throat. He couldn't say or do anything as the baron reached along his hairless sex toward the one thing Derik couldn't afford to be found.

Unconsciously, as the baron's finger started down the smooth line of his folded back cock, Derik quickly dropped to his knees. He whimpered as he crashed on the pillows, but the baron's fingers drew up to stop at Derik's throat.

The baron quirked up one white eyebrow, then smiled. "Eager, I see."

His voice rumbled playfully, and Derik shook as he stared back up at the giant man. Every centimeter of his skin burned with a flush, no doubt down to the very tip of his cock, but he couldn't tear his eyes away from the baron's piercing gaze.

Spreading his fingers, the baron brought his hand up to the side of Derik's face, cradling it as he chuckled again. "Well, my eager blackbird, go on."

Derik blinked, wondering what he got himself into.

The baron reached down with his other hand to stroke along the hard bulge at his crotch.

Derik's eyes followed, then he realized what the baron had in mind. Gulping, he stared at it as the cloth-covered member twitched and swelled even as he watched it.

"Go on," repeated the baron.

The trembling thief swallowed again and looked up, but the blue eye was even more demanding. Saying nothing, the baron's presence seemed to glow in Derik's eyes. There was no way to escape the hand that gently cradled his face.

With shaking hands, he reached up to run his own palms against the massive member. Under his touch, it was more like silk over steel. The heat pulsed through it with the steady drum of the baron's heart. Breathing heavily and feeling the world spinning, he started to work the line of buttons that kept the baron's manhood trapped underneath the fabric. Every second that passed, Derik both feared and anticipated what he would find.

His fingers fumbled with the buttons and he winced as he caught a cracked nail on one of the buttons. Finally, he managed to ease the first one out from its hole and worked on the second. Derik got his first sight of the baron's cock and drank in his smell.

It was warm and powerful, like the rumble of his voice. He didn't have the words to describe it. That the baron smelled... strong. His fingers worked at the second, then the third button. Finally, he released the fourth and stared at the gash of fabric and the swollen cock beyond.

"Go on."

Biting his lip, he delved his hands into the baron's pants, marveling at the heat that rolled off the hard flesh inside. His delicate fingers wrapped around the thick member, and he pulled, easing out the lord's cock.

When it popped out, Derik froze in surprise and shock. It was thick, thicker than he thought possible. His hands looked like a child's wrapped around it, the tips of his fingers not even touching. The thick member stretched out from the baron by at least four hand spans. At the tip, a rounded, wedge-shaped head already glistened with pre-cum. Derik gasped, feeling his body burning hotly and his own pre-cum dribbling down his inner thighs.

Only a strangled whimper escaped his lips as he stared at the immense manhood. His ass clenched tightly at the though but his mind focused on the hardness, like silk-covered iron, that rested heavily in his hand. A thick patch of hair, also white, grew from the base.

"Oh... my... lord."

The baron laughed, the deep rumbling shaking his cock from tip to base. "It is a pleasure to see that first wide-eyed stare. Go ahead, pull out my balls too."

Derik glanced up with surprise, then pushed his hands back into the baron's pants. At the first touch, he thought he found a pair of grapefruits, but the baron's balls twitched as he ran his fingers along their surface. Long hairs teased his fingertips as he worked out one, then the other, large testicle from his pants.

Seeing the full set, the immense cock and balls, stole Derik's breath away. He whimpered loudly, his lips parting with shock. "Th-They're huge!"

His whisper brought another roaring laugh from the baron. The large hand against the side of his head held him tightly as the baron stroked his cheek with his thumb. "They are, Blackbird, and they are very full. I would very much like to see them pressed against your lips then," he paused, "somewhere lower."

Derik trembled and brought his eyes up to the sapphire gaze above him. His stomach tightened painfully as he thought about being speared by such a thick, long member. Even Madre's wrist wasn't as big but somehow, he knew that it could be buried to the balls inside his trembling body. He let out a tiny whimper.

A whimper of need.

"Go on," encouraged the baron.

Derik needed no other commands as he wrapped his fingers around the baron's cock, holding it tightly as the thick member bobbed in front of his face. Taking a deep breath, he leaned forward and drank in the powerful smell of the baron. It left his stomach churning from anticipation, but the heat that rolled off it was easily matched by the searing inferno between his own legs.

After the weeks in the harem, he knew what to do, but staring at the throbbing cock in his hand, trepidation filled him. Closing his eyes, Derik leaned forward and brushed his lips against the side of the baron's large cock. Warm and soft, silk on steel, he moaned at the taste of it. Still strong, he decided, and to his surprise, he was kissing up and down the shaft. His tongue peeked out to lap at it, moaning as he moved. Derik's heart pounded in his chest and pre-cum dribbled down both of his inner thighs as he kissed and slurped up and down the shaft.

He reached the base and buried his nose in the soft skin of the baron's scrotum. His mouth opened against the grapefruit-sized balls and he blushed hotly at the thought of him sucking on another man's nuts. But kneeling in front of the baron, he couldn't and didn't want to stop. Releasing the heated shaft, he cupped both balls with his hands, working his lips along their hairy surface until they glistened with his saliva.

Pulling back, he realized what he had done, and the flush blossomed even hotter on his cheeks. Guilty, he looked up past the baron's hard spear to look into that single piercing blue eyes staring down at him.

The baron nodded. "The tip."

Derik whimpered and shame rose up to drown him. Here he was, acting like nothing but a whore. Lips trailing along the silken steel shaft, he held the baron's balls as he kissed and lapped up the length of the shaft, losing himself in the hardness. He could taste the hot pre-cum on the shaft and lapped at it, tasting it at the back of his tongue. Realizing he was tasting another man's cum, pre-cum actually, almost set him off again, and he clamped hard on his trapped cock to prevent it from soaking his panties.

It took forever to reach the end, and he pulled back again, to look at the glistening tip. Larger than his mouth, the thick swollen head drooled with excitement. Clear, slick fluids oozed out of the hole at the tip, soaking the entire head and dripping down the bottom. His heart beat frantically in his chest as he pressed his lips against the tip, like sucking on Teri's strap-on, and opened his mouth.

Hot.

Searing hot and wet.

His lips stretched around the baron's cock and he spread his jaw as far as it could until the spongy head pushed into his mouth.

The baron's hand, still cradling his head, tightened his grip and powerful muscles pulled the two together to guide the throbbing hardness past Derik's lips.

Derik gasped, breathing hard through his nose as he tried to pull it further into his mouth. His tongue lapped at the head, tracing the tip along the baron's hole and on the swollen wrinkles that he could taste. It was hot and warm and strong. He moaned and forced his jaw open even more. His lips stretched out tautly around the cock head and he could imagine something so thick burying into another part of his body.

At that thought, he finally lost control and his cock surged, splattering hot cum into his silk panties. His blush burned brightly as he looked up at the baron, lips stretched around his head.

The baron chuckled, not apparently realizing the reason for Derik's blush. He reached down with both hands. Holding Derik's head firmly with a massive palm, the baron forced his shaft deeper.

Still coming hard between his legs, Derik leaned into the baron, moaning as his lips stretched painfully around the cock head, then with a slurp, the wedge-shaped head slid into his mouth, lodging itself in the tight ring of his lips and teeth. He gasped, still staring at the baron, but the more powerful man just chuckled and rocked back and forth, plunging it in and out in tiny strokes.

"Now," he breathed in a low, husky voice, "I shouldn't come in your mouth yet, but seeing your lips stretched like that, makes me want to so badly."

Derik moaned around his shaft, feeling the baron's balls clenching and tightening. He stroked them with his hands, feeling how they seemed alive in his palm, hot and swollen with seed. He could taste pre-cum flooding his mouth, a river pouring out of the baron and filling his senses. Slick and hot, he swallowed it, drinking from the baron's cock.

The baron just watched him, breathing heavily as he kept Derik's head still. His cock pulsated inside the tight ring of the thief's mouth.

Derik whimpered around it, feeling the last of his cum dribbling hotly down his inner thighs. A surge of embarrassment filled him, both from his shame and his orgasm.

The baron pulled him closer, keeping the hardness in his mouth. Derik rose slightly to meet him. He wondered what was happening until the throbbing length of the cock pressed firmly into the valley of his breasts. Without really thinking, Derik released the massive balls and clutched his own breasts, thumbs on his sensitive nipples. His smaller shaft surged again, adding a bit more to his panties. He pushed his mounds together, wrapping them around the baron's cock.

The baron moaned with approval, thrusting up into his mouth. The baron released his head as Derik rocked his body against the baron, sliding the slicked shaft in the channel of his breasts. The cock head swelled even more, flooding his mouth with a thick torrent of juices that he had to swallow constantly to avoid drowning. He swallowed and stroked.

To his surprise, the baron eased his cock head from Derik's mouth. Derik opened with hunger, confusion and tears on his face, but he kept sliding up and down, fucking the baron with his breasts.

The baron moaned with pleasure and leaned into Derik.

Derik stroked harder and faster, soaking his cleavage with the baron's lubrication.

Breath coming hard and fast, he pumped the baron to an orgasm. He was unprepared when the baron actually came. Instantly, the shaft swelled up to almost double its width and seemed to grow even longer, then there was a hot, searing splash of liquid that plastered Derik's throat, chin, and face. He caught a bit in his mouth, the same tangy taste as his own, but there was a musk to the flavor that made him realize there was a difference between him and real man.

Rivers of cum oozed down Derik's face as he stared up with surprise. A second blast never came, just a single one with the volume of a pitcher, splattering his face and soaking his chest instantly. He released his breast and held up a hand, staring at the white cum that oozed down his wrist.

Without thinking, he brought it to his mouth, sucking on his fingers and properly tasting the baron. Hot and tangy with an intense flavor of man on it. He cleaned two fingers, then blushed with the realization of what he was doing.

Above him, the giant moaned with pleasure. "I can see why Madre liked you."

Derik flushed hotly as he stared up again. The baron's cum oozed down his stomach, soaking his panties and mixing the two men's cum together. Derik pressed one hand between his legs, holding his throbbing cock in place as he found himself staring at the blue eye of the baron. "I-I—"

The baron chuckled. "You might want to learn how to speak though."

"S-Sorry, lord."

He laughed and ran a thumb along Derik's jaw, ignoring the cum that soaked his face. "You can speak, Blackbird. I was afraid that Teri-cat frightened the words from you too."

He glanced over, and Derik followed the gaze. With a rush, the world just returned to him and he found himself looking at Teri, staring in shock with her mouth agape. One hand stroked hard and fast between her legs as she leaned against the wall, her eyes riveted on Derik. He could see her inner thighs glistening with her juices, dribbling down even as his own cum soaked his.

"I think she likes you too."

Derik blinked and used his other hand to wipe the cum from his face. His eyes slowly scanned around the room, looking at the women who stared at him with surprise, shock, and more than a little lust.

The baron chuckled himself. "I've never seen them this speech-less."

His eyes turned back to Derik and his gaze burned Derik's skin. Looking up, he blushed again as he stared into that single memorizing eye. "You must be rather special, Blackbird."

Derik couldn't speak, caught by his gaze. The baron hooked his chin and pulled him up into a standing position.

Derik obeyed silently, one hand pressed against his crotch and the other hanging limply. He whimpered softly, his body shivering at the touch. He had been used and soaked. Somehow, he was also more excited than any other time of his life.

"I'd like to find out why."

The words broke his pleasure. "W-What?"

"Take off your clothes, I want to fuck you properly," he said with a throaty growl.

"I-I... you can't, you just came!"

He laughed loudly.

"Came? That was foreplay! And this," he reached down to wrap his meaty fingers around his cum-soaked shaft, "is now properly lubricated."

Derik let out a long whimper that turned into an unwitting moan.

The baron leaned forward. "Come on, I want to feel you from the inside."

His words filled Derik's ears and he stared in shock. His fingers curled tightly in his crotch, trying to find some way to escape his fate.

"Go on," commanded the baron.

Fuck, thought Derik. He shrugged off his robe, letting it spill to the ground. Black and covered in seed, it looked like a slash of a muddy pool. Blushing hotly, he stood almost naked in front of the baron who just nodded in approval.

Turning around, he started to push down his panties. Derik's mind furiously flew in all directions, preparing for the guards and spears but unable to do anything but obey the giant man's order. His fingers trembled as he looked in the crowds for Madre, but the older woman wasn't visible.

Despair filling him, he reached down to pull his shaft from between his legs and bending over slightly to push his panties down to his knees.

The baron cleared his throat. "Madre spanked you?"

Looking over his shoulder, Derik nodded in silence. The baron had a strange look on his face as he reached out, stroking his palm against Derik's tender and still red ass. The thief could feel the heat still there as the baron stroked it.

"Change of idea, I never could resist fucking a properly reddened ass."

He nodded toward the nearest pillar. Slipping out of his panties, Derik followed with one hand covering his cock and walked to the pillar. The baron reached out to stroke his hair, pulling it into a long tail of black and gently pushed Derik against the pillar. Derik gasped and planted one hand against the cool stone, leaning forward and exposing his red ass to the baron.

Looking over his shoulder, he could see the cum-slicked shaft bobbing as the baron stood behind him, positioned for only one thing. Derik swallowed, his anus clenching tightly, and his fingers gripping his own shaft tightly.

He watched as the baron stroked a finger down his spine, trailing along the marked tattoo that Hime left on him. Derik arched his back, the electric connection of the baron and him sending more pleasure through his body and bringing his aching cock back to life. He gasped as the baron's finger ran down the crack of his ass, slipping through cheeks lubricated with Derik's own cum.

"Already wet, I see."

The finger dipped lower and Derik clutched his balls tightly, hoping the baron wouldn't find them. At the last second, the baron just brought his finger back up to press against the tight opening of his anal ring. Derik gasped, looking forward to the intruder sliding in.

"And loose enough for me."

The baron spoke in a rumble, hungry and lustful.

Two hands clamped over his hips and held him still. He could imagine the cock lining up, aiming for his most private of openings, but nothing could prepare him for the feeling of that slick, rounded head pressing against the crack of his ass.

He let out a long, drawn-out moan as the baron nestled the tip of his thick cock into the line of Derik's ass. He could feel the hot, soaked spear pressing against his asshole, the pressure building up with every passing heartbeat. Shaking his head, he realized there was no escape and shook his head.

"No, no," he whispered, half to himself, but the baron just held his hips tightly and pushed forward. Derik's whispers turned into another moan as he was stretched open, the ring resisting with all his might as the cock head eased its way into him.

Lust burned through Derik's body as his cock swelled in his palm. His anal ring parted underneath the thick member, screwing up even as he tried to bear down. Every iota of his focus grew on that feeling of it stretching, stretching, stretching.

The baron's cock pushed harder into Derik's tiny little ass, forcing it open as the head continued to violate the ring, stretching it open.

Just as he thought he would snap, the ring of his opening reached the crest of the baron's cock. The head lodged itself into his ass and he let out a shuddering gasp that turned into a moan as his asshole sealed around the flared ridge of his baron's glans.

"Oh, Bridget…"

The baron chuckled at Derik's whispered prayer.

Derik blushed hotly as he realized whose name he called. But then his world returned to the cock easing into him. The cum-slicked shaft began a slow, irresistible slide into his rectum.

He gasped and sobbed from the intensity of pleasure. His asshole stretched around the throbbing member, and his inner sheath tightened around the baron's member. Hot and hard, it pierced him and he shuddered with the feeling. His cock surged, splattering his palm with juices as he tried to escape it, tried to pull away. But the baron's hands, tight around his hips, pulled him back, impaling him on the largest cock he had ever known.

His rectum stretched around the thick member as the baron leaned into him, impaling him even further. The thick wedge of the head plunged deeply, filling him more than he could image. Hot tears of pleasure ran down Derik's cheek as he slid further back on the hot trunk of a cock filling him.

Shaking from the power, he let out another shuddering breath as the baron grunted louder, driving his cock into Derik. It slid a hand span in, stuffing him to the brim. Derik could feel the cum soaking his insides as the baron sank into him. Trembling, he stretched out his lower hand to press against his stomach, feeling something deep and hard shifting in his bowels.

When the baron had half of his cock stuffed into Derik's tight ass, the rouge started to whimper. He whispered to no one, begging and praying. "Please, no more, no more, no more—"

But every whisper, the baron just drove in deeper, a slow powerful impaling that consumed Derik's senses. Every ridge brought a new wave of pleasure as the baron buried himself.

Just as the pressure of his insides reached their limit and his breath came in labored pants, the baron bottomed out inside Derik. Derik gasped, struggling from breath as he tried to comprehend the powerful hardness buried inside him. Every movement seemed to be a pleasurable agony, searing with intensity and leaving him yearning for more.

The baron breathed deeply as he held his throbbing shaft inside Derik, his hands holding him in place as Derik squirmed on the pole. He tried to relax, but the cock impaling him was too thick and too hard. Everything sent a pang of pleasure coursing through his body, and he moaned almost deliriously.

"Now, my little blackbird, you might scream."

That was his only warning as the baron's hand tightened painfully on his hips and the baron pulled his cock out.

Derik let out a low, guttural moan with every stroke of the immense cock.

When the baron pulled almost completely out, Derik couldn't help but feel hollow. To his relief, the emptiness was short-lived as the baron paused for a single heartbeat with only his head in, then slammed forward, driving his slicked shaft deep into Derik.

This time, Derik let out a scream of pleasure. His body spasmed, assaulted by the feeling of the pole penetrating him, but he was helpless as the baron drew out and slammed it back in, slapping his hips against Derik's tanned ass.

Hard and powerful, the baron pumped into Derik, opening him further than any toy ever had and driving the immense cock down the tightly stretched sheath of his passage. Derik's head reeled with the storm of his body reporting unexpected pleasures, the rapid power of the baron and the complete control he had over Derik's body. He was helpless and ravaged, beaten into submission by the hard shaft that drove in and out, slapping with hard blows against his tender ass.

Derik gasped and whimpered, crying as the baron slid out of him and gasping when he was filled once again. His body shook with every blow, and he clung to the pillar with his cracked fingernails. Tears ran down his cheeks, but he didn't know if it was from the pain, the pleasure, or the humiliation. It didn't matter any more as he drove back, pushing against every thrust as he tried to take in more of the immense shaft dominating him.

Then, between the powerful thrusts that left him breathless, the baron's hand slid around his hips and worked their way toward Derik's crotch.

Desperate, Derik released his cock, his hand dripping with his cum and slapped it against the baron's hand, pinning it in place. The baron just held on tighter, increasing his speed that he drove into Derik.

Derik's body burned with pleasure. His cock, nipples, and ass seemed connected by a single flaring line of ecstasy. As the baron drove forward, he could feel it in the breasts that Hime gave him. Every time the base of that immense shaft nestled into the crack of his ass, his cock would squeeze out more cum to dribble down his length. He wanted to scream out, to thrash around, but he was tautly stretched in an orgasm that would never end.

The baron's other hand slid around his hips, moving with every thrust. He could imagine the baron trying to slide his fingers into a pussy he didn't have and finding an spurting cock instead. He whimpered, his eyes tightly closed as he counted the millimeters of the fingers as it reached for his manhood. The baron, unaware of his terror, continued to drive forward, plunging in and out until Derik could feel the slurping of pre-cum as it violated his insides.

Two centimeters.

A powerful thrust forced Derik to step forward, one leg bracing against the ground. It curved his ass more so the second one drove even deeper, finding some new place to pound pleasure into his body. He came hard, splattering the wall with his orgasm.

One centimeter.

He was almost caught, and he couldn't stop coming. Hot and flushed, his fingernails dug into the baron's other hand, holding him tightly as he screamed out from the pleasure that had beaten him into submission. He strained for one more orgasm before his secret was revealed.

The baron's fingers plunged between his legs and Derik had the most powerful orgasm of his life. It grabbed him up by the senses and shook him violently, his entire vision and hearing turning into a field of white static as he spasmed tighter and harder than he ever thought possible. As it slammed into him, he couldn't even feel his body and wailed out at that single moment of loss.

He came too after only a few seconds, but to his surprise, the baron's cock continued to pound into him, fucking him hard and fast as the thick member swelled inside him. He gasped, confused and dazed, as the baron reached up to grab his hair. His back arched as the baron began to pound even harder, thrusting his cock so hard into Derik the thief thought his hips would break. With every stroke, the pressure increased on his cock. It took him a a dazed moment to realized the source; someone had swallowed him whole to protect him from the barons' fingers. He released the baron's hand and clutched down, running his fingers through Sherrel's hair as the baron redoubled his speed.

Wet and slurping, his entire world focused on that immense shaft driving into him with endless strength and power. He wanted it deeper, wanted to feel it tearing him open as his orgasm continued to pump seed into Sherrel's mouth. Clutching her hair tightly and pulled back by the hand that held his hair, he orgasmed again and again.

He reached his very limit and went beyond it, a crack forming in his mind as he went numb from overloaded ecstasy.

In that single change, the baron came inside him. A single hard burst that flooded his insides with at least a liter of cum. His guts swell as the baron drove hard into him and held the vibrating, silken steel shaft deep inside Derik's body. Soon, the thief's insides were cramped with agonizing pleasure.

Panting heavily, the baron pulled Derik back away from the wall, grinding the shaft deep inside the smaller man's rectum. His breath was hot and sweaty, but happy, as he rumbled into Derik's ear.

"Welcome to the harem, Blackbird."

Derik spasmed again, then moaned pitifully as the baron withdrew. The cock slid out, leaving him with a feeling of remorse and emptiness. Behind it came a sloshing of cum pouring down his legs, but Derik didn't have the strength to stand anymore. He slowly collapsed forward, bending over Sherrel who guided him to the ground.

He didn't care if anyone knew if he was male.

He didn't care if the guards would come.

Derik was dominated by the baron's cock.

Above him, in a world spinning away, he heard the baron turning away. "Who's next?"

Derik let out a soft sob, trying to release the senses that vibrated beyond his ability comprehend them. He couldn't imagine how much cum poured out of his gaping ass. He could only shake violently and clutch Sherrel for comfort as it emptied out of his aching body.

She cooed to him, stroking his hair. "Now, my dear Dora, you are truly the baron's woman. You were beautiful, so beautiful, Blackbird."

Shadows

As much as the powerful orgasm crashed into him, the afterglow sucked the strength from him. As the baron walked away, Derik just curled up on the ground, cum pouring out of his ass and his body shaking.

Sherrel held him until the baron called for her and she had to leave.

Alone, he didn't get up. A sob caught in his throat at the empty void that had grown inside his heart. The power of the orgasm blew away his senses, and he mind had shattered from the intensity. Tears, hot and salty, coated his cheeks as he remained in place.

He found his strength some time later and managed to stagger to his feet. Over at the pile of pillows, the baron fucked Sherrel and Teri, his fingers buried in both of them while two other girls sucked on his cock.

Derik tried to smile, but couldn't find the energy. Instead, he grabbed his robe, slipped it on, and fled to the darkness of the massage room. Just to wait out the night from the baron, he told himself.

Derik felt alone, so terribly alone. Tears kept pouring down his cheeks, but he was helpless to stop them. Clutching himself tighter, he sat near the cool pond and just waited, rocking back and forth as he tried to sort through the storm of emotions dragging him into some pit. Underneath, he could feel lust burning for the baron, a hunger to feel filled once again. The wet dribbling from his gaping sphincter didn't help. It was a terrible contrast of despair and hunger, and he sobbed as if torn in half.

Hoping that sleep would help, he curled up on one of the padded tables and closed his eyes, praying for darkness.

"Dora, are you okay?"

Sherrel's voice rang out in the darkened massage room.

Derik, his face wet with tears, sobbed and held his legs tightly to his chest. He couldn't see the entrance from where he sat, nestled behind one of the waterfalls in the back, but he could hear her moving. He couldn't remember when he moved, but the gnawing emotions still burned inside him. He tried to shift further away from her voice but Sherrel brought the lights up with a wave of her hand over the magical rune.

Warm light, orange and subdued, filled the room, and he whimpered, clutching himself even tighter. Everything was wrong, a terrible feeling deep inside the pit of his stomach. Shivering from the cool water he sat next to, he closed his eyes and prayed that Sherrel would go away.

"Dora? Derik?"

She moved closer. He could hear her padding across the room, circling around as she looked under the tables.

He shivered again, then fought back a sob as a wave of despair filled him.

Then, he couldn't hear her. Only the pattering of water splashing down and the shivering of his body. He cracked one eye open to see Sherrel sticking her head through the water. It cascaded around her neck and poured down her shoulders, soaking the flowered robe that hung on her curves. He could see her nipples through the fabric, but it was those soft eyes that he couldn't stand. Closing his eyes tightly, he whispered sharply. "Go away."

She laughed, "You know I won't."

He shivered and turned his head away. The water soaked his body, plastering Madre's robe to his skin, but he didn't want to leave.

"Come on, you haven't been out of here in two days."

Darkness rose up in his thoughts and he tightened his arms until his joints creaked. "That long? I thought it was just a...." His voice trailed off as he remembered the long hours of crying in the dark.

"Yes, you were hiding in here and Madre has been in a meeting with the baron all day. Otherwise, it would be her in here. Actually," she paused sadly, "she should have been there as soon as the baron pulled out of you, but she was fighting with Nightingale."

He said nothing, his jaw tightening at the guilt that cut his heart.

Sherrel sighed and crawled into the pond, settling down next to him and wrapping her soft arms around them.

He wanted to dive into her arms, but he couldn't find the energy.

"This happens every time, you know."

He didn't want to listen, but she whispered in his ear. "The first time the baron fucks a girl. They get depressed and withdraw. I cried for four days."

Derik let out a shuddering breath, but said nothing.

"We usually give them some time alone and keep an eye so they don't do anything stupid. But it gets better, it always gets better."

"W-Why didn't anyone tell me?"

"It makes it worse when you know about it. A lot worse. And I never expected you to actually fuck the baron like that."

She stroked his long black hair, pulling a few water-logged strands away. Her hands brought his chin up to kiss him lightly on the lips. Her voice was soft and subdued. "Madre says the baron drains life force when he comes. An energy transfer. That is why he has so many girls. It isn't because of ego, it's to keep us healthy."

Derik sniffed and trembled. Even as he withdrew into himself, he listened to Sherrel.

"You feel numb, don't you?"

He nodded.

"Kind of a despair in your pit, gnawing away at your insides?"

Another nod.

"Fear?"

He nodded again.

"A desperate urge to give me head?"

He looked up surprised and Sherrel giggled.

Blushing, he ducked his head back against his chest but Sherrel slipped an arm around him, wrapping herself around his neck and holding him tight.

Her large breasts ground against his own and he shivered at the sensation. She stroked his head. "Still want him inside you?"

He suppressed a moan at the thought. "Oh yes. I want him so much. But, I'm so scared now. I've never been like this before."

"It will pass, Dora. It always passes."

"It hurts, not my ass but... my heart hurts," he whispered into her neck.

"I know, I've been there. Teri bawled like a baby for two days before Madre decided she was milking it and spanked her ass silly. They say the only person who never did this was Madre. Something about being a mage, I guess. Shields, whatever they are."

"I-I'm not a mage."

She laughed and kissed him again. "No, you aren't. You are something special."

He blinked at the water clinging to his eyelashes. "I'm a bad man."

She shook her head, "No, you aren't."

"Y-Yes, I am. I did something terrible."

Sherrel sighed softly and pushed the hair from his face. "I know."

Shocked, he stared at her. Ice ran in his veins. "Y-You know?"

"I know you did something. I don't know what but I think Madre can sense it too. You have a secret, a very deep secret."

"I-I can't tell you."

She smiled sadly. "I wish you would."

"W-Why?"

She cocked her head as she admired him. He shivered and looked away again. She leaned against him, arms still wrapped around his neck. "Because, it hurts you. I don't like when someone hurts inside. You know, I was there when my father gave me to the baron as part of a deal. For a while, I saw him growing more bitter with every day, he made the decision months before but couldn't tell me. And it gnawed him out from the inside."

Derik froze as Sherrel continued.

"I was so angry at him convinced I was nothing but property to him. His own daughter, third born but still. If he told me first, maybe I wouldn't have been so angry. If he just was honest with me, maybe I would have willingly gone to the baron. It was that night, that very first night, that the baron took me in his bed. It was a difficult night, even with my three handmaids also pleasing him."

Her voice got softer as she remembered, "He was so big, and I was a virgin then, a princess. That's what he calls me here, his Princess. Like he called you Blackbird and Teri is his cat."

"D-Does that mean I have a new name?"

"Only if you want it. Nightingale took the name he gave her, but I didn't. I liked Sherrel, it was the name my late mother gave me."

"W-What happened?"

Sherrel said nothing for a long moment, and they both listened to the water splattering down on them. He realized she was crying, but he couldn't roust himself from his despair to withdraw his question and comfort her.

She answered him in her soft, sad voice. "They died. Father, mother, my sisters and brothers. The baron lent his military force, but Papa insisted on leading. It was a slaughter."

"I'm... sorry."

She squeezed him. "The baron once told me that he knew it would fail. He said he knew that my father's kingdom couldn't last, and every one of us was going to die."

Derik sobbed, trying to imagine it.

Sherrel squeezed him tightly. "I was the one he saved. It wasn't only sex, he had enough trophies and girls for that, but it was the only way to save someone from my father's pride."

"W-What about his troops?"

"The baron trained very good men. Not to mention the magically bred war dogs. However, he wouldn't let my papa split them apart, his army took very few casualties, but they couldn't be everywhere at once. It just took one wrong move, and the palace was undefended."

She sniffed and wiped the water from her face. "He was right, you know. Papa was a proud man, he fought to the last man, woman, and child to save his kingdom. The amount of drive it takes to carve something out of there.... It's scary how much it takes but it also blinds you."

He listened to her words, staring out into the dimly lit massage room. His own thoughts were dark and morose, but he couldn't imagine that came from anywhere but his own guilt and despair.

"They sent an assassin after me, the next year. Cleaning up loose ends, they said. It was during one of the baron's picnics. Twenty girls, fucked almost constantly over a week right in the middle of the prettiest glade you have ever seen. The baron was having his way with me on the edge of a pond, just the two of us."

"What happened?" He didn't want to ask, but he couldn't stop her.

"The assassin came in and tried to buy my life. A thousand marks to kill me. The baron just laughed and killed him. Broke the man's arm, then his back. He was so powerful, he almost glowed in the daylight. Then he kept me close to him for the rest of the day. It was a scary time, but around him, I feel safe."

"I-I... he hurt me."

She hugged him again. "Yes, but next time it won't be so bad. I think the entire harem orgasmed when he entered you. It was so hot I almost didn't catch him to do my little part. And I can't believe you managed to hide yourself when he fucked you that hard."

"I guess."

"And you haven't thanked me yet."

Derik said nothing.

Someone called out in the other room and Sherrel cocked her head. A frown flickered across her face. "Madre is making an announcement."

"I don't want to go."

"Yes, but when she calls the harem and you don't show up, your ass will burn for a week."

Shivering, he let her pull him from the waterfall and into the room. The drenched robes were plastered to him, but they only had a few seconds to towel dry before entering the main room.

As soon as they returned to the main room, he noticed the cold air around him.

Madre stood in the front, with red-rimmed eyes and a dark expression on her face.

A cold shiver ran down his spine.

She was looking right at the massage room, not moving her eyes away from the opening.

"I have a-an announcement," her voice broke as she spoke. The room silenced as they stared at her, waiting.

Derik's despair rose from his gut just seeing Madre.

There was a sorrow around her as she stepped a bit to the side. "Night... Night..." She sniffed and wiped the tears from her face. "Nightingale is no longer with the harem."

A ripple of shock filled the room.

Madre waved her hand for silence but it was obvious she was fighting back the tears. "You all know what she did to Dora, but that was just one of many things. S-She had a chance to go to the baron, but she decided to handle it on her own."

She sniffed again. Tears ran down her cheeks. She scratched one of her scars and Derik saw blood oozing from the wound. "Terrible things were said when I brought her before the baron. She asked to leave, demanded actually. Hamel made a de... decision and..."

Her voice trailed off as she struggled to speak.

"... and, she goes on sale tonight."

Everyone else in the room focused their attention on him and their gaze caused his skin to squirm.

Madre shook her head curtly. "No! This isn't about Dora. This is about Nightingale and me. I-I am Madre, and even for the on... only woman I loved, there has to be rules. And she broke that rule so many times. She had the chance, she always had the chance to report Dora directly to the baron."

Teri spoke up softly, her voice echoing in the room. "What about Dora? Does the baron know?"

"He doesn't know anything new. Dora is still one of our girls and will be for as long as I can make it so."

Teri, Sherrel, and Derik all breathed a sigh of relief.

Derik watched Madre as she looked at him. At the sight of those sorrow-filled eyes, his heart lurched and he looked away, tears in his own eyes. Madre look away herself before speaking. "I love Nightingale and... and..." she took a deep breath, "I need some time alone."

Without looking back, she left the room.

Derik stared at her, tears on his own face and darkness filling his heart. "Fuck."

Sherrel hugged him. "It isn't your fault, she was angry."

"If I wasn't here, this would have never happened."

"Probably, but Nightingale made her choice, and the baron made his. Madre made her choice, and you made yours. We all made a choice. I haven't regretted a single day since you came to be one of my sisters."

Derik sighed sadly, the claws of guilt clutching his heart. He turned away from the room. Stopping, he reached over and kissed Sherrel on the lips. "Thank you for saving me."

She turned to watch him heading back to the massage room.

"I'll be back. You can't hide forever."

He stopped at the door, feeling the despair raging inside him but somehow knowing where it came from helped a little. He smiled the best he could, even if he didn't feel it yet. "Then I'll thank you for saving me again."

And he returned to the darkness of the massage room.

Disobedience

It took him three more days to shed the despair that filled him. However, knowing his energy was drained gave him strength to fight it.

Even Teri showed surprising compassion, sitting with him as he sobbed. She told him stories of her own first time which occasionally made him smile. Her tale of Madre spanking her reminded him that Madre took care of her own. She also described his own fucking by the baron in graphic detail. That brought a different emotion to the fore and a blush to his cheeks. When she apologized for not telling him, he broke down again and began to sob. She just held him until the tears stopped coming.

Finally, he needed to move. The guilt for what happened with Nightingale still hung over him, but he couldn't avoid the world forever.

Staggering out of the massage room, he stared at the sleeping women. Above him, the morning light streamed in through the window. They would be sleeping for hours more but he answered his own calling. Stepping over the sprawl of bodies, he made his way to the bathrooms before heading to Madre's room.

At the door, he held up his hand and knocked.

"Go the fuck away!" came an angry voice inside.

He knocked again, shivering as he clutched the black robe around his body. "Madre, I want—"

"I said fuck off!"

The door shuddered as something powerful hit it, and he saw a flash of light from around the cracks.

He sighed and turned away. He walked down the hall to Madre's room, a walk he had taken several times now. At the corner, he leaned against the corner and stared out across the sleeping room. He looked up and whispered to the ceiling. "Bridget?"

He didn't know why he called out the god. Somehow, knowing that even a minor god watched out for him gave him a comfort and Bridget seemed as good as any other.

"What do I do?"

Naturally, he didn't get an answer. He chuckled dryly to himself and leaned against the corner, letting the sharp tiles dig into his hand. "Fuck, why can't the gods just give clear answers?"

He glanced down the hall at Madre's room. He said nothing as the world passed on by for a few more minutes, then he sighed. Letting his hand trail along the tile, he returned to the main room.

Finding Teri and Sherrel, he slipped off the robe and cuddled into them.

Teri opened one eye, "Back?"

He nodded and smiled.

She wrapped her arms around him, holding him tight. "Good, I missed you."

Sherrel held him from the other side. "We both missed you." She kissed him on the ear.

Derik smiled and kissed them both before they drifted back to sleep. Just as Sherrel dozed off, she whispered something that woke him up. "If Madre would get out of her room, we would all be happy."

He gasped, "She's been in her room all that time?"

"Yep, five days," came the sleepy response, "drinking herself in a stupor and crying when she thinks we can't hear her."

Hearing those words, any desire to sleep fled away. Instead he stared up the ventilation shaft and the skylight, letting his mind wander. He could imagine the Eye of Hamel above him, laughing its crystalline symmetry off at his misfortune.

A pressure released from his heart and the darkness evaporated, leaving him at peace for the first time in days. Not enough for him to blurt out a confession, but something lifted. He also realized that he was worried about Madre. There were two losses that night in the harem.

An hour passed as he just watched the ceiling. Then, he looked up at a strange sound. It was sobbing, but muted. Curious, he slipped to his feet.

Teri moaned and clutched for him, but Derik slid Sherrel's arms into hers, and the two women pulled each other together.

He padded carefully around the room wearing nothing but his thong. The sounds came from Madre's room. Whisper quiet, he remained as silent as possible until he could press his ear to the door.

Inside, he heard the clink of bottles and another strangled sob. He leaned against the door, resting his forehead as the guilt rose up. His bare feet only made a whisper of noise as he headed back down the hall. He made it just past the corner when he stopped. Looking back, he heard another sob coming from Madre. Shaking his head, he made up his mind. "She better be worth it. This is a fucking stupid idea."

Reaching up, he gathered up long black hair and knotted it once. It would be a bitch to unravel, but he guessed he needed it tight. Turning around, he headed back down the hall. His feet scuffed against the ground until he stopped by the door.

"Go the fuck away!" came through the door.

"Madre, I'm coming in."

"I'll burn your ass so go the hells away!"

Taking a deep breath, Derik disobeyed her and threw open the door.

He saw the flash of energy of a spell bursting out from the bed. Kicking off the door frame, he launched himself into the darkness of the room and into a roll that brought him near the tub. The spell impacted the door with a shudder and a burst of fire, but he was deep in the room, blinded by the darkness.

Spinning up to his feet, he laid out the room in his mind just like it was one of his jobs. His bare feet almost slipped on scattered papers and bumped up against a bottle. He managed to get to his feet before the second spell went off, screaming through the air. He ducked down, snatched up the bottle, and threw it with all his might. It tumbled through the air, shattering as it hit her bolt of force. In the mere second he had, Derik launched himself across the room, grabbing a bottle he spotted in the light from the door and throwing it before him.

Madre's third spell caught the bottle, but he managed to jump through the shards of glass to land heavily on her body, pinning her clumsily.

"Get off me, you bastard!"

Her entire body ignited with flames as she grabbed him.

He gulped as she squeezed his arms tightly using supernatural strength and threw him straight up into the air. Blind, he desperately flipped in the air, catching the ceiling with his toes. As gravity took hold of him, he kicked himself off and brought his hands down in an attack of his own.

He saw Madre's glowing hands, reaching up with some terrible spell, and he prayed he wouldn't miss.

The sound of his slap cracked the very air.

The silence that followed was deafening.

Madre's breath blasted across his face as her body flickered with anger. He could feel her body, naked and covered with sweat. She trembled with barely controlled rage.

"What, in name of the Seven Gods, did you just do?" she growled.

Derik's body came to a rest, and his hair plastered itself to his back. Looking down, he could feel himself straddling Madre's body like a lover. One hand caught her wrist, but he could feel her already twisting for freedom. His other palm stung from his slap and he had no doubt Madre's face also stung.

He had to calm his own shuddering breath before he could speak. "I slapped you. Why?"

She moved with blinding speed. Twisting her wrist out of his grip, he saw her hand flare up to a brilliant white. Then his world exploded in pain as she slapped him back. The force of the blow threw him off the bed and across the room; his back slammed against the cabinet with her toys. Sliding down, he groaned and shook his head to clear it. Looking up, he watched the outline of her body as she staggered out of the bed. Her body ignited into light to reveal her nakedness.

Her voice was strong and murderous as she walked toward him. "What gives you the right, Derik?"

He staggered to his feet, panting from his efforts. His hand cracked open the door to the cabinet, fumbling around for anything useful. To cover up the sounds from her magical hearing, he spoke loudly. "You are Madre."

"So!?"

"Aren't you supposed to be the strong bitch here?"

She didn't say anything, but Derik kept on talking, speaking in far more anger than he felt. He needed the noise to drown out his fumbling in the closet. "Why didn't you tell me about that damn drain? Why the fuck didn't you stop him? You knew damn well I was in the massage room all this time. You knew what was happening to me. And where were you? You were cowering in your room."

"I lost my Nightingale!"

Her voice shook the room as she used power behind her scream. Her presence slammed into him, crushing him against the wood.

A pair of locking cuffs caught underneath his fingers. An idea blossomed in his thoughts. It was stupid and foolish, but why not go with his strengths? He took a breath to calm himself, watching as Madre circled around him.

"If it wasn't for Sherrel and Teri, I'd still be sobbing in that room. Damn it, why the hell didn't you tell me that the baron is a vampire?"

"I do care, damn it! And he isn't a vampire! He's a—"

She paused but he snatched on her phrase and raised his voice to drown out the clinking of the cuffs. "He's a what? What kind of man drains the life out of every person he fucks!? What if I did something stupid?"

"You wouldn't understand."

"Why not? For a man who tells the truth, he sure as hell has a lot of them himself."

Madre stepped forward. The light around her grew brighter. She snarled, "I think you better shut up now."

Derik planned out his movements even as he stammered for the words. "Or what? Sell me? Throw me in prison? Damn it, you're suppose to take care of me."

"Then why won't you tell me your damn secret!?"

He froze, the guilt slashing through him.

He saw Madre moving, the halo of her body blurring as she attacked. He almost missed it, but he managed to bring his hand up, spinning and ducking into her blow as he grabbed her wrist. She twisted it, but this time he held on as he flipped over. To his surprise, he managed to get the cuff locked over her wrist as he hit the ground.

Her foot flashed as she went to kick him and he jumped up, twisting frantically to latch the cuff to her other wrist.

He missed as he heard the flagstone of her office crack from the blow.

She spun around, dragging him, and he lashed out again, desperately thankful when he heard the cuffs latch to her other wrist. There was a brief scream of rage, then a dull thud as Madre hit the ground, breasts first and arms bound behind her back. He slumped to the ground next to her, panting hard.

Madre's eyes flashed as she glared at him. "You are so fucking dead."

He sighed, fighting back the sob of despair that rushed inside of him. "Damn it, Madre, listen. Those girls need you. I need you. I needed you."

She froze, but he could feel her glare burning his skin.

"Damn it, it wasn't suppose to be like this. I wasn't suppose to want it. I mean, that baron gave me the best fucking orgasm I've had in my entire life. A man!? Even the despair, all I could think about was fucking him. I want it, craved it, but hell, I feared it too. He ripped out my damn heart and left a gaping hole in there."

Her shoulders slump.

"Damn it, I really needed you, Madre."

"I-I," her voice brimmed with anger, but it cracked, "I'm sorry."

"You should be."

"Damn it, you're right. I should have been there for you. Okay!? I'm sorry!"

He groaned, "This is all wrong. I shouldn't be here, I'm just a th
—"

Derik froze in mid-word. He swallowed before correcting himself quickly.

"—a guy hiding in a harem from Rick. Now, I'm becoming rather fond of you and the girls, which makes me do stupid things like attack Madre when she's drinking herself into a stupor."

"And the baron?"

His body heated up at the thought. "Except for the life-sucking cock—which for some fucked up reason I still want inside me—he seems like a nice guy."

Madre let out a short laugh. "Welcome to my world. Now let me go."

He glanced around the room. He noticed a shadow of someone standing outside of the door, and an evil thought crossed his head. Smiling in the darkness, he shook his head slowly. "One more thing."

"What?" came the wary response.

"You didn't do your job, did you?"

"I said I'm sorry. Now let me go."

He leaned forward. "So, just call it five?"

She froze and the world seemed to plunge into silence.

The air grew tense and tight.

His heart pounded in his chest as he stared at her, watching the battle aura growing brighter along her body. In the light of her spell, he could see her twisting in her bounds; he had no doubt that his seconds were numbered before they snapped.

Then, Madre spoke in a very deliberate voice, promising pain on his very soul. "Don't you dare."

He swallowed at the terror rising inside him, but he spoke anyways. "You are also holding secrets about the baron, despite all that honesty crap. Why don't we call that ten more?"

"I will break that ass of yours. I will fuck you so hard that your spine will snap!"

"And not being there when I was drained by the life-sucking cock? Another ten? Frankly you could have done a lot more." He was terrified and playful at the same time.

She said nothing, but her glare could strip off paint off the walls. He heard the metal twisting as she flexed her spell-fueled strength into breaking free.

"And, one more thing, making me like the baron's cock. Oh, that's worth twenty. Okay, ten, Teri says I'm a slut anyways."

"You touch me and you won't walk for a week."

Her voice was hard and brutal, threatening everything from pain to death. He thought about it, his cock rising up to the occasion.

He chuckled despite the fact death breathed on his neck. "Sorry, Madre, but I think it will be worth it. Thirty-five it is."

His hand came down hard and the slap against her naked rear rang out across the room.

He got to twelve before she snapped her cuffs.

He almost made it to thirteen before she pinned him roughly against the ground. Before he could move, she flipped him over her own lap and began to beat his ass.

It was worth it.

Even if he could barely walk after.

Heels

Derik moaned around the ball gag and closed his eyes as his body jerked forward. He focused on the feeling of the large, smooth strap-on plunging deep into his ass and the slap of Madre's hips against his still-smarting cheeks. Her hand cracked down, and he jerked forward again, this time from the pleasure and pain mixing in the cauldron of his loins.

As she withdrew, sliding the thick hardness from his body, he smiled around his gag and opened his eyes again. His wrists, cuffed to the railing above Madre's headboard, twisted so he could stare at his fingernails. Freshly painted, trimmed, and sparkling, they were still wet from where Madre finished painting them only a few minutes before. In the twelve days that passed, they finally healed enough to be shaped and painted. He smiled as he stared at the white crescents and deep sapphire color. He would blow on them to dry, but the gag in his mouth prevented everything but the moan escaping his throat.

Madre slammed forward, and he closed his eyes, anticipating the slap against his ass. Her hand impacted against his right cheek again, redoubling the heated pain and pleasure as the thick dildo sank to the hilt inside him.

He moaned again, a long shuddering one of ecstasy, and his cock bobbed against her soaked blankets.

She grunted and planted her hands on his hips, yanking out and driving into him as she switched to hard, powerful strokes that sent bolts of pleasure bursting inside him and his head bumping up against the headboard.

He twisted his wrists to keep from marring the fresh paint on his nails.

As the thickness plunged in and out, fucking him almost as deep as the baron, he waited for the next smack against his red ass. It never came, only the rapid pumping of Madre reaching her own orgasm. He pushed back against the headboard, using his elbows, to let her plunge deeper into it, to feel the friction of his more than willing body around her strap-on. Her breath came out in grunts with the first signs of an orgasm; tiny releases of her magic set the hairs on his neck on end. He closed his eyes tightly as she gave him two, then three hard pumps, then buried herself completely in him, pinning the thick pressure as she swept through her orgasm.

Pinned against the wall and a rubber cock, he marveled how much he enjoyed his predicament. The toy wasn't the baron's real cock, but he could never turn down a chance to have either stuffed into his asshole. His place in the world was on the bed, beneath Madre's body with his ass impaled.

Panting, Madre plastered herself against his back, her sweaty breasts rubbing against his shoulder-blades. She gasped as she spoke curtly but with a voice filled with an afterglow of an orgasm. "And that was two thousand swats over twelve days."

Her hips rocked slightly and he grunted, unable to speak around the rubber ball in his mouth. Her fingers worked the strap, and he gasped as she eased it out of his jaw. "And, Dora, what did we learn?"

Derik moaned softly, pushing back on the cock. "Spank faster?"

When she grabbed his hair and pulled back, he gasped. Her hand came down, this time flaring with magic. Energy ripple shot through his body. The electric shock sent him over another edge of an orgasm. He groaned with pleasure, squeezing his inner muscles around her strap-on as he splattered her sheets once again with his seed.

Madre raised her hand and a searing light glowed from her fingertips. He could feel the magic pooling in her palm.

He gasped in the feelings of helplessness and terror. He cried out quickly, "I don't ever spank Madre!"

The second magical blow didn't come and she released his hair.

He leaned forward, feeling the strands of his hair slipping through her fingers.

"Good. Even if I do something wrong?"

Derik said nothing, thinking about the feel of his hand against her ass and also the thousands of swats he got since. His cock, despite his release just seconds before, twitched and drooled more cum into her blankets.

She pulled his hair again. "I said," she growled, "even if I do something wrong?"

He spoke softly, half moaning as he spoke. "I won't do it again," she started to release his hair, but he kept on speaking, "unless I think its important. Then, I'm going to do it again and you will tan my ass even more."

For a second, he thought she was going to smack him again, but she just let the hair slip from her fingers. "Fair enough. Next time, it will be two hundred spankings for every time you do it, and I won't spread it out over a week."

She pushed against his hips, withdrawing her cock, and leaving him with the feeling of emptiness.

He slumped to the bed, ignoring the squelch of his own cum that plastered itself to his stomach. Sated, he just smiled and looked up to his drying nails.

"Are they done?" asked Madre.

"I think so, but kind of hard to check."

"You should know by now how long it takes."

He thought back to the time she fucked him and nodded.

She reached over to release his cuffs and he sat up, smearing his juices but still staring at his nails. "Thank you for fixing them."

Madre at on the edge of the bed, sweaty but smiling herself. "It was the best I could do. They'll grow over the next week and I'll re-shape them."

He smiled to her. "Thank you."

"I guess," she glanced away, "I should thank you also. I didn't realize how much I was withdrawing until you came in."

Her head snapped back to stare at him, "But! That doesn't mean you have permission to lay your hand on my ass again."

He giggled, then froze at the sound of it.

Madre smirked and held out her hand. "Come, you need to get cleaned up, we are doing something different today."

"Is that why I'm up at seven in the morning?"

"Yes."

She drew him into the bath, and he was relived to find out his nails were dry as they washed each other. Later, sitting at her desk, he leaned forward as she brushed out his hair.

"What made you come in here? It seems rather bold for you."

Derik sighed and closed his eyes. "I... I had a lot of reasons, I guess."

"Such as?"

"My mother and Nightingale."

She froze in mid-stroke. "Nightingale?"

"I-I never realized you loved her that much."

Madre sighed and continued brushing his hair. "It's difficult being Madre. I can't have favorites otherwise the girls complain. But, when I was just Rachi..." She sniffed. "...I was so much in love with Gale. Neither of us dated or went out because we had each other and the baron. I didn't need anything else. If I knew what would change when I became Madre, I may have never done it."

She set a brush to his hair and he leaned into her to enjoy the stroke of the bristles and the softness of her breath on his bare skin. A tear formed in his eyes at the thought of Madre's loss, trying to understand how much that could have hurt. "Why did you?"

"Become Madre?"

"Yes."

"The baron asked me to. I was the first to really understood what he was doing to the girls. I could help that first time after they ride his shaft. That 'life-sucking cock' as you put it."

"What is it?"

She hesitated, but finished her brushing before answering Derik. "It isn't my story, Dora, and I don't exactly know. But, I trust you to never tell anyone about it. He isn't a danger to anyone as long as we are here, but it is his secret. If it gets out, many people will be hurt."

"But, it hurt me already."

"Yes, it always does the first time."

"Not for you."

"No, even for me. I just hid it better than others. And I had my Nightingale. But now, you are his woman. Next time," she paused as she set down the brush and picked up the long blue cord he used for braiding, "next time, it will feel like he's fucking your body and your mind. Its an orgasm you will never forget."

He shifted at the thought, his body still craving that hardness inside him. His manhood rose at the memory and she chuckled.

"I can feel you thinking about him, that speeding of your heart and the heat coming off your body."

He sighed himself, rapping his head on the desk. "Why do I want him so badly?"

"Because you belong here and to him, body and mind."

As she braided his hair in his now favorite style: a complicated five strand that integrated the cord as the sixth and always made him feel like it was part of some magical spell.

He smiled and remained still, listening to the palace and her body. "Why your mother?"

He jumped as she asked her hesitant question. He closed his eyes as a dagger seemed to spear his heart. "She drank herself into Oblivion."

"I'm sorry. How old were you?"

The memories were still painful, but he managed to speak about them. "I last saw her when I was five, just over twenty years ago, and a few months before she was killed."

Madre's hands faltered, "I thought she drank herself to death."

New tears ran down his cheeks. "No, I said to Oblivion not to death. S-She was killed by a guard."

"I don't understand."

"She was a whore on the south side of the town. Drank away the money her pimp let her keep. I had to steal to find enough food to eat. But, she drank too much one day and passed out at the Buggered Unicorn. She woke up long enough to make a deal with a mage, a Dimensional-something, when he decided to pay for one more use of her body. She never came back."

Madre's hands fell away as Derik spoke in a monotone. He heard her gasp and speak through her hand. "Seven Gods!"

"He used her to open the rift to Oblivion. Twenty years ago, when the demon invasion came pouring into the city. I didn't find out until I was ten, when I met the captain of the guards who finally killed her and sealed the gate."

He sniffed, remembering the pain of that second memory, of a black-haired thief sitting in cuffs on the edge of a chair and listening to the captain tearfully apologizing.

"Oh, Derik!"

Her arms wrapped around him tightly, holding him as she pressed her head against him. He pushed back the memory of it, only letting a few tears roll down his cheeks as Madre held him.

He cracked and let out a sob, fighting it every way, but soon he could let the memory fade again. Sniffing, he wiped the tears from his face. "After that, I became a proper th—"

He started to correct himself but Madre interrupted him. "A thief?"

Derik froze, his heart pounding. He tried to think of a thousand things to say, but he just nodded. "Yes."

Madre leaned back, turning his head to face her. "Did you steal anything here?"

"I haven't taken anything from the palace."

It was truth but not the full truth. He thought about the burning sapphire orb above the main room, then pushed his thoughts away from that also.

Madre's lips tightened and he cringed, waiting for her to call the guards.

"Were you going to?"

He sighed, turning away from her as shame burned on his cheeks. He spoke before he could think about it. "Yes."

Inside, he screamed out at rage, at himself for speaking and for everything that led up to that moment. He found new tears, but it was that hand on his chin that forced him to look back at Madre. He stared into her brown eyes and saw tears shimmering in them.

"Why didn't you?"

It was a low, almost whispered question. He struggled with his answer, opening his mouth then closing it. He tried to look away again, but Madre held his chin in place, her eyes boring into his very soul.

"I-I," he swallowed hard, "I'm happy here. Happier than I ever been. I-I," the tears were burning down his cheek, "I want to stay."

Madre's eyes flickered as she focused on him.

He sniffed, waiting for the guards or for him to attack him.

"What?"

"Huh?"

"What were you going to steal?"

Panic rose up inside him and he clamped his mouth shut.

Madre, listening to his heart as she always did, sighed. "Don't keep this a secret, Dora. Just let it out."

He came within half a heartbeat of confessing. Then, he flung himself away, ripping his chin from her fingers. "I-I don't want to go."

His chest hurt from the tightness that squeezed him. Hot tears splashed down on the desk as he trembled.

Madre said nothing then she hugged him again sightly. "Someday, Dora. Just tell me before its too late."

"I-I'm sorry."

"I know, but thank you for being this honest."

He was shocked that she didn't call the guards.

After a tight hug, she returned to his hair, braiding it in silence. He remained still, fighting with a storm of emotions and memories that her questions brought up. It hurt to think about his mother, but those memories had faded over the years, worn smooth with time. Instead, he just thought about the Eye of Hamel and berated himself for not telling Madre. He even opened his mouth once to tell her, then closed it out of cowardice.

Working himself into a deep funk, he jumped when Madre finished and set a box on the desk in front of him. It was wrapped in brown paper and had his name neatly written on the top.

"What is this?"

Madre chuckled and sat on the edge of the desk. "Many people call it a present."

He looked up, stunned. "What for?"

"Many things, I guess: becoming the baron's woman, pulling me from my sorrow, being honest with me. Turning everyone on?"

"Oh," as he spoke with a growing blush.

Madre chuckled and stroked her fingers along them. "You blush so pretty. It's nice you do it so often. Now open your present."

Still shocked, he reached over and delicately opened the package, careful of his nails. The paper tore loudly as he pulled it off. The box was inlaid with gold trim and made of polished wood. Gasping, he ran his fingers over the smooth surface. "It's beautiful."

She smiled and gestured. "Open it."

Fingers trembling, he worked the latch and opened it up to find a pair of sapphire shoes inside. Gasping, he stared at them nestled into the black velvet. They had short heels, maybe three or four centimeters, but the tiny row of sapphires that ran along the edge to the narrow tip stole his breath away.

He sobbed with surprise, delight, and confusion.

Madre chuckled and reached out, taking one out and holding it with her fingers. "I've never given a girl her first pair of shoes, but after seeing you move, I think these would be perfect for you."

"I... I... I don't know what to say."

She answered by setting another box down in front of him.

He gaped at her until she gestured for him to open it. This one was also stored in polished wood, but with a different color and symbol on the seal. Shaking, he worked the latch and pushed it open. It took him a moment to realize he was looking at a dress of the purest dark blue he had ever seen. It was shimmering and soft on his fingers, as sensual as his silk underwear. Tears ran down his cheeks as he stroked against it. "I can't."

"Funny, I don't recall asking you."

He just stared up at her, tears on his cheeks.

Madre slid off the edge of the desk and stood up. Pulling him to his feet, she said, "Come on, we need to teach you how to walk like a woman before we go shopping."

"S-Shopping?"

Madre grinned, "Yes, I need new boots and you need to get out."

He stammered as she pulled him into the center of the room.

She helped him slip on his first pair of heels and stand up. It was intense, a feeling of standing higher, but also his feet perfectly fitting into the silken sheath of the shoes.

He shivered at the sensations and at the feeling of the backs of his legs tightening. His calves tightened like springs as he balanced on them, using his acrobatic training to find his center despite the change in posture.

Firmly, Madre walked him through crossing the room, guiding and holding him until he could balance. It only took two tries before he could move without help. Then, she worked on the sway of his hips and the bob of his movements. Wearing nothing but the shoes, his manhood stood up straight and drooled pre-cum with every step.

Soon, Madre gave her approval. "You are very aware of your body, Dora. I didn't think you'd pick it up so fast."

He circled the room, feeling very sexy as he grew comfortable with moving. In many ways, it wasn't that different from the stilts he used for a while as a clown to get a few silvers. "I got this idea when I saw you bouncing off the ceiling. I knew this one battle mage, the class victor actually, who fought in heels and you moved like her. That was the nastiest fight I ever had; bitch took me out with a powered jump and a flaming fist to the head. Shift your weight a bit more, there, that's good. And, damn, Hime did a great job with you. With a dress and you tucked back, I bet no one could tell you were anything other than a woman."

He blushed hotly as he came to a stop. His legs trembled only slightly but he could feel his juices dribbling down the side of shaft and his thighs.

Madre caught sight of them and sighed playfully. "You get wetter than any girl I know though."

"Sorry."

"Don't be. Now, get out of the heels, time to get you into your dress."

His dress. It sent a tiny thrill through his loins as he slipped out of the shoes, almost sad to part with them. When Madre pulled out more clothes, the passing faded as he stared at a new pair of underwear, a black thong that looked very snug. It wasn't until she pulled out the corset that he realized he had a desperate ache in his balls.

Madre chuckled.

"Go on, masturbate, but clean up with a rag, we don't have time for me to fuck you again if you try to lick it up."

He did so, a quick and hard orgasm against her sheets before he returned.

Madre helped him slip on the thong, tucking back his cock and balls into place and settling the fabric over his hips. He panted at the feeling of being delightfully exposed while still being held firmly. The line of fabric up his ass sent a tiny shiver up his spine as she circled him.

"I hate that priestess some days. Well I don't, but I do, you know what I mean. Bitch did everything right and I have no doubt I'm not going to hear the end of it."

"Is she coming back, Madre?"

Madre nodded. "Yes, she cashed in her favor yesterday. The baron agreed to replace Forbis with her and to maintain the marks on his harem. Including yours."

"Just for me?"

Chuckling, Madre patted him before wrapping the corset around his chest and underneath his breasts. "Not entirely you. The baron pays good money for caring for his harem and her church needs the money. There aren't a lot of cross-dressers, you know."

"Oh."

She gave his ass a playful spank, sending another bolt of pleasure coursing through his system as her palm connected to the red cheek. He moaned, but she snatched her hand away. "Better not turn you on anymore, I'd have to call in Teri and Sherrel to drain you, and they aren't ready to see you yet."

The corset was tight, with its many straps. It held his chest in, making breathing a bit uncomfortable. However, when he looked in the mirror at his breasts cupped in the corset, he was stunned at his appeared. "I-I'm beautiful?"

"You will be," came the cheerful reply.

Finishing up the lacing, Madre helped him slip the dress over his head, snuggling into place. It clung to his body, hugging his hips and reaching down to his mid-shin. Two slits ran up both sides, stopping only inches from the curve of his waist. Underneath, black satin trimmed the edge so he could see tantalizing glimpses of his thigh as he turned around. His corset, with the same satin trim, peeked out of the front of the dress, giving him a deep cleavage and breasts that ached to be touched. The sleeves were short, but also trimmed in the same black. His waist looked tiny in the mirror, and he was stunned at his own appearance.

Madre stepped back and nodded again in approval. "Hold on."

Opening her door, she called to Teri.

A few seconds later, Teri ran to the door, then stopped just inside it, her mouth opening in surprise. "Holy fucking gods!"

"Teri!"

Gulping, Teri stared at Derik and he blushed even hotter at the sight of her lustful gaze. Turning around slowly, he looked at her through lidded eyes, holding his hands against the fabric that still sent tiny shivers through his body.

Neither said anything for a long time before Madre cleared her throat.

Teri jumped and looked sheepish. "Sorry, Madre."

"You are better at makeup—"

Derik let out a soft whimper.

"—and would you please put some on Dora? We are going out."

Teri, still surprised, came up to Dora and sat her down in front of the mirror.

As soon as Madre began to dress herself, Teri leaned forward and whispered in Derik's ear. "I want to fuck you so hard right now."

Her hand slid into the slit of the dress, stroking a finger along the thong and sending a hungry moan to erupt from Derik's lips.

Across the room, Madre snapped out. "Teri! No molesting her. Just do her makeup."

Snatching her hand from Derik's wet crotch, she giggled and pulled out a dazzling array of makeup. He lost himself in her commands as she applies eye color and lipstick, mascara and even blush. Derik struggled with his image of the woman being dolled up in the mirror to the memory of his life before the harem.

Finally, he was ready. Standing in his heels and looking every inch a woman, he couldn't tear his eyes away from the mirror.

Teri leaned against the bed, one hand pressed against her pussy as she watched.

Madre smiled warmly and took Derik's arm, peeling him away from the mirror. "Come on, I need new boots."

She was also beautiful, but Derik kept trying to look at himself in the mirror as she pulled him out of her room.

Shopping

After an embarrassing round of applause, whistles, and catcalls walking through the harem, Derik followed Madre out of the harem with a hot blush on his cheeks. Heading down the hall to the exit, he heard his new heels tapping against the tile, a pattern of movement that made him want to sway with the motions. He did and Madre patted his arm approvingly.

"Just relax and don't rush it."

He nodded and closed his lips. They tasted differently, but he could still remember the sight of his own painted lips, a deep sapphire that was striking as the blue and black that adorn his body. However, he wasn't expecting his movements to rub his sensitive nipples against the edge of the corset. Every movement sent pleasurable tingles along his shape-shifted breasts and down between his legs.

By the time they walked out the front door of the palace, he could already feel a dampness between his legs. Outside, in the sunlight that he hadn't seen in a long time, he stared at the elegant carriage awaiting them. Two guards, without armor but wearing heavy shirts and pants with the baron's symbol, stood on either side of the carriage door.

Derik blushed even hotter as he followed Madre down. One of the guards opened the door. Madre hopped in easily, but Derik suddenly panicked when he almost lost his balance. His hand reached out for the door handle, knowing he would miss it. To his surprise, his fingers wrapped around someone's hand and he used it for balance. Looking up, he found himself holding hands with one of the guards. His piercing green eyes admired Derik and Derik's stomach twisted with strange emotions. Unbidden, a heat grew on his cheeks as he held the hand of the guard.

"Uh... thank you."

He gave Derik a little bow and held up his hand to help him into the carriage. Clinging the handle, Derik slipped into the leather-bound cushion. The green eyes burned against his skin as the guard shut the door and Madre let out a chuckle.

"It really doesn't take much, does it?"

"What?"

He blushed hotly at Madre's smirk. "Oh, nothing."

The carriage jerked and then headed down the paved road leading to the palace. Derik watched it moving out the window, but every time he glanced at Madre, she was smirking. He quickly turned back to the window.

"You are very pretty, Dora."

"T-Thank you."

He turned back to the window, watching places he had never seen from the ground. He'd only seen the palace grounds rom views on top of buildings, as he planned out his heist. Now, he was wearing a dress with damp thighs and being ridden out in a carriage.

Life was strange.

The palace grounds lead into the estates of the rich, then into the merchant areas of the city. He spotted familiar stores and beggars and let a smile lift his spirits.

"Um, where are we going?"

"Haston's Leathery, it's a small place..."

As she spoke, Derik thought back to the store. He stole from it, one of his earlier jobs. It was for a set of leather tooled belts, but it was one of his first jobs as a thief. He chuckled, reliving how he fumbled through it, then thought to the other stores in town.

With a flash, he remembered one of Wendi's favorites. It was a small, tiny-looking leather shop at the end of an alley right on the edge of the merchant district. He didn't know why, but she always dragged him there. He once stole a pair of gloves for her and she gave him one of the longest blowjobs in his life for it.

"Um, what about Tiv's?"

"Tiv's? I'm not familiar with that."

"It's off Golden Swan, right next to Marble Court. It's in," he paused for a second, "at the end of an alley."

Madre quirked an eyebrow.

"An alley?"

"Yeah," he blushed hotly, "but it has boots that you'll like. With all the lacing. And Wen... a friend I know likes it."

Madre hummed, but she leaned out the window to give the directions. When she came back, she sat back herself and watched Derik.

He blushed hotly and fiddled with his hands for the long minutes it took to reach the small shop.

As he left the carriage, he was surprised when the guard held out his hand for Derik. He took it gratefully, but frowned at the blush that burned his skin as he did so. Settling in his heels, he walked delicately across the cobblestones and gestured down the alley. Madre didn't seem convinced and gestured for the guard to go first. He did and Derik let out a tiny sigh of relief when the green eyes no longer watched him.

"This is a very strange place for a boot shop, Dora."

"It has, um, a lot more things. She liked it a lot, back... then..."

His voice trailed off and he looked away to hide his discomfort.

Madre stepped next to him and slid her arm around his waist. Derik jumped, but she just smiled up at him. "Relax. No one is going to bite you."

"I-I know, Madre, it's just I feel so exposed."

Madre chuckled, "It's the thong."

Derik managed to forget that tiny strip of darkness that held in his dick, but at mention of it, he instantly became horribly aware of how exposed he was under the dress. He gulped as his cheeks burned once again.

Madre chuckled. "You are easy, Dora, you know that?"

"S-Sorry."

"Don't ever be."

The guard stood outside the alley and gave Madre a nod.

She tugged Derik, and together they walked down the alley.

As they stepped off the street, Derik caught sight of a few men staring with more than a little lust at them. He blushed even hotter when he realized it was his body they were undressing. At the plain door that Derik remembered well, they stopped.

Madre cocked her head as her eyes unfocused for just a second. Then a slow smile stretched across her lips. "How did you find this, Dora?"

"Um, that... um, friend I told you about."

"Really." It wasn't a question nor did Madre wait as she rapped on the door and stepped inside.

The guard with the green eyes turned at the entrance and pressed his back against the wall.

Derik blushed looking at him and followed Madre.

Memories of Tiv slammed into Derik as he stepped over the threshold. The smell of aged leather, warm and comforting, surrounded him as he entered the shadowed store. From floor to ceiling, hundreds of shelves brimmed with leather-work of all types.

Madre stood just inside the door, looking around with parted lips and an expression of joy. "Oh, Dora, it's perfect!"

The man who ran the store, a retired fighter covered in scars, looked up from his tools and watched as Madre pushed past some leather coats and cloaks and headed straight for the vast array of boots that lined the back wall.

She let out a tiny cooing noise as she found them, her fingers trailing along the seams.

Derik turned away from the proprietor, not wanting to be recognized from his time with Wendi. Idly, he played with a pair of gloves that resembled the same ones he stole a year before.

As he waited, he heard Madre let out a gasp. "Oh, these are more than perfect!"

He glanced over to see Madre holding up two pairs of boots, one was pink leather and distinctly cute while the other looked exactly like a pair he pulled off her feet just the night before.

"Brother? Can you give me something in this style, but with this enchantment?"

Derik froze at the strange address. A cold sparkle dripped down his spine as he turned to watch the storekeeper join Madre.

"But, of course, sister. Do you want this exactly one? I have a stronger set, let's see, this pair here."

"Oh, those would be even better. But I prefer the cross-stitch, they last longer. And I love this lacing."

"Of course, my sister. With your figure, I would highly—"

Derik's hand began to shake as he realized he'd made a terrible mistake. This wasn't a tiny store for expensive leather boots. It was a hidden store for mages. He gulped and carefully set down a pair of bracelets he was inspecting, suddenly thankful that he wasn't struck deaf, blind, and dumb for his thievery. He also finally realized why Wendi fucked him for a day solid after he gave those gloves to her. And then wore them pretty much every day since.

The tiny, quaint leather shop became claustrophobic with his realization. Gasping for breath, he made his way to the door and fled for the sunlight outside.

"Something wrong?"

Derik jumped, then guilty looked over at the guard outside. "Oh! No, I'm just not really into leather."

He chuckled, "You never can tell. To me, you seem very delicate to be into all that. But I just assumed I was wrong about you."

Somehow, the way the guard spoke sent a powerful heat rising in Derik's body. He became instantly aware of the piercing gaze and its effect on his hardening nipples. Looking away, he took a deep breath as he found a sudden rise of emotions.

Then froze solid as he saw three people enter one end of the alley. There was no way to forget how Wendi walked, the way she purposefully headed toward Tiv's with her two massive brothers in tow.

Derik swallowed and spoke without thinking. "Oh, fuck."

"Something wrong?"

The guard's tone turned hard and Derik looked around to see his hand on his sword.

Stammering, Derik held up his hands. "Oh, no, no! Its, um, I know her."

"A threat?"

Only to me, Derik thought. Instead, he shook his head. "No, no, s-she and I don't like each other. I-I need to get out of here."

The guard looked around, then gestured with his head down the other end of the alley.

Sweating, Derik stepped off the stone that marked Tiv's and hurried down the alley. To his surprise, Derik heard the guard following him. Together, they followed the alley until it came out to a wider street lined with stores. Panting, Derik glanced back to see Wendi had paused at the door of Tiv's. She was watching him.

Squeaking with surprise, he stepped out of sight. Seeing a few looks directed at him, he forced himself to slow down and walk along the store fronts.

The guard followed smoothly.

Derik blushed as the guard matched step with him. "A-Aren't you suppose to guard Madre?"

He shook his head, "I'd rather watch you. Madre can defend herself."

"Oh."

"I'm Tornsin."

"Uh..., I'm D... Dora."

When Tornsin said nothing else, Derik's heartbeat calmed down. They walked in silence until Derik paused at a perfume store. His nose picked up the incredible array of perfumes, but he could pick out the individual scents of the ones used in the harem. Curious, he slipped into the store and looked around until he smelled the apple one Madre gave him.

"Apple Orgasm."

The name brought a smirk to his painted lips. The guard chuckled discretely and Derik rolled the bottle in his fingers, considering stealing it.

Instead, the guard cleared his throat. "Do you want me to get it?"

Derik froze, staring in shock, but the guard blushed hotly himself and stammered. "N-No, not from me, I mean from the baron. He pays for things like this."

The older woman behind the counter cackled. "Using the baron's money for your girlfriend?"

The guard blushed.

Derik guiltily stared at the brother of a man he accidentally killed. His fingers slipped on the bottle, and Derik whimpered as it crashed to the ground. The glass shattered, spraying perfume everywhere. "Oh! I'm so sorry!"

Tornsin chuckled and pulled out his wallet. "I guess the baron is paying for it after all."

The old lady pushed him aside to glare at the perfume, then hissed in annoyance. Then, she lifted her eyes up to Derik for a long count before she gave Tornsin a grin. "Good choice for this one."

"S-She's not for me!" he stammered.

"Oh?"

"She's the baron's. I swear!"

The older woman chuckled evilly. "Don't mean you can't get a taste of forbidden pussy."

Both the guard and Derik blushed hotly. He paid for the perfume and they both hurried out. Reaching the freedom of the street, Derik had to stop to balance on his heels again.

Tornsin chuckled and scratched his head. "Sorry about that. I didn't... know that some of them just assume... we'd... be together."

Derik smiled bashfully. "It's okay, I'm kind of new to this."

"Really?"

He seemed relieved as he took a deep breath.

In response, Derik nodded shyly, wondering why his stomach jumped.

The guard scratched his head, then shyly pointed down the street. "Do you like sweets? I know this place that has the greatest spiced muffins."

Derik's stomach rumbled. "That would be very nice," he said bashfully.

They made it back about an hour later, to find Madre waiting by the carriage.

Their laughter died off immediately.

The other guard stood sternly next to the vehicle, glaring at Tornsin as he stuffed two large packages into the chest at the back.

Madre's eyes narrowed as she watched Tornsin and Derik returning to the carriage. She sniffed and her eyes grew suspicious as Derik stopped in front of her bashfully. "Have fun?"

Derik nodded, embarrassed and blushing.

Tornsin said nothing as he stood next to her.

Madre stared at the both of them, then she gestured to the carriage. "I got my boots. Why don't we head back?"

"Yes, Madre."

"Tornsin, in the carriage too," she commanded.

"Yes, madam."

Tornsin helped Derik into the carriage. Unsure where to sit, Derik sat down on the far edge where Madre had sat. Madre slipped next to him and Tornsin sat opposite of them, obviously uncomfortable inside the carriage.

As it began to move, Madre started with her questions. "So, what did you do?"

Derik stammered when he answered. "Just walked around."

Madre regarded both of them, then asked more questions. Both he and Tornsin answered just as awkwardly as she grilled them. Finally, the questions trailed off, and they rose in silence.

They were reaching the edge of the richer estates when Madre leaned over to whisper in Derik's ear. "You fancy him?"

Those three simple words brought a flush to his cheeks. He looked at Tornsin through his eyelashes but said nothing.

Madre chuckled and kept on whispering. "A little cat told me he's been asking about you for close to a month now. Discretely, but he's kept his eye on you. I think he fancies you."

Derik's cheeks grew hot. Between his legs, his manhood stirred with the thought of being wanted, even before he was shaped like a woman.

"And, I was thinking maybe you'd blush less if you got out a bit more."

Cheeks burning, Derik whispered back even as his own body stirred. "What about the baron?"

Madre grinned, "It wouldn't be the first time one of the guards enjoyed one of the harem."

"But, I can't! You know..."

She started to lean back, then she leaned forward and looked at Tornsin. "Tornsin?"

He jumped, "Yes, madam?"

"Do you fancy Dora here?"

"Madre!" Derik exclaimed, wondering if he could die of embarrassment.

Tornsin flushed hotly himself as he gulped.

Madre gestured with her hand at Derik. "Well, do you?"

"Y-Yeah, I guess."

"You guess or you do?" came Madre's wry reply.

"I... yes."

"Good, now that we got that over with, you two can stop making doe eyes at each other. You have my blessings to date."

When Madre leaned back, Derik whispered sharply at her. "Madre! What are you doing?"

Madre closed her eyes and grinned. "I'm being the strong bitch, like you said."

Derik froze, mouth open. He closed it with a snap and had to swallow as he realized that his cock began to ooze pre-cum at the thought. He whispered under his breath, so she couldn't hear. "Oh, you bitch."

Madre cracked open one eye.

Derik shivered at the glare, suddenly remembering her magical hearing.

Instead of saying anything, she just closed her eye again. After a second, she spoke without opening her eyes. "Get on your knees."

"What!?"

This time, it didn't come out as a whisper. His blush refused to go away and his cock ached between his bare legs. His hardness strained the fabric of his little black thong.

Madre repeated herself. "On your knees, Dora."

"Madre—"

"That's... thirty-five, wasn't it?"

He froze, staring at Madre who just rested there, eyes closed. She smirked and stretched out more, pretending to go to sleep.

Derik looked over his shoulder at Tornsin who was also blushing hotly and had his hands pressed against his crotch.

Derik opened his mouth to say something, then he turned to face Tornsin. As the guard gulped loudly and his own heartbeat slammed against his chest, Derik lifted himself from the padded leather seat and sunk forward, lowering himself to his knees.

"Um, madam? I don't think—"

Madre interrupted him, "I didn't ask you either, Tornsin."

"I—"

"Just enjoy it, that's an order."

"Y-Yes, Madre," he said, his voice indicating he wasn't really opposed to the idea.

Derik found himself breathing heavily as he looked into those piercing green eyes. His stomach twisted as he thought about his actions. With trembling fingers, he reached out to pull Tornsin's hands away from his crotch. Through the fabric, he could see the bulge and smell the apple perfume that doused his jeans. Panting, he shifted forward so he was kneeling between the guard's legs.

Looking up, he knew he needed no permission seeing the lust-filled eyes of the guard. With delicate fingers, Derik enjoyed his heart pounding as he worked the buttons open to pull out Tornsin's cock. It was thick but not huge, barely longer than Derik's own shaft. But, he could feel the heat on it, spreading through his fingers as they both breathed as one.

While the enjoyment of cock had only come to him recently, Derik couldn't help but appreciate the soft-clad hardness of the guard's shaft.

Closing his eyes, Derik leaned forward and pressed his lipstick-painted lips against the base, right where the patch of hair dusted his testicles.

Tornsin gave out a long groan of pleasure. His cock jumped in Derik's grip.

Derik moaned softly, kissing down the shaft and leaving tiny red stamps of his lips along the hard member until he could nuzzle along the two tightly-held balls. The smell of man, a real man, filled his senses. His cock surged hard, soaking his thong and inner thighs as he slid his lips up to the top of Tornsin's swollen shaft. Through parted lips, he took Tornsin's head in his lips and slid down it. Every ridge and pulse of heat brought him joy as he lapped at it, sucking on the length until it slid past his tongue and teased the back of his throat. Swallowing, he pushed down until his nose pressed against Tornsin's thatch of hair and his lips wrapped around the throbbing base of the guard's cock.

Derik sneaked one hand down between his legs to stroke his cock through the silk fabric as he pulled the hard cock from his lips. He fisted his own cock before bobbing down on Tornsin's. It wasn't much different than pleasing Teri's fake cock, but there was something about the living hardness that made it more intense. His fingers plunged past the slicked head of his own cock and teased his asshole, circling it as he imagined Tornsin's cock plunging inside.

Moaning, he worked his mouth up and down for the long carriage ride. Neither seem to hurry as they enjoyed the slow, pleasurable building of an orgasm.

Derik came first, soaking his thong as he fingered his ass.

Tornsin came a few minutes later, grunting loudly as he began to come.

Derik swallowed the salty seed flooding his mouth, moaning even louder as he gulped at it. Hot as it dribbled down his throat, the feeling brought another orgasm soaking his thighs. Lost in pleasure, he almost forgot to clean the green-eyed man's shaft, but he left is glistening with only a dark red ring of lipstick around the base. Smiling, Derik lapped at the tip to clean it of the last bit of cum and carefully tucked it back into his pants.

When the carriage came to a halt, they were all sitting back in their position. Derik couldn't look at Tornsin as the guard excused himself practically fleeing the carriage.

Madre finally opened her eyes and sat up. She pretended to yawn before kissing Derik on the cheek. "That was pretty good, girl."

"Madre! What are you doing?"

Madre shifted to the other seat, grinning. "I thought I was cutting through the courting. He was turning you on, and you were turning him on."

"But—"

"But what? Besides, I think it would be healthy for you."

Derik sniffed, feeling the flush burning his cheeks, "But, I l-love the baron."

His heart skipped at those words, but it was the right to say.

Madre smiled at that, then spoke softly. "Yes, and you still need to date someone else."

"Why?"

"For two reasons. One, I said so."

"But—"

"And two, because having a second sexual partner helps you recover from the baron's 'life-sucking cock.'"

Derik froze, mouth open.

Madre chuckled as she stretched again. "Imagine that, Madre knowing what she's doing. Yes, dating has a purpose here. It recharges your energies so the baron doesn't drain your—I'm not sure how to explain this to you—your innermost energies. If you don't date, it takes longer to recover and eventually you'll get hurt or sick."

Only a whimper slipped past his lips. Madre continued as she played with her laces.

"Plus, it doesn't hurt to know what it feels like to have someone not hung like a horse and thinks that coming only three dozen times in a night is 'taking it easy'. The girls tease Tornsin pretty badly, I figured it was time that he got to enjoy a bit more than a hand-job or a flash of tit."

"But, I can't date him!"

"Why not?"

Derik's flush grew hotter, "I'm... I'm..."

Madre leaned and brushed her fingers against Derik's lips. He silenced himself as she held it up, showing a tiny bit of the guard's cum on the tip of her finger. Without asking, she pressed it against his lips and he sucked it clean; below, his cock jumped again at her touch.

"You will always be the baron's girl, and for that to happen, I need you to obey me. The baron talked to me last night and he only had compliments for you. He also expressed interest in having you for the night in his room tomorrow."

Derik coughed and sputtered, but Madre just slowly slid her finger from his lips. Whimpering, Derik shook his head.

"The baron!? I can't, he'll find out!"

Madre cocked her head as she dispassionately spoke. "Maybe, but he's my lord. And if he wants you in his room, then I'm going to tell you to go to his room. Then, it will be up to you to decide if you obey me or leave the harem. Remember my Nightingale, Dora. I don't love you like I still love her. I will throw you on that auction block for the sake of my baron."

The temperature of the carriage grew icy for a moment.

Derik whimpered, then closed his mouth. He shivered for a long moment. "I'm sorry, Madre."

She reached over again to stroke his cheek, smiling softly. "Don't worry, a lot of girls have trouble the first couple of times. He is a very powerful man."

Derik warmed at the thought of the baron's dick inside him, filling him.

Madre chuckled knowingly and slipped out of the carriage. Standing in the door, she peered inside. "Besides, why don't you worry more about your date with Tornsin?"

"But, I can't date him. He'll find out I'm a..."

"Well, my dear Dora, then you better learn how to be the greatest cock-tease this world has known because I say you are dating. And when it comes to you, there is me then the baron. If you don't agree, you can go directly to him."

She walked away, her boots crunching the gravel as she headed into the palace.

Derik sat for a long time, thinking about her words. He considered running away and worked out how to escape in his head. But, the plans fell apart when he realized he couldn't come back. He didn't have a choice anymore, he had to stay.

Carefully, he followed Madre's path into the palace. To his surprise, she was waiting inside the door for him.

Seeing him, she smiled broadly. "I was half afraid you were going to flee."

Derik blushed, "No, Madre."

"And Tornsin?"

"Do I have to?"

"Yes."

He blushed and whimpered softly. "How can I do it?"

She laughed. "What? You want easy answers?"

"Well, yeah, that would be nice for once."

She sighed and looked around.

Derik followed her gaze, seeing no one.

Madre turned back to him, stroking her hands along his bare hands. "No."

He jerked slightly. His jaw opened with his surprise. "What?"

"No, I refuse to give you an easy answer. Figure this one out on your own. Just remember, you are the baron's woman and think about what you have here. You'll make the right choice."

Despair plucked at his heart strings. "You don't make things easy."

Madre shrugged and grinned evilly. "Well, I'm nicer to the girls who don't spank me."

His mouth opened in shock as she smirked. Then, the evil mistress of the harem spun on her heels and headed into the palace.

Soaked

Derik padded down the hallways of the palace with a skip. He smiled to himself as he bounced along the tiles, his slippers tapping lightly as he returned to the harem after delivering a message for Madre. His black silk robe fluttered behind him, contrasting with the sapphire blue silk shorts around his hips and a tank top that clung to his curves—he hadn't had time to put on his thong or bra because Madre was in a hurry. His nipples, still sensitive from Hime's transformation, peeked out through the taut fabric over his breasts.

Outside, the sunlight streamed through the late summer clouds and the smell of the storm that recently passed filled the hallway of the palace with the smell of wet grass and stone.

It was a good day.

He padded around a corner and skidded to a halt. At the far end of the hallway, standing in front of a conference room, he spotted a guard standing in position. The breath caught in his chest as he peered a little closer, then backed up as he realized it was Tornsin.

Blushing and worrying his bottom lip, he spun around to go down another hallway and found himself looking at the broad, powerful chest of the baron.

"Blackbird!"

Derik's heart pounded faster as he looked up at the baron. His palms tightened against the powerful chest, fingers curling to stroke along the cords and ridges. The pulse of the baron, the man he still ached for in his dreams, sent a hammer slamming into his body. The slow breathing of the older man seemed to counterpoint the rapid panting as Derik struggled for air.

His vision blurred as he focused on the baron's face, seeing that single blue gaze piercing into his soul. The baron's form shimmered and twisted for a moment before solidifying into a soft, easy smile.

The baron wrapped his arms around Derik's thin waist, holding his hips tightly with his large hands. "Happy to see me?"

Derik opened his mouth to say something but no words came out, only a squeaking noise.

The baron chuckled and released Derik's hip long enough to hook his finger under the thief's chin and close his mouth. "I like your lipstick."

Derik whimpered, still unable to speak. The pounding in his ears drowned out the words until the rest of the world melted away into darkness and only two people remained.

"Can you speak?"

Trying harder, Derik managed to regain control his vocal cords. "Y-Yes, baron."

"Good, it would be sad to have a mute blackbird. I seem to recall you had a pretty song the last time I enjoyed you."

Derik blushed hotly, his hands trembling against the baron's chest. The baron looked down, breaking the spell he had on Derik's body. Derik gasped and followed the gaze down, staring at his hands pressed against the man's chest. He started to pull them away, but the baron shook his head.

"It's okay. I plan to have more of you pressed against me."

He squeaked again.

The baron laughed, "You do that a lot, don't you?"

"Sorry! Sorry, baron."

"No matter," he smiled broadly and stroked his hand down Derik's chin, tracing the line along his collar and igniting a flame searing down Derik's spine to pool between his legs. His manhood, barely caught between his legs twitched and started to grow, unfolding as it began to tent his shorts.

Frantically, he ducked slightly to press one hand between his legs, forcing his cock back before it could give away his true deception to the most powerful man he knew.

The baron chuckled wryly. "I remember you did that last time also. I make you wet thinking about me?"

Derik whimpered as he looked up, then slowly trailed his eyes down to stare at the growling thickness in the baron's pants.

The baron leaned forward to whisper playfully. "I also seem to recall I rather enjoyed it."

Unable to tear his eyes away from the baron's cock, Derik shook with the memory of it impaling him. His cock twitched even hotter, and pre-cum oozed down his inner thighs.

"Can't speak again?"

Blushing, he looked up, one hand buried between his legs and one pressed against his chest. "Sorry! H-How may I serve you?"

The baron chuckled, "I have this annoying meeting with some bureaucrats and I needed a little pick-me-up."

"Baron?"

His hand raised up to take Derik's hand from his chest. Derik's heart surged for a moment, then he moaned as the baron drew it down to his crotch, pressing his palm tightly against the throbbing mass buried in his pants.

Derik needed no other command as he pulled his other hand up, discretely wiping the moisture on his robe, before working his fingers on the baron's imprisoned cock.

He moaned loudly as he freed the thick hardness, his lips parting with a hunger that redoubled with every heartbeat he stared at it. It was hot and hard, silk over steel. The shaft dominated him, and he almost came with the thought of it once again burying itself in his ass. His cock jerked once, and luckily, he didn't come at the thought of it. Instead, he drew it up to his body. His mouth parted around the head, working it into his mouth until the baron's breath quickened with pleasure.

"Oh, that is exactly what I had in mind."

Derik stroked down the shaft to ease out the huge balls. His fingers stroking and rolling it in his palms, feeling how they twitched with the heavy seed churning inside. He gasped and mouthed the rounded end, sucking on the flood of juices pouring out of it.

The baron was strong. It vibrated through every iota of the man and Derik breathed in the scent of his strength and masculinity.

Muscles flexed as the baron turned Derik up against the wall, hands cupping his naked breasts with his fingers. The size of the man meant that Derik's lips never left the throbbing cock. Powerful digits teased his sensitive nipples, pinching them until Derik writhed with the storm of pleasure and pain.

As Derik mouthed and lapped at the massive member, the baron slid his top up to reveal his rounded breasts. The cool air and powerful fingers against his tits was intense, and he drew the baron's shaft into the valley between them. The baron sighed with pleasure and Derik took it as approval as he squeezed his breasts around the slicked, iron-hard member.

Derik's eyes lifted up as he bobbed his body up and down, using the wall for balance, and stared up into the baron's eye. The feelings of pleasure grew with the silken hardness sliding up and down, the ridges of the baron's shaft against the inner skin of his breasts ignited the flames deep between his thighs. Unable to pull his hands away, he whimpered as his own length tented the silk shorts as he bobbed faster and harder. Grinding down, he squeezed his own nipples and pumped the baron's cock until the shaft surged with heat and desire.

They came together: Derik soaking his silk shorts and the baron's cum spraying against Derik's chin and chest, overflowing the valley of his breasts and pouring down his front. Searing hot and liquid, it soaked him as the baron let out a long, satisfied moan.

Derik, panting hard, released the throbbing shaft from his body and quickly planted one hand on his crotch to push his cock back into place. Cum oozed down, splattering wetly on the tile as he looked up at the baron. It only took a second for a large puddle to form underneath him.

The older man nodded in approval, then lifted one hand to cup Derik's chin. Bringing his gaze into Derik, the thief found himself once again caught in the blue stare, losing himself with the intensity of it. The baron stroked a thumb through the slick edge of Derik's chin. "Always pleasurable, Blackbird."

Derik moaned, his hips rocking slightly as he stood there. His heart crashed loudly against his ribs. "T-Thank you, baron."

"I think..." He paused. "Sadly, I need to go to a meeting. But, tonight, I want to see a pretty kitty, my princess, and my little blackbird on my bed."

Even as he wanted to crawl into a shadow, his mouth moved without thinking. "O-Of course, my lord."

"Good. Because," he smiled as his finger trailed down the side of his cum-soaked breast and tweak the dripping nipple, "I can't wait to see you spread out naked on my blankets. I have a lot of plans for tonight."

Derik nearly fainted at that very moment.

The baron chuckled and reached down to brush his lips against Derik's.

At his first kiss from a man, Derik's knees grew weak from the electric surge that coursed between them.

Hamel drew him close, and he squeaked as he used his hand to shield his manhood from grinding on the baron's leg as the kiss deepened.

When the baron's tongue pressed against his lips, Derik moaned hungrily and accepted the baron inside his mouth. His body surged hotly and cum splattered into his palm. It splattered to the ground along with the rivers that poured down his thighs.

The baron held him close, kissing hard and powerful until Derik could no longer breath.

Then, the kiss broke and Derik swayed as he watched the baron turn on his heels and walk down the hall. Derik reached out for the wall, but slipped as his knees collapsed and he sank to the ground, splattering in the puddle of cum from the baron's orgasm.

It hurt to breath from the tightness in his chest. Derik pressed one dripping hand against his chest, feeling how his heart pounded under the skin and his breath came out shuddering.

When the baron walked out of sight, tucking his immense cock back into his pants, Derik regained control of his body and he slumped forward. "Oh, fuck."

He remained there, soaking in the baron's seed, until boots stopped in front of him. Derik shivered as he looked up to see Tornsin holding out a towel. There was a strange look on Tornsin's face.

Blushing hotly, Derik gratefully took it and used it to pat at the cum that soaked his entire front. He couldn't look up at the piercing green eyes as he sopped up as much as he could, thankful the baron's orgasm overwhelmed his own juices dribbling down his thighs.

Even though he took as long as possible, he ran out of cum to towel off. Finally, he sighed and looked up.

Tornsin held out his hand.

Trembling, Derik accepted it and let the young guard help him into standing position.

Derik shivered, looking away. "S-Sorry."

"The baron always does that."

Derik gulped and glanced over at Tornsin, feeling a blush growing again. "What?"

"Comes all over his girls. The maids really hate cleaning it up. It's even worse for his nights, practically a lake in his room. You can smell it from the great hall on his 'good' days. It was worse before they put in a drain under his bed."

Derik giggled with the thought, then pulled the robe tighter around his breasts to hide the embarrassment at how the fabric clung to his breasts and curves. He knew the dripping cum only highlighted his new features. When he looked up, he saw Tornsin's eyes following his gaze and a slight smile on the guard's lips.

"Come, I'll walk you back to the harem."

"Thank you."

The guard didn't release Derik's hand, and the thief didn't want to pull away. Together, they walked down the hall toward the harem. He didn't say anything, half afraid that—

"Are you avoiding me, Dora?"

Derik stumbled.

"Um, no, no, I'm..." his eyes caught sight of the piercing green gaze, "I'm sorry, Tornsin."

"Why?"

"I..." he stumbled over the words, "I... don't know."

"Do you like me? Like Madre said?"

Searing hot, his cheeks reminded him of his embarrassment. "I love the baron."

"But that isn't what I asked."

Derik stopped, looking at Tornsin.

The guard shrugged, but there was a hint of sadness in his green eyes. "I've been a guard for the harem most of my life, since I was fifteen. I don't have anything beyond the baron, and my mother of course, and I... I would be willing to share, you know. I-I've never really been interested in any of the girls before, but there is something about you. Madre was right, I was asking about you, and I do, um, fancy you."

Derik's lips parted with surprise.

Tornsin laughed nervously. "And now, I feel foolish. But, there is something about you that I find attractive. I don't know why, but when I first saw you standing outside the harem, it felt like you were special."

Swallowing hard, Derik just wrapped his fingers tighter around Tornsin's. He stumbled over the words, trying to fight past a fluttering in his stomach. "I'm just confused, Tornsin. I don't understand all... of Madre's... rules and stuff. This dating and the baron, I'm not sure this is right for me. I-I'm just so confused."

"I see."

Tornsin's fingers slipped from Derik's, and the thief fought back a strange and sudden sob from an intense feeling of rejection. He let his hand trail back to his side as they walked down the hall, no longer touching. At the entrance of the harem, they stopped.

Derik looked around, feeling like the world focused on him, before speaking. "Well, thank you. This is, um, my place."

Tornsin bowed curtly and turned away.

Derik watched as Tornsin walked down the hall and disappeared around a corner. He worried his bottom lip for moment then grunted with frustration, "Well, fuck."

Choices

"Madre!"

Her door slammed open as Derik rushed inside. Madre looked up from her desk, surprised but she didn't look like she even jerked with his cry. One eyebrow quirked up as she lifted her pen. "Dora?"

He froze, the words faltering on his lips. His eyes slid across the room to her bed, where Teri writhed on the blankets, naked and blindfolded. Her skin shimmered with sweat as she arched her back, fighting with the cuffs that bound her wrists behind her back. He could hear one of Madre's dildos humming between her legs as the slender woman gasped around a ball-gag.

"The, um, sorry, I didn't mean to burst... in...."

"But you did."

Blushing, his eyes couldn't move away from Teri's sweat-slicked skin. "I..."

"Spit it out or you'll be joining her," said Madre with a hint of annoyance.

"Oh, the baron asked me to join him tonight, with Teri and Sher-rel."

Madre cocked her head. "So?"

"W-What do you mean? I can't go up there."

She stood up smoothly and came around her desk. "What's the problem?"

"What's the problem!? I'm a guy! The baron is going to lynch me if I show up."

Madre stopped in front of him, trailing her fingers to part his robe, exposing the cum-plastered clothes on his body. She clicked her tongue. "I see he was in a good mood."

"Oh, I," he blushed hotly, "he was."

She chuckled and ran her finger along the bottom hem of his top, pushing it up to expose one glistening nipple. She traced her fingernail along the tip and it crinkled with a little spark of pleasure. "And the problem?"

He fought back a moan before he managed to speak. "W-What do I do?"

Madre's eyes looked up. "You choose."

"What? Choose what?"

The battle mage gestured to the door.

"Dora," she sighed, "Derik, you are now at that point you've been rushing into ever since you fell into this harem."

He whimpered, but she kept speaking.

"You have two choices: either you join the girls in the baron's room tonight, or you flee."

"B-But, I don't want to go."

She smiled, motherly and compassionate, "I know, but this is the point where that is finally put to the test. How much? What would you give up to remain here?"

"H-He'll have me arrested."

"Do you know that?"

Derik sniffed, wiping tears from his eyes. "No."

"And do you trust me?"

"Y-Yeah, I guess?"

Her voice grew icy, "You guess?"

Derik blushed, "I trust you, Madre."

She smiled, "Then, go to the baron. Do what you think is right, but be honest when it comes down to it."

"He won't hurt me?"

"I can't promise that. But, I can promise you this: if you lie to him or if you flee, this harem will never be your home again."

Derik shivered with the thought. "I don't want to go. I like it here. You are also so... wonderful."

"I know, and I trust you to make the right decision."

The world spun around Derik as he nodded. He tried to breathe in deeply, but couldn't. There were only hours before his life changed for an unknown that he couldn't even comprehend.

Madre searched his face for a long moment, then she tweaked his nipple, causing him to jump from the explosion of pleasure that burst in his manhood. "Come on, you have plenty of hours to worry about that. I'll give you up to the moment we leave for his room; I'll walk you up today. Until then, would you like to help me play with Teri?"

He gulped at the thought of being presented to the baron, but his cock twitched at the thought of enjoying Teri. He grinned sheepishly.

"What did she do?"

"Nothing, I just think she needed a good orgasm. I was about to stuff her pussy with my strap-on with the hummer in her butt, but I bet she would really love you to fill her up instead. Interested?"

He moaned at the thought.

Madre grinned happily and gestured to her bed.

Derik flung his clothes to the ground as he stripped naked, his body still glistening from the baron.

Madre padded before him, rolling Teri on her back as the slender girl writhed with pleasure. Her stretched lips drooled on both sides of the gag, soaking her face as she blindly wiggled in place. He stopped at the edge of the bed, staring at the splayed open lips, dripping with her excitement, and the fragrance in the air.

"Go on, just have fun. Tease her good and proper."

His cock bobbed in the air as he slipped out of his slippers, crawling on the bed. Moving his head around, he knelt between her legs and brought his mouth down against her heated sex, giving it one lick from asshole to clitoris.

Teri jumped, moaning loudly as her legs clenched together.

Madre caught them, pulling them to the edge and hooking a loop around her ankles to keep her spread open.

Derik grinned and lapped again, tracing her folds with the tip of his tongue as he found her opening and slurped at it. She tasted excited, he thought, and he dove into her cunt, slurping and lapping until she screamed out with the need to come. He pulled back as she started to buck with a growing orgasm. Ignoring her whimpers, he waited for her to calm down.

As soon as her hips lowered to the soaked blankets, he lapped at her again, then held back. Teasing, he worked her up until her juices frothed on her lips, her begging clearly heard around the sphere in her mouth, and her body arched desperately for release.

He added one finger, then a second, to pump in and out of her clenching tunnel and applied his lips to her clitoris, sucking and nibbling on it as her moans turned into hungry screams for release. Grinning, he added a third finger, but slid it into her lubricated asshole and stroked all three into her two holes with the effort to bring her to the edge of orgasm before pulling away.

Finally, his own needs forced him to change, and he knelt higher up and aimed the swollen length of his member toward her hungry pussy. Without giving a second moment, he drove it into her, plunging to the very hilt in a single thrust.

The sound of their skins slapping rang out clearing in the room, then Teri's scream as she orgasmed and nearly ripped her legs from the bed. He grinned and pumped into her, riding the waves of her passion as he enjoyed the liquid velvet feel of her pussy spasming around him, milking his cock. He quickly found the crest of his own pleasure and started to pump harder and faster.

Then, Madre stopped him with a hand on his back.

He froze, cock half buried in Teri's pussy, and looked at her. At the sight of her strap-on, his eyes widened.

"Didn't say I wasn't going to fuck something," she said with a grin. "Interested?"

Derik answered by spreading his legs apart. His knees slid under Teri's as he opened up his own ass, preparing to accept the thick intruder in his own body. As Madre crawled on the bed, he moaned and plastered himself against Teri's writhing form, focusing on the feel of Madre aiming the lubricated cock up against his ass and easing it inside.

He let out a long moan from having his ass filled. His cock twitched in the slick vice of Teri's pussy.

Fully impaled, Madre began to pump into him. As she drove forward, he ground deep into Teri's pussy. When Madre pulled out, Derik slid out until only the ridge of his cock remained inside Teri.

As one, he became Madre's cock as Madre fucked Teri. He mirrored every movement of the thick dildo with his own shaft. The submission fueled his lust and soon he gasped out with a growing orgasm.

She pumped harder, fucking him until he came hotly inside Teri and soaked her pussy with his seed.

Panting, he remained inside her as Madre grabbed his hair, forcing him to arch his back, and redoubled her speed to fuck him hard and fast, plunging in and out. The vibrations of his body transmitted into Teri and she came hard around his throbbing shaft.

A few minutes later, Madre reached her own orgasm and she slowed down for all three of them to enjoy it.

Panting, Madre slipped out. "Just have fun," she said before turning to her desk with a smile.

Derik grinned and reached up to remove Teri's gag and blindfold. Her eyes took a second to focus, then she smiled.

"Slut."

He responded with a smile, "Bitch."

She squeezed down on her inner muscles, massaging his length. "That was very powerful."

"Madre helped."

"Oh?"

"Strap-on."

Teri cooed, "Oh, double fucked and I didn't get to see it."

"You want to?"

She seemed surprised as she worked her wrists in her cuffs. "What?"

"The baron wants you, me, and Sherrel tonight. I, um, there is a chance you'll get to see it."

Her body shuddered with desire.

He also shivered with anticipation, the same lust grew inside him.

She gaped for a moment. "And you are going?"

"I... yes."

"Why?"

"I trust Madre."

Her eyes glanced over to Madre who nodded.

Teri looked back, then leaned up to kiss Derik on the lips. "And then I will be there. I'm looking forward to seeing the baron ream you out again."

She giggled.

He kissed her again, then they just touched and talked and kissed before fucking again and going back to cuddling.

They were lost in touching each other's bodies when Madre interrupted them by clearing her throat.

Derik looked up with a grin.

"Why don't you release her and get cleaned up. Get pretty for the baron and help Dora with her dress."

"Yes, Madre."

The next two hours spun past as the three had fun dressing, putting on makeup and perfume. By the time early evening darkened the horizon, they were standing in their best dress.

Teri had a white dress that clung to every curve and showed off the dark shadows of her nipples. It wrapped around in a complicated pattern that would come off with a single tug of the bow right above her naval. Her white stockings rode up to her hips, but she wore nothing between them but a dab of perfume.

Next to her, Sherrel had a stunning red dress that supported her amazing breasts and left her belly bare. Through the deep slit up the front and back, he could see her thong that nestled in the folds of her sex.

Together, they were absolutely stunning. The cheers and compliments of the rest of the harem left a blush on his cheeks and a feeling of pride that swelled his heart. He danced back and forth until Madre came to them, then forced himself to calm down as she admired them.

"My three lovely ladies. The baron is never going to forget tonight."

"Yeah, when he finds boy cock in his bed," smirked Teri.

Derik blushed hotly.

Madre leveled a glare at Teri. "And when he does, I expect you two to make sure it is the best cock he's every enjoyed."

"Yes, Madre," said both Teri and Sherrel.

Madre padded over to Derik who was finding it hard to breathe. "Ready?"

"Y-Yes, Madre."

"You'll be fine."

"I'm scared."

She smiled and stroked a strand of his hair. "I know, but just trust me. The baron is going to love you."

Derik sighed, "I'm still frightened."

"You'll be wonderful. You will all be wonderful—"

Madre's words were interrupted when the baron spoke from the hallway in his deep, booming voice. "I already think so."

Derik stumbled backwards at the sound of his voice, but quickly found his balance. Blushing hotly, he stared at the hallway as the baron stepped out of the shadows. He wore a military uniform and the sight of it took Derik's breath away.

Surprised, Madre turned to him. "My lord! I wasn't expecting you!"

The baron entered the room, filling it with his presence. He stopped in front of Madre and took her hands. "I was called away at the last minute, my dear, and unfortunately my night of passion will have to be postponed."

Derik let out a sigh of relief, feeling the executioner's blade passing but somehow wishing that the deception would finally past.

Madre sounded disappointed as she spoke. "I'm sorry, is it serious?"

"One of the outlying villages needs me. They have some information I've been looking for. I shouldn't be gone for more than three days or so, but when I get back, we'll resume this."

"Yes, my lord, I know you were looking forward to tonight."

He smiled and then sighed, "I have been too. I couldn't wait to try all of Blackbird's holes in one night."

The baron kissed her warmly, almost passionately, then walked over to Teri. He gave her and Sherrel a kiss. When he came up to Derik, the thief's chest fluttered in his presence. He moaned as he melted into the baron's arms, parting his lips as the baron kissed him powerfully. His cock, safely caught in the black thong, surged with heat as the pleasure coursed through him.

When the baron released him, he panted for breath and fought with the flutters in his stomach. He fanned himself and giggled at the look Teri gave him.

Together, they shared a smile.

Which faded instantly when the baron stepped aside and Derik noticed someone standing behind him.

Rick Thrantas.

Joy turned to acid in his stomach as he froze. The wide smile on Rick's face betrayed all emotion as the king of the underground stared fixedly at Derik. Without acknowledging him, Rick slowly turned away from Derik and he beamed at the baron. "Thank you, old friend."

The baron, seeing him, chuckled. "Sorry, Rick, about tonight, but love and lust take second place to certain obligations."

Hamel turned to Madre who stared at Rick with surprise, "Madre?"

She focused on the baron. "Yes?"

"Rick asked if he could borrow one of the girls while I was gone. Make sure he has everything he wants."

Madre looked worried as she glanced over at Derik, then at the baron. "Of course, my lord."

The baron and Rick spoke as they left the hallway, leaving the others alone.

Derik backed up, swearing. "Oh, fuck, oh, fuck, oh fuck."

The acid burn in his stomach just grew as Madre came over to him. Behind him, both Teri and Sherrel looked confused as they gathered closer.

Madre held out her hand. "I didn't know, Dora. I swear, I didn't know."

"I-I-I got to get out of here," he whimpered as he looked around.

From the shadows, Rick's voice carried out with an evil chuckle.

"Going somewhere, Derik?"

Derik's heart nearly leaped into his throat as he stared wide-eyed at the shadows. The boss of the underworld stepped out with a cruel smile and nodded toward Madre, but his eyes never left Derik. "Don't worry about presenting the girls, Madre, I already know which one I want."

Derk whimpered in fear.

Madre stepped in front of Derik as she scowled. "Master Thrantas."

Her voice was black ice as she stood between them. On the very edge of his vision, Derik could see curls of power rising up from her short form, of arcane spells filling her frame.

Rick just nodded curly, his eyes finally breaking away from Derik's to stare fixedly at her. A fake smile lit up on his face. "Madre, good to see you again."

She spoke sardonically, "Really? Because I'm not really feeling it right now."

Rick grunted and his smile faded. "I can imagine why. A lot of drama in this last month or so. And I see you have a new..." He paused to smile with relish and Derik cringed, "...girl."

"Yes, my ward. Not yours."

He chuckled, "I seem to recall Hamel just saying I could enjoy any one I want."

The muscles in Madre's jaw tightened. "Not her."

"Really? What makes him special?"

"You damn well know why."

His eyes roamed over Derik who hugged himself tightly, feeling naked and exposed. Only Teri and Sherrel stood next to him, their arms wrapped around Derik, but he couldn't escape. In his mind, he already planned how to flee the pillar.

Rick slowly focused his gaze on Madre and chuckled dryly. "Isn't he the baron's girl?"

Madre's eyes flashed with anger, but she closed her mouth with a snap.

Triumphant, Rick walked around her to stand in front of Derik. He reached out for him and Derik stepped back, his heart pounding as strongly as the twisting in his stomach. "Don't worry, Derik... excuse me, Dora. We are just going to have a nice three days together. Just to get to know each other again, don't you think?"

Everything inside Derik screamed out in fear as he stepped back.

Madre spoke up. "Don't do this, Rick."

"Do what? It's my right. Hamel gave him to me."

"Don't take Dora."

Rick turned on Derik, glaring back at Madre. "Does he know? Does Hamel know that he's got a little dick in his harem?"

When Madre didn't answer, he chuckled again. "He doesn't, does he? Why don't we tell him? Why don't just the three of us go catch up with him and we'll have a long talk about why his little pussy boy shouldn't go home with me?"

His words didn't frighten Derik as much as the evil, triumphant tone of a man who had Madre pinned to a wall. Derik shivered at the thought, terrified to even move.

Rich gestured to the hall. "Go on, let's see how the baron handles this."

Madre's eyes slid away from Rick to look at Derik. He could see the frustration, compassion, and the storm that tore her up from the inside.

"Dora?"

Derik's heart pounded but he forced himself to step forward, his heels rapping against the ground. Fear burned inside him and it took all his effort not to bolt for freedom.

"Y-Yes, Madre?"

Her eyes bore into him, then she sighed before glaring back up at Rick. "I guess you have another choice to make."

"A-A choice? I made one."

She smiled sweetly, but her eyes never left Rick's.

The crime lord focused on her gaze as their personalities rose up against each other.

"Yes, and no matter what happens, I'm very proud of you for that. But this is the other one, the one I talked about in the hallway before Hime."

Derik hesitated. Then, he remembered her conversation, the promise she made to stand up to Rick. Slowly, his hand pressed against his pounding heart.

Without looking at him, Madre nodded. "That one."

"Madre..." it came off as a terrified whisper.

She turned to face him. "Your choice."

Rick looked back and forth between Madre and Derik, a slow grin stretching across his face. "Mask of Shadows! You mean you told her?"

Derik cringed.

He roared with laughter. "Why kind of fucked-up thief are you?"

Derik squeaked as the entire room erupted in ripples of gasps and whispers. His face turned red as he looked away from everyone as shame burned on his cheeks. He couldn't bare to look at Teri and Sherrel more than anyone else.

Rick's laughter boomed off the walls as he slapped his thigh. "Oh, this is rich! Did you actually tell her what you were going to steal before you decided to become the baron's girl?"

Derik shook his head, still unable to match anyone's eyes.

Rich roared again. "Oh! Should I tell them, Derik? Silk Spider?"

In the sudden silence of the room, Derik's stomach lurched. He shook his head, a tear rolling down his cheek. "No."

He laughed loudly, "Maybe I should tell her anyways, just to see that betrayal in Madre's eyes. I bet you kept that a secret, didn't you?"

Derik's shoulders shook as he closed his eyes tightly. Tears on his cheeks, he shook his head.

When Madre's voice cut through the air, he froze. "If you do, then I promise we will be having that talk with the baron."

Rick jumped and Derik's head snapped up with shock.

He stared at Madre who glared at Rick. Her eyes were glowing and the air wavered around her. Cracks formed in the tiles below her feet as she ground her teeth together.

The larger man cleared his throat. "W-What?"

"If you tell me, or anyone else in this room, his secret, then you will never touch a finger on him."

He shook his head in slow surprise. "You don't know what he was here for?"

"I don't care if he was trying to steal the baron's balls, but that is Dora's secret to tell. If it comes out of your lips, you will not lay one finger on her. I made a promise and I don't break them."

The air grew icy and small snowflakes appeared around her, dancing in the waves of sudden cold of her aura. Her eyes flashed with anger as she stared at Rick.

He glared back at her.

Both of them held as the air grew tenser by the second.

Derik swallowed and glanced around; Sherrel had a profoundly hurt expression on her face but Teri just stared at him with slack-jaw surprise. He blushed and spoke in a whisper. "I'm sorry."

Before either could respond, he stepped forward. As one, Rick and Madre turned to face him. He blushed hotly, feeling the corset around his chest squeezing the life out of him. Taking a long deep breath, he struggled with the consequences of his confession or three days with Rick. It came fast when he balanced the two. Three days of pain verses leaving the harem forever.

He was a coward and took the easy way out.

"M-Madre…"

She looked at him hopefully as he struggled with the words.

"I-I'm sorry."

She glanced at Rick with a confused and worried look on her face, then stepped in front of Derik. Her hand pressed against his heart, feeling his heart slamming into his ribs, crushing his lungs with the fear that coursed through him.

"Dora, are you sure?"

He sniffed and wiped at the tears. "Y-Yes, I am."

She frowned and stared at him. He could see compassion and fear shimmering in her eyes. Fear for him and what would happen.

"It can't be that serious, Dora. Is it?" Madre's voice cracked slightly.

He sniffed, the tears streaming as he nodded. He tried to speak, then closed his eyes as he slumped into her, hugging her tightly, pressing his tears against her shoulder.

Madre held her hand against his chest, feeling his pulse as her other wrapped around his bare back. "Dora, it can't be. No matter what you say, it can't be that bad."

No matter how much he tried to open his mouth, to confess his crime, the words refused to go. Instead, just a sob ripped out of his throat.

She held him for a long moment, then helped him stand again. Sadly, she wiped the tears from his face. "You ruined your mascara."

"I'm sorry."

She sighed, "I wish you'd trust me, Dora."

"I'm an idiot, I know."

She nodded, the tears not quite leaving her eyes and her voice filled with regret. "Yes, you are."

Behind her, Rick chuckled in amusement.

Madre's concern turned to a flash of anger as she snapped around, her hand reaching out to point to Rick at the same time her fingers ignited into flames. "And you, Master Thrantas, you better fucking take care of Dora. If there is one scratch on her body, I will yank off your balls and shove them down your throat."

A repressed anger glowed in Rick's eyes, but he held up his hands with a false smile. "Don't worry, Madre. I'm not going to ruin the good," he almost spat out the word, "friendship I have with your lord and master, Baron Hamel. When Derik leaves my front door, there won't be a single scratch on his body. I'm looking forward to having many more of these days. I know the long game as well as you do."

Madre said something under her breath.

When Rick reached out for Derik, the thief cringed away. Madre took him in arm and headed toward the hallway. "Come, Dora, I won't have him touching you in my harem."

She shot a glare at Rick.

Rick followed, chuckling to himself.

She held him tightly as they walked down the hallways and then out to the front of the palace. As they walked, two and then four of baron's guards joined in.

Rick's carriage, a massive vehicle trimmed in gold and pulled by four black horses, waited in the front as the sky began to rumble with a summer storm. A large thriban, female and wearing skimpy armor, held the door open with a smirk of her own.

Derik shivered with fearful anticipation as Madre stopped by the door.

"Dora, please just tell me."

Derik shook his head, "I-I want to stay."

"And you are willing to do this, just to stay with the baron?"

He sniffed, feeling the tears drying on his face. "Y-Yes, Madre."

She sighed sadly, "Damn you. Rick has you until noon on the third day. If you aren't here by then, I will send someone for you. And remember, it will end."

Derik smiled, still trying to decide if he did the right thing, and kissed her as gently as he could.

She gave him a quick hug, then stepped back.

Rick gestured for the carriage, and Derik did the one thing he never thought he would do willingly since that fateful day in the tavern room.

He got into that carriage.

Rules to Hell

Author's Note: *While I typically don't feel the need to include content warnings on my work, the following three chapters have been called out as being more extreme in term of violence, abuse, and degradation compared to the rest of this story. If you are into it, great. If you aren't, that is also wonderful and I suggest you skip ahead to chapter thirty-seven, titled Kerlis.*

"You owe me a lot of money, Derik."

Rick's voice burned with danger and hatred.

Derik shivered as he sat on the opposite side of the spacious carriage, his hairless legs pressed together and tilted slightly to the side. He struggled to control himself, to remain sitting straight, even as a storm of fear burned brightly inside him. His heels clicked on the wooden floor of the carriage as it rolled down a hill and out of the baron's estates. Part of him wondered if he would ever return.

Slowly, Derik nodded, unwilling to match the deep, dark eyes of the evil man.

"Even if I was generous, which I'm not, that hundred thousand marks was due close to six weeks ago, wasn't it?"

Derik couldn't figure out the math, so he just nodded and tightened his lips. He prayed it was just a bad dream, and he was about to wrap his lips around the baron's cock. The thought of the baron fought with the fear and he swallowed as his body heated up slightly, despite the terror.

The carriage bumped as it crossed into the paved roads of the richer area of town.

Derik fought with his emotions, struggling to contains the tears.

Rick, leaning back on his side, spoke in a hard, powerful voice. "This is no longer about money. It's personal."

Derik's heart skipped as he risked a glance at the scowling man. Rick's eyes were shadows and hidden. His arms, bulky and powerful, wrapped over his chest as he stared at Derik.

The frail man shivered at the sight, unable to tear his eyes away.

"This isn't about that family silver you stole from the Anasai family."

He shivered at the thought, but Rick wasn't even done.

"But if you just gave all that silver to me a year ago, like you were hired to do, you wouldn't be here now, would you? I need leverage on the Anasais and their assassin guild ties but you just had to stick your dick in it."

He didn't continue. Instead, he looked at Derik and waited for an answer.

Derik shook his head, terrified that if he spoke, only sobbing would come out. His body shook with the efforts and he folded his fingers tightly in his lap.

Rick only grunted.

Derik watched as he lifted his hips slightly and leaned forward, changing his position. He closed his eyes, trying to think about anything but where he stood. There was a scuffing sound in the carriage, then something crashed into him.

His world exploded in pain as Rick's fist slammed into his stomach.

Derik's mouth flung open, but no sound came out as he folded in half over the large hand and bent over the heavily muscled forearm.

Rick, who had covered the distance from one seat to the other in a blink, leaned against him, talking into Derik's ear in his dead voice. "Do you know why I told Madre you would have no scratch on you?"

Derik's world continued to ignite in pain as he struggled to catch his breath. His hands flung to his stomach, but the hard fist of Rick just ground down, pinning him even as bile rose up in Derik's throat.

"Because I'm going to have you healed before you leave. The best healers money can buy."

Derik froze, tears of pain burning in his eyes. He tried to breathe, but his lungs refused to work. His feet scratched the floor as he struggled to move his body away from the hard knuckles that continued to grind into his stomach, redoubling the pain as the crime lord spoke in his hard, impassive voice.

"And if you tell Madre, the baron, or anyone else, finds out, do you know what I'm going to do? I'm going to take a quarter million marks and hire the Spiders of Steel, maybe even Falasi Anasai herself, to assassinate you."

The image of Falasi, Wendi's mother, flashed through his mind. He remembered the powerful woman sitting on the altar while yanking his cock into her hot, soaked pussy. He didn't find out she was the mistress of the assassin's guild until after he ran off.

"Oh, you remember her, don't you? Well, I bet a quarter million marks will make her forget that you are a good fuck and you stole her grandmother's silver."

Derik's shoulder sagged, and he folded tighter over Rick's fist, trying to escape the pain that radiated from his insides.

Rick followed him down, his voice deep and rumbling. "I'm going to rape you. Do you know that?"

When Derik didn't answer, he grabbed Derik's long black hair and yanked him back, baring his throat and slamming him against the wall of the carriage. With a twist of strength, he forced Derik to look into his dead blue eyes.

"Do you know that?" he repeated.

Derik's fragile desire not to cry shattered as he tried to breath and wrap his mind around the pain exploding from his stomach and along his scalp. He started to sob with hot tears rolling down his cheeks. Unable to do anything else, he gave a small, terrified nod.

"You really are a fucking idiot. All this because you want to be the baron's bitch? You want to spread your legs for that tree he calls a dick?"

Swallowing, Derik nodded. Hot tears rolled down his cheeks, following the curve of his bared and vulnerable throat.

Rick let out a disgusted snarl and threw Derik against the side of the carriage.

Derik caught himself so only his shoulder slammed up against it, but he cringed at the pain. Released from the grinding fist in his stomach, he curled up, his dress pulling along the seat, as sobs wracked his body.

Rick snarled as he leaned back, glaring at Derik. "You are so fucking pathetic."

They rode in silence. Derik clutched himself, pulling up his knees to his chest. He could feel the air of the carriage teasing his ass, but he fought with his own inner terror to find the energy to pull his dress down.

The carriage bounced violently as they entered the poorest area of town. Derik's heart fluttered at the realization of their destination. They wouldn't be going to Rick's fancy home in the rich area of town. Instead, he was being taken to one of the many safe houses, where Rick took people meant never to see the light of day again.

Rick cracked his knuckles and Derik jumped at the sound of it. When he spoke, it was a deep growl of anger, frustration, and cruelly. "All right, enough whimpering and whining."

Derik started to peek up when he saw Rick reaching out for him. He yelped and tried to curl into a ball, but Rick just grabbed his hair and yanked, pulling him off the padded seat and shoving his face into the floor.

"Rule one. Aw, fuck it, I'm not going to number these. But, if you disobey one, I'm going to hurt you even more."

Derik whimpered, one foot still caught on the seat and the other pinned under his leg.

"First rule, for the next three days, your head will never go above my waist." He spoke in a hard, cruel voice, "That means if I'm standing, you are kneeling. If I'm sitting, you are on the ground. If I'm laying down, you better be under me. Do you understand?"

Derik started to nod but Rick slammed his head again on the bottom.

"Second rule, no more of this timid little nodding crap. You aren't a fucking noble lady, you are nothing but a thieving whore! You say, 'Yes, master' or 'No, master.'" If I can't hear you, I'm going to assume you aren't answering. If I don't hear 'master', you haven't answered. If I hear my name, you didn't answer. Got it?"

Derik sobbed and tried to get to his feet. Rick snarled, and Derik wailed quickly. "Y-Yes, master!"

Rick's hand barely lifted off his head, giving him a bit of breathing room.

Derik panted, whimpering at the pain that cataloged itself across his body. He curled up his feet, one shoe slipping off as he did so.

"Third rule... damn it, I'm numbering. Fine, third rule. If you hesitate, I will beat you. If I tell you to tear out your own hair, your hands better be bloody and you better be bald! Do you got it?"

Derik looked up at shock, his hand reaching for his hair.

Rick's face darkened. Derik realized he needed to answer, but Rick was already moving. Yanking up Derik's head, he pulled him into position and slapped him hard with his other hand.

Derik let out a scream of pain and held one hand against his burning face. "Yes, master!"

Still holding his hair, Rick leaned down to stare at Derik. "This is no longer about money. This is about making a point. I'm going to make you an example of all the other thieves out there who think they can steal my money and get away with it."

Derik whimpered and tore his eyes away from Rick's angry glare.

Rick grabbed his face, turning it back. "Another rule, you look at my face. You don't look away, you don't look down. If I'm in front of you, I want to see that broken look in your fucking eyes. If you can't handle that, you better be looking at my dick like it is a god. Got it?"

"Y-Yes, master."

He smiled humorlessly, "Good, you do learn."

Derik had to fight the urge to look away. "Yes... master."

Rick released his hair and Derik slumped back to the floor of the carriage.

"On your knees," he commanded.

Mutely, he kept his eyes locked on Rick's face as he curled his aching legs underneath him.

Rick shifted position, moving to sit in front of Derik. Derik, without thinking, looked down to see that Rick's knees were on either side of him, then looked back up as he remembered the rules.

Rick grunted with approval. "Still need some training, whore, don't you?"

He blushed with humiliation, "Y-Yes, master."

Rick leaned forward to smile evilly at Derik. "After three days, you won't. I'm going to teach you how to be a proper slut."

Derik shivered with fear and realized that even being thrown in prison wasn't anything compared to what he was about to experience.

Rick looked out the window for a moment, then brought his gaze back down to Derik.

Derik shivered at the hard look in the nearly black eyes and he clutched himself. His legs tightened as he kept his eyes locked on Rick's.

"You like cock, don't you?"

The question surprised Derik, and he struggled with an answer. When he saw Rick's hand raising, he blurted you an answer. "Yes, master!"

"Do you like it up the ass?"

The memory of the baron's length buried inside him brought a heat to his lips and Derik almost looked away before answering in a whisper. "Yes, master."

The slap came hard, throwing him across the carriage and into the side.

Derik, hand on his cheek, struggled to get back up, then dropped to his knees. Rick motioned him to come closer. As Derik crawled toward him, he reached over to grab the long black braid and yank him back into position.

"Kneel!"

Derik obeyed.

Rick kept his hand holding the braid tightly.

Tears on his cheeks, Derik looked back into his face.

Rick repeated his question. "Do you like having a dick up your ass, whore?"

"Y-Yes, master."

"Do you want my cock in your ass?"

That was an easy one. "No, master."

The blow that came threw him against the back wall and Derik folded from the pain that caught him in the stomach. Whimpering, he struggled back into the kneeling position when Rich pointed at the floor between his legs. He reached down and grabbed the front of Derik's dress, pulling it up until the fabric began to rip.

"Look, fuck hole, the baron might like honesty, but when I ask a question like that, there is only one answer: yes, master. Got it!?"

Derik whimpered loudly, "Y-Yes, master."

"Good. Now, do you want my fucking cock in your ass or not!?"

Rick's hand twisted, tightening the fabric around Derik until the seam gave out, tearing open to expose the black corset below. Derik wailed out his answer. "Yes, master!"

When the hand released his dress, Derik slumped back down to his knees. Hot tears burning on his face, he glanced down to see it torn from throat to crotch and exposing the corset and skin below. At the very edge, he could see the black line of his thong. He sobbed, then forced himself to look up at Rick, to take in those piercing dark eyes that pinned him to the ground.

"Take it out."

Derik's eyes widened.

Rick growled and started to stand up, his hand reaching for Derik's throat.

With a yelp, Derik had to look away from his face to reach down to Rick's crotch; he could already see the hardness that strained the fabric. At the first touch of his manicured fingers, Rick settled back down, watching him.

Soft whimpers vibrated in his throat as Derik worked out the buttons. He could feel the moist heat rising through the fabric as he peeled it open. Underneath, he could smell Rick's musk, a powerful smell that nearly choked him. He trembled as he dug his fingers into the gaping opening of the pants and worked out the throbbing length of meat.

He remembered it from the hotel room, but kneeling before Rick, with it in his hand, memories slammed into Derik. It was huge, nearly twice the length of his own meager length but a third shorter than the baron's. It was hot, iron under silk, and it burned his palms as he wrapped his hands around the length. His manicured fingernails just touched on the other side. At the base, there was a thick brier patch of pubic hair, deep and coarse—Derik couldn't even see the skin at the base.

Up close, he didn't realize that Rick had so many ridges and bumps along his length. Derik shivered at the thought of it being rammed into his being, a shiver of anticipated fear. The shaft swelled out thickly as it pulsed with the heat in his fingers and Derik shook as he brought his eyes to look at the large, flared head of the crime lord's manhood.

"Go on."

Derik jumped, his hand slipping away until Rick snatched his wrist and slapped it back against his cock. Derik's fingers wrapped around the shaft again but his eyes looked up with an unasked question.

"Well, you're a whore. What the fuck do you think a whore should be doing?"

Whimpering at the sound of Rick's voice, Derik closed his eyes and leaned forward.

"Open your fucking eyes!"

His eyes snapped open, his body trembling as he was forced to stare at the hard shaft in his hand. A bit of pre-cum oozed out of the tip and Derik shift his hand to avoid the droplet that ran down his length.

Rick snarled, "Well, get on with it, cock slut."

Shaking, Derik forced himself to take the side of Rick's cock in his mouth. He could feel it hot and slick in his mouth as he kissed the side of it, his hands reaching down to cup his balls. His eyes flickered up to see Rick scowling at him, his hands clenching into fists. Suddenly terrified, he licked harder.

A hand grabbed hair, yanking him away from the hard shaft.

A strange sense of helplessness pierced him; it started a tiny flame of something in his gut.

"Are you dating it?"

"W-What, master?"

A slap, hard and powerful.

Derik tasted blood on his mouth as he forced his eyes to look up at Rick. "N-No, master!"

"Then suck it like a whore!"

As Derik started to frown, trying to figure out what Rick commanded, the more powerful man sighed. His hand snatched his cock and he yanked Derik down toward it. Using both hands, he smeared the pre-cum against Derik's face, then shoved the swollen head right up against his lips. "Suck it like you are being paid by the fucking hour!"

Shame burned on his lips as Rick forced his head between Derik's painted lips, bumping it against his teeth.

At the feeling, Rick snarled with a deep voice. "And if I feel teeth..." He let the sentence hang.

Derik sobbed as humiliation wrapped around his flicker desire. He had to force his mouth open to the insistent cock head.

As soon as his jaw parted, Rick yanked his head down. Terrified, Derik opened his jaw, then gagged as Rick rammed half of his length into his mouth. His jaw screamed out in pain as he flinched from the skin of the dick, terrified to mar it with his teeth. The thick cock head buried itself right at the back of his throat.

Instantly, Derik began to choke. His hands flailed around, trying to pull himself off the thick intruder in his mouth, but Rick just bore down on him, his iron-tight grip preventing Derik from pulling back.

"Oh, we aren't done yet, slut."

Derik screamed out as the pressure on his head increased. Rick's finger dug into the back of his head as the pressure built up in the back of his throat. The cock head ground against his gag reflex and he choked on it but Rick refused to relent.

Grunting, Rick released his cock and slapped his other hand on Derik's head, holding it tightly as he bore down, forcing the thick cock head into the tight ring of the rogue's throat. His scream of pain and shock grew muted as the cock tore into his throat.

He couldn't respond fast enough as Rick's powerful muscles drove the shaft deep into him, ripping down his throat and smashing his nose in the forest of pubic hair at Rick's base.

Derik's world spun around as he flailed, pushing at the thickly muscled legs of Rick, but the more powerful man kept bearing down, forcing the cock deeper into Derik's throat. In a sense of blind panic, Derik realized he couldn't breath and his frantic efforts redoubled.

Rick groaned. "Oh, fuck, yes. That where you belong, on the base of my cock. You always had a face for fucking."

He moaned again as Derik gagged and writhed. His foot kicked out as he tried to pull himself off, but he couldn't find the strength to free himself. A burning seared his lungs. It grew with every passing and with terribly clarity, he could feel Rick's cock growing hotter with every second he struggled to breath.

Just as a ringing sounded in his ears, Rick pulled him off.

His lips stretched as they slid down the ridges of his length, leaving a thick sheen of saliva coating it. He choked and had to force himself not to close his mouth until the thick head slipped out of his lips. Derik took a deep breath, bringing cool air into his lungs. He started another, but Rick suddenly yanked him back on the shaft. He barely got a yelp out before the thick member punched inside, scraping along the back of his throat and driving deep. His nose bent as it was crushed against Rick's hard stomach and all he could see was thick curls of hair on the man's chest.

Shame and humiliation burned brightly, shame at being so easily commanded and humiliation at the growing flame inside him, a terrible feeling of his body responding to this torment.

To his horror, the searing in his lungs started sooner than before, and he began jerking with a desperate need to breath. Rick groaned with pleasure, grinding him down hard on his cock and choking him until finally releasing him. Derik desperately gulped for a single breath of air before Rick slammed him down again, impaling his throat and tearing him more open.

Rick refused to give him respite. His powerful hands yanked him off enough for a single breath of frantic air before slamming him back down, fucking his throat hard and holding it there until the world grew dizzy and his body screamed for air.

Derik sobbed at the taste of blood in his mouth, but his futile attempts to free himself were useless. Rick fucked him brutally, suffocating him with every blow as his cock just grew thicker and harder, ripping his throat open with every brutal thrust.

Soon, even the air he could breath in wasn't enough to stop the searing pain in his lungs. Rick growled as he jammed him down, then started to use his head to skull-fuck himself.

Derik sobbed with the realization he was nothing but a hole to Rick. A throat to rape. And Rick didn't relent. Each thrust crushed Derik's nose and smack the thick hair against his victim's lips. He slammed down again and again, pounding Derik's face into his crotch.

Then, the cock surged inside his mouth and Rick pulled Derik off, leaving the head inside his lips and pumping hot, searing cum into his mouth. Derik started to close his lips, but Rick snapped sharply.

"Don't you fucking swallow."

Shocked, Derik forced his tongue to the back of his throat just as hot jets of seed flooded his cheeks. The taste was strong, powerful, and sharp, but he didn't care spit it out either. Instead, he suffered as Rick came in his mouth, filling him until his cheeks started to puff out.

Panting, Rick smiled fiercely. "When I pull out, it better be clean."

Derik's eyes widened, but he wrapped his lips tightly around Rick's cock. He could feel every ridge and bump as the crime lord pulled out. When the massive member bobbed in front of him, Rick nodded.

"You can be trained."

He stared down at his cock. Mouth still full of cooling sperm, Derik worked the shaft back into Rick's pants and closed it up. He sat back, unsure what to do.

Then he realized something more humiliating than anything else.

He was hard. Trapped in his black thong, he could feel pre-cum soaking his length. Flushing hot, he squeezed his legs together and prayed that he wouldn't be turned on.

Humiliation heated his cheeks as he closed his eyes. When Rick cleared his throat, he opened them, staring up into the evil dark gaze for long minutes. Minutes stretched out even further and Derik had to fight a growing desperation to swallow. He couldn't help tasting it as it imprinted in his senses. His tongue reflexively swirled around it and he shuddered at the feeling of the slimy liquid that filled his mouth.

After twenty long minutes, the carriage finally came to a halt. Derik jerked, then stood up straight. Tears blurred his eyes as Rick glared at him.

"Tilt back and open your mouth."

Shame. Shame caught his lungs as Derik forced his head back, opening his mouth to show the creamy liquid that still filled his mouth. It was cooler and congealed, but the feeling of the slime on his tongue sent disgusted shivers down his spine.

"Now, swallow," came the command.

Derik's shoulder shook as he closed his mouth and swallowed. Sodden mass of cum oozed down his throat, searing along the torn insides and pooling in his stomach. When Rick commanded, he obediently opened his mouth to show it was empty.

Rick grunted as he grabbed Derik's hair again. "Every time I come in your mouth, you don't swallow until I tell you to. I don't care if it is an hour or a day, when you open your mouth, it better be full."

Still sobbing, Derik managed to answer. "Yes, m-master."

"And if anything leaks out of that slutty mouth of yours, I'll put in something far worse than my dick."

"Yes, master," he said through a sob.

Rick reached over and shoved open the door with his foot.

Derik glanced out and froze, terrified by the tower outside the door.

Rumors called it the Tower of the Silent Screams.

A tower that no person had ever left alive.

Rick took people there and turned them into "examples," where they suffered very short, but painful, lives to make a point to everyone else. Above the door, skulls had been mounted to show off Rick's victim. Sixty-three examples. His eyes caught sight of an empty spike near the top, a spot that he knew was reserved for him.

A slap threw him out of the side of the carriage, and he slammed into the gravel outside. The sharp rocks cut at his hands and knees. He opened his eyes to see a long strip of his torn dress fluttering in the wind. From behind him, he heard Rick snarling. "I told you to look at me!"

The gravel shuddered as Rick jumped out, then yanked Derik up by his hair, to stare at the tower with tear streaming down his face.

"Welcome to your home for the next three days."

Derik realized, beyond all doubts, he should have just been honest when he had the chance.

Reaching for the Door

Rick dragged him into the tower, and Derik could barely keep his head below waist level as his bare feet skittered across the gravel. His beautiful dress tore even more. He was dimly aware of the wet air and ground soaking into his skin Rick tossed him through the door. The cabin plunged into darkness as a peal of thunder rumbled through the stone. A moment later, a light flared up as the female thriban, who guarded the carriage, set her burning finger on a torch to light it. Grinning evilly at him, she lit three other torches before snuffing the flame in her palm.

Rick smiled to her before turning his gaze to the huddling Derik on the floor. "You know what, Derik? You are going to be the first person who survives this tower."

Derik forced his eyes to look up, trembling as he clutched at the torn remains of his dress. The stone, cold despite the summer, stung at his ass with only a black thong to protect it.

Rick chuckled dryly. "This time. Because, even if Madre somehow convinces the baron, sooner or later, you'll be back."

Shivering at the thought, Derik forced himself to calm down, fighting the twisting in his stomach and the tears in his eyes.

Rick chuckled at his efforts, then turned to the female. She wore a suit of chain armor that held in her large, watermelon-sized breasts and clung to the wide curves of her hips. He could see just as many muscles as Rick in her bare skin, but there was a sense of pure physical power in her frame as she turned to the crime lord.

"Yes?"

"Anything you want?"

"The corset."

Rick raised an eyebrow, "The corset? Isn't a bit small for you, Truk?"

Truk looked down at her large frame and then at Derik's frail one. She shook her head, "Well, yes, but it has an enchantment on it, I'm curious."

"Well, then."

Rick turned his attention back to Derik. "Strip."

The idea of being naked in front of Rick scared him, but his face still stung from the impact of his blows. Trembling violently, he forced himself to his knees and started to pull off the sapphire dress, stripping down to the black corset and thong. He looked for his heels, but he couldn't find them. Instead, he looked up at Rick as his hands reached behind him to unlace his corset.

Rick rumbled with amusement and backed up against the wall, rubbing his crotch.

A hot blush rose on Derik's cheeks as he worked the final lacing free, then hooked his fingers on the lace cup to pull it down, exposing his breasts to Rick's hungry eyes. Looking up to see a lust burning there brought back the flame inside him; the feelings of humiliation that flared inside Derik warmed his body.

Rick chuckled, still rubbing himself, "You are a slut, aren't you?"

Derik held out the corset for Truk.

She stepped forward and snatched it from his hands.

He winced, then turned his eyes back to Rick.

The crime lord gestured with a finger. "You aren't done."

Still shaking, Derik lifted his hips to work his cock out. It was only semi-hard, but he could see his pre-cum glistening on his length and the feeling of humiliation rose even further.

He wasn't suppose to enjoy this. He wasn't suppose to find any pleasure being being choked on Rick's cock.

At the brief memory of it, the feeling of being helplessly impaled by the hardness, a shiver raced down the length of his cock. It swelled into a heat that burned in his balls. Whimpering, he tore his thoughts away and stared back up at Rick as he slipped off his thong and set it aside.

Rick grunted and turned away from Derik to look at the thriban. "So?"

Her fingers danced over it, tiny sparks of light flowing up from the black corset. "Madre's work."

"Damn, one of her sensors?"

"No, protection. Temporary enhancement, but it could probably turn away a knife."

Rick made a curious noise, then turned back to Derik. He took the two steps forward to stand in front of him.

Derik looked up, shaking with fear, but said nothing.

"Madre really cares for you, doesn't she?"

"Y-Yes, master," came the frightened response.

Rick reached down to grab his hair, pulling it up until Derik was forced to raise up on his knees, his head barely below Rick's belt. The powerful man turned him away, forcing him to look at a rust-stained door. "See that door?"

"Yes, master."

Derik saw blood stains along the bottom edge, and fingernail scratches on the frame. "That's the slaughter room. If you go through that door, you will never come back."

He let out a sob before he could control himself.

Rick twisted him back to face him, holding his head to force him to look up. "We are going to start at the top. I was hoping for a week or more, but the baron is in a hurry to find those rumors about that curse of his. So, I don't have much time to properly enjoy you, so call this a preview of what I'm going to do next time I get to borrow you."

Derik said nothing, just kept his eyes locked on Rick's.

After a few seconds, the man dropped him back to his knees. "Go upstairs."

Looking around, Derik saw stone stairs going up. He started to stand, but Rick slapped him across the room.

"You don't need feet. Crawl!"

Fighting the stinging pain that coursed through him, he crawled along the ground, naked and helpless. Knowing Rick watched him did nothing to help the spark burning inside him. At the bottom of the stairs, he looked up and began to crawl up the stairs, hooking his feet on the edge. He made it five steps before Rick shoved him hard against the stone.

"Don't go above my waist," he warned.

Derik whimpered and looked around, seeing how Rick grinned as he stood a few steps below. He turned back, then whimpered loudly as he tried to figure out how to get up the stairs.

Finally, he plastered himself hard against the edge and crawled up, almost slithered. His nipples and cock bumped against the harsh stone as he inched up the stairs.

Rick followed, giving him orders and calling him a whore or slut.

It took him nearly twenty minutes to climb the three stories, scraping his stomach, breasts, and manhood against the stone until he finally spotted the top. His body shook with the effort to remain low and flat, but it was the burning humiliation that hurt more than anything else. His manhood never softened at Rick's words.

"Mask of Shadows, you are a fucking slut. I bet you'd get off on this, wouldn't you?"

Derik swallowed, "No, master."

"Really?"

Hands jammed between his legs, pulling them painfully part before they grabbed his cock.

Rick grunted, then squeezed hard on his balls until Derik let out a scream of agony.

"Don't lie to me, whore."

Derik sobbed and slumped against the hard, stone stairs. They scraped at his knees and hands, but he still sopped to reach one shaking hand back to feel his cock.

He tried to close his legs tightly, but Rick's hand shoved back between his legs. His four fingers ground against Derik's balls and manhood while the thumb pressed against his asshole. Derik shivered, freezing in place as the thick digit pressed down.

Rick leaned forward to growl at him. "What is getting you off? Crawling on the floor like a bitch or the idea of me beating you? Or fact I'm going to rape you for three days?"

Derik couldn't answer it, but he yelped as Rick pushed the thick thumb into his anal ring, forcing it open as he squeezed him tightly.

"I asked a question."

"No... master."

Rick jammed his entire thumb into Derik's ass, and the thief's cock surged to full height in a single instant. Heat burned inside him as the thick digit plunged into him.

Rick stopped just past the second knuckle.

Derik whimpered at the feeling, both of being filled from behind but his cock oozing pre-cum into Rick's hand.

"You are fucking lying, whore. You want your ass stuffed so badly, don't you?"

Derik started to answer, but Rick jammed his thumb in deeper and tightened his fingers around Derik's balls. "Don't you!?"

Letting out a sob, Derik nodded frantically, "Yes, master!"

Rick shoved his thumb hard in between his cheeks, fucking him with hard, brutal strokes that were almost punching, would have been punishing if not for his training in the harem.

Derik was shoved against the stairs. He braced himself with his hands and held himself still, fighting the feelings both pleasurable and shameful. His cock continued to grow hotter, leaking as Rick pumped his ass with just a thumb. A thick, powerful thumb.

"Beg for it."

"M-Master?"

"Beg for my fucking dick, you fucking cunt!"

Derik sobbed as he leaned against the stone, feeling how Rick's humiliating words brought a disgusting desire to the fore, a hunger for submission that the harem had brought out was now being used against him. His cock, hot and hard, ground against Rick's fingers. "F-Fuck me, master."

"What?" came the hard reply and another hard thrust.

Derik swallowed, the shame on his cheeks as he begged for something he never wanted. "Please fuck me. Fuck my ass. F-fuck your whore."

The thumb that drove into him pounded in a bit softer as Derik spoke. His breath came hard as he growled. "Louder! Scream it. I want Truk and everyone else in this tower to hear it. I want the whole neighborhood to hear you!"

Derik tried to gain the courage, but he took too long and Rick reached out with his other hand to grab his hair. A bolt of pleasure and pain coursed through his spine, pooling in his balls and tightening his asshole around the plunging finger.

Rick snarled, but just pulled harder. "Fucking beg for it!" His voice echoed off the stone walls.

Derik sobbed but he screamed out. "Fuck me! Fuck me master! Fuck me so hard I scream, fuck me until I come, fuck—"

He kept on crying out, begging for it blindly. Every scream caused his breasts to grind against the stone. Every word that escaped his throat seemed another nail in the coffin of his pride. Every thrust of the thick thumb into his guts reminded him of the pleasures his body hungered for.

Rick grunted. His thumb yanked out of his ass and Derik let out another sob. The hand wrapped around his hair didn't relent and he was forced to arch his back to keep the pressure.

Then, he heard Rick clear his throat and spit; a hot glob of saliva splattering against his tail bone and oozing down the crevice of his cheeks. As it dripped against his clenching asshole, the thick swollen head of Rick's manhood pressed into it and lodged itself right at the entrance of Derik's rectum.

Derik stumbled with his litany of begging, then let out a scream of surprise, shock, and pain as Rick drove his cock into him. The hard, ridged length plunged deep into Derik's ass with only a bit of spit for lubrication. Before his body could catalog the pain, Rick bottomed out with his large balls crashing against Derik's smaller ones.

Rick held it there, just as he held the entire length of his cock in Derik's throat.

To his surprise, Derik was choking again, this time from the explosion of nerves that screamed out in shock, a storm of pleasure at being penetrated mixed with the brutal pain of the brutal thrust filling him. He sobbed and plastered his face against the stone, his shoulders shaking as Rick pulled back on his hair and ground deeper.

The hot pole of the crime lord's cock vibrated deep inside him for a moment before Rick yanked it out. The cock head burst out of Derik's asshole with a popping sound and Derik slumped forward.

"Please stop—"

His word froze as Rick slammed into him again, forcing his swollen head into the tight ring of Derik's being and driving deep until his balls once again slammed into Derik. The slender thief's voice cracked as he wailed, helpless to stop as Rick grabbed his shoulder with one hand and tightened his grip on the long braid. With powerful muscles, he yanked himself completely out with a slurping noise. After only a half a heartbeat, barely a chance to inhale a single breath, Rick impaled him again, ripping open the tight ring and slamming deep.

Derik's shoulders shook violently as Rick began to assault him, punching his cock with brutal thrusts that ground the hardness deep inside him and pulled all the way out, stretching open the tight ring until it was no longer a barrier to the thick member that dominated him.

Hard strokes jammed into his inner organs, filling his depths with hard length. As the stroking grew faster and stronger, slamming Derik against the stone with every thrust of Rick's powerful hips, Derik lost more of himself in lust. Pre-cum dripped loudly against the stone underneath him. He wanted to stroke himself, and then he sobbed with the realization that he got even a small amount out of pleasure from Rick's rape.

He silently prayed that it would end soon, but the massive member kept plunging into him, stretching him open and leaving the opening of his being gaping, would remain until Rick found his orgasm.

After many long minutes, Rick came, and hot jets of sperm flooded Derik's burning insides. Rick bellowed out with rage and lust, yanking back on Derik's hair as he forced the thief to bend backwards.

Derik's shoulder blades ground against the heavily muscled chest as he came. It was a humiliating orgasm born by only the pleasure of being fucked.

Rick jerked as he came again, his body shoving forward with every hot surge of seed that flooded Derik's insides. Then, panting hard, Rick shoved Derik back down and released his hair.

Derik sobbed, not only for the burning pain of his rape, but the realization that he hungered for the feeling of something, anything, inside him. His body jerked as a final splatter of cum oozed out of his cock and splashed down on the ground.

Rick yanked his cock out.

Derik looked over his shoulder to see cum dripping off the angry red length. Rick looked down with an expression of disgust and... lustful excitement. He pointed to his shaft.

"Clean it."

Derik's eyes widened, but he didn't respond fast enough for Rick. The powerful man grabbed his hair and yanked him back, twisting him around until Derik was sitting in his own cooling seed, staring at the dripping shaft.

"I said, fucking clean it!"

The moment Derik opened his mouth, Rick jammed the hard cock into his mouth, trying to force it in. Derik got half of it into his mouth, tasting cum but nothing else. Utterly thankful for the magical containment rune, he bobbed up and down.

Rick moaned and reached down to grab his head. Derik tried to pull off, but Rick forced him down hard, shoving his swelling cock into Derik's throat until the thief's nose buried itself into the hard muscles and thick pubic hair of Rick's stomach.

"Whores belong on the bottom!"

Hands held him there until the desperate need to breath seared his lungs. Rick released him slightly but then he began to fuck Derik's face like before, hard strokes that slammed the cock deep into Derik's aching throat and holding it there until he needed air.

After only a few strokes, Rick came in his mouth while growling a warning for Derik not to swallow.

Derik held it there, tasting the slimy liquid and keeping his lips tight as Rick pulled out his glistening shaft. His jaw ached from the pressure, but he leaned back to open his mouth to show Rick he obeyed the rules.

"Swallow and clean up the damned floor," came the immediate command. Derik's cheeks burned as he swallowed Rick's cum, feeling it slide down his throat and fill his stomach. He sat up, keeping his head below Rick's waist and looked down at the puddle of cum on the stairs.

It wasn't anything different than what he did for Madre, he told himself, and started licking the floor clean.

Unfair Commands

It took nearly thirty minutes to crawl up the last five stone steps. As Derik bent over the stairs, lapping up the cum with his tongue, with his ass in the air. Cum dripped down his thighs, reminding him of what had happened.

Rick groaned with lust and tightly grabbed his hips.

He barely managed to lift his head up when the hard shaft impaled him again, driving deep and filling him to the brim. The second time, Rick pounded him brutally, and Derik sobbed into the stairs from the pain and pleasure tearing into him. He tasted cum on the pulsating shaft when Rick ordered him to clean it with his mouth. When Derik didn't bob down far enough, Rick grabbed the back of his head and raped his throat repeatedly, tearing his throat open even more.

Finally, Rick shoved him up the last few steps and forced him to kneel in front of a heavy door. The top steps smelled of piss, fear, and blood. The ancient wood stood darkly at the top, stained with age. Derik whimpered, feeling the hot cum running out of him and the ache inside. His own member, sore after coming again, drooled on the ground.

Now, he knelt in front of the torture room. Rick chuckled dryly as he reached over Derik's head and flung open the door.

Rick turned his head to look at his new home for three days. Derik expected an array of torture instruments, but found a room filled with crates and barrels. Two chairs sat near the door, facing the center. Looking up, he saw a long chain hanging from the ceiling with a pair of manacles at the end. Confused, he looked up at Rick who just laughed.

"Expecting something more?"

"Yes, master."

A kick slammed into his side and he slammed against the side of the door. Rick gestured.

"Well, get the fuck in there."

Frightened and wary, Derik crawled into the room, his breasts swaying along with his half-hard manhood. He didn't know where to go, so he crawled into the center. Rick followed him, stripping out of his clothes and dropping them in the corner. When Derik came to the middle, he turned around and knelt. A long shuddering breath came out of him, almost relief, as he stared around the plain room.

He remembered one of the rules a few seconds too late and Rick's kick caught him in the stomach, folding him in half and crashing him into the boxes behind him. He screamed out in pain as he collapsed to the ground, clutching himself. Rick's bare feet slapped across the ground as he stormed up to Derik. Derik saw the shadow and tried to flinch away, but Rick grabbed his hair and yanked him up, holding him up until Derik managed to get his knees underneath him.

"One fucking orgasm, and you forget everything!?"

Clutching his stomach, Derik shook his head, then spoke clearly. "No, master."

Rick yanked back his hair and forced him to look up. "You are nothing but a fucking cock whore."

After the faintest pause, Derik stammered. "Yes, master."

"And like all whores, you need to be taught your place. Something you obviously don't know."

Another pause, but Derik couldn't fill it. Tears filled in his eyes as Rick snarled, then yanked him higher up, pulling him completely off the ground. Derik grabbed his hand, trying to gain some relief from the pain in his scalp. His feet kicked off the ground until his soles gripped the stone and he could stand up. Rick dragged him over to the center and grabbed both wrists with one hand. His large fingers squeezed down painfully, grinding the bones together, as he reached up to pull at the chain. Tiny runes flared up along the surface of the pitted iron manacles and it came down easily.

Without saying anything, Rick yanked Derik's wrists above his head and clamped the manacles into place. It clicked. A second later, the thin line of the join glowed before it melted over to form a solid band of iron. Rick tugged on it and the chain drew up from a magical command.

Derik stared at it in shock, then a yelp escaped his throat as the chain yanked him off the ground, bearing all the weight on his wrists as his feet kicked in the air.

Rick watched him dance for a moment, then chuckled. "Be thankful I didn't wrap it around your neck."

Derik whimpered, his eyes widening. He was struggling to breathe with the fear pounding in his veins.

Rick snapped his fingers and pointed down. The chain ratcheted down until Derik's toes touched the ground, then Rick held up his hand. The chain stopped with the man's hand gestures.

Rick circled, his naked form a startling contrast to Derik's. He was larger than most men and heavily muscled. Thick coarse hair covered his entire body, leading down to a half-hard shaft that jumped despite raping Derik three times on the stairs.

Derik forced himself to look up, to keep his gaze on Rick's face as he circled.

"You won't enjoy this."

Derik answered immediately, his body tensing with the thought. "Yes, master."

"Do you know why this room is so plain?"

"No, master."

"Because I don't need fancy tools to rip off your arms or legs, or to hold you still. I need only one thing to break most people."

As he spoke, he dragged one of the barrels in front of Derik. Pulling on a rope through the lid, he set it aside and pulled out a long, thin switch of wood.

"This is a cane."

He snapped it, and Derik winced at the whistling sound it made as it cut through the air.

"It hurts, right?"

"Um—"

Rick cracked it across Derik's chest.

A sharp pain exploded from Derick's breasts, and he screamed out in pain. Looking down through the tears, he saw a red line forming just above his hard nipples.

The crime lord chuckled and walked up in front of Derik, closer than a lover would stand. His hand reached up to trace a line from Derik's cheek, along his jaw, and down to his throat. "There is a danger, you know, of having breasts like these."

His hand caressing Derik's right breast, stroking along the sensitive curve and then teasing along the red score line.

Derik's lower lip trembled.

The touch was a sharp pain but it wouldn't last. Rick dropped his finger down to the dusky nipple, teasing it until it puckered and grew sensitive.

When the thumb and finger caressing both sides of the nipple, he shook his head, begging with his eyes.

Rick just smiled, then twisted it hard, sending a sharp pain to slash through his body.

Derik let out a strangled yelp, then another as Rick released it.

A slap caught him right along the breast and he grabbed the other nipple. "I'm going to make you regret getting those tits."

"I-I didn't—"

The words slipped out before Derik could stop them. Rick's face grew stormy, and he stepped back, cracking the whip across his breasts again. This time, it caught both of his nipples, and he screamed out as his world exploded into white stars.

A third blow struck him, diagonal across his taut stomach and he almost folded in half as he twisted away from it. A fourth strike caught his side, the thin wood wrapping around his ribs and leaving a painful welt to rise to the surface.

Rick snarled. "In this room, if you disobey the rules, you get struck."

"Yes, master," cried Derik. His body trembled with not only the pain but the anticipation of many more rules being broken. He tried to force himself to focus and stare up at Rick as Rick came close again.

With a false tenderness, Rick stroked his hands against Derik's left nipple, where the hard, sensitive nub rolled in his palm. Derik whimpered softly, crossing his legs as he prepared for the pain. "These belong on a high-class whore, Derik, not a thieving slut like yourself!"

He twisted hard, grinding his fist into the soft mound. Derik's scream rose into a shrill sound as he writhed from the pain, trying to escape. Rick grabbed his other breast, digging his fingers into the thick meat and twisting the entire mound until the dual pains nearly made Derik faint.

Rick released him, and he slumped forward, putting the weight on his wrists as he panted for breath. He looked up too late and saw Rick raise his cane.

"I said look at me."

Derik cried out, "No!", but the blow came hard, scoring a red line across his thighs and nearly hitting his manhood. Rick snarled and struck again, this time across Derik's back as he spun around. Three more blows came across his chest and Derik sobbed from the pain that radiated from each one. Looking down, he saw one of them oozing blood right above the valley of his breasts.

"You're hard, slut," rumbled Rick.

Derik focused his bleary eyes between the soft, scored mounds on his chest and down to the hard cock between his legs. Derik shook his head, as if could deny the angry red cock and the hot feelings that coursed down his entire length. Droplets of pre-cum already formed at the tip and he watched as one splattered down on the clean stone below.

"Are you a slut?"

He resisted answering for a moment, then winced as the cane slammed across his shoulder and catching his forehead. In the burning pain, he fought back his tears. "Yes, master."

"And when I'm done, are you going to beg for my dick?"

He wanted to say no, but he knew the right answer. Despite the pulse that jerked his manhood. "Yes, master."

"Do you want to choke on it?"

"Yes, master."

"You also want it in your ass, don't you?"

He suppressed a moan, "Yes, master."

Rick chuckled and reached down to grab Derik's balls. Squeezing them, he twisted until Derik threw back his head and screamed out. Rick leaned forward, his hairy chest pressing against Derik's slick one.

"And we are going to. Three days I'm going to do that. And when I'm done each time, I'm going to seal you in a barrel and pack you in so tight that you won't be able to move. If you are lucky, I won't accidentally pack you in salt for the many wounds you'll be wearing."

Derik shivered at the thought, then looked up at Rick's face.

The powerful man chuckled. "But, I think you need a slightly differently position, don't you think?"

"Y-Yes, master?"

"Good."

Rick set the cane on the barrel and dragged another one next to Derik's hips. He walked around and brought a second one to his other side. On top of each one was a rope sticking out of a hole.

Rick walked behind him, then grabbed Derik's balls tightly.

"Kneel on those."

Derik cried from the squeezing pressure. He was forced to bring one knee up on the barrel and then the other. As he settled into position, he realized he couldn't pull his obscenely spread legs together and his balls were dangling above the stone floor. His ass hovered right at the level of Rick's cock. He could feel it bobbing right below the curve of his ass and shivered with the thought of it impaling him.

Rick's hands yanked his knees further apart, pulling him apart until he moaned out in protest. Then, the harsh rope wrapped around his ankles, pinning him to the two heavy barrels. Derik whimpered at the pressure on his inner thighs and back, his position utterly helpless and exposed.

His cock dripped hotly to the ground, splattering it with pre-cum and humiliation.

Rick's fingers stroked along his shaft. He moaned, then yelped as Rick twisted his balls. "I'm going to make you stop enjoying this."

He stepped back, and the cane whistled through the air, smacking him across the ass. He jerked forward, but the barrels didn't even move, and he couldn't escape them. Another blow followed the first, scoring parallel lines across his butt. Derik gasped at the pain of it, his back arching to try drawing his buttocks away, but Rick just laid into them, slamming blow after blow along the tight ass and up along his back. The wood cut into his skin, tearing pain along his nerves as Rick bent his weight into it.

Derik screamed out, writhing to try escaping the cane, but the blows kept coming, slicing into him. Rick stayed behind him, grunting as he cracked it across his skin.

After an endless period of agony, the blows slowed, then stopped. Derik slumped forward, unable to see Rick, and stared at the ground as he panted with an effort to clear his head. Something hot and wet rolled down his back, then followed the curve before splattering down. He stared at the crimson splashes, mixed in with the cum that still dripped from his rectum and his manhood.

Rick's presence grew as the powerful man stepped forward and impaled him on a hard, throbbing shaft. Derik inhaled sharply, feeling it sliding deep inside his slick channel, but the hiss turned into a whimper of pain as Rick grabbed his hips and the welts raised along his surface. One hand grabbed his hair, pulling on his head, but Rick used the other to slap him across the back, igniting the pain of the cane marks and sending bolts of pain through him.

Derik's asshole tightened around Rick's cock, and the larger man ran his fingernails across the wounds as he pounded hard and fast.

Crying from the pain and moaning from the pleasure of being filled, Derik lost himself in a storm of sensations that tore him from the inside. His tears splashed down on the floor as Rick pounded into him, his massive balls crashing into Derik's smaller ones with every stroke and sending bolts of lighting up his spine.

Rick came with a grunt, flooding Derik's insides with hot cum before pulling it out. It oozed out of him, splattering to the ground. Derik panted from almost reaching an orgasm.

Rick leaned forward, grinding his fingernails into the welts. Derik whimpered, then froze as Rick spoke directly into his ear. "Why is your head above my waist, slut?"

Derik's mouth opened. He looked down at his position, bound in the air and ankles spread why.

"I-I can't! I can't get down."

Rick chuckled, "I'll give you to the count of twenty before I punish you then."

Derik wailed as he tried to twist out of the manacles. The long seconds counted down as he struggled against his bounds.

Rick stepped back, switching the cane in the air as he counted down. "Five."

Jerking harder, Derik broke the skin around his wrist as he tried to slip out.

"Four."

His body tensed up as he strained against the ropes and chains, yanking them desperately as he tried to bring himself below Rick's waist.

"Three."

Derik sobbed as he wailed in fright, "Damn it, Rick, you know I can't get down!"

"Tw... what did you say?"

The cold, hard voice rang out in the room. Derik flinched and closed his eyes tightly.

"I'm sorry, master."

"One," snarled Rick.

Then a single blow came, right up between his exposed legs. The cane struck the entire length of his cock and he let out a high-pitched scream as the agony slammed into him with the force of an orgasm, cutting through his senses and leaving him breathless. Rick wasn't finished as a second one came up, slicing a red light right on the junction of his hips and waist. The third caught his left testicle and Derik nearly blacked out from the pain.

Rick rushed up to him, reaching through his legs to squeeze the agony-filled balls and cock. "Too bad I don't do that too often. Even a healer can't help if I break these."

Derik sobbed, his body shaking from the after spasms of the pain. Rick just toyed with his nuts, squeezing them and tracing the welt with his finger as Derik twisted with the effort to escape. His shoulders shook as the sobs wracked his body.

Rick breathed hard as he continued to abuse him. "But, when you come back, when that baron of yours isn't protecting you, there is no limit of what I can do. And I will castrate you with this cane if I have you. Can you imagine how many blows that would take?"

Derik shook more violently, tears splashing down his cheeks. Rick squeezed his balls again, then released them to hold up his hand, coated with a thin sheet of blood and clear fluid.

"I'm going to break you, Derik. And they are going to hear your screams from the palace."

Struggling to control himself, Derik could only shake as Rick aimed his cock once again at his opening. "Beg for it. Whose cock do you want in your ass?"

Derik begged for it, begging for Rick to rape him.

Rick did, with hard brutal thrust that buried his entire length. Then, his hand reached around to play with the abused balls, squeezing and rolling them in his fingers as he fucked Derik hard and fast.

When he came, he stalked around Derik and started to whip him from the front. Hard, powerful blows alternating with fucking his throat. The hard blows split skin and ignited it with pain. Even when the cane didn't whistle in the air, he could feel every puff of air or movement that scraped across his wounds.

Hours of whipping, he was covered in blood and cum. It ran down his front, channeled through his cleavage and dripped off his hardness. His ass trembled with red welts and he struggled with the pain and ache to be fucked once again. It was a terrible pain, a knife's edge of pleasure and pain when he was just too far over the edge.

As the blows came down, he suddenly remembered Nightingale. A single clear image of her lying on Madre's bed, cooing happily with the same red lines across her ass. He shuddered at the thought, but as the next blow came across, he focused on them, wondering how she could take so many and still be turned on.

With every blow, his body jerked violently forward and more blood dripped down his back and front. He closed his eyes, breaking one more rule but it was too late. The blindness made each blow more intense, and he focused on that image. The words that Madre said, and even the time she used magic to spank him. The blow that caught him right in the right tit shook his body violently, but it wasn't for the pain, but from the memory of her spell, the one that made him feel like every bone in his body was broken. He gasped, sobbing at the intensity of it, then jerked as the next one caught him.

He gasped as he focused on the images of being spanked by Madre, forcing his will into those memories. As Rick slammed into him, his cane cutting skin apart, he found the balance of pleasure and pain shifting, sliding over the knife's edge as he focused on the pleasure that came after the pain, the wave of agony and the ecstasy in that moment of respite. Even as Rick rained pain down, he only let his body feel the pleasure between the blows. Relief became his pleasure.

Then he came.

Between one blow and another, his cock surged with heat and sent out a long stream of white into the room. Rick paused for a second, confused, then crashed the cane up between his legs. It hurts, a blossom of pain, but he finished coming as Rick beat him.

"Damn it!"

The cane whipped harder, but Derik found that he could survive it. The tears dried on his face as they came. When Rick mounted him and yelled for him to beg, Derik did, not because he wanted the pain to stop but because of the hard brutality, that pounding that seemed to fill him so hard, was now pleasure for him. He craved that feeling of being filled, that gasp of pain that rippled away as Rick scraped his fingernails against the countless welts across his back.

The cuts across his breasts only magnified the intensity of the feelings when Rick grabbed them, twisting and mauling as he came deep inside him. Derik's lips parted with a moan and a sob, still feeling the pain but finding pleasure in every one.

"Whose cock do you want, whore? Whose!?" he roared. His hard, throbbing shaft buried deep into his body and Derik moaned into it. Rick's balls slammed into his cock, crushing them for a second. Swallowing at the cum he held in his mouth, he gasped as he started to come. Dribbles ran down both sides of his mouth as he panted, struggling to get the word out.

Derik tried to say master, but an image of something new flashed through his mind. Of Hime in the sunlight of the conference room, standing with her smile and the raw presence that clutched his heart. His mouth cracked as Derik called out, but not Rick's name or even master, but something entirely different, something entirely unexpected. "Bridget's!"

It came out as a burst of noise from his throat, barely understandable.

Instantly, the tension and fear popped. In the space left behind, a strange sense of peace eased into his thoughts. Stunned, he wondered why he even said a god's name.

He didn't believe in gods.

Right?

Kerlis

After that single word, as confusing to Derik as it was to Rick, Derik's life exploded into pain as Rick rained down blow after blow. He screamed and writhed as he begged for mercy. Even with the pleasure of it, he found his limits reached and shattered with the wave of agony that crashed into him, but it was nothing compared to the tsunami of pleasure that tore him apart every time Rick slammed his cock into his mouth or asshole.

Every time the agony speared through his thoughts, he focused on the girls of the harem: Nightingale's ass on the bed, Sherrel purring on Teri's lap, and even Madre as she rode his burning red cheeks with her strap-on.

He would find new limits of pain, where his body screamed out in agony, and he realized he couldn't take more. Then, Rick would shatter them with the cane, and he found himself being pushed further, harder, and deeper into a world where pleasure and pain turned into a single tornado of sensations.

Then, it stopped.

Derik cracked open one eye, looking through the dried sweat, cum, and blood. Rick's chest was just in front of him as the man unshackled the manacles and released Derik. The thief slumped forward, balancing on the barrels as he panted. His breath came hoarsely, whistling as it passed his ruined vocal cords. Everything burned, every inch of his skin and even his bones. He tasted Rick on his lips. Panting, he looked up as his breasts heaved with his effort to breathe.

Rick looked down, saying nothing, but Derik was surprised to see dark shadows under his eyes. The crime lord panted as he glared down at Derik. One hand rose up, balling in a fist and shaking. His cock bobbed right in front of him, but when Derik opened his mouth, as he had for many hours, Rick just spun on his heels. Grabbing his clothes, he yanked open the door and stormed down the stairs.

Still panting, Derik stared at the door in confusion. His legs trembled from the effort to hold himself up and he fumbled with the ropes that bound his ankles. His fingers were clumsy, and he cracked a nail trying to get the harsh rope removed.

A knife appeared next to him and he jumped, but it was only Bruk—or Gluk, Derik couldn't tell—cutting the ropes. He stared, parched lips open in surprise, but the thriban didn't look at him. Derik swallowed and tried to speak, but only a hoarse whisper came out.

"W-What's happening?"

Bruk sighed and walked around to work at the other rope. "You're done."

He whimpered, biting his lip. His eyes looked down, where his body bled red over the welts and bruises. "I have two more days of this?"

Derik gave Bruk a pleading look, but the thriban shook his head. He spoke in a growl, "No, you are done."

"I-I—" it hurt to talk, but Derik grew confused with every passing second.

Bruk sighed with annoyance. "Either you did something amazing or something stupid, but Rick hasn't left this room in three days. He beat you solid, I've never seen that. When Truk suggested he take a break, he lashed out at her. She's a big girl, but her face is going to take a bit to heal. Rick... damn, Rick's obsessed with you now."

Eyes widening, Derik gaped with surprise.

Stepping closer, Bruk picked him up.

Derik set down one trembling leg, then the other. He stared down at his feet, marveling at the circle of drying blood and cum beneath his feet. Nausea rose up but something Bruk said caught his attention. "Three days?"

The thriban frowned, "Yes. He didn't leave for food, sleep, or even to go the bathroom."

"Is," he swallowed, "is that normal?"

Bruk shook his head, "No. But, we need to get you to the healer now."

Unsteady, Derik had to lean against the larger man as he was lead out of the top torture room. He whimpered with his steps. "Are you Bruk?"

The thriban chuckled, "You can't tell?"

They walked down the stairs, as fast as Derik could manage but probably slower than the enforcer wanted. He grabbed on the belt tightly and just took each step, one at a time.

At the bottom, Bruk aimed him for the door.

"Gluk has a notch in his right ear, I have a broken nose. Truk has tits, can you remember that?"

Derik looked up and saw how the large creature's nose was obviously broken a few times. He ducked his head and sighed. "Why is this happening to me?"

"Well, you fucked with the wrong person, Derik."

"Damn it, I should have just told the truth."

Bruk chuckled, "Or decided not to keep the silver. All of this wouldn't have happened if you just did your job properly."

Derik groaned, "I hate that silver. Why did I ever steal it?" He sighed as he walked over to the door. "I'm an idiot."

"Yes, you are."

He said nothing for a moment, then cleared his throat, "Um, Truk gave you a present for the corset."

Surprised, Derik stared at the package in Bruk's hand. Then he tried to unwrap it but his fingers wouldn't work.

The thriban grunted and unwrapped it, revealing a white cotton dress.

"She enchanted it so it wouldn't soak blood, it should hide most of your wounds until we get to the brothel."

Derik froze, "B-Brothel?"

"Kerlis Palace. I think you know the place."

His lips parted and a tear formed in his eyes. "T-That's my mother's place."

"Yeah," he sighed, "I know."

"Do we have to go there? I hate him."

"Rick says yes."

At Rick's name, Derik started to sink to his knees in memory of the rules, but the thriban just pulled him back up.

"Oh, damn it, just keep standing. Can you dress yourself?"

Derik shook his head, and Bruk rolled his eyes.

The thriban grunted. "Okay, but no kissing. I'm not in the mood to date a guy, even if you have a nice set of tits."

That got a chuckle out of Derik, breaking the mood, and he lifted his hands as the thriban helped him into the simple dress. It flowed down his skin, the smooth fabric scraping against his wounds and bringing a hiss of pain to Derik's lips.

Bruk ignored him, tugging harder, but true to his word, the few wounds that still bled didn't soak into the fabric.

"Come on, we are running out of time."

Barefoot, Derik limped after him and to the waiting carriage. Inside, he saw Rick slumped in the seat, glaring at Derik as he came into view. The crime lord seemed exhausted, and knowing this made Derik hesitate before crawling into the carriage. He got to his knees, holding his position in front of Rick and looked up into the dark eyes.

The door closed, and Derik leaned into the motion as the carriage started forward. He kept his eyes focused on Rick, waiting, but the crime lord said nothing. As the seconds stretched into minutes, Derik decided to respond. Reaching out, he pulled open Rick's pants and worked the half-hard penis out. Rolling it in his hands, he brought it to his mouth and swallowed it, bobbing up and down until Rick grew thick in Derik's mouth. Feeling it tease his throat, he bobbed down on it, swallowing it deep until it cut off his breath. Eyes still locked on Rick, he bobbed down harder, then up when he needed to breath. Breathing quickly, he bobbed down again and tasted the hard cock, blowing him like Rick wanted.

Rick's eyes closed as he moaned and continued to impale Derik's throat. It ached, but not as much as before, and he found he could take the entire length easily, even when his nose ground into the forest of pubic hair at the bottom.

Derik went slow, taking his time as he choked himself on Rick's cock. For twenty minutes, he gave a long, deep blow job until Rick came hard, a grunt filling the room and seed filling Derik's mouth. He held it there, staring at Rick for the remaining of the carriage.

When they stopped at Kerlis, Rick only gave a single command before getting out. "Swallow."

Derik swallowed, almost enjoying the taste of it before he followed Rick. He started to crawl out, but Rick sighed. "Just fucking stand."

Getting to his feet, Derik looked around the brothel where he had grown up. The Kerlis Palace was a massive complex that filled half a city block. Clad in marble and the single cleanest building in the entire area, it bridged the poor and the rich districts. Ten guards, all heavily armored, stood in front as a steady stream of customers poured in and out of the doors. He shivered at the memory of his childhood. Then he noticed Rick entering the main entrance and followed. The crowds parted around Rick, and Derik blushed as he followed, feeling self-conscious in his white dress and nothing else.

They entered the back rooms, and Derik could only follow as he shivered in the memories. He grew up there, for the first few years of life, visiting his mother whenever he could. When she died, he got the offer to keep on working there by the most disgusting man in the world, Kerlis.

"Oh, my. I know that beautiful hair anywhere. Is that our little Derik?"

Derik froze as Kerlis came up. He was a thin man with large hands and bulging eyes. His beard looked more like fuzz from a whore's crotch, but the grin sent a shiver of revulsion down his spine. The higher pitched voice sounded like a fop's, but Derik knew the terrible mind that spun underneath. Kerlis grabbed Derik and hugged him tightly, then slid his hands up the openings of the dress to stroke against the side of his breasts. "Oh, my Derik, I heard you joined the baron's harem. Does this mean you finally decided to become a whore?"

Rick shook his head, "No, he's here to get healed."

Kerlis looked surprised, then inspected Derik, a frown crossing his face. His hands brushed against the wounds and Derik shuddered at the dull pain that followed.

Holding him firmly, Kerlis tilted up his head and pulled the dress down a bit. "Oh, Rick, Rick, Rick," he clicked his tongue, "You shouldn't hurt the boys like this. Makes it hard to heal and harder to sell their bodies."

"Heal him."

"Healing is expensive."

"I said he'll heal!"

Kerlis ignored Rick's roar as he pulled Derik's dress up to inspect his legs. He wrapped one hand around Derik's manhood for a quick stroke along a deep cut before releasing it.

Derik shivered, then clutched himself as the brothel owner stepped back.

"But people remember the scars, they brand the soul. Bodies heal, but don't break the girl."

Rick snapped back, "Kerlis, shut the fuck up."

Kerlis sighed dramatically. He hooked his arm with Derik's. Derik shivered, but let the thin man drag him forward. "Come, come. I bet you'll enjoy this. We have one of your good friends here."

Friend? Curious, Derik followed Kerlis into the furthest wing, the one wing he didn't want to go. He tried to slow down, but Kerlis dragged him forward and didn't him the chance. When they reached his mother's hallway, Derik tried not to remember walking down it as a young boy of five. He tried to force his head down, but his eyes rose up to seek out his mother's old door. Each room had a necklace or bracelet on it, adding a bit of personality to the stark hallway. When they passed his mother's room, he could still see the raven necklace she always wore. Now, it was a series of beads with some rune on the end of it. Memories crushed him, but Kerlis only slowed slightly before walking around the corner.

"Lot of memories in here, Derik."

Derik pulled back the tears and nodded.

"You were always welcomed here, you know."

"I'm not a whore."

Kerlis chuckled and glanced at him. "Yes, you are. You just didn't want to admit it. But, the baron's shaft got to you, didn't it?"

Derik's lips parted slightly as he thought about the baron. His body warmed up, then he blushed hotly as Kerlis reached down at pressed his hand right against his hardening crotch.

The thin man grinned. "You will always be a whore, Derik. Just like your mother."

Derik looked away angrily, but Kerlis just laughed and pulled him forward. It took a moment to reach the medical rooms, where the city did its monthly inspections and Kerlis kept a small staff of healers and mages to treat his brothel.

Reaching one of the larger rooms, he pushed open the door and guided Derik in. Derik gasped as the mage Forbis looked up with a scowl. In his hand, he clutched his black bag ringed with protective runes.

Derik froze, but Kerlis just pushed him forward, somehow managing to strip off the dress as he moved.

Naked and covered from head to toe with red and bleeding welts, Derik could only whimper as Kerlis pressed him down against a padded table and ran a finger down his ass crack before stepping back.

"Now, lie still and let Forbis heal you."

Forbis grumbled angrily as he took Kerlis' place.

"I remember you. You were the one Madre pulled her favor for. Ungrateful bitch, she got me kicked out the next week and had me replaced by some faggot priestess."

The mage pulled tools from his bag. He pressed one against an angry welt.

Derik jerked from the rough pain.

"And I think you stole something of mine. I don't know how, but I know you did. For that, I'm going to make you feel it."

That was the only warning before the mage leaned forward, grinding the edge into the cut, and energy poured into him.

Derik let out a gasp of pain from the sharp burning but it slowly faded.

Forbis chuckled. "Hurt? Good, you deserve it. One down, thousands to go."

The heat from the mage's tools increased, spreading out through his back as the wounds healed supernaturally fast but still slower than Derik wanted. Forbis worked roughly, making no effort to relieve the pain. Derik could feel his cuts sealing up and the bruises fading away, but every healing came with another flash of pain, like the wound being inflicted in reverse. He gasped and clutched the edge of the table, whimpering as the healing stretched into minutes, then into hours. By the time the last of the injuries faded into nothing but memory, he was slick with sweat and trembling once again.

When Forbis stepped back, Kerlis replaced him and ran his hands over Derik's naked body. He shivered as the thinner man probed and prodded, sliding his fingers into his ass and stroking along his length. Despite the revulsion of being inspected like cattle, relief flooded through his body at the release of his pain; he couldn't feel a single cut or bruise as Kerlis groped him.

Derik heard Forbis and Rick speaking quietly, too quietly for him to normally hear it, but Kerlis slowed down as he eavesdropped himself on their words.

"Master Thrantas, I can't reverse the shaping effect. His priestess wrapped a blessing around it and combined it with the three marks. I could remove the marks, quickly, but I can't replace it without ruining my tools. I could also separate the energies, but that will take at least half a day."

Rick grumbled, "Damn, I was hoping to send him back as a man, give the baron a real surprise."

Derik rolled over, blushing, as Kerlis flipped him over and resumed his slow, distracted inspection.

Forbis said, "I'm sorry, Master Thrantas, I can't help there."

"Oh, well, I'll still pay you."

"Thank you from the bottom of my heart."

The footsteps of the mage faded, then Derik froze as Rick called out.

"Forbis!"

"Yes, sir?"

"Actually, there is one thing."

"Anything."

"Can you prevent him from speaking about a topic?"

"Yes, it will only last a few months."

"Oh," Rick chuckled, "That should be enough. Two things, actually."

"Sir?"

Derik could feel Rick's eyes on his skin and he shivered. Kerlis' hands pressed down on him, pinning him with one hand on his balls and the other on his throat. Derik looked up at the thinner man who just shook his head.

"Make it so he can't talk about the Eye of Hamel. Or about anything that happened since he left the palace."

"Oh, very good, sir."

Kerlis' hands pressed down as Derik started to struggle.

Forbis glided up to him, grinning, and Derik thrashed harder with his efforts to escape. Forbis shook his head, then said a single word of power.

Even if he lived a hundred years, Derik would never be able to understand those terrible syllables, but his body froze into solid place, every muscle in his body tensing until his bones creaked.

Helpless, he could do nothing as Forbis pulled out a long stick and began to trace tiny runes on his throat. He struggled against the magical bounds, but only a single tear dripped down his face. When he finished, only a few minutes later, Forbis snapped his fingers and Derik slumped to the table gasping for breath.

Rick grunted, "Done?"

"Yes, sir."

"How long?"

"Three months, maybe, after that-"

"I only need a month or so. Thank you."

Forbis grinned at Derik, then closed his bag tightly. "Good, if you excuse me, I don't trust this thief."

"Go on," commanded Rick.

Derik listened to the mage walked out of the room and down the hall. His body trembled with a feeling of humiliation and helplessness and he tried to say "Eye of Hamel" but no words came out of his throat. The panic look on his face brought a fierce smile to Rick's lips.

Rick stood closer and wrapped his powerful fingers around Derik's manhood and balls, squeezing firmly but not tightly. His hard voice sent a pang of terror through Derik as he stared up into the dead, blue eyes. "I want you, Derik."

It wasn't a good want either, Derik suspected.

"I want to break you. I want to hear you scream. I want to make you suffer for this. You got out easy because I have to return your whore's ass to the baron unharmed, but if I had but one more day, I would have shattered your bones and then paid Forbis to heal you in the most painful way possible."

Derik swallowed, unable to escape as the pressure grew on his testicles.

"But, you got lucky. This time."

Rick leaned forward, rage burning in his eyes. "Sooner or later, you'll end up on that auction block. Or, you'll stop being the baron's little whore for some other reason. And when that happens, I'll be there. It doesn't matter if it costs me every mark I have, I will own your ass, and I will make sure that no one..." He roared as he ground down hard.

Derik screamed out shrilly, folding in half as he tried to grab his tortured balls.

Rick released them and shoved him down. "No one will ever fuck with me again!"

The hard voice slammed into him as Derik clutched himself, curling up in the fetal position on the table. Rick snarled, panting with anger, then spun around. Storming out of the room, Derik just sobbed.

Kerlis clicked his tongue as he slithered back up. Pushing Derik out, he inspected his manhood carefully with his fingers and a bit more than needed stroking. "He didn't bruise anything, good. Healing is expensive, you know. Forbis is good, but thinks too much of himself."

There was something comforting about talking to the man who ruined his mother, Derik thought.

Kerlis smiled and helped him up. "Come, do you want to meet your friend?"

Derik nodded hesitantly, then held up his hands as Kerlis dressed him in his white dress, stroking and pinching through the fabric until it settled down on his flawless skin.

Derik swallowed, "Friend?"

"Yes, your friend."

Curious, Derik got to his feet, feeling a wash of pleasure coursing over him with the realization he didn't hurt anymore. He was stronger and could balance without limping.

Kerlis smiled happily and hooked his arm into Derik's, pulling him out of the room and down the hall.

They came up to one of the observation rooms, rooms that stood against one of the solid walls of the expensive suites for the prostitutes. Derik frowned, but Kerlis ushered him in and set him down on one of the large padded chairs that faced a blank wall. Derik blinked but Kerlis slid over to a small bar and started to pour himself a drink.

Derik sighed and opened his hand, looking at five small gems he stole from Forbis' bag. A small smile crossed his lips as he closed his fingers over it.

"Always stealing, Derik. Even as a child."

Freezing, Derik watched as the pimp unfolded his fingers and pulled out one of the larger pieces. He held it up to the light, a brilliant blue sapphire, and then pocketed it.

"You know I always get my cut."

Derik closed his mouth as Kerlis slid into the chair next to him, sprawling his legs across Derik's pinning him down. In his hand, he held a large glass half-filled with ice and Carium rum. He smiled as he drank, then reached out to stroke Derik's breasts.

"They made you very pretty, boy."

Derik pressed an arm across his breasts, but Kerlis' fingers slithered around it to tweak one hard nipple. "I'm amazed that they look just like your mother's. She was very pretty."

Derik had to swallow before he could speak. "Please don't talk about her."

"Why? She was one of my girls. A good paying one. She made me a lot of money in eighteen years. A good investment was my dear Raven."

Derik looked away, afraid of what would come out.

Kerlis stroked him a bit. "I know, boy, it's hard to lose a parent. I've seen it a lot, but remember, I offered you her rates when she died, and the offer stands. Leave the baron and be my whore. You'll get all the cock and pussy you want."

"I'm not a whore."

Kerlis laughed, "Yes, you are. You always were. From the womb of a whore and you'll die a whore. The only difference is the baron got you before I did."

A blush rose up on his cheeks but Derik just tightened his lips.

Kerlis watched him for a moment, then took another drink. "Oh, your friend."

He barked out a command word and the wall before them faded into translucency. Curious, Derik peered into a richly, but tacky, decorated room. In the center, a large four poster bed dominated the space. Hundreds of rings and hooks adorned the heavily carved posts, no doubt to latch ropes and chains for whatever bondage the client had in mind.

In the bed, a large fat man pumped in between the sprawled legs of some women. Derik could see her wrists chained above her, but couldn't see anything besides a flash of hair and naked skin.

His eyes drifted over to the door, where two guards stood at attention, watching without looking like they actually cared about the rutting on the bed.

"Recognize her?"

Derik shook his head. When Kerlis insisted, he peered harder through the transparent wall with a flash of guilt from being a voyeur.

On the bed, the large man pumped harder, pulling her back up and arching her painfully against his cock and the chain on her wrist.

Then he saw it.

A star-burst around her navel.

Gasping, he pressed a hand against his mouth.

"Nightingale!?"

Kerlis chuckled and drank again. "Ah, you do see it. Yes, my angry little Nightingale."

Whimpering, Derik stared at her with unexpected intensity.

Nightingale's eyes burned with a suppressed rage, but the fat man just kept on pounding into her, grunting as he mauled her breasts.

"She has a lot of spirit, Derik. Got into fights with three customers already. I had to put a guard in with orders to put her down before she would stop attacking them."

Numb, he stared at the former harem kitten. The fat man roared and yanked out. Flipping her over, he spread her trim thighs and plunged his short, thick cock into her ass.

Nightingale's face flickered with some emotion and Derik's stomach soured.

It wasn't pain that filled her eyes. He knew that she could take the baron's pole easily. What he saw on her face was rage, sadness, and regret. He had known that last one too painfully in the last three days. He closed his eyes tightly.

"Turn it off, Kerlis."

"Are you sure? The ambassador is about to finish."

"Turn it off!"

The brothel owner snapped out the command and Derik cracked open one eye to see the scene fading. He struggled to speak, but finally managed to get the words out. "H-How?"

Kerlis drained the glass before answering, "Rick. He buys most of the girls from the baron, either directly or through one of his men."

"C-Can you let her go?"

"Don't you want to see her suffer for what she did? I heard she almost ruined everything for you."

Derik searched his feelings, but he didn't feel any joy in seeing that face. He shook his head. "No, just let her go."

Kerlis shrugged and set the glass down on the table. He shook his head. "I can't and I won't."

"Damn it, Kerlis, why not?"

"Because I bought her from Rick and it cost me a lot of money."

"Not even for me?"

Kerlis' eyes hardened as he reached over, pulling Derik's gaze over to him with a finger under his chin. "You know that answer.

Do you know what I would have done if you became my girl tonight?"

"What?"

"I would strip you down naked and have you two fight it out. Winner gets fucked by the client who won the most money. Loser gets plowed by everyone else. It would be good money for me. She cost me a lot of money and there is only way she can earn it back."

"Damn you."

"I know, Derik. I was damned long before you were born."

Derik sighed and looked down. He said nothing as Kerlis watched him. Then, a scream cut out through the walls and then an impact.

Kerlis rolled his eyes and barked out a command. The wall faded before them, revealing the suite.

Derik gasped as he saw Nightingale on top of the ambassador, trying to strangle him as her face twisted in a mask of rage. His mind fought a new mixture of emotions as he passively watched her. Fear won out at her expression. It was as if she wanted Derik below her straining body.

A guard sprinted across the room and slammed her into the wall.

Kerlis' finger reached out to stroke Derik's nipples as they watched the guard pin Nightingale to the transparent wall. Her breasts crushed against the invisible barrier and she screamed into the wall in blind fury. The ambassador screamed dire threats as the guard dragged her out, kicking and screaming.

"She has a lot of fight, Derik," said a cheerful Kerlis. "A lot like your mother when she first came here."

Derik bit his bottom lip before looking away. "Don't talk about her."

"Why? They are whores, property. Both of them. They'll live out their life making back the money I sink into them, then they'll make me a profit. As they lose their looks or their will breaks, I'll just move them down to poorer customers until they are doing nothing but trolling the streets for customers."

"This isn't right."

Kerlis shrugged, "It doesn't matter about right and wrong. She got sold and I bought her from Rick. It's a good investment. You grew up with this, though you won't admit you are the son of a whore. You came from the same diseased cunts that I did."

Derik glared at the door through the wall. Through the door came two more prostitutes to placate the ambassador, one of them immediately dropping to her knees in front of him.

He whispered angrily with the effort to not remember his childhood. "She didn't deserve this."

Pausing, the brothel owner ran his fingers long Derik's nipples for another second before pulling them back. "Which one are you talking about?"

Derik frowned before glancing over to Kerlis. "Nightingale, of course."

The thin man shrugged, "I wasn't sure. Both Raven and Nightingale came from the same place, but I never knew if your mother told you that."

Something clenched inside Derik as he stared in shock.

"W-What do you mean?"

"The baron's harem. Both of them. Nightingale recently but your mother was... oh, almost forty years ago. She was," Kerlis spoke softly in his own memories, "a fighter, that girl. Lot of money she made me as she went from a high-classed slut to a whore who begged for liquor money."

Derik swallowed, suddenly finding it hard to breath.

Kerlis picked up his glass, then sighed at the single ice cube at the bottom. "She killed someone, actually. One of the other harem girls. I remember that, mainly because of what she made you promise."

Derik started to shake as memories slammed into him. Of a bitter, drunk women with short, black hair, a bruise on her face, and a bottle of vodka in her hand. They were sitting in the medical room as one of the healers did his best to heal the knife cuts in her back. Derik, only four years at the time, sat next to her, confused why she was damaged.

"Never kill someone, Derri. No matter how much it hurts inside, no matter how much it burns. Even when you think there is no answer, just," she sniffed, "just don't do it. That blood never washes from your hand."

Kerlis' fingers against his throat broke him from his memory and he looked up, tears burning in his eyes. Kerlis gave him a false smile. "I heard you never killed anyone in all these years. Even when you got arrested or in all those fights."

Derik sniffed, a new wound forming on his heart, "I-I killed two people."

Kerlis shrugged indifferently, "I don't believe you."

"It was," he sniffed, "an accident."

"We all make mistakes."

Derik glared at him and Kerlis shrugged. "Okay, you make more than me. But, I'm a killer and you aren't. You managed to keep that heart of yours while I lost mine somewhere in the bodies of whores, customers, and nobles."

"Y-You're a bastard."

Kerlis shrugged and slipped off Derik to get up. "I always get my cut, Derik, don't forget that."

As the thin man refilled his drink, Derik leaned forward and began to sob. He cried for his mother and Nightingale and for the terrible future that stood before him. His shoulders shook as they wracked him, tearing him apart with the guilt and fear.

Kerlis came back to him and wrapped one arm around him as he sobbed. It was a tiny gesture of compassion from a man with no morals, virtues, or compassion, but it was something.

Derik leaned against his shoulder and just let the tears flow.

Just a Shirt

After the tears had dried, Kerlis left him to find Rick to take him home.

Derik sat there for a long time, then snatched a bottle and padded out of the room. No one paid him any attention to what looked like a barely dressed women walking down the hall with a bottle in her hand. He slipped out the side door and stood at the street, ignoring the guard that watched him.

Popping the top, he took a swig of the vodka and it burned down his throat. Making a face, he realized he didn't care for it anymore. "Aw, fuck," he muttered.

Handing it to the guard, he turned around until he oriented himself by spotting flag over the baron's place. Carefully stepping over the curb, he walked away from the brothel and the men within.

He had gotten several blocks before he realized he only had the white dress and the four gems he had stolen. The gems would be worth something at a fence but not enough for a carriage to return to the palace.

A tear burned at his face but he kept pushing through the crowds with a dogged attempt to return to the one place that made him happy: the baron's harem. He considered going along the roofs but changed his mind. The idea of the nails and tar and garbage that always gathered on his preferred method of travel stopped him. He stole a pair of shoes, then put them back when he thought about Madre's expression when he came back.

Still barefoot, he worked his way into the merchant area. In the middle of the day, there were large crowds, and he fought the urge to pick pockets as he was shoved aside with glares and elbows.

He passed a shop and the smell of spices sent a rumbling in his empty stomach. Slowing to a halt, he backed up to stare into the glass of the place Tornsin had taken him. It felt like years ago as he licked his lips. He could still taste them and remember the guard's laughter.

Three days. Three days with only beatings and cum for food.

Clicking his tongue like Kerlis, he reached up and ran his fingers through the long black strands, working them back behind his ear and using a bit of spit to wipe a smudge from his face.

On the other side, the baker caught sight of him and gave him a glare and a gesture to move away.

Derik focused back on his reflection and saw what he did, a common whore in nothing but a dress.

And a man watching him.

He gulped as he turned away. Peeking at the reflection, he focused on the guy, then frowned as he realized it was a familiar face. It took him a second to place it. Gaol, a common mugger and rapist. The bastard focused on the bottom rungs of society, but only rarely went into the merchant areas.

Derik flushed, then realized he looked exactly like Gaol's mark: appearing female, alone, and poor enough to do anything to save his life. In his mind, he recalled Gaol's victims and the guys who hung around him. They traveled in a pack which meant there were others in the crowd no doubt considering him as their victim.

"Fuck," he muttered again.

Being as discrete as possible, he made a show of using the glass for a mirror while inspecting his surroundings. There was an alley less than a block away with another one in the next one. Above him, there were roofs; he wished he kept the shoes he stole.

He thought furiously for a moment and then made a plan for ducking down the second alley. Hopefully, he could get him clear of Gaol and his friends.

Derik jerked into movement, ducking his head as he raced for the alley.

A yelp rose behind him and a swear, Gaol was charging.

Derik redoubled his speed, his bare feet slapping against the stone.

Passing the first alley, he spotted one of Gaol's friends standing there, waiting.

There was a flash of movement and soon he had two men on him.

Biting his lip, he ducked into the second alley, ready to scramble up the first ledge he found.

And rammed right into the chest of Gaol's other friend.

He yelped as he plummeted to the ground, ripping his dress. Scrambling to his feet, he spun to flee, but Gaol and the other mugger stood in the alley.

"Where you going, my pretty?"

"Fuck, fuck, fuck," whispered Derik. Fear ran down his spine as he looked for some way to escape. There were two men in front of him and one behind. He was trapped.

Gaol grinned and stepped forward. Derik backed up as the mugger pulled out a short dagger and ran it along his palm. The man behind him just backed away, drawing him deeper into the alley.

He grinned even more as he drawled slowly. "Oh, I'm thinking we are going to do a bit of that."

"Fuck, Gaol, I'm not in the mood."

Gaol stopped with a confused look on his face. "Do I know you, my pretty?"

Blushing, Derik nodded, "It's me, Derik."

Gaol peered at him, then the grin grew bigger. "When you get the tits, pretty? You look like a whore."

Derik pressed one arm against his breasts, then jerked as the man behind him ran a hand up his thigh to grope him. He pulled away and spoke to Gaol, "Damn it, just let me go."

"Oh, not sure I want to do that, pretty. Rick has a bounty on your head, you know. Anyone who can get you away from the baron, oh, and a hundred thou can go a long way."

Derik's blood ice ran cold as he stared at the knife.

Gaol chuckled and hands grabbed him from behind. He squeezed Derik's wrists.

Derik screamed out in agony.

Gaol didn't let go of the knife as he covered the distance to Derik and ran one lustful hand along his thigh.

Derik shuddered with revulsion and the twisting feeling in his gut.

Gaol grabbed one breast painfully. "Now, he didn't say anything about being unspoiled, you know."

"I'm a fucking guy, damn it."

"You always had a pretty mouth, and my friends here don't care what hole they use. You got two, that's good enough for us to take turns."

Derik shuddered and opened his hands, letting the gems falls from his palm to the ground.

Gaol caught one of them, then knelt down in front of Derik to grab the others.

Derik tensed up and then lashed out with his foot. His blow caught Gaol, but it wasn't enough to push him back more than a foot. Derik kicked behind him, connecting to the man's knee.

Behind him, the guy yanked Derik's arms up above his head and slammed a knee into his back.

Gaol regained his balance. "Oh, that was a mistake, pretty."

Derik cried as he lashed out again.

This time, Gaol grabbed Derik's nipple and twisted hard until Derik screamed out in pain. Releasing it, Gaol slapped Derik once and then grabbed the collar of the white dress. "Don't worry, think of this as the last loving touch you'll get before Rick gets you."

Grabbing the front of the dress, Gaol cut down, sliding it open. The sharp point scraped along Derik's stomach but it was a shallow cut. The cold air around Derik's naked body sent a shiver of fear. It was moist as it curled around his nipples, breasts, and manhood.

Gaol looked down at Derik. He had a mixture of lust and disgust on his face. "Hate the dick, love the tits. Well, can't have everything."

Derik screamed as they dragged him further into the alley. His hair thrashed in all directions as he lashed out, but missed his rapists.

Gaol worked the belt around his pants and chuckled. "Going to enjo—"

The word hung in Gaol's throat as a strange look went across his face.

Derik whimpered as he looked, then saw a crimson blade shove out through his chest.

A muted gurgling noise rose up as bubbled formed in Gaol's lips, then the rapist collapsed to the ground.

Derik gasped as Tornsin stepped around Gaol. His long sword dripped with blood. He glared at the man holding Derik. "I believe she is one of the baron's women."

Tornsin didn't have armor, just a white, button-down shirt, and trousers. But there was no mistaking the sword nor the baron's symbol he wore around his neck.

The thief not holding Derik whipped out a dagger and slashed at Tornsin.

The guard stepped back and swung low, only to be parried by a second dagger.

Derik trembled as he tried to twist free. He reached back as he did and deftly snatched the man's dagger from its sheath. Twisting around, he slammed it into the rapist's thigh.

The man holding him suddenly shoved him aside. Staggering back, he clutched at his sheath but came up empty.

Derik stumbled back, the stones cutting into his bare feet. He slammed against the wall of the alley but pushed away while brandishing his attacker's dagger.

The larger thief chuckled and drew a sword from the other side. "Come on, pretty, Ersto will handle the guard and I'll make sure you never sing again," he growled.

Derik searched the walls for somewhere to climb, but found none. Turning back, he saw a flash of steel and dodged out of the way. The blow struck the wall and sent chips of stone flying in all directions.

Down the alley, Derik saw Tornsin fighting with Ersto, blades whistling through the air as they grunted. He returned his gaze to his own attacker in time to see the backhand coming toward his face. He ducked under it and slashed out with the dagger.

His promise to his mother rose in his mind. He couldn't kill any-one. He hesitated, hand outstretched and helpless.

The thief had no such compulsions and punched him in the stomach.

Folding over, Derik rolled backwards and his dress tore off his right shoulder. He whimpered as he scrambled back, crawling through the garbage and muck.

The thief towered over him, jagged blade rising up. He swung down. The blade caught Derik's shoulder, bouncing off the bone. An explosion of agony exploded along his senses and he bit back a scream as he tried to back away.

In his wild attempt to escape, he saw the thief crumpling to the ground. A cloud of dust and broken shards of stone cascaded from his head and face. His body crunched among the debris.

It took Derik a heartbeat to calm himself enough to look around.

Tornsin stalked down the alley toward him, blade dripping with blood and two dead rapists behind him. He didn't hesitate as he stood over the third attacker and rammed the length of his sword into the body. He twisted the blade twice. The wet sucking noise when he pulled out sickened Derik.

Derik clutched his breasts with one hand as he held on the wall for balance. Fear surged through his veins, a dance of terror and adrenaline.

Tornsin looked at him, breathing heavily. He started to say something, then his eyes flickered down.

Derik blushed at the welling of despair and humiliation. Trembling, he pressed one hand against to hide his exposed manhood.

The guard swallowed with an unreadable expression on his face. "Y-You're a guy?"

The surprised voice echoed around Derik, and the thief trembled, tears running down his cheeks as he curled his fingers around himself, suddenly wishing he was protecting a pussy.

Tornsin let out a long, shuddering sigh before reaching down to clean his blade on the clothes of the rapist. With a flick, he sheathed his blade and sighed again, a sad look in his eyes.

Derik sniffed, his stomach twisting violently as he looked up at the guard and only saw rejection in his face.

Tornsin surprised him when he held out his hand. "Come on."

Shaking, Derik took the hand and used it to stand up. He clutched the remains of his dress around him, trying to cover up his sex.

Tornsin watched him for a second, saying nothing but his eyes burned along Derik's skin. "Hold on," he said in a softer voice.

Derik looked up to see him unbuttoning his shirt, pulling it open to reveal a powerful chest with a dusting of hair. He slipped it off and then held it out to Derik.

Derik blushed and turned away from him, pulling off the dress and slipping on his shirt. He breathed in the smell of sweat and musk, an intoxicating scent that would fade as soon as he exhaled. Holding his breath, he buttoned up the shirt but had to finally release it. Turning around, he sniffed a few times trying to build up the courage. "I-I'm sorry," he finally whimpered.

"Does the baron know?"

"No."

"Madre?"

Derik responded in a whisper, "Yes."

Turning around, he looked down at the shirt. It hung loosely on him, brushing his mid-thighs with the length and tenting over the twin peaks of his breasts. He burned with the humiliation and the shame of finally being revealed to one of the few men he desired.

Tornsin looked up from the body of the rapist and pocketed their identification. He spoke in a curt, almost impersonal, voice. "I need to report this, but I can do it at the castle. My duty now is to get you to safety."

Derik's lip trembled as Tornsin guided him out of the alley. He flagged down a guard with a whistle, then gave short instructions before bustling Derik down the street. They cut through a park to head toward one of the carriage places in the city.

As they followed the beaten path, Derik swallowed. "T-Thank you."

"For?"

"Coming for me. How did Madre know?"

Tornsin slowed down and sighed angrily, "Damn it!"

Derik looked around sharply for someone attacking. "What!?"

Tornsin blushed and shook his head. "No, nothing. I... Madre didn't send me, I was doing personal errands, actually."

A profound sense of relief filled him and Derik couldn't figure out why. "Oh."

"I," Tornsin swallowed before speaking, "I was in the perfume shop. To, um, get... you... something."

Derik's mouth opened in surprise, and he looked at the blushing guard.

His hands clenched at the shirt as Tornsin fumbled with his pouch. He pulled it open and handed Derik a small box. "I couldn't find that stuff, um, Apple Orgasm. But the lady said that this would be a nicer match."

Staring at him for a second and feeling a flush burning his cheeks, he opened the box and pulled out a crystalline vial, a perfume named Apple's Summer Love. His hands trembling, he spritzed a small amount on his wrist and breathed it in. The scent of it, jasmine and apples, sent a tiny shiver down his spine and he sniffed at the sweetness.

Tornsin made a grunting noise.

Derik looked up.

The guard blushed even hotter. "You, um, were the first woman I was ever attracted to."

Derik ducked his head, "I'm sorry."

Tornsin chuckled dryly, "I just left the shop when I saw you running down the street. Then I saw that guy chasing you and, well, I knew you were in trouble. I mean, I knew you were when Madre told me what happened, but then you were there."

Bashfully, Derik smiled. "T-Thank you."

They walked together through the park, listening to the birds. Derik held the bottle tightly, unwilling to let it go as he walked next to Tornsin. They reached near the end with Derik spoke again.

"I'm sorry I'm not a woman. I didn't want to ruin your first time."

Tornsin chuckled, "I never said you were the first person I was attracted to, you were just the first woman."

Derik froze and Tornsin walked a few steps before stopping.

He turned around with a wry smile.

Derik swallowed as the heat rose. "What?"

Tornsin sighed before he answered. "I thought I was going straight for you, Dora."

"Y-You're gay!?"

Scratching his head, he chuckled. "Yeah. I guess I saw something special about you. Guess I did. Mom will be disappointed though, she always hoped I'd find some nice girl."

Derik clutched the perfume bottle. "You mean?"

Tornsin walked back to him. "I mean a lot of things, and, well this probably isn't the best time to ask. But I would be honored if you were to go out to dinner with me some time. You know, like Madre suggested."

Happy tears splashed on Derik's cheeks. "I-I would love to."

Tornsin held out his hand and Derik took it. He pulled Derik close and slid an arm around his waist, holding him firmly as they headed toward the carriage.

Derik couldn't talk, feeling a strange sense of elation, like the wave of pleasure after being struck, and he rode it.

They stepped down from the carriage at the first palace gate. Derik looked at the shirt and saw that the cut in his shoulder had soaked through the fabric. A large crimson stain ran down both sides. He blushed as he pointed it out. "I-I'm sorry, I ruined your shirt."

Standing next to him, Tornsin shrugged. "It's just a shirt."

Derik looked up at him, then shook his head. "No, it will never be just a shirt."

Before the guard could respond, he reached up with both arms and wrapped them around his neck. Pulling him tight, he brought his lips up to Tornsin's and kissed him.

Tornsin gasped, then opened his mouth as they embraced in front of the baron's palace.

Derik could feel the eyes of the other guards and servants on him, but he realized he didn't care anymore. He was safer than he ever felt before. When Tornsin slipped his hand around to press one palm against his back and the other on his hip, his heart almost burst with joy.

Heaven-Bound

Derik huddled under the waterfall in the massage room, sitting in the darkness as he clutched himself. Tornsin's shirt plastered against his naked skin, and the warmth of their kiss still burned bright, but he couldn't go out to face Madre.

When he finally reached the harem again, Derik found that he was an hour earlier than Madre expected; she had sent out a carriage to pick him up.

At the first sight of him—he surprised her in the middle of a game of strip poker—she rushed up and hugged him tightly. Concerned, she started with a battery of questions, but the spell that sealed his throat prevented him from saying anything. Instead, they both grew frustrated by his lack of communication. She thought he was being difficult, not because some spell silenced his voice, making it more terrible.

Tornsin walked in wearing a fresh shirt, coming to his rescue. He gave a dispassionate description of where he found Derik, the attempted rape, and the attack. He left out the perfume and the kiss, but Derik knew Madre would find out about that soon enough.

He blushed hotly, standing between the two of them.

When Tornsin finished, Madre drew her attention at Derik and he cringed. "Why couldn't you tell me that! You were almost raped!"

Derik whimpered and stepped away, feeling heat and energy rising up from Madre. He opened his mouth to speak, but the spell silenced him, and he closed his mouth again.

Madre shook her head. "Damn it, Dora, just tell me what he did!"

He stepped back another step, afraid of the rage that burned in her frame.

She stalked closer as flickers of magical flame became visible. "Did he hurt you?"

Derik whimpered, still backing up. Tears burned in his eyes.

Madre took another step, then froze in mid-step. She set down her foot, then stormed over to him, pressing one hand against his heart and her eyes probing. "He hurt you?"

Despite the spell that stole his voice, there was nothing to prevent him from reliving the memories of his caning. He looked down to watch Madre listening directly to his heart, the rapid pounding of a fear-fueled heart. Looking up, he saw her staring at him with eyes that pierced his soul.

Madre choked as she looked away for a second, the presence of her gaze fading. "You still have healing magic in you. Why did he have to heal you, Dora? And why are you so frightened?"

Unable to speak, Derik just looked away. He tried to speak, but the words refused to come.

Madre's voice grew dark as she growled, "I'll kill him."

The sound of her anger scraped like claws against his spine, and Derik closed his eyes tightly as Madre pulled away from him. He slowly peeked to see her storming out of the room, angry flames burning visibly around her body.

Tornsin looked back and forth for a moment. He sighed. "I better stop her. The baron won't be happy if she kills anyone."

He gave Derik a quick kiss on the lips, then ran after Madre.

Derik blushed hotly, a hand on his lips. When he turned around, a smirking Teri stood only a footstep away. "So, Dora, why is Tornsin now kissing you?" she drawled.

He blushed and fled past her, fleeing for the massage room to avoid the uncomfortable questions he knew would follow.

Crawling into the waterfall, he clutched himself as he waited for Madre to return.

Sherrel made a brief effort to talk, but he refused to even look at her until she promised to bring him food later and left him alone.

Derik sobbed, not for the man he hated more than anything else, but for Madre's anger. He had never wanted to see that anger again, and somehow the idea of Madre attacking Rick made him sick to his stomach.

He heard someone enter the massage room. He clutched down tight and prayed they wouldn't turn on the lights. To his surprise, no illumination flooded the room and he breathed a tiny sigh of relief. Then, he heard footsteps on the tile, moving closer as the visitor circled around the tables and walked toward the waterfall.

It wasn't Sherrel—she knew where he was. Derik muttered softly.

"Go away."

Two hands came for him, two large hands that sliced the streams of the waterfall as they hooked under Derik's armpits and easily picked him up. He let out an inarticulate yelp as large thumbs caught on the ribs below his breasts. Water splashed down his face, blinding him. The hands set him down and he wiped the droplets from his eyes to find himself staring at the chest of the baron.

Derik's mouth opened with surprise as he looked up, feeling the raw presence of the baron sending a flush through his body. He shivered and focused on that sapphire-colored gaze that seemed to glow in the darkness.

"Hello, Blackbird," his voice rumbled deeply.

Derik's nipples grew harder with every word that caressed his senses, pouring hot lead into his manhood. It twitched, coming fully to life and he pressed one hand discretely against it as he listened. "B-Baron?" His voice could barely rise above a whisper.

Hamel smiled and brushed one hand along Derik's jaw. An electrical connection coursing through him and had to curl his fingers tighter against his sex to prevent it from sticking up through the seam of his dripping shirt.

The baron chuckled. "I have never had anyone cause this much trouble in my harem or in my barony."

Derik shivered and a whimper rose to his lips.

The baron continued to speak as his hand stroked Derik's jaw. "Thankfully, Tornsin found me on my way home. Only two people in this world could have stopped Rachi from storming out of the palace and slaughtering Rick and everyone who worked for him."

Whimpering louder, Derik pulled away from the baron to retreat back to the waterfall, but Hamel reached down with one hand and pressed it against his ass, drawing him up against his hard body.

Derik gasped, splaying his fingers across the powerful chest and feeling the swollen manhood of his baron against his belly.

"No, no, little blackbird."

Derik twisted, trying to pull away. He begged the baron, but trying to talk about Rick just left him speechless.

The baron held him tight, talking in a low, soothing rumble, "He won't have you. Not tonight, not tomorrow. Before I had Rachi arrested, she told me what you and Tornsin told her. I didn't know about you and Rick, otherwise, I would never have brought him to the harem that night."

Derik trembled but kept squirming. He couldn't let the baron know he was a male.

The baron seemed unconcerned as he easily kept Derik in place. He stroked Derik's long black hair.

Unable to escape, Derik tried to ask a question to distract the powerful man. "Arrested?"

Baron chuckled, a rumble that shook Derik and brought the heat boiling inside him.

"It won't stop her, just enough to let her punch some stone walls, carve me out a new prison cell with her bare hands, and calm down long enough to talk logically. There is something about battle mages that really turns me on, but when they get pissed, you have to have a pretty strong house to survive it."

"She scared me."

Baron stroked his back, then reached down.

Derik whimpered, his hand holding the shirt down, but the baron just hooked his hand under his ass and picked him up. He sat down on the padded table and leaned back slightly. The muscular ridge of his thigh was only centimeters from Derik's manhood.

Derik shifted position so his legs were hanging off the left side of the baron. He tried to slip off but the baron guided his head to rest on Hamel's opposite shoulder.

"You want to know a secret? She scares me too." His voice was even deeper when Derik's body was pressed against it. It seemed to fill him and his body betrayed his growing excitement. Discretely, he rested his hand over his crotch.

Gulping, Derik said, "S-She said she would kill him."

The baron nodded, "And she probably would have. And all the men and women that worked for him or anyone who got in her way."

"W-Why did you stop her?"

"It was the right thing. There are laws in this country, laws I've swore to uphold. I cannot break a promise. She'll calm down, apologize for slapping me," Derik gasped but the baron laughed, "and then, we'll find an intelligent way of handling this."

Derik breathed softly, closing his eyes at the relief that Madre wouldn't suffer consequences for slaughtering Rick. Then, a memory of Rick's shaft buried inside him came up and a heated desire bubbled up. Blushing, he tore his thoughts away and nestled closer to the baron.

The baron reached down and hooked Derik's chin with his hand, sending an electric arc through his body, before drawing him up to him. "I promise you this, Blackbird, if he hurt you, then I will break him."

"T-Thank you."

He chuckled, "It isn't only for me. Rick is a powerful man who has too many fingers into crime. I call him a friend because it is better to keep your enemies close. I suspect he knows this also, but he has a lot of influence here and with the duke, which makes it difficult for anything to happen to him."

"I-I know."

"I heard, but then again, aren't all blackbirds also thieves?"

Derik blushed hotly and tried to pull away.

The baron refused to release his chin and kissed him lightly on the lips. It was powerful and dominating. The caress send whorls of pleasure racing along Derik's veins.

When they broke, Derik was breathless and desperately needed to change the topic away from his own thieving ways. "Why? Um, why does Madre scare you?"

Chuckling, Hamel shrugged. "Rachi said that you know I'm not human, right? With the life-sucking cock?"

Derik ducked his head, blushing.

The baron grinned. "She figured it out in a couple of days. Bright girl and she had the grace to bring it up to me private. Over three hundred years of hiding and some girl notices after getting screwed once. I'd rather you not tell anyone though, won't go well with the general populace."

Whispering, Derik asked the question he posed to Madre. "What are you?"

The baron sighed, his chest swelling and rubbing against Derik. "I'm... alone. Last of my kind, I think, but I did something I should have never done. And then made a promise I should have never made."

"That is very confusing."

The baron chuckled and stroked Derik's hair.

The gesture calmed Derik. Moments later, he arched his back minutely to press his breasts against the man's chest. Even seconds away from being caught, he couldn't stand being separated.

The baron reached over with his other hand to stroke a hand up the line of Derik's breasts.

Derik shivered as his breath came deeply. At the hard fingers caressing his nipples, Derik shifted his position so he was almost lying on his back, balanced on the baron's shoulder and his buttocks against his lap. He kept one hand over his crotch, holding it down against the soaked fabric.

"I can't lie, Blackbird. I won't tell you why or how it happened, but just say, to explain it is to surrender the one secret I have left."

Whispering softy, Derik said, "I have a secret."

He said nothing for a moment, but worked the top button of his shirt open.

Derik's breath came harder as his breasts heaved, feeling every movement as the baron parted the fabric at his damp throat.

"I know, Blackbird, but you never have to tell me."

"Then why," he sniffed, "do you let me stay?"

The baron worked a second button open, trailing his fingertips along the top of Derik's breasts and leaving an electrical trail of pleasure along his recently healed skin. "Because everyone has secrets. I doubt yours are as terrible as my own and you've already proven yourself."

"How?"

"Madre told me that you went willingly to Rick, just because you were more afraid of being removed from the harem than what he would do."

Derik shivered and the baron curled his right arm around Derik, cradling him more.

"I know Rick is a sadist. More than once, I'd reminded him to leave my girls uninjured. I also told him I will never accept him using magical healing to cover it. In the last few years, not even the pain kittens wanted to go to him; everyone else is afraid of him."

The thief's mouth opened to say something, but the prick of Forbis' spell silencing him. He closed it, then sighed. "I'm sorry."

"For what? Knowing that Rick hurt my blackbird? I know you aren't into pain, not the type that needs healing, which means you were serious about wanting to stay."

The remembered rape brought another flush, he hated the hungry craving of Rick's shaft buried deep and the anticipation of pleasure after the pain. A tiny part of him started to ache for it, but he shoved down on it, hoping it would go away. "I want to. I mean, I want to stay."

"And you will," Derik's heart blossomed like a flower opening up at those three words.

The baron hugged him tightly, then leaned back, "As far as I'm concerned, you are now officially part of my harem. Even if you fell into all of this."

Derik sniffed at the sudden tears of happiness.

Hamel chuckled and ran his finger down Derik's throat and along the parted seams of the shirt. Finding the next button, he worked it open and spread his large hands over one of Derik's breasts. Droplets of water ran down Derik's stomach and pooled in his navel.

When the powerful hands touched him, Derik let out a long breath. The thief moaned, his back arching and his hand clutching himself even tighter. Blood pounding in his ears, he still didn't know what to do when the baron reached the seventh button and found something other than a slick pussy.

Neither said anything as the baron cradled Derik and unbuttoned his shirt. The feeling of a countdown shook Derik and he had to fight to keep his hardness down between his legs. It was hot and sensitive, the pulse of it pounding against his palm.

"I see that Tornsin has fallen for you."

"Oh, I, um," Derik stammered.

"I was wondering why he returned without a shirt, but I see it on you. We had a bet, these last few years, most of the guard staff and the harem."

The baron worked his hand along Derik's stomach, tracing a tiny circle around his navel before working the sixth button.

Derik whimpered as he started to pant. "A-About what?"

He chuckled as his fingers released the fabric and spread it apart. "If he was gay. Well, lost that one. Never hear the end of it from Madre, she was right as usual."

Whimpering, Derik whispered at the thought of Hamel finding out he was right. "Oh, Bridget."

The baron didn't hear him and trailed his fingertips along Derik's bare, clenching stomach to brush against the fingers protecting the last button. Derik's heart pounded hard as he froze, his hand covering over his manhood. Knowing that only a single button remained, he couldn't move away from the baron's embrace.

The baron's hand slid down, then along his fingers.

Derik clenched hem tightly against his hard manhood, protecting them and not wanting things to ever change.

"Going shy on me now?"

"I, um, will Madre be back soon?"

Grinning, the baron worked his fingers into Derik's. He pushed the thief's digits aside to work at the button. "Not for another hour or so, why?"

The fabric slid off his hips, parting and bringing the cool air to his aching manhood. His body shook as he tried to bring his hands back, but the baron's arm blocked him.

"You're trembling, Blackbird, why?" Hamel said huskily, his breath hot against Derik's face.

Derik looked up in the darkness, only able to see the glint of the blue eye.

The baron's hand pressed against Derik's aching length. He slid it down his palm to curl his fingers around Derik's balls and tease his asshole.

Weeks of anticipation and ecstasy exploded in a single heartbeat, bursting out as he came in the baron's hand with a shuddering gasp. His hands clutched at his wrist as he arched back, wailing out as the orgasm ignited into an electrical storm that raged inside him.

Derik couldn't move as he began to sob, the release of everything and the anticipation of what came next refined the pleasure even more, until it became a single diamond of intensity, filling him and consuming his thoughts until he slumped down in the baron's arms with a smile.

Lips brushed against his. Surprised, he opened his mouth and arched up as the baron kissed him, the powerful lips standing the hairs on the back of his neck up. With a gasp, hungry and desperate, he wrapped his arms around the baron's neck, feeling the large fingers stroking his cum-slicked cock along his palm.

He came again, nestled in the arms of a man he truly loved. Like reaching into the heart of a god, he drowned in passion. Sobbing, Derik could only cling to the baron and pray that he could breath again when it ended.

The baron broke the kiss and held up his dripping hand. He chuckled, then looked down at Derik, his lips brushing against Derik's as he whispered huskily. "You are the most beautiful man I have ever seen, Derik."

Derik didn't think he could come again. His body proved him wrong as his world exploded in the white heat of an orgasm born of nothing but those mere words.

Apologies

Derik slumped down in the baron's arms, feeling boneless and vibrating at the same time. His body floated with the afterglow of his orgasm. Cum and moisture from the waterfall mixed together as they slowly ran down his chest and belly.

Panting, he closed his eyes at the sensation of his breasts heaving, then opened them up to look up at the baron. He felt so small in the large man's eyes, but the warm blue eye that regarded him sent another quake of pleasure through his body. "When did you, um, find out?"

Hamel chuckled, his hand stroking along Derik's cleavage. "The night Rachi found you. We discussed it after you went to sleep."

Derik's lip trembled, thinking back to the sacrifice he made to go to Rick and feeling as if it was in vain. "Y-You mean, I didn't have to go to Rick? That you already accepted me?"

He curled up, but the baron set his hand down on Derik's breasts, pushing him back into position.

"No, Blackbird, there is a lot more involved, and I think that is why you went somewhere you should have never have gone. And, I think, all three of us are at fault for what happened."

Derik shivered at the prickle of fear but also the electrical touch of the baron holding him so tightly. "What do you mean?"

"Three days before Rachi told me about you, I had a visitor. A rather curvy and attractive one, but also one that seemed to have a fair amount of spite and anger. In fact, I think she was getting excited just talking to me about you."

Derik frowned, trying to remember which of the many people he annoyed in his life. The baron expanded on the description.

"She wore long leather gloves and brought along her two brothers. I remember the gloves because she wouldn't take them off and they set the hairs on my arm on end, which means they were probably enchanted."

"Oh, fuck, Wendi."

The baron chuckled, his fingers curling around Derik's breasts to tease one hard, slick nipple. "I didn't know her name, but she told me that a thief named Derik was going to steal something from me."

Squeaking, Derik cringed, but the baron just twisted his nipple playfully until he relaxed. The feeling of pleasure and pain mixed through his elated body, simmering the heat that filled him from the baron's closeness.

"D-Did she say what I was going to steal?"

"Yes," said the baron in his rumbling voice. He continued to tease and twisting his nipples. His other hand slid along Derik's manhood, teasing it as the seconds passed by.

"I-I'm sorry."

The baron said nothing.

Derik whimpered softly, his back arching as the baron plucked at his sensitive ridges.

"You know, I waited for the Eye to disappear. Every day, every morning I came into my hall, expecting to see it gone. I knew you were there, but didn't know if you were biding your time or if you had something else in mind."

Derik's lips cracked with surprise.

The baron continued to speak softly in his deep voice that resonated with the flame in the thief's loins. "Rachi watched you pretty closely too. I didn't actually tell her you were going to steal the Eye, she would have probably killed you, but she knew you were stealing something important to me. She enchanted that blue cord you used for your hair with a seeking spell, hoping you'd wear it when you ran away."

He chuckled softly, "I even had extra guards posted for the last six weeks, just waiting for it to happen."

Derik realized he had tears in his eyes. Sniffing, he wiped them with the soaked sleeve of Tornsin's shirt. "W-What happened?"

The baron chuckled again, then drew Derik up until their lips were almost touching. "Nothing. Nothing happened. You didn't even try to get into the hall, even when she sent you out on errands in the palace. You didn't try to escape, check things out, or anything we would expect a thief to do."

The air grew thick around him, a tenseness that made him shiver.

Derik drew up one legs and worked it below him, straddling the baron's hips and settling back down.

"Then, when Rachi locked herself into her room, because of Nightingale." He sighed sadly. "You broke her out."

"I had to, b-because of Nightingale and my—"

"Raven," Derik didn't think the baron could sound sadder with a single word. He shivered at his mother's name, then rested his head on the powerful shoulder of the baron.

"She's my mother."

"I didn't know until Rachi figured it out. I can't tell you how upset I was when I found out how she died."

Hamel stroked his hair, holding him tightly. His eye probed into Derik's before he said, "I never wanted that, Blackbird. I love all my girls but love could never change the fact: Raven was a fighter. Even as a kitten, she was always fighting."

He sniffed, desperately not wanting to know but, at the same time, hungrily needing it. "What happened?" he whispered.

"A guy. His name was Gorvin. He was the captain of my guards, and ironically, Tornsin's uncle. She and another girl, Raccoon, fell for him hard. They started to fight but it kept getting worse until Esali got involved."

Derik sniffed, already guessing what happened.

"It wasn't pretty. When I managed to shove my way through the crowds, your mother had already strangled Coon and injured Esali. She fought off the guards until Gorvin came. He stopped her, not with words but fighting. It was brutal, seeing their love torn apart that way, but it had to be done."

Derik shook as the tears came, dripping on the baron's shoulder as he clutched him tightly. The baron said nothing, just held him tightly as the sobs wracked the thief's body. The sobbing stretched into minutes but eventually they faded.

"It's a strange world, Blackbird, when you fall into the harem that your mother grew up in."

Derik chuckled sadly, wiping his eyes. "Ironic."

"Lucky, I think."

"Lucky?"

"I hated how I handled Raven. I beat myself up that I didn't talk to her before it blew up into something serious. When I saw you in that harem, with your long black hair and blue eyes, I actually thought Rachi played a joke on me and brought Raven back. I feel like I was given a second chance to... I guess not make the same mistake twice. You, Blackbird, look just like her. No doubt, Hawk's little trick helped. That girl is more annoying than anyone else I've known. Always doing fucking stupid things that end up being the right thing in the end."

Derik giggled and the baron smiled, stroking his thumb along Derik's jaw. He sighed for a moment, then drew Derik into a long, lingering kiss that stole the thief's breath away. He moaned into it, pressing his body against the hard ridge of the baron's manhood. When they broke, they were both gasping for breath.

"You are so pretty, but I think you heard it before."

Derik blushed, "I-I like it when you say it."

"And I like saying it, Blackbird."

"Call me Derik, please?"

The baron smiled warmly and pulled him into a kiss, holding Derik's waist with one hand and a hand against his back as they embraced. When they broke, the rumble of the man's voice filled Derik with an intense feeling of lightness. "Derik."

He nearly came again, just hearing his name. He cooed softly and hugged him tightly.

The baron chuckled and shifted his position, moving the long hardness tighter against Derik's stomach and manhood.

Derik shivered at the feeling.

"Rachi finally decided to trust you. The dress-shopping, the corset, even that night was going to be her present to you, to let you know that I'm happy to have another pretty thief in my harem."

Derik moaned softly, imagining how it could have been.

Hamel playfully teased him as he said, "I was going to tease you a little, bend you over my bed, then right before I entered you, I was going to lean over and whisper your name."

Moaning louder, Derik's hands reached down to stroke the hard shaft between them. The baron breathed deeply, then inhaled as Derik pulled out his shaft, sliding his fingers down the slicked length.

Hamel swallowed, his eyes watching the movements. "I wanted to make you come hard, just with that. It was the point I wanted you to know I wanted you to be mine."

Derik breathed deeply, "I want to be yours."

"On my bed?"

Gasping, he nodded, his fingers working up and down the steel-hard shaft and feeling it in his palms. His body ached for it to be inside him and he lifted himself up, dragging the baron's cock along the junction between his balls and thigh.

"Oh, yes..."

"Bent over the pillows, ass up in the air?"

The heated head sliding across Derik's balls and he gasped at the inferno that surged to fill him. His breasts teased the baron's face until his lover caught one with his strong lips. Derik moaned with pleasure.

The lips slid off as Derik positioned himself right above the cock, swollen head pressed into the only hole he could give the baron.

"I want you, baron."

"And I want you, Derik. Please forgive us?"

Derik lowered himself down on the hard spear of pleasure, feeling the thick head pry him open. It buried deep inside him in a single stroke, as if he was born for it.

A long shuddering gasp filled the room as he sank down, centimeter by centimeter, aching for the baron even as he was filled. The baron's breath came hot against him, making him glow with such warmth and love and passion that he came all over the junction of their beings before he settled down. His cock jumped and jerked, still pumping out hot fluids, but Derik just leaned into the baron, rocking back and forth to enjoy the rod of ecstasy swirling his insides.

The baron just held him, hands on his ass, as Derik impaled himself, rising and dropping down, tracing each ridge as orgasms grew inside his body. They were white hot and intoxicating, something he now craved more than anything.

The baron came quickly, his balls tightening up and the feeling of the entire length swelling before exploding inside Derik.

The thief let out a long gasp of pleasure, unable to come from the afterglow, but grinding down with a desperation to be the baron's lover.

Hot cum dripped from his tightly stretched rectum, but he just continued to rock and pump, riding the shaft until the baron came again and again. Their combined juices splashed loudly to the floor beneath them.

Panting, he swayed for a moment before pulling himself off the still-hard cock. A shudder filled Derik, a long withdrawing of energy as it slipped out of his body. He knew what it was now and it followed with an intense sense of pleasure, like fingernails down his back and he finally came hard against the baron once again, emptying his balls before slumping against the baron.

Hamel, panting from their love-making, stroked his hand along Derik's back.

Derik purred softly, his breasts heaving as he enjoyed another afterglow of pleasure. He found the words. "I forgive you, if you forgive me."

"Always."

The baron's arms wrapped around him, holding him tight as they just held each other. A soft time of pleasure and just enjoying the comfort. But, it ended too soon when the baron stirred. "Come on, I hear Rachi talking to the girls outside."

Derik slipped off Hamel and stood up, wearing nothing but an open shirt and dripping cum. It splattered to the ground between his thighs. He blushed and started to button his shirt, but his lord stopped him.

"No, no reason to hide. Not to mention, you are probably just getting out of it in a moment anyways."

He blinked. "Um, what?"

"Well, I think Rachi needs closure also. She knows as well as I do that she should have broken the ruse the second Rick came in, instead of holding on to that promise of hers. She won't admit it, of course, but she needs your forgiveness."

"I'll forgive her."

He chuckled, "I plan on that, but just saying it isn't enough. So, I'm going to have a talk to her and then I'm going to have you spank her in front of everyone in the harem. You didn't need to suffer than much pain, just because you wouldn't admit to trying to steal the Eye of Hamel."

Derik's breath got tight again. He remembered all the pain that Rick did to him, but he couldn't say anything. Instead, he pushed it down and resolved to forget it as fast as possible.

The baron chuckled and ran a finger along Derik's cleavage. As Derik's manhood woke up, so did the baron's. His smile filled the room as he spoke playfully. "I know, but it's important to me that we can push this behind us. So, you are going to spank Rachi for her apology. Then, I'm going to apologize, and you are going to spank her again on my behalf."

Derik looked up in surprise.

The baron shrugged with a grin. "I'm the baron, you don't spank me. I spank you."

Derik blushed which turned into a moan as the baron slipped arm around his waist, holding him tight.

The baron's fingers stroked the side of his hip. "In addition, I'm going to tell you this, I'm only interested in sticking my dick in you, not the other way around. Understand? I'm in charge. The only thing that goes in my mouth is your nipples and no one gets my ass."

It never occurred to him, but Derik shivered and nestled closer at the thought. A faint smile and a blush crossed his lips as he thought about being happily impaled on Hamel's shaft.

"Yes, sir."

Company of Thieves

Derik stepped out of the carriage with a beaming smile and a twist of his hips. He stepped down, his sapphire heels hitting the gravel and Tornsin gently took his hand with a smile of his own. Letting a tiny blush reach his cheeks, he let the guard draw him away as Teri, Sherrel, and Madre filtered out of vehicle.

Teri gave him a playful grin and skipped over, easily balancing on her own heels. She wrapped her arms around Derik's waist and pulled him back. "Come on, you can visit your boyfriend later."

"Teri!" Derik grinned, then blushed as the slender girl reached up to grab his breasts. The leather of his new corset flexed underneath her fingers and Derik shivered at the warm sensation against his bare skin. The tickle of lace trimming the corset added another layer of pleasure.

Chuckling, Teri started to pull open his dress in front of Tornsin until Madre cleared her throat.

"Come on, we need to get inside. Its going to rain soon."

Slipping away from Teri, Derik looked up to the storm clouds above. The feeling of lighting in the air brought a shiver to his spine and he ducked his head back down. One hand stroked against the leather and lace of his present. It smelled new, of magic and leather.

"You like it?"

Looking up, he admired the relaxed Madre. "It's wonderful, Madre, but why Tiv's?"

Madre slipped one arm in Derik's, squeezing it for a moment, then leading the thief up the stairs. "I wanted to. You really look gorgeous in a corset, even if everyone knows you are a male, you are still dressing like a female."

Teri spoke up, her heels tapping against the stone steps leading to the balance. "I like you as a woman, makes you all," she grinned evilly, "submissive."

Madre raised an eyebrow, "You saying women are submissive?"

Teri shook her head and giggled. "No, it makes Derik submissive. He likes to be the pussy, don't you?"

Derik blushed hotly, but said nothing.

Madre chuckled, and Sherrel leaned over.

"Don't worry, Teri-cat gets all submissive when the baron teases her with that log of his. Just wait, you'll see her beg."

Teri blushed herself, "I don't beg."

"Oh really? I guess we'll find out in two days, won't we? Little cat purrs loudly when he's waving that over her."

Derik let out a soft moan with the thought of their night with the baron. Only two days before he would spend the entire night with Hamel, with only Sherrel and Teri to warm the bed. His lips parted as he wondered how it will be to finally lie in the baron's bed as one of his harem girls.

Sherrel's breath tickled his ear as she whispered. "Thinking about how the baron took Madre?"

Derik's blush seared his skin as he remembered the scene after he spanked Madre. The baron took her, right in the middle of the harem. It wasn't tender or playful, just jaw-dropping powerful. A rapid-fire pounding hammer that slammed into Madre so hard, he thought her bones would break. Hungry and desperate, the baron threw everything into his fucking, and Madre took everything he gave her. He could still remember the blurred shaft and cum pouring out of her with every stroke. A part of him hungered to feel that same inhuman pounding.

He moaned again, his eyes closing at the thought, and his cock strained against the dark blue thong he wore.

Sherrel's hand teased him, trailing down his front and stroking against the swollen member that pushed up against the front of his dress. She chuckled softly, "Don't worry, I bet he would do that for you, in his bed."

Swallowing, Derik panted with anticipation. His corset's tightness resisted his chest and the binding only added to growing desire.

Sherrel giggled and traced his length with one finger. "Soon, Dora, soon," she whispered before trailing away.

He cracked open one eye and gave her a mock glare. "Slut."

"Trap," she replied with a smile.

Derik grinned but then froze as he realized Madre had stopped. Looking around, he realized that the air of the palace had become tense. Feeling a prickle of something down his spine, he stared at the serious guards standing guard and the pair that guarded with the main hall with drawn swords.

Teri grunted, then looked up with confusion. "What's going on?"

Madre frowned, "I don't know."

After a few more seconds, she amended herself. "Teri, Sherrel, Dora, go to the harem. I need to check on this."

Teri pouted, "Madre—"

"Now," came the uncompromising command.

Jumping at the hard voice, Derik fled the hall and headed for the harem.

Teri and Sherrel joined him and they talked about the sudden change as they walked.

In the harem, all three of them stripped out of their dresses and slipped into their more comfortable clothes. Derik almost purred as he pulled on Tornsin's shirt, buttoning it down and leaving it teasing his knees. Teri rolled her eyes, but Sherrel giggled. Teri flipped up the hem as she pulled on her silk robe.

"Are you going to ever give that back?"

Derik blushed and held it against his skin. He could feel the fabric teasing his nipples and he breathed in the scent of the guard. "He said I could keep it."

Teri snorted, "He just wants to get in your panties."

Bashfully, Derik looked away, but Teri grabbed him and snaked her hands to grip his buttocks.

"And you want him to get into your thong, don't you?" she teased.

Derik started to say something, then grinned. "He is cute."

"He is gay."

"He likes me."

"You are gay."

Derik gaped for a moment. "I am not!"

"You are too, when was the last time you had some pussy?"

"Last night! When you decided you wanted sex in the middle of the morning and thought my tongue made a great dildo!"

Teri grinned and wormed a finger between his buttocks.

He moaned softly, parting his legs as his hardness pressed against her cleavage.

"Oh yeah. That was fun."

"And I'm not gay."

She giggled and drew her body up, pressing her breasts against his. "Fine, you aren't gay. You are a little submissive slut with a dick."

He was still trying to find an appropriate response when Madre spoke seriously from the bathroom entrance. "Dora? Can you come with me?"

Looking into those dead eyes, the good mood evaporated like the morning mist. He slipped out of Teri's grasp and started toward her.

Madre shook her head. "Get dressed and hurry, please."

Fear filled him as he slipped on his thong and pulled a long dress over his hips, tucking Tornsin's shirt into it. Madre seemed in a hurry as she guided him back to the hall. This time, the doors were closed tightly and the feeling of unease grew with every passing second. His slippers scuffed against the ground as one of the guards cracked open the door, then he gasped as he stared into the main hall.

Glass.

Broken glass across the entire floor. One of the statue arms rested on the ground and he realized where the blue glass came from. Stepping forward, despite the feeling of him walking into a collapsed building. He looked up for the bright light of the Eye suddenly remembering that the fake would shatter long after he was suppose to be gone. He shook like a leaf as his eyes focused in the center of the hall.

Except for a brilliant beam of light that speared down through the rest of the room, only shadows filled the great hall. The map of the barony broke on the floor, shard everywhere. In the center, under the light, a pool of molten glass oozed out slowly. Where the brilliant orb of light used to be, or more accurately where the fake sphere used to glow, there was nothing.

Panic filled him as he stared at the missing sphere. His mouth opened up, but Forbis' spell silence even the gasp that slipped out of his mouth. He started to shake, sweat forming on his forehead. His stomach lurched to the side and plummeted into a sick feeling near his feet.

He looked around, finding the exits, but then jumped as Madre grabbed his arm. She whispered sharply. "Relax, I know it wasn't you."

Derik let out a long shuddering sigh, but the knot in his stomach refused to relax. She didn't know he had already stolen it.

Madre glared at him for a long moment, then gestured across the room.

Derik followed her movement to see Hamel frowning at his throne and some guards standing around something that could only be a bloody corpse.

He swallowed and let Madre lead him across the room.

Hamel spotted him and stood up, meeting him at the knot of guards. They parted and he found himself looking at the body. The sight of the puddle of blood, sword wounds, and massive burns sickened Derik and he had to force himself not to vomit.

"W-What happened?" it came out as a strangled whisper and he looked pleadingly up at the baron.

Hamel sighed and shook his head. "Someone stole my Eye."

The familiar rumble became a funeral bell, a looming that caused Derik to cringe from guilt. Sweat dripping down his neck, he looked at the terrified face of the corpse and whimpered softly in fright.

At that moment, he wished he could speak. Looking up at the baron, seeing the pain in his face, he just wanted to confess to having the real Eye above the harem. His mouth opened and he tried to say the words, but no sound came out. Tears forming in his eyes, he tried to say it again and again, screaming out but the spell silenced him. In the long moments that followed, with Hamel and Madre glaring at the corpse, Derik tried to confess again and again until the tears dripped down his face with frustration.

Hamel glanced up and immediately looked concerned. Stepping around Madre, he took Derik up in his arms. Even the electrical feeling between them couldn't push away the sickening feeling that grew in Derik's gut. "It's okay, Blackbird. It's okay."

Derik sobbed, trying to force the words out. Tears dripping off his face with the desire to scream at Hamel, to tell him it was all his fault.

The baron didn't understand, couldn't understand. He cleared his throat and ordered the guards out of the room. They gave him curious looks as they left, sealing the doors after them. Hamel held him until the sound of the doors closing sounded across the room. Then, he held her tighter. "I know it isn't you, Blackbird, I trust you."

Derik tried to shake his head, but the spell froze him in place. He just sobbed again, leaning against the baron's powerful chest as he tried to find some way of explaining and confessing.

It just wouldn't come.

Finally, he gave up and just slumped against the baron, letting the tears soak the expensive cloth over his love. Hamel stroked his hair, just whispering to him.

"It's okay. It's okay..."

The frustration tore him apart, but there was simply no way of getting around the spell that silenced him. Derik sighed as he forced himself to stop sobbing, to stop trying to confess.

The baron held him until the shakes ended, then looked into his eyes. "I know it isn't you. But, I was hoping that you would tell me who did this."

Derik sniffed and wiped the tears from his eyes. He found his voice when he spoke again. "I-I shouldn't. They kill thieves who tell people like you." If he couldn't confess, at least he could give the plausible lie of self-preservation. Despite his attempts at a confession, the words stumbled out of his mouth.

The baron nodded, his hand slipping off.

Derik whimpered, afraid of losing him.

The baron sighed. "I understand."

Derik worried his bottom lip, then he whispered. "I'll try."

Hamel looked up with surprise.

Derik blushed. "I guess," he paused sheepishly, "I'd rather be your harem girl than a thief."

With Madre and Hamel staring at him in shock, Derik blushed and pulled him his skirt to kneel above the bloody corpse. With a shaking hand, he pushed the body over and frowned at the expression on his face. "This is Opir, he's a boxer from the merchant area."

Derik surprised himself with the steady, soft voice he gave. He looked at the thief impassively, remembering the arguments they had, frequently over their individual shares.

"What's a boxer?"

Nodding, Derik stepped back and let his skirt slide back into place. "A boxer is a thief who specializes in safe cracking and locks."

Madre frowned, "There weren't any safes here, and the hall was unlocked."

Derik nodded for a moment, remembering Opir's friends. "He's part of a team of four others. There is, um, Xerim who is the acrobat, Billet and Moose are the brutes, and Gif who is a face."

Madre shook her head in confusion, "What are those? Brute?"

Derik sheepishly explained, half afraid an assassin would come out as he spoke. "Thieves here have their own titles. A brute is a thug or enforcer. Face is a seducer or a con-man, someone who preys on emotions. Acrobats are the ones who do the climbing and acrobatic jobs. We, they, um, also use the title 'master' to mean they've done a number of high profile jobs."

"How many?"

"Usually twenty jobs where they hear about rumors across the duchy or one job if the entire country talks about it."

"And my Eye?" grumbled Hamel.

"Master if they get away with it."

Madre shook her head, "Battle mages had a ranking system, based on battles and specialties, but I never knew thieves were organized that well."

Derik said nothing, still feeling numb from his effort to confess. He looked at the corpse on the floor, imagining himself in the same position.

Hamel sighed angrily and looked down at Derik. "You know what, I'm so glad you didn't steal my Eye. And, from the bottom of my heart, thank you for telling me who did this. I will have them hunted down."

A horrible wrenching twisted his stomach as Hamel looked down at him with misplaced trust and love.

The baron stroked a thumb along his jaw and sighed. He looked at Madre. "Rumors are already out about this, and I have to make an announcement soon, otherwise I'll look weak."

"What are you going to say, my lord?"

Hamel slipped away from Derik.

"I have an idea. When I put," he paused to swallow, "the Eye up there, I had trust that no one would ever get away with stealing it. I knew they would try, but it has enough protections to avoid all but the most talented of thieves. Regardless, I thought it might happen."

The baron turned to look at both Derik and Madre. "I going to swear to hunt down whoever stole my Eye. It doesn't matter how far they run or how fast they do it. I'm going to hunt them down and inflict the worse possible torment I can. I will make them suffer for years if possible, to even dare—"

He glanced at Derik and corrected himself, "Sorry, Blackbird. They will suffer for actually stealing my Eye."

Derik swallowed as the terrible feeling in his stomach tore him in half. The look in the baron's eye, hard and angry, sent a horrible spear through his heart. He opened his mouth one more time to confess, but the words refused to get out.

Both were unaware of Derik's struggle to speak.

"And a reward?" asked Madre.

"Start with a hundred thousand marks. We'll go up from there. I want my Eye back."

"Yes, my lord."

The baron came back.

Derik looked up with tears in his eyes.

The baron smiled, sweetly, and stroked his hand back along Derik's chin. The electrical touch warred with Derik's guilt, but the baron just leaned down to kiss him unaware of the storm inside the thief's head.

Derik accepted it, but he didn't feel the passion of the embrace. Just the sickening feeling of guilt strangling his throat.

After a few more minutes of speaking, the baron thanked them and hurried off to make an announcement.

Derik clutched himself as Madre walked him back to the harem.

"What are you?"

Derik jumped at her sudden question. "W-What?"

"Thief ranks. What are you?"

Derik didn't say anything as they turned a corner.

Madre gave him a few moments, then stood in front of him, forcing him to look at her.

"Dora, what are you?"

He tried to look away, but she cleared her throat.

"That's five."

"I," he swallowed, "I have a few."

"Really? Which ones?"

He blushed as he looked at her with sad eyes. "I've, um, been called acrobat, boxer, finger, wolf, ghost, and, um, clover."

As he listed his thief ranks, Madre's expression with from concerned to surprise and finally incredulously. "All that?"

He nodded, "I guess. I'm a master acrobat, wolf, and clover."

"What are those?"

"Wolf is lone wolf, someone who works alone. Most of my jobs were solo, so I got credit for that. And," he sighed, "clover is someone who steals from mages."

"You stole from twenty mages?"

He blushed, "A lot more, over the years."

"H-How?"

Derik looked away, "I'm very good at it."

"I see. What is a finger?"

"Pickpocket. And, well, ghost means I'm very good at stealth jobs."

It hurt to explain his thieving ways to Madre, but his confession eased the knot in his stomach. She asked a few more probing questions. When he finished going into more details, Madre wryly grinned at him. "And a face?"

He shook his head.

"Even if you seduce the baron?"

His blush deepened, "I-I didn't—"

Madre chuckled and gave him a hug. "I won't tell anyone, Face."

He chuckled and wrapped his arms around her. They held each other tightly for a long moment before parting.

"Come, we should get back. Can you really steal from mages?"

"Yes, Madre."

"Steal from me."

"What? I can't do that!"

Madre walked along him for a moment. "Well, you have until we get to the harem, or I'm going to spend the next two hours tanning your ass, thief."

As they continued walking, he noticed how she focused on every movement he made. Her attention almost grated on him. He considered just accepting the swats, but at the last moment, just as they entered the hallway, he caught a mere microsecond where she relaxed her guard.

Madre didn't even flinch.

They reached her door and she turned around to look at him. "Well? Can't do it?"

Derik sighed and shook his head, already knowing he lied.

Madre smirked then opened her door.

"Go on, I'll get the paddle."

"Yes, Madre."

As he walked through the door, he toyed with a small piece of metal he stole from her pocket. Looking down, he was surprised to see a brass star-burst, identical to the one around Nightingale's navel.

Behind him, Madre shut the door and chuckled playfully. "Don't worry, thief, I'll be gentle."

Derik passed by the desk and carefully set down the metal.

Madre's chuckle stopped with a strangled sound, and Derik had to fight the smile that tweaked the side of his mouth. He turned around to see her gaping at him.

"H-How did you do that!?"

Sitting down on the edge of the bed, he shrugged. "I don't know. It just kind of happens. Kerlis used to say I was a natural, and he tried to get me to steal from his customers."

Madre didn't respond as she quickly walked over to the starburst and picked it up. A sad look crossed her face as she flipped it up. Silence filled her room for a long moment before she spoke. "She gave this to me."

"Nightingale?"

Madre nodded sadly, "She said it was the closest that we could ever get to marriage."

Derik pressed his hands in his lap, just listening.

Madre sniffed. "I miss her, Derik. Every day, I wonder how she's doing."

He tried to tell her, of Kerlis and the brothel, but the words refused to come. Only the feeling of his silence, the gift from Forbis that he hated with every passing second of his life. After a moment, he closed his mouth.

"It was scary, at the time. She asked me to brand her."

Derik's eyes widened with surprise. Madre looked up with a soft chuckle. "It isn't a tattoo around her button, Dora, it was a brand. She begged me for a month to do it, and I refused for so long, but then, one day, I realized I loved her so much and did it."

"H-How?"

"Magic. Heated up the metal with a spell and pressed it right again her stomach. She didn't even flinch, told me it was love that shielded her from the pain."

She sighed again. "The first time I ever used a combat spell for pleasure."

Madre looked up after a moment, then waved her hand. "Go on, Derik, enjoy a bit of fun with Teri and the others. I'll get your five later."

"I'm sorry," Derik said suddenly.

"For what?"

"That you lost Nightingale. I... know you love her."

Madre nodded and put it back in her pocket. "Thank you, Derik, you are sweet. I'm sure she'll find a way of being happy. I just know it."

Somehow, his magical silence was worse hearing those words. Even if he tried to say something.

Dancing

"What's wrong, Derik?"

Teri's voice stirred Derik from his thoughts, and he looked up with surprise. She tugged on his perfectly brushed hair and he grinned.

"Oh, nothing."

"Well, you've been thinking about nothing for two days. Being sullen makes wrinkles, don't you know that? I mean, come on, we're going out to dinner and dancing with the baron! Shouldn't you be more worried about keeping that dick of yours in your panties?"

Derik smirked, "Shouldn't you be wearing them?"

Giggling, Teri hooked her arm into his, then snuggled closer. They walked along the cobblestones of the richer area of town.

In front of them, the baron held Sherrel's arm in the same way as they made for their destination. Their path took them through an elegant garden, smell of fresh rain and cut grass.

Derik glanced up to the sky, where the recent storm passed only hours before and left the sky a brilliant purple. He smiled happily.

"I can't believe you planned to steal the Eye."

Derik's smile faded. A sourness burned in his stomach as sweat prickled his brow. "Um—"

"You got lucky, trap," grinned Teri, "someone else did it before you. Which is good, because then you'd be in the dungeon, and I wouldn't be getting ready to have a hot threesome right on the dance floor."

"D-Does the baron dance?"

Teri shook her head, "No, but Sherrel does. It will be just us three on the dance floor."

The thief blushed, "Um, I don't know how to dance."

Teri stopped and Derik turned around to prevent his arm leaving hers. She stared up at him in shock. "Seriously?"

He nodded, blushing. His dress shifted in the wind and the breeze brought the scent of his apple perfume—from Tornsin of course—and the clean smell of a summer rain. Nodding again, he shrugged. "I never really dated."

"But, you fuck so well," she seemed shocked.

His blush deepened and he glanced at Sherrel's back for a second. "I paid for a lot of whores, um, prostitutes when... before the harem."

Teri purred louder as she pressed up against him. Their breasts ground together as she wrapped her fingers around his tight ass. Pulling him close, she spoke huskily, "Then, you are going to get lucky on the dance floor. And you won't pay for it either."

Derik blushed hotly, but he still brought his lips to hers, kissing softly and gently. Slipping his arm around her narrow waist, he held her tight until they both moaned from the building pleasure.

"And that is what I like to see," rumbled the baron playfully.

Derik stepped back, but Teri kept her hands on his ass as they looked over to the grinning man.

Sherrel smirked, but Derik spotted a faint flush to her cheeks too.

With a hop in her step, Teri slipped away and wrapped her arm around the baron's other. "Well, my lord, we know how much you like the girl on girl action."

Hamel's eye glinted with amusement and he let it remain on Derik for a long moment before turning around. "I prefer man on girl, you know."

"And man on boy?"

"Oh, I'm getting to enjoy that too. I might need to see a bit more tonight, just to make sure."

Derik's body warmed up at the baron's answer.

"Oh sure," came Teri's playful response, "I can't wait."

Derik hurried up, his heels tapping on the cobblestones, and hooked his arm into Sherrel's. Together, the four of them made their way along the pathway until they reached their destination.

To Derik's surprise, it wasn't a fancy restaurant but a night club. Guards stood on both sides of the door and a long line snaked along the side of the building. A painted sign declared the group inside as "Phoenix Falling" but he didn't recognize it. As they walked across a narrow street, a ripple of surprise filled the street and people stopped to gawk at the baron and his three girls. A blush rise on Derik's cheeks but the others strode forward.

They didn't even stop at the door. The crowds parted, and one of the guards held it open as the baron swept into the building.

Derik lingered for a moment, then followed in the wake of the man he loved.

Behind him, the baron's guards followed and spread out discretely.

Inside, smaller tables surrounded a large dance floor in a typical club layout. On the stage, Derik spotted a group of musicians setting up. He froze in culture shock.

They looked like barbarians, but something seemed wrong. Dressed in the Emberkan style, the band consisted of three men with soft, feminine features and two women who looked just as pampered. They all wore leather and feathers, but one of the women caught Derik's attention. Almost as long as his, her hair was bound with a leather strap, her hair had been braided so it almost looked like wings as she hopped around. They chatted to themselves as they set up a dazzling array of drums, disks of metal, and even a pair of water-filled buckets.

"Derik?"

Derik jumped, then slid over to stand next to Sherrel. "Sorry, I never saw anything like that."

"It's a band from Emberka."

"I thought they were all barbarians."

"They are, but these are, um, they call them Softins, or kept people."

"Softins?"

Sherrel grinned and slipped her arm around Derik's waist.

He did the same, holding her tightly as they worked their way around the gathering crowds.

"Emberka has Haros and Softins. Haros are the warriors and fighters, like those two large men."

She pointed to a pair of huge men with bulging muscles standing on the edge. They scowled at the crowds, but looked more more than capable of defending themselves.

"And the Softins are their singers, dancers, makers, and breeders. The pretty boys and girls. In that country, the Softins are constantly being stolen and moved from tribe to tribe, which they use to keep their culture together."

She nuzzled his ear, "All of us would be Softins and Hamel would be our Haros."

Derik blushed and ducked his head, then climbed a short set of stairs to a large table in front of a padded bench.

The baron already sat in the center, chuckling as he ordered enough food for a small army. When he finished, he looked at Derik and the others. "Do you want anything?"

Smirking, they ordered and settled down. The baron chatted with the two girls and Derik, but allowed himself to be interrupted by various people in the club.

Derik took one opportunity to whisper to Sherrel. "I thought the baron would be into classical music or opera or something. Isn't that what all the nobility like?"

She nipped his ear and giggled, "He likes to try new things, just like certain boys in his bed."

Derik blushed, but Sherrel continued to whisper to him, "When he took Madre and Nightingale out, they went to the opera or Carium Classical concerts and wine tastings. With us, he takes us to Emberkan Tribal because Teri really gets into it. If it is just me and him, we go to softer venues, and if it is just him and Teri, I heard they go to the faster stuff, like the battle bands."

"B-Battle bands?"

Sherrel shuddered for a moment, and Derik spotted the baron's hands sliding between her legs even as he spoke to someone else. Parting her legs, she closed her eyes and leaned against Derik. "Battle bands are really hard... fast rhythm but I can't understand a damn thing they scream out. It's just a wall of noise to me, but Teri loves it."

Her words faded off as she moaned, then kissed Derik.

He kissed her back, feeling her body shifting as the baron fingered her discretely.

She whimpered, and Derik held her, teasing her nipples as Sherrel reached a fast orgasm.

Then, the baron slipped his slick fingers from her pussy and held them up with a silent command.

Derik blushed as he leaned over Sherrel. Holding the baron's wrists, he brought the dripping fingers to his painted lips and sucked on them. He could feel the burning gaze of people watching, but it wasn't shame but excitement that filled him as he finished cleaning Hamel. When he released them, he had to adjust himself before sitting straight up.

Sherrel giggled and passionately kissed Derik on the lips. Her tongue flicked in his mouth and he moaned at the soft hand against his hardness.

"I love tasting myself on your lips," she whispered.

"D-Did I do okay? I-I didn't really think and just did it... in front of that man."

"Oh, yes. That was hot, just watching you," she kissed him again, "The baron likes to do this in public. By the end of the night, I bet at least one of us will be on this table being ridden in time with the music. One reason Teri likes the pounding beat, because he fucks just as hard and just as fast as the music."

Derik moaned at the memory of how hard and fast the baron rode Madre's body.

Sherrel kissed him again, whispering as she grinned. "It's the only way he dances, you know."

"I-In public?"

"Something to be said about the most powerful man in town bringing some of his harem out for a night of politics, sex, and having a good time. You'll be amazed how many deals will go down."

She grinned, "And the occasional time when he lends one of us out for a favor or two."

Derik warmed up to the idea of being fucked to the time of some drum beat and wondered what type of music they were about to listen to. He blushed, realizing he never really paid attention to any music, except for commoner music in the brothel and random bars. He lost himself in thought until the food showed up and then just gaped as Hamel inhaled his food, easily polishing off everything in front of him in less than fifteen minutes.

"I... I've never seen anyone eat so much."

Sherrel giggled, "He eats a lot, but look how much he fucks. It takes energy to stay up all night and we'll be here long until the club stops for the morning. Oh, the band is starting!"

She nestled into Derik, slipping one arm around his shoulders and draping her fingers so her tips just slipped under the front of Derik's dress and teased his nipples.

He inhaled sharply and peeked around, seeing more than a few gazes directed toward him.

Sherrel purred in his ear and rolled the hard nub between her fingertips until Derik moaned from the growing pleasure.

Then, the music forced itself to the foreground. The air throbbed as the three drummers threw themselves into the first set, pounding the drums in a rapid, complicated rhythm that almost hurt Derik's head to follow. Sherrel moved effortlessly in time with it. The singer, the woman with the long hair, jumped in front of the stage and started with a sing-song that blended with the music. He couldn't understand the words, but their music together perfectly, becoming powerful.

Having Sherrel tweaking his aching nipples and rocking against him didn't help.

Nor the fixated gazes of the others in the club.

Derik squirmed under the attention, his blush growing hotter with every passing second and his body aching for release.

He thought Sherrel would give him some relief when she stood up and pulled him off the bench. "Come on."

Instead of the bathrooms or to shelter, she dragged him out to the dance floor.

At the wave of heat from bodies already in motion and the gathering attention, he cringed and let out a little yelp of discomfort.

A small space spread out around them, a hush despite the pounding beat that punched the air with the music.

"S-Sherrel! I can't dance!"

Sherrel ignored his wail and pulled him close. Her arm wrapped around his waist and her hips ground into his. Even over the wash of sound and darkness, he saw her painted lips stretching into a smile, then her body shifting in time with the music.

He resisted, then he started to rock into her, grinding his body against hers as she held him tightly, leading him into his first dance. He stumbled, feeling shame, but Sherrel could be as tenacious as Madre, and soon he adapted.

Derik experienced pleasure from moving with music before, but as he rocked his hips and shoulders in time, mimicking Sherrel's movements and grinding his body up against her, he felt more than just a beat. His heart pounded hard, and he smiled, working tighter against her until their breasts ground against each other and fingers danced along shoulders.

When Sherrel slipped her fingers up his side, he moaned and rocked against it. She peeled back the front of his dress, exposing his nipples to the air.

He knew everyone was looking at him. It added to the growing lust in the air. He relented and pressed tighter to her body. He wanted to lose himself in the music before he came again.

She teased him as they danced, sliding her hands to his dress and tugging them up, sliding them until his bare buttocks teased the hot hair and he groaned with the feeling of exposure. Just as his manhood was about to be shown, she let it slip down.

Derik grinned, finally moving easily, and did the same. One hand on her ass and the other sliding up her cleavage to tease her nipples, tugging them out as their bodies moved closely together.

Sherrel grinned evilly as they pressed their lips together, kissing as this moved as lovers in the middle of the dance floor.

Daring, he pulled up Sherrel's dress, sliding his hands against her naked ass and bringing a moan to his and the surrounding voyeurs' lips. He grinned as he kissed her, then slid one finger between her cheeks to tease her pussy.

Sherrel moaned, then clutched him as she came hard and fast.

Sex on the dance floor.

Their movements didn't even slow as he released her dress. They danced from one song into another, then a third. By the time Derik regained his senses, they were drifting to the edge. An afterglow of being watched and his orgasms pounded inside him and he couldn't help but notice his inner thighs were wet.

"Not," Sherrel gasped, "a bad dancer."

"Thank you, coming from the slut."

Sherrel grinned then pointed up at the baron's semi-private spot. Teri was bobbing up and down on his lap, her legs spread as she took his hard cock into her soaked pussy. Hands clutched his shoulders as the baron watched her with a happy smile on his lips.

Around them, various supplicants watched while trying not to appear interested.

"Remember, Derik," Sherrel whispered, "part of our job is to keep the baron occupied so he doesn't make the mistake of sticking his life-sucking cock into someone who can't handle it."

"W-Why doesn't he just not do this?"

She slid a hand up his thigh, exposing his ass cheek and bringing a finger down his crack. "Because music turns him on, silly. And he's a slut in his own way, he likes to show off."

Derik watched as the baron came inside Teri, his cum pouring out of her pussy to the ground. Someone had piled up some towels on the floor already. He shivered at the thought of being there, in front of everyone, then mounted the steps to reach him.

"Blackbird," the baron rumbled as Teri slipped off with a grin and a kiss for Sherrel. Behind her, a larger man watched Sherrel's breasts with obvious lust. The baron caught sight of him, then leaned over to Sherrel. A few whispered words and Sherrel grinned. Her eyes rose silkily to the man, then she crawled over the table to him.

Derik watched with an open mouth as she spoke a few short words, then drew him down to the dance floor.

Teri disappeared herself, and Derik found himself alone with the baron.

And somehow, he could imagine himself a virgin again.

Hamel grinned and patted the bench next to him. As daintily as he could, Derik slid along it and pressed his body against the baron. A large arm wrapped around him and Derik moaned at the feeling of power that surrounded him.

"Enjoying yourself?"

"Yes, my lord," he gasped.

"Bet you thought I was just going to take you to my bed, weren't you?"

Derik blushed, his body heating up and his cock twitching. "Yes, my lord."

Hamel chuckled and slid his hands between Derik's breasts, teasing one nipple with a large hand and tracing the bit of sweat that formed in his cleavage. "Teri-cat thought you'd enjoy dancing a bit, and nothing says I can't use this table as my bed later."

Derik's body lurched. "B-Baron?"

"When everyone else goes home, I'm going to bend you over this table, whisper your name, and ride you until the band stops singing."

Derik shuddered with pleasure and ground against the baron. He ran his hand along the swollen length of the slick cock and purred at the thought of the end of his night.

As he snuggled, a man came up and started to talk to the baron. Derik tried to pull away, but the baron kept him there, stroking and teasing as they spoke about business and politics. Then, a woman came up, discussing a crisis in the religious quarter and how it impacted the factories. Derik couldn't follow the politics, but he could focus on the fingers that teased him, flashing everyone with his body and driving him to a burning crest of an orgasm that wouldn't subside.

When she left, Derik blushed at the look she gave him.

The baron chuckled. "I think she likes you, Blackbird."

"I-I don't have to fuck her, do I?"

The baron laughed and hugged him tightly. "Never. You never have to fuck anyone you don't want to, except maybe me. Sherrel and Teri like to do it."

"Why?"

"Because it garners favor with those with power. They get the forbidden chance to sleep with one of my girls, and I get a bit more power or knowledge. It's a dance too, you know, politics."

Derik blushed hotly, then moaned as the baron's hand dropped to his legs, sliding between his parted thighs and stroking his cock through the thong he wore.

"Besides, right now, there is only two dicks I want in my blackbird. Me and Tornsin's. And just because Tornsin knows he'll never get any from me... ever. He has too many muscles for this old man."

"You aren't that old, baron."

The baron laughed and drove one finger up between Derik's cheeks, penetrating his asshole to the second knuckle and sending a bolt of pleasure through Derik and bringing him dangerously close to cresting his orgasm.

"I'm old enough to know who rules this body."

"Oh, baron, you do," gasped Derik.

The baron's lips teased Derik's ears, and he fought back the electrical shiver that filled him. "Good, because I want to feel your body wrapped around my dick right now."

Derik finally came, soaking his thong as he stared out at the crowds. The baron ran his finger through the hot liquid that splashed against it, teasing Derik's asshole with it and fucking him with a few strokes. Then, with a playful grin on his lips, he brought it up to Derik's own mouth.

Moaning, Derik kept his eyes locked on the baron as he wrapped his lips around the dripping fingers, tasting Teri, Sherrel, and himself on it. Swallowing, he nearly came again as he saw the emotions burning in the sapphire gaze focused on him.

When the cleaned fingers slipped from Derik's lips, he heard the baron give a command.

"Now, please."

"Yes, my lord," he breathed.

Derik's pulsed race as he slipped over to the baron, straddling his hips as the larger man let his cock stand up straight. As he started to lift his dress, he knew that he was exposing himself. His fingers faltered with nervousness.

The baron just watched, grinning at that knife's edge of public exposure.

Changing his mind at the last minute, Derik leaned forward and brought his legs between the baron's. With a smile of his own, he slipped between his legs and under the table.

Stretching his knees over the puddle of cum, he brought his mouth to the baron's shaft. Kissing and sucking, he worked his way down to the grapefruit sized balls and up to the tip. The silk over steel feeling of the hardness brought another tiny orgasm shaking through his body, but he couldn't stop worshiping the massive member that brought him so much pleasure.

Under the table, he could still feel eyes staring at him. He knew that his behind couldn't be missed under the table, but he just pushed it aside and let his dress hide his secrets. His mouth opened as he took the swollen head of the shaft into his mouth. It filled him and stretched his lips.

Just like Rick.

He had to fight down the excitement that came from Rick's degradation. But, the heat rose and he forced himself to suck on the baron's head, sliding it back and forth in his mouth. It was thick and hot and wonderful as it drooled thick pre-cum down his throat.

Derik opened his eyes to look up at the baron, keeping his gaze fixed as he pushed down harder. The cock head bumped up against the back of his throat, teasing his gag reflex, but he just kept on pushing with a hunger to feel the baron in his throat.

To his surprise, the baron actually looked shocked as Derik opened his throat and took more of the baron. It stretched out his insides, but Rick already already pushed Derik beyond that point. The hardness invaded his throat and cut off his breath, but Derik could only feel the infernos of pleasure building rapidly.

Swallowing, he bobbed up and took a quick breath before taking more into his mouth. His jaw ached being pried so open, but he managed to slide down a few more centimeters. Their eyes never breaking, Derik lifted his hips to giving the hardness a straighter path into his throat, and he forced it deeper.

Holding it until he needed to breathe, he slid up with a moan that shook the baron's length. The baron's eyes closed slowly and

Derik nearly came at the expression of pleasure. Grinning, he bobbed deeper and harder. He had to push against the tightness of his throat. The girth resisted the tight confines, but he aimed for the bottom. His fingers held the shaft tightly, using it for balance as he continued to drive deep.

He barely paid attention to Teri slipping into the bench next to the baron, then the gasp of lust that came from the girl's body as she saw Derik taking the baron's cock deeply. His eyes flicked to the side to see her pulling up her dress to finger herself and he found inspiration for a few more centimeters.

Derik's blood rushed in his ears as he took more and more. When his lips kissed the baron's base, his nose had buried in the thick forest of pubic hair. Lips stretched painfully, he could barely pull himself up for air before his world grew dark. The baron stared down at Derik, his lips parted with surprise, as Derik slammed down, taking the entire length into his throat and feeling the hardness heating him up from the inside. His painted lips worked at the base for a long moment before he drew up slowly, leaving a glistening shaft behind.

Bobbing deeper, he stretched himself open for the baron and each stroke became easier than the one before it. Rick already ruined his throat, but Derik couldn't imagine what pleasure he could feel when he was completely buried in the baron's base, working his lips like a good whore around that swollen base.

Then, as he started to draw up for air, the baron's shaft suddenly swelled. His jaw creaked as he pried it open even further. That was his only warning before a hot load of searing cum exploded into his stomach, filling him instantly as the baron came inside him. Derik's ears rang with the need for air, but he came too, so hard that his cum now soaked the floor.

It took Derik a few seconds to regain his wits, and he slid himself off, leaving a long streamer of cum connecting his lips to the baron's shaft. Sitting back, he panted desperately for breath and smiled happily.

It was something.

Something that Rick didn't ruin.

And he wanted to do it again.

The baron held out his hand and Derik took it, letting the powerful man pull him up between his legs.

The baron growled with pleasure. "Where did you learn that?"

"I—" but he couldn't get another word out because of Forbis' spell.

He didn't need another word as the baron picked him up and sat him down on the edge of the table. Powerful muscles flexed as the baron pushed the table back and stood up. His hands pushed Derik's dress up, exposing the thief's hardness to the world. Ripples of surprise and shock ran through the spectators, but the baron only had his eye on Derik as he aimed the dripping shaft to Derik's ass and shoved forward.

The massive cock impaled his sphincter in a burst of pleasure. The thief came again from the intense wave of pleasure. It was magnified by the realization others were watching. Cum splattered his exposed belly and slid down to the table, but he didn't care. The dress didn't stain, thanks to one of Madre's spells, and he was already lost in pleasure by the baron's mastery over his body. He shook in time with the music as the baron began to fuck him hard and fast, matching the beat of the dance and the rapid pulse in Derik's ears.

Enter the Hunter

Derik purred to himself as he stretched out on the pillow. His ass smarted from Madre spanking him for an inappropriate swat of his own, but it was always worth it. In his fingers, he rolled a strawberry between two painted fingertips before popping it into his mouth.

He wore Tornsin's shirt and he sniffed the lapel, enjoying the scents of the apple perfume and the strong man. A smile crossed his lips and he grabbed another strawberry.

"So, you look like the cat who ate the mouse."

Derik peeked up through the curtain of his black hair at Teri who stretched out on a pillow with her legs spread. Tucking his hair back, he scooted closer to slide his lips against her labia and use his tongue to part them. Her moans sweetly teased his senses and he dove into her, lapping and tracing her slick folds. He found the knot of her pleasure and teased it until she moaned.

"Oh, fuck, I never miss this."

Teri moaned again and Derik ignored his platter of fruit to hold her buttocks tightly, lapping and tasting her until she came with a shuddering scream that filled the room. He sucked her juices and enjoyed the feel of her body writhing under his lips.

When he finished, he pulled her down and pressed his aching cock against her pussy, entering her with a moan of his own.

Teri wrapped her legs and arms around him. He jumped at the feeling of her thighs against his red cheeks, but Teri just grinned and clamped her hands right on the tanned part of his buttocks, using that to guide him into hard, fast strokes that left them both breathless and gasping happily.

He came slowly, after coming twice on Madre's floor and cleaning, but Teri didn't seem to rush it. When he flooded her, he slumped against her and nibbled on her ear.

Teri giggled and grabbed a strawberry, eating it herself. "This is good, isn't it?"

Derik purred, "The best I've ever had it."

"Oh? Didn't I hear that Tornsin asked you out?"

Derik's cock burst to life again and Teri giggled.

"Oh, that is a yes. When?"

"Right after he gets back, in two weeks."

"The anticipation. What are you going to do?"

Derik blushed, "He asked me out to dinner and dancing. I-I didn't know where, so I asked him to take me to Phoenix Falling again. I liked that dancing," he finished with a blush.

Teri stroked her hands against his face and then fed him a strawberry. A few droplets of juice dribbled down his chin which she kissed off his skin. "And to think you never danced before."

"I like it, it isn't as boring as classical."

"You should listen to the faster stuff. Oh, better yet, let the baron fuck you to that rhythm. You'll come so hard, it won't be silly."

Derik blushed hotly but his shaft throbbed at the memory of dancing the week before. It was hot and pleasurable, even with half his clothes off and his secret being exposed to the entire barony. To his surprise, the baron only got a few letters about it and, in a private conference, told Derik that he needed to shake things up anyways. That led to Derik enjoying being plastered face down on the leather blotter of the baron's desk, being fucked with hard strokes in memory of that night.

Teri cooed softly, "You keep on remembering that, you are going to come again."

Derik grinned and moved his hips, sliding his cock in and out of her soaked pussy.

Teri moaned and arched her back, pressing one nipple against his lips.

He sucked on it, nipping lightly until they both came again.

Once his heart stopped pounding, Derik asked a question that hung in the back of his head, "So, what is this visit?"

Teri giggled, "A nap, actually. I'm tired."

"And my strawberries."

"Well, you're the thief, might as well steal from you," she batted her eyelashes, "for the good of society, of course."

"And the sex?"

Teri grinned, "For the good of my pussy. Of course."

Together, they laughed and settled in to drift to sleep. Feeling her breath on his breasts, Derik let himself smile and he drifted to sleep.

"Derik?"

He half-woke up as Teri whispered into his ear. He smiled and kissed her. Teri yawned and clutched at him.

"Promise me something?"

"Anything," he whispered back.

"Promise me that you won't go gay. I want you to keep liking the pussy."

Derik grinned and kissed her again. "I'll never give up on your kitty, Teri."

"Or Sherrel's?"

He spoke in a mock-serious voice, "Well, I'm more interested in her breasts."

Teri purred and held him tightly, her breasts grinding against his own. "Good, I was afraid I'd have to grow a dick to keep loving you."

"Never, my Teri-cat."

"Trap."

"Bitch."

With a giggle, they drifted back into their nap. Derik dreamed of many things, some pleasurable and others less so. He writhed with discomfort.

Then he was awake with Sherrel holding his finger.

Derik sat up. "Don't hit me!" Images of his nightmare, of Rick and the baron fighting over his body with cane and cock.

"What!?" Teri snorted.

Sherrel giggled and pushed him down. "Relax, Dora."

Slowing his pounding heart, he blushed hotly and looked down.

Teri grinned and stretched out like a cat.

"You were having a bad dream," said Sherrel.

"Sorry, it was weird."

Sherrel looked concerned as she stroked his hair.

Derik blushed. "Um, what?"

"You know the baron would never cane you, right?"

Derik gasped and his blush deepened. "I, I didn't mean that!"

Sherrel hugged him. "Well, you whimpering with a nightmare wouldn't be good with Madre and the bounty hunter here."

Ice ran through his blood. "B-Bounty hunter? What bounty hunter?"

Sherrel sat down and pulled her robe on tighter. She pointed to the entrance of the harem where Madre spoke to a woman Derik had never seen before.

The newcomer was the same height as Derik. Despite having delicate features, there was something hard about her. She had very short, reddish-blond hair that spiked up in all directions. It looked more like she cut it with a rusty knife than actually had it properly trimmed. He could see her pointed ears peaking out from her head, long and elegant, and pierced at least three times on one side.

Teri whispered as she sat up, "She's a Silfae?"

Sherrel grunted, "Sivlir probably. Supposed to be some hot shot bounty hunter."

Derik's stomach twisted as he stared at the hunter. She wore a leather outfit, pulled tightly over her small breasts and narrow hips. Between the two, she had a very tight, muscular abdomen crossed with bands of throwing knives. On her back. a hilt of a sword as tall as herself rose above one shoulder; as she rocked back and forth, the sword tip would almost scraped the ground and. More knives graced her arms and legs, strapped down with more leather and chains. He spotted even a rusting dagger against the small of her back.

"Mask of Shadows, how many knives does she have!?" Teri exclaimed.

Neither Sherrel nor Derik said anything. Instead, they just watched the new female. The hunter held one of the baron's bottles of wine in her hand. As she spoke to Madre, she drained half of it, then polished it off before tossing it on a nearby pillow.

Madre frowned, but said nothing. She rubbed her arms unhappily as the hunter yanked open another bottle and started to drain it.

Mid-bottle, the hunter sniffed, then pulled the bottle from her lips. A few droplets splashed on her chest, but she ignored it as she turned around, sniffing the air. Her head swiveled back and forth for a moment, then her eyes focused on Derik and the others.

At the sight of the one blue eye and one green one, the ice forming in his gut turned into sharp spikes. "Oh, fuck, Shiel."

Sherrel stared at him, "Who?"

Sweat formed on Derik's brow as he remembered the rumors about the brutal silfae. Swallowing, he backed away from her but Shiel had already caught sight of him. With a grim smile on her lips, she stalked toward him on bare feet.

"Um, crap."

Shiel shoved her way past Teri and Sherrel to chase Derik.

He backed away until he pressed up against one of the columns in the harem. Shiel matched him in height but her violent presence made Derik feel only a meter tall. Shaking, he closed his eyes as she sniffed at him, right along the sensitive part of his neck and shoulder.

Fighting back a whimper, he tried not to think about her breath against his skin.

Then, she pulled back.

"Ya smell like the thief." She had a thick accent and breath that smelled like wine.

Derik shuddered and waited for something to happen.

Shiel growled for a moment. "No, not quite. Smells like ya but isn't ya. The thief is a man."

"Derik's a man," slipped out of Teri's mouth, then she clapped her hand over her mouth, blushing.

Derik's eyes flew open to see Shiel only a centimeter away from his face, staring at him with her mismatched eyes.

She sniffed again. "No, mean a real man. Not a little cunt boy for the baron. Even with that apple crap you have on, you aren't the same thing. You smell more," she paused to come up with a word, "you smell like a girl. A pussy boy."

Derik whimpered, unable to pull his eyes away from her gaze. They were piercing his soul with the intensity of her look. She rocked back on her heels and took a swig from the bottle. Derik noticed it was one of the baron's private stock; he helped clear out a few of them from Madre's room.

"Got a bro, pussy?" There was no mistaking the disdain in Shiel's voice. Nor was there any mistaking the slightly slurred voice of someone buzzed on alcohol.

Derik, clutched himself, and shook his head. "No."

"The thief smells like your bro. You mom sleep around?"

"S-She's dead."

"So, doesn't mean you ain't got a bro. The thief is related to ya, I know that now. What about your pa?"

Derik felt pinned under glass. He shook his head. "I-I don't know."

"Why not?"

"I don't know who he is."

"You form fully grown from your ma's cunt?"

Madre cleared her throat, "Shiel."

The bounty hunter turned away from Derik to look at her.

Derik followed her gaze to the obviously uncomfortable Madre.

Shiel drawled as she stepped back. "You pay me to find that Eye. I don't care if it be you, da baron, or even the pussy boy. For a hundred grand, I'll find anyone. For a quarter mil, I'll kill anyone."

"Yes, but don't pressure poor Dora like that."

"Why not? He's a pussy."

"She's one of my girls."

"He's a he and you are a deluded old bitch if you think otherwise."

A shocked silence filled the harem as everyone stared at the bounty hunter.

Madre's jaw tightened as her hair started to rise up. She cleaned her hand and a ripple of power rose from her grip.

Shiel just barked out a laugh. "Go ahead and try, bitch. I'll take you down faster than you can snuff me."

Madre opened her mouth to say something, but Shiel's head snapped up. Her eyes probed the ceiling and then fixed on the duct that Derik originally fell through.

His heart jumped as she spoke curtly over Madre's words. "Thief was right here."

Without waiting for a response, Shiel launched herself straight up and clutched the column for a mere moment before kicking off to a second column. She bounced off that, her bare toes curling for a grip, then leaped across the room to slide right into the ventilation opening. Sherrel's and Madre's mouth opened in surprise, but Derik was impressed that she only needed two launching points to reach that high; he was the only other one he knew who could jump so far.

And the fact that the Eye was just inside the opening.

He whimpered and started to slip around the column, but Madre's head came down to focus on him. Blushing hotly, he found that he couldn't move from the steady gaze. Swallowing, he glanced up and spotted Shiel crawling across the opening.

The next minute became a terrifying moment on a knife's edge. Derik's heart pounded, waiting for the famed bounty hunter to reveal the Eye and ruin everything. He swallowed and sweat dripped down his brow. Clutching Tornsin's shirt tighter around him, he waited.

And waited.

The minute turned into five, then ten. Finally, it hit twenty before Shiel came down the hall of the harem with a scowl. She walked straight over to Derik, stopping only a millimeter from his noise. "I'll find your bro, pussy. And when I do, I'll snap him in half and bring him to da baron."

Her eyes snapped over to Madre. "The Eye was up there, top, but not anymore. Someone crawled along the ducts from the hall. Scorch marks everywhere, but it ain't there. But, there is no doubt about it, there was only one thief, and it was pussy's bro. Not that corpse in the dungeon."

Derik swallowed hard, but said nothing. Even if he wanted to, spell or no spell, his voice remained silent.

Shiel gave him another glare, then stalked out of the harem. She tossed away the empty bottle to the side and grabbed a third one before disappearing down the hall.

Teri let out a gasp, "Wow, Madre, if you weren't here, that could have gotten nasty."

Swallowing, Derik desperately wanted to agree, but he said nothing.

Madre glanced over at Derik, then spoke in a soft voice. "Don't be too excited, that would have not been an easy fight."

"Why?"

"Shiel must hunt mages a lot. She has enough disruptive magics on her to stop most mages in their tracks. Battle mages focus their spells in themselves, but she has protections against most of my spells too."

"So, what does that mean?" said Teri with a hint of growing discomfort.

Madre looked at her. "I don't know who would win a fight between us. If it came down to it, that is. Actually, she would win since I don't really fight anymore."

"Oh, fuck."

"Fuck indeed. Shiel is a nasty person, that much is true. But she's never missed finding her mark, and the baron knows that. Whoever stole the Eye, she will find him." Her eyes focused on Derik, and he thought he saw a doubt behind her gaze.

That didn't didn't help Derik's mood.

Improvised Gags

Derik used his hip to push open the door to the baron's study and helped himself inside. Walking in his heels, he set down a tray of wines and cheeses on the corner of the desk. He wore his favorite dress and corset and felt prettier than normal. The sapphire blue accented his curves and the folds of the dress teased his half-hard cock.

His heart sang as he circled the massive wooden desk. His fingertips trailed along the edge of the blotter, and a flush rose in his cheeks at the memory of his body bent over it. The thrill of clutching the desk while Hamel had fucked him hard brought a heat to his body and an ache between his legs.

For the briefest moment, he considered looking through the drawers but then withdrew from his old thoughts. He didn't steal, not when he was so happy. Instead, he glided across the room and pressed one ear against the far door.

Beyond, he heard the baron speaking with the ambassadors from Emberka and Carium and some delegates from the Shattered Kingdoms. Hamel, as a man honored by his war experiences, housed the talks with the threat of neutrality and his own personal army to enforce his will.

Derik shrugged, not really understanding the politics, and circled back the room to set up the wine glass and bottle.

One of the doors opened, and he looked up in surprise. When he saw Tornsin slipping into the room, Derik parted parted his lips slightly and licked the black lipstick on them. His lover wore full dress uniform that day, and he looked handsome.

Tornsin turned around, then caught sight of Derik.

Hurrying around the desk, Derik flung himself into Tornsin's arms. His guard caught him, sweeping him up in a tight hug and a passionate kiss that stole Derik's breath away.

"Tornsin!" Derik whispered as excitedly as he could.

Tornsin held his official satchel in one hand and pressed his other against the small of Derik's back, pulling him closer until their manhoods brushed against each other in their respective outfits.

Derik purred and kissed him again.

"Oh, Derik, I missed you."

Tornsin turned Derik around and pressed him to the door.

With a hungry growl, Derik arched his back and lifted his legs, wrapping them around Tornsin's waist and feeling the hardness pressing against the ridge between his asshole and manhood. He kissed back passionately, mouth opening as their tongues teased each other lightly.

"Well, I see Tornsin is already being debriefed."

The baron's amused rumble froze both lovers, and Derik blushed hotly as he watched the baron enter through the other door, shutting it behind him.

Slowly, Derik lowered himself to the floor and straightened out his dress as Tornsin spun around, snapping to attention.

"Sorry, sir."

The baron shrugged. "I know what lovers do when no one is looking. Plus, you've been both separated for a few weeks now. Speaking of which, got a report?"

Derik didn't know what to do, so he slid around Tornsin and walked to the side of the baron. Holding up one of the wine glasses, he asked a silent question.

The baron glanced over at Tornsin. "Wine?"

"I wouldn't mind, if you don't."

"Two please, Blackbird."

Derik blushed happily and poured the wine for his two loves. As he did, they spoke between themselves.

"Any luck, Tornsin?"

"No, sir, but we did get more information, which may have been of use. The group calls themselves the Maces of Submission. A group of transformers who specialize in shape-shifted creatures.

They dominated a group of werewolves and rat-gaunts in two cities before we scared them off."

"Damn, did you catch any?"

"Yes, one of them, but he killed himself by turning his chest inside out. It was," Tornsin swallowed, "not the most pleasant way of going."

Hamel made a face, "No, I assume it wouldn't be. Are they still threatening me?"

"Yes, sir. They claim you are a monster in human guise, and they plan on wiping the world of your existence. A lot of proclamations but no proof. They just appear to be searching for your fatal weakness, which no doubt you keep in the bottom drawer of your desk or something."

The baron grunted without amusement.

Derik ducked his head as he handed them each glass of translucent red wine, then stood quietly as they finished.

Hamel took a drink of wine and spoke. "Send a company over to the Eldarvast Woods."

"Sir? Aren't those woods haunted?"

"Yes, by a rather territorial Copir silfae who will kill anyone who enters. We have an agreement, him and me, we must not harm any plants, trees, or even weeds. Ask the master of arms, he has the rules for that woods."

"May I ask why?"

"It is a day's travel from where I was born. If I sent the company there directly, this cabal would figure it out. No doubt they hope I'll panic and rush to defend the obvious places they can find something. Hopefully, they'll be stupid enough to rush into the woods and make the mistake of harming a tree."

"Should I watch your home?"

Hamel shrugged. His hand reached out to stroke along Derik's buttocks and the thief bit back a moan as he leaned forward. Fingertips stroked along his inner thighs, working the dress up to tease the dark blue strip of fabric between his cheeks. The baron chuckled. "No, not you. Send... the Silver Wolf company. They need to be rotated in. But, I lived there a long time ago, no one resides there anymore. Leave it alone, no reason to even consider it anymore. They are obviously heading there so a bit of misdirection could help, I'll just defend the wrong place obsessively."

Tornsin saluted, "Yes, sir!"

The baron's hand pushed him forward.

He stood up on his toes as the powerful man wormed one finger between his legs to stroke the length of Derik's member. His lips parted with pleasure, and he pressed his fingertips against the blotter for balance.

Tornsin looked away with a blush, and Derik flushed even hotter, but he couldn't and wouldn't move away from the baron's questing fingers.

"Very good. I know you have plans, but why don't you take a few days off? We have a longer meeting after this one. I need to convince the ambassadors to get off their asses and relax some of the embargo against the Shattered Kingdoms."

"Sir."

"Oh, and Tornsin?"

Derik's guard turned back around, curious but also blushing.

The baron chuckled. "I heard you are taking Blackbird out for a night on the town."

Tornsin and Derik ducked their heads.

"Yes, sir. By your leave, of course."

"What are your plans afterwards?"

"I-I," stammered the guard, "I was going to bring her back."

"Why?"

Tornsin blushed and scratched his head. "I, um, the barracks isn't an appropriate place for, um, stuff."

The baron slipped his hand from between Derik's thighs and pulled out his wallet. "Look, both of you need a bit of fun. Take this, um, one, two... make it four hundred marks and spend the next two nights in a good hotel."

Derik gaped and Tornsin shook his head.

"I can't, sir!"

"Funny, I just told you to."

"Why?"

"Because Madre told me," he paused for the shortest moment, then continued dryly, "in no uncertain terms that Blackbird needs to recover from me, and you earned a vacation."

"Sir—"

"Listen, take this money, get a hotel, have fun with Blackbird, and come back in three days. If I see either of you on the palace grounds, I'll throw both of you in my bedroom and have Madre watch over you. And trust me, if either of you have any pride, dignity, or something taboo remaining, you won't after her."

Blushing hotly, the guard nodded and took the money. He stared at it for a moment, then shoved it into a pocket. "T-Thank you, sir."

"No, thank you. This cabal thing is important to me, and you are the only man I trust to handle it discretely. You are a credit to your uncle and your mother."

Tornsin bowed. When Hamel said nothing, he turned to leave the room.

"Oh, one more thing," said the baron.

Tornsin turned back around, his cheeks still red.

Hope and fear rose inside Derik. He couldn't anticipate what the baron would say.

"Yes, sir?"

"I'm about to bend this fine piece of ass over the arm of that couch over there and was wondering if you would do something for me?"

Derik gulped, his cock rising up to full mast and his legs parting with the hunger that burned inside him. His eyes locked on Tornsin's, feeling the discomfort but also the lust.

"Y-Yes, sir?"

"Well, we both know that Blackbird is very noisy, and I have a bunch of politicians in the next room. A bunch of stuck-up morons who don't appreciate attractive young men like this."

Chuckling at the thought, the baron continued, "So, would you be willing to gag her as I have a little fun before dealing with the soul-crushing politics? No reason for them to know I'm enjoying myself here."

"Gag?"

"You know," the baron said with a wry grin, "shove your dick in his mouth so I can do what I enjoy best—fucking."

Tornsin stammered as he looked back and forth.

Derik started to say something, but the baron stood up and guided him over to the bench. The overstuffed end never looked as promising as when Derik planted his hands on it, closing his eyes as the baron drew up his dress and exposed his bare ass to the cool air to the room. A flip of the finger brought his dress up and a sensual stroke down pulled his thong away from his buttocks. With a moan, Derik slid his legs apart.

When Tornsin came in front of him, Derik looked up and licked his lips.

Moving nervously, the guard worked his hands on his belt until Derik reached over to unbuckle it. Bent over the end, he moaned at the finger that explored him and the pre-cum that dripped down his thighs.

It took Derik's full concentration to unbuckle, then unbutton, Tornsin's fly. Licking his lips, he held onto his guard as Tornsin knelt on the couch, his cock bobbing in the air right before his lips.

The slick hardness of Hamel's shaft lined up to his opening. The thick head teased Derik's wrinkled pucker.

Derik opened his mouth widely and pulled Tornsin in. The heated length tickled the back of his throat, but didn't cut off his breath. To Derik, it was the perfect length as he tasted Tornsin again. Sweat and musk, the manly scents of a working guard, filled his senses and he nearly came from the scents alone. He worked his mouth open even further, then shoved forward as the baron drove into him.

A muffled moan filled the room and Tornsin gasped as Derik gulped at his cock, teasing it with his tongue. The baron impaled him deeper, sliding in and out until his entire length easily penetrated Derik's body. Derik let out another muffled moan, jerking forward as his lips ground against Tornsin's base. The feeling of being filled at both ends set him on fire, and his own cock drooled hotly against the side of the couch. One hand reached around to hold the tight, muscular ass of the guard while the other reached up to grab Tornsin's hand, bringing it to the back of his head. Tornsin hesitated, then held Derik tightly, grinding him down on his cock as the baron started a hard, powerful stroke against every nerve inside Derik's body.

Hamel's hands gripped Derik's hips tightly and the speed of the cock drove faster into him, slapping against his ass and sending bolts of pleasure that connected his muffled throat, cock, and nipples into a fiery line of pleasure.

Derik writhed with the growing sensations, swallowing and gulping at the shaft that pulsated in his mouth.

Tornsin's hand tightened on his head, pulling him down harder and faster. The dual sounds of slurping cocks sin wet holes echoed in the room as the baron grunted, slamming his length into Derik until the couch creaked from the impact.

Derik came from the dual assaults of ecstasy. His orgasmic scream would have been easily heard if it wasn't for the impromptu gag muffling him. His own dick surged and soaked the side of the couch, but he didn't care. He just rocked back and forth, moving from cock to cock as the world spun around him. The baron grunted and drove deep, coming hard and soaking his insides with volumes of cum.

Tornsin grunted, but didn't come.

The baron withdrew, he left the two lovers alone and cleaned himself up.

Derik just clutched tighter to Tornsin, lathering the throbbing shaft with his tongue until Tornsin came in his mouth, flooding it with the hot, salty taste of pleasure. Purring to himself, Derik swallowed every drop before looking up.

Tornsin gulped himself, his cock still hard and pulsating. "I'll never understand that man."

Derik slid his lips off Tornsin's shaft, leaving it clean and glistening. He grinned. He could feel the cum pouring out of his ass, splashing down his thighs and soaking his shoes. The tingle left him feeling flushed but excited. With the smile on his lips, he purred happily.

"Me either," he replied with a grin, "but I'm not going to complain!"

Inappropriate Dancing

Derik's heart fluttered happily as he leaned against Tornsin. They stood outside of the club, looking up at the "Phoenix Falling" sign. Derik forced himself not to think about all the people in line before him.

A much different experience than the baron sweeping in with three women on his arm. He grinned and turned back to Tornsin, reaching up to kiss him on the lips. He smiled in the kiss and wrapped his arm around Derik's waist, holding him close.

It was a new night for many things, including a new dress. Sapphire blue, like everything else he owned, and trimmed in black. However, instead of a long sweeping bottom, it has a short skirt that flared up if he spun too quickly. The hem rippled against his thigh, and he felt horribly exposed and even more turned on as Tornsin glanced down more than a few occasions. The top of the dress had a high collar, but a keyhole opening right above his cleavage, showing off the deep shadows that Teri drooled over. She had said something about it looking like the proper place to put a fake cock. Derik smiled to himself and held on Tornsin's arm tightly, just enjoying the feeling of anticipation and hard muscles underneath the soft shirt he already planned on stealing.

Tornsin's fingers cupped Derik's chin, and the former thief automatically raised his head. His lips parted to Tornsin's kiss, warm and cool at the same time, the early fall night being held back by the heat that smoldered inside the thief.

In middle of their embrace, someone tapped on his shoulder. Settling back into his heels, he peered around to see one of the massive bouncers that guarded the gate.

"You the baron's?"

He spoke in a deep voice that drew the attention of everyone around him.

Derik gave a tiny, bashful nod.

The bounce gestured with his head and walked to the front of the line. Blushing, Derik followed with Tornsin in his hand.

At the door, he took a deep breath as the bouncer opened the door.

"Won thirty marks on you, figured you were shaved but not a guy. You are pretty hot, you know." The bouncer grinned with only a little forced effort.

Derik didn't think he could feel any more heat on his cheeks.

Tornsin chuckled, wrapping his arms around Derik's waist.

The bouncer's eyes rose up to the guard, then back down.

"If you get tired of the baron's scout here, look me up. That was probably the hottest show I've ever seen. Go on in, both of you."

"Thank you," Derik let out a sigh of relief.

The bouncer winked and Tornsin gripped a bit tighter before they both entered the club.

The air pounded with the band's music, already in full bloom and swamping Derik's senses with its intensity. He bobbed in time with the music, rocking his hips like Sherrel did and relieving his impromptu dancing lesson.

They stopped briefly at one of the tables to deposit Tornsin's sword and Derik's gift from Sherrel, a new matching purse. A nod from the guard who watched the area ensured both would be safe. Drinking in the sight of the dance floor, Derik spotted a perfect spot. Filled with the heat of memory of the last time, and the pulse of the music, Derik reached out for Tornsin and pulled him to the floor. His ass rocked against Tornsin's crotch as they threaded their way toward the center. Reaching his goal, Derik turned around with a smile.

Words were impossible on the floor, so Derik just pressed against Tornsin. His breasts ground against the muscular chest, and he started to move in time with the music. Hips swaying, he smiled up at the guard and lowered himself, dragging his breasts down the chest, he reached the point his mouth hovered just centimeters from the guard's cock. The feeling of his hard nipples peeking through the fabric of his dress, sent a delicious thrill of pleasure and he brought himself back up.

Tornsin let out an unheard moan as Derik moved against him, teasing him with breasts and thighs. Lips brushed against his own as Derik turned around, keeping his eyes locked on Tornsin as he backed up against the obvious hardness and traced it along the crevice between his buttocks.

Tornsin's hands snaked around to hold Derik right along the bottom of his ribs. With a playful grin, Derik set his hands on Tornsin's and pulled them up to cup his breasts. The sensation of the guard's hard palms against his aching nipples redoubled the pleasure he gained from dancing and he pumped harder on the guard's shaft. Tornsin's fingers cupped his breast tightly as his hips thrust up against him, driving the clothed manhood in a wonderful hint of how the night would end.

Derik moaned and narrowed his eyes, feeling the others watching him but no longer caring. He sank into his excitement and enjoyed how his hardening shaft poked slightly from the front of his dress.

Ignoring his maleness, Derik spun back around and ground up against Tornsin, holding him tightly as he just rocked his hips in circles, playfully teasing even as they shared a lustful gaze. Closing his eyes, Derik reached up and wrapped his arms around Tornsin's neck, pulling himself up into a passionate kiss.

He almost came as their lips touched.

They danced for hours, losing themselves in the rhythm. Derik needed only a few short breaks for water before the band drew him back out. The music was a drug, made more potent by moving in time with it. The sensual music drove him, and lust burned inside him. His thighs dampened from his excitement, and moist heat rose up from Tornsin's cock.

Finally, the band's rapid fire music slowed to a ballad, a softer, almost crooning song. The singer perched herself on a stool as she sang. Her body swayed in time with the music and sweat dripped off her body from the heat of the lights. Behind her, the drummers beat in time with her smoldering singing.

Derik held Tornsin tightly around the neck, and Tornsin held him around the waist. Kissing, they swayed back and forth on the dance floor, moving in the shadows of the ballad.

"I want you," whispered Tornsin.

Derik moaned, his eyes half-closed as burning embers of lust waited to explode into fire inside him.

"I want you too."

"I don't think I can wait."

Derik smiled and let one hand slip from his neck.

Tornsin frowned for a second, then gasped as Derik reached between them and into his pants to stroke his painted fingertips along his throbbing length.

"I can feel," Derik purred.

"Now?"

Derik shook his head and whispered. "When the song ends."

Inhaling, he ground his hips against Tornsin's. Seductively, he lifted his leg to hook on the back of the guard's and held his cock tight against the swollen hardness he found. Giving a sly grin, Derik worked his fingers along Tornsin's fly and opened it, fishing out the pulsating cock and tucking it under Derik's dress.

"What are you doing?" Tornsin sounded shocked but his cock was hot in Derik's hand.

Not saying anything, Derik rocked his body, guiding Tornsin's slick shaft up along his own. The thick hardness easily fit in the gap between Derik's cock and his thong. The feeling of their manhoods intertwining stole his breath away, but he just continued to sway to the movement, moving lower with every beat until their balls pressed against each other and he could feel both of their juices soaking his underwear.

Tornsin started to say something, but Derik pulled him tight, thrusting forward like a lover and silencing him with a word. He humped Tornsin until his lover's strong hands grabbed his ass, guiding him as their hips pumped into each other.

Half-closing his eyes, he turned his head to the side and rested it on Tornsin's shoulder. He moaned into Tornsin's ear, nipping on it as their shafts slid up and down each other.

Beyond the profile of his lover, he saw the singer watching him with a smile. He smiled back, then moaned as she started to sing slightly faster, a smirk on her lips and a twinkle in her eyes.

Derik matched the beat of her song, thrusting into Tornsin as their manhoods swelled with excitement. The singer accelerated her beat, and Derik panted as he kept up, matching her beat for thrust.

When Tornin's shaft almost slipped into his ass, Derik whimpered. Wonderfully close to his opening, it drove intense bolts of pleasure from where their manhoods ground against each other, dripping pre-cum and excitement to the ground below.

He didn't know how long they made out, but soon Tornsin's thrusting grew faster and more erratic. Around them, the pounding drums matched every beat of their hips, filling the air with the frantic pulse of love-making. Then, as if reading them, the drums grew hot and hard, punching the air. Helpless to do anything else, Derik obeyed the music.

They came together, so hard that Derik almost fell to the ground, but Tornsin's strong hands held him tightly as their orgasm soaked the inside of his thong and dress. The burning cum dripping off his stomach and he cooed with pleasure.

In an instant, a sudden silence of the song gave away to two drums matching the final, weakening surges of their orgasms.

Panting for breath, Derik relaxed and slipped to the ground. A hot blushed burned on his cheeks as he looked up at Tornsin.

The water drum splashed loudly, and he jumped. Looking sheepishly up to the stage, he caught sight of the singer smiling wryly at the couple. Then, she blew Derik a kiss and launched herself into the next song, a rapid beat to drown every other sound.

The thief could only stare for a moment, then a slow smile stretched across his lips.

Without saying anything, he pushed Tornsin's cock back into his pants and pulled him away from the dance floor. Quickly getting their belongings, Derik wound his way across the club and they burst out of one of the side doors into the alley next to the club.

Spinning around, he grabbed Tornsin at the same time the guard grabbed him. Hungrily, they kissed, mouth and tongue exploring as they clutched each other hungrily. Derik happily drowned in the embrace, but he didn't want to be anywhere but losing his breath to the lover before him.

He jumped when Tornsin pressed him against a brick wall, but he just used it to balance as he wrapped both legs around the guard's waist and clung on. Tornsin stole his breath away, his hands pulling up the short skirt and his hand grabbing the slick hardness and pumped it.

"Oh, Tornsin."

Their lips broke and Tornsin kissed down the side of Derik's neck, sending terrible waves of pleasure through his body as he writhed with the growing ecstasy.

He clutched against his lover and gasped, "Oh, I want you. I want you so badly in me."

Tornsin looked up, "No."

Derik whimpered but Tornsin wasn't finished.

"This time, I want you in me."

In that moment of shock, Derik could do nothing as Tornsin lowered his body.

Derik whimpered, his breasts heaving as he leaned back. Ignoring the moisture in the air, Tornsin came down on his knees and eased Derik's dress up.

The guard smiled up at him, then brought Derik's dripping shaft to his lips. Watching with wide eyes, Derik trembled as Tornsin took his manhood in his mouth. The liquid heat and the caress of lips ran down his length and Derik threw back his head and gasped. His hands clutched the bricks as Tornsin bobbed down, taking more of his length until lips pressed against his hairless base.

"Oh, fuck," moaned Derik.

Bobbing up and down, Derik enjoyed the first blow job of his life from another man. Lips that held his shaft tightly, pulling it into the hot depths of his lover's hungry mouth. Strong hands grabbed his ass, holding him tightly and pulling him deeper. Derik whimpered as his lover's lips bobbed up and down. When Tornsin's reached his base, Derik didn't know if he could take too much. A lap at his hairless balls brought more surges of pleasure. Derik thrashed back and forth, his hair flying in all directions, as he gasped and moaned again, whimpering with the intensity as his balls clenched with a quickly rising orgasm.

"Fuck, yeah! Make him earn it, babe!"

Derik's head snapped up to see a couple at the entrance of the alley. The woman, obviously drunk and half-dressed, called out with a beaming smile on her face. Her male friend whispered sharply, giving Derik an unreadable gaze.

Both a blush and his orgasm rose sharply.

To his surprise, the girl shrugged then called out just as happily. "Oh, sorry! Suck that man shaft, boy!"

Giggling, Derik leaned back and just rocked into the slurping mouth, enjoying every pleasure as his orgasm rose up. He arched his back, whimpering as he tried to hold back.

He failed.

His cock exploded into Tornsin's mouth, spewing hot liquid against the back of his lover's throat.

Tornsin slurped and sucked at him, cleaning his shaft as he clutched tightly.

When Derik slid down the wall, Torsin caught him and brought him close. "That was wonderful."

Tornsin kissed him and Derik tasted his cum on the guard's lips. It was hot and wonderful, filling his body with such pleasure with the fading afterglow.

When he broke, Derik grinned. "The song is finally over. Let's go to the room."

The Last Morning

Morning brought a smile to Derik's lips as he cracked open his eyes and looked out the window to the park beyond the hotel. The sky boiled with clouds but no rain came splattering down. His smile broadened as he stretched out, then froze. Realizing Tornsin was spooning him, he snuggled back into place. His bare skin stroked against the muscular chest of his lover and the half-hard cock nestling between his legs. A soft purr escaped his lips and he settled back into place.

Tornsin shifted in place and kissed Derik on the back of his neck. The slender man moaned softly, pulling his long black hair from between them and holding it in his hands to bare his nape. Tornsin sleepily kissed it, trailing his lips along Derik's shoulder as both of their manhoods rose to full mast.

A hand reached around Derik to cup his breasts, pulling him back as the kisses grew more passionate. Derik turned his head, his lips seeking out Tornsin's. They met and Derik moaned as he let the guard dominate him, holding him tight and kissing until the slender man couldn't breath anymore.

When they broke, he just remained in position, pinned up against Tornsin and looking into the guard's eyes.

"I'm happy," he announced.

Tornsin kissed him again, then shifted position to slide his cock into a better place.

Derik closed his eyes for a moment, feeling the aching hardness, but made no effort to raise his own hips.

"I am too," murmured Tornsin, "but I don't think I can have sex anymore."

Derik giggled, "Aww, why?"

"Well, it's a bit sore."

Wiggling his hips, Derik had to agree. His own shaft and holes felt a bit abused—happily used but aching. "It was a wonderful three days."

"Yeah, and nineteen times is pretty good for one date."

His blush grew hotter and he grinned. He still had pre-cum oozing down his length, but he was content to not coming again. "Good enough for me. Besides, we can do this again, right?"

"Maybe not in such a fancy hotel. I can't believe the baron paid for all this."

Derik looked around the room, marveling at the rich decorations and expensive linens. As a thief, he made more than enough money to sleep in a place like the room, but he just blew it on whores and drink. Moaning, he stretched in place, teasing Tornsin playfully as the man tweaked his nipples and plastered tiny kisses along his back.

It trailed off, then Tornsin announced he needed the bathroom.

Derik followed and did his own thing before crawling back into the bed.

Tornsin settled down next to him, and Derik slid his body over the guard, straddling Tornsin's hips and pressing his manhood against his lover's. Tornsin reached up with his hands, one on Derik's breasts and the other holding both of their shafts together.

Derik purred and rocked his hips, "It doesn't matter if you take me to a hotel on the south side, a date like this will make me the happiest... man I know."

He surprised himself with that sudden question of his gender, a feeling that he wasn't exactly male nor was he female. But, Tornsin just smiled and Derik leaned forward to kiss him.

Tornsin kissed him back, stroking the intertwined cocks but he said nothing.

Derik cocked his head and just admired him. But, his smile faded when he saw a flicker of some emotion crossing Tornsin's face. "Tornsin? Did I say something wrong?"

Tornsin looked guilty and sighed, "Sorry, no, you have been nothing but wonderful this day, um, this entire date actually."

Derik frowned and leaned forward again, sliding his shaft in the hand and pressing his breasts against Tornsin's chest. Fear and concern bubbled, but Tornsin's weren't directed at him. "Something I can help with? Did I do something? Say something?"

Tornsin said nothing, working his lip silently. Then, he let out a shuddering breath. "I feel terrible."

"About what, love?"

"A-About not trusting you."

Derik inhaled sharply as he continued to frown. His hand reached up to stroke Tornsin's face. "What do you mean?"

Tornsin closed his eyes tightly, his hand squeezing their members for a moment, before he opened them. "When I heard you were a thief—"

Derik's heart managed to skip a beat.

"—and you were stealing the Eye—"

Derik's heart decided that it wanted to break a rib or two. Sweat prickled along his skin and his cock withered.

"—and that you fell into the harem the night my brother died."

Derik decided that his heart already gave up in this conversation and just concentrating on fighting back the sob that rose in his throat.

Tornsin struggled with his own words, then he let it out. "I asked a seer if you were the one who killed my brother."

Derik imagined some ghost reached out and grabbed his spine, freezing it in place as his blood ran to ice. He tried to speak and found that the words wouldn't come out until he forced each one from his lips. "What... did he... say?"

Tears formed in Tornsin's eyes as he sniffed. His hands still held Derik, and the thief could feel his lover trembling.

"H-He said," the guard had to take a deep breath to continue, "that you were there, that night and in that hall."

Derik bowed his head and he resisted the urge to press a hand against the burn in his stomach. Closing his eyes tightly caused tears to drip down his face. Hands clenched into fists against Tornsin's chest and he let his shoulders shake with the sobs and guilt that tore through him. "I told you I did terrible things."

He cried for a long moment.

Then, a hand pressed against his cheek.

Opening his eyes and peering through his blurry vision, he saw Tornsin looking up at him with his own sorrow.

"No, Derik, I can't imagine you ever doing something terrible like that. I-I asked, because I was afraid it was you. I," Tornsin sniffed, "I wanted to know. But, the seer said that it wasn't you who killed my brother."

Derik gaped as another shock tore through his system. "W-What? I-I didn't?"

Tornsin shook his head and smiled sadly. Tears ran down his face as he spoke in a broken whisper. "No, it was the men who repaired the ceiling of the hallway a few months ago, after one of the nasty storms. I got some names, and the baron is going to bring them in for questioning. It, um, I think they cut corners and it could have come down at any moment. It was just luck," he sniffed as his shoulders shook, "...luck that only two guards... If it had fallen during the day, hundreds would have died."

Derik's breath came out suddenly, and it felt like a weight on his shoulders just burst into flames. A sob caught in his throat and for a moment, he just held himself over Tornsin. Then, it finally ripped from his throat and he slumped against his lover. "Fuck, fuck, fuck."

Tornsin's hand slipped from between them, and he wrapped his arms around Derik.

Derik just sobbed from relief, that incredible sensation of finding freedom from the guilt that tore into him for months. He managed to push it aside in the sex and romance, but it bore down on him. And it wasn't until he heard those words that it finally lifted. After the pain, relief from agony tore through him like an orgasm.

He wailed from the agony of release.

Tornsin just held him as he cried, lost in the emotions that ripped through his soul.

Derik managed to regain his senses after a few minutes and lifted his head to see Tornsin's concerned expression. He could feel the last of his tears dripping down his neck, following the lines of his breasts. "Why does everyone know everything? I keep finding out that you figured out things I've been keeping secret, and for some damn reason, you all seem to keep on liking me. Why? What did I do?"

Tornsin chuckled and stroked Derik's check, "There is something about you. An innocence or just a feeling like you belong no matter what you were before. There are a lot in the harem who found happiness there once they cast off their old lives. Madre or the baron might be able to explain, but you are so... wonderful. That look on your face, that vulnerable shiver you have, or just your bright blue eyes. Every time I see you, I just want to protect you and take care of you."

Derik sniffed, "I-I didn't need protecting before."

"Rick?"

He had to sniffle the flash of memory of Rick's time, the sudden heat that always rose up at the memory of his debasement. "He's different. Um, he was different."

Tornsin's eyes sparkled, "And you really needed a knight in that alley."

Derik blushed and smiled bashfully. "You were my knight."

The guard smiled and kissed him on the lips. "Thank you. You are a fresh flower in the harem, and as everyone keeps telling me, you belong there. Heart and soul, that harem is your home. Seeing you in these last months, thinking about you while I'm alone in my bed or even on duty, everything I've seen tells me you belong in the baron's and my arms."

Derik swallowed, finding it suddenly hard to breath again.

Tornsin kissed him again. "W-When you came here, when I first saw you, my heart started beating faster just looking at you. A frail, trembling young woman. I mean, a woman," he chuckled, "I was falling for a woman. Not a guy. Then, I found out you were a man, but you were more woman than any lover I've ever imagined. You were wonderful and kind to me. That isn't a thief, that isn't a murderer, D-Derik. And, well, even sharing you with the baron has made me the happiest man in this world."

The thief sniffed and smiled through the tears.

Tornsin wrapped one arm around him and cupped Derik's chin to kiss him. "And I want those thieves to be found. I want them to find the Eye and to have it placed back. T-Then, there won't be any more guilt or question that you stole anything. I know, absolutely know, you didn't steal that Eye. But, I also know that it hangs over you like a shadow, guilt by association."

Derik nearly choked as he closed his eyes tightly. He tried to confess right then and there, but Forbis' spell still kept him silent. He tried again and again but the spell bound him tightly. Giving up, he sobbed and pressed his cheek against Tornsin's chest and listened to the beating heart and compassionate words.

"For as long as you'll have me, I want to be your knight."

Sobbing, Derik managed a false smile on his lips to cover the new guilt that burrowed deep. He swore to keep it hidden, in the deep place, so he would never lose Tornsin or Hamel or anyone else.

"My knight of shirts?"

Tornsin hugged him tightly, "And I'll let you steal every one, if you want."

Derik nodded and wiped the tears from his eyes.

"I do."

Three Months Gone

Marking day.

Three months since the last one.

Three months since Hime gave him breasts.

Three months since the baron took his ass.

Three months since he became the happiest slut in the world.

Derik sat back against the wall outside the massage room and hummed to himself. Like the rest of the girls in the harem, he was forbidden from going out with Tornsin or the baron for the last few weeks because of the fading magic keeping them safe. The time without his lover had planted a growing ache for something hard and throbbing to be buried in his body.

Teri's strap-on didn't always fill him the right way. She was willing to try repeatedly and he enjoyed when he was bent over the pillows with his ass in the air.

He smiled to himself and let his thoughts drift back to the weeks as the harem grew more and more anxious. Teri resumed her favorite task at night: forcing Derik's head into as many pussies as she could find. His jaw and tongue ached, but it was a good ache. Just like his aching shaft between his legs.

Leaning back, he took a deep breath and just smiled.

Teri hopped out of the massage room with a giggle and pranced up to Derik. He looked up from his position on the floor and chuckled as she spun around, showing off the freshly inked markings at the base of her spine. "I can fuck you again!"

Turning around, she spread her legs on both side of Derik and bent over. Reaching behind her, she parted her cheeks and exposed the swollen folds and tiny opening of her ass. With a giggle, she waved her rear above his head. "And look, no worries of nasty stuff coming out of my butt."

Derik reached up with his hands, leaving a feather-light touch on her inner thighs and caressing the soft lips of her pussy.

Teri moaned and settled back, her breathing coming faster as Derik eased apart her labia and slid a finger around the opening of her sex.

He smirked while he ran his fingers along her moist slit. "Doesn't matter, the nasty stuff comes out of your mouth, anyways."

Teri's hips lowered further to aim her wrinkled opening near his mouth

"Shut up and lick it," she commanded.

Derik set a towel on his lap, just in case, and reached out with both hands. Holding her hips, he pulled her close and ran the tip of his tongue from clitoris to ass and back again.

Teri let out a tiny moaning sound and pressed back.

Derik circled around her rosebud. He increased the pressure as he spiraled down to the very center, pushing his tongue in and swirling it around.

"Oh, fuck."

He slid his hand around her ass to finger her.

Someone loomed over him.

Looking up, his tongue still buried in Teri's anal ring, he saw Hime beaming down.

"Hiya, Blackbird. Your turn."

Teri whimpered, looking up with pleading eyes and pressing back on Derik.

Hime shook her head and smirked. "You can play with him later, but I need him now."

"Hime? Please? Just a few more seconds." Teri moaned. "I'm... I'm almost there."

"Now."

Reluctantly, Teri stepped away from Derik, and he scrambled to his feet.

Hime continued to grin as the towel hung on his hardness and he blushed briefly before taking it off. Following the statuesque blond, he padded into the dimly lit massage room.

Sherrel passed him on the way out, kissing him playfully. He followed her with his eyes and she wiggled her ass, completely with a new marking, before disappearing.

Hime circled around the center table and pulled out the corrupted marking sticks. Tapping the table, she waited for Derik to settle into the padded surface, face down. "You seem to have come a long way, Dora."

"Thank you."

She traced her fingers along his spine, following the curves of his ass before spreading his legs along the cool surface. "Found out the baron is into cute, submissive guys?"

Derik purred, his body warming at the thought.

"I heard you found a cute boyfriend too. Bridget, I remember when Tornsin was born. Damn it, now I feel old."

He shivered as she spoke, then she tapped his back. "So, at this important junction of your life, you have to answer but one question."

Curious, Derik looked up.

The priestess grinned. "Do I mark you as a male or as a female?"

Derik's jaw dropped. "W-What?"

"Well, its obvious you still aren't ready for a permanent change."

He choked in surprise.

Hime giggled and pressed her hand against his back. "Don't worry, I knew that before I asked. But, I'm giving you a choice. Do I use the sterility mark for a male or the one for a female?"

He swallowed, "What will happen?"

"Well, you got through the emotional hurdles of the female mark. If you stick with that, nothing will really change. As a male, you'll go through different ones, but you'll be like you were before you came into this harem."

"A-And my breasts?"

Hime smirked again, "You like those?"

Derik lifted his body up off the massage table and looked down at the mounds. They were a part of him now. With one hand, he ran his fingers down the curve and teased his nipple. The feeling of pleasure rose up inside him and he looked up with pleading eyes.

Hime smiled warmly and hefted the marking sticks. "Female it is, my dear boy."

"T-Thank you."

She patted his shoulder and ran her finger down his spine. "You know, if you keep this up, you'll end up worshiping Bridget."

Derik's shoulders tensed up.

Hime froze. For a moment she said nothing, then she ran the first stick along his back, starting into the lines of the various runes. He took a long breath and tried to relax. Instead of the previous pain, the marking sticks were just a faint sense of uncomfortable but nothing compared to his time with Rick or even Madre's affections.

He smiled, happy for mild discomfort, and closed his eyes.

Hime worked in silence until she switched back to the first one. "Do you have a god? I didn't think you did, I thought you were agnostic last time."

Derik though for a moment, through everything he lived in the last three months and everything beyond. Not sure how to answer, he nodded. "I guess."

"It's Bridget now, isn't it?"

"Yeah, I think it is."

Hime paused and reached over. Her breasts trailed along his back as she kissed him between the shoulder blades. Her whisper tickled his ear, "Welcome to the brotherhood."

A tiny shiver pooled in the center of his back.

Frowning, he started to look up, but she pushed him gently down. A few seconds later, she was working on the markings again. "What happened?"

Derik started to open his mouth, but Forbis' spell caught him.

Hime stopped and he slumped down, saying nothing. Then, her hand trailed along his back and she spoke in a hard, sudden voice. "Turn over."

He obeyed, his shaft half-hard and bobbing as he settled down.

Her bright eyes focused on his face, then down toward his throat. "You have a compulsion on you?"

Hope and fear rose inside him. He wanted to nod, wanted to say anything. He opened his mouth to explain and to his surprise, the words came out in a rush. "Forbis did—"

He froze in mid-word, surprised at the sound his voice made. With a trembling hand, he reached up and caressed his throat, trying to feel something but couldn't. "Forbis did that. S-So I wouldn't talk about Rick. How? Why can I speak now?"

Hime grinned and caressed his throat again. "I'm pretty good at dispelling spells on worshipers of Bridget. And it means you gave yourself to Bridget before he cast his spell."

"I'm a worshiper? Why? How?"

"Do you call his name when you are in trouble? Hand him your soul?"

Derik thought back to that moment during his torture with Rick. That single moment when he called out for Bridget's cock, not Rick's. Blushing hotly, he nodded.

Hime's eyes glittered. "A blush and you got hard remembering it? Yeah, you prayed to Bridget."

Her eyes glittered and she wryly grinned, "Did you give a god a lap dance?"

He blushed even hotter as she ran a finger along his length. He shook his head.

Hime's eyes rose back to catch his gaze. "Tell me. What happened?"

Derik hesitated, then he rolled over and started to tell her from that night, when Rick selected him. Hime prompted when he faltered, but her hands worked steadily on his back. Telling of her of the pain of the rape and his caning brought relief. He avoided any mention of the Eye but included everything else.

Hime froze when he mentioned Raven. "Y-You're Raven's boy?"

Wary, he nodded, "I never knew, until Kerlis said something."

She sighed sadly, "Well, fuck me, Bridget."

Brushing his hair off his ear, Hime smiled sadly at him. "I guess it should have been obvious, now that you mentioned it. You have her eyes and hair."

Derik sighed, "I never knew about this part," he swallowed at the tightness in his throat, "of her life."

"Well, she loved as hard as she fought. The problem was, well, she," sigh, "we all made mistakes that night. The baron tortured himself for months after that. I saw her twice, when I left, but..."

Hime's voice trailed off and she lifted the tools.

Derik turned his head to look at her and saw a single tear rolling down her cheek.

"I wish I could have said something then. But, there was so much anger between us that we just turned around and went our separate ways. I never saw her again, until I... I..."

She sniffed, then bowed her head. "I was one of the people who found her body... as the demon gate."

Derik sat up. He didn't know what to say, so he just rested on his heels. Hime sobbed as the tears splashed down.

"Damn that bitch, I couldn't help her and she knew it. Even then, with all that pain, she just couldn't forgive me."

Feeling tears in his own eyes, Derik held out his hands and Hime fell into them.

"I wish I could apologize. I wish I could have turned back the clock. I wish we were still here, in the harem, giving Rachi a hard time because she's control freak and I'm a tattletale. Even when the guard killed her, Raven wouldn't take her eyes off me. That anger kept that gate open and even in the final breaths of her life, she still couldn't forgive me."

Derik held her tight as the tears slammed into her. He didn't know what to say, so he just said whatever came out of his mouth. "I forgive you."

She sobbed something, but for a moment, he thought she called him Raven. Then Hime stood up and wiped the tears from her eyes. She smiled under her sorrow and sniffed loudly. "Damn it, I'm a mess. Besides, I'm not suppose to be the one crying. I mean, you fell in love with the baron after stealing his Eye. And then, Tornsin falls head over heels... for... you... what's wrong?"

Derik couldn't answer as he stared at Hime in shock. His body shook as he tried to stand up, lie down, do anything other than stare at her. His heart started up again, pounding hard in his chest as she looked at him curiously, still sniffing.

"What did I say?"

"H-" his voice was a strangled gurgle, "h-how did you know?"

Hime frowned for a moment, then she cocked her head and shrugged. "I don't know, actually. I didn't really think about it. I just said it. But, it's true, isn't it?"

Derik didn't answer.

Hime sighed and grumbled to herself. "Maybe I always knew, I don't know. Sometimes, I just say things. Part of being an intuitive and what makes me a priestess. I do what I think is right and let Bridget and the world work out the details."

"W-Why didn't you say something?"

She patted the table.

Derik started to move, then froze. "What are you doing?"

"Finishing your marks, silly."

"Y-You mean, you don't care?"

Hime thought for a second and shook her head. She looked as she patted the table again. "Actually, I do care. I care more than you can understand, but my intuition tells me to finish marking you so we can talk. So, lie down."

Confused, Derik rested back on the table and Hime resumed her work on his back, drawing the marks as if he never stole the most precious item in the barony. She hummed softly as she drew.

The knots in Derik's shoulders grew while he struggled to find words to say. "Hime?"

"Yes, Dora?"

"I don't understand. Why?"

Hime tapped lightly, then switched sticks. "Well, I can't really explain it. I don't seem to see the world like most people. Madre called me an intuitive, since I just do what I think is right. I don't really think about the consequences and in the end, it seems like I usually make the right choice."

"No, about talking."

"Well, its obvious you are past one of the major choices in your life and all you have right before you are relatively minor decisions and major consequences. Your path has been set and there is no escaping it."

Derik shivered and clutched the table tightly. "I... I don't want to leave. I love it here."

"I don't think you have that option anymore, Dora," she sounded sad as she switched marking sticks. She worked for a few seconds, then spoke up again. "You have to tell Rachi."

Derik pressed his face tightly against the table. Tears ran down his face, burning his face before soaking into the towel on the table. He was almost ready to throw up. "She will be angry at me."

"Yes. More than you can imagine."

"She might hurt me."

"Might kill you, actually."

"And then," he sniffed as he fought back the tears, "the baron will send me away."

For a moment, he wondered if it would ever come to that, if Madre would honestly kill him, but then he pushed both ideas away sharply.

Hime sighed and ran a finger up his spine. Spreading out her fingers, she stroked against his shoulders. "He has to know. At this point, he must do what he promised to do."

He lifted his head and wiped some of the tears from his face but they kept pouring down. "I love it here, I don't... I didn't mean to."

"I'm sorry."

"W-Why?"

"Because of Hamel's curse. He cannot tell a lie. That also means if he promises to send the thief into a hell on this world, then he must," she empathized the word strongly, "do that. Anything else would be a lie. It is his, and now your, curse."

"Fuck."

Neither said anything as she finished her spells on his back, marking him. He spent the silence in thought, trying to get past the tightness in his chest that came not from shaping spells but a sudden fear of the future.

She tapped his back once. "And there you go, little brother. Three more months of markings and a heap of trouble to burden your soul."

He sniffed, not feeling the humor. Groaning, he pushed himself up off the table. "Thanks a lot. Got any suggestions for a, um, brother?"

Hime helped him into a sitting position. She looked him straight in the eye. Her mouth opened, and for a moment it looked like she would close it. But, Hime spoke with the same conviction she said everything else. "Be honest."

"That's it?"

She shrugged. She ran her thumbs along Derik's jaw. "Well, might not hurt to beg like your life depended on it. But, I can tell you this: I think you should do this. I think you have to be honest, to stand up to the baron and face the consequences of what's happened."

"W-What if he kicks me out?"

"Then, you get kicked out."

"What if he kills me."

Her eyes shadowed in sadness, "Then I'll pray that Bridget comforts your soul."

Derik shivered and clutched himself. "Doesn't sound like really good options."

Hime swept him up in a tight hug.

Derik didn't feel tears, but he held her tightly as he tried to find something positive about his sudden future. His entire body ached with agony as dread loomed over him. "H-How can you just tell me this? Just to tell the truth, knowing that I'll lose the best thing that ever happened to me?"

She released him and kissed him on the cheek. "I'm a priestess."

"What does that... I-I don't understand."

"Do you know the difference between a priestess," she tapped her chest between her breasts, "and a worshiper?"

Tapping Derik between his breasts, she waited for him to respond.

He shook his head.

Hime smiled and rubbed her left wrist. "A worshiper asks for answers. They call to the god when they are in trouble or when they need something. A priestess called on her god when she doesn't need something. When she's in trouble, she knows there won't be an answer. Instead, she does what she thinks is right and trusts that it works out in the end."

"I-I'm not a priestess, am I?"

Hime chuckled, "No, my dear brother, you are not. But, you believe in her and that is where we all start."

Derik let a soft smile cross his lips. "So, would you give up everything if you were in my position?"

"Yes, in a heartbeat."

"Why?"

"Because I have absolute and utter faith that Bridget will see me through every trial I face. No matter how much it hurts, I'll know that she'll lead me through it."

"Even being caned and raped by a brutal man?"

He could see the pain in her eyes as she nodded slowly. "Even when I saw one of my former friends as a gate to Oblivion. I had faith, Derik. I also trust Bridget with my life. If he puts me somewhere I'll be raped, at this point, I will go into it willingly. If I am killed, then I know he will be waiting for me. A-After so many years of being who I am, it isn't a matter of wanting to do this, it just, well, me."

Sniffing, Derik shook his head. "I don't think I have the courage for that."

Hime sighed. "You don't have many other choices, Derik. You either have to tell the truth, run away, or hope to keep on lying."

"Why can't I do that? Just keep on lying?"

She smiled bitterly as she kissed him on the nose. "Because, in the baron's palace, lying never works. Sooner or later, someone will figure out all of your secrets, and the longer it goes on, the more it will hurt everyone."

He shivered again.

Hime watched him for a moment, then held up his chin to kiss him on the cheek, not like a lover but a sister. "You'll do the right thing, Derik, I know you will."

Derik took a long shuddering breath. "I wish this was easy. I was... I was so happy here." More tears ran down his cheeks and his joints ached.

Hime chuckled, "I said that myself. But, if anything was that easy, would it be worth it?"

Thinking for a few minutes, he shook his head. "I guess not."

"Trust me, please? Your trials are always worth it. And, seeing that you are about to experience a difficult one, I would be honored if you would let me show you how to pray to Bridget."

He nodded, unable to speak. He watched as Hime took up his left hand and rotated his wrist until his palm faced up. She smiled and kissed him right at the meeting of his palm and arm.

Looking up, she whispered slowly and surely. "We are the shadows between man and women. We are the lovers of his life and the keepers of his passion. We are Bridget's blessed."

A different type of sensation rose through him, like a clear liquid being poured into his body from the very tip of his head. It filled him with a rushing sound, and he gasped at the feeling of it. Blinking back sudden tears, he saw a faint imprint of her lipstick against his skin. He blinked again, and it was gone. Surprised, he looked up to see Hime slip out of the massage room, leaving him with his thoughts.

The Truth

For two days, Derik didn't sleep. He moved in a daze, sleep-walking through his life as he struggled with a choice he didn't have to make. From the bottom of his heart, he knew he must make a choice, and he also knew the choice his heart told him to take. But his intellect didn't want to give up everything he never realized he needed.

In those moments between the waking and dreaming world, the nightmares reached up to clutch him, threatening terrible dreams if he would just relax. Terrified, Derik just closed his eyes and waited for the exhaustion to take him, but it never came.

He could feel Sherrel's concern for him and later Teri's and Madre's, but none of them seemed to do anything. It twisted inside him and he fled to the rest of the palace, remaining in the shadows until the last possible moment.

When Teri managed to corner him, he snapped out at her, then ran in the shocked silence that followed.

Derik knew it wouldn't last.

The look in Madre's eyes told him he only had hours before she intervened, no doubt as he did when she was drinking so many months ago. At that moment, right as the harem grew silent with the coming morning, he decided on an answer, a coward's answer but was the only one that he could live with.

He would return the Eye.

But, he wouldn't return it in front of everyone. Instead, he decided to find the Eye and just leave it in the hall, in hopes that someone would stumble on it, and he could stay where he so desperately wanted to remain.

Slipping from between the sleeping Sherrel and Teri, he padded into the bathroom. He was exhausted and tired. Even after thinking about it so long, he still wasn't committed to returning the Eye. Some sadistic little part of him screamed at him to confess, to march down to Madre's room and tell her. A larger part bellowed for him to run, with the Eye of course. A bit of him just want to run away, abandon the Eye entirely and everything else. That was the worse part of it, he choked with the thought of losing everything.

Chest and throat tight, he slipped into a bra and panties to cover at least some of his body. He didn't have his stealth outfit, but the dark colors would help in the shadows. Slowly, he unwound the blue cord in his hair. Looking at it sadly, he rolled it up and set it in the tub. It swirled in the water and he nodded with satisfaction; it would be moving just in case Madre followed it.

Sweating from the flutters in his stomach, he walked around the harem to the fountain he had fallen into, all those months ago. Closing his eyes, he prayed softly for Bridget. "Bridget, please? I don't ask for much, I guess, but I want to stay. Just help me out, okay?"

No answer came, but he didn't expect any. Taking a deep breath, he jumped along one column and held there as gravity took its hold, then launched himself to a second, then a third before smoothly sliding into the ventilation. It wasn't as impressive as Shiel's jump, but he managed to do it without a whisper of sound.

Crouching down, he waited for his eyes to adjust to the darkness. As he pictured himself sneaking around the shafts months ago, his breath came harder and tears blurred his vision. Swallowing, he thought about his plan.

Of course, trying to find the Eye would be a more difficult task.

As his eyes cleared, he spotted an empty wine bottle near the entrance. One of the many wines Shiel no doubt stole. He made a face and looked around at the scorch marks from the flaming sphere. To his surprise, they actually criss-crossed the dust multiple times and traveled in both directions, far beyond what he thought possible. Shiel's bare footprints scuffed the dust and he could see how she followed the various scorched trails up and down the tunnel.

Derik frowned.

Crawling forward, he spotted the marks of his own struggles. The original path of the flaming sphere and his own body. Moving softly, he followed one, then a second path but it quickly became apparent that Shiel would have found the Eye, if it was still inside the ventilation.

With an annoyed sigh, he realized that Shiel must have taken the Eye herself. Shaking his eyes, he swore softly. "Damn that bitch."

He heard a sound. The sound of crystal rolling through the darkness. His head snapped up as he saw a flickering of light in the distance. It steadily moving toward him. Fear clutched his heart as he remained still, watching the light grow brighter with every breath that escaped his lips. Trembling, he watched as the Eye of Hamel just rolled along the side of the shaft and then come to a halt right at his foot.

Derik looked up, trying to find the person who rolled it to him, but the only sounds he could hear was the faint whistle of wind blowing past him and his own breath. Everything about his situation screamed a trap, so he waited for many minutes for a hint of anything: someone breathing, the shifting of air, or even the scrape of metal.

Nothing happened.

Trembling, he looked down at the Eye and reached for it.

It twitched, rolling back for a second, then settled back into place against his foot.

Derik froze, staring at it as the Eye stopped moving again.

Flame flickered on the inside of it, rolling around for a moment, then it winked out and plunged the ventilation shaft into darkness.

With only his heartbeat pounding in his ears, he forced himself to move forward with his plan. Reaching down, he picked up the remarkably warm crystal. It was heavy in his hand. A flame flickered in its depth for a moment, lighting up the world around him, then snuffed back into darkness.

Derik swallowed, struggling to move his suddenly dry throat.

Fear coursed through him, and he set the Eye back down in the dust. Blood rushed through his ears as he stared down into the darkness. The sphere flickered to life, a faint blue flame deep inside the sapphire. His hand trembled as the sphere began to move on its own, rolling a few centimeters away from him and then rolling back, bumping against his naked thigh.

With a start, Derik suddenly realized why Shiel never found the Eye. "Fuck me, Bridget, you can move yourself!?"

His whisper was far louder than he wanted, and he clamped a hand against his mouth as he stared at the sphere.

The Eye of Hamel, the artifact he despised and hated three months ago, just rolled away and then back to bump up against him.

He didn't know what to feel. At first fear, then relief, and finally anger took place. He glared at the flickering sphere. All the frustration he gathered in the last few days, all the pain as he struggled with a decision, it came down to a single thing. Trying to return a sphere that apparently could just meander back whenever it wanted. His rage only grew as he watched the sphere rock and forth, moving on its own. Leaning over, he whispered in a hard, quiet whisper. "Then fucking take yourself back!"

The sphere didn't respond.

He shook his head before whispering again. "Damn it, I don't want this. I want to be happy with the baron, Tornsin, and everyone else. I want to be in love, and I want to keep being... used, loved, damn it, I don't want anything to change! If you can just go back, then we can just pretend this never happened."

The Eye of Hamel rolled away for a mere moment, then bumped up against his leg.

Derik choked with his emotions. "Go! Just go! Damn it, stop doing this to me! I want to be happy."

Rolling back, the Eye suddenly grew dark as Teri's voice rose from below.

"Dora? Where are you?"

Derik gave the Eye a glare before whispering at it. "Fuck off."

The sphere didn't respond and Derik peered down quickly before jumping out of the gate. This time, he flipped once and landed neatly on the edge of the fountain as Teri came around the column with a concerned look on her face. His hair came fluttering down around him, spreading out in a cloud as she spotted him.

Even in the dim light of the harem, her smile lit up the world.

"Dora!" she whispered and rushed over to him, hugging him tightly as the last of his hair settled into place over her shoulders.

Heart pounding, Derik wrapped his arms around her tightly.

She let out a sigh, then looked up with her eyes shimmering in the light. "I-I thought I heard you whispering. You sounded so angry, a-and I never heard that before. I was afraid you got in trouble with Madre."

Derik let out a long sigh. His mind pushed aside the Eye once again and he ran his fingers through Teri's hair. "No, I'm just a bit stressed."

Teri sniffed, "I know. Since you got marked, you've been no fun. Did Hime tell you something horrible?"

She faced him strongly, her eyes glaring at him. "Don't tell me you are going gay. You promised!"

A smirk quirked his lip, "Sorry."

"You should be. I mean, you weren't around when I wanted to plow your booty. My guy is rather busy lately, so I want something to abuse."

Derik chuckled and rested his cheek against her own. He stroked his palms down her naked shoulders. "I've been a bit of a bitch, haven't I?"

"I can fix that," came the playful grin.

Derik chuckled and slid his hands along hers as she reached around him. Teri purred against him as her fingers found the crevice of his buttocks and teased them apart. He moaned at the feeling of the fingers against his most delicate of openings.

"First, I'm going to get my strap on and open you up properly. Then I'm going to fuck your ass in the tub until you scream. And your only break is going to be when I ride that pretty mouth of yours."

His shaft grew to full hardness against her belly. "How is that going to help?"

"Well, for starters, I'll be happy." She grinned, "And when I'm —"

He didn't hear her next word as something smacked him hard against the shoulder. The crystal sphere rolled down his back. He gasped and Teri yanked her hands back. However, despite her movement, the sphere somehow landed loudly into her palm as if it was aiming. The smack of crystal against flesh echoed across the room.

The world froze.

Curious, Teri frowned as she stepped back away from Derik. Her eyes were locked on the crystal in her hand.

His hand slid off her. He shook violently as he struggled with his inward screaming. He glared at the Eye of Hamel and tried to come up with some reason for it landing in her hand.

Teri gaped as she pulled it to her, looking at it as her mouth remained open. "D-Derik!?" her voice came out as a strangled whisper.

His stomach twisted in two as she looked up at him, her eyes reflecting the glow of the enchanted sphere.

"T-This is," she swallowed with surprise, "this is the Eye of Hamel!"

Derik started to nod, but Teri grabbed his hand and dragged him away from the fountain and behind the columns. A sense of déjà vécu filled him as she pinned him against the stone. Her eyes flashed. "Why the fuck did you steal this!? Why did you fucking steal it!?"

He winced at the hard whisper and fought with his emotions while trying to speak. "I didn't steal it!"

Teri brandished it, "Then why the fuck do you have this!? We weren't good enough!? What about the baron!? Damn it, you were suppose to be the good girl here!"

Derik took a quick, deep breath. "I was trying to return it, damn it!"

She froze and her mouth gaped open again. "Y-You mean, you already stole this!? You mean, not tonight?"

Derik whimpered at the realization that everyone was spinning out of control. He closed his eyes as a tear ran down his cheek. He choked before he managed to get the words out, "Yes. Fuck, yes. I want to stay here. I've never been so happy in my entire life. So, I was going to return it before anyone knew I had it."

Teri stepped back, releasing Derik.

He struggled as he stood up. "Look, something Hime said a few days ago pointed out that I needed to get rid of it. I was going to just roll it in the great hall and then pretend this never happened. Then that fucking sphere decided to ruin my life."

She hefted it, looking confused. "What do you mean 'it' ruined your life?"

Derik shook his head, whispering harshly, "Damn it, I want to stay. I love you and everyone else. I just want it to go away and for me to be happy!"

Teri frowned, but he could see the worry in her eyes. She hefted the crystal before taking a long, deep breath. "When did you steal this?"

He opened his mouth to say something, but something halted the word in his throat. It was the tiny whisper of wind and the feeling of hairs rising on the back of his neck. A quake shook his limbs, and he turned to the column to see the nearly transparent flares of Madre's aura and two glowing eyes filled with more rage than he could ever comprehend. He whimpered and stepped back as Madre stalked in front of him.

She wore her robe and nothing else, but the fierceness of her gaze negated any illusion of vulnerability. Waves of power rolled off her, and his hair shifted from the energy surrounding them. She spoke in the silky voice of death and with a tone of anger barely held in check. "Yes, Derik, when did you steal it?"

The Consequences

"Um, hi."

Madre snarled and lunged forward.

Derik tried to let out a shriek, but his world exploded into white-hot pain as she slapped him across the face. The impact of her spell, the one she used to spank him, short-circuited his nervous system, and he blanked out for a second.

When he recovered, Madre held him by his throat against the column.

Her body shook with rage as she snarled again. "When did you take the damn Eye!?"

Her voice rumbled with power and the mirror behind her shuddered with the force.

He couldn't speak and his ears rang with a high-pitched ringing as he clawed at her hand. His fingernails cracked, but he couldn't even scratch her skin. His mouth gaped open, trying to get air into his lungs, but Madre's inhuman strength pinned him helplessly against the column.

"Um, Madre?" came Teri's hesitant voice, or what he thought was her voice. The ringing in his ears continued to rise in pitch and he saw stars floating in his vision.

"Madre?"

Derik's lungs burned with the desperate need to breath. He kicked out. His toes impacted against Madre's stomach but the hard muscle felt like kicking a stone wall.

"Madre!"

Madre squeezed tighter, and he heard his bones grind, then she suddenly released him.

He collapsed to the ground and heaved forward, struggling to stay awake as blood flowed into his brain and he drank in the cool air. Trembling, he closed his eyes and waited for the killing blow.

Madre snarled, her voice rumbling as the air beat around her. "Teri, give me the Eye."

A pounding heartbeat passed.

"Go back to bed."

"Madre?"

"NOW!"

Derik winced as the power of her voice slammed against him. It rumbled through the harem, no doubt waking everyone, but he struggled to keep his balance. Before him, he saw Madre's toes curling and crackling energy coursing along the marble tiles. His world shook, but he heard Teri's bare feet fleeing and he closed his eyes tightly.

When he opened them, Madre crouched before him, holding the Eye of Hamel in her hand in front of her face. "When did you steal this, Derik?"

He struggled to speak but Madre had no patience. Her palm smacked down on the tile and it shattered into dust. When the dust settled, there was a half-meter crater underneath her palm.

"I said," she growled, "when did you fucking steal the Eye!?"

"T-The first," he gasped, "the first night."

"After the girls found you?"

He shook his head, "The night I fell into the fountain."

Her voice grew low and violent. "You mean to tell me, you've been hiding in my harem, stealing my affection, and betraying my trust from the very beginning!?"

Madre's growl started low, but the end of her question slammed into him.

Collapsing to the ground, he whimpered and curled into a fetal position, unable to look into her terrible eyes. Sobs tore through him. He tried to crawl away but she yanked him up by his hair, pulling him completely to his feet and slamming him back against the column.

The impact drove the breath from his lungs and he choked on the marble dust that poured down his face. Madre's eyes glowed with some terrible spell and her body burned with flames of rage.

He whimpered and flinched but couldn't escape.

Madre froze for a long moment and he counted the last seconds of his life in his rapidly beating heart.

"You mean," she took a long, shuddering breath, "I lost my Nightingale because of you?"

Light pooled in her right hand as she pulled it back from his hair. Through the curtain of black that cascaded down, he saw wisps of energy condensing into her hand. It formed into a ball of burning energy as the world seemed to warp around her. Twisting energies tore at his skin and pulled at his hair as he saw a few strands ignite as they touched the killing spell.

Madre's face became a mask of rage and anger as she drew her hand back.

Derik whimpered and clutched himself, unable to move from the spot as she stepped back, then punched forward. He screamed as the air ignited into flames. The air pressure burst around him, but no concussion slammed into him and, a heartbeat later, he still breathed.

Whimpering, he cracked open one eye to see the Eye of Hamel hovering in front of him and the energies of Madre's spell evaporating around it. Gasping, he stepped back, then caught sight of the surrounding columns.

Or, more accurately, the gaping holes where the force of her spell vaporized the columns.

His chest ached as he stared at the destruction that tore up the floors and scorched the walls in a straight "V", centered right on the sapphire sphere.

Madre growled and slashed her other hand toward him, the hand bursting into flame as it came screaming through the air. A flash of sapphire and the Eye of Hamel block it without appearing to move in the intervening space.

The air that blasted into him threw him back a foot. Bare feet skittering on the ground, he looked for an escape.

She started toward him, then froze. He watched as her eyes took in the destruction and the cowering girls on the other side of the column. For a moment, her glare returned, then she stepped back.

The Eye, the damned artifact, zipped around her once then came to Derik. He automatically held out his hand and it dropped into it with a heavy slap. A moment later, the burning light inside the sphere snuffed out and it was once again just a normal sapphire sphere.

Madre stood there, trembling with rage.

Derik stepped back.

She started for him, then stopped. Her eyes glittered in the light. With a growl, she waved toward the door. "Leave."

"Madre—"

"Leave!"

"Please—"

"LEAVE!"

Her voice shattered the skylights and tore tiles off the ground around her. Marble dust exploded in all directions as she took a single step toward him.

The others screamed and backed away quickly.

Before she could attack, he fled the harem and the accusing eyes of everyone who trusted him.

He wondered if he would ever stop crying.

Ten minutes later, he stood on the roof of the palace. The Eye of Hamel rested heavily in his hand, quiet and inert, but he already knew better. Twenty meters away, he could see the shattered glass of the harem and the voices that rose from it. He could hear the feelings of betrayal, shock, and anger from almost everyone he spoke.

Tears ran down his cheek. Shaking his head, he started across the roof and toward a thin wire for hanging flags during the holidays. It stretched from the roof to one of the guard towers near the entrance of the palace. It might have been considered a security threat, but no one could climb the pencil-thin wire. Much less on a windy night.

Derik just hopped on it and started to walk down its length. Though he was sobbing as the wind picked at him, he easily balanced himself.

"Fuck it, Bridget and Hime, I'm just running. Let Rick or Shiel find me, I don't really care anymore."

It hurt to walk down the wire.

The pain didn't come from the sharp wire on his bare feet or even the winds that tugged at him, but the pain of leaving the harem. The look on Madre's face and the sounds of the women he grew to love as they spoke about him. He betrayed them and the guilt of it cut him to the bone.

Every step down the line reminded him of a beat of a dirge. It took him nearly twenty minutes of walking before he almost reached the tower.

Then the Eye stopped.

Derik nearly lost his balance as the Eye refused to move, locked into position by some mystical force. He released it and spun around, glaring at the hovering sphere.

"What the fuck is wrong with you?" he snapped.

All the frustration burst inside him, and he threw up his hands. "You know what? Fuck it. I don't need them, and I don't need you."

It was a lie, but he couldn't take it anymore. Abandoning the sphere, he spun back around and raced toward the tower.

The Eye of Hamel spun around, flaring to life as it stopped in front of him.

Derik came to a skittering halt, nearly losing his balance again. He crouched down and the Eye lowered itself.

Tears burned in his eyes. He sobbed before bowing his head. "Damn it, why are you doing this?"

The Eye moved closer, burning with its flickering light.

Derik stepped back, but the Eye followed him.

He stopped and so did the sphere. It inched forward and bobbed against him, bumping his thigh. Derik shivered at the warmth that came from the sphere. He brushed it again but when his knuckles impacted the surface, his world exploded into color.

Derik was suddenly in the great hall, standing at the points of the four arms as he looked down. He could see Hamel sitting in his padded chair, staring down at Derik as Derik pleaded silently for his life. Derik frowned, shivering at the sight of the cuffs that bound his hands behind his back and the six guards that watched over him. The entire scene was ethereal as he argued with the baron.

He realized he wasn't the one kneeling before Hamel.

His mother.

Anger burned in her eyes as she screamed at him. He could see sword cuts crossing her body. Her shift—blood-stained and torn—moved constantly with the rage as she snarled at the baron. Every movement, he could feel the sphere's feeble intelligence trying to enforce the illusion that he was his mother. He resisted, but the sphere stubbornly kept giving him the impression they were the same person.

Finally, the baron stood. He appeared to roar, but not a sound came through the strange vision. The guards dragged Raven from the room and Derik was stunned how much he looked like her. Long black hair, burning sapphire eyes, and similar body shapes. But, there was something different. An aura or sense around her.

In a flash, he realized his mother was a fighter. She lashed out, kicking at a guard. The first collapsed, and she spun around, the back of her heel catching another in the throat before a teenager stepped from the shadows. Derik gaped at the young Rachi. The battle mage took a step forward, her hand bursting into light, and she punched Raven out with a single blow. His mother collapsed to the ground, and the guards dragged her out.

Hot tears splashed down Derik's cheek as he focused on the baron. As soon as the door shut, parting him from Raven, he dropped to his knees and buried his face in his hands. The guards and Rachi stared for a long time, then backed out of the room. As the door shut, the vision faded.

Derik gasped, swaying on the wire. He snatched his fingers back from the sphere. Somehow, he could feel the sphere seeing him as his mother, a gut reaction passed on by the image.

"I-I can't do anything. That's my mother."

The sphere just bumped against him.

"What? I can't forgive him, that isn't me!"

It tapped him again.

"Damn it, Bridget, I can't go back!"

To his surprise, the sphere sagged in the air. The flame flickered out and it dropped straight down. He reached out to grab it, but missed. It landed on the wire and stopped moving. Balanced perfectly on the line, like it was welded in place.

"Look, I can't go back. The baron will kill me, Madre will kill me, and T-Tornsin... damn it, how can I face him?"

The sphere did nothing.

Derik glared for a moment, then cautiously stepped forward. When the sphere didn't move, he stepped over it and took another step. This time, nothing stopped him, and he raced down the line, his heart pounding until he reached the roof of the guard tower. Lightly ghosting across the surface, he spun around and crouched down.

In the distance and the darkness, he could see the sapphire sphere still on the line. Beyond it, the palace.

He sobbed at the idea of leaving it. Slowly, he turned his back on the palace and looked out over the city. He tried to plan his escape from the town of his birth, any path away from the baron, the palace, Rick, and everyone else. He took a deep breath and prepared himself for a new life.

Then choked on the bitter taste in his lungs.

Closing his eyes, he dropped to his knees. Tears ran down his cheeks, splashing on the tile of the tower. His heart fought with his mind, the voices of Hime and everyone else echoing in his head as he considered the unthinkable. He fought against himself until his broken fingernails cut into his palms and he shook from the effort.

He hated himself when he stood up. Looking into the dark sky, he whispered angrily. "Fuck you, Bridget."

Turning around, he walked back up the line, toward the palace and his betrayal. Everything about him ached, from his heart to his joints. Inwardly, he screamed at himself with imagined punishments, but he knew that it was love that urged him forward.

He had no words for it. He just stepped over and picked it up. Inert, it just settled into his hand as he padded back up the wire. "What the hell are you?"

In a flash, another vision slammed into him. A sense of time long past crashed into him. He stood in a clearing of a forest. A tiny Copir silfae, his elfin figure barely a meter in height and as old as the trees, stood in front of a young man, handsome but unfamiliar to Derik. His face was a mask of determination and sorrow as he agreed with the silfae about something. Somehow, Derik knew the young man had agreed to some terrible oath, but nothing could prepare him to see the man gouge out his own eye using nothing but his fingers. Derik wanted to scream as the man held out his bloody orb and the Copir elf whispered over it. Strange symbols floated around it, encasing it as the eldritch magics solidified into a perfect, flawless sapphire sphere.

The Eye of Hamel. The literal eye of Hamel.

The point of view for the vision changed. He looked up at the man who mutilated himself. Derik's heart skipped as he recognized the man as his lover.

The baron.

Hamel.

The vision ended with a crash and Derik froze at the very top of the line, one foot resting on the roof.

"Y-You," he gasped, "you really are his eye!?"

The sphere did nothing, but he knew it was true.

Any chance of turning back evaporated with the idea of stealing part of the baron himself. Silently, Derik steeled himself and walked back into the palace. His heart ached as he took the hallway the last time, winding his way around the harem and toward the main hall. He could feel, through the Eye, Hamel standing in his den. Tears ran down his cheeks as he walked up to the door and knocked.

"Come in."

The rumbling voice of the baron didn't give him comfort as he pushed open the door. Inside, two guards stood along the walls.

The baron looked up from his desk, then a slow smile crossed his lips. "Blackbird!" Madre had apparently not told him yet.

"H-Hello, baron."

He came around and swept Derik up in a hug.

Derik held the Eye in his palm but the baron hadn't noticed. He leaned against the baron for a moment, then pushed himself away.

Hamel frowned, his one eye narrowing.

A sob rose up as Derik imagined the baron with two eyes, and shook his head.

"What's wrong, Blackbird?"

"A-About," he had trouble saying the word, "your eye."

The baron's face fell.

"I just found out. We caught the group you told us about. They didn't have my Eye, instead it was a glass sphere. Right size and color. In fact, it was quite fractured from heat and stress, but they gave up their lives to defend it. I think they thought it was real. But, it wasn't my Eye."

There was no way to avoid it.

Derik's chest ached from his sorrow. He shook violently as he struggled with his own will. Slowly, he lifted his hand and held out the Eye of Hamel.

It ignited from the inside, a flickering flame that burned warmly in his palm. Slowly, it rose in the air as the baron gasped in surprise.

"I know," sobbed Derik. He swallowed hard and said the words that would implode his entire world, "I'm sorry."

Imprisoned

Derik brushed the hair from his face and tucked it behind his head. He looked around at the dungeon cell and sighed unhappily. Leaning back, he rapped his head against the smooth cut stones that made up the wall and regarded the solid steel bars in front of him.

He said, "Well, this sucks."

He wore only a simple shift, uncomfortably similar to the one he saw his mother in the Eye's vision. Looking down, he wondered why his nipples were hard from the texture of the fabric when the rest of his world continued to plummet into the depths of hell with no escape.

Reaching over, he grabbed his shackles and swung them from his finger. They were on him less than a few minutes before he managed to pick the lock and cast them aside. Now, they were the only source of entertainment as the long night stretched into the morning.

Not like he could sleep.

Groaning, he leaned back again and tapped the back of his head against the stone.

The cool stone was comforting, despite the flickering pain, and it was something. Somehow, revealing his last and final secret brought relief. No one told him they already knew... well, Hime did, but the priestess really didn't think about anything. He chuckled bitterly and rapped his head again.

"You know, Derik, you could hurt yourself doing that."

He looked up to see Teri sadly watching him. She wore her robe tight around her body.

The sight of her red-rimmed eyes sent his heart in a lurch.

He closed his eyes tightly. "Go away."

"No," came the choked reply.

"Why not?"

"Because, I want, um, need to know something."

Derik sighed and opened his eyes.

Teri leaned against the bars and held her arms tightly around her stomach.

He sighed, still feeling the sensations of being dropped into a pit. "Sorry, Teri, I think I'm a bit stressed."

She chuckled dryly. "Can't imagine why, Madre tore into you pretty well, I'm surprised you are still standing."

Teri stroked the bars of the cell. "I'm also surprised you went to the baron."

Derik said nothing about the Eye protecting him.

Teri looked uncomfortable in the silence, then she whispered. "Why you do it?"

"I owed Rick—"

"No, I know why you stole it. I mean, why did you return? Why did you go to the baron? That was the worse thing you could have done."

He said nothing.

Teri wiped a tear from her eyes. "I mean, Madre sent you out by yourself. Y-You are a thief, you could have just run away. Could have taken the Eye with you, and we... we would have never seen you again."

Derik slumped his head forward, feeling the same pain in his heart. Looking down, he flexed his fingers and set them purposefully down on his slender thighs. "Love, I think."

Teri sniffed. "I don't understand."

Tears rose as he spoke, "I love the baron and Tornsin... and you and Sherrel," he sighed, "damn it, I love even Madre. You have," he sniffed himself, "you have all be so wonderful to me. And..."

His voice trailed off as he lost himself in though. The tears dripped down his face as the world imploded a bit more.

Teri banged her head against the bars and clutched them. "Fuck you, Derik. Why did you have to ruin this?"

"Because of love?"

She banged on the bars. "Love doesn't get you thrown in prison!"

Her shrill voice echoed in the hall of the prison cell.

Derik looked away as he struggled with the tears and sorrow. "I-I, I couldn't do it. I couldn't have that Eye hanging over me with everyone trusting me. My date with Tornsin, it-it was perfect and so sweet. He confessed to things, but then he said I was a good person. And I know I'm not, I did terrible things."

"You are a good person."

Derik snapped loudly, "I'm a fucking thief, Teri!"

"You... you tried to return it!"

"Yes, and that is why I'm here! I can't live without you! I don't want to leave, but every choice I made tore me away."

"Then, just take the Eye and run, that way you wouldn't—" Her voice stopped suddenly.

The silence cut Derik like a knife in his gut. There was fear in her face and he could see her avoiding some topic. Morbidly, he had to know what it was. "I... I what?"

Teri sniffed, the tears streaming down her face. "Then, I wouldn't see you on the auction block. Not like the other girls."

Pushed over the abyss into Oblivion, he swallowed against the sudden tightness in his throat. "Is... is that was the baron is going to do?"

Teri sobbed and nodded. "Storn, um, someone said that they saw the notice this morning. A-And Madre said that you had to suffer otherwise the baron would lie. S-So, you go on the block tonight."

Derik whispered as the darkness formed over him. "Oh, fuck me, Bridget."

"A-And Rick," she sniffed and looked away, "Rick is bidding on you. He's gathering up the deeds to most of the, um, places he owns. Word on the street is that he's going to buy you at any cost."

Memories of that horrible tower and his torture crashed into him. Derik opened his mouth to say something, then all the strength flooded out of him. He sobbed and buried his face in his hands.

"Fuck, fuck, fuck..." he swore softly. The dread that filled him pooled in his stomach, like a solid block of icy lead. For a moment, throwing himself on the nearest knife or dagger seemed like a viable option. He pushed it aside, he couldn't inflict that on his friends. Sniffing, he struggled to control his emotions. "I-I can't go back there."

This time, Teri said nothing and they remained in silence, with nothing but their tears for sound.

Derik shuddered at the remembered pain and agony, the haunted look on Rick's face. Even as his cock twitched to life from the hunger of abuse, he struggled to breath.

Teri broke the silence. "I-I'm sorry, Derik."

Derik let out a soft whimper, then smiled bitterly. "I know, kitten."

He heard her turn on her feet and start up the stairs. As she hit the second stairs, a tiny prick of something caught his memory. "Teri!"

Teri froze and padded down. "Derik?"

He looked up, pained at her expression.

"How do you know Storn?"

Panic filled her eyes, "Um, who?"

Derik rolled his eyes, "Damn it, how do you know Storn or the word on the street?"

She struggled with her words, then glanced up the stairs. For a moment, he thought she would flee, but Teri leaned against the bars. "Aw, fuck it. Can't be any worse than you telling the truth." She took a deep breath, "I've been moonlighting as a thief."

"What!?"

Teri flinched and motioned him to be quiet. "You know my date, the old scholar?"

"Yeah?"

"He can only get it up every few months. So, I told Madre that I was going out when I was actually, um, stealing things."

Derik stared at her in stunned silence. His mind spun furiously, then he remembered a conversation with Storn in a different life. "Shadow Wasp?"

Her face turned bright red, telling him everything. For a moment, Derik just sputtered, then he started to laugh. A bitter and angry laugh, that nonetheless broke some of the sorrow inside him. "Well, fuck, you were the one who stole all my jobs. I had to go after the Eye because there was nothing else."

Teri whimpered. Her face paled and she gripped the bars tightly. "You mean, this is my fault?"

Derik thought for just a second, then he stood up and padded over to the bars. His shift clung to his legs as he reached out to stroke his hand along her back. "Yes, it is."

Teri's lower lip trembled.

Derik struggled for the words and the effort to crawl out of the darkness filling him. "Its your fault that I'm a slut."

It took her a heartbeat to understand his words. "What!?"

Derik rolled his eyes, "If it wasn't for you stealing my jobs, I would have never been in that harem. I wouldn't have found out where I really belong and I wouldn't have found love. I also wouldn't have ever known that my mother was part of the harem herself. So, that part is your fault. But, me stealing the Eye, that wasn't your fault."

She reached through the bars to hug him and Derik leaned into it. He breathed in her smells, feeling that he would miss them soon enough. For as long as he could miss something.

"Trap," she muttered sullenly.

"Bitch," he smiled back.

They held each other for a long moment before Derik whispered.

"Teri-cat, can you do me a favor?"

"What?"

"Tell Storn something? Or ask him something?"

"Anything."

"I have a safe in the old bell tower, right off Gladius and Dove, where I kept random stuff I never fenced. C-Could you ask him to sell it off and, maybe, buy me? There might be enough to out-bid Rick."

"What's the combination?"

"Its a key lock and I heard you're the master boxer."

Teri sniffed and looked up at him with a quizzical look.

Derik grinned sheepishly. "I lost the key years ago, but it has my old stuff in it. I liked the box, so I just picked it every time."

She nodded, "I-I'll do that. I have a bit myself, just in case, I'll add it."

"I can never pay you back."

She sniffed and giggled through the tears. "I'll take it out of your ass. Your... sweet ass."

He answered by kissing her. It was soft and tender as their lips touched. She stole his breath and he stole hers and they both were crying as they parted.

Teri ran her hands down his chest, sweeping around his breasts to tease him. "I love you, Derik. Be safe, please? No matter what."

"I love you, Teri, but you know that I love the baron too, right?"

Teri smiled sadly, "I know, and Tornsin and Sherrel and everyone else. That is one of those things I like so much about you, you have so much love in your heart. I guess I can see why you came back. Even if you are an idiot."

When she left, he could still feel her lips against his. He smiled sadly and caressed his fingertips along the tingling before returning back to his seat. Settling down, he took a long deep breath.

"Well, this sucks," he repeated.

The faint hope of Storn and Teri rescuing him helped push back the black cloud of Rick. He shivered at the memory of his abuse and clamped one hand down on his crotch in hopes that it wouldn't rise. Clutching himself, he curled up into a ball and let himself drift to sleep.

He slept uneasily, with nightmares of the Eye's vision and the baron's betrayed look as he held his eye. When it grew too dark, Derik whimpered and clawed himself into wakefulness.

A hand rested on his shoulder.

Yelping, he sat bolt up. He blinked and then saw Tornsin waking up next to him. Surprised, Derik cried out. "Tornsin!?"

The guard scrambled to his feet and blushed. It was the alley again, even more so when Tornsin picked him off the bench and swept him into a tight hug. Derik hesitated, then he wrapped his arms around the powerful man and rested his head on Tornsin's shoulder.

"Do you hate me?"

Tornsin shook his head.

Derik sniffed, "Why?"

"Because Hime is very good at calming people down."

Derik froze, "Hime?"

"After you were thrown in prison, I was pulled from guard duty into a conference with baron and Madre. They were talking about what to do. Then, Hime came sweeping in and made a mess of everything. Madre almost killed her but then it was over, just like that."

"You mean, I won't go on the block?"

When Tornsin said nothing and just held him tighter, Derik knew he wouldn't escape Rick. Numb and terrified, Derik forced himself to enjoy every second he had with Tornsin. He shifted his head and brought his lips to his lover's.

Tornsin whispered softly and sadly. "I'm sorry."

"Its okay, Hime said so. Or I think that is what she told me."

Tornsin started to say something, but Derik just kissed him. Even with everything happening, their passion still rose up and the guard's love for him washed over his aching heart. Derik wanted to melt in his arms and held him tightly. They broke with a soft gasp.

"Don't worry, Tornsin, I would never ask you to choose between me and the baron."

"I-I don't want to."

"I know, which is why I did this."

Tornsin nodded, "Hime said that. She asked the baron for forgiveness."

"Are you it? My forgiveness?"

Tornsin chuckled, "No, I'm just going to be in trouble for being in here, but I had to see you one more time."

Derik sniffed, "I may never come back."

"I don't care, you are the only women I loved."

Somehow, those soft words brought tears to his eyes. Derik hugged him again, his lips seeking Tornsin's. Powerful hands stroked up his flanks, pushing him back the stone wall pressed against his back. Derik whimpered, lifting his feet to hook behind Tornsin's leg, but the guard pushed him away. Derik whimpered and looked up with pleading eyes.

"I, um, got you something."

Frowning, Derik looked around as Tornsin picked up some folded cloth. Derik's world brightened as the guard unfolded it, revealing one of his shirts. The same shirt Derik slept in for the last three months.

"It, it isn't much, but please take this."

Derik couldn't speak as Tornsin set it down and gathered up Derik's shift. Pulling it over his head, he exposed Derik's nude form before slipping the shirt on him. The smells of Tornsin and apple perfume surrounded Derik but the thief could only stare at his lover and cry.

Tornsin smiled sadly and started to button the shirt, his fingers teasing along Derik's breasts. "Look, I know that I can't afford you. Even if I wanted to, but keep this with you as long as you can. And... if you ever need to, send word and I'll give you another. And another. No matter what, no matter where."

The thief's lower lip trembled as Tornsin finished the buttons.

The guard clasped Derik by his hips. "I can't say I'm happy about this, but if you trust Hime, then I will. Someday I hope... someday I'll be your knight in shirts again."

Derik finally found the words. "Y-You'll always be my knight. Always."

The Auction Block

Derik shivered as he stood in the center of a hurricane. Activity swirled around energetically as servants arranged dozens of chairs in a fan pattern, all aimed directly at his vulnerable body. His feet rocked back and forth on a wooden platform which raised him above the floor. More servants set up tables of food and wine while a pair arranged a large table in front of Derik. He watched with a dread feeling in his gut, but hung on to the warmth of Tornsin's love and the hope that Storn could save him.

Taking a deep, shuddering breath, he wrapped his arms around his breasts and hugged himself. The fabric of his favorite shirt caressed his naked skin, reminding him that he wore nothing under the button-down shirt smelling of apple and man. The feeling of vulnerability increased as he looked out at the rest of the room, where dozens of guards stared at him impassively. Shivering with growing discomfort, he looked up at the Eye of Hamel situated right above his head.

"I hate you," he whispered in a voice only he could hear, "I hate you so much."

He could almost imagine what the Eye saw, the silent vision looking down and a dim intelligence seeing him and his mother as the same person. Worrying the bottom of his lip, he took another breath.

"You are an idiot," said Madre as she hopped up on the wooden platform that raised him above the chairs.

Derik stepped back at her glare until his bare feet caressed the edge.

Madre reached out for him, but she only grabbed his waist and pulled him back to the center of the platform. Her eyes looked sad, Derik decided, as she spoke softly. "And I see Tornsin violated the ban on visiting you."

Derik warmed up at the memory of his lover. He cleared his throat. "I'm sorry. I'm sorry for everything."

"You should be, despite everything you do, everyone seems to still love you."

Her eyes were glittering. She reached out and straightened down his shirt, smoothing it over his breasts and tucking it along his narrow waist and broader hips. He blushed at the touches, his nipples growing hard, as cotton caressed his body.

"E-Even you?" he asked with a bit of hope.

Madre smiled sadly, "Yeah, I love you too. But, you better remember, I respond poorly to surprises of this nature. I almost killed you, if it wasn't for the..."

Her eyes flicked up and Derik followed the gaze to look at the Eye. After a second, he looked down to match her gaze.

"And now?"

"Well, you are damn lucky you got that fucking blonde priestess on your side. She can be most convincing when she cares about something. Though, I almost hit her as hard as you."

He thought back to the destroyed columns and laughed curtly. "Point made, next time, I'll find a way of telling you when I stole a priceless artifact."

Madre's lip curled into a smile, then dropped instantly. "Hime told me about Forbis' compulsion."

Derik said nothing.

Madre finished and brushed her fingertips along his thigh before she stepped back to the edge of the platform to admire him. "I've made too many mistakes with you, Derik."

"It isn't your fault," he said quietly.

"No, it is my fault. I am your Madre and I should be the one taking care of you."

"You do fuck me rather hard,"

She grinned, "You are still the hottest submissive I had ever met. And," she paused for a moment, "I don't regret a single second I spent with you; except maybe losing my Nightingale."

"I never meant for all of this."

"I know," she reached up and kissed him on the lips, "but Hime is right, this is where you are now."

Derik fought the urge to whimper. "What is going to happen?"

"In about a half hour, everyone will come in. They'll poke and prod you, probably grope you a bit, then they'll start bidding. He is changing one thing, but otherwise it will be the same bidding as Nightingale, Raven, and everyone else who left the harem this way."

"I-I never been to an auction."

"Well, the baron runs things differently than most of them. See that table in front of you?"

He nodded but didn't look at it.

"They'll bid on you by throwing something on the table. However, once its on the table, it stays there."

"Which means?"

"Basically if someone puts a thousand down, even if they lose, the baron keeps the thousand."

"Why?"

Madre shrugged, "I don't know, its one of those things I don't understand about Hamel. Probably cuts down on people driving up prices or something. Or he uses it for some strategic reason."

He let out a long breath. "Damn it."

She kissed him again.

"Derik," he looked at her and saw tears in her eyes, "I really mean it. If there was some way to save you from this, I would."

"I know. And... it isn't Hime's fault."

Madre snorted with harsh amusement. "That bitch doesn't think enough about her actions. Of course it is her fault, but we all have some guilt in this. Despite how close I came to killing you, I also felt relief that we have no more secrets between us."

Her eyes narrowed, "Right?"

Derik held up his manacled hands. "I swear, you know every secret I held. Not that anything can beat stealing the Eye."

Madre gave him a hug. "The baron is coming soon, so I'm going to go. Just remember, no matter what he says, He was crying when I walked into that office. He won't say it, but I think he loves you as much as you love him."

"I wish—" The image the eye had gave him came back and he knew that she was right. The baron no doubt loved him but he was bound by restrictions that Derik could not escape.

"Don't. It will only hurt you more. Right now, just focus on your future. This harem," a single tear finally ran down her cheek and she balled her hands into fists, "I'm sorry, but the harem will never be your home again."

Derik sniffed, "I love you, Madre."

Madre sniffed and wiped her tears away. He could see her steeling herself against her emotions, and her face grew tight as she took a deep breath. Her hands stroked against his arms, smoothing the fabric. "Write, if you can. Don't ever forget us."

Derik leaned forward, reaching up.

Guards around him stepped forward in concern, but he just rested his bound wrists behind her head and hugged her as best he could. Closing his eyes, he rested his head on her shoulder, then kissed her on the cheek. "Thank you for showing me my true self, Rachi."

Her body stiffened for a moment, then a sob escaped her throat. She fought it down and hugged him tightly. They held each other for a long time before she slipped away. Without looking back, she hopped off the platform and quickly padded out of the room.

He straightened up and stood tall. It was only a little thing, but he had to survive through this. Even if he knew only one path remained before him.

Rick.

He breathed slowly to calm his beating heart. When he looked up, he saw the man who held his life in his hands. The cruel smile and powerful frame sent a conflicted shiver of fear, terror, and hunger through him. The world spun as Derik watched the crime lord casually drifted across the room, circling like a shark.

Behind him, Derik spotted the thin form of Kerlis and three guards. They held two large leather cases. Kerlis smiled happily, a little wave of his fingers, and plopped himself down in one chair. The guards remained with Kerlis, but Rick just drew closer until he was looking up at Derik.

Derik's heart screamed out in agony, and his body trembled at the presence of the man. He couldn't help remember the torture and abuse, the rape that haunted his dreams. He hated how the flush rose in his cheeks and his manhood twitched to life, desiring the humiliation and helpless that stood before him.

Rick said with a deep growl, "Hello, Derik."

Derik shivered, and he clamped down on his muscles to fight the sudden weakness that slammed into his knees. His body trembled, but he managed to say nothing.

Rick chuckled.

"You'll make plenty of noise later. I knew you would be on this block. I have almost my entire personal fortune in Kerlis' hands. Nothing will save you from me and you will be worth every mark I drop down."

He leaned forward, his face twitching into a snarl. The dark eyes caught Derik's, and he couldn't tear his gaze away. "I will make you an example, I promise you this."

Derik closed his eyes tightly and tears ran down his cheeks. He could feel his breasts heaving from the tightness in his chest. It hurt to breath and hurt to swallow.

At the touch of Rick's hand sliding up his thigh, to cup his cock and balls, he finally broke and let out a whimper as rough fingers caressed his already hard shaft. "You really are a fucking whore."

One finger wormed between his thighs, and despite Derik's effort to clamp down, he circled the wrinkled opening of his anus. "And there is only one use I have for a whore. I'm going to rape you until you suffocate on my cock, then I'm going to take you down to my butcher room and—"

"Rick." The baron's hard voice interrupted the terrifying speech.

Rick pulled his fingers away and turned to face the baron.

Derik's eyes rose. The tightness in his chest increased from the pain of seeing the baron up close. His love didn't even look at him. Instead, he focused on Rick.

"Don't torture the boy."

"He's mine, you know."

"Only the bidding will tell."

Rick chuckled dryly. "You already know I'm going to win."

The baron's voice vibrated with frustrated sorrow. "I know, but there are rules and we follow them."

Rick just grunted, but he did walk away leaving Derik alone with Hamel.

Hamel turned to watch him and Derik could only look down. He was too terrified to speak to him and even more terrified that the baron would just walk away. For a long moment, neither moved.

Then, the baron turned around and looked up at Derik. Even with this height, the angle of looking down gave Derik a strange sense of being the Eye itself, watching the world from above.

The baron's eye shone the brightest blue as he stared at Derik. Then, the deep rumbling voice spoke up, filling Derik with both hope and despair at the same time. "Damn you."

All the strength drained from Derik in a rush. Hope blow away, he collapsed to his knees from just two words. His body shuddered with the impact of the platform, and he let out a long wail of rejection and sorrow. He tried to fight, to be strong, but sobs tore out of him with the force of a hammer. He collapsed forward, his head smacking against the wood as he made only the feeblest effort to catch himself. Nothing could stop his tears.

He could hear Rick laughing in the distance, and his world imploded completely. His heart ached with the terribleness of a knife being jabbed into his gut. Helplessness tore through him. Everything he wanted, everything he didn't realize he needed, ripped away from his life because he finally told the truth.

Months too late.

Gasping for breath, he could do nothing as the baron walked away from his life. In that moment, Derik finally lost everything he loved.

The tears kept on coming.

Sobbing, he crouched on the table for the longest time, until one of the guards poked him with the hilt of his sword. He didn't want to respond, but the poking grew more insistent. Finally, Derik lifted his head to see the hall had filled in his sorrow.

The baron watched from the back of the room, his gaze hard against the skin. Merchants, ambassadors, and the rich arrayed themselves out on chairs, watching him with amusement and greed.

Derik slowly rose himself to his feet, but he couldn't take his eyes away from the man right before him.

Rick Thrantas.

The auction was a joke. He knew who would win. The baron knew it, Rick knew it, and Derik knew it. It was just a dance, a decision already passed and the consequences laid out before him.

He stood up straight. It felt like when he willingly went with Rick for those three nights, but this time, there wasn't some truth that would save him. Fighting back the rising terror, he stood up straight and took a deep breath. His breasts rose up against the shirt and he waited.

A priest of some sort walked up and looked at him. Derik didn't know the symbol that he wore, but there was something about the man's distracted gaze that sent a shiver down his spine. He turned around and stood in place. Another guard joined him, standing next to the table.

To his surprise, there was already a small amount of money setting in the center of the table before him.

The room grew hush as Madre stepped in front of Derik. She looked stunning in a formal dress and with a hard look on her face. Derik opened his mouth to say something, but she just gave him a determined shake. He stepped back and fought back a sob.

She already said goodbye. He didn't realize that she would still be there.

He sniffed and forced himself to stare forward at the baron who glared back at him. Matching his gaze was terrible but better than looking down at Rick.

"Good evening. This is the auction for Derik, a former member of the Baron Hamel's harem. Due to the crimes of stealing the Eye of Hamel, which has been now recovered, deceptions against the nobility, and all other crimes, he has been pardoned by the grace of Baron Hamel." Her nearly monotone voice that cut like a knife.

Derik couldn't close his eyes. Instead, he trembled and held his arms over his breasts, waiting.

"He has been banned from the harem and the palace, baring a pardon of the Royal Court of Franome. He will now be sold as a slave to the highest bidder."

She went on to explain the bidding process, including the rules of leaving everything on the table.

Derik shook at the words. His eyes flickered down, and found Rick grinning darkly.

Madre paused for a second. "There is one difference from prior auctions. Due to a conflict of interest with the baron's auditor," Derik saw Rick's eyes widen, then narrow with anger, "the baron has agreed to use the services of the College of Galifren for calculating worth of any non-monetary bidding."

The priest next to Madre stepped forward and bowed. Derik couldn't see his face, but Rick's face turned stormy, a snarl forming on the edge of his lip. The priest cleared his throat. "Good evening. My name is Brother Jilim, and I am part of the extended research network of the college. Galifren is a religion of knowledge and collecting information in attempt to understand the true nature of the world around us. Our brothers and sisters spend the first thirty years of their lives in the world, traveling constantly and recording their experiences. Once this journeyman period is over, they spend the rest of their life studying their findings and integrating them into the libraries of our colleges. They find connections between all aspects of life and society. This also gives us the ability to identify the true value of something, not only in terms of physical cost but in the worth to an individual."

Rick snarled, "So, what? A spy network?"

The brother answered smoothly. "Our priests do not hide themselves, Master Thrantas. We use no disguises, and we make no deceptions. We are public and honest about our goals. Most of our information comes from public records, verified from multiple sources, and rated according to our documented standards."

Rick got more agitated as he asked a series of questions. Derik winced at the anger burning in his voice, but the priest answered each one calmly. Occasionally, another bidder would ask a question. Neither Hamel nor Madre asked anything or stopped the questioning.

Finally, it ended as the priest bowed again. "If we have no other questions, I assume we can begin. And remember, as I mentioned in the questioning period, if you wish to have written proof of any assessment, any priest can provide it for a small fee."

He bowed again and stepped back.

Madre took a deep breath and stepped forward. Derik's eyes lowered to watch the short, curvy woman stand in front of him, her blood-red dress swirling before settling into price.

"The bidding for this slave will now start. One bid has already been placed on the table for a hundred thousand marks."

"Whose?" Rick asked.

After a short hesitation, Madre answered smoothly. "From the person who recovered the Eye and brought Derik to justice."

Derik frowned, suddenly confused.

Rick opened his mouth, but Madre interjected. "And it is for his freedom."

Rick chuckled, "That's easy. One fifty."

One of the guards reached into a bag and pulled out a sheaf of marks. Another guard took it and delivered it to the table.

Derik shook violently his body as the bidding started and the pile on the table grew.

Rick matched every bid with a snarl.

Derik's eyes focused on him, like a whore in the carriage, and he couldn't take his eyes from the dark, angry look. The bidding increased quickly. The casual way the numbers were thrown around reminded Derik that he had become less than a living being. He was property, something to be sold.

Whenever Derik shifted in position, the guards around the room would twitch. Two already had their swords out, holding them casually but with an implied threat. He looked at them, struggling with the fear that stormed inside him. But, as his gaze wandered, it would return back to Rick's, and he would lose himself in the terrible anger.

The bidding slowed down as it reached almost two million marks, an unheard of amount for anyone, much less a thief such as Derik. He closed his eyes tightly at the triumphant grin on Derik's face.

"H-Hold on!"

His eyes snapped open as Teri ran into the room. She panted for a moment before racing up to Madre. Madre looked confused for a moment, but Teri just handed her a single piece of paper a writ of funds, guaranteed exchange from one of the many banks in the city.

Derik could see Madre's eyes narrow as she read it.

"We'll talk later, Teri," she whispered with a curt voice.

Derik could see a few strands of Madre's hair starting to rise up with the woman's emotional state.

"Yes, Madre." Teri glanced up at Derik and gave him a hopeful grin before backing up.

Madre handed the check over to the priest who closed his eyes for a moment, then nodded. He set it down on the table carefully. "The bid for Derik's freedom is now set at five million eight."

Derik nearly collapsed again as he stared in shock at Teri's retreating back. She gave him another grin, then jumped as the baron called her. Turning away from Derik, the harem kitten ran to her master. Derik's eyes dropped down to Rick and stepped back at the mottled red that burned in his face. He started to say something, but then closed his mouth. The arm of the chair he sat in creaked as his knuckles turned white, then he snarled. His head snapped over to Kerlis, and he whispered frantically at him.

Watching them, Derik let himself a tiny smile, suddenly thankful for an apparent rescue from the crime lord.

Kerlis flipped through the other bag and pulled out a short stack of larger pieces of paper. One of the guard delivered it directly to the priest who paged through it for a moment. He stepped over to Madre while setting them on the table.

After a whispered conversation, the priest gave Derik a brief look.

Madre cleared her throat.

"Rick Thrantas. Twelve properties with an estimated value of four million twelve. This brings his bid up to six million forty-one."

Derik couldn't breath. He stared helplessly as Rick grinned at him fiercely.

"I told you, Derik, I won't lose you."

Whimpering, Derik looked up at Teri who stared back with shock. Then a tear ran down her cheek and she turned away from him to press her face into the baron's shoulder.

The baron stroked her hair, talking quietly to her, but there was nothing left for him at the throne.

"Any other bids?"

Silence.

A terrible silence.

"In that case—" Madre's voice stopped instantly and her body ignited into flames as two shadows dropped down from the ceiling. A ripple of surprise filled the room as the guards drew their weapons and ran toward the shadows. The intruders picked themselves up from the floor, moving smoothly as they stood up.

Clad from head to toe in black, Derik could see one was male and the other female. They wore stealth suits but drew no weapons. The only symbol on their pitch-black outfits was a spider impaled by a sword.

Spiders of Steel.

Assassins.

Derik found it a lot harder to breath as the guards surrounded the two killers. They took a defensive position but made no attack. They stood just behind the chairs, between the bidders and the baron.

Hamel stood up and yelled out angrily. "What is the meaning of this!?"

The assassins said nothing and didn't move.

The baron repeated himself, his rumbling voice echoing against the walls of the hall.

The assassins suddenly turned to face him, standing up straight in almost a salute. Between them, the world began to warp. Tiny cracks formed in the air, black as death and dripping some foul liquid.

Madre stormed forward, her body flaming bright as she stood between the bidders and the assassins.

The cracks stretched together, forming a circular rent in reality. Darkness poured out of it, the black mist spreading out across the floor. A sickening scent of death choked Derik as he whimpered, unable to flee the platform.

Two figures stepped through the darkness, the mist clinging to their faces and bodies for a moment. Behind him, the tear in the universe quickly sealed up and the mist evaporated to reveal—

"Storn!?"

Derik's voice echoed in the hall, shrill and frantic. Storn, the bartender and his life-long friend, didn't look at Derik. Instead, he turned to orient himself and faced the baron. Next to him, Derik focused on the sight of the first woman he betrayed: Wendi.

Her body vibrated with rage as she clenched her hands into tight fists. Tiny motes of water formed around her, hovering like a cloud, and Madre stopped in front of her. The air crackled as the two battle mages faced each other.

The baron raised his voice, the power of it clutching Derik's heart. "What is going on!?"

Storn smoothly spoke, "Please forgive me, my lord baron."

"Who are you?"

"I am Storn Anasai and this is my sister, Wendi."

"What is the meaning of this?"

Storn bowed again. "I'm sorry for the dramatics, but mother's assassins are far more effective at interrupting than my father's teleportation spells."

Hamel said nothing, but Derik noticed his eye flashing up to the Eye above Derik, then back down.

"I am here to bid for the life of," he gestured at Derik, "that slave."

Derik shivered at the suddenly hard voice of Storn.

The baron's eye narrowed. "As a friend?"

At Storn's bitter laugh, Derik wondered what had happened to his friend. "No. I want to kill him."

Derik's heart stopped.

"And then I want my father to bring him back to life and do it again."

The sudden silence that filled the room brought a new terror to Derik. He whimpered, his eyes moving from person to person and he suddenly found himself in danger from more than one person.

"Why? If you don't mind."

"Derik," Storn struggled with his words and anger, "was once engaged to my sister in marriage. Due to poor decisions on his and my mother's part, the marriage was called off. When he fled, the bastard stole our family silver."

Hamel nodded, "I heard some of this. But, I remember gossip that Derik was a friend."

Storn's hands tightened into fists. "That silver was important to us. Made from the remains of our family founder, it has been in our blood line for centuries. It is priceless... to us."

"And?" prompted the baron.

"I could forgive Derik if I thought he just sold it before he realized its worth. I held back the assassins because I was convinced he didn't have it. Our friendship remained because it never showed on the market."

Derik realized what was happening. He had kept the silver in the chest that Teri had just opened. His knews grew weak and he struggled to remain standing.

Storn's voice broke and he turned to glare at Derik. "But, when opening his cache in the old tower, I found that he didn't. Instead, he kept it there, knowing its full worth, and never gave it back. The coward knew and refused to do anything. There are some things that are forgivable," growled Storn, "and there are others that we'll use necromancy to keep making a point for the rest of the pathetic existence of his soul."

With a rush, Derik suddenly remembered shoving the silver into the safe, unsure what to do with it. He lied to his friend and just pretended it didn't exist. Another lie. It had ruined his life once again. He collapsed to the platform, hitting the wood hard as his last hope crumbled.

"Fuck," he whispered. He looked up to see Madre and Teri staring at him, asking a question with their eyes. It hurt him more than anything else to nod.

Madre closed her eyes and shook her head.

Teri started to cry and ran from the room.

Blood rushing in his ears, Derik forced himself to stand up. Breathing hard and bleeding from his heart, he struggled to stand up.

"I'm sorry," he said quietly.

Storn spun around to face the baron. "Can I bid?"

Emotions burned across the baron's face. He nodded curtly and sat down.

Madre swallowed and returned to her position. Her battle aura faded as she stood in front of Derik and refused to look at him. Her fingers ran through her hair to straighten it.

In front of him, Storn and Wendi remained standing, but the two assassins were gone.

"T-The bid is Rick Thrantas at six million forty-one," said Madre.

Storn's voice cut across the ripples of noise and whispers. "I bid my sister's life in servitude."

Silence strangled the room.

Derik nearly collapsed again.

Madre froze.

"Y-You do realize that once you bid, it cannot be taken off the table," asked Hamel.

The brother and sister nodded.

Madre looked at the priest who held up a finger, his eyes growing distant as he queried the telepathic network of his peers.

As the silence stretched into minutes, the baron finally spoke up. "Is that silver this important?"

Wendi spoke up, "Yes, your lord. I would take on the entire guild to earn the right to kill himself. When we win, I only need four seconds and then you can have me forever."

The baron focused on her with his sapphire eye. "And you'd give up your life for revenge?"

"Yes."

"Why?"

"Because your reputation precedes you. You are a good warrior and tactician. I am a battle mage and I'll willingly let you use me as one of your weapons."

"Come here."

Wendi gave her brother a single, unreadable look and padded up to the throne.

Derik watched as they spoke for a moment, but his thoughts were interrupted when the priest spoke up.

"Twenty-two million, including tactical and military uses, synergy and cross-training with the baron's other battle mage."

Derik and the others gasped, but Rick just snarled. The crime lord turned to speak to Kerlis and their conversation grew more heated for a long moment.

Derik couldn't tear his eyes away from them as the brothel owner and crime lord argued.

Then Kerlis stood up sharply, pointed to the priest, and spoke.

"You, how much is my business worth if Rick bids it?"

The priest thought for a moment, then spoke. "Thirty-one million."

Kerlis gestured to the guards who pulled out a third bag and flipped through it.

Rick stared in confusion as Kerlis dug into the bag and began to shuffle through it. The confusion turned to anger. "What are you doing, Kerlis?"

"Buying my palace, Rick."

"You what!?"

Kerlis' eyes shone as he glared at the crim lord. "This is not good business, Rick. I will not lose everything because you are obsessed with that boy. No pretty face is worth good business."

He yanked out a large handful of papers and slapped them into Rick's hand. He grabbed a single piece of paper from Rick's bag and shoved it into his own bag.

"Here, forty million marks, and I'm taking my deed."

Rick stood up straight, holding the papers tightly. His face turned purple with rage. "I'll kill you!"

Kerlis stood up to his narrow height and stared at one of the most powerful men in the city. "This is bad business, and I am a businessman. All I care about is money, and Derik isn't worth more than ten million, even in the best of days. Anything above that is just pride and anger. Neither of which pays me marks. You are already a fool but I refuse to join you beyond this point."

Then, Derik saw the man who abused and pimped his mother, the man with no morals or compassion, shove his way past Rick and leave the room.

The three guards handed Rick his two bags and followed after their true owner.

Rick screamed out in rage. He started after Kerlis, then turned to face Derik. Something bordering on insanity seared through the gaze and chilled Derik to the bone. Storming forward, Rick threw the stack of marks on the table. "Forty fucking million."

Storn spoke from the back. "Ten assassinations by the Spiders in the next two years, no limitations."

The priest spoke up, "Fifty-eight million which bring—"

Rick didn't wait for the number to be called out as he grabbed a handful of deeds and threw them on.

Storn countered with necromantic services.

As Rick threw more of his resources on the table, Derik couldn't help but feel that he was being torn apart by two irresistible forces. Tears ran down his cheeks as he watched Rick and Storn bidding for him. On one side, he knew he would have a short, painful life of torture and rape before being dragged to the slaughter room of the tower. On the other, it would be an even shorter life, but a never ending un-life.

He couldn't take it, and he trembled violently. Tearing his eyes away from the two, he looked up to the baron.

And saw something that hurt even more.

Wendi, on her knees and worshiping the baron's cock, legs spread as she knelt. She had her back to him, but there was no hiding the hardness in her hands. The baron didn't look at him. He looked down at her as she did everything Derik wished he could be doing.

And, for the first time in Derik's life, a new emotion rose up: jealousy.

He saw how she sucked on his balls. He watched as Hamel pulled open her front, hefting her large breasts and holding them as she bobbed up and down to take his cock head into her mouth. He saw the flickers of power rising up around her as he moaned, echoing powerfully across Derik's senses as he wished desperately to be in her place.

The tears that came were not from the fear of his life. They didn't come from the threat of pain and torture. He would have easily accepted either to never see Wendi having what he once loved.

"Fuck this!" bellowed Rick.

Derik's sorrow tore away from the terrible sight of Wendi and Hamel to look down at the crime lord.

Rick flung open his bag, grabbed three pieces of paper, and then threw them at the priest.

Madre's hand flashed out to catch it in mid-air. Casually, she handed it to the frightened man.

The priest swallowed and paged through it, his eyes unfocused as he spoke with the others in his college. "Two hundred, seventy-six businesses. Um, four thousand, three hundred, eighty-nine residencies. Including secondary services of Master Thrantas' spy and criminal networks, fencing operations, and everything else, this comes out to seven hundred, fifty-three million marks."

Derik tried to swallow, his body freezing.

Rick glared up at him, breathing heavily. Every exhalation, he heard the enraged crime lord growling and his hands twitching with his thoughts.

As one, they looked at Storn. The bartender's face looked like stone as he pulled out a list from his pocket. With a pen, he casually marked off a few lines. Then, he raised his eyes to look at Rick. "That's past my limit and the family honor."

His eyes rose up to Derik in the stunned silence. There were tears of anger and frustration in his gaze. "Goodbye, Derik. I wish you the longest, most painful agony of your existence. I'm only saddened I have lost a sister for the chance to kill you myself but neither of us will ever regret our attempts to have you."

Turning around, he simply walked out of the hall. He had sold his sister into the harem and gave away half a million marks work of services only to walk away.

Rick barked out a laugh, panting and growling, then he did it again. His laughter boomed in the room, balancing right on the edge of madness.

"Anyone else!?"

Everyone remained silent as Rick growled, turning in a slow circle to challenge everyone. "Anyone? Anyone!?"

Derik couldn't tear his eyes away from his dark gaze. He could see the same shadows under his eyes, the same rage and violence as Rick pointed at him. Derik's stomach lurched violent as he struggled to breath. Still laughing, the crime lord growled with all the triumph in the world. "You are mine, Derik. For the rest of your life. And I will take out every Shadow-damned mark I spent from your hide!"

His New Owner

Derik whimpered, shaking like a leaf, as Rick reached out for him. He tried to pull away, but the powerful hand grabbed him by the shirt. For a moment, Derik pulled back, but the sound of the ripping shirt terrified him and he let himself be pulled off the platform.

Stumbling forward, he yelped as Rick grabbed his shoulder and shoved him down to his knees. Snarling, Rick shoved his face into Derik's. "You thought you could escape," he growled.

Derik whimpered, tears in his eyes

"You thought you could win, didn't you?"

He couldn't respond, he couldn't even breath as rage poured into him. Derik tried to move, but the hand squeezed down on his shoulder, sending bolts of pain through his system.

"I almost broke you, whore. I almost had you begging for your life. But, then you called on that god, that fucking whore of yours. After that, you had that god-damned hope and I couldn't break you. But this time, this time, I will, break you. And you will beg. And no faith will ever save you."

Derik's lips started to repeat the name, but Rick slapped him hard. The force of the blow threw him across the room and he crashed into some chairs, shattering them.

Derik managed to get to his knees, looking around for help.

He saw Madre. The battle mage had a look of horror on her face, but she just closed her eyes as tears ran down her cheeks.

Derik sobbed. He turned to Hamel, hoping to find some mercy. He started to focus on the baron when Rick grabbed his long black hair and yanked him back. He screamed from the pain that exploded in his world, then he hit the ground hard and lost his breath.

Rick loomed over him. "I didn't give everything away, cock whore. I still have my tower and that is all I need for you. And I still have my family farm. It doesn't matter if I have no more money left, I'll rebuild."

His owner panted as he growled, his eyes darkening.

"But you'll suffer. You'll take the blows, you have nothing else. And, right now, I have nothing to do but to break you. I will shatter that will of yours, I will," he screamed out at the top of his lungs, "shatter that hope you have in your Shadows-damned god!"

Derik scrambled back, but Rick wrapped his hair twice around his hand and yanked him back.

"I'll fucking break you and make sure they'll talk about you forever!"

Derik screamed as Rick yanked him up by his hair. A powerful hand clamped around his throat as Rick hefted him above the ground. Screaming and flailing, Derik hoped he would be die quickly.

"I said 'Oi!'" A new voice broke through his struggles a heartbeat before a wine bottle exploded into the side of Rick's face.

Rick paused, his hands squeezing down on Derik's throat.

Derik, gasping for breath, managed to look over Rick's shadow at a slender woman throwing two more bottles of wine. Each one tumbled in the air before slamming into the back of Rick's head. The blows staggered the man forward.

Rick snarled and spun around in time to catch the fourth bottle of wine in his face. It shattered, alcohol and glass flying in all directions. He dropped Derik to wipe the remains from his face.

"WHAT THE FUCK DO YOU WANT!?" Rick's roar echoed against the walls.

"I said 'Oi' you fucking bastard!"

The voice sounded familiar, but Derik could barely hear it over the pounding in his ears. He staggered to his feet and wiped his face, seeing a bit of blood where the glass shards cut him. Wiping his face clear, he managed to focus on Rick's attacker.

"Look, psycho, I was asking da baron if I could bid on the pussy boy, and he say yes. So, stop fucking with the pussy until I buy him!"

It took Derik a moment to realize who was speaking. It was Shiel, the bounty hunter. She stepped forward as she snatched another two bottles from the table of wines. Popping off, she staggered forward. "Now, shut the hell up and let me bid!"

Rick struggled to contain himself. Growling, he let out a long struggling breath. "You can't afford it."

He almost sounded sane as he spoke.

"Like I fucking care what you say, thriban-fucker, but that pussy," she pointed at Derik with a glare at a bottle, "is the only bastard who ever escaped me. And I'm gonna get my due and you'll fucking wait for me to bid!" Her voice was slurred with drink but her body didn't even have a hint of sway or dizziness.

Derik whimpered and stepped away from Rick, thankful for a few more seconds of life before he was taken away. He looked around to see Madre, the baron, and even Wendi staring at the tiny bounty hunter with surprise.

The priest of Galifren stood behind Madre, obviously frightened but staying his ground.

Except for the guards, the rest of the room was empty.

Rick took another deep breath, then a third. His eyes focused on Derik. "Whatever. You can't afford it."

Shiel shoved past him and stalked right up to Madre and the priest of knowledge. "Ya, knower, you know things?"

The priest stood up, "I'm a priest of Galifren. We are part—"

"I don't fucking care if you are sleeping with your sister and banging her horse. What is the most expensive thing I got?"

The priest started to say something, but Shiel just snapped off the neck of a bottle of wine and chugged it.

He swallowed in fright, then walked around her.

Madre followed, her eyes never leaving the bounty hunter. There was fear and wariness in her gaze.

It took the priest a moment.

"Um, your dagger and its sheath. The one on your back."

Shiel shrugged and yanked it off her back. It was a harmless-looking dagger with rust dripping off it. She hefted it one hand and made to toss it on the table when the priest spoke up. "I can give you an appraisal, for a fee."

Shiel favored him with a dirty look. "You damn well know that the price is, asshole. I've been picking my nose and shaving my cunt hairs with it, don't give a flying fuck what he does with it."

With that, she just tossed it on the table.

Derik couldn't decide if he was honored or insulted by her valuing his life with a rusty dagger.

Rick started forward, then laughed. "A dagger!? That's all you think he's worth."

Shiel snarled, "Well, at least I ain't giving up the entire fucking criminal underground for a pussy boy!"

Rick snarled, then calmed himself again. "I didn't give up everything. I have enough to recover and I will. Property isn't the only thing of worth. I still have loyalty and I still have fear. I own this city and there is nothing that can stop me."

"Yeah, I heard you got a sack and a limp dick too, bet that would make a pretty penny at the sausage factory," came the crude reply.

Shiel drained the bottle and tossed it aside. Derik flinched as it shattered on the floor. She stormed around him to grab three more bottles from the table, popping off the top of two of them and draining each one in turn. She swayed as she finished. "Oh, fuck, da baron got good wine."

Rick growled and spun around. "Move it, priest, I want my fucking slave!"

The priest jumped, his eyes unfocused. "P-Please wait, we are discussing the value."

"It's a fucking dagger! How much can it be worth?" He stepped forward angrily, "I can get ten of them for two—"

"Two billion, three hundred twenty-one million, eight thousand marks," interrupted the priest as his eyes snapped into focus.

The silence that filled the hall was deafening. Derik realized part of it was his heart and plastered a hand against his chest until he could feel it pounding against his ribs.

Rick stumbled as he stopped, then he stared. "What. Did. You. Say?"

The priest swallowed, stepping back in the suddenly angry voice. "I-I said: two b-billion, three hundred twenty-one million, eight thousand marks."

Rick's face grew dark and mottled.

The baron stood up. "Explain, please."

The priest kept his eyes focused on the enraged crime lord. He was pale as a ghost as he stammered. "T-The dagger was the only known possession of Prince Vissolis when he disappeared thirty years ago. Since no item of his has ever been found, this is the only known object that could be used to locate him or his corpse for the Royal Family of Franome. There is a ten million mark reward for such a thing. However, the political power alone from that favor, coupled with the baron's documented mastery of court politics, could be used to elevate his position to a count or duke. The value comes from the estimated taxes over the next hundred years of reasonable life by the baron as a count over this territory."

More silence.

The priest cleared his throat. "And the Temple of Galifren will waive the assessment fee for the dagger in exchange for the right to inspect it for a month," he finished softly.

Shiel interrupted the uncomfortable quietness in the hall. "Fucking dagger was dull. I used it to scratch my ass."

"Yes," the priest said with distaste, "we excluded that from the assessment."

Rick blinked and looked around. "W-What? I lost? I can't lose! I can't fucking lose that whore!"

His voice roared loudly and he lunged for Derik.

Derik flung himself back, but two forms appeared in front of him, blocking Derik.

Madre and Wendi. Wendi had her blouse off and cum dripping down her breasts and thighs, but both mages were glowing with fire as they stood in front of him. Madre snapped the heels of her shoes to stand on the ground and Derik watched slivers from the broken chairs started to shake.

Rick snarled and tried to storm around them, but they both blocked him again.

"Rick," came the baron's voice.

Rick spun on the baron, his face purple with rage. "NO! I can't lose him! I can't give him up. Not after all this. I gave everything! Everything! Give me a chance! I'll get more!" His voice bounced from rage to pleading and back to a bitter, festering anger.

The baron stood up tall in front of Rick. "Rick, you lost him."

"Never!"

"Rick," Hamel repeated himself and spoke carefully, "you have been a stain for far too long. I promised Blackbird I would break you and I think it is time for me to fulfill that promise. Rick Thrantas, I'm placing you under arrest for the crimes you have committed in my town and my barony. I am seizing every property, building, and business you have remaining within my control. Not that you have much left."

"Y-You? Never!"

The baron folded his powerful arms over his chest. "Including your family farm."

A dozen more guards appeared behind him. Wendi's form blurred and reappeared next to Hamel. Derik could see the flush on her cheeks and the cum that coursed down her thighs.

The jealousy rose, but then Shiel stood in front of him, blocking his vision. "Pick yourself up, pussy."

She didn't offer him help up.

Derik winced at the bruises and aches covering his body. Standing up, he took a deep breath. The baron and everyone's attention focused on Rick. With a flash of insight, Derik realized he was truly no longer part of the baron's hall.

Shiel shoved him toward the hall entrance. She was stronger than he could imagine, and he almost fell a few times.

There was no question who owned him now. As he left, the last he heard of Rick was bellowing. "This isn't over, whore!"

Shiel rolled her eyes, "Yeah, yeah, I got a big old cock too. Got it stuffed on my mantle." She grumbled, "Stupid thriban."

Derik frowned, half confused as she pushed him roughly toward the door. "W-What? What's happening?"

"What do you think, pussy? I bought you, and now I want to go back to sleep!"

He struggled, but she easily shoved him along the hallway and toward the entrance of the palace. After a few moments, he turned around and let her roughly shove him out the front door. He could feel her blue and green eyes glittering with annoyance, coupled with the cloud of wine-flavored breath that surrounded him.

Outside, she left him to stalk toward one of the guards. He stepped back, but she just snatched a filthy bag from his hand and turn around. Digging inside, she pulled out a thick iron ring and brandished it at Derik.

His whimpers grew louder as he saw the ring. Something about it frightened him, and he turned on his heels and ran back for the door. His bare feet slapped against the skin, but he didn't even make it two meters before she tackled him and threw him to the ground.

Screaming, he tried to fight back, but she grabbed his hair, rapped his head hard against the ground, then snapped the iron ring around his throat as he struggled to clear the stars from his vision.

Shiel knelt on his chest, crushing his breasts as she looked down impassively in your face. "You run, I kill you, 'kay?"

When he didn't answer, she said some word that he didn't catch because his body ignited into white-hot pain. He had experienced the same, overwhelming pain, but Madre's spanking spell was nothing more than a memory now.

"'kay?"

"Y-Yes."

"Good, now get up, I'm going home."

Six guards ran into the palace as Derik scrambled to his feet. In the cool wind blowing outside, he shivered with just Tornsin's shirt wrapped around his body. A few rents tore the fabric and he distinctly felt every blast of wind.

Shiel didn't have a carriage. She didn't have a horse. Derik found out the hard way as the bare-footed silfae just started walking down the drive of the palace.

He followed, wincing at the sharp gravel cutting into his feet. He struggled and she called to him. He tried to keep up, but she didn't even slow down. Another spark of pain slammed into him and he dropped to his knees with a whimper.

The gravel crunched as she returned and knelt in front of him. "Keep up, pussy."

Spinning around, she kicked some gravel into his face.

He got up and tried to follow, whimpering in pain as he hurried to keep up.

She kept a brutal pace as she strode out of the palace and right down the cobblestones. No words were exchanged.

He just limped after her. When he fell too far behind, panting from the effort and struggling against the agony in his delicate feet, she activated the collar, and he found himself writhing in pain in an ice-cold puddle.

Grinning, she waited for him to stand up and activated it again in spite.

An hour later, he could barely keep up. They made it almost half way through town and a fall storm picked up the wind. It yanked at his clothes, pulling them up to reveal his nakedness to anyone watching. He could feel the eyes of people watching, the shock and surprise. He clutched himself, one hand holding down the shirt.

Shiel didn't seem to care about her discomfort as she took a long swig from a bottle she bought along the way.

Stumbling, he hit a sign when his unbound hair whipped around. He yelped as he fell to the ground, his shirt riding up so his bare ass slapped against the street.

The collar ignited in pain and he screamed, spasming on the ground. When his vision cleared, he saw Shiel looking down.

"You are a pathetic little fuck, aren't you?"

Struggling with the words, frustration and anger built inside him. "No."

"Oh, really?"

She grinned as she whispered the activation words and the collar shocked him again.

He thrashed on the ground, clawing at the stones until it passed.

"Now, I believe I have your attention."

Derik shivered from the cold. "Sorry."

"Not yet. You are nothing but a pussy. I don't know how you managed to change your scent to throw me off, but it probably has to do with those tits, huh?"

She stabbed his breasts with one hard finger.

He winched and covered them protectively. "Only pussies want tits. Pussy boys have little cocks, big tits, and whimper because they can't walk."

Derik's lips trembled, and he shivered.

She rolled her eyes. "Don't know why I bother. Come on, get up."

He got to his feet, feeling the aches and pains of the night before.

"Give me your hair."

Her sharp command sent a bolt of something. He pulled his hair down, gathering it in his hand before handing her the thick bundle.

Derik's world burst into white as Shiel grabbed his hair and slammed his face against the sign he had hit.

A moment later, she released him and he pushed himself away.

In a brief moment of disorientation, he tried to identify the strange sensations that surprised him. He struggled for a moment, then he saw her releasing hair, the severed strands plummeting to the ground in a thick curtain of black and blowing across the street.

The cloud of hair hit the face of a meat vendor, and he swore at them, shaking his fist.

When Shiel glared back, the swearing stopped instantly.

Trembling, Derik lifted both hands up to his head. When his touch only found short, ragged hairs, tears blurred his vision. The trembling grew into sobbing shakes as he fell to the ground, clutching at the remains of his hair.

Shiel just flipped her dagger back around and shoved it into the sheath along her forearm. "There, now you can see where you're going!"

Derik wailed.

Shiel gave him a moment, then grabbed the collar around his neck. Twisting, she forced him to look up at her. "Long hair is for whores and harems. You aren't either now, so get on your damn feet and get over it! I'm tired, and if I get cranky, more than your feet will be bleeding!"

Broken, he stood up. Head held low, he limped after Shiel as she walked quickly down the street. Behind him, he could imagine the remains of his long, beautiful hair blowing in the wind, a life that he had finally left behind.

It took two more hours to make it to the small mansion Shiel called home. The wooden siding was desperately in need of paint. The long driveway had grasses and thistles that cut Derik's bare feet. He left bloody footprints behind him as he followed her up the stairs. Shiel just kicked at the door, which swung open, and he got a look at his new home.

A pig sty. There were more empty bottles than he thought possible on every flat surface. Shields, weapons, and artifacts laid scattered everywhere, covered in more bottles. A broken window let in the breeze, which shuffled through a stack of scrolls held down by a thick made. Which had a bottle on it.

"I'd say welcome, but fuck if I know what to do with you."

Derik just shivered, staring around at the room. Trickles of blood ran down his thighs and he didn't try to think about the bone-deep cold that had blasted them during the entire walk.

Shiel hummed for a moment, then motioned for him to follow.

He did, limping as he did.

She took him into a musty basement, tapping on a magical light to cause it to glow.

He hesitated on the splintered wooden steps, but followed, wincing at the pain that coursed up his legs.

Shiel had packed her basement almost solid. Crates and boxes, mostly empty wine racks, and even the remains of weapons were stacked everywhere. She took him through a narrow path before stopping in front of a cage the size of a large dog. "Strip and get in."

Derik's eyes widened as he stared at her.

Shiel's face darkened. "Look, either you strip or I tear it off you."

Frantically, Derik unbuttoned the shirt as fast as he could. He shivered as he stood naked at her but Shiel just made a face.

"Hate the tits, and your dick is really small."

He blushed hotly as she snatched the shirt from his hand.

"Get in."

Whimpering, he hesitated and she activated the collar.

He curled up in a ball for a moment, then she activated it again.

"Get in."

This time, he crawled into the cage with his face burning with shame and humiliation. It was tight but Shiel didn't seem to care as she slammed it shut. A lock clicked into place and Derik shuddered at the sound. Turning around, he could barely stay on his hands and knees as he looked up from the claustrophobic confinement.

Shiel sniffed at his shirt and made another face. She made to throw it away and Derik whimpered.

Her eyes fixed on him, then she cleared her throat. "Look, pussy. You behave and do what I say, and you can keep the shirt. You piss me off, and I'll piss on it, then burn it, k?"

He focused on the shirt, the last shred of his happy life. "Y-Yes. I-I'll do anything."

For a moment, Shiel glared at him, then she threw the shirt on a stack of Melkuth tribal masks and stormed out.

Derik shivered with fear, feeling horribly naked and exposed. His eyes locked on Tornsin's shirt, and he ran his fingers through his trimmed hair.

Then the basement plunged into darkness.

He yelped at the suddenness, then curled up on the floor of his cage. His body shook as he stared through the inky void to where his lover's shirt hung. He couldn't see it, but he just imagined he could.

It helped as he drifted to sleep, to dream of nightmares and to try to puzzle out how fast his life changed.

House Sitter

Derik couldn't get comfortable. The bar pressed into his spine no matter which side he rolled on. Every time he shifted, it pressed against his thighs or the back of his head before he could curl himself into a tighter ball and try not to think about his situation.

Only four days had passed since he admitted his betrayal, and the baron auctioned him off. He could still remember the terror that sung through his veins when he watched Rick continue to outbid everyone. The man had snapped in his obsession with Derik, a fury that drove him to abandon everything to get his hands on Derik's body.

Derik shivered at the memories and hated how his cock grew hotter. If Rick had one, Derik would be in a much different place at the moment. Instead of being trapped in a metal cage, Rick would no doubt be raping his ass or beating him with a cane. Between the agony, there would be the brief moments of pleasure as Rick stuffed his cock deep into Derik's ass or choked him on the length.

He hated how his body grew hot with the idea of submission. At the same time, he craved how he surrendered to Hamel, Madre, and even Teri over the last wonderful months.

Fresh tears threatened to leak from his eyes. He sniffed and wiped them clear before rolling over. His naked body shivered in the cool air of the basement.

He finished turning over and rested his knees against the bars as long as he could. The cage wasn't quite big enough for him, but it wasn't impossible.

Shiel had continued to cruelly shove him into it every night. The rest of the time she had him cleaning the house or shoveling out the incredible number of empty bottles that littered every surface and furniture.

With a sigh, he rolled on his back and lifted his soles up to the top of the cage. That forced his ass to stick out, millimeters from the end of the cage, but it relieved the pressure in a different way.

It also made him think of being bent in half by a lover with his sensitive sphincter exposed to be penetrated.

His cock twitched and grew along his belly. He ignored it at first but his mind kept moving back to Hamel's immense cock and the many strap-ons that were used on him. This was Teri's favorite position, on his back and exposed, because she said it let her see his eyes.

Derik smiled and reached down to stroke his length. His hardness jumped at the touch. He traced the tip of his cock, running his finger underneath the ridge of his glans. It didn't take long for the head to grow swollen underneath his touch, the wrinkled head smoothing out into a slick hardness.

He breathed hard as he trailed his manicured fingernails down his length. He had to pull three cracked nails away, but the remaining fingers were enough to bring more pleasure prickling along his skin.

Below, his balls contracted against his body. It was cool enough, but it also gave them a strange sensation as he delved his other hand between his legs to fondle them.

Derik moaned softly and continued to tease his cock and balls. Slowly, he moved further down until he rested one hand against his asshole and the other along his length. Grabbing the hardness lightly, he jacked it while playing with his ass.

Pleasure sparked along his senses, teasing. He wasn't horny, but the idea of an orgasm appealed to him. Maybe it would help relieve the anxiety he felt for being caged nightly and being bound to a woman who was a cruel and mean drunk.

His cock began to drool pre-cum. He smeared it on his shaft and used it to lubricate his fist to move faster. Soon, his fingers caressed every centimeter of his length as little bursts of pleasure danced across his vision.

In the darkness, it was his only focus.

His shaft continued to ooze pre-cum and soon it splattered against his belly. He used his lower hand to scoop it up and transfer it to the ring of his sphincter; it wasn't tight after Hamel's cock, but it still felt good when he started to slide one finger in and out of with firm strokes.

The pleasure increased, and his shaft grew rock-hard in his grip. He panted and braced himself on the ceiling of the cage to thrust harder, rocking his hips as much as he moved his hands. The wet slurps of his masturbation filled the basement. He didn't care.

Moaning, he pounding his fist on his cock, thrusting clear to the base. He could almost imagine it sliding Sherrel's pussy or Teri's ass. The heat and warmth of his memories pushed him closer, and he grunted with the last few moments before his orgasm exploded.

Derik shoved three fingers into his ass and thrust hard. It was tight and sensitive with just a little lubrication from his drying pre-cum. It didn't matter, the pressure pushed him into an orgasm.

With a long sigh, he came hard against his belly. Hot ropes of cum splattered his breasts, stomach, and even his face. It burned with the intensity of his orgasm, but he kept squeezing and pumping until his shaft finished dribbling across his belly.

Derik slumped back with a moan. The orgasm relaxed some of his fear, and he enjoyed the pulse of an afterglow seeping through his nerves.

It didn't last long, but then he was cool and sticky from his own cum.

With a grin, he reached down and scooped some of it up off his belly. Closing his eyes, he brought it to his mouth and sucked it clean. It wasn't any different than licking it off the ground and he could almost imagine Madre ordering him to clean himself up.

It took almost as long to clean up as it did to masturbate, but soon every part of his body was slick with his saliva and his stomach gurgled from swallowing his seed.

He smiled and closed his eyes. He could feel exhaustion reaching up for him, beckoning for him to sleep away the night.

The light turned on.

Derik groaned, the relaxation snapping instantly.

"Oi," Shiel said as she stumbled down the stairs. She shoved some boxes aside to reach his cage.

Derik looked up at her and cringed.

"You gotta get dressed." She kicked the lock on the cage and then shoved it open. "Come on, ya pussy. Get dressed and hurry up."

"W-Where are we going?" He rolled on his knees and eased out of the cage. He missed enjoying his afterglow, and his cock hung half-hard from his hips as he got to his feet.

"I got a job."

He didn't know how to answer nor what she had in mind.

"You cannot be staying here. It will be a week at least and you'd probably starve."

Derik blanched. "A week?"

"I can't get a sitter, no one can find this house unless I let them. So, get dressed, you are coming with me." She reached into a box and pulled out half a dozen bottles of wine. Snapping the end off one, she drained it in five gulps before tossing it aside.

The bottle rang out as it landed on the cage. A few droplets of wine poured onto the floor of the cage. It mixed with a small puddle of cum that Derik had missed.

He gulped. "What are you going to make me do?"

Shiel shrugged and headed up the stairs. "I don't know, sit in the room and look like a fucking pussy? I'll find some way to make you useful. Apparently your ass is worth something."

With a feeling of dread, Derik followed after her.

His True Calling

Walking down the side street of some small city, Derik held himself tightly. His heels rapped against the wooden boardwalk through the few motes of snow that dusted the ground before melting. More drifted around him, but the wind storm that took the city passed a few hours before, just as the sun dipped below, and the shadowed streets were silent.

For once.

Despite the weather, he wore a short miniskirt that did nothing to help the wind blowing against the thong that rode up between his legs. His top, a skimpy thing of garish pink, hurt his eyes but it was the only protection he had from the coming winter winds. His short hair stuck out in all directions, courtesy of Shiel's indelicate fashion sense.

He stopped at one of the stores and glared at his reflection. Snow caught on fake eyelashes and he could see where she slathered makeup on his face. He sighed and almost drew away, but stopped. Instead, he dried his fingers on the shawl he wore around his neck and started to smooth out the lines. It reminded him of Teri's expert application of makeup and the memory of it choked him.

Determined not to cry, he smoothed out the color until he didn't quite look like a cheap whore. The blending almost accented his face properly and gave him a bit more class.

"Yeah, just a middle-priced whore," he muttered.

He heard someone walking toward him and turned around to see a city guard patrolling the streets.

He looked bored, but seeing Derik in his skimpy outfit, a slow smile crossed his lips. "Haven't seen a crotch digger out on the streets for a couple days. Desperate for money?"

Derik nodded, terrified out of his wits as his heart beat powerfully against his chest. His barely covered breasts heaved in the cold light of the night. "Y-Yes, sir."

The guard stopped in front of him with a grin. He was slightly overweight, a career guard from the looks of it, but he held the sword easily and his eyes were admiring as they scanned up Derik's exposed legs to focus on the breasts.

Derik flushed, feeling like meat to him, and arched his back to thrust them higher up.

The guard chuckled happily. "'Sir', I like that. Been a while since the street walkers had respect."

Derik blushed bashfully and looked over the guard. He wasn't Tornsin but his old lover still brought a pang of longing to his heart. However, it also brought his manhood to life and a flush to his cheeks, so he focused on the feel of hard muscles against his skin as he watched the guard.

The man watched him for a moment. "How much for a quick blow job?"

Derik smiled and rocked on his heels, "N-Normally I'd charge fifty, but since you are keeping me safe, how about forty?"

The guard nodded in approval, then gestured toward an alley. His eyes scanned the street before slipping his arm around Derik's waist and pulling him close.

"You better believe it. There is a monster out here that is picking off women. Must be hard on a girl like you."

"Yes, sir," Derik breathed softly. His heart pounded as he forced himself to relax. His heels rapped against the walk, then along the stones of the alley as the guard let him into the shadows.

When he reached far enough in, he turned Derik around. In his hand, he held half the marks for the favor and Derik pocketed it before lowering himself to his knees.

The guard let out a guttural moan as Derik worked his fly open, pulling out his reasonable size shaft and rolling it in his fingertips.

"Oh, be gentle."

Derik looked up and smiled, his painted lips parting with the flush of humiliation and excitement rising. "Yes, sir."

The cock grew in his hand. Keeping his eyes on the man's face, he lowered his lips and parted them for the tip of the shaft. It was musky and warm, the smell of man and excitement. Derik let out a soft moan as his body heated up quickly at the thought. The taste of pre-cum flooded his mouth, and he bobbed down, enjoying the feel of silky hardness against his lips while another man filled him. One hand dipped between his own legs to stroke his growing hardness.

Languishingly at first, then faster, Derik slid down the hard shaft, taking it clear to the base and burying his face into the tiny curls of the guard. The man let out a loud moan of his own, shuddering with the sensations. Derik slid the full length a few times before pulling off the hardness. He looked up with a smile, a hunger burning inside him.

"Fuck my face, please?"

Above him, the man looked surprise, so Derik reached up with his hands, took him by the wrists and pressed his fingers into Derik's short hair. After a second of smiling, Derik returned his mouth to the guard's cock, sliding it into the hot depths of his mouth.

The guard groaned and fucked Derik's face, shoving his shaft into the base and plunging it deep inside him.

Derik stroked his customer's hairy balls, moaning as he felt the wonderful feeling of being debased and used coupled with the hardness that impaled his mouth.

The man came hard and fast in his mouth, and Derik gulped at it, swallowing and enjoying the sparkle of pleasure as it slid down his throat. He bobbed up and down on the shaft, feeling the spent energies of the guard, before sliding up and leaving it glistening.

Panting, the guard gasped. "Damn, you... wow, you are a great cock-sucker."

Derik blushed happily, "Thank you, sir."

Pulling out his wallet, the guard tugged out a few more marks.

"Here," he grinned, "an extra thirty. If you are still working in three hours, come find me down at the Dove's Cafe, I'll pay for a warm bed, if you know what I mean."

Still on his knees, Derik enjoyed how the flush of lust sank into his groin before suffusing across the rest of his body.

Which sensation evaporated instantly when a shadow crossed over him. The guard caught it too and they both looked up to see the sky blotted out by something straddling the buildings on each side of the alley.

"Tom's Shield!" swore the guard as he yanked on his pants and reached for his sword.

A tentacle slashed through the air, catching the guard in the chest and throwing him ten meters out of the alley.

He hit the ground hard. Rolling over, the guard tried to scramble to his feet.

Derik watched the guard from the corner of his eyes but his attention was on the tentacles. His heart pounded faster as he stood up, his eyes wide as he saw more tentacles reaching down for him. They dripped with slime and the very tips had rounded ends pulsating with inner muscles.

Two of them coiled up, and Derik tensed. As the tentacles shot out, he dove to the side and sprinted toward the end of the alley.

"Shiel! Move your ass!" echoed his shrill voice. Two tentacles slammed down at the entrance of the alley and Derik slid hard against the ground before kicking down on the ground. Flipping up, he managed to avoid another one that shot at waist level and bounced off one side of the alley to the other. Another leap and he cleared the top of the alley and got his first look at the monster that preyed on whores.

It looked like a horse, except it had a mass of tentacles for each leg and its tail. It howled at him, the sound of a fog horn mixed with a neigh. He could see a thick tendril writhing underneath the horse creature; it was nearly a meter in length and thicker than Derik's thigh. He staggered, then two of the creature's limbs burst out from the alley to spear at him.

Tapping on the edge of the building, Derik sprinted across the rooftops. His heels snapped, and he let them slip off as he dodged through the garbage and nails, jumping from edge to gutter. He heard the creature following him, spearing the ground just behind him with tentacles that punched through tile and tar.

Heart beating, he raced along the side street toward the nearest park. It was a terrifying race, and the cold wind that snapped at him was nothing compared to the thick tentacles that reached out, caressing his back with the threat of something far worse.

He almost made it.

Between one building and another, he jumped the width of the street. The wind whistled in the air, but he jerked violently as the creature caught his leg.

Two more tentacles speared out, wrapping around his other leg and waist, yanking him back to the roof.

He let out a scream of surprise before he hit the tile.

The tentacles lifted him up and spread apart his legs. He tried to force them together, but the powerful limbs easily held him as more tendrils wrapped around his arms and wrists. They slid under his clothes, then bulged out. The fabric around his chest tightened for a minute, then tore through his shirt as easily as wrapping paper.

"Shiel! Fucking help—"

He was silenced by a thick tentacle driving into his mouth, stuffing it. He tried to bite down, but it shoved deep into his mouth, burying its length into his throat. His body ignited into heated flames of sexual fire as more tentacles wrapped around his breasts, coating them in the sticky slime and stroking them.

A pressure ground against his asshole.

He moaned as his body accepted the slick, rounded end of the inhuman member. It thrust deep, filling him to the brim. His manhood burst to full life, hard and aching as it thrust into him brutally fast.

The tentacle inside him plunged deep, following the curves of his inner organs and pumping with meter-long strokes that left him feeling dizzy with euphoria. The tentacle in his throat started the same long strokes, barely giving him a chance to draw in air as it raped his throat, plunging deep into his gut with every stroke.

The horse creature loomed over him as the immense cock, the one that killed so many women aimed up between his legs.

He wanted to scream out as tears burned in his eyes.

The creature thrust, and he jerked violent as the tip of the immense cock slammed against his balls. It slid hotly down the length of his shaft to touch the bottom of his ribs. The horse creature drew back and thrust again, but Derik had no more openings for him to rape.

A powerful feeling of being helpless and filled at the same time set off an intense orgasm to ravage Derik's body and mind. His cum splattered hotly against his chest.

The horse creature paused. A curious growling neigh filled the world as Derik was pulled in front of the slobbering mouth of the enchanted beast.

Derik spasmed again, coming against the creature's face until splatters of cum covered it.

It sniffed loudly, then growled with impotent rage. Its jaw cracked open and teeth pushed out of its mouth. The lower jaw gaped open and long streamers of drool steamed in the air.

Derik tried to scream, but the tentacle that continued to rape his throat, stopping him from making any noise.

With a flash of light, the horse's head fell to the ground heavily.

Derik came as the tentacles spasmed inside him, and white-hot lighting burst around him. He hit the ground in a puddle of slime and shuddering tentacles. He shook as he pulled the invader from his throat and took in deep, icy breaths.

Shiel stood before him, cackling happily as she sliced the horse creature in half, easily defending against its tentacles and teeth. In a matter of seconds, it slumped to the ground—dead. Severed tentacles, slime, and blood showered down around them as she turned around.

Derik ignored her as he rolled over on his hands and feet, the one tentacle still buried deep in his rectum and bowels. He fought against the afterglow of his orgasm and the humiliating situation of his rescue.

She laughed as she jumped to him, splattering him with the viscera of the creature. "Why is it that every single damn creature wants to fuck you? You are a fucking pussy trap to monsters, aren't you?"

Derik glared at her, shuddering as he caught his breath.

Shiel grabbed his hair to hold him still and then caught the tentacle embedded in his body. Wrapping it twice, she prepared to pull.

He shook his head frantically. "No, give me—"

Muscles flexed, and the entire length of the tentacle slid out of him in a single heartbeat. Every sense of his body, hypersensitive from his orgasm, burst into stars, and he came again, slumping into the puddle of slime.

She threw it aside and chuckled gleefully. "You are the best bait I've ever had, pussy. I've caught so many fucking horny monsters because of your ass."

The Final Mark

Months passed in a whirlwind of fighting, fucking, and abuse.

Sweat on his brow, Derrik carried another handful of bottles to the kitchen. His stomach twisted sharply, and he stumbled, almost dropping his load. He managed to make it to the sink and dumped the bottles in, flinching at the loud sound they made.

The pain in his stomach doubled and he bent over the edge, wishing he could throw up and relieve the agony. After a few moments, the pain subsided and he stood up.

Automatically, he pulled the fabric of his shirt to his nose and drew in a deep breath. He wore Tornsin's shirt around his body and smiled as the muted smells of his lover rose to his senses. It melted away some of the exhaustion and he picked up the nearest bottle and upended it, draining the last centimeter from the bottom before tossing it into a large crate. It crashed against the hundreds of bottles already inside. Grabbing another bottle, he turned it on the side, then felt a wave of nausea slam into him.

Clutching the side of the sink, he fought against the wave of dizziness and struggled to remain standing. Concern slammed into him as he realized he had something more serious than a cold brought on by the winter.

When the second wave crashed into him, he leaned over the sink and vomited loudly. It splashed against discarded bottles, and he slumped to the floor.

Shiel grumbled as she got up from the other room.

Derik tried to stand up but his legs felt weak, and he slumped against the ground.

"What's your problem, you fucking cunt?"

Derik moaned and reached out for her, but Shiel made no effort to help him. He managed to scramble to his feet, then he felt his body twist painfully from the inside. He collapsed and started clawing at the pain in his chest. It felt like bees were stinging him from the inside out and his hips were being crushed. He spasmed on the ground, writhing in agony for the endless time. He felt his body being torn away.

As fast as it hit him, the pain passed between heartbeats. Derik gasped for breath but remained on the floor, blinking back the tears as he stared up at the ceiling. A sob tore through him and he cried as the aftershock of agony coursed through him.

Shiel just grunted.

Rolling over on his back, he gasped for breath. "W-What is happening?"

"Lost your tits," came the bored answer. Shiel drained her bottle and tossed it into the crate with the others.

Derik's eyes snapped wide open, and he sat up quickly. Slamming his head against the bottom of the table, he yelped and crawled out from under the table.

He clutched his chest. Instead of the soft, rounded breasts he had grown used to, he only found the smooth chest. Whimpering, he looked at Shiel pleadingly as he rubbed against his nipples. He didn't get the intense bolts of pleasure, and his panting grew louder.

Trembling, his hands reached down to his hips and he felt where the bones reshaped themselves back into his own boyish ones. Hyperventilating, he rushed to a mirror in the kitchen and stared at himself. Only the short-haired man looked back, the body he had when he first fell into the harem.

It was like a stranger looking back.

Shiel shrugged and walked to him as he began to panic. She grabbed Derik's and forced his wrists apart to stare at his body.

He blushed at the hard gaze she gave him from head to toe.

With a grunt, she released his hands. "No, still ugly as shit."

Derik gasped, but she smacked him hard across the face, shocking him back to his senses.

He gulped the air, struggling to move, then did a double-take. "What!?"

Shiel shrugged and took another swig. "I was hoping when that damn shaping spell wore off, you'd actually be good-looking. But all I see now is a soft pussy boy without tits."

Used to being attractive to everyone, he wrapped his arms around his chest and winced as the arms slid down before he caught himself.

Shiel casually sat down on the end of the table, her weapons clinking as she settled into place. Even in the house, she remained armed. She even wore weapons to bed, hurting Derik more than once when he tried to wake her.

She glared at him. "I hate shaping spells. You never know how someone looks without it. I mean, you look a lot better without tits but that isn't saying much. Could we hope your dick got bigger?"

He blushed hotly. She gestured to her tiny breasts underneath her leather top and band of daggers. "I mean, I can't stand anyone with bigger boobs that me. Looks unnatural."

She glared at Derik, "And on a pussy boy, well, that is just fucked up. Whoever did that had some serious issues in their head."

"S-She was a transvestite."

"Okay, see? There is some fucked up problems."

"Hime is not fucked up!"

"A transvestite and she wasn't fucked up? Pussy, look, everyone is screwed up. Your bitch, that lady with all the magic? Oh yeah, she's got problems. Thinks she's all hot stuff but hasn't killed any-one in years. Just uses her magic to spank her girls. Bah, that's a waste of skills. Da baron? He's got problems up the kazoo and has that shaping spell on him and that big old magical sphere in his room. He's fucked up more than you and me together."

Derik started to say something, but Shiel wasn't done.

"And you? You are a little pansy-assed pussy who wants some-thing shoved up his butt and to be beaten until he comes. You are as submissive as they come. One reason you are so good at being bait, you smell like slut."

He flushed hotly because she wasn't entirely wrong. "I'm not a slut!"

"What about that dragon-kin?"

"He tried to rape me!"

"And the dwarf clan?"

"You told me to get them outside, I did."

"With an orgy? Don't tell me you didn't enjoy getting reamed out. I found your face in that skanky lady's cunt!"

Derik blushed again and looked away. "I'm not bait."

"You are bait, the ultimately fuckable monster bait, and everything in this damn county seems to want to get into your pants. If it isn't your ass, then they want to fuck that face of yours."

Derik pouted, "Except you."

She chuckled happily and opened a new bottle by ripping off the top. "Well, yeah, you're a pussy and I have standards."

He grabbed the bottle from her hand and took a swig himself. The wine burned down his throat and he handed it back. "Why are you different?"

Shiel shrugged, "You ain't my type."

"What is your type?"

"Oh," she grinned and rocked back and forth, "someone with lots of muscles and power. And a really, really big sword. You know what I mean, something that hurts when he shoves it in. You know, the type of bastard who can throw you up against the wall and bang you so hard you can make cheese with your cunt juices."

She sighed happily. "I want a guy who considered a bloody fight to be foreplay, where really good sex means that five or six people die, and you just go at it, right in the middle of the blood and gore. I want him to use a fucking arm as one of those... those things you shove in your cunt?"

"Dildo."

Her smile brightened. "Yeah, I want a fucking bloody dildo shoved into my snatch as fucking foreplay."

Derik felt nauseous.

Shiel practically purred as her large ears twitched. "Oh, I want a man who takes me. You know, really takes me, even if I fight back.

And isn't afraid if I bite, kick, or stab him a few times in the process. Oh, that would be..."

Her voice trailed off, and she squirmed on the chair.

"You scare me, Shiel."

She beamed happily. "Thank you... Derik."

It took him a second to realize she had used his real name for the first time.

t'Sade

Rooms

Derik shoved open the door to Kerlis' Palace with a snarl on his lips.

Behind him, Shiel trailed behind with a red mark on her face from where he slapped her.

She grumbled as she kicked the door shut behind her. "I said I was fucking sorry!"

One of the guards reached out for Shiel's weapons.

Shiel stopped and looked him over with scathing glance. Her shoulders turned to face him and a slow smile crossed her lips. "I will rip your fucking balls off."

The guard gulped, and his hand shook.

Shiel stepped toward him with a grin. "Go on, I'm in a pissy mood. Bet I can get off by beating your skull into the wall?"

Suddenly deciding that life was enjoyable, the guard stepped back.

Shiel grinned and hopped after Derik as the former thief made his way to the bar.

He sat down on the stool and tapped the counter. "Give me something red... no, white."

Shiel grunted, "Give me... um... that row," and pointed toward the top.

The bartender's eyes grew wide, and Derik felt a blush rising as he watched the bartender's eyes drift down his face, to focus on his neck. Bashfully, he pulled up the shirt over the two puncture marks on the side of his neck and glared at Shiel.

The bounty hunter beamed happily and grabbed the nearest bottle from someone sitting next to her. When the bartender held out a glass, she snorted and just chugged it directly from the bottle.

Derik sullenly chuckled. "Don't worry, a few years ago a necromancer granted her liver immortality."

The world grew dizzy, and he slumped against the bar for a moment. Groaning, he held out his hand and the bartender gave him a glass. Making a face, he drained it.

As he set down the bottle, someone ran a bony palm up his spine while another palm curled down the curve of his ass to cup his balls.

Derik jumped with a yelp.

"My dear Derik! I thought you were dead."

Squirming from Kerlis' grip, Derik pointedly looked away.

Kerlis reached up to caress Derik's collar before kissing his ear.

Metal scraped against metal, and Kerlis jumped back as Shiel shoved her sword between them. The massive blade hummed loudly as enchantments warped the air around it. In her other hand, she drained the bottle before looking over at the pimp. "Gonna pay for that ass, old man?"

Kerlis shook his hands, then shooed away the guards that appeared around them. He shook his head. "No, not me. As lovely as Derik is, I have no sexual interests in him. I just miss him, its been over a year since he was last here."

Derik perked up, frowning. Its already been a year? He looked out the window of the brothel and into the late summer morning. His mind spun for a bit, then he shrugged. Taking a deep breath, he set down his glass.

Shiel, on the other hand, didn't even pause as she snapped back. "Why you grabbing his jewels?"

He smiled, "Call it a bad habit, checking up on former employees."

"Yeah, right. Derik was never one of yours. I could have smelled that."

"One could hope."

"One could hope that this turns into a bloody slaughter," supplied the cheerful bounty hunter. "Bring those guards back, I'll show you what I mean. I mean this is a pleasure place right? A good murder would please me."

She held up a finger and chugged another bottle. She slammed the empty bottle on the counter. "Okay, now bring them back."

Kerlis blinked and turned his attention back to Derik. He frowned and reached out for him, then stopped as Shiel kept her huge blade between them.

"You look pale, Derrie."

Derik sighed and looked away again. "Had a bit of trouble, making my head fuzzy."

"Trouble?"

For a moment, Kerlis sounded concerned, but it passed as he looked around at the booming business.

Shiel chuckled, "Yeah, found a nest of vampires just now. Staked them out in the sun really good too."

"You mean," Derik snapped, "you cut them up into tiny pieces, then remembered you left the stakes at home."

Shiel beamed, "And Derik here helpfully supplied me with a few and we killed them. Neat and pie!"

Kerlis beamed, "Oh! I put out that request. Six, you said?"

In response, Shiel yanked up a large sack and emptied out the six still-bleeding vampire hearts across the bar.

The bartender's eyes grew very wide, then rolled back into her head before she collapsed.

Kerlis swallowed and gestured for someone. "Very, um, uncouth."

With a groan, Derik shook his head and pushed one of the hearts away from him, it was still beating. "You should be glad I talked her out of keeping the lungs attached."

Shiel chuckled. When Kerlis looked at her, she shrugged. "You didn't pay me to be pretty."

"No, no, I didn't. I take it poor Derik here was bitten?"

"Yeah, yeah, I made sure he wouldn't turn into one. Garlic and blessed silver, I know that rule."

"Yes, but blood loss might cause some problems. Did you lose any blood, Derik?"

Derik chuckled. "Shiel managed to get all six to feed on me at the same time. Used it to line them up for the kill."

"Oh dear... six? All six?"

He could feel the pimp's eyes scanning over him. Derik pulled the shirt down to show the mark on his neck. In the growing silence of the bar, he unbuttoned Tornsin's shirt, bloodstained and with jagged rent in it, to show another on his shoulder and a third on his nipple. Kerlis looked impressed.

"And the other three?"

"Both legs, right at the crotch, and the base of my dick."

Shiel giggled, "He is good bait. Everyone loves him."

Kerlis shook his head. "You should take care of your boys, young lady. They last longer."

"Blow me."

Clicking his tongue, Kerlis gestured for one of the servants to clear the hearts from the bar and ordered cheese and crackers. He pushed it in front of Derik. "Eat, it will help recover the blood. A good shower would help too."

Derik looked at Shiel for permissions and then realized he didn't need it. He bowed his head to Kerlis. "Thanks."

"No problem, I have to thank you for getting my palace back from that horrible man, Rick. That was bad business, you know."

Derik shivered at the memory.

Next to him, Shiel giggled at her own memories of the night.

Drawing his thoughts away, Derik looked around the room. Just as he remembered it as a child, but for one thing–when he looked up, he saw half a dozen naked women hanging from rings with gags in their mouths. Their arms and legs were stretched out in a cross. The six rings spun around lazily but it didn't look comfortable.

"New?"

"Oh yeah, I thought it set the mood much better. The girls who don't behave get sent up there for a few hours. I made a game about it. If something drips in your drink, you get an hour with her when she is pulled off. But, sometimes clients pay to have a girl hung up there for a few hours to soften them up. Breaks the spirit, they say."

"You're a bastard." Derik didn't have the energy to be offended.

"But a rich one, my boy. Life has been good with not having to pay a percentage to criminals. Well, smaller percentages."

The thin man patted Derik on the shoulder, stroked his chin, and disappeared into the crowds.

The cheese and crackers helped Derik's head. He relaxed and started to enjoy himself. Familiarity made the Palace strangely comfortable. Also, Derik felt more relaxed any time he wasn't being used as bait. He turned around to see Shiel balancing her empty bottles on top of each other. He grinned and set one on top of hers.

Her eyes glittered as she grabbed the bottom one; Derik plucked his from the air before setting it neatly down on the bottom. She set hers on top and let go; a second later, Derik grabbed his from the bottom and pulled it out. It went on for a few minutes before Shiel finally dropped one.

"Damn it. Beat me again."

"You are slow."

"And you are still a pussy without tits."

"Yeah, it seems like that. But, no more vampires, please?"

Shiel chuckled, "For a hundred thou, we'll hunt anything. For a quarter mil, I'll kill anything." It was her favorite thing to say.

Derik chuckled.

Shiel turned around and looked over the nearly naked men and women strolling in the entry area of the brothel. "You know what? I want to get laid."

Derik raised an eye, "Kerlis will steal back every mark you get on this job."

"So?"

"We made a lot on the job."

"So?"

"Don't care?"

"Didn't care about losing billions on a dagger, why would I care about a lousy thirty thou? I have a scratch, and I want a big old dick in it."

At the mention of money, Kerlis appeared with a smile. "Anything I can do to help?"

Shiel yawned, "Yeah, I wanna get laid."

"Oh, I can be very helpful there. What interests you?"

"Someone rough."

"I have some excellent masters, would they work? Or do you wish to dominate someone submissive?"

"I guess, but no bitches. Can't stand cunt."

"Well, we have a great selection—"

"Kerlis," Derik interrupted.

Kerlis looked up.

Derik chuckled and leaned over Shiel resting his hand on her arm. "Look, give her two all-night specials. Grab two of your guards, you know the ones you use to collect on debts. Dress them up in armor, give them swords. Then, tell them to go into her room and rape and kill her."

Kerlis looked concerned. "Derik, are you sure?"

"Oh yeah, I bet she'd give up her weapons for that. But, you better put some regeneration spells on them and keep your healer on call, she's probably going to break both of them."

"Two brutal men verses an unarmed woman, that seems..."

Kerlis voice trailed off as he looked up to Shiel, who had a blush on her cheeks and fingers plunging between her legs. Soft coos of pleasure echoed as she looked out with unseeing eyes. The broad smile on her face answered Kerlis question.

The pimp swallowed carefully. "Is she going to kill them?"

Derik shrugged, "Might want to add more, but she is only paying for two. And the special is 'no questions asked of the whore', remember?"

Kerlis looked away from the masturbating Shiel. "Two all-night specials? That is two rooms for the night. I'm not going to let her drench one room in blood."

"Yeah... she's going to ruin the room anyways but probably sleep on the bodies. The other is for me. I just want a shower and a soft bed that doesn't have bars."

"You could have just asked for a room."

Derik grinned, "And you would have charged me double for it. This way, we all win. Besides, the specials include the food."

"True, true, even for you, I can't resist. Come, let me show you to your room and make arrangements for your... master? Mistress?"

Derik fingered the iron collar and nodded. His relationship with Shiel had become complicated. She used him as bait, but he fought next to her as often as she abused him. The collar was just a reminder of his previous life. A dark cloud draped over his thoughts.

Kerlis gestured for Derik, who followed. They left Shiel at the bar, and Kerlis slipped his arm around Derik's waist. Resting his head on the thief's shoulder, they headed into the depths of the brothel. "Are you happy, Derik?"

Derik thought for a long moment, watching as they headed toward his mother's hallway. "No, not really. Well, maybe? I was happier in the harem."

"You seemed very happy there. Why don't you go back?"

He shivered at the memory. "No, I can't ever go back."

"Do you think about it?"

"Every night when I pray."

"You pray? I thought you didn't believe in gods."

Derik smiled sadly, "Bridget has plans for me."

"Never had a love for gods."

"Money is your god."

"Yeah, maybe. But, you are... stronger now. Not as fragile but still as beautiful."

"Shiel is a harsh mistress."

"What is it like, being a slave to that... thing?"

"Shiel's a bitch, but she's okay. I mean, it's like living with a drunk berserker who thinks the funniest thing in the world is seeing an orphanage collapse."

"And you with her?"

Derik sighed and worked his arm around Kerlis' waist. "You know what? She still throws me in a cage every night, but she means well. Manners of an alley cat, morals of a sewer rat, but in the end, she takes care of me. This last few months, I'm almost her companion instead of a slave."

"Sex?"

He shook his head, "I just told you to send two men in to rape her, knowing that she will probably break them and have the orgasm of her life at the same time. Can you see me surviving that?"

Kerlis chuckled. "I guess not. Well, I have two guards who are currently in trouble for roughing someone up too much. This would be a good lesson in humility, and she'll pay well."

"Give her thirty thou worth, okay?"

Kerlis froze and Derik turned around.

The thin man frowned. "She is blowing her entire reward on tonight? For one night of sex?"

Derik nodded, "Shiel really isn't into money, fame, or fortune. She is just... Shiel."

They entered a familiar hallway. To his surprise, Kerlis stopped in front of his mother's room.

Derik's eyes looked up to the number, but no symbol or necklace hung from the door.

Kerlis cleared his throat and dug into his pockets. "Look, I know you'll never be one of my whores. But," he held out something, "I don't have the words to say this. I-It isn't my nature, look, enjoy the night, and I'll take care of your mistress."

The thin man shoved something into Derik's hands and walked quickly away.

Derik frowned and looked down, unwrapping his fingers around a raven necklace. His mouth gaped open as he stared at his mother's necklace, then up at the retreating back of the pimp. "Kerlis!"

The old man came to a halt. Derik could see his knuckles turn white as he clutched the wall.

"Thank you, you bastard."

Kerlis didn't look back. He just hurried around the corner and was gone.

Tears burned in Derik's eyes as he reached up and wrapped the necklace around the hook, just as he remembered it as a child. Opening the door, he entered his mother's room one last time.

Hot Shower

Turning both handles completely around, Derik stepped into the steaming hot shower and let out a soft moan of relief and pleasure. Mud, blood, and grime sheeted off him as he just stood there, head bowed. His short, black hair had been soaked and the sloppy mess dripped down his front. The tiny, liquid caresses ran down his skin brought life to his manhood and a soft smile to his lips. He rested one hand against the tiled wall of the shower and rubbed at the vampiric wounds on his neck.

Shiel's healing potion, even mixed with red wine, did its job, and the seductive vampires had only inflicted shallow cuts instead of deep punctures.

He chuckled dryly and let his hand trail down his tight belly to wrap his fingers around his hairless cock.

His chuckle turned into a smirk as he teased his length, feeling it growing in his palm. Madre never told him that the cream they used was permanent. Even after a year, he was as smooth as a harem kitten.

Lips parted, he let his memories drift back to the harem. Most of the girls faded, but he managed to hold the image of Teri, Madre, and Sherrel tight in his thoughts. He couldn't remember their taste, but he stroked himself as he focused on one scene after the other.

He came in the shower. It was a brief orgasm that left him happy but wouldn't ease the pain of losing his loves.

Turning off the water, he let it cascade down his skin and closed his eyes so he could pretend he had breasts again. But the water dripped in the wrong direction, and after a year, those memories had started to fade. Without opening his eyes, he brought his left wrist up to his lips and kissed it before whispering Hime's prayer to Bridget.

He just stood there for a moment, then opened his eyes. Grabbing a towel, he dried himself and wrapped it around his waist. Barefooted, he padded back into the tiny room that his mother used to work in.

And froze at the sight of someone else standing at the door.

She stood slightly taller than him and had a deep red tan across her entire body. Her tawny hair nearly reached the ground except for two braids looping back up to the top. Feathers and leather peeked out of her hair as she looked around curiously. Derik's eyes scanned down her, both looking for weapons and admiring the soft curves of her breasts and hips and the trim lines of her thighs. She wore moccasins, and he recognized the leather and scale pattern as being from a young thorny fire drake.

He cleared his throat.

She turned and looked at him with eyes like liquid wood, shifting in a strange whorl that seemed to move when he didn't focus on them. "Sorry, I didn't know this was your room."

She looked around a bit more before smiling at him. "Isn't it yours?"

The stranger had an Emberkan accent, soft and seductive in the clear tones. It was the voice of a singer, one that prickled his memory.

"No, well, yes, but only for the night."

She smiled, "I didn't think this type of place would have guest employees."

Derik blushed, "No, no, not that. I'm not a who—", the word froze in his throat so he found a different way, "I don't work for Kerlis."

Gliding up to him, she lifted a hand to cup his chin.

He shivered at her caress, a touch he could never resist.

Her eyes probed him for a moment. "No doubt. You are far too beautiful for this humble place."

"Thank you. But, um, I'm not for sale."

Laughing musically, she released his chin. "Everyone is for sale."

Derik shivered and fingered his iron collar. "I'm already owned."

"I can imagine, but I'm interested in spending the night with you anyways."

Derik shook his head, "I can't, sorry, you are beautiful and I'd be honored, but not here, not in my moth... not here."

The cultured barbarian turned away from him and drifted to the door. As her hand brushed the handle, she turned back. "Are you sure? I can pay."

"I don't need the money."

"I wasn't talking about cash, Raven."

Derik froze for a moment, staring at the calm, unreadable face of the woman. The world spun for a moment from a wave of something different about the world. He shook his head and looked away. "I-I'm not Raven."

"Short black hair, incomparable beauty, and a shining spirit. And the raven necklace outside. Seems like the Raven I heard about."

He shook his head. "Raven is my mother, she... died."

She walked back and then hooked her finger on his chin. He wanted to keep looking away, but she turned his head toward her. Her touch seemed intense, like a building orgasm from the very bottom of his soul. "Then who are you?"

"I-I'm," he struggled with the words. His many names flashed by but only one passed his lips, "Blackbird."

"Ah, the thief."

"Not anymore," he muttered. Everyone in town knew about the Blackbird who betrayed the baron.

She smiled, "Oh, I think you stole something."

Derik opened his mouth to say something, but she leaned into him and kissed him on the lips. It was soft and delicate, something he had missed for so long. His voice turned into a moan as he shuddered with the pleasure of it. Her hands rested against his chest, one palm against his suddenly pounding heart. Her hands felt hot against his skin as she turned him around, pushing him back until he caught the edge of the bed with his knees. Sitting down, he broke the kiss and she smiled warmly.

"Just one night."

"I can't take your money," he whispered.

"I won't give it."

"Why?"

"Because you need something far more than cash."

"What?"

She straddled his legs and sat down. She was soft and warm. The feeling of the trim legs and delicate features stole his breath away. His body grew hot with desire and his hardness pushed up against the towel. Her eyes trailed down before she wrapped her fingers around his shaft through the towel.

She spoke softly, "Love, of course."

He breathed against her. "Love is hard to find here."

"Your mother was here. Didn't she love you?"

"Yes."

"You must have grown up here. Would you say Kerlis loved you?"

Derik started to laugh, but remembered the look on his face as the thin man pressed the necklace in his hands. He frowned for a moment, then sighed. "Yeah, as much as he can."

"So, what is wrong with me loving you tonight?"

"Nothing, nothing I guess."

The woman grinned, "Then, let us love the night away and in the morning, drift away like the mist on the plains."

Derik hesitated, but she drew him into a kiss, grinding her breasts against his naked chest as they embraced. He moaned and trailed his fingertips along her smooth skin, cupping the soft mounds. Her tongue teased his lips apart, sliding in and he explored her mouth. His fingers worked their way under the leather top to tease the hot nipples and roll them in his fingers. Her body shuddered with pleasure, and he removed her top, setting it aside. She broke the kiss with a smile, and he ducked his head to suck on her nipples.

The throaty moan that vibrated through her body spurred him on. She leaned back and he held her with one arm and stroked against her skin, working the perfect nipple in his mouth. His fingertips caught under the hem of her short skirt and ran up her thigh, teasing one side than the other. Then, he switched to the other nipple as his hand slid up between her legs caressing...

He found hardness where he expected softness. His body tensed up for a mere moment as he realized she had a cock, then he just smiled with the memories of his own body and stroked her length.

"You don't mind?" came the soft question, distracted with pleasure.

"No," he breathed. "I like cocks."

When she smiled, he pulled her clothes open. He ran his fingertips from the tip of her shaft to the dimple of her opening. It was hard and slick, and he lost himself in pleasuring her with his fingertips. As she began to shudder, he removed the rest of her clothes and let them fall to the ground.

Looking down, he beheld the most beautiful manhood he had ever seen. It was thick and long with a dusting of hair at the base. He almost purred as he ran his hand down it, stroking as he worked his mouth down her skin.

In the middle, they managed to switch places so he was kneeling between her legs and her hardness rested on his throat. Teasing it, he kissed it and caressed it, teased it until it swelled thickly. Then, he took it in his mouth.

She let out a guttural whimper of her own as he bobbed down. He tasted cinnamon and musk in his throat and nearly came from the exquisite flavor. Fingers danced on his hair, and he looked up into her liquid eyes.

"Trust me?" she asked.

He nodded.

She gripped his hair and gently pulled him down.

He relaxed and closed his eyes, letting the memories of everyone rising as she pumped into his mouth.

Her cock slid down his throat, blocking his breath, and she held it there. A mere heartbeat before it grew uncomfortable, she gave him a breath, then pulled him down. Pleasure grew inside him, filling up from the very bottom of his feet as she fucked his face, masterfully reading him to keep him right on the edge of helpless pleasure and growing ecstasy.

The world disappeared around him. His eyes gazed into hers, and she smiled as she continued to drive him harder and faster on her cock until he thought he would explode. Nothing else existed except his submission, and he burned with the ache to come. His hands dropped down between his legs, tossing off the towel, but she shook her head.

"I want you to come inside me, Blackbird."

He nearly came at her words, but managed to control himself.

She just pulled him down, her fingers running through his ragged black hair with every stroke.

Her shaft swelled in his mouth, teasing the back of his throat. He whimpered at the stuffed feeling, a hunger dancing on the edge of euphoria. The silky hardness that impaled him brought to life the old pleasures of serving Hamel, and he struggled to contain himself.

Then, she came. She drew back to come in his mouth, filling it with the searing hot seed. He almost swallowed, then decided to hold it there, like Rick taught him. She let out a long, shuddering sigh as she came, then pulled out her glistening shaft. Her smile broadened.

"Show me?"

Leaning back, he opened his mouth to show her his filled mouth.

She cooed softly and closed his mouth. "Don't swallow, Blackbird."

He obeyed, the flush of being commanded bringing the edge of an orgasm to a knife's edge.

She leaned back and spread her legs. "Don't come until I come in you again."

He frowned for a moment, looking down as she pulled her legs up, exposing the tight ring of her asshole. She grinned. "Me first."

Grinning, he said nothing as he stood up more. His cock bobbed and drooled pre-cum on the floor. A streamer of it waved back and forth as he aimed the angry red tip against the ring of her being.

His lover let out low moan of pleasure as he slid into her, feeling the incredible tightness and smooth insides milking his length. He had to struggle to avoid coming instantly, but it was difficult to resist the heavily tightness of her body as he worked his member deeper into her. He stroked her length as he slid in.

When he bottomed out inside her, she shuddered.

"Fuck me," came the command. He was all too willing to do so. His hips rocked back and forth, and he pumped inside her, silently fighting the orgasm that raced up inside him. She moaned and teased her nipples. He used his free hand to grab one breast, pumping and stroking as he made love to her.

After a year of only his hand, he couldn't last long. He let out a muffled groan of pleasure as he came, filling her insides with hot cum and shuddering to breath. It was an intense release and stars floated across his vision as the orgasm crashed into him.

He slipped out of her and nearly swallowed.

She purred as a droplet oozed out of her rosebud.

"My turn," she said. "Please?"

Derik crawled up on the bed, on his hands and knees. She positioned herself behind him and her swollen member entered him. The strokes were gentle as first, then harder and faster until her flesh slapped against his. He kept his eyes closed, imagining the days when he was in the harem, hands on his breasts and gasping from the pleasure.

A hand cracked down on his ass, and he jerked forward. His body spasmed and he came again.

She spanked him again, then reached up to grab his hair. With a sharp tug, she forced him to arch his back. Derik came hard a third time, his body swamped with pleasure and memories. They seared through his mind and body, and he just kept coming.

She pulled him back until he was balanced on the thrusting shaft, plunging deep into his body with every stroke. Hot and wet, he couldn't escape it. He didn't want to escape, he craved everything more than he could imagine. The hunger of submission, the feel of a spanked ass, and even the comfort of being in the harem.

He started to cry. Soft sobs, muted by his filled mouth, but she just drove into him again and again, her hardness impaling him and sending off more orgasms coursing through his body. One hand still holding his hair, her other slid around to press against his chest, cupping his nipples. He could feel her hot breath against his ear and the feel of her breasts on his back.

Grunts of pleasure filled his senses as her shaft swelled.

He kept on coming, splattering the sheets as his body shook. He couldn't move, he couldn't scream, he couldn't do anything but let her dominate him. All that matter was that hardness that impaled him with nothing but pleasure, the feeling of being filled and emptied in wet, hot strokes.

"I'm coming," she whispered between the grunts.

Derik tried to feel every part of his body, clinging to that intense pleasure.

Then, she came inside him. At the first hot jet of pleasure, he swallowed her seed.

Instead of a salty taste, her cum felt more like the purest light somehow pouring down his throat. A thousand pleasurable sensations filled him up from his stomach before it flooded the rest of his body.

Another burst of brilliance exploded from the junction of their bodies where she continued to come inside his ass.

The dual stars of flame and lust filled him set off an intense orgasm that tore through his senses and scrambled his thoughts. He let out a scream of pleasure as the ecstasy grew and grew, filling him with a sense of something far beyond and then pushing his limits further. He shook violently as he lost himself in the onslaught of ecstasy beyond anything he had ever experienced before.

When he recovered, he was sprawled out on the bed, and she was dressing silently.

With her back to him, he could admire the feminine taper of her waist and the hair that plastered against her back.

"W-Who are you?" The roughness of the last year had burned away, leaving his voice soft and delicate.

She looked at him over her shoulder. "Are you sure you want to know?"

"Why?"

"Because, the answer to that question changes everything."

"How? Its just a name."

She just smiled for a moment. "You are at a junction of your life, Derik. You have two paths before you, the final two paths I have for you. And it comes down to that question."

Weak from his orgasm, he managed to push himself up to a sitting position. His eyes scanned across her, confused and feeling that the words she said were true. "What will happen?"

"If I remain nameless, you will keep on moving forward. Your time with Shiel with continue, and you will grow to love her as a sister and a friend. You will... be happy."

Derik gaped, "How do you know our names?"

She giggled and finished tying her top back on. Standing up, he saw her cock bobbing for a moment before she pulled up her skirt. "And if I answer you, then something will change. I can't tell you how it ends, but I can promise you this, it will change."

"How, how do you know this?"

She smiled, "I used to sing for a band called Phoenix Falling. About a year ago. I remember you, I remember that black-haired girl learning how to dance on the floor. Later, she learned how to love on the dance floor and found herself. When I saw you tonight, seeing your strength to be be yourself, despite everything you experienced. It was then, I realized that you were finally ready. And maybe its time for you to go back?"

Tears ran down his cheeks. He didn't know why, but the idea of returning to the harem broke the sorrow. "I-I can't go back, ever."

She tugged up her skirt and then pulled on her underwear. Tucking in her manhood, she smoothed it down. "Never is a long time."

"It feels like that."

"Who am I to change your mind?"

He looked up, balling his hands into fists of frustration. "Who are you?"

"Are you sure? You may lose everything."

He nodded.

She smiled sweetly and reached down to wipe the tears from his face. He trembled as the world spun around him, but she just took him by his left wrist and turned it so his palm faced up. With a smile, she reached down and kissed him on the wrist, just as Hime did.

His heart thumped loudly as she looked up and whispered, "You are the shadows between man and women. You are the lover of my life and the keepers of my passion. You are my blessed, and I love you, Derik."

It hit him with the force of a bat to the head. He had whispered the same words to himself almost every night before sleeping. The world spun around him, and he clutched the bed for balance. "Oh, fuck me, Bridget."

"I just did."

He started to laugh but it turned into a bawl. His body shook as he sobbed loudly, feeling a terrible release of so much at once.

She took him up in her arms, and Derik buried his head on the shoulder of his god. She just stroked his hair and held him as he cried. He clutched at her, holding her tightly in fear she would fade away like a bad dream. But, she didn't go. She didn't leave. She was there, and he could feel her love in his heart.

The tears slowed, then stopped. He looked up with red-rimmed eyes and she smiled. Tenderly, she kissed him on the lips.

His voice broken, he whispered, "Why?"

"Because you needed it."

"I did? I needed Rick? I needed to lose," he sniffed and she wiped away the tears, "why did I need to lose them all?"

Bridget smiled, "If you knew you were to marry Wendi, would you have slept with her mother?"

He shook his head, "No."

"And, if you knew that you would fall into the harem and turned into a woman, would you have gone?"

It took him a moment, "No, probably not."

"But, it was Madre's spanking and your time with the baron that helped you survive Rick's torture."

"Why?"

She kissed him again. "Because, I need you to be strong for what comes next. I need to you to know that pain, I need you to be able to fight for all those you love."

"I don't understand."

"And I can't tell you. Knowing the goal doesn't help, knowing how I want it to end won't help you. I can't tell you the path to take because that is your choice. You have free will, I can only help you along it. But, if you trust me, then you will find love again. I won't tell you who, I won't tell you where. You just have to trust."

He sniffed, "I trust you, I really do. This last year... I couldn't have done it without my faith in you."

She smiled, "I know, and that is why you have a beautiful soul, Derik."

Bridget stood up and tugged on her shirt. "How do I look?"

The idea of a god asking Derik about appearances made him laugh and she joined him. He managed to gasp out. "You look beautiful."

She beamed happily, and his entire body fluttered in her smile. Turning on her heels, the divine singer opened the door.

"Bridget?"

Turning around, he could almost feel that she knew the question he wanted to ask. His mouth opened, then closed.

She smiled. "It won't be tomorrow, my love, in fact it will be years. I won't tell you how many or what happens until then. But, just trust me. In the end, you'll do the right thing and I will be so, so proud of you."

She reached around the door and pulled the necklace off the hook. Tossing it to him, she smiled. "You have only one real master now."

Bridget smiled brightly. "And you have done your mother proud."

Derik looked down at the necklace, staring at the carved raven. In his hand, the stone melted and flowed, working on the will of the god and reformed into a blackbird. Nearly identical but somehow different. Below the necklace, he saw the imprint of Bridget's lips against his wrist. A mark that would never fade. With tears in his eyes, he slipped the necklace on. He looked up to thank her, but she was gone.

Somehow, he knew she would be.

He dressed back into his outfit of Tornsin's shirt and the black skirt he preferred. Padding out of the room, he left his mother's room behind and sought out Kerlis.

He found him in one of the observation rooms. The thin man sat alone in a padded chair, watching the scene through the transparent wall. Derik slipped inside and closed the door. His eyes sparkled as he saw a dozen men: three of them unconscious against the wall and the others piled on top of a struggling body. He spotted Shiel's legs lashing out as they struggled to hold her down.

She was laughing and screaming and had bruises and cuts everywhere.

Four swords were buried in the ceiling, another lay in pieces on the ground, and one blade was bent completely around the bed post. Most of the guards were heavily injured, with cuts and scratches of their own, but there was no mistaking the two cocks that drove into his friend's pussy and ass, splitting her open as she fought and came and fought some more.

Derik chuckled and slipped into the chair, worming under Kerlis.

The old man jumped, then lifted himself to settle on Derik's lap. "She is a monster, Derrie. I have three healers just trying to keep up with her. I needed two more from the hospital to keep one of them alive. That poor, poor man."

He sounded shocked and surprised. Kerlis gestured to the center of the transparent wall, where a crack snaked up the entire length. "She broke my wall. That's half a meter of enchanted rock."

Derik smiled and nodded with approval. "Looks like she's happy. I see you gave her thirty thousand dollars' worth of pleasure."

"I have to. I'm afraid that if she doesn't come enough, she'll tear apart my business."

Derik laughed cheerfully. "She's a good friend. Rough but good."

Old eyes looked at him, admiring and inspecting. "You seem happy. A shower help?"

For a moment, they looked at each other. Then Derik reached over and kissed him on the cheek.

Kerlis frowned and pressed his fingers against the kiss. "What was that?"

"I found something, and I wanted to give you your share. You always get a cut, remember?"

Blooming Flowers

Kneeling in the dirt of a late spring morning, Derik frowned as he read the directions on a packet of seeds. He didn't know why, but while he could still climb to the third story of a building in a few seconds, he couldn't understand how to make things grow. Grumbling, he jammed one of Shiel's daggers into the dirt and carved out a hole. Picking a few seeds, he dropped them in and shoved it back into place. Nothing happened, so he did it again and again, drilling a neat line across a patch of overturned dirt.

He chuckled and looked over to Shiel's enchanted sword. She had dug up the ground for him, using the massive blade to slice huge chunks of earth and sod, tossing it into the air, and obliterating the clods until they rained down in a fine shower of dirt.

He smiled and dug a few more holes to plant the rest of the seeds. He finished the packet and frowned; his efforts only covered a quarter of the upturned earth.

Shrugging, he hopped to his feet. He let out a sigh as his bare feet sank into the cool earth. Brushing out the deep blue skirt he wore, he twirled around for a moment, then hopped lightly out of the garden. His shirt, a thick flannel one clung to his body.

He couldn't wear Tornsin's anymore. After three years, it had become so thread-bare and torn that Shiel forbade him to wear it. She didn't want to see his naked skin through the rents. Instead, he just used it as his pillow in his cage—memories of an old life he refused to abandon.

Half-remembered fantasies bubbled up and wafted across his mind. Then, as they always did, he found his mind heading toward his new life. He turned his wrist to look at the kiss mark still on his wrist. Two years had passed since that night, and it still shimmered against his skin. He reached down and kissed it lightly. It was a prayer, of sorts. He knew something would happen, he just needed patience until Bridget called him.

Flipping the dagger, he threw it into the earth next to the enchanted sword. It thunked into the ground point first, sinking to the hilt. He sat admiring the freshly made garden.

From inside the house came the sounds of Shiel sleeping off her latest round of binge drinking. This time, she downed an entire a cask of Dragon Gut, and the snores rattled the walls.

He rolled his eyes and played with a strand of grass. He tensed as he heard someone walking up the path leading up to the house. Without looking back, he tapped the ground and listened to the hesitating movements.

Then, a familiar voice spoke up. "I'm no expert, but I don't think it will grow if you watch."

Derik chuckled as Storn sat down next to him. It had been years since they had seen each other. The last time was the night of the auction.

The old man looked nervous and uncomfortable.

Derik nodded to him. He didn't know what he was supposed to feel, but there was no anger or rage left. "Hey."

Storn grunted but still looked nervous.

Derik sighed and gestured to the garden. "I never tried to grow something, you know."

"Won't grow if you watch it. Takes weeks. Wendi liked to grow flowers."

"Yeah, I remember. She always made it look easy."

"Not really, father helped. Necromancy does wonderful things to dead flowers and it was a secret she didn't have to know."

Derik nodded but couldn't think of anything else to say.

Storn stared at him.

Derik said nothing but the fence eventually spoke.

"You seem, um, domestic."

Derik chuckled, "Not really. Shiel is sleeping off some booze and tomorrow we leave for the coast. Got a job to hunt a river dragon causing trouble with some boats. I, I just felt like planting a garden last night."

"Going to be difficult? The dragon?"

"Probably not. I'll probably end up naked and either swallowed or fucked, then Shiel will hop up and kill it. I'd rather get a dragon cock up my ass than swallowed. Digestive juices ruin more of my clothes than anything else."

"Okay, that sounds just wrong."

Derik laughed happily. "Yeah, but its where I need to be."

"That sounds worse."

Neither said anything for a long moment, then Storn cleared his throat. "Don't you miss it?"

"Stealing?"

"Yeah, being a thief."

"Not really."

"What about the rest of it?"

"Not really. Last week, I got to climb a twelve story tower in the rain, swing down and distract a wizard while Shiel fought her way up the stairs."

"I heard about that one, heard you got hurt pretty badly."

Derik shivered at the memory of the acidic spell that peeled back his flesh. And then the pain of it being healed while Shiel bitched him out. "Yeah, but I heal."

Storn struggled with his words and Derik just looked at the garden. He already knew it would fail, but he needed to try something new. He finished painting the house right before winter the year before, and he needed something to do with his hands.

"Look, about, you know, the auction. We were so damn angry at you."

Derik closed his eyes, but said nothing.

Storn cleared his throat. "I heard you got it pretty bad, with Shiel and Rick and everything. And, well—"

"I wrong you, Storn. You were my friend and I betrayed you. I'm surprised you even considered coming back after all that."

"...I would kind of- What?"

Derik smiled at his old friend. "I fucked up. At this point, I'm not going to pretend I did anything else. Your family was rightfully angry. And, well, I can't say I shouldn't have done it, but I will say I'm sorry that I hurt you."

Frowning, Storn ripped up some grass and stared at him. "What happened to you?"

"Well, after a few years of being used as bait, I had enough time to think about things. I'm here and, at the moment, this is where I am suppose to be."

"You seem..." He hesitated. "...so confident now. Most people would be terrified to be the slave of Shiel. I heard she broke Maston's leg last month."

"Both actually, and a pair of ribs, and his hand. Bastard shouldn't have tried to stab me."

Storn swallowed hard. "I also heard she dressed you up as a nun for that one."

Derik grinned, "Yeah, she did. But, it was my idea. Got a bunch of outfits in the basement now. Shiel thinks its great fun to dress me up inappropriately for our jobs. I just like being pretty." He lifted his blue skirt and let it drape over his bare thigh.

"You are fucked up."

Leaning back, Derik looked up at the sky. He grinned, remembering Shiel's words. "We're all fucked up, Storn. Some of us are just happy about it."

"Yeah, well I couldn't do it."

Storn set down a heavy packet on the ground. "Look, I didn't know where to find you, then when I did, I kind of sat on it, but this came for you about a year ago. From my sister and the harem."

Derik turned to look at him curiously. "Me?"

"Yeah, sorry it took so long. At first I thought she was being ironic, still mad at you for stealing the silver."

Surprised, Derik looked at the paper-wrapped package. He reached out to stroke the edge of it.

Storn watched him, then spoke cautiously. "Do you miss the harem?"

"More than you can imagine, Storn."

"Ever thought about going back? Even with Wendi there?"

"Every day and every night."

"Why don't you? You are probably the best thief in the country now. I'm sure you'll find a way in."

"It isn't time."

"How will you know?"

Derik turned his wrist to bring the kiss mark to the sunlight. "Faith."

Storn grunted. After a few minutes of silence, he scrambled to his feet.

Derik hopped up lightly, leaving the package on the grass.

Storn looked around at the neatly trimmed walk, the painted house, and the fresh garden that would fail. "Look, I know you say you forgave me, but... well, I felt like coming out here today. I-I'm not angry at you anymore. We got the silver and you, well, you got what came to you. It wasn't death, but I heard the stories and I think you got more than you probably deserved."

"I wasn't going to sell it, you know."

"Yeah, but you didn't return it either. But... as you said, forgiveness, right?"

Derik smiled and nodded.

"You have best damned luck to make the worst person in the world your friend."

He thought about Rick and shivered. "Not the worst. Not even close."

"Yeah, sorry. Speaking of that, watch out. I heard Rick is back in the area and asked about you."

Derik's heart beat faster. "Is he still in charge?"

"No, he retreated to his family home after the duke sprung him from prison. Haven't seen him in a few years, but the word is that he's back."

"I'll stay near Shiel then."

"Yeah," his friend distractedly, "you should do that. She will make a good guard that even the triplets wouldn't consider attacking."

Together, they walked down the path toward the house and on the road. Derik's eyes scanned around, but Storn was honestly alone.

At the intersection, the fence turned to him. "Oh, one more thing. As the guild master of the thieves now, I'm here to give you a new rank."

"I'm not a thief. Oh, and congratulations."

Storn chuckled, "You'll always be a thief, Derik."

"What rank?"

"We created a new category for you. Um, 'bait.'"

Derik's eyebrow rose with a question.

"I'm now a bait?"

"Actually, a master bait. Also, after the thing with the baron and that bit with stealing the princess from the merchant's guild, you are also now a master boxer, bait, and face. Adding to your official titles as master acrobat, wolf, and clover you are tied for the most ranks in this entire region. You are getting pretty famous, despite the fact, people can't seem to find this place."

Derik's lip quirked as Storn said it like "masturbate." "Got a lot of time to think, now that you are guild master?"

Storn grinned, "Yeah, but mainly I wanted to see if there could be a friendship between us again."

Derik nodded and patted his shoulder. "No more anger, but no promise that Shiel won't be dragging me to be bait."

"Good, you have no clue how hard it was to come here like this."

"You are always welcomed, just bring a cask to distract Shiel."

Storn held out his hand. "You are always welcomed in my bar, Derik, day or night."

Derik took the hand and shook it. "As a friend?"

"As a brother."

With a smile, Derik dragged Storn into a tight hug. Storn resisted for a moment, his stomach clenching, but Derik just squeezed him once and released him.

After a few short words, Storn headed back up the road and Derik watched him disappear into the distance. Feeling light, he padded across the grass and looked down at the package on the ground. Picking it up with his feet, he flipped it up and carried it into the house.

In the kitchen, he picked up a bottle of mead, which Shiel refused to touch, and popped it open as he sat at the table. The package sat in front of him, and he seriously considered just leaving it wrapped. After a few minutes, he pulled it to him and ripped it open.

He found two letters, both perfumed, and set them aside. His fingers trembled as she pulled open the paper and picked up his corset, the one from Tiv's. Tears sparkled in his eyes as he brought it to his nose and breathed in the smells of the harem. The memories that slammed into him brought the tears down on his face.

Shaking, he set it aside and picked up the long blue cord he used to tie up his hair. He fingered it before setting it aside.

The third and final item stole his breath away. It was a simple white shirt, but he already knew who gave it to him as the tears streamed down his face. Picking it up, he buried his face in it and lost himself in the smells of Tornsin and apple perfume. It was faded, but his heart hurt to be reminded of so much. He was crying before he realized it, his sobs muted by the soft fabric of a lover.

Still crying, he set down the shirt long enough to remove his flannel one and slip into his gift. Anticipation set his body on fire and his manhood came to life. It pulsed with every button he closed on the shirt. As he fumbled with the last button, he was panting for air and crying at the same time.

Finished, he buried his face in the fabric and stroked his shaft. He was hot and hard and burning with lust, the memories crashed into him as he soaked the shirt with his tears. His hands fumbled with his skirt, yanking it up and freeing his manhood. Stroking it with both hands, he bent over the table and pumped himself, his eyes closed tight as he imagined Tornsin coming behind him, filling him as only a true lover could.

Frustratingly, he couldn't reach his orgasm. His fingers dripped with his juices, but his mind refused to give him the release he craved. Letting out a gasp of lust, he plastered his face against the table and bit his lip, begging his own body to come.

"Oi! What the fuck?"

Derik froze and blushed. He opened his eyes to see Shiel standing in the door, rubbing her eyes. She gathered her enchanted sword but she stared at him with an expression of disgust and surprise.

Derik's blush grew hotter as he released his dripping shaft and stood up, tugging the skirt down over his exposed buttocks.

Shiel sniffed. "Yuck, you got more of that apple crap?"

Bashfully, he plastered his hands over his hardness and nodded.

Shiel staggered into the room and dropped the wooden cask into the crate near the door. Grabbing a narrow bottle, she leaned against the kitchen and looked at him. "Getting all hot and bothered thinking about your boyfriend?"

"I, um, Shiel—"

She snapped her fingers. "Come here."

He hesitated for a moment, then blushing hotly, he walked over to her, his hand still covering the hardness below his skirt. Shiel looked at him, her blue and green eyes piercing. Then she grinned evilly. He swallowed, knowing she was about to do something he didn't like.

She grabbed him and spun him around. Before he could response, she bent him over the table and kicked apart his legs.

"Shiel!"

"Ya, shut up. Look, you ain't that pretty, but you need this."

"What!?"

In answer, she yanked up his skirt to expose his ass. He tried to pull away, but she shoved his head down on the table. At the touch of something smooth sliding up his thigh, he let out a whimper. Glancing over, he realized it was the thick end of the bottle in her hand.

Shiel worked it between his ass cheeks and pressed it right against his hole. "You know you can't get off unless someone is doing da pumping."

He whimpered, but the strength flew out of him as her rotated the smooth glass against his anal ring.

Shiel grunted as she muttered. "Pretend I'm da baron or something. Got a big old glass cock."

A moan escaped Derik's lips as he plastered his hands against the surface of the table. His body burned with hunger, and he heard pre-cum dripping to the ground. The thick end circled around, easing him open, then she jammed it into him. With the stretching came memories and then he almost lost control.

As she pumped it, the orgasm built up quickly. Derik closed his eyes and imagined it was Tornsin or the baron taking him, and the heat flushed even hotter. He gasped and opened his mouth, his bottom lip caressing the table as he pushed back on the bottle. It was so thick and hard as it drove into him.

Shiel said nothing as she gripped it tightly, driving it in and out with hard, powerful strokes. It wasn't love-making, she was fucking him. Hard and brutal, at first it didn't seem like it was for his pleasure, but Shiel knew him as well as he did and the feelings of helplessness, being pinned to the table and almost raped sent him over the edge.

He let out a scream of pleasure as he came. He shuddered violently as Shiel continued to drive into him, the glass slick against his insides and setting off every tiny mote of pleasure to course through his system. He whimpered and wailed, begging for more and she gave it him. He lost himself in his fantasies and in the scents of his gifts as she buried the entire length into his rectum and forced out another mind-blowing orgasm.

When she was finished, she pulled out the bottle from his body and tossed it in the air.

Derik slid off the table and slumped to the ground, a smile on his lips and his body shivering with pleasure.

He looked up to see Shiel washing off the bottle. Then, she broke the end off and drank half of its contents. Gasping for breath, she wiped her mouth and pointed at him. "We ain't doing this again, we ain't lovers, and I don't like you."

He let out a happy, shuddering breath. "Thank you, Shiel."

Her eyes drifted to the table, then she grinned. Reaching over, she grabbed the corset. "Oh, this would be perfect. Mine."

Derik chuckled, then nodded. "Might as well, I don't have breasts."

"Damn right. And it's magical. So is the cord."

"Locater sensor on the cord, and I think the corset is protective. It's from Tiv's."

"Never heard of it."

"Store for mages."

Shiel purred as she looked at the corset. "Fair enough, you keep the cord, the corset is mine."

She growled playfully and Derik just laughed.

Shiel hopped over the table and ran out of the room to try it on.

Derik reached up and grabbed the cord and letters. "Shiel?"

From upstairs, his mistress and friend yelled back. "Yeah?"

"I'm growing my hair long again."

"Yeah, whatever."

Wincing as he got up, Derik headed to his own room, the area around his cage, to read the letters in peace.

Just Friends

"Hey, Derik?" It was Shiel.

Derik's eyes snapped open as he stared out into the darkness of the basement. His body trembled with the sudden waking, but it took him a few seconds to find his voice. "Yeah?"

"I can't get off. I can't come."

Derik frowned in the darkness and shifted his position, his hands clawing at the bars of the cage as he flipped on his back. Tornsin's shirt tugged as he arched his back to release the pressure. He ran his fingers through his hair to stall as he struggled with the concept of Shiel masturbating. "Um, what?"

"You know, what you do all the damn time when I'm not watching."

Derik blushed and reached up. He smiled as he pulled out a pin and removed the latch in the darkness. His hands moved with the familiarity of picking the lock every morning for over three years. A faint click shot through the darkness and he rolled out of his cage.

He crawled out and stretched. "Anything I can do?"

She didn't response for a long time, and he began to think Shiel had gone back upstairs. He sighed and started back toward his cage when Shiel spoke softly.

"No, sorry, never mind. Cage."

Derik frowned as he listened to Shiel climb the stairs, her bare feet slapping against the steps and faded into the distance. He listened to the darkness for a long time, then considered crawling back into the cage as she commanded.

Tapping the ground with he toes, he made a decision. Padding through the darkness, he wound his way around the piles of weapons and artifacts before reaching the stairs. Moving silently, he mounted up the stairs and looked out in the shadows of the mansion. His eyes focused on the windows, half-covered with snow and ice. More drifts piled up against the side of the house and he didn't want to think about shoveling off the porch.

Reaching up, he pulled his hair back and bound it with the dark blue cord from Madre. He smiled at the feel of it and padded up the stairs. At the top, he could hear Shiel grunting in frustrating. Silently, he covered the last few meters and peered through the cracked open door to her bedroom.

Shiel slept in a massive bed that filled the entire room. Velvet comforters piled up in mountains of blankets. A dozen pillows—each one larger than both of them—were balanced on the edges of the mountains. Derik could barely see her body, but there was no mistaking Shiel's naked form as she plunged both hands between her legs, fingering her pussy with a desperate speed. He could see her weapons thrown around the best, a land mine field of magic and blades.

Derik watched her as she screamed out with frustration and slumped back.

Stretching out, she snarled into the ceiling. "Fuck."

He chuckled silent for a moment, then pushed open the door.

She snapped up into position, her long ears twitching. "What the fuck?"

Derik didn't say anything as he crawled up on the bed.

Shiel glared at him and crossed her hands over her small breasts. "Go away."

He stopped and let a ghost of a smile cross his lips. Backing up, he slid off the bed and worked his way back to the bed. Shutting it behind him, he slowly walked down the hall toward the stairs. In his head, he could almost count the seconds.

"Hey, Derik?"

Returning to her room, he peeked inside. "Yes?"

She blushed as she knelt up on her bed, peeking over the mountains of blankets. "Um, you remember that time, a few months ago? In the kitchen with the bottle."

He already knew the answer. At a strange urging, he unbuttoned his shirt.

She gasped and watched him with bright eyes.

The shirt puddled to the ground and he removed the blue cord and let it join the floor. A few seconds later, he was naked in front of her, wearing nothing but an iron collar.

Shiel blushed hotly, "Look, that isn't it. You know what?" She gestured violently, "Just go back."

Derik chuckled and crawled up on the bed.

Shiel pulled back, her blush crawling down the front of her body and bringing heat along the cleavage of her bare breasts. "W-What are you doing?"

Seeing her bashful surprised him, but Derik pushed it aside. He whispered, "Returning the favor, obviously."

"Hey, I didn't ask you."

He reached out and caught one wrist. She could have shattered his bone with a twist, but she made no effort to free herself as he brought her fingers to his mouth. He could smell her juices on the tips, a sour mixture of wine and woman. His eyes glittering, he sucked on her fingers and she trembled at the touch.

For the briefest of moments, a soft look crossed her face. Then she dredged up some of her anger. "Oi!"

Derik grinned, his body warming as he sucked on her fingers, cleaning each digit one by one.

"I don't like you," she said.

"I know," he purred and sucked on her thumb. Releasing her wrist, he caught her other wrist.

Shiel let out a soft, girlish whimper as his lips caressed her finger, tasting the slick juices drying on her tips. She moaned, shuddering as he slipped his lips around her finger, bobbing down to the second knuckle. "I don't like pussies."

"I don't have one," he whispered.

He sucked on the next finger, tasting wine. It somehow fit with everything he knew about her. As he moved to the third, she stammered.

"I-I don't like submissives pussies."

He said nothing for a moment, "I know."

She blushed hotly as he sucked on her fourth finger.

"I, um, I don't like you."

Derik cleaned off her thumb, then crawled forward. Shiel tightened her jaw as she leaned back and he brought his lips down to kiss her right between the breasts.

"You don't have to like me, Shiel."

"I don't."

"Good," he chuckled, then kissed her right along the sternum. His lips caressed her skin, tapping tiny kisses down her tight, muscular stomach and around her naval.

He heard her fighting back moans, her body trembling as she panted for air. Derik chuckled and kissed her right along the pubic bone and she shuddered almost violent.

"This doesn't mean anything."

Derik looked up at the emotion-filled eyes of his friend. "I know, this is just a friend helping another friend. Sometimes, Shiel, you just need it sweet."

She bristled, "No, I don't—"

He silenced her by pressing his lips against the swollen lips between her legs. At his touch, her muscles tightened until they were as hard as rock. He darted his tongue out, delving between the slick wine-flavored folds to curl around her clitoris. He buried his nose in the sparse hairs that sprouted along her lips, drinking in her heady smell and lapping her from the base to the tip with his tongue.

Shiel gasped, her back arching as she let out a whimper. It sounded like a mix of pain and confusion, but Derik just lapped against her again, parting her and drinking from the juices that clung to her petals. He pressed his hands on her knees and spread her legs apart. She resisted, but he managed to ease her apart, delving deeper into the wet depths until the bounty hunter let out tiny gasps of pleasure.

Her body vibrated. Under his hands, she lifted herself off the blankets using nothing but her feet and head. She arched her body while gripping his hair tightly. Her pussy ground against his mouth.

Derik just lapped harder, sucking on her clitoris and her opening. He released one hand to ease a finger into her tight channel.

At the first touch of her slick tunnel, Shiel let out a high-pitched shriek and locked into position, her body vibrating intensely.

He almost suffocated against her pussy, her hands grinding him down until the afterglow of her pleasure died down. As fast as she came, Shiel slumped to the bed and released him.

Derik chuckled and wiped the juices from his face.

Shiel glared at him, the flush hot on her cheeks and breasts. "When the fuck did you stop being my slave?"

Derik sat up on his heels and shrugged. "No idea, actually. A while ago, I think."

"Cocky bastard."

He looked down at his hardness, "Well, yeah."

"Well, um, thanks."

Her eyes looked away from him, "We're even now, k?"

Derik bowed and crawled off the bed. Gathering his shirt and hair cord, he slipped out of the room and closed the door behind him. Feeling the flush, he headed down the stairs for a well-deserved masturbation and sleep.

"Derik?"

He froze half-way down the stairs. His head cocked at the small voice that echoed down. Looking up, he called out. "Yeah?"

"Come back?"

Turning around, he padded back up the stairs and set the shirt and cord outside her door before opening her bedroom door.

Shiel sat in the middle of her blankets, looking uncomfortable. Her hair leaned to one side, messier than usual.

"Yes, Shiel?"

"We're friends, right? Not slave and master?"

"Yeah, Shiel, we're friends."

She worried the bottom of her lip. "Um, about that..." her voice trailed off.

Derik slipped through the door and shut it behind him. His bare feet stepped carefully around the murderous weapons and empty wine bottles to crawl back up on the bed.

Shiel watched him and clamped her hands between his knees. She looked nervous for a moment and reached over to grab a bottle. Rocking it to hear the level, she took a deep swig and handed it to Derik.

Derik, as naked as her, curled up his feet and took it. Swallowing the burning liquid, he handed it back silently.

Together, they finished the bottle before Shiel found the courage to speak.

"I-If you are a friend, y-you really should... um, you shouldn't be sleeping in the cage." She blushed hotly and flung up a hand between them. "But, we ain't fucking!"

Derik laughed loudly, and Shiel joined him, grabbing another bottle to share. They finished it off, feeling a bit of buzz as they threw it aside.

Derik looked around. "Um, Shiel, where am I sleeping then?"

She gestured to the large bed. "Here works."

"Are you sure?"

Swallowing, she nodded, "Yeah, just as friends though."

"Of course."

"And... I'm tired now."

Derik nodded and found a comfortable spot on the bed, slipping under the blankets as his heart pounded against his chest.

Shiel burrowed under the largest pile of blankets until only her toes and head peeked out. With a curt word, she commanded the lights and the room plunged in darkness.

He waited for a long moment, getting used to the soft blankets holding him and the soft, irregular breathing of another woman in bed. It was like the harem and he smiled, feeling the beginnings of something new changing in his life.

After a hour, he heard Shiel sigh and roll over. "Damn it, I can't sleep," she muttered.

Derik chuckled, still awake himself. "Why?"

"I keep feeling like you gonna attack. Then we'll fight, I'll kill you and I'll feel bad since I don't know how to grow flowers."

He grinned. "I won't attack."

"Yeah, I know. You're a pussy."

"See, nothing to worry about."

"Not used to this. I never slept with someone."

Derik thought for a moment. "If it makes you feel better, just think me as someone to kick while you are sleeping."

There was a brief moment, then his world exploded in pain as Shiel kicked him in the gut.

He groaned and curled up under the blankets, in time for her foot to catch him right under the chin. "I said while you sleep."

Shiel said, "I'm sleeping."

Derik scrambled under the blankets. They flew up and he lunged for Shiel.

She grinned, the insane berserker coming back to life. There was a brief struggle and he found himself pinned to the blankets and Shiel straddling him. "I win."

"I thought you were sleeping," he grinned.

Then, he saw Shiel realize her position. Her eyes drifted down as she leaned on his wrists, seeing his hardness pressed against the cleft of her pussy. "Um."

Derik looked up with hooded eyes. "We're just friends, right?" His heart beat in his chest as his cock grew harder.

Shiel sighed, "Yeah."

She lifted her body and Derik held his breath.

She trembled as she knelt up, then looked down with a hunger that burned in her eyes.

"D-Derik?" her voice cracked.

"Go ahead."

"I don't like you."

"Prove it."

She impaled herself on him, her pussy crushing Derik's cock. They moaned together at the penetration. She ground down, forcing him deeper into her painfully tight sheath. He tried to move his hands, but she pinned him down as his aching length slid up. Her nether lips clung to his member and his cock disappearing into the hot liquid depths.

Derik thrust up with his hips, burying the last of his cock into her pussy. She let out a tiny whimper and pulled up with her body. He let out a soft moan and she ground down, slamming down and driving him into the blankets.

Except for the whimpers, they were silent. Their bodies moving in time, rocking up and down, her hips sliding the shaft up and down inside her. Unlike everything else they did in three years together, there was no fighting, no arguing, no playing. Just two friends moving to the beat of something only they could hear.

Sweat sheened against their skins as she moved. He could feel her struggling with unfamiliar emotions and sensations. Her body twitched with the reflexes of a warrior not a lover. He just lifted himself. Her arms seemed to lose her strength and he freed himself. Sitting up, he wrapped his arms around her waist, pulling himself up against her sweat-slicked breasts.

She seemed to jerk, her blue and green eyes wide as she stared at him. Gasping, she said, "I still don't like you."

"I know," he whispered and kissed her.

They came together, his cum splattering her insides as she squeezed down on him until his bones ground together. In her eyes, he saw her struggling with a sob, then she closed her eyes tightly and buried her face on his shoulder. They held each other and said nothing.

Hours later, they lay in the bed. Shiel slept away from him, with just their hands touching.

He smiled with a strange sense of contentment. Stretching out, he kept his fingertips against her palm and let out a soft sigh of pleasure. His eyes closed slowly and he drifted toward sleep.

He dreamed of the harem but there was something dark inside. A monster or beast hiding in the darkness. The sorrow and fear rose up as he paced through the still familiar walls. It had been years since he had experienced such a longing to go back, and even then, it was never as clear as in his dream.

With a start, he had an epiphany.

He was ready to go home.

And someone was coming.

His exhaustion peeled away, and he was utterly awake. Every tiny part of his body vibrated with a powerful burst of energy and he sat up.

Shiel grumbled and curled away from him, wrapping her body around an empty bottle of wine.

Derik slipped out of the bed, carefully working his way around the weapons and gathering his shirt and cord outside the door. Shutting the door, he held still. Something tugged him down the stairs. Following the pull and curious of its destination, he dressed and wrapped his hair in the cord.

Intuition drew him to the front door. With steady fingers, he unlatched it and opened it. His eyes peered through the door into the winter night. Outside, the snow piled deep across the porch but his eyes were drawn to one thing.

Teri stood shivering in the snow. She whimpered as she reached out for him, her hand shaking violently. Underneath a cloak, she wore only her harem outfit and heavy boots. "D-Derik? Is-is that you?"

"Teri!"

She flung himself into his arms and he caught her, pulling her into the warmth of the house. She kissed him frantically, clutching to him as she shook violently. Her teeth chattered as she swooned.

"Teri!"

Her body collapsed in his arms, and he knelt to slow her fall. Her eyes flicked open as she clutched at him, fear burning in her eyes.

"R-Rick, he's attacking the baron!"

Brothers

Despite waiting three years for this point, panic gripping his heart. He clutched Teri tightly.

Her eyes rolled back into her head. The slender girl shivered violently and he grabbed her hands. They were icy.

Whimpering, he rubbed them to warm them.

"Don't," said Shiel behind him. "If you move her, the cold blood will flow into her heart. She'll be dead before you can blow her again."

He looked up as silfae came down the stairs, fully dressed and armed. She had a serious look on her face as she regarded Teri and Derik. She gestured up the stairs. "Throw her in the shower, I'll get the healing potions."

"What about those warmth potions you made when you made me seduce the ice monster?"

"Good idea."

Derik nodded and picked up Teri. He easily carried her body up the stairs. Stripping off their clothes, he didn't give himself a chance to think until he set her in the shower and activated the magically heated water. He wasn't sure how hot, so he set it to right above his own temperature, warm but not searing.

As the water sheeted over them, he held her up and gave himself a chance to look at her. Three years were kind to her. She had the same soft look to her face and her body kept its youthful trim, but he could see that her breasts hung down a bit more, and she had a few lines in her face. Her toes and fingers were dusky, and he found scorch marks on her right hand.

He also realized he still loved her.

Clutching her to his body, he held her until she started to stir. "T-Teri?"

Moaning, her eyes rolled for a moment before she focused on him. A pained smile crossed her lips. "Derik? Is it really you?"

He lifted his hand to her cheek, holding her. Tears mixed with water as he pulled her into a kiss. He could feel the sorrow in her, but she flung her arms around him as they embraced, their lips seeking each other out. He couldn't stop kissing, even if he tried.

She clung to him tightly, their bodies intertwined and clutching, but not fucking.

"Oi!"

Derik jumped and pulled apart.

Shiel glared at him. "Plowing her won't help either!"

She jammed two wine bottles into the shower with them. Identical to the endless other bottles in the house, the tips were painted a bright red to remind Shiel not to drink them. She added another bottle of the thick fluid that warmed Derik before.

Derik's fingers fumbled with the top of the warming potion before pulling out the cork and handing it to Teri.

The young woman tore her eyes away from Shiel and looked at it.

"Drink this, its a potion to warm you," said the killer and handed her an open potion.

"And then chug this. It tastes horrible but will help with your toes."

Her body shaking from the frostbite, she took it and held it with both hands. Raising it to her lips, she took a long swig.

Then gagged.

"Mask of Shadows, fuck that hurts!"

Derik giggled. He realized he was falling into his old ways at the harem in a matter of minutes. "Well, Shiel cuts it with vodka. Drink."

She hesitated and he repeated himself in a firm command.

"Drink!"

Still shivering, Teri made a face and drained the bottle as fast as she could. Derik held her, wiping the water from her face as she stared at him. He smiled back and fought against the urge to kiss her again. To his surprise, his heart beat faster at the sight of her after all those years.

A few minutes later, the shivering slowed, and she clutched herself.

Derik pushed the soaked hair from her face. "What happened?" he asked quietly.

"Rick, he invaded the palace. She... I... we..."

"Out with it!" snapped Shiel.

Teri jumped and stepped back.

Derik glared at Shiel. "Be nice."

"Blow me."

Derik chuckled, "Teri?"

"We were dancing for the winter festival. It... it was me, and the baron, and Sher.. Sher... Sherrel."

Derik saw a flash of emotion, then Teri burst into tears. "He killed her! Rick just killed her!"

Shock slammed into him, but he managed to retain his wits long enough to hold Teri as the thief collapsed to the ground. Tears ran down his cheek as an icy numbness filled him.

Teri sobbed, clutching him as they knelt in the shower.

Shiel sighed and reached in to turn off the water. "What happened?" she snapped. "Details, you little cunt! Details!"

Derik stared out into nothing, his mind crushed by the memories of Sherrel. He wallowed in them until a new emotion rose to erase them: rage.

Teri sobbed loudly, clutching to him.

Shiel reached in and grabbed her by the hair, yanking her up to a standing position.

Derik looked up at the annoyed bounty hunter, his eyes flicking past the shaved slit of the harem kitten before he stood up.

"What. The. Fuck. Happened?"

"We were dancing and Sherrel was laughing. Then, she stopped. I looked over as saw her... her just standing there, a sword sticking out of her chest. R-Rick twisted it and yanked it out. S-She was crying when she collapsed and t-then the baron told me to run. And I ran. I ran so hard I hurt myself. T-They already surrounded the harem and I could hear Madre and Wendi fighting; there were bodies everywhere, but I crawled through the ventilation."

She sobbed, and Derik pulled her from the shower. Grabbing a towel, he wrapped it around her and started to dry her hair, listening as the tears ran down his cheeks. He could feel an incredible desire to crawl back in his cage, but there was no escaping his fate. Instead, he just dried Teri as she finished.

"M-Madre saw me and shoved t-this compass thing in my hand. And she told me to find help. I-I didn't want to leave, I didn't! Oh, Derik, please forgive me!"

She wrapped her arms around him, hugging him until it hurt. Derik held her and walked her backwards into Shiel's bedroom before he sat her down on the bed.

"How did you find us?"

Shiel grunted, "Yeah, this place is protected against strangers."

Shaking violently, Teri held up her burnt hand. "I-I followed the compass. U-Until it exploded in my hand. Then I just kept on walking in the same direction. My hands and feet hurt for a long time, it was so cold, but then it stopped hurting and I was getting worried. I-I saw this house and thought I would find some blankets to warm up or something."

She sniffed, the tears still streaming down her face, "A-And then you were there. It was like an angel came down, with your black hair fanning out behind you. I-I thought I died."

Derik smiled sadly and wiped at the tears.

Shiel grunted. "How many?"

"I-I don't know. They had at least a thousand in the palace and I saw some fires in town. And there were some strange robed guys coming into the hall when I ran along the roof."

Derik looked up at Shiel. "I have to go there."

Teri whimpered and clutched at him. "Take me!"

Shiel shook her head curtly. "Like fuck you are! You are injured and weak. You'll make a mistake and someone will die."

"No, please, I have to go," Teri screamed out, standing up.

Shiel took a step forward and punched her hard across the chin.

Derik just stared as Teri collapsed to the ground. He glared at her. "Shiel!"

"What! She's gonna fuck you up, and you know it."

Derik picked up Teri and set her on the bed. He shook from the inside, feeling emotions burning through him. His hand trembled as he wrapped her in blankets. "She'll be okay?"

"Yeah, yeah, I'll watch her."

Derik froze. "Shiel?"

The bounty hunter shook her head. "Not this time, Derik. This isn't a job. This isn't for fun." She swallowed hard, "Look, we're friends, right?"

Derik nodded numbly.

"I have a bad feeling about this. This isn't a good fight and people are going to die tonight."

"I thought that is what you do?"

"Well, yeah, but something is wrong. There is nasty magic going on and... well, I won't do this."

He turned to her and looked at the blue and green eyes that stared back at him. He refused to pull away from the path Bridget gave him. "I still have to go. That is my... my family. They are in trouble."

"I know."

Sweeping her up in a hug, he held her tightly while managing to avoid being cut by her endless weapons. "You are more than a friend, Shiel."

Leaving her behind, he quickly dressed in his winter gear: a long leather duster, Tornsin's shirt, and his pants. He ran to the basement to grab the blackbird necklace and wrap it around his neck, settling the cord under the iron collar that suddenly weighed heavily on his shoulder. Grabbing the blue cord, he looked back into the house he lived in for three years.

Shiel grabbed two bottles of wine and disappeared back into her bedroom.

Derik shook his head for a moment, then closed the door.

The winter night burned his skin. A storm was building up, but he had a long way to run. Jumping, he sprinted across the snow and ice toward the lovers who needed him.

It only took him an hour to reach the city limits, and he smelled smoke long before he saw it. Part of the southern quarter burned brightly in the night. Patrols of men, all heavily armored, walked around the walls but Derik easily scaled the icy barrier and jumped down into the shadows. A few leaps later, he was sprinting across the rooftops.

He almost made it.

Jumping across the street, he caught a patch of black ice and his ankle twisted painfully. Biting back a yelp, he scrambled to regain his footing, but his fingers missed a ledge and he plummeted to the street.

Fortunately, he landed on the cooling body of a peasant, breaking the impact of his fall and driving the air from his lungs. As he scrambled to his feet, he heard someone chuckling.

"Well, looks like we got ourselves another one."

Derik's head snapped up to regard six warriors standing in front of him. They wore white and black. Up close, he saw they also had a symbol–a tower with skulls around it. At the very top, the row of heads had a missing spot. There was no question in his mind for whom the space was reserved.

"Rick," he whispered.

The lead warrior stepped forward and held up his blade. Fresh blood steamed as it ran down the length. "No survivors. That's the rules."

Derik's heart pounded painfully as he watched the murderers spread out. His eyes flickered to the leader's bloody blade, then back to all six. Blood rushing in his ears, he lowered himself into a crouch. Years of being bait taught him some combat skills, even if he still refused to kill, he could defend himself.

As one, all six charged. Derik snapped forward, ducking under the lead warrior's slash and stole his dagger. He rolled into the ground and spun around. Seeing a flash of movement, he dove back as two arrows slammed into the ground at his feet. Surprised, he looked up to see an archer reloading from a second-story window.

"Fuck!"

With a snap, he threw the dagger at the archer's bow. It snapped the string but he was jumping away from two swords that slashed out at him. Kicking off an icy wall, he winced at the pain of his aching ankle and slid past his attackers. Two kicks against the back of their knees and they dropped and he accelerated across the ice. As he passed the third, who snapped the tip off his blade against the ground, he grabbed his sword belt and yanked hard. The buckle snapped from the force and the fighter spun into the wall, hitting it with a sickening crunch. Rolling backwards, he kicked himself off the ground and jump over the fourth and land on the fifth warrior's head long enough to kick up again to the second story. He caught sight of a second archer and landed next to him, wrapping the belt around his bow, wrist, and the railing before pulling it tight.

The archer struggled for a moment, then lashed out.

Derik's ankle twinged painfully. He fell back toward the ground and landed heavily on his knees. As he started to get up, he saw a sword centimeters away from his throat.

"Pretty jumping, pretty face, but my boss says kill the pretty boys. And he said if I want to fuck a guy, kill him even faster. I don't know about you, but I want to really fuck your skull now."

Derik swallowed, a snarl on his lips.

Then, a flash of light lit up the street.

Derik jumped back as Shiel came down, her sword slicing the man in half and splattering the street with blood. The runes of power on her blade hummed violently as the gore showered down around her. She had an insane look on her face, a look of rapture. "Why the fuck is the pacifist fighting!?" she yelled.

Without waiting for an answer, she spun on her bare feet and punched the sword into one man's chest, shattering bone. With a twist, she ripped off the top of his body and threw it at the last warrior who screamed in agony. His scream cut off as Shiel covered the distance and slammed her sword down. It cut through the man and the wall behind him as easily as butter.

"S-Shiel!?"

She wore the same outfit as she always did. Thin leather across her breasts and hips and covered in weapons. The blood that splattered her steamed as it cooled, but she glared at Derik before helping him up. Looking him over, she shoved a healing wine at him. "Look, I lied."

Derik drained it, feeling the burn of the vodka and the flush of healing coursing through his veins. "Lied?"

"Yeah, I like you more than a friend too."

He laughed with relief.

She snapped back. "But there better be some fucking money in this! I mean it, I want to get paid. Then I'm going back to Kerlis and getting properly laid by someone who isn't a pussy! All the fucking muscle guys for me to beat up!"

Derik laughed as the pain in his ankle faded. Taking a deep breath, he thought furiously for a moment. Then, he had a flash of insight. A grin crossed his face. "I know someone willing to give you a quarter mil."

"Well, let's go see him."

Together, they raced back into the southern quarter. They encountered more bands of warriors, but this time the thief and the warrior did what they did best: bait and slaughter.

The Buggered Unicorn was under siege. Fifty men pounded on the doors and windows. Corpses were piled three deep around the blood-stained snow and ice. Derik spotted two captains and a mage directing the attack against the bar.

"T-This? A bar?" Shiel seemed unimpressed.

"Yeah, this bar. It is important."

Shiel grumbled, "Fine, any other ways in?"

"There is a small trap door near the back gutter. Its very small though."

"Won't fit, mind if I go through the front door? Aw, fuck it," Shiel snapped forward, her blade humming as she charged fifty men by herself.

Derik watched her cut the mage in half and bury her blade in the leader. He chuckled grimly and scrambled up the side of the alley, hopping lightly on the top and sprinting toward the bar. Finding two archers overlooking the bar, he grabbed their bows and used them as a vault to leap across the street. The bows snapped but he managed to hit the roof and slide up it. Moving quickly, he slid down the other side, but he was ready. Catching the gutter, he prayed they didn't move it and swung blindly under the gutter and into the Buggered Unicorn's attic.

Whisper quiet, Derik dropped to roll along the rafters. His heart pounded hard as he heard the screams outside and the insane cackle of Shiel, laughing as she slaughtered men unprepared for her berserker assault. He focused on the task at hand and looked for the trap door leading into the bar. Cracking it open, he looked inside to see Storn below him and behind the bar, a short sword in his hand as he stared at the door. A dozen other thieves, assassins, and rogues stood in the room, looking nervous as they waited.

Derik slipped through the opening and landed lightly behind Storn. For a moment, he resisted his need to show off, but a smirk crossed his lips, and he leaned over the guild master's back. "Boo."

Storn screamed and spun around.

The other thieves charged, but then slowed as Derik laughed.

"Sorry!"

"Derik!" Storn grabbed him in a tight hug. "Why the fuck are you here?"

"The baron."

Storn's face was pale as he took a deep breath. "The baron is further to the north, you know."

"Yeah, but I have to bribe a friend to help."

"Shiel?"

"Yeah, I need a quarter mil."

"I can't afford her, don't have that cash."

Derik's lips tightened, then the room shuddered as someone pounded on the door. "Oi! Let me in, its cold! My tits are snapping off!"

The members of the thief guild stared at the door in shock. One crossed his heart while another circled hers, two signs of praying for a god.

Then Shiel pounded on it again. "Oi!"

"Let her in," said Derik.

One of the brutes turned him. "Are you fucking nuts? There are fifty out there!"

"There is one, and she's pissy. Open the damn door!"

The brute looked at Storn who nodded cautiously. Shaking, the brute inched up to the door and flung it open.

Shiel, coated from head to toe in blood, stepped into the bar and shook herself like a dog. Derik managed to duck under the bar in time to avoid being splattered, but everyone else made various noises of disgust until she stopped. Behind her, the street was a slaughter house of bodies, blood, and gore.

Bouncing happily, Shiel stepped further into the bar, then her eyes grew wide. A squeal escaped her lips as she gestured to the bar. "Wine!"

Derik stood up and turned Storn toward him. The older man looked nervous as he glanced back at Shiel.

"Look, Storn, you remember three years ago, when all that shit went down?"

Storn nodded and stepped back to lean against the counter. "Yeah?"

"You said there were two ways for me to make some money. One of them was the Eye of Hamel. The other was avoiding Shiel for a month," Derik winced as Shiel cracked the top off an expensive bottle. He didn't look at her.

Storn swallowed hard, sweat dripping down his brow. "Yeah?"

"I think it was two hundred?"

Storn frowned, then swallowed again. "Two-twenty, for the two months. No, please not the Ruffo 56."

He winced as Shiel shattered another three bottles.

Derik let himself follow the gaze and groaned.

Shiel stood with one foot on the bar and the other on a shelf, plucking bottles from the top shelf with a gleeful look. She glared at him and tossed a bottle aside. In her hands, she held a dozen bottles easily as she continued to inspect the expensive, dust-covered wines.

Storn groaned and turned away, there was a tear in his eyes. "Yeah, I remember that bet."

"Who put out that job?"

"Why?"

"I told you, I need a quarter mil."

Storn frowned. "Why are you doing this?"

"Trust me, please?"

He nodded, "I did say any time, didn't I? Fine."

Storn turned around and looked up at the stealing silfae. "Excuse me?"

"Yeah? What the fuck do you want?"

"Money?" Storn held out his hand.

Shiel glared at him, then at Derik. Then, she shrugged. "Didn't think I'd need it, he never asked for it."

Derik froze, then glared at his friend. "You put up that bounty?"

She grinned, "Yeah, wanted the challenge. Figures a cross-dressing pussy was the only one to make it."

"Fine, then write an IOU."

"Yeah, whatever, I owe you."

Storn turned back. "What is this about?"

Derik tapped his fingers against the bar. "Say, Storn, can I borrow some money?"

"Let me guess, forty thou?"

"Um..."

Storn chuckled, "I do get ten percent of your bounties, you know that."

Derik struggled for a moment, but then nodded. "Yeah, I'll pay you back. I promise. Forty. Hurry?"

"Fine, that I have on me." He dug behind the bar and pulled out a thick bundle of marks. Some of the bills were stained with blood.

Derik hugged him tightly. "Thank you."

"Going to explain this?"

"Yeah, really easy."

Derik slipped around the guild master and walked up to Shiel.

She dropped a bottle at his feet, which shattered and splattered him with wine. "Crappy stuff."

"Shiel?"

"Yeah?" she said distractedly.

He held up the money from Storn.

She tucked a bottle in her mouth and grabbed it. Looking down, she muttered around the glass. "What for?"

"With your IOU, that is a quarter mil."

"Yeah, so?"

"Shiel, I want to contract you to kill Rick Thrantas."

Shiel's head slowly turned to look down at him as the thieves gasped in surprise.

A bottle fell from her hand, splattering Derik with wine.

Then another.

And a third.

Then, he heard a tiny, familiar squeal of pleasure as Shiel orgasmed.

Being Tender

"So, got a plan, Derik?"

They raced along the rooftops, him and Shiel. He led the way, his hair streaming behind him, finding the safe spots for the slightly less agile Shiel to land. "Not really."

She said nothing for a few buildings, then they came up to the palace walls. A dozen men guarded the gate, with weapons drawn and torches to push back the winter darkness.

Both Shiel and Dark stopped in the shadows, neither of them breathing hard from their efforts.

Shiel dripped blood on the snow, staining it with the taint of death. None of it was hers, but he suspected some of it was wine.

Derik stared at the guards.

"People are going to die, Derik."

"I know, Shiel."

"You will probably die."

He closed his eyes and nodded.

"Why do this?" she grumbled.

"Love."

"Heard of it, overrated emotion that turns your brains to shit."

"And yet you are still here," he grinned.

Shiel glared at him. "I don't love you."

Derik smiled at her. "Prove it, you soft-hearted bitch."

In the shocked silence, he ran toward the palace wall.

Shiel let out a growl and leaped high into the air. Her strength easily carried her into the midsts of the guards and brought her enchanted sword down hard on the heads of two of them. Before she hit the ground, her daggers flew out to impale the throats of three more defenders.

Derik focused on his own task, jumping to the wall and scrambling up. He spotted an archer in one of the towers and slid behind him, grabbing him and twisting his wrist hard. The man screamed as his hand broke and Derik jumped out, plummeting to the ground on the inside of the walls.

Beyond the heavy wooden door, he heard the screams of agony and bloodshed. Then, the archer from the second crashed to the snow-covered cobblestones. Derik swallowed at the sight of his broken face and the helm next to him, with a second head sticking out of the opening. The look of horror would have given anyone nightmares but Derik had seen Shiel fight before.

He forced himself to lurch forward and throw the gate lever. With a grumble and squeal of gears, the gate opened to reveal the blood-drenched warrior grinning happily. She cut the last man's throat and stormed forward.

"I want a challenge," she declared. "These guys are pathetic."

"Don't worry, Rick is inside."

"Finally, a real man to beat up. Then maybe we'll hate fuck?"

Derik was pretty sure Shiel was talking about Rick, not him.

It took them a few minutes to reach the palace itself. As they crested a hill, their feet crunching ice-covered gravel, they heard fighting. Derik scanned the battlefield and then froze.

Only four people were left standing. Truk, looked on as Bruk and Gluk fought one of the baron's guards. The lone warrior fought with surprising skill, but Derik could tell that he was exhausted and losing.

From a thirty meters away, he recognized the warrior as his lover: Tornsin.

Derik's breath came out in a fog of ice. He stumbled forward.

Shiel let out a disgusted noise and charged forward, screaming at the top of her lungs as blood splattered in all directions. She left behind a trail of gore.

Gluk knocked Tornsin to the ground, and Bruk raised his bloody sword to strike, but Shiel slammed into him, throwing him ten meters.

Derik's heart stopped, but he raced forward as Tornsin scrambled out of the way of Gluk and raised his shaking weapon.

Truk watched the fight for a moment, then stepped back. As Tornsin and Shiel attacked her brothers, she raised her hands and began to chant. Tiny symbols appeared in the air around her, forming a circle of flickering flame. The air warped around her body as she chanted quickly, powering some eldritch spell. The snow melted in a circle around her, and he skittered to a halt.

He desperately looked for a way to distract her, but he found only bodies and swords. Swallowing, he considered grabbing one of them, but his body shook as his mother's promise bound him far tighter than the fear of death.

Shiel cackled happily, slamming her sword toward Bruk with brutal grace. The wall behind him shattered as he managed to parry most of her blows. A few lines streaked his dark skin.

Tornsin, on the other hand, struggled to defend himself against the other brother, and Derik wished he could help the desperate, fighting man.

He made a decision. Grabbing a dead guard's still-sheathed sword, he yanked the blade out. His body burned with conviction as he tossed the blade away. Snatching the wire used to peacebond the weapon, he twisted it. The wire bit into his fingers, drawing blood, but he ignored the pain and kept working until it broke off. Working desperately, he jammed it into the pin hole of his iron collar and started to pick it.

Truk's eyes focused on him as she chanted, more of the circle filling in with the arcane symbols as power rolled off her body.

Derik, sweat dripping down his brow, worked frantically at the collar. He had an idea of how to stop her, but he wasn't entirely sure it would work.

It became a race between the two. As they worked, the melee centered between them, blocking a direct route between mage and thief.

When the lock clicked, he nearly fell over. Yanking it off, a sense of relief flooded through him. He had forgotten what it was like not to have the weight around his collar.

Both thriban brothers blocked his route to Truk, but Derik charged between them. "Shiel!" he yelled.

The warrior spun around and saw him running into battle. It only took her a second as she jumped straight up and slammed her sword down into the ground. It vibrated loudly as her hands left it. Leaving it behind, she spun around and punched Bruk hard in the gut. Metal armor peeled back from the blow, and she brought up her bloody fist with a grin.

He shuddered as his feet scraped the gravel.

She didn't give him a chance to recover as she jerked forward and started pounding him with hands and fists, cackling just as happily as her body blurred with her rapid-fire series of attacks.

Derik hopped on the hilt of the sword and jumped straight up. His body flipped as he leaped over the upper edge arcane ring of power. His duster caught fire as power scorched him. Landing heavily behind Truk, he reached out and snapped the collar around her neck.

"Shiel, activate this!"

Truk spun around, her yellowed eyes wide with surprise.

The warrior looked up, punched Bruk across the throat and screamed loudly. "Shock!"

The collar in Derik's hand ignited into a terrible force, throwing him back as Truk let out a terrible scream. Her body shuddered as she collapsed to the ground. Her spell wavered for a moment, then tore itself apart into a hell storm that brought more screams from the mage.

At the same time, Bruk and Gluk both let out terrified screams of their own as they collapsed to the ground. A spiderweb of energy connected the triplets as the collar's power rippled through their telepathic connection.

Shiel stepped back, panting. Then, she grinned. "Shock!"

All three screamed out as the collar activated and lighting arced between the three thribans.

She bounced for a moment, giggling as she clapped her hands like a little girl. Her mouth opened and she screamed out as loudly as she could. "Shock! Shock! Shock! Shock!"

The three thriban's let out an inhuman scream as their connection tore into them. The collar sparkled and burned, searing Truk's flesh and sharing the pain between all three of them.

"Shiel!"

"Shock! Fuck, yes! Shock!"

"Shiel! Stop it!"

"Shock! Burn you bastards! Shock!"

Derik snarled as he stormed forward. Jumping over the spasming form of Bruk, he slapped her hard across the face.

Shiel didn't seem to notice the blow. She blinked and looked at him. "What?" she asked as if it was a normal to have her face slapped.

Derik spun around as Bruk tried to push himself up. His face was bloody and bruised. Two ribs stuck out of his armor, where Shiel had tore apart the metal. Ignoring Shiel's moan of pleasure, he knelt down in the snow and blood. "Bruk."

The thriban shuddered, right on the edge of consciousness.

"You were nice to me once. You showed me a bit of kindness. I'm returning the favor. Go home."

"I—"

"Go home," commanded Derik, "or I'll let Shiel kill you and your siblings right here and now."

He nodded once, and Shiel glared at him disappointedly.

Derik stood up, not looking at his friend. He spoke in a hard voice. "Shiel, Rick is inside."

In a flash, he saw her sprinting inside, her enchanted sword flashing behind her.

Derik stood up painfully to watch Bruk crawling toward his sister.

Gluk groaned with pain.

Derik turned and realized Tornsin was holding the sword over the thriban back. "Tornsin!" he gasped, "Love? Please don't."

Tornsin looked over at Derik, then did a double-take. "D-Derik?"

Opponent forgotten, Tornsin dropped the sword and ran to Derik. Derik let out a sob as he opened his arms to catch his lover in a tight hug.

"Derik!"

Tears ran down their cheeks as they embraced, holding each other tightly.

"I thought I would never see you again."

From inside the palace came the sound of stone shattering and a scream of rage drifted through the broken windows.

Derik shuddered and squeezed his lover tightly. "Not now, we have to save the baron."

Tornsin nodded and wiped the tears from his eyes. He opened his mouth, then ran his finger down the side of Derik's chin. "You are still so beautiful. I missed you so much."

Derik's heart floated into the heavens. He wanted to kiss Tornsin, to strip him and fuck him right there. Three years of longing condensed to a single moment of relief with the power of an orgasm.

Then Shiel ruined it by flying out of the palace door and slamming into them. Snarling, she screamed loudly as she scrambled to her feet. "You don't fucking throw me!"

Blurring, she sprinted back into the palace. At the door, she grabbed her sword and yanked it out of the stone wall before disappearing inside.

Alarmed, Derik raced after her.

Behind him, Tornsin snatched his weapon from the ground and followed.

Inside the hall, Derik stumbled. The first thing he saw was Sherrel's body, sprawled out on the floor in a puddle of blood. Grief crashed into him as he saw her torn open gut and the tears that still soaked her terrified face. Then, his eyes beheld the terrible battle.

Shiel's blade cut through the air, leaving glowing streaks of magic. Rick's blade left a burning trail as it snapped up, catching the blade and shoving her back. In that moment between strikes, Derik could see dark flames along the blade and ghostly, screaming faces in the embers. The entire thing stank of death and magic.

Derik swallowed as Tornsin raced up to him. His eyes locked on Rick himself. The former crime lord looked both stronger and more enraged than Derik had ever seen him. His plate armor glowed with the same necromantic fire as his sword. Every strike against

Shiel's weapon brought ghostly flames in gouts of energy. Despite the weight, he moved easily as he jumped and bobbed around her attacks, matching her own with his own terrible speed and force.

Behind the terrible battle, he saw Hamel standing in the center of a ring of power. Six men in dark robes chanted loudly, surrounding him and holding him in place.

Derik's heart leapt at the sight of the baron, but he hesitated when he saw Hamel's skin rippling and boiling, like some terrible creature was trying to burst from the baron's chest.

Fighting back the tears, he spun to look at Tornsin. "We have to stop them."

Nodding curtly, the guard broke right around Shiel and Rick. Derik sprinted around the left side. As he passed the fighters, he looked up to see the Eye of Hamel glowing above. The glass map was destroyed, and one statue slumped against the wall. What remained carefully balanced on the other statues.

Shiel sheared through another column, and Rick left a bleeding line across her side. Screaming out in rage, she punched her sword clear through the meter-thick column and slammed it into Rick's side. Metal screamed out in agony as the enchanted blade cut deeply.

Derik forced his attention to the mages. They chanted loudly, their attention focused on the baron.

Hamel bellowed in anger and pain as he collapsed to his knees. Claws shoved from his chest, deforming his body before sliding back inside. The brilliant sapphire eye glowed brightly, searingly intense as the Eye above the battle.

Even with his promise not to kill, Derik still knew how to stop a mage. Padding up to the first one, he reared back and kicked with all his might into the back of the wizard's knee. The sound of snapping bone rang out loudly in the room and the mage collapsed to the ground, screaming in agony.

Rage burned in Derik as he stormed toward the next mage.

The robed figure glanced at him, then did a double take. Yanking himself away from the spell, he spun to face Derik.

Raw magick burst around them as the spell shattered. Black lighting, backlash, shot out to a third mage. It lit her up from the inside, her bones briefly visible before she burst into flames. The fourth mage ignited at the same time, but the last two remained standing.

One of the surviving mages, his body smoking, bellowed out a quick spell and three spheres of force slammed into Derik.

Derik staggered back and snarled as he recovered. "Shiel hits me harder than that!"

He sprinted forward as the mage backed away in fear. Grabbing the mage's arm, Derik twisted hard and threw him over his shoulder. As the body hit the ground, he wrenched with all his might until he heard the muted pop of the limb being dislocated.

Derik stepped back to kick him, but Tornsin blocked him and drove the sword into the man's throat, killing him instantly.

Seeing death so close, from someone so tender, brought a wave of nausea. He fought against it, panting hard. "I always hate that. Setting them up for the kill."

His eyes drifted toward the baron as Tornsin looked around. Then, the guard shoved him roughly to the side as a body blew past them, slamming hard into the wall behind them.

Derik spun around as Shiel slid to the ground, her body covered in fresh blood. "Shiel!"

Without looking to see what Tornsin would do, he raced toward his friend. At her body, he dropped to his knees in fear.

Shiel was hurt.

The bounty hunter opened one eye, her other sealed shut from a cut that ran down her face. "Well, fuck, that stings."

Derik patted her, looking for a healing potion, but he couldn't find any. "Shit, shit. Shiel, stay with me."

The slender berserker coughed, and blood splattered against Derik.

He whimpered. "S-Shiel?"

"Figures. I'd find the perfect guy," she coughed violently and tried to stand up. Her leg slipped and she slumped down to the ground, "and he ends up killing me."

Tears burned at Derik's cheeks. "You aren't dead yet."

"Y-Yeah, I know," she shuddered, "but between the death magic, curses, poison, that damn dagger in my gut, and the bruises, I think I'm losing."

She closed her eye as a shudder slammed into her. "Oh yeah, the sword cuts hurt too."

Derik screamed loudly, "Damn it, don't die on me!"

Her eye snapped open and she glared at him. "You're such a fucking pussy."

"Yeah, I know," he sniffed.

"I don't like you."

"You lie."

He pressed his hands against her, trying to find some way of picking her up but his hands just slipped off from her blood.

Shiel coughed violently and clutched her side. "Fuck, that hurts!"

"Shiel?"

Her green eye focused on him. "Why the fuck did I fall for you?"

Derik froze, "W-What?"

"You are a submissive little pussy, why do I love you?"

"No, no," he whispered, shaking his head in denial, "you don't love me."

"You lie," she choked out.

"Shiel!"

He held her tightly as the tears burned hotly down his face. Sobbing, he shook with the grief that plunged him into darkness.

Shiel coughed suddenly, "You're doing it wrong."

"What?"

"Healing."

He pulled back, feeling her blood hot on his cheek. Looking down, he saw a flickering yellow-green light forming around his hands. "Fucking priest, can't even heal right."

Hope and shock stunned Derik as he stared at his glowing hands. "W-What? How?"

"Oi, maybe. I-I heard they say you have to be a gate, to just let it," she coughed violently, pressing her slender, shaking body to his palms, "let it flow through you. Not that I know what healers do. I just buy potions."

Derik whimpered as he knelt in her blood, trying to release himself. When the healing energies flowed and her wounds slowly knitted together, he let out a sob of hope.

Shiel's body shuddered violently as she was jerked out of his hands.

He looked up to see Rick's necromantic blade buried in Shiel's chest, right through her heart. His mouth opened as surprise, shock, and terror wracked his body. Trembling, he followed the blade up to see Rick snarling above him. His body vibrated with rage. Rick's face was coated in blood, hundreds of cuts that scored clear to the bone. His jaw worked powerfully and the thief could hear teeth grinding together as he panted.

"O-Oi!"

Derik's head snapped back to look at Shiel. She glared up at Rick as she shook. "I-I was," her voice started to grow soft, "I was being tender here... asshole."

"I don't care," came Rick's growl.

"W-Well, I do." She swallowed. "S-so, fuck off!"

Derik could only watch as Shiel wrenched herself to the right, tearing open her own heart. With a grunt of rage and anger, she punched the side of his sword with the last of her strength. Her hand shattered on the blade but the weapon cracked from the impact. Flames hissed out of the fractures that formed along the steel. With a snarl, she drew back and punched it again. The force of the blow shattered the enchanted sword, and Derik's world turned black as the necromantic blade exploded.

Bitter Memories

He couldn't breathe.

He couldn't speak.

He couldn't see.

Derik fumbled in the aftereffects of the explosion: the acidic wind tore through his duster, magic popped and hissed all around him, and his heart continued to pound in his chest. He bit his tongue against the pain and forced himself to rage against it. The tears of Shiel's death ripped from his face but he managed to stand up.

Something cold plunged into his chest.

He opened his eyes.

In the maelstrom of power streaming out in all directions, he saw ghostly faces rise from the shattered remains of the blade. Spectral hands reached out for him, the claws of the dying sinking into his skin. Derik shuddered as the icy cold fingers disappear into him.

He looked down but saw nothing as the distinct sensation of having a sword yanked out of his chest and then plunged into his stomach branded across his senses. Despite being unable to see it, his nerves reported with terribly clarity the spilling of his organs out across his fingers and a weakness that sucked away his life.

Confused, he bent over in pain as the spectral blade cut into him again. Every blow was a fatal one, but only across his mind's eye. Somehow, he managed to survive each attack but his sanity began to crumble under the onslaught.

A shifting brightness caught his attention. He looked up, straining with every movement, to see a translucent Sherrel before him.

She smiled at him, tears sparkling in her ethereal body. Moving in silence, she reached out to bring his lips to hers, kissing him softly as she grew more transparent with each passing second.

"S-Sherrel?" His voice choked.

Hands reached around to take her wrists. A kiss flared up along her left wrist as a body interposed itself between Derik and the spirit. He looked up to catch a brief sight of liquid eyes the color of the warmest wood, then Bridget drew Sherrel away to safety.

Derik reached out for them, the grief consuming him, and shuddered as he felt another sword pierce his body, tearing him in half. Looking down, he saw another ghost passing through them, then a second. Each one forced Derik to relive their own death before they scattered to the five winds. In his mind's eye, he saw the heralds of the gods taking the faithful away and those without gods just fading into nothing.

Tears splashed down his cheeks as he watched them.

Then, one last ghost stood before him.

Shiel glared at him for a moment, her mouth working as she tried to find the words. Then, she flicked him off. Reaching down, her ghostly fingers wrapped around the hilt of the shattered necromantic sword. Picking it up, hellish flames of red seared up the blade and colored her spirit with the rage of a berserker. Her eyes glowed a blood red and she stepped forward, raising the blade to strike at Derik.

He tried to stumble back away from her. His body almost collapsed with Shiel's death searing across his mind and memories. There was no time or memories to fade the startling clear feeling of her heart being pierced, then torn in half.

Shiel spun on her heels and stalked away. Unlike the others, she didn't fade into nothingness and no herald came for her spirit. She just... walked away.

Suddenly he couldn't breathe again.

Reality rushed back to slam into him. Someone had a bar across his throat and he struggled to breathe. His feet kicked against the ground.He kicked out and winced at the pain of his ankle hitting solid metal.

"Hamel!" roared Rick from behind Derik. His armor burned into Derik's skin.

Derik's eyes snapped open as Rick hauled him forward.

The baron looked up from where he crouched over Tornsin's body.

When Tornsin rolled over, there was blood everywhere. The sight of it ripped at Derik's heart and he choked louder as sorrow flooded his mind.

"Hamel!" repeated Rick.

Hamel stood up, a mask of rage burning on his face. His one eye glowed brightly, a searing light that no mortal could have.

"We end this, baron. We end this now."

Hamel reached down and picked up Tornsin's blade.

Derik watched him with bright eyes, feeling the pressure grinding down on his neck, choking off his breath.

Hamel circled.

Then, the tip of a blade pressed against Derik's neck, right against the pounding artery in his throat. "Stop," commanded Rick.

Hamel froze.

Rick grinned. "We aren't fighting, Hamel. No, I'm not going to risk it. I saw what a monster you are."

The baron's face tightened as he squeezed the hilt of his blade until his knuckles popped.

Rick just chuckled. "I found the body of your wife too, or should I say your... mate. I saw what you did to her. I saw that corpse, and she gave me the blade that bitch just broke."

Derik whimpered and looked up.

Rick glanced down and his face spasmed as he glared at Derik. "To think I lost everything for you."

He snarled and bore down on Derik's throat, threatening to crush it. "I will never make that mistake again."

Rick's eyes snapped back to Hamel. "No, she made me promise this. Hamel, kill yourself."

"Never!" roared the baron.

Derik whimpered as the blade jabbed him in the throat. "Yes, or you'll see me cut the throat your lover. And you'll see him bleed to death before your eyes."

Staring at the baron, Derik tried to break free. His foot snaked around to catch Rick's but the larger man just ground down on his throat until he gasped for breath. The familiar burn in his lungs and tears in his eyes returned as he struggled for air.

"Now!"

"You'll just kill him too, Rick." Hamel's voice was hoarse and wheezing.

"Do you want to see another of your loves dying? Do you want to see the second of your true loves die with their throat ripped out?"

Hamel snapped back, "He isn't my true love!"

Despair tore into Derik. Rick wrenched him back, but then froze as Hamel let out a terrible scream. His eye burst into sapphire flames and his skin peeled back. Clawing at his face, the baron's body swelled suddenly, then peeled like a banana. Derik had the impression of some terrible creature bursting out of the baron's body, with shocking white fur and a large, curled horn in its forehead.

The creature stepped forward, swelling up to three meters in height, then four. Its head turned down to glare at Rick and a deep growl rose from its throat. One eye burned with sapphire flames and the other was a gaping wound. Derik whimpered as he stared up at the terrible face, suddenly realizing that the Eye of Hamel wasn't a magically created sphere, but the actual eye of the baron, the creature who pretended to be his lover.

The baron's voice came from the beast, deeper and rumbling. "No!" His roar contained the same power and presence that made Derik's insides twist with lust and fear. He grew hot inside, but instead of focusing on his cock, it spread out to his limbs. Flames burst along Derik's body, not touching his clothes but growing rapidly hotter.

Rick swore and loosened his grip.

Kicking back violently, Derik caught him in the knee and slipped out, sprinting away as the warrior stared up at the powerful form of Hamel.

Huge claws, the color of the finest marble, stretched out of massive paws. Derik stumbled and fell, twisting backwards to crawl away from Hamel as he stood up to his full height of five meters. His eyes glanced down to see the massive shaft that hung between his legs, swollen and half-hard.

Hamel stepped forward, and the entire room shook from the impact.

Rick laughed angrily. "All those fucking mages, all those spells to find your true form, and all I had to do was make you lie!? If I knew that, I would have done it years ago! Everyone knows you love Derik. Everyone knows you've pined over that cock whore ever since you kicked him out!"

He laughed, the same insane cackle Derik remembered from his auction.

Derik shivered at the memory of it and looked around. He didn't know what to do.

Returning his attention to the center, he watched as Rick tossed aside his short sword and snatched Shiel's blade from the ground. It hummed violently, but he twisted his hands around the hilt. "Now, I can kill you, Hamel. In this form, you are mortal."

With a scream of rage, Rick attacked the creature. The blade flashed and it cut deep.

Hamel roared, shaking the walls and ceiling. He slammed his hand down.

Rick parried it, but the force of the blow drove him to his knees. With a surge of strength, he threw off Hamel's claws and punched forward, burying the blade to the hilt in the creature's wrist. He twisted the blade and yanked it out. Blood, sapphire and black, burst out from the wound, and Hamel staggered back.

Derik couldn't focus on both fights. He looked back and forth rapidly until he caught sight of Tornsin. With his throat tightening, he ran to his lover and slid to his knees. He checked for a pulse. To his surprise and utter relief, Tornsin was alive and breathing raggedly. Derik closed his eyes and opened himself up to Bridget, feeling the healing energies rising and flowing through his palms. His body grew hot as the energy sank into the guard, but as he thought about it, it sputtered then stopped. Whimpering, he looked down to see Tornsin relaxing as he fell unconscious.

The battle raged across the hall, shattering columns and tearing apart the ceiling. The white creature Hamel slammed down, slashing open Rick's armor, but Rick's attack cut clear to the bone of the immense monster.

As Rick jammed down into Hamel's side, Hamel threw him up into the air. The blade left a streak of light behind it as Rick flipped over and landed heavily. However, Derik's eyes focused on the flickering light of the Eye of Hamel. He saw it vibrating angrily, burning with flames inside.

He didn't know why he started, but he raced for it. Climbing up the broken statue, he steeled himself for when the acidic trap activated, but little could shield him from liquid that burned his feet. He staggered as he found purchase, then jumped with all his strength to catch another statue, then a third, before flinging himself over the battle to grab an arm. The greenish-yellow flash that coursed along the arm warned him of the trap, and he screamed as acid burned into his fingers. Gasping for breath, he forced himself to crawl up on the statue's arm. The acid burned at his legs, thighs and hands as he staggered to his feet. Faltering and nearly losing his balance, he reached out for the Eye. It burned brightly, rocking back and forth as it screamed out in rage. The magical light that speared through scattered everywhere.

Derik hesitated before grabbing it, feeling the burning heat from the sphere and the acid eating away at his soles. He snarled and grabbed it with both hands.

A memory of himself.

A silent image of him grabbing the sphere, swinging across the room to replace the Eye of Hamel. Derik forced the sphere's memories away and then gasped as he lost his balance.

Spinning in the air, he plummeted to the ground. As the floor raced up to him, he saw a flash of black and flame as Rick knelt below him and jammed up with his sword.

Derik screamed out as he saw the tip of the weapon right before it punched into his stomach. Agony tore through him as he slid down the blade to land heavily at the hilt.

Images of Shiel's death ran through his mind as he fought against the pain, feeling the blade twisting in his gut. He sobbed as he tried to do something.

Rick smiled grimly. "I told you I would end you, Derik."

His hand grabbed the burning Eye of Hamel.

Derik pulled it back despite the heated crystal melting flesh and bone. It was more pain than he had ever experienced, but he locked his hand tightly on the sphere.

Rick's triumphant smile faltered as he tried to pry the Eye from Derik.

Derik glared at him, blood flecking his lips. "Fuck off."

Rick chuckled, "Not from you."

He twisted the blade in Derik's gut.

Derik shuddered from the pain, then forced himself to work past it. It wasn't much different than being caned by Rick or being abused by monsters when Shiel used him as bait.

The Eye flashed. The memories in his head grew hazy.

Suddenly, Rick shuddered. A flicker of surprise crossed his face, and he twisted his back as if he was in sudden pain. The moment passed. He tightened his grip and tried to yank it out again.

Derik's blood poured out of his gaping wound. It sheeted down the blade before splashing on the ground. He stared at it, dazed and confused.

A strange thought drifted through his mind, an interruption of a happy moment from Rick's point of view as the man cheerfully planned the attack. He was about to draw something on the map when he knocked over his soup. The hot liquid scalded his hand.

Derik shuddered as his own hand burned. He looked down to see a red mark appear right where Rick had burned himself in the memories.

A wave of nausea and weakness crashed into him. He choked and blood poured out of his mouth, the coppery taste sticking to the back of his throat.

He thought about the image and wondered if the Eye could transfer memories and sensations. His thinking fell into a groove, as if the Eye was guiding his thoughts.

The Eye flashed and a new memory came flowing from Rick and into Derik. It was some night in an inn. Rick had just penetrated a whore's cunt and his cock was firmly sheathed into her clenching pussy. Her cries turned him on as he grabbed her hips and prepared to thrust.

Derik couldn't tell that the memories were any different than his physical body. His cock grew wet as if he was buried inside her pussy. He could feel the curve of her ass and hips in his palm.

He smiled then coughed again. It could be the blood loss but he was willing to try. Taking a deep breath and choking on the coppery stench, he focused on the most painful memory he could recall.

A memory rose, the agony from the shock of Shiel's collar. The echoes of her voice screaming "Shock!" burned through him.

A bolt of agony coursed through him.

Then Rick shuddered from the same memory. His body jerked violently as a black scorch line formed around his neck. He had never worn Shiel's collar, but Derik could feel the electric surge coursing through their bodies.

The memory faded but the dark line remained.

Derik's mouth gaped open as he stared at the angry eyes. He let a fierce smile cross his lips as he held on the sphere tightly with both hands and buried himself into his memories. The world growing dim, Derik focused on the three days when Rick tortured him. Thanks to the Eye, he could recall every blow of the cane and cut that scored his body. He sank into them, his body heating up as he relived the torture.

The sphere grew brighter, the light spearing through both of their hands until their bones were visible.

Rick shuddered again as a line appeared on his forehead, bleeding sluggishly.

Derik gasped with the effort. He coughed up more blood and then snapped at Rick, "Fuck off."

With all his willpower, he threw himself into the nightmares. He forced himself to relive the pain of his rape, the constant beatings of the cane. Three days of agony as fast as he could handle it. As he did, lines of red appeared across Rick's face and body. The warrior shuddered from the pain, and Derik just dredging up more memories, the memories of being torn open and having his skin being split open. He added brutal choke-fucking and anal rape. He layered the countless memories of his balls being crushed, whipped, and beaten.

Rick screamed out as Derik let the floodgates of suffering rip open in his mind, and they both relived everything that had happened to Derik over the years.

He didn't focus on the gentle touch or spanking, Madre's attempts to fist him or even Teri's fucking him. He just went directly into the pain and agony. He forced Rick to feel the humiliation and hunger of being raped, tearing him from the inside. Days of memories compressed into a single second. As he passed through them, Derik just found more. Pain of his time with Shiel, the fighting and the monsters. The sensations of being drained to an inch of his life by vampires and the acidic spells that burned his skin.

Rick's body suffered the same wounds he did. Every passing second, the Eye of Hamel grew brighter and Derik just fed it more memories.

Rick gasped at the pain, his face and body bleeding from the inside. He started to whisper a spell, his incredible will keeping his voice steady as his insides tore. Hellish flames rose around his body.

Derik drew up more memories. Of Rick's cock choking him, tearing open his throat as he was raped. Tears splashing down his cheeks, Derik held that memory in his head and held his breath, hearing Rick choking as his face turned to fear then blue with the need for air.

Derik shuddered from the intensity, but he could stand it. He could handle more pain than Rick.

Then, he let the new memories drive into him. The exact pain of Sherrel's death, the feeling of her gut being ripped open by his sword. He tugged on the memories of the ghosts, the people who

Rick slaughtered, and shoved them into his rapist. Blood splashed down as Rick was torn apart, pouring out of the cracks of his armor and hissing as it hit the ground.

Just as the world grew dim, Derik pulled on one final memory. The memory of Shiel's death, the terrible recollection of having her own heart torn out.

Rick froze, his mouth gaping in shock and pain. Blood burbled up from his lips and his eyes grew unfocused. With painful slowness, Derik's rapist fell back to the ground, yanking the sword from the former thief's stomach as he died.

Derik clutched his side as he staggered to his feet. He could feel the hot blood pouring down through his fingers. He struggled to force words from his broken throat. "Damn my promise. Rick, I will never wash your blood from my hands."

He spat on Rick's corpse. Then, his eyes rolled up into his head, and he crumpled to the ground.

True Love

Curling up in a fetal position, Derik gasped for life as it poured out of his stomach. The fierce joy of killing Rick passed quickly as he worried about surviving. Panting, he forced himself to push everything aside, asking Bridget silently for healing.

Warmth flooded through him, pooling in his torn stomach as he smelled the cinnamon and tasted Bridget on his tongue. A song drifted right at the edge of his hearing, Phoenix Falling, and he smiled.

He was going to live.

Derik knew he wasn't healing himself right. He could feel his organs twisting and sealing into place, a stuffed feeling that should have been and a pressure where the blood pooled inside him. Flesh stitched back over his fingers, hiding away bone but he could feel scars forming as he healed himself inexpertly.

When Bridget gave him enough strength, he shuddered violently trying to straighten. He could feel things tearing inside him, healed in the wrong place, but he just let the yellow-green glow fill him, repairing himself as he struggled to his hands and knees.

Looking up, he saw Hamel screaming. Claws scraped against the ceiling and fists pounding against the walls. Insane, the creature slammed against the columns, shattering one, then the other. The burning blue eye stared out into nothing as he grabbed one of the statues. The flash of the acid trap activated and smoke rose from the white fur, but the creature just threw it down.

Derik swallowed as it crashed less than a meter away from him. Dust and gore blew past him as it crushed Rick's form, but he couldn't move to avoid it.

Gasping for breath and choking on the dust, he saw the Eye of Hamel roll toward him. Reaching out with his hand, it bounced once and flew up into his palm.

Memories.

A vision slammed into him, and he found himself in a deep forest, staring into the endless green with furious rage in his heart. This time, he heard the same anger-filled howl assaulting his physical ears in the present. The vision turned around, looking at a path of destruction meters across. He could see shattered stones and the bodies of animals in Hamel's wake.

The vision blurred, moving back rapidly in time until it focused on Hamel again, this time ripping the throat out of a black-furred creature just like himself. They fought with furious rage, tearing at each other. The battle in reverse time was terrifying, both in the sheer power and also the senseless destruction.

The memories of the Eye blurred again, this time running forward, year after year, the seasons flashing by as Hamel raged across the earth. Then, the short Copir silfae from before. The old man found him as Hamel perched on a mountain, sobbing crystalline tears. Derik heard them speaking, somehow knowing what they said but not understanding the words.

A promise.

Forgiveness.

Finding love again.

And a terrible curse.

The Eye tried to bring Derik into the memory of being plucked from Hamel's eye socket, but the vision snapped when powerful claws picked up Derik like a rag, shaking him violently.

The pressure ground down, and Derik opened himself to Bridget for healing, regenerating as fast as the creature crushed him. His insides tore as the insane monster drew back and threw him with all his might into the ceiling of the palace.

Derik screamed shrilly, expecting his body to be nothing but bloody paste in a heartbeat. He threw his hands forward, and the Eye sliced air to hover in front of him. It flared brightly and a beam of light poured out of it, incinerating the ceiling and clearing the path for Derik. Derik's scream faded, echoing painfully as he shot through the searing tunnel to burst out through the palace roof.

Winter wind cut at his naked body as he shot high into the air. He briefly spotted someone in blue racing inside the palace, a magical light following them as they disappeared inside. Then, it was too late to see anything as the darkness enveloped him.

He heard the wind screaming as something loomed from below. He threw his hands in front of him, and the Eye of Hamel shielded him as a chunk of the ceiling hurtled toward him. It shattered on the Eye, dust and shards of stone cutting his face, chest, and legs.

He panted, unable to hear himself through the whistling wind.

A second, then a third hunk of ceiling flew at him, each one as large as a house. Each one shattered on the Eye as it blocked the blows. When Derik held up his hand, the Eye responded.

Gravity tugged on him, and his ascent slowed. Then, came the terrible sensation of hanging in air, far above everything, blind and naked in the darkness.

He fell.

The Eye raced down after him, turning into a streak of blue as he plummeted.

Derik started to curl up in a ball, to protect his face from the wind slashing at him, but then just forced himself to ignore the pain.

Something he was getting good at.

As he accelerated, the wind cut across him and opened up his wound.

He crashed through the falling debris of the ceiling. He covered his face, then screamed out loudly. "Bridget!"

Time slowed for a brief moment, then muscles in his back ripped and pulled away, a pain like nothing he ever experienced grabbed him and violently stopped him in mid-air. He gasped and shuddered. Blood poured from his body.

The Eye of Hamel came to a rest before him and brightened.

He felt his body moving but without his conscious thought. Every twitch and gesture brought a fresh agony. He could feel it as a burning across his chest.

Raising one shaking hand to his neck, he tried to find the source of the pain. His fingers brushed against his blackbird necklace as it melted into his skin, briefly adding to his torture.

Derik caught movement in his periphery, and turned. He gaped as he saw two huge black wings sprout from his back, glowing with divine energies of transformation. Every beat rippled through his back. They were attached to him.

"F-Fuck me, Bridget," he gasped.

His mind filled with understanding: how to fly, how to move, and how long he had before his energies ran out. He plummeted again. He also got the feeling that someone was in trouble, far below.

Biting his lip, he breathed a prayer to Bridget and dove. Seconds flew by as he accelerated, his new wings crashing against the air as wind and snow cut at his face.

As the light formed below, he could see Hamel tearing the entire ceiling off the great hall, throwing it aside as he demolished his palace. But now, he stood over a brightly glowing form. Derik's eyes focused on it, and he whimpered as he saw Hamel about to crush Hime as she healed Tornsin.

Her body shone from the inside, her hair rising on the waves of power, and the entire hall reflected the light of her divine healing.

Derik flew faster, holding out his hand as the Eye shifted in front of his palm. Curving out, he struggled with the unaccustomed limbs and flew in a low arc that brought him through the gaping entrance of the hall.

As Hamel's clawed fist came down, Derik and the Eye hit him the chest, throwing him back with incredible force and shattering the back wall of the hall with the impact. The creature rolled to his feet and howled in anger.

Derik snapped out his wings to stop and beat powerfully to keep himself aloft.

The life drained from him, sucked out by the energies needed to maintain his wings.

He released it and fell to the ground, gasping for breath as a wave of dizziness crushed him. The ground shook underneath him and he looked up to see Hamel charging.

Flinging his hand up, he directed the Eye of Hamel to block the coming blow. It did, but he and the sapphire sphere were thrown back ten meters to crash into the remains of a column. Derik peeled himself off, leaving more blood and skin on the stone.

He held out his hands, palms facing Hamel. The Eye positioned itself, glowing brightly as he prepared to defend himself from the creature who was once his lover.

Hamel jumped up, disappearing into the darkness.

Derik threw his hands up and braced himself as the white furred fists slammed down. His knees buckled, and he was driven into the tiles of the floor. Muscles screamed out in agony as Derik tried to recall some memory to stop him.

The pain of torture was gone, drained by Rick's death. The pain of the ghosts' deaths and even Shiel's final moment had become emotionless thoughts, there but with no more fire. As his knees began to buckle, Derik screamed out and tried to find some memory to use, the only weapons he had left.

He focused his thoughts on the baron himself. The man who he fell in love with. The not-insane lover that he fell for at first sight. He remembered that first night he saw him, the way his heart pounded frantically as he stood in front the baron. The shaking that consumed him as he lifted his eyes to look into that brilliant blue eye.

The creature froze in place.

With the last of his energy, Derik plunged into his thoughts, plundering every feeling of worship, awe, and lust for the baron. His body ignited with desperate desire as he recalled the club, being thrown in the table. The feelings of humiliation and excitement as the baron yanked up his dress, taking him without a concern for anything. He relived the time in the massage room, when the baron stroked his shaft for the first time. His breath came out as a fog as Derik closed his eyes and remembered.

The pressure of the creature released, and Derik slumped forward. Looking up, he saw the monstrous form shrinking.

It took all his energy to dredge up the memories. They were already worn thin from the years apart, the hunger fading as he relived them night after night, masturbating frantically in his cage.

He gave the baron those memories, the pang of loneliness and the desperate need to return.

The baron's form softened as the fur fell off and the claws disappeared into his palm. The injuries remained, bloody and angry, but it was the man he loved, not the creature he feared.

As he watched, barely able to stand, he saw the baron's body seal back up over the monster inside.

Derik ran out of thoughts. He just slumped forward, unable to take his eye away from Hamel as he sobbed. The horn on the man's head froze in place for a long time, then it withdrew as Hamel opened his eye and looked down at Derik without anger or rage, without hatred or insanity.

He knelt down in the rubble and gore to sweep Derik into a tight hug. Derik whimpered from the pain. He pushed it back to wrapped his arms around his one true love. "I-I don't want to leave."

Hamel let out a shuddering breath. "I don't want you to, ever... B-Blackbird."

"Promise me? Please?"

His lover only tensed for the slightest of moment. "I swear to you, Blackbird, I will never stop loving you. I love you, Derik, and I always have."

They held each other tightly despite the pain and agony. The feeling of being loved and comforted filled Derik. It was intense, a relief after so many years of pain.

Only a single emotion remained inside Derik. It burned as bright as Bridget's love, and it burned with the sapphire glow of his passion, his love, his destiny.

Choices

As he laid in the soft, comfortable bed, Derik decided that while winning back the man he loved was more than wonderful, combat healing should only be practiced by someone who actually knew how the body worked. He groaned in discomfort, trying to move his body, but his spine and lower muscles fused themselves into a single block and he had to be carried to the bed in Hamel's arms.

That part wasn't so bad.

He smiled as he remembered the kiss the large man had placed on his lips, but duties pulled him away, and he was left alone for hours. He couldn't move. He couldn't even scratch the maddening itch on his nose.

Every ache and pain reporting itself against his senses, he peered into the room. It smelled new and old at the same time, like a room set aside and never used. He frowned, feeling pretty useless.

"Well, don't you look comfortable."

Derik jumped and then winced as his body exploded in pain again. He whimpered and forced himself to relax as Madre and Wendi came into the room.

Both battle mages were injured, with bruises and cuts, but they had a glow about them as they circled the bed. Each one sat down next to him and Derik looked back and forth.

He tried to smile. "Um, hi."

Madre smiled warmly. She reached out to stroke his cheek. "I heard I have you to thank for all this."

Derik smiled up bashfully and scrunched his nose as the itch redoubled.

Wendi surprised him by reaching over and scratching her nails against the itch.

He smiled at her thankfully. "I hurt."

Madre chuckled, "I can see. You have enough regenerative damage going on that I felt the glow outside of the room."

Wendi rested her hands in her lap before she spoke in an unaccustomed softness. "Most battle mages never figure out how to use combat healing, I sure haven't"

Madre grinned, "And the first and only time I used it, I ended up in a brace for a month until they could chip my knees apart again."

Derik's eyes widened, "A-A month?"

Madre shook her head, "No, probably not. I heard Hime is coming up. There is a world of a difference between battle mages and healers. Just as you'll find there is a universe of difference between mages like us and a priest like you."

His mouth opened and Madre rolled her eyes before reaching over to close it.

"Yes, you are a priest. Between the Eye of Hamel floating outside your bedroom door, trying to be let in, and the blessings covering your body and the healing magic that you are still channeling, there really isn't a doubt."

"I-I, um, what?"

He looked over to Wendi, who nodded.

"Who would imagine that shitty little thief would end up a priest of a cross-dressing god," said his former financée with a wry smile.

"Look, Wendi, I'm—"

"Forgiven. Storn told me you talked. I agree with what he said."

He sighed, "I didn't mean for any of this."

Wendi leaned over him and kissed him on the lips. "Yet, I'm utterly thankful for everything you did. I'm falling for the baron as hard as you did, and once Rachi and I figured out our differences, I found a friend who finally understands me."

Madre rested a hand on Wendi's thigh. "Yeah, and has the same size corset too."

The two women shared a grin.

Derik found himself enjoying the sense of belonging. Then he looked up with a surprise. "Madre, what about Teri?"

"I had a location sensor on her, and I sent some guards with a compass to find her."

"Shiel's home resists location. Teri said the compass blew up and Teri burned her hand pretty badly. She also almost died of exposure."

Madre looked surprise and got up. "I better get her myself, is she okay?"

"Well, she got nasty frostbite, healed, and then Shiel punched her out."

She looked concerned as she hurried out of the room. She paused at the door, a smile quirking her lip. "That's ten."

Wendi followed casually after her, but she stopped halfway to the door. "Hey, Derik?"

"Yeah?"

"Thanks."

"For what?"

"For everything, I guess. I hated you so much, and then everything just changed."

"Yeah, I'm getting that a lot."

She turned and padded over to him. Reaching down, she kissed him on the lips.

He gasped at the touch, and she stroked his chest. "Maybe later, you and me will play again."

"That would be nice," he smiled.

She glared, "But if you fuck my mother again, baron or no baron, I will castrate you."

He could tell by her tone, the threat was serious. It didn't matter though, he has his baron. "Deal."

He watched as his former fiancée left him alone. As she closed the door, the Eye of Hamel swung into the room and hovered up to him. He groaned as he moved, patting the bed next to him. It streaked over and landed next to him. Rolling around, it bumped against him and settled into place.

Derik chuckled as he regarded it.

It rolled back and bumped him again.

"Okay, I forgive you too."

The flame in the sphere lit up for a second, then went dark.

"I never saw it do that," said Hamel from the door.

Derik looked up and his heart soared. He wanted to reach for him, but his joints locked up and he just contented himself with smiling. "Hel... hi."

Hamel walked into the room, his presence filling Derik with a hot warmth. "Good morning. I only have a minute, but I had to see you."

"How bad is it?"

"About a thousand dead, eight of the harem, and forty of my guards. Tornsin's mother—the captain of my estate guards—was killed in the battle, so I just promoted Tornsin in her place. He earned it."

"Is he okay?"

Hamel nodded and leaned over to kiss Derik.

The thief bent his head back, and then moaned from the electric surge coursing through him. It filled him with such passion and his body heated up quickly at the thought.

The baron chuckled in the kiss and rested his hand along Derik's chin.

Derik shivered at the touch, helplessly ecstatic that he couldn't escape until the baron released him.

When he did, Derik let out a sigh of pleasure and settled down.

Hamel pulled up a chair and sat down. "I, um, feel I owe you an explanation."

Derik shook his head, "You don't need to."

"Yes, I do. You gave up your final secret all those years ago and I was so angry. It is time you knew my own secret."

"The Eye?"

The Eye of Hamel rose, flickering for a moment, then settled down.

Hamel shook his head. "More than that. You deserve all my secrets."

Derik said nothing, but he watched Hamel fighting with his own emotions.

"I-I don't know our name. I don't know what we were, but I've been around since before Franome was founded but long after Carium was born."

Hamel sighed sadly.

"We were cursed, me and my mate, the last or only of our kinds. We were just filled with this... rage that wouldn't go away. We pulled apart for so long, but came together every few years in this attempt to have a child. One time..." his voice trailed off.

"I killed her. She tried to kill me, and I tried to kill her. We couldn't really stop ourselves, but when it was over, I was utterly alone."

Derik sniffed with the tears rolling down his cheeks. He remembered the vision he saw from the Eye. "I-I saw."

Hamel looked up, a frown furrowing his face. "How?"

Derik gestured with his nose to the sphere next to him. "The Eye remembers."

"I never thought it would. I never thought it was anything other than my... eye."

"I saw a Copir silfae, and y-you plucking it out."

Hamel chuckled, "Sounds like you figured out my secret before me. Sounds familiar. Deep secrets don't stay hidden, do they?"

Derik chuckled, "Yeah, seems to happen in this place."

They started laughing until Derik winced from the pain.

Hamel reached over to hold Derik's hand. "Hime will be here soon. She says that you'll live."

Derik smiled, enjoying the touch of his baron against his skin. "I-I have one question."

"Anything, I will never keep anything from you now."

"Why did you take out your eye?"

Hamel chuckled bitterly.

"That Copir. I asked if I would love again. He said the 'unfettered eye would find the made woman.' So, in my hot-headed desperately for someone, I just ripped it out."

Derik made a face. "Seems... drastic."

"Well, after a few centuries, I agree. I was stupid then, but... I guess it worked out. I didn't realize he meant 'made' not 'maid.'"

The problem with insane prophets is that most of them don't write down crucial spellings," he said with a grin.

"D-Do you," asked Derik bashfully, "really love me?"

"I never stopped, Blackbird. Even when I saw you on the auction block, when I had Storn looking for you, or even when I saw myself through your memories, I realized I always loved you. From that very first day that very first time that trembling young man stood before me."

Derik sniffed. "I wish I could kiss you."

Hamel leaned over to kiss him, tenderly and softly.

Derik giggled. "I wish I could fuck you now."

From the door, Hime spoke sharply. "You do that and I'm not healing you until next week."

Hamel snapped into a standing position, a blush forming on his cheeks.

Derik already turned bright red as he looked at the amused priestess.

"Baron, out," Hime commanded.

Hamel kissed Derik again, slowly and lingeringly, then stood up. Walking past Hime, his hand snapped out to spank her hard on the ass cheek.

She squeaked as she jumped forward, then glared playfully at him. "Hamel!"

"Good to see you, Hawk."

He closed the door behind him.

Hime stroked her fingers against the frame, then turned around. "You," she said, pointing a finger, "fucked a god. I can smell Bridget on you."

Derik blushed even hotter.

Hime chuckled and sat down on the edge of the bed. She pulled out a small roll of tools. "But, I think that is what you needed."

"Thank you?"

"No thanks needed, my brother. You are truly a priest now and my equal in every way."

Derik smiled and blushed. "Except for anatomy lessons. As you prepare for your marriage, you better come to me for lessons so... we... can teach... what?"

"M-Marriage?"

"Well yeah, you're marrying the baron, aren't you?"

The room spun around him. "Um, what?"

"Damn, I thought he just proposed. Oops, well, pretend I didn't say anything."

"T-The baron is going to propose!?" Derik's voice rose shrilly.

Hime rolled her eyes and shrugged. "I don't think he knows it yet. Actually, I'm pretty sure he doesn't know it, but he's going to. I think you're too shy to ask the question, besides, you're the girl in this relationship."

Derik's heart fluttered with excitement. Anticipation and desire swirled inside his thoughts.

Hime's eyes trailed down his body to stare at the tent his manhood formed under the blankets. "Okay, put that down and stop thinking about sucking off the baron. Healing you is difficult enough without the distraction. You have a very pretty cock."

Derik yanked his thoughts away and regarded Hime.

The blond tucked some of her hair back and Derik noticed a few white streaks between the golden strands. She sighed and she turned back to him. "You really damaged your back muscles and some of the bones; though it was an excellent example of divine flight. I see you also managed to get your inner organs all messed up, so I'm going to have to fix the damage you did."

"I'm—"

"You say you're sorry, and I'm smacking you."

Derik blushed.

Hime reached over and kissed his cheek. "You did what you thought was right, I'll do what I think is right. And that is to ask you probably the most important question of your entire life."

Derik blinked, "I-I thought Bridget said I only had two paths left."

"Well, yeah, what does he know? So, the question you must decide now."

She held up both of her hands. She had a stylus in each one. "Do you want to be the baron's wife or the baron's husband?"

Goodbyes

The winter wind blew hard against the bare ground, kicking up clouds of snow and ice. Frozen dunes rolled across the graveyard and piled up against ancient tombstones and crypts.

Derik watched as the snowflakes caught on his long black hair whipping in the breeze, a smile on his face as tears ran down his cheeks. He shivered under his duster and curled his arms underneath his breasts. He smiled and looked up at the baron next to him.

Hamel looked down and then wrapped his arm around Derik's waist, shielding his love from the cutting wind. On the other side of Derik, the Eye hovered brightly, flickering with an internal fire as it bobbed and weaved to block individual snowflakes.

The former thief's smile faded as he looked across the eight graves in front of him.

Around them was the entire harem, crying and shivering. They were all broken from their loss.

Madre and Wendi stood in front, side by side. They knelt together, setting a bright red rose on each mound of upturned earth.

Sniffing, they stepped back, and one by one, the rest of the harem set down eight roses, one on each grave. Tears and sniffing drifted through the howling wind.

Derik's heart sank as he watched dark-rimmed eyes of ruined mascara and the sorrow crossing their faces. Fighting the tears that burned inside him, he turned away to watch the other funeral for the estate guards who died. Tornsin stood as their commander, giving a speech as he laid his own mother to rest, right next to his uncle.

A hot tear ran down his cheek.

Turning back, he watched the last of the harem pay their respects. Then Hime walked up, wearing a black habit and holding eight roses. She gave Derik a sad smile and set down her own respects.

Standing up, she sniffed. "Feels strange, you know, paying respects for the dead in a life you left behind."

Hamel held out his hand, and she took it to stand up.

"You can come back, Hawk."

Hime shook her head and smiled.

"No, my dear baron, I gave my heart to Bridget, and he isn't planning on giving me up. I'm a one god woman now. Even if you could give Bridget's a challenge in the bed."

He chuckled.

Hime gestured toward the line of carriages outside the graveyard and cleared her throat.

Hamel rolled his eye. "You were always bossy, Hawk."

"Well, always being right does that. Now, shoo."

Hamel kissed Derik, then walked past Hime. She stepped aside to protect her ass from being spanked. Hamel's eyes glittered with amusement, then he swept her into hug, his lips kissing hers passionately for just a second, then setting her back into position.

"You... bastard," she grinned and adjusted her cock.

Hamel laughed as his boots crunched down the path. "Once a kitten, always my kitten."

Derik giggled and shifted under his duster. His sensitive nipples teased against the silk of his dress. He let out a tiny shiver; it took some time to adjust to breasts again.

Hime held out her hand, and Derik carefully walked forward, his heels balancing easily on the snow and ice. Reaching her, he slipped his arm around her waist as they looked down at Sherrel's tombstone. It gave her full name, the date of her birth and the day she died. And, carved below, a symbol of Bridget and one additional word: "Sister."

Sighing sadly, Hime sniffed. "Never thought I'd see someone else buried here."

"Didn't know there was a harem graveyard."

"I did, but that doesn't mean I wanted to remember. Everyone lives, everyone dies. No reason to argue with that."

"One of those things I never thought of. I mean, it makes sense, but I thought they would be buried with their families." Derik sighed. "Most of them don't have those anymore, do they?"

Hime sniffed again, rubbing her hands against her tears. "Well, you are young, got a lot of life to live."

Derik turned to the priestess. "Thank you, Hime, for everything."

She grinned, "Don't forget Bridget."

"I was going to tell him in person."

"Hey! You only get to fuck the god once, that's the rules."

Derik quirked an eye, "No threesomes?"

Hime leaned over and kissed him on the cheek. "No threesomes, unless its you, me, and Bridget."

"Deal."

They stood in silence in front of Sherrel's grave. Tears ran down both of their cheeks, but there were no more words.

Finally, Hime stepped back and pulled her hands from Derik. "Coming? There is always an orgy for the dead after these funerals."

"I have plans, but I have one more grave to visit."

"Don't be long, they'll miss you."

"I'm not leaving," he said with a smile.

As Hime walked down the path, Derik jumped up along a snow bank and balanced on his heels, finding the spots where the ice could hold his slender form. His duster rippled in the wind and the Eye followed in silence.

In the furthest corner of the harem graveyard, behind a bare tree, he found the final grave. The earth steamed slightly from being turned, and the tombstone said only one thing: Shiel.

No dates, no words, no symbols. She believed in no gods and no one knew anything about her life. No one knew anything about her, so Hamel made her an honorary harem member to bury in the private grave.

It would have pissed her off to no end.

Derik's tears came faster as he pulled a wine bottle from under his coat. "Hey, you bitch. Sorry about having you buried in the harem graveyard. Know you don't like cunt, but someone has to watch over us."

He popped off the top and upended the bottle, pouring the blood red wine into the fresh earth. It steamed as it soaked into the ground.

"I can't thank you for everything you've done for me. You already knew that. We couldn't really speak, but you were probably my best friend."

Derik shook the last few drops out, then just casually dropped it in the earth. "I love you."

Tears mixed with the wine. He sobbed for a long moment before wiping the tears away. "I'll be back. Can't keep up with your drinking, but I promise you, every year I'll find the best bottle Storn can get me. Then I'm going to chug it. I promise."

He smiled sadly, then headed back to the carriages. By the time he reached there, there were only two carriages. The horses exhaled icy clouds as they waited. Next to them, sheltered from the window, she spotted her two men, Hamel and Tornsin. They were talking to each other as Madre, Wendi, and Teri hugged each other.

Feeling the comfort of being a family, he covered the last short distance and stood before them.

Madre, fresh tears in her eyes, rushed over and hugged her tightly. "Congratulations, he just told me."

She sniffed and kissed Derik on the lips.

He hugged her back tightly, enjoying the embrace.

When they broke, she sniffed sadly. "I've never been so happy to lose someone from the harem."

"I'm not going anywhere."

"Yeah, but you're done being one of my girls."

Derik grinned, "Maybe I'll get my own."

"And who would be in charge?"

A flash of an idea burst in his head. "Oh, I have an idea."

"Not Teri, please not Teri." Madre looked pained.

Teri perked up, "What?"

Derik shook his head and fought a smile. He already had a harem planned but they were still looking for the woman he wanted to be his Madre. "I know someone far better than Teri."

Madre frowned and looked over at Wendi.

Derik chuckled and shook his head.

Pushing it aside, Madre turned to her. "Come on, you were my girl long enough to join us. A prayer for the dead, an orgy for the harem."

"No, I got other plans."

"What other—"

Hamel interrupted, "Rachi and Wendi with me."

Confused, Madre turned from Derik and followed the baron. Hamel got into the carriage, smiled at Derik, and then it rolled off.

Teri and Tornsin joined Derik as it rolled over the hill.

Teri cleared her throat, "Um, not to be a spoiled sport, but what is going on? I thought Madre and Wendi were going with you."

"Well," Derik smiled at her, "I want to go somewhere else."

"Where?"

"My new summer home, Shiel's old house. Going to spend a week there."

"And...?"

"Going to make you two do whatever I want."

He got into the carriage and the others followed. As it rolled down the path, their eyes focused on him. He smiled, happier than he had been in a long time. The Eye rolled once, then lodged itself into the roof of the carriage, growing dark as it went to sleep.

Teri and Tornsin sat stiffly, unsure of what to do.

Derik smiled at them, feeling his body trembling with warmth, excitement, and happiness. "Just trust me. I'll be a wonderful baroness."

Teri took a deep breath to relax, "You'll always be a trap to me."

Derik chuckled. "Well, you know the rules, right? No taking my virginity, I'm saving that for the baron. I'm only going to have this one pussy and it is entirely his."

"Are you sure? I could really open you up," came the grinning reply.

"No, I want to lose it like Sherrel did. Just the baron and me." Teri pouted.

Derik focused his attention on Tornsin.

The guard swallowed, his hands tight in his lap.

Taking a deep breath, Derik hiked up his dress and knelt forward, positioning himself between the man's legs.

Tornsin gasped, then let out a soft moan as Derik opened his pants, breathing hard as he pulled out the wonderful hard shaft.

With a smile, Derik looked up. "Tornsin?"

"Y-Yes, madam."

"I want you to do something for me."

"Of course."

"I want you to grab my head and fuck my mouth."

Tornsin's shaft surged in his hands and Derik lowered himself, sliding his soft lips around the swollen head and bobbing down. Tornsin's hands curled into Derik's long, black hair.

With a moan, Derik said, "And I want you to be as rough as you want."

"What about me?" whined Teri as she pulled up her dress.

Derik just cocked his hips and wiggled his ass.

Teri grinned. In a flash, she hopped to the other side of the carriage.

Derik turned back to the cock in her hand, then gasped as Tornsin pulled him down, impaling his mouth and throat with his throbbing hardness.

As the guard fucked Derik's mouth, Teri's fingers slid up his thighs and pushed the dress up to expose his buttocks to the cool air of the carriage.

Delicate fingers caressed his aching hardness, the long length of his cock already wet with juices. Her fingertips circled around his hairless balls, then Derik moaned louder as Teri ran her fingers along the seam of his being, his womanhood. New sensations, terrible and wonderful at the same time, flooded through him as she played with his sexes.

He came from that first touch against the slick folds, soaking the insides of his thong and bringing a giggle from Teri.

She caressed it again, a new toy for her to admire and to tease.

It was a gift from Hime and a blessing of Bridget. A shadow of man and woman, a priest of the cross-dressing god.

Teri called it his pussy.

Shiel would have called it his cunt.

The baron called it something else: his luck.

Epilogue

Nightingale had many titles in her life: harem kitten, lover, slave, and whore. And, less than a day ago, she got a new one.

Murderer.

She sobbed as she twisted in her bounds, feeling the bruises that covered her body and the warm wind of summer beating against her skin.

They laid her out on a cross. Two heavy beams of wood in the shape of an "X" with locks and manacles at each end. Her wrists bled from her efforts to escape and semen dried on her thighs from the guards raping her.

So much changed since the night before. After all those years of struggle, fighting back the rage, she finally surrendered, not to the constant demands for her submission, she could crawl on the ground and suck dicks like the best of them. She had balanced on the edge of anger and acceptance since she stood on the auction block. No, she had surrendered to her burning rage.

She finally lost control and killed someone, strangling him with his own belt. Nightingale remembered panting heavily when the guards came, skidding to a stop as they stared in shock.

She had looked up at them, her face a mask of rage.

It didn't matter if he tried to strangle her himself. All that mattered was she killed the only son of a Shattered Kingdom warlord, the king of some tiny country. He was, beyond a doubt, pissed and sentenced her to death as soon as the sun touched her feet.

She sniffed bitterly as she watched a flock of blackbirds pulling apart a roll of bread dropped by one of her rapists. They seemed so carefree as they chirped at each other, and she was forced to remember the happy days of the harem. She smiled, the tears dripping down her face.

She missed those days.

At first, she blamed Blackbird for everything. Derik, the man who invaded her harem and stole her lover, an intruder who was up to no good. But, Rachi and everyone else were blinded by his looks, that sweet innocence, and those fragile, compassionate blue eyes. She shook her head, tearing her thoughts away.

Derik hadn't gotten her traded from that bastard Kerlis to the ambassador. It was her fault for trying to kill him. She knew why she was given to this king, her victim's father. It was something far more mundane: Sherrel.

Her eyes looked down the path before her. She was on a cliff top, her cross mounted above a raging river that would be her body's final home. A winding path led down to the courtyard of the keep. It was Sherrel's old home, the castle her father built and died defending. She looked at it with sadness, finding a small shred of compassion for what her fellow harem member went through.

The king couldn't get Sherrel, but he would get her.

Nightingale shook her head sadly.

She was fucked.

The blackbirds shot into the air as a large shadow passed over her. She didn't even look up. Through bleary eyes, she saw men run across the court, their voices just noise as they rushed to the gate.

She felt every bruise and ache as she prepared for the end.

The gate opened and someone walked through. She stared at the stranger for a long time, confused at the colors. It looked like the baron's colors. Blinking past the tears, she focused on the face, remembering him despite the years that parted them.

Tornsin.

The baron's man stood in the center of the courtyard and yelled out. Lights flared to life inside the castle and soon the keep's warriors poured into the yard, surrounding Tornsin as he stood there. He had a weapon but it remained sheathed. She watched as the king, the bastard who abused her as much as his son, came out with his honor guard. More men poured into the yard, taking position on the walls. Archers, crossbow men, half of the warlord's army, over a thousand men, surround Tornsin as the baron's man spoke curtly with the king. She shivered as they both pointed at her angrily.

Closing her eyes, she gave up. "Well, fuck me," she whispered to herself.

A shadow draped over her, but didn't pass. As she opened her eyes, she found herself staring at two bright blue eyes, like the purest sapphire. Inhaling sharply, she stared at the upside-down woman before the newcomer spoke.

"Let me guess. You're wondering which god hates you enough to put you here." The speaker had a soft, amused tone in her voice.

Nightingale frowned in confusion, then recognized the woman. The shock felt like someone shoved a sword in her gut. "D-Derik!?"

Derik smiled warmly and kissed her on the nose. "Yeah, sorry for the excitement."

Nightingale looked up with surprise. He wore a dress with a slit up the side. His bare thighs were braced against the wooden cross; she didn't even feel him standing there. Her eyes roamed across his body, remembering the hips and the breasts, but not the bird tattoo that stretched above his breasts or the strange kiss mark on his left wrist.

Derik flipped over and landed in front of her, his bare feet smacking the ground. Turning around, he looked up at her sheepishly. "I have a favor to ask you," he said as he knelt down to her ankle. Pulling out a thin length of wire, he began to pick the lock.

Nightingale could only stare in shock as he moved quickly. Behind her, she heard someone breathing hard and tumbling rocks falling off the cliff.

"I-It isn't fair, Derik," gasped Teri, "I can't fly like a fucking bird."

Derik grinned but didn't take his eyes off the lock.

Nightingale tried to turn around, but Teri walked around and knelt to the other manacle around her ankle. "Give me a Gebo Ten?"

Derik handed her a notched length of metal and Teri began to pick her own lock.

"T-Teri? What are you doing here?"

From below, Nightingale heard an angry cry. Snapping her head up, she saw a hundred men charging up the path at them. On the nearest wall, archers spun around and pulled back their bows. "D-Derik!"

"I see them," said the distracted thief. Her manacle snapped open as the archers fired, a cloud of arrows rising in the air toward them.

Nightingale whimpered and shuddered, trying to escape.

Derik stood up smoothly and smiled at her. Then he held his hand out behind him. The air screamed as a sphere of blue shot from the sky to hover right before his palm. Derik's eyes glittered with amusement. A curved shield of sapphire energy formed in front of his palm and the arrows simply shattered against it.

"Sorry, kind of in a hurry," he said without looking up.

Releasing his hand, he reached up for her right wrist and started picking the lock. As he did, he winked at her and said, "Nightingale, this might be coming as a surprise, but would you be willing to be Rachi's date for my wedding ceremony?"

Nightingale looked away from the floating sphere that resembled the Eye of Hamel and stared at him in shock. "W-What!?"

Derik smiled bashfully, "Well, Rachi is going to be there, and she asked which girl I thought could be her date. And she only loves one woman. So, the baron sent me to buy you from the king."

Teri chuckled as she popped open the lock. "Yeah, except then we heard you killed someone, so we rushed here to free you."

Nightingale stammered, "I-I-I—"

Derik opened the lock on her wrist and she slumped forward. His arm, surprisingly strong, caught her and pulled her into a hug as Teri worked on the final binding.

Nightingale inhaled sharply. "R-Rachi?"

Derik's face was centimeters from hers as he spoke softly. "She loves you, you know."

"I-I miss her," came the broken whisper. "I'm so sorry."

"Then, is that a yes?"

As Teri removed the final lock, she snapped at Derik. "Of course, its a yes. Why the fuck would she want to be executed?"

Derik rolled his eyes. "Give me a dramatic moment, could you?"

"Stop being a fucking cunt and tell her."

Nightingale ignoring their bickering as she looked out at the castle. The hundred men charging would be there in moments, but her eyes caught the sight of a woman standing on the battlements, a familiar flame burning across her body.

A voice, one she thought lost forever, echoed powerfully across the castle and the cliff. "Where is my Nightingale!?"

The magically enhanced voice rumbled like thunder and Nightingale began to cry.

Derik chuckled. "Madre is here. I thought we'd have a few more seconds with her going the long way."

Rachi's body exploded into flame as she jumped into the courtyard. Her hands clamped together as she hit the ground and the earth exploded in all directions. A cloud of dust rose up in the air, but Nightingale saw as her lover charged forward, her body a streak of flame as she cut through warriors like butter.

A moment later, the entire front gate exploded as another mage stepped through the smoking remains. It was another female battle mage. Fear lurched in Nightingale's heart as the other woman charged forward, spheres of water and dust shooting out in all directions and a flash of a dagger cutting a swath through the armored men.

The terrified woman stared at the flashes of light as the two battle mages tore into the army, killing dozens in seconds and spreading out to do the most damage.

Tornsin's blade flashed twice and Nightingale focused on it to see the king falling to the ground, dropping his weapon as he died.

"Um, Derik?" asked Teri.

"Yes, Bitch?"

"We have company."

Nightingale snapped her head down to see Derik's hand against her breast, glowing with a yellow-green light as healing energy poured into her. She saw movement and looked up to see a huge group of warriors charging up the path. One of them was in the lead, with the red plume of the commander. She shivered in fear, knowing he would give her no mercy.

Derik spoke distractedly as he concentrated on healing. "So?"

"You are a pacifist, she is naked, and I'm a crappy fighter."

"Nothing we four can't handle."

"There are a hundred... wait, four?"

Derik smiled as he pressed his hand against Nightingale's stomach, healing her from the inside and sending uncomfortable sensations through her skin. "Found an old friend last night. Had to bribe her though. Her price went up and a quarter million marks wasn't enough."

Nightingale screamed as the commander slashed forward, his blade sparkling in the summer morning.

Derik's hands held her tightly, seemingly unaware of the attack.

Then he exploded in a shower of blood and gore.

Hot liquid splattered across Nightingale's face and she screamed.

"Oi!"

Blood boiled up from the ground. Droplets that flung into the air snapped down to form into a slender woman with long ears and short, ragged hair. Nightingale couldn't see her face, but she could feel the stranger's voice like fingernails scraping against her spine. A blade appeared in the woman's hand, black with hellish flames running up the surface. Necromantic runes glowed brightly along the surface of the blade and on the skin of the woman.

"Oi, I said, that's my cunt licker!"

Teri whimpered, "Oh fuck; it's Shiel. I thought she's dead!"

"Yeah, drunk on thirty thou worth of wines too." Derik smirked. He pushed his black hair over his ear. "Ston's bar may never recover."

"How is she here!? She's dead!"

Derik grinned. "It's amazing how an immortal liver can keep a ghost in this realm."

Nightingale just stared as Shiel charged forward. She left a cloud of steaming red mist behind her before slamming into the front ranks of the guards. Her blade flashed, and men died.

Derik chuckled as he pulled back his hand.

He looked up at Nightingale, then hooked his finger under her chin to turn her to him. "I have one other favor," said the former thief while ignoring the slaughter meters away.

Nightingale whimpered, unsure of how her life could change so fast, "W-What?"

"I'm starting a harem—"

Teri let out a squeaking noise.

"—and I need someone to be in charge—"

Nightingale's heart pounded in her chest, feeling the blood rushing in her veins.

"—and you came highly recommended by the baron's Madre. Are you interested?"

Teri whimpered, "What!?"

Nightingale shook her head in shock. "B-But, I don't like you."

Derik just smiled. "You don't have to like me. I just want you to be a bitch and keep the girls in line. And, you'll have to work with Madre since you'll be sharing the space for a while."

"I-I... Madre?"

"Well, I figured I'd call you Padre or something, but yeah."

Teri growled, "Why does she get to be in charge?"

Derik's eyes slid over to the other woman. "Well, do you see the baron fucking Rachi all the time?"

"No. She's too busy."

"Do you fuck the baron?"

"Well, yeah. Every few weeks."

Nightingale couldn't breathe. Her eyes rolled as she looked back and forth in growing confusion and frustration.

"And does Rachi get to have as much fun as you?" Derik said with a grin.

"No," came the sullen reply.

"And do you want to fuck me?"

Teri hesitated, then grinned. "Okay, Nightingale gets to be Padre, but I still get to spank you."

"Deal," grinned Derik.

He turned back to Nightingale. "Gale?"

She couldn't speak. Her eyes stared into the battle.

Shiel sprinted down the path, carving a trail of blood and death.

The gruesome sight was nothing compared to the woman walking up the path. Madre's magic warped the air around her as she stepped over corpses without ever staining her leather boots.

Battle mage and psychopath passed either other without even a nod.

Nightingale stared at her lover and saw love reflected back. Tears glittered on Rachi's cheeks as she broke into a run toward her.

Derik snapped his fingers. "Gale? Be my Padre?"

Nightingale sobbed as she stared at her lover. "Yes, fuck yes."

Yanking herself from Derik's grip, she ran to the woman she loved.

About the Author

t'Sade has been happily using third-person singular since the late eighties. Besides that strange quirk, they enjoy writing a brutal combination of sex and violence for decades. Most of their stories explore the fringe edges of sexuality in the epic quest of trying to write a story for every fetish and turn-on known to the human libido.

It's going to take a long time.

Their writing can be found on their website, tsade.com. Most of it is free to read and enjoy. Subscribers have access to the rest, including digital versions of all published works, a few additional series and stories. Patrons also get fresh chapters every month and have the opportunity to vote on what comes next. If that interests you, please consider becoming one at tsade.com/subscribe. On the other hand, if you prefer only more polished versions, then head over to Curious Cabbit Press (curiouscabbit.com) which has both the print and ebook versions of select works.

The Mummy's Girl

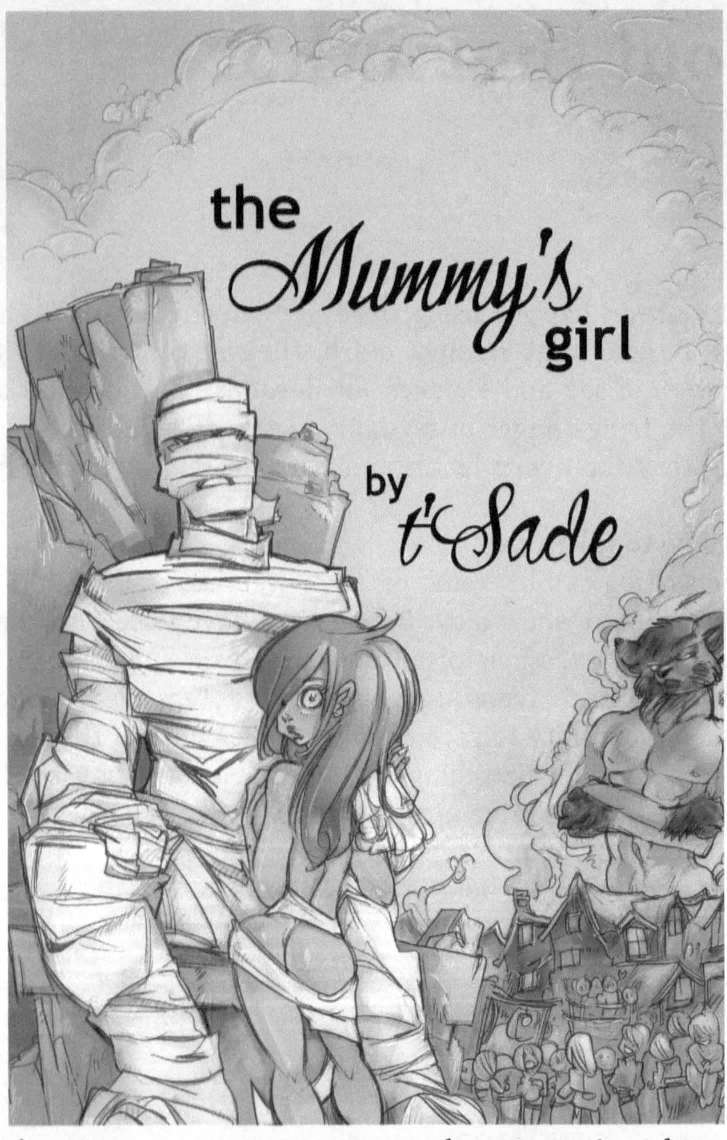

In a love story spanning centuries, The Mummy's Girl is an epic, erotic tale set in a land of pure fantasy. A cruel master with a warm heart punishes a new slave in the temple of a wolf-god, discovering that it is more for her pleasure than her pain, and gradually finds himself falling in love with her. They are not destined to be together when death by betrayal tears them apart. One sacrifices her soul to bring her master to life, cursing him to walk the earth as a mummy, a creature of death, sex, and magic. But, even as they are torn apart, the games of gods scheme to reunite the star-crossed lovers.

The Mummy's Girl is extremely and sexually explicit in nature, and this leads a heightened sense of anticipation to the drama of the plot. Many variations of fantastic BDSM and sexuality blend together in the twisting reincarnations of two souls as they seek each other. When they finally become one, it is only through divine submission and sacrifice of mind and body that gives them that final chance to be reunited.

Eliza and the Raptor

The only crime Third Lieutenant Eliza committed was stealing a few precious minutes of her patrol to pleasure herself. On the *FCM Quantor Generation Ship*, where reproduction occurred in test tubes and an active libido was a crime, she was found guilty of treason. Her superior officer sentenced her to a life of hard labor in the mines with a threat of execution if she touched herself even once more.

In the midst of her personal hell, salvation came when they pulled her from the depths of the asteroid ship and assigned her to aid the newly encountered sentient dinosaurs and their massive fleet of war ships. Unspoken was the hopes that she would die while spying and the FCM would use her death to steal the fleet's technology.

No one could expect that Fleet Master Kraken would see something else in the former prisoner. She not only appealed to his joy of Machiavellian plots, but also to his more primal lusts. And Kraken wasn't opposed to exploring beyond his own species and satisfying his own curiosity of what humans did when they stole a few moments of pleasure.

Eliza and the Raptor is a sci-fi set in a rich universe of pulp science, intellectual eroticism, and hope that there is always a chance to discover love.

Credits

There are a number of people who have helped make this book a possibility.

Forums

7chan/elit and 99chan/elit

Editor

Shannon Ryan

Illustrator

Mamabliss (http://www.mamabliss.com/blog/)

Support

My patrons and subscribers, both past and present

www.ingramcontent.com/pod-product-compliance
Lightning Source LLC
Chambersburg PA
CBHW031924110726
47902CB00001B/29